PRAISE FOR
We Need to Talk About Kevin

"It's always a challenge for a novelist to take on front-page events. A guilt-stricken Eva Khatchadourian digs into her own history, her son's, and the nation's, in her search for the responsible party, and her fierceness and honesty sustain the narrative; this is an impressive novel." —*New York Times*

"Sometimes searing . . . impossible to put down . . . brutally honest. [*We Need to Talk About Kevin*] drives home its chilling point. There are no answers here, no pat explanations. Shriver doesn't take an easy way out by blaming the parents. Instead, the novel holds a mirror up to a whole culture. Who, in the end, needs to talk about Kevin? Maybe we all do." —*Boston Globe*

"Terribly honest. Ms. Shriver takes a calculated risk . . . but the gamble pays off as she strikes a tone of compelling intimacy. This is heavy material, but Ms. Shriver tackles it with admirable panache, turning a sensational story into a troubling one." —*Wall Street Journal*

"An underground feminist hit." —*New York Observer*

"[A] fascinating, painful mediation on motherhood-as-regret." —*Time Out* (New York)

"Impossible to put down. . . . Witty. . . . Balletic." —*Philadelphia Inquirer*

"Furiously imagined. . . . A pleasure to read." —*Seattle Times*

"Shriver's searingly intelligent story bristles with suspense—an amazing accomplishment. . . . Uncomfortable yet utterly mesmerizing." —*Rocky Mountain News*

"A number of fictional attempts have been made to portray what might lead a teenager to kill . . . but Shriver's is the most triumphantly accomplished by far. [Shriver is] gifted . . . she brings to her story a keen understanding of the intricacies of marital and parental relationships as well as a narrative pace that is both compelling and thoughtful. A harrowing, psychologically astute, sometimes even darkly humorous novel, with a clear-eyed, hard-won ending and a tough-minded sense of the difficult, often painful, human enterprise."

—*Publishers Weekly* (starred review)

"In crisply crafted sentences that cut to the bone of her feelings about motherhood, career, family, and what it is about American culture that produces child killers, Shriver yanks the reader back and forth between blame and empathy, retribution and forgiveness. Never letting up on the tension, Shriver ensures that, like Eva, the reader grapples with unhealed wounds."

—*Booklist* (starred review)

"Gutsy."   —*Slate*

"What adds to the horror of *We Need to Talk About Kevin* is the fresh way it examines the cosmic gamble of having a child, how producing a new life introduces an unquantifiable variable into life's equation."   —*National Post*

"Startling. . . . A book about the dangerous distance that exists between what we feel and what we are actually prepared to admit when it comes to family life. . . . Shriver's satire on child-centered families captained by adult buffoons whose intellectual, not to mention erotic, life is in pieces could not be more timely."

—*The Guardian* (UK)

"[A] fierce, taboo-breaking book."   —*The Week*

Terri Gelenian-Wood

About the Author

LIONEL SHRIVER is a novelist and has written for *The Econo-mist*, the *Wall Street Journal*, and the *Philadelphia Inquirer*, among other publications. She lives in London and New York.

We Need to Talk About Kevin

A Novel

LIONEL SHRIVER

A complete catalogue record for this book can
be obtained from the British Library on request

First published in 2003 by Counterpoint, a member of the Perseus
Books Group, New York

First published in the UK in 2005 by Serpent's Tail,
4 Blackstock Mews, London N4 2BT

website: www.serpentstail.com

Printed in Great Britain by Mackays of Chatham plc

10 9 8 7

For Terri
One worst-case scenario we've both escaped.

A child needs your love most when he deserves it least.

—ERMA BOMBECK

Dear Franklin,

I'm unsure why one trifling incident this afternoon has moved me to write to you. But since we've been separated, I may most miss coming home to deliver the narrative curiosities of my day, the way a cat might lay mice at your feet: the small, humble offerings that couples proffer after foraging in separate backyards. Were you still installed in my kitchen, slathering crunchy peanut butter on Branola though it was almost time for dinner, I'd no sooner have put down the bags, one leaking a clear viscous drool, than this little story would come tumbling out, even before I chided that we're having pasta tonight so would you please not eat that whole sandwich.

In the early days, of course, my tales were exotic imports, from Lisbon, from Katmandu. But no one wants to hear stories from abroad, really, and I could detect from your telltale politeness that you privately preferred anecdotal trinkets from closer to home: an eccentric encounter with a toll collector on the George Washington Bridge, say. Marvels from the mundane helped to ratify your view that all my foreign travel was a kind of cheating. My souvenirs—a packet of slightly stale Belgian waffles, the British expression for "piffle" (*codswallop!*)—were artificially imbued with magic by mere dint of distance. Like those baubles the Japanese exchange—in a box in a bag, in a box in a bag—the sheen on my offerings from far afield was all packaging. What a more considerable achievement, to root around in the untransubstantiated rubbish of plain old New York state and scrounge a moment of piquancy from a trip to the Nyack Grand Union.

Which is just where my story takes place. I seem finally to be learning what you were always trying to teach me, that my own country is as exotic and even as perilous as Algeria. I was in the dairy aisle and didn't need much; I wouldn't. I never eat pasta these days, without you to dispatch most of the bowl. I do miss your gusto.

It's still difficult for me to venture into public. You would think, in a country that so famously has "no sense of history," as Europeans claim, that I might cash in on America's famous amnesia. No such luck. No one in this "community" shows any signs of forgetting, after a year and eight months—to the day. So I have to steel myself when provisions run low. Oh, for the clerks at the 7-Eleven on Hopewell Street my novelty has worn off, and I can pick up a quart of milk without glares. But our regular Grand Union remains a gauntlet.

I always feel furtive there. To compensate, I force my back straight, my shoulders square. I see now what they mean by "holding your head high," and I am sometimes surprised by how much interior transformation a ramrod posture can afford. When I stand physically proud, I feel a small measure less mortified.

Debating medium eggs or large, I glanced toward the yogurts. A few feet away, a fellow shopper's frazzled black hair went white at the roots for a good inch, while its curl held only at the ends: an old permanent grown out. Her lavender top and matching skirt may have once been stylish, but now the blouse bound under the arms and the peplum served to emphasize heavy hips. The outfit needed pressing, and the padded shoulders bore the faint stripe of fading from a wire hanger. Something from the nether regions of the closet, I concluded, what you reach for when everything else is filthy or on the floor. As the woman's head tilted toward the processed cheese, I caught the crease of a double chin.

Don't try to guess; you'd never recognize her from that portrait. She was once so neurotically svelte, sharply cornered, and glossy as if commercially gift wrapped. Though it may be more romantic to picture the bereaved as gaunt, I imagine you can grieve as efficiently with chocolates as with tap water. Besides, there are women who keep themselves sleek and smartly turned out less to please a spouse than to keep up with a daughter, and, thanks to us, she lacks that incentive these days.

It was Mary Woolford. I'm not proud of this, but I couldn't face her. I reeled. My hands went clammy as I fumbled with the carton, checking that the eggs were whole. I rearranged my features into those of a shopper who had just remembered something in the next aisle over and managed to place the eggs on the child-seat without turning. Scuttling off on this pretense of mission, I left the cart behind, because the wheels squeaked. I caught my breath in soup.

I should have been prepared, and often am—girded, guarded, often to no purpose as it turns out. But I can't clank out the door in full armor to run every silly errand, and besides, how can Mary harm me now? She has tried her damnedest; she's taken me to court. Still, I could not tame my heartbeat, nor return to dairy right away, even once I realized that I'd left that embroidered bag from Egypt, with my wallet, in the cart.

Which is the only reason I didn't abandon the Grand Union altogether. I eventually had to skulk back to my bag, and so I meditated on Campbell's asparagus and cheese, thinking aimlessly how Warhol would be appalled by the redesign.

By the time I crept back the coast was clear, and I swept up my cart, abruptly the busy professional woman who must make quick work of domestic chores. A familiar role, you would think. Yet it's been so long since I thought of myself that way that I felt sure the folks ahead of me at checkout must have pegged my impatience not as the imperiousness of the second-earner for whom time is money, but as the moist, urgent panic of a fugitive.

When I unloaded my motley groceries, the egg carton felt sticky, which moved the salesclerk to flip it open. Ah. Mary Woolford had spotted me after all.

"All twelve!" the girl exclaimed. "I'll have them get you another carton."

I stopped her. "No, no," I said. "I'm in a hurry. I'll take them as they are."

"But they're totally—"

"I'll take them as they are!" There's no better way to get people to cooperate in this country than by seeming a little unhinged. After dabbing pointedly at the price code with a Kleenex, she scanned the eggs, then wiped her hands on the tissue with a rolled eye.

"*Khatchadourian*," the girl pronounced when I handed her my debit card. She spoke loudly, as if to those waiting in line. It was late afternoon, the right shift for an after-school job; plausibly about seventeen, this girl could have been one of Kevin's classmates. Sure, there are half a dozen high schools in this area, and her family might have just moved here from California. But from the look in her eye I didn't think so. She fixed me with a hard stare. "That's an unusual name."

I'm not sure what got into me, but I'm so tired of this. It's not that I have no shame. Rather, I'm exhausted with shame, slippery all over with its sticky albumen taint. It is not an emotion that leads anywhere. "I'm the only Khatchadourian in New York state," I flouted, and snatched my card back. She threw my eggs in a bag, where they drooled a little more.

So now I'm home—what passes for it. Of course you've never been here, so allow me to describe it for you.

You'd be taken aback. Not least because I've opted to remain in Gladstone, after kicking up such a fuss about moving to the suburbs in the first place. But I felt I should stay within driving distance of Kevin. Besides, much as I crave anonymity, it's not that I want my neighbors to forget who I am; I want to, and that is not an opportunity any town affords. This is the one place in the world where the ramifications of my life are fully felt, and it's far less important to me to be liked these days than to be understood.

I'd enough of a pittance left over after paying off the lawyers to buy a little place of my own, but the tentativeness of renting suited. Likewise my living in this Tinkertoy duplex seemed a fitting marriage of temperaments. Oh, you'd be horrified; its flimsy pressboard cabinetry defies your father's motto, "Materials are everything." But it is this very quality of barely hanging on that I cherish.

Everything here is precarious. The steep stairway to the second floor has no banister, spicing my ascent to bed with vertigo after three glasses of wine. The floors creak and the window frames leak, and there is an air about the place of fragility and underconfidence, as if at any moment the entire structure might simply blink out like a bad idea. Swinging on rusty coat hangers from a live wire across the ceiling, the tiny halogen bulbs downstairs have a tendency to flicker, and their tremulous light contributes to the on-again, off-again sensation that permeates my new life. Likewise the innards of my sole telephone socket are disgorged; my uncertain connection to the outside world dangles by two poorly soldered wires, and it often cuts off. Though the landlord has promised me a proper stove, I really don't mind the hot plate—whose "on" light doesn't work. The inside handle of the front door often comes off in my hand. So far I've been able to work it back on again, but the stump of the lock shaft teases me with intimations of my mother: unable to leave the house.

I recognize, too, my duplex's broad tendency to stretch its resources to the very limit. The heating is feeble, rising off the radiators in a stale, shallow breath, and though it is only early November, I have already cranked their regulators on full. When I shower, I use all hot water and no cold; it's just warm enough that I don't shiver, but awareness that there is no reserve permeates my ablutions with disquiet. The refrigerator dial is set at its highest point, and the milk keeps only three days.

As for the decor, it evokes a quality of mockery that feels apt. The downstairs is painted in a slapdash, abrasively bright yellow, the brushstrokes careless and aerated with streaks of underlying white, as if scrawled with crayon. Upstairs in my bedroom, the walls are sponged amateurishly in aqua, like primary-school daubs. This tremulous little house—it doesn't feel quite *real*, Franklin. And neither do I.

Yet I do hope that you're not feeling sorry for me; it's not my intention that you do. I might have found more palatial accommodation, if that's what I wanted. I like it here, in a way. It's unserious, toy. I live in a dollhouse. Even the furniture is out of scale. The dining table strikes chesthigh, which makes me feel underage, and the little bedside table on which I have perched this laptop is much too low for typing—about the right height for serving coconut cookies and pineapple juice to kindergartners.

Maybe this askew, juvenile atmosphere helps to explain why yesterday, in a presidential election, I didn't vote. I simply forgot. Everything around me seems to take place so far away. And now rather than pose a firm counterpoint to my dislocation, the country seems to have joined me in the realm of the surreal. The votes are tallied. But as in some Kafka tale, no one seems to know who won.

And I have this dozen eggs—what's left of them. I've emptied the remains into a bowl and fished out the shards of shell. If you were here I might whip us up a nice frittata, with diced potato, cilantro, that one teaspoon of sugar that's the secret. Alone, I'll slop them in a skillet, scramble, and sullenly pick. But I will eat them all the same. There was something about Mary's gesture that I found, in an inchoate sort of way, rather elegant.

Food revulsed me at first. Visiting my mother in Racine, I turned green before her stuffed dolma, though she'd spent all day blanching grape leaves and rolling the lamb and rice filling into neat parcels; I reminded her they could be frozen. In Manhattan, when I scurried past the 57th Street deli on the way to Harvey's law office, the peppery smell of pastrami fat would flip my stomach. But the nausea passed, and I missed it. When after four or five months I began to get hungry—ravenous, in fact—the appetite struck me as unseemly. So I continued to act the part of a woman who'd lost interest in food.

But after about a year, I faced the fact that the theater was wasted. If I grew cadaverous, no one cared. What did I expect, that you would wrap my rib cage with those enormous hands in which horses must be measured, lifting me overhead with the stern reproach that is every Western woman's sly delight, "You're too thin"?

So now I eat a croissant with my coffee every morning, picking up every flake with a moistened forefinger. Methodically chopping cabbage occupies a portion of these long evenings. I have even declined, once or twice, those few invitations out that still jangle my phone, usually friends from abroad who e-mail from time to time, but whom I haven't seen for years. Especially if they don't know, and I can always tell; innocents sound too roisterous, whereas initiates begin with a deferential stutter and a hushed, churchy tone. Obviously I don't want to recite the story. Nor do I covet the mute commiseration of friends who *don't know what to say* and so leave me to spill my guts by way of making conversation. But what really drives me to make my apologies about how "busy" I am is that I am terrified we will both order a salad and the bill will arrive and it will only be 8:30 or 9:00 at night and I will go home to my tiny duplex and have nothing to chop.

It's funny, after so long on the road for Wing and a Prayer—a different restaurant every night, where waiters speak Spanish or Thai, whose menus list seviche or dog—that I should have grown so fixated on this fierce routine. Horribly, I remind myself of my mother. But I cannot break with this narrow sequence (square of cheese or six to seven olives; breast of chicken, chop, or omelet; hot vegetable; single vanilla sandwich cookie; no more wine than will finish exactly half the bottle) as if I am walking a balance beam, and with one step off I will topple. I have had to disallow snow peas altogether because their preparation is insufficiently arduous.

Anyway, even with the two of us estranged, I knew you would worry about whether I was eating. You always did. Thanks to Mary Woolford's feeble revenge this evening, I am amply fed. Not all of our neighbors' antics have proved so anodyne.

Those gallons of crimson paint splashed all over the front porch, for example, when I was still living in our nouveau riche ranch house (that's what it was, Franklin, whether or not you like the sound of it—a *ranch house*) on Palisades Parade. Over the windows, the front door. They came in the night, and by the time I woke the next morning the paint had almost dried. I thought at the time, only a month or so after—whatever am I going to call that Thursday?—that I couldn't be horrified anymore, or wounded. I suppose that's a common conceit, that you've already been so damaged that damage itself, in its totality, makes you safe.

As I turned the corner from the kitchen into the living room that morning, I recognized this notion that I was impervious for codswallop. I gasped. The sun was streaming in the windows, or at least through the panes not streaked with paint. It also shone through in spots where the paint was thinnest, casting the off-white walls of that room in the lurid red glow of a garish Chinese restaurant.

I'd always made it a policy, one you admired, to face what I feared, though this policy was conceived in days when my fears ran to losing my way in a foreign city—child's play. What I would give now to return to the days when I'd no idea what lay in wait (*child's play* itself, for example). Still, old habits die hard, so rather than flee back to our bed and draw up the covers, I resolved to survey the damage. But the front door stuck, glued shut with thick crimson enamel. Unlike latex, enamel isn't water soluble. And enamel is expensive, Franklin. Someone made a serious investment. Of course, our old neighborhood has any number of deficiencies, but one of them has never been money.

So I went out the side door and around to the front in my robe. Taking in our neighbors' artwork, I could feel my face set in the same "impassive mask" the *New York Times* described from the trial. The *Post*, less kindly, depicted my expression throughout as "defiant," and our local *Journal News* went even further: "From Eva Khatchadourian's stony implacability, her son might have done nothing more egregious than dip a pigtail in an inkwell." (I grant that I stiffened in court, squinting and sucking my cheeks against my molars; I remember grasping at one of your tough-guy mottoes, "Don't let 'em see you sweat." But Franklin, "defiant"? I was trying not to cry.)

The effect was quite magnificent, if you had a taste for the sensational, which by that point I certainly didn't. The house looked as if its throat were slit. Splashed in wild, gushing Rorschachs, the hue had been chosen so meticulously—deep, rich, and luscious, with a hint of purplish blue—that it might have been specially mixed. I thought dully that had the culprits requested this color rather than pulled it off the shelf, the police might be able to track them down.

I wasn't about to walk into a police station again unless I had to.

My kimono was thin, the one you gave me for our first anniversary back in 1980. Meant for summer, it was the only wrap I had from you, and I wouldn't reach for anything else. I've thrown so much away, but nothing you gave me or left behind. I admit that these talismans are excruciating. That is why I keep them. Those bullying therapeutic types would claim that my cluttered closets aren't "healthy." I beg to differ. In contrast to the cringing, dirty pain of Kevin, of the paint, the criminal and civil trials, this pain is *wholesome*. Much belittled in the sixties, wholesomeness is a property I have come to appreciate as surprisingly scarce.

The point is, clutching that soft blue cotton and assessing the somewhat slapdash paint job that our neighbors had seen fit to sponsor free of charge, I was cold. It was May, but crisp, with a whipping wind. Before I found out for myself, I might have imagined that in the aftermath of personal apocalypse, the little bothers of life would effectively vanish. But it's not true. You still feel chills, you still despair when a package is lost in the mail, and you still feel irked to discover you were shortchanged at Starbucks. It might seem, in the circumstances, a little embarrassing for me to continue to need a sweater or a muff, or to object to being cheated of a dollar and fifty cents. But since that *Thursday* my whole life has been smothered in such a blanket of embarrassment that I have chosen to find these passing pinpricks solace instead, emblems of a surviving propriety. Being inadequately dressed for the season, or chafing that in a Wal-Mart the size of a cattle market I cannot locate a single box of kitchen matches, I glory in the emotionally commonplace.

Picking my way to the side door again, I puzzled over how a band of marauders could have assaulted this structure so thoroughly while I slept unawares inside. I blamed the heavy dose of tranquilizers I was taking every night (please don't say anything, Franklin, I know you don't approve), until I realized that I was picturing the scene all wrong. It was a month later, not a day. There were no jeers and howls, no ski masks and sawn-off shotguns. They came in stealth. The only sounds were broken twigs, a muffled thump as the first full can slapped our lustrous mahogany door, the lulling oceanic lap of paint against glass, a tiny rat-a-tat-tat as spatters splattered, no louder than fat rain. Our house had not been spurted with the Day-Glo spray of spontaneous outrage but slathered with a hatred that had reduced until it was thick and savorous, like a fine French sauce.

You'd have insisted we hire someone else to clean it off. You were always keen on this splendid American penchant for specialization, whereby there was an expert for every want, and you sometimes thumbed the Yellow Pages just for fun. "Paint Removers: Crimson enamel." But so much was made in the papers about how rich we were, how Kevin had been spoiled. I didn't want to give Gladstone the satisfaction of sneering, look, she can just hire one more minion to clean up the mess, like that expensive lawyer. No, I made them watch me day after day, scraping by hand, renting a sandblaster for the bricks. One evening I glimpsed my reflection after a day's toil—clothing smeared, fingernails creased, hair flecked—and shrieked. I'd looked like this once before.

A few crevices around the door may still gleam with a ruby tint; deep in the crags of those faux-antique bricks may yet glisten a few drops of spite that I was unable to reach with the ladder. I wouldn't know. I sold that house. After the civil trial, I had to.

I had expected to have trouble unloading the property. Surely superstitious buyers would shy away when they found out who owned the place. But that just goes to show once again how poorly I understood my own country. You once accused me of lavishing all my curiosity on "Third

World shitholes," while what was arguably the most extraordinary empire in the history of mankind was staring me in the face. You were right, Franklin. There's no place like home.

As soon as the property was listed, the bids tumbled in. Not because the bidders didn't know; because they did. Our house sold for well more than it was worth—over $3 million. In my naïveté, I hadn't grasped that the property's very notoriety was its selling point. While poking about our pantry, apparently couples on the climb were picturing gleefully in their minds' eyes the crowning moment of their housewarming dinner party.

[Ting-ting!] Listen up, folks. I'm gonna propose a toast, but first, you're not gonna believe who we bought this spread from. Ready? Eva Khatchadourian. . . . *Familiar? You bet. Where'd we move to, anyway? Gladstone! . . . Yeah, that Khatchadourian, Pete, among all the Khatchadourians you know? Christ, guy, little slow.*

. . . That's right, "Kevin." Wild, huh? My kid Lawrence has his room. Tried one on the other night, too. Said he had to stay up with me to watch Henry: Portrait of a Serial Killer *because his room was "haunted" by "Kevin Ketchup." Had to disappoint the kid. Sorry, I said, Kevin Ketchup can't no way be haunting your bedroom when the worthless little bastard's all too alive and well in some kiddie prison upstate. Up to me, man, that scumbag would've got the chair. . . . No, it wasn't quite as bad as Columbine. What was it, ten, honey? Nine, right, seven kids, two adults. The teacher he whacked was like, this brat's big champion or something, too. And I don't know about blaming videos, rock music. We grew up with rock music, didn't we? None of us went on some killing frenzy at our high school. Or take Lawrence. That little guy loves blood-and-guts TV, and no matter how graphic he doesn't flinch. But his rabbit got run over? He cried for a week. They know the difference.*

We're raising him to know what's right. Maybe it seems unfair, but you really gotta wonder about the parents.

Eva

Dear Franklin,

You know, I try to be polite. So when my coworkers—that's right, I work, at a Nyack travel agency, believe it or not, and gratefully, too—when they start foaming at the mouth about the disproportionate number of votes for Pat Buchanan in Palm Beach, I wait so patiently for them to finish that in a way I have become a treasured commodity: I am the only one in the office who will allow them to finish a sentence. If the atmosphere of this country has suddenly become carnival-like, festive with fierce opinion, I do not feel invited to the party. I don't care who's president.

Yet too vividly I can see this last week through the lens of my private if-only. I would have voted for Gore, you for Bush. We'd have had heated enough exchanges before the election, but this—this—oh, it would have been marvelous. Loud, strident fist pounding and door slamming, me reciting choice snippets from the *New York Times,* you furiously underscoring op-eds in the *Wall Street Journal*—suppressing smiles the whole time. How I miss getting exercised over bagatelle.

It may have been disingenuous of me to imply at the start of my last letter that when we conferred at the end of a day, I told all. To the contrary, one of the things that impels me to write is that my mind is huge with all the little stories I never told you.

Don't imagine that I've enjoyed my secrets. They've trapped me, crowded me in, and long ago I'd have liked nothing more than to pour out my heart. But Franklin, you didn't want to hear. I'm sure you still don't. And maybe I should have tried harder at the time to force you to listen, but early on we got on opposite sides of something. For many couples who quarrel, just what they are on opposite sides of may be unformed, a line of some sort, an abstraction that divides them—a history or floating grudge, an insensible power struggle with a life of its own: gossamer. Perhaps in times of reconciliation for such couples the unreality of that line assists its dissolve. *Look*, I can jealously see them noting, *there is nothing in the room; we can reach across the sheer air between us.* But in our case, what separated us was all too tangible, and if it wasn't in the room it could walk in of its own accord.

Our son. Who is not a smattering of small tales but one long one. And though the natural impulse of yarn spinners is to begin at the beginning, I will resist it. I have to go further back. So many stories are determined before they start.

What possessed us? We were so happy! Why, then, did we take the stake of all we had and place it all on this outrageous gamble of having a child? Of course you consider the very putting of that question profane. Although the infertile are entitled to sour grapes, it's against the rules, isn't it, to actually have a baby and spend any time at all on that banished parallel life in which you didn't. But a Pandoran perversity draws me to prize open what is forbidden. I have an imagination, and I like to dare myself. I knew this about myself in advance, too: that I was just the sort of woman who had the capacity, however ghastly, to rue even so unretractable a matter as another person. But then, Kevin didn't regard other people's existence as unretractable—did he?

I'm sorry, but you can't expect me to avoid it. I may not know what to call it, that *Thursday. The atrocity* sounds torn from a newspaper, *the incident* is minimizing to the point of obscenity, and *the day our own son committed mass murder* is too long, isn't it? For every mention? But I am going to mention it. I wake up with what he did every morning and I go to bed with it every night. It is my shabby substitute for a husband.

So I have racked my brain, trying to reconstruct those few months in 1982 when we were officially "deciding." We were still living in my cavernous loft in Tribeca, where we were surrounded by arch homosexuals, unattached artists you deplored as "self-indulgent," and unencumbered professional couples who dined out at Tex-Mex nightly and flopped about at the Limelight until 3 A.M. Children in that neighborhood were pretty much on a par with the spotted owl and other endangered species, so it's little wonder that our deliberations were stilted and abstract. We even set

ourselves a deadline, for pity's sake——my thirty-seventh birthday that August——since we didn't want a child who could still be living at home in our
sixties.

Our sixties! In those days, an age as bafflingly theoretical as a baby.
Yet I expect to embark to that foreign land five years from now with no
more ceremony than boarding a city bus. It was in 1999 that I made a
temporal leap, although I didn't notice the aging so much in the mirror as
through the aegis of other people. When I renewed my driver's license this
last January, for example, the functionary at the desk didn't act surprised I
was all of fifty-four, and you remember I was once rather spoiled on this
front, accustomed to regular coos over how I looked at least ten years
younger. The coos came to a complete halt overnight. Indeed, I had one
embarrassing encounter, soon after *Thursday*, in which a Manhattan subway attendant called my attention to the fact that over-sixty-fives qualified
for a senior discount.

We'd agreed that whether we became parents would be "the single
most important decision we would ever make together." Yet the very mo-
mentousness of the decision guaranteed that it never seemed real, and so
remained on the level of whimsy. Every time one of us raised the question
of parenthood, I felt like a seven-year-old contemplating a Thumbellina
that wets itself for Christmas.

I do recall a sequence of conversations during that period that lurched
with a seemingly arbitrary rhythm between tending toward and tending
against. The most upbeat of these has surely to be after a Sunday lunch
with Brian and Louise on Riverside Drive. They no longer did dinner,
which always resulted in parental apartheid: one spouse playing grown-up
with calamatas and cabernet, the other corralling, bathing, and bedding
those two rambunctious little girls. Me, I always prefer socializing at
night——it is implicitly more wanton——although wantonness was no longer
a quality I would have associated with that warm, settled Home Box Office scriptwriter who made his own pasta and watered spindly parsley
plants on his window ledge.

I marveled in the elevator down, "And he used to be such a cokehead."

"You sound wistful," you noted.

"Oh, I'm sure he's happier now."

I wasn't sure. In those days I still held wholesomeness to be suspect. In fact, we had had a very "nice" time, which left me bafflingly bereft. I had admired the solid oak dining set seized for a song from an upstate tag sale, while you submitted to a complete inventory of the younger girl's Cabbage Patch Kids with a patience that left me agog. We commended the inventive salad with ingenuous fervor, for in the early 1980s goat cheese and sun-dried tomatoes were not yet passé.

Years before we'd agreed that you and Brian wouldn't get into it over Ronald Reagan—to you, a good-humored icon with easy flash and fiscal ingenuity who had restored pride to the nation; to Brian, a figure of menacing idiocy who would bankrupt the country with tax cuts for rich people. So we stayed on safe topics, as "Ebony and Ivory" crooned in the background at a grown-up volume and I suppressed my annoyance that the little girls kept singing tunelessly along and replaying the same track. You bewailed the fact that the Knicks hadn't made the playoffs, and Brian did an impressive imitation of a man who was interested in sports. We were all disappointed that *All in the Family* would soon wrap up its last season, but agreed that the show was about played out. About the only conflict that arose all afternoon was over the equally terminal fate of M*A*S*H. Well aware that Brian worshiped him, you savaged Alan Alda as a "sanctimonious pill."

Yet the difference was dismayingly good-natured. Brian had a blind spot about Israel, and I was tempted to plant one quiet reference to "Judeo-Nazis" and detonate this affable occasion. Instead I asked him about the subject of his new script, but never got a proper answer because the older girl got chewing gum in her Barbie-blond hair. There was a long maunder about solvents, which Brian put an end to by lopping off the lock with a carving knife, and Louise got a little upset. But that was the single set-piece commotion, and otherwise no one drank too much or took offense; their home was nice, the food was nice, the girls were nice—nice, nice, *nice.*

I disappointed myself by finding our perfectly pleasant lunch with perfectly pleasant people inadequate. Why would I have preferred a fight? Weren't those two girls captivating as could be, so what did it matter that they were eternally interrupting and I had not for the whole afternoon been able to finish a thought? Wasn't I married to a man I loved, so why did something wicked in me wish that Brian had slipped his hand up my skirt when I helped him bring in bowls of Häagen-Dazs from the kitchen? In retrospect, I was quite right to kick myself, too. Just a few years later I'd have paid money for an ordinary, good-spirited family gathering during which the worst thing any of the children got up to was sticking gum in their hair.

You, however, announced boisterously in the lobby, "That was great. I think they're both terrific. We should be sure to have them over soon, if they can get a sitter."

I held my tongue. You would have no time for my nit-picking about how wasn't the luncheon a little bland, didn't you have this feeling like, what's the point, isn't there something flat and plain and doughy about this whole *Father Knows Best* routine when Brian was once (at last I can admit to a guest-room quickie at a party before you and I met) such a hellraiser. It's quite possible that you felt exactly as I did, that this to all appearances successful encounter had felt dumpy and insipid to you as well, but in lieu of another obvious model to aspire to—we were not going to go score a gram of cocaine—you took refuge in denial. These were good people and they had been good to us and we had therefore had a *good time.* To conclude otherwise was frightening, raising the specter of some unnamable quantity without which we could not abide, but which we could not summon on demand, least of all by proceeding in virtuous accordance with an established formula.

You regarded redemption as an act of will. You disparaged people (people like me) for their cussedly nonspecific dissatisfactions, because to fail to embrace the simple fineness of being alive betrayed a weakness of character. You always hated finicky eaters, hypochondriacs, and snobs who turn up their noses at *Terms of Endearment* just because it was popular. Nice eats, nice place, nice folks—what more could I possibly want? Besides, the good life doesn't knock on the door. Joy is a job. So if you believed with sufficient industry that we had had a good time with Brian and Louise in theory, then we would have had a good time in fact. The only hint that in truth you'd found our afternoon laborious was that your enthusiasm was excessive.

As we spun through the revolving doors onto Riverside Drive, I'm sure my disquiet was unformed and fleeting. Later these thoughts would come back to haunt me, though I could not have anticipated that your compulsion to manhandle your unruly, misshapen experience into a tidy box, like someone trying to cram a wild tangle of driftwood into a hard-shell Samsonite suitcase, as well as this sincere confusion of the *is* with the *ought to be*—your heartrending tendency to mistake what you actually had for what you desperately wanted—would produce such devastating consequences.

I proposed that we walk home. On the road for Wing and a Prayer I walked everywhere, and the impulse was second nature.

"It must be six or seven miles to Tribeca!" you objected.

"You'll take a taxi in order to jump rope 7,500 times in front of the Knicks game, but a vigorous walk that gets you where you're going is too exhausting."

"Hell, yes. Everything in its place." Limited to exercise or the strict way you folded your shirts, your regimens were adorable. But in more serious contexts, Franklin, I was less charmed. Orderliness readily slides to conformity over time.

So I threatened to walk home by myself, and that did it; I was leaving for Sweden three days later, and you were greedy for my company. We roistered down the footpath into Riverside Park, where the ginkgoes were in flower, and the sloping lawn was littered with anorexics doing tai chi. Ebullient over getting away from my own friends, I stumbled.

"You're a drunk," you said.

"Two glasses!"

You tsked. "Middle of the day."

"I should have made it three," I said sharply. Your every pleasure rationed except *television*, I wished that sometimes you would let go, as you had in our salad days of courtship, arriving at my door with two pinot noirs, a six of St. Pauli Girl, and a lecherous leer that did not promise to hold off until we'd flossed.

"Brian's kids," I introduced formally. "They make you want one?"

"M-m-maybe. They're cute. Then, I'm not the one who has to stuff the beasties in the sack when they want a cracker, Mr. Bunnikins, and 5 million drinks of water."

I understood. These talks of ours had a gameliness, and your opening play was noncommittal. One of us always got lodged into the role of parental party pooper, and I had rained on the progeny parade in our previous session: A child was loud, messy, constraining, and ungrateful. This time I bid for the more daring role: "At least if I got pregnant, something would *happen*."

"Obviously," you said dryly. "You'd have a baby."

I dragged you down the walkway to the riverfront. "I like the idea of turning the page is all."

"That was inscrutable."

"I mean, we're happy? Wouldn't you say?"

"Sure," you concurred cautiously. "I guess so." For you, our contentment didn't bear scrutiny—as if it were a skittish bird, easily startled, and the moment one of us cried out *Look at that beautiful swan!* it would fly away.

"Well, maybe we're too happy."

"Yeah, I've been meaning to talk to you about that. I wish you could make me a little more miserable."

"Stop it. I'm talking about story. In fairy tales, 'And they lived happily ever after' is the last line."

"Do me a favor: Talk down to me."

Oh, you knew exactly what I meant. Not that happiness is dull. Only that it doesn't tell well. And one of our consuming diversions as we age is to recite, not only to others but to ourselves, our own story. I should know; I am in flight from my story every day, and it dogs me like a faithful stray. Accordingly, the one respect in which I depart from my younger self is that I now regard those people who have little or no story to tell themselves as terribly fortunate.

We slowed by the tennis courts in the blaze of April sunlight, pausing to admire a powerful slice backhand through a gap in the green mesh windbreaks. "Everything seems so sorted out," I lamented. "Wing and a Prayer has taken off so that the only thing that could really *happen* to me professionally is for the company to go belly-up. I could always make more money—but I'm a thrift-shop junkie, Franklin, and I don't know what to do with it. Money bores me, and it's starting to change the way we live in a way I'm not totally comfortable with. Plenty of people don't have a kid because they can't afford one. For me it would a relief to find something of consequence to spend it on."

"I'm not of consequence?"

"You don't want enough."

"New jump rope?"

"Ten bucks."

"Well," you conceded, "at least a kid would answer the Big Question."
I could be perverse, too. "What big question?"

"You know," you said lightly, and drew out with an emcee drawl, "the
old *e-e-existential* dilemma."

I did not put my finger on why, but your Big Question left me unmoved. I far preferred my *turn of the page*. "I could always traipse off to a
new country—"

"Any left? You go through countries the way most folks go through
socks."

"Russia," I noted. "But I'm not, for once, threatening to ransom my
life to Aeroflot. Because lately . . . everywhere seems kind of the same.
Countries all have different food, but they all have *food*, know what I
mean?"

"What do you call that? Right! Codswallop."

See, you'd a habit back then of pretending to have no idea what I was
talking about if what I was getting at was at all complicated or subtle.
Later this playing-dumb strategy, which began as gentle teasing, warped
into a darker incapacity to grasp what I was getting at not because it was
abstruse but because it was all too clear and you didn't want it to be so.

Allow me, then, to elucidate: Countries all have different weather, but
they all have weather of some sort, architecture of some sort, a disposition toward burping at the dinner table that regards it as flattering or rude.
Hence, I had begun to attend less to whether one was expected to leave
one's sandals at the door in Morocco than to the constant that, wherever I
was, its culture would have a custom about shoes. It seemed a great deal of
trouble to go to—checking baggage, adapting to new time zones—only
to remain stuck on the old weather-shoes continuum; the continuum itself
had come to feel like a location of sorts, thereby landing me relentlessly in
the same place. Nevertheless, though I would sometimes rant about globalization—I could now buy your favorite chocolate-brown Stove brogans
from Banana Republic in Bangkok—what had really grown monotonous
was the world in my head, what I thought and how I felt and what I said.
The only way my head was going truly somewhere else was to travel to a
different life and not to a different airport.

"Motherhood," I condensed in the park. "Now, that is a foreign country."

On those rare occasions when it seemed as if I might really want to *do it*, you got nervous. "You may be self-satisfied with your success," you said. "Location scouting for Madison Avenue ad clients hasn't brought me to an orgasm of self-actualization."

"All right." I stopped, leaned on the warm wooden rail that fenced the Hudson, and extended my arms on either side to face you squarely. "What's going to *happen*, then? To you, professionally, what are we waiting and hoping for?"

You waggled your head, searching my face. You seemed to discern that I was not trying to impugn your achievements or the importance of your work. This was about something else. "I could scout for feature films instead."

"But you've always said that's the same job: You find the canvas, someone else paints the scene. And ads pay better."

"Married to Mrs. Moneybags, that doesn't matter."

"It does to you." Your maturity about my vastly outearning you had its limits.

"I've considered trying something else altogether."

"So, what, you'll get all fired up to start your own restaurant?"

You smiled. "They never make it."

"Exactly. You're too practical. Maybe you will do something different, but it'll be pretty much on the same *plane*. And I'm talking about topography. Emotional, narrative topography. We live in Holland. And sometimes I get a hankering for Nepal."

Since other New Yorkers were so driven, you could have been injured that I didn't regard you as ambitious. But one of the things you were practical about was yourself, and you didn't take offense. You were ambitious—for your life, what it was like when you woke up in the morning, and not for some attainment. Like most people who did not answer a particular calling from an early age, you placed work beside yourself; any occupation would fill up your day but not your heart. I liked that about you. I liked it enormously.

We started walking again, and I swung your hand. "Our parents will die soon," I resumed. "In fact, one by one everyone we know will start pitching their mortal coils in the drink. We'll get old, and at some point you're losing more friends than you make. Sure, we can go on holidays, finally giving in to suitcases with wheelies. We can eat more foods and slug more wines and have more sex. But—and don't take this wrong—I'm worried that it all starts getting a little tired."

"One of us could always get pancreatic cancer," you said pleasantly.

"Yeah. Or run your pickup into a concrete mixer, and the plot thickens. But that's my point. Everything I can think of happening to us from now on—not, you know, we get an affectionate postcard from France, but really happen-happen—is awful."

You kissed my hair. "Pretty morbid for such a gorgeous day."

For a few steps we walked in a half embrace, but our strides clashed; I settled for hooking your belt loop with my forefinger. "You know that euphemism, *she's expecting*? It's apt. The birth of a baby, so long as it's healthy, is something to look forward to. It's a good thing, a big, good, huge event. And from thereon in, every good thing that happens to them happens to you, too. Of course, bad things, too," I added hurriedly, "but also, you know, first steps, first dates, first places in sack races. Kids, they graduate, they marry, they have kids themselves—in a way, you get to do everything twice. Even if our kid had problems," I supposed idiotically, "at least they wouldn't be our same old problems . . . "

Enough. Recounting this dialogue is breaking my heart.

Looking back, maybe my saying that I wanted more "story" was all by way of alluding to the fact that I wanted someone else to love. We never said such things outright; we were too shy. And I was nervous of ever intimating that you weren't enough for me. In fact, now that we're parted I wish I had overcome my own bashfulness and had told you more often how falling in love with you was the most astonishing thing that ever happened to me. Not just the falling, either, the trite and finite part, but being in love. Every day we spent apart, I would conjure that wide warm chest of yours, its pectoral hillocks firm and mounded from your daily 100 push-ups, the clavicle valley into which I could nestle the crown of my head on those glorious mornings that I did not have to catch a plane. Sometimes I would hear you call my name from around a corner—"Ee-VA!"—often irascible, curt, demanding, calling me to heel because I was yours, like a *dog*, Franklin! But I was yours and I didn't resent it and I wanted you to make that claim: "Eeeeeee-VAH!" always the emphasis on the second syllable, and there were some evenings I could hardly answer because my throat had closed with a rising lump. I would have to stop slicing apples for a crumble at the counter because a film had formed over my eyes and the kitchen had gone all liquid and wobbly and if I kept on slicing I would cut myself. You always shouted at me when I cut myself, it made you furious, and the irrationality of that anger would almost beguile me into doing it again.

I never, ever took you for granted. We met too late for that; I was nearly thirty-three by then, and my past without you was too stark and insistent for me to find the miracle of companionship ordinary. But after I'd survived for so long on the scraps from my own emotional table, you spoiled me with a daily banquet of complicitous what-an-asshole looks at parties, surprise bouquets for no occasion, and fridge-magnet notes that always signed off "XXXX, Franklin." You made me greedy. Like any addict worth his salt, I wanted more. And I was curious. I wondered how it felt when it was a piping voice calling, "Momm-MEEE?" from around that same corner. You started it—like someone who gives you a gift of a single carved ebony elephant, and suddenly you get this idea that it might be fun to start a *collection*.

Eva

P.S. (3:40 A.M.)

I've been trying to go cold turkey on sleeping pills, if only because I know you'd disapprove of my using them. But without the pills I keep tossing. I'll be worthless at Travel R Us tomorrow, but I wanted to get down another memory from that period.

Remember having soft-shell crabs with Eileen and Belmont at the loft? That evening *was* wanton. Even you threw caution to the winds and lurched up for the raspberry brandy at 2 A.M. With no interruptions to admire dolly outfits, no tomorrow is a *school day*, we gorged on fruit and sorbet and splashed immoderate second shots of clear, heady framboise, whooping at each others' top-this tales in the orgy of eternal adolescence characteristic of the childless in middle age.

We all talked about our parents—rather to their collective detriment, I'm afraid. We staged an unofficial contest of sorts: whose parents were the most bonkers. You were at a disadvantage; your parents' uninflected New England stoicism was difficult to parody. By contrast, my mother's ingenious contrivances for avoiding leaving the house made for great hilarity, and I even managed to explain the private joke between me and my brother Giles about "It's very convenient"—the catchphrase in our family for "They deliver." In those days (before he was reluctant to let his children anywhere near me), I had only to say "It's very convenient" to Giles, and he guffawed. By the wee-smalls I could say "It's very *convenient*" to Eileen and Belmont and they cracked up, too.

Neither of us could compete with that interracial vaudeville team of been-around-the-block bohemians. Eileen's mother was schizophrenic, her father a professional cardsharp; Belmont's mother was a former prostitute who still dressed like Bette Davis in *Whatever Happened to Baby Jane?* and his father was a semifamous jazz drummer who had played with Dizzy Gillespie. I sensed that they'd told these stories before, but as a consequence they told them very well, and after so much chardonnay to wash down a feast of crabs I laughed until I wept. Once I considered bending the conversation toward this monstrous decision you and I were trying to make, but Eileen and Belmont were at least ten years older, and I wasn't sure childless by choice; raising the matter might have been unkind.

They didn't leave until almost 4 A.M. And make no mistake: On this occasion I'd had a wonderful time. It was one of those rare evenings that had proved worth the bustle of rushing to the fish market and chopping all that fruit, and that should even have been worth cleaning up the kitchen, dusty with dredging flour and sticky with mango peel. I could see being a little let down that the night was over, or a little heavy with too much booze, whose giddy effects had peaked, leaving only an unsteadiness on my feet and a difficulty in focusing when I needed to concentrate on not dropping the wine glasses. But that wasn't why I felt dolorous.

"So quiet," you noticed, stacking plates. "Beat?"

I noshed on a lone crab claw that had fallen off in the skillet. "We must have spent what, four, five hours, talking about our parents."

"So? If you feel guilty about bad-mouthing your mother, you're looking at penance until 2025. It's one of your favorite sports."

"I know it is. That's what bothers me."

"She couldn't hear you. And no one around that table assumed that because you think she's funny you don't also think she's tragic. Or that you don't love her." You added, "In your way."

"But when she dies, we won't, I won't be able to carry on like that. It won't be possible to be so scathing, not without feeling traitorous."

"Pillory the poor woman while you can, then."

"But should we be talking about our parents, for hours, at this age?"

"What's the problem? You were laughing so hard you must have wet yourself."

"I had this image, after they left—the four of us, all in our eighties with liver spots, still boozing it up, still telling the same stories. Maybe tinged with affection or regret since they'd be dead, but still talking about weird Mom and Dad. Isn't it a little pathetic?"

"You'd rather anguish over El Salvador."

"It's not that—"

"—Or dole out cultural after-dinner mints: Belgians are rude, Thais disapprove of groping in public, and Germans are obsessed with shit."

The tinge of bitterness in such jibes had been on the increase. My hard-won anthropological nuggets apparently served as reminders that I'd gone on an adventure abroad while you were searching suburban New Jersey for a tumbledown garage for Black and Decker. I might have snapped that I was sorry my travel stories bored you, but you were mostly teasing, it was late, and I wasn't in the mood to scrap.

"Don't be silly," I said. "I'm like everyone else: I love to talk about other people. Not *peoples*. People I know, people close to me—people who drive me crazy. But I feel as if I'm using my family up. My father was killed before I was born; one brother and one mom make for pretty slim pickings. Honestly, Franklin, maybe we should have a kid just to have something else to talk about."

"Now *that*," you clanged the spinach pan in the sink, "is frivolous."

I stayed your hand. "It's not. What we talk about is what we think about, is what our lives are about. I'm not sure I want to spend mine looking over my shoulder at a generation whose lineage I'm personally helping to truncate. There's something nihilistic about not having children, Franklin. As if you don't believe in the whole human *thing*. If everyone followed our lead, the species would disappear in a hundred years."

"Get out," you jeered. "Nobody has kids to perpetuate the species."

"Maybe not consciously. But it's only been since about 1960 that we've been able to decide without joining a nunnery. Besides, after nights like this, there might be poetic justice in having grown kids talking for hours to their friends about *me*."

How we shelter ourselves! For the prospect of such scrutiny clearly appealed to me. *Wasn't Mom pretty? Wasn't Mom brave? Gosh, she went to all those scary countries all by herself!* These flashes of my children's late-night meditations on their mother were gauzy with the very adoration so signally absent from my savage dissection of my own mother. Try, *Isn't Mom pretentious? Isn't her nose huge? And those travel guides she grinds out are sooooo booooooring.* Worse, the deadly accuracy of filial faultfinding is facilitated by access, by trust, by willing disclosure, and so constitutes a double betrayal.

Yet even in retrospect this craving for "something else to talk about" seems far from frivolous. Indeed, I may have first been enticed into the notion of giving pregnancy a go by these tempting little imaginative packages like movie previews: of opening the front door to the boy on whom my daughter (I confess I always imagined a daughter) has her first crush, soothing his awkwardness with easy banter, and assessing him endlessly—playfully, ruthlessly—once he is gone. My yearning to stay up late with Eileen and Belmont for once ruminating about young people whose lives lay before them—who made *new* stories, about which I would have *new* opinions, and whose fabric was not threadbare from retelling—was real enough, it wasn't flip.

Oh, but it never entered my head what, once I was finally provided my coveted fresh subject matter, I would have to say. Much less could I foresee the aching O. Henry irony that in lighting upon my consuming new topic of conversation, I would lose the man that I most wanted to talk to.

Dear Franklin,

This carnival in Florida shows no signs of picking up stakes. The office is up in arms about some state official who wears a lot of makeup, and a number of my overwrought coworkers are predicting a "constitutional crisis." Although I haven't followed the details, I doubt that. What strikes me as people in diners rail at each other at the counter when before they ate in silence is not how imperiled they feel, but how safe. Only a country that feels invulnerable can afford political turmoil as entertainment.

But having come so close to extermination within living memory (I know you're tired of hearing about it), few Armenian Americans share their compatriots' smug sense of security. The very numerics of my own life are apocalyptic. I was born in August 1945, when the spoors of two poisonous mushrooms gave us all a cautionary foretaste of hell. Kevin himself was born during the anxious countdown to 1984—much feared, you'll recall; though I scoffed at folks who took George Orwell's arbitrary title to heart, those digits did usher in an era of tyranny for me. *Thursday* itself took place in 1999, a year widely mooted beforehand as the end of the world. And wasn't it.

Since I last wrote, I've been rooting around in my mental attic for my original reservations about motherhood. I do recall a tumult of fears, though all the wrong ones. Had I catalogued the downsides of parenthood, "son might turn out killer" would never have turned up on the list. Rather, it might have looked something like this:

1. Hassle.
2. Less time just the two of us. (Try *no* time just the two of us.)

3. Other people. (PTA meetings. Ballet teachers. The kid's insufferable friends and their insufferable parents.)

4. Turning into a cow. (I was slight, and preferred to stay that way. My sister-in-law had developed bulging varicose veins in her legs during pregnancy that never retreated, and the prospect of calves branched in blue tree roots mortified me more than I could say. So I didn't say. I am vain, or once was, and one of my vanities was to feign that I was not.)

5. Unnatural altruism: being forced to make decisions in accordance with what was best for someone else. (I'm a pig.)

6. Curtailment of my traveling. (Note *curtailment*. Not *conclusion*.)

7. Dementing boredom. (I found small children brutally dull. I did, even at the outset, admit this to myself.)

8. Worthless social life. (I had never had a decent conversation with a friend's five-year-old in the room.)

9. Social demotion. (I was a respected entrepreneur. Once I had a toddler in tow, every man I knew—every woman, too, which is depressing—would take me less seriously.)

10. Paying the piper. (Parenthood repays a debt. But who wants to pay a debt she can escape? Apparently, the childless get away with something sneaky. Besides, what good is repaying a debt to the wrong party? Only the most warped mother could feel rewarded for her trouble by the fact that at last her daughter's life is hideous, too.)

Those, as best I can recall, are the pygmy misgivings I weighed beforehand, and I've tried not to contaminate their dumbfounding naïveté with what actually happened. Clearly, the reasons to remain barren—and what a devastating word—were all petty inconveniences and trifling sacrifices. They were selfish and mean and small-minded, so that anyone compiling such a catalogue who still chose to retain her tidy, airless, static, dead-end, desiccated family-free life was not only short-sighted but a terrible person.

Yet as I contemplate that list now it strikes me that, however damning, the conventional reservations about parenthood are practical. After all, now that children don't till your fields or take you in when you're incontinent, there is no sensible reason to have them, and it's amazing that with the advent of effective contraception anyone chooses to reproduce at all. By contrast, love, story, content, faith in the human "thing"—the modern incentives are like dirigibles, immense, floating, and few; optimistic, large-hearted, even profound, but ominously ungrounded.

For years I'd been awaiting that overriding urge I'd always heard about, the narcotic pining that draws childless women ineluctably to strangers' strollers in parks. I wanted to be drowned by the hormonal imperative, to wake one day and throw my arms around your neck, reach down for you, and pray that while that black flower bloomed behind my eyes you had just left me with child. (*With child:* There's a lovely warm sound to that expression, an archaic but tender acknowledgment that for nine months you have company wherever you go. *Pregnant*, by contrast, is heavy and bulging and always sounds to my ear like bad news: "I'm *pregnant*." I instinctively picture a sixteen-year-old at the dinner table—pale, unwell, with a scoundrel of a boyfriend—forcing herself to blurt out her mother's deepest fear.)

Whatever the trigger, it never entered my system, and that made me feel cheated. When I hadn't gone into maternal heat by my mid-thirties, I worried that there was something wrong with me, something missing. By the time I gave birth to Kevin at thirty-seven, I had begun to anguish over whether, by not simply accepting this defect, I had amplified an incidental, perhaps merely chemical deficiency into a flaw of Shakespearean proportions.

So what finally pulled me off the fence? You, for starters. For if *we* were happy, you weren't, not quite, and I must have known that. There was a hole in your life that I couldn't quite fill. You had work, and it suited you. Nosing into undiscovered stables and armories, searching out a field that had to be edged with a split-rail fence and sport a cherry-red silo and black-and-white cows (Kraft—whose cheese-food slices were made with "real milk"), you made your own hours, your own vista. You liked location scouting. But you didn't love it. Your passion was for people, Franklin. So when I saw you playing with Brian's children, nuzzling them with monkey puppets and admiring their wash-off tattoos, I yearned to provide you opportunity for the ardor that I myself once found in A Wing and a Prayer—or, as you would say, AWAP.

I remember once you tried to express, haltingly, what was not like you; not the sentiment, not the language. You were always uncomfortable with the rhetoric of emotion, which is quite a different matter from discomfort with emotion itself. You feared that too much examination could bruise the feelings, like the well-meaning but brutish handling of a salamander by big, clumsy hands.

We were in bed, still in that vaulting Tribeca loft whose creaky hand-worked elevator was forever breaking down. Cavernous, sifting with dust, undifferentiated into civilized cubicles with end tables, the loft always re-minded me of the private hideout my brother and I had fashioned from corrugated iron in Racine. You and I had made love, and I was just swoon-ing off into sleep when I sat bolt upright. I had to catch a plane for Madrid in ten hours' time and had forgotten to set the alarm. Once I'd ad-justed the clock, I noticed you were on your back. Your eyes were open.

"What is it?"

You sighed. "I don't know how you do it." As I nestled back to bask in another paean to my amazing adventurousness and courage, you must have sensed my mistake, for you added hastily, "Leave. Leave all the time for so long. Leave *me*."

"But I don't like to."

"I wonder."

"Franklin, I didn't contrive my company to escape your clutches. Don't forget, it predates you."

"Oh, I could hardly forget that."

"It's my job!"

"It doesn't have to be."

I sat up. "Are you—"

"I'm not." You pressed me gently back down; this was not going as you planned, and you had, I could tell, planned it. You rolled over to place your elbows on either side of me and touched your forehead, briefly, to mine. "I'm not trying to take your series away. I know how much it means to you. That's the trouble. The other way around, I couldn't do it. I couldn't get up tomorrow to fly to Madrid and try to discourage you from meeting me at the airport three weeks later. Maybe once or twice. Not over and over."

"You could if you had to."

"Eva. You know and I know. You don't have to."

I twisted. You were so close up; I felt hot, and, between your elbows, caged. "We've been through this—"

"Not often. Your travel guides are a runaway success. You could hire college students to do all the grubbing around in flophouses that you do yourself. They already do most of your research, don't they?"

I was vexed; I'd been through this. "If I don't keep tabs on them, they cheat. They say they've confirmed that a listing is still good, and don't bother and go get slammed. Later it turns out the B&B has changed hands and is riddled with lice, or it's moved to a new location. I get complaints from cross-country cyclists who have ridden a hundred miles to find an insurance office instead of a hard-earned bed. They're furious, as they should be. And without the boss lady looking over their shoulder, some of those students will take kickbacks. AWAP's most valuable asset is its reputation—"

"You could hire someone else to do spot checks, too. So you're going to Madrid tomorrow because you want to. There's nothing awful about that except that I wouldn't, and I couldn't. You know that when you're gone I think about you all the time? On the hour I think about what you're eating, who you're meeting—"

"But I think about you, too!"

You laughed, and the chuckle was congenial; you weren't trying to pick a fight. You released me, rolling onto your back. "Horseshit, Eva. You think about whether the falafel stand on the corner will last through the next update, and how to describe the color of the sky. Fine. But in that case, you must feel differently about me than I do about you. That's all I'm getting at."

"Are you seriously claiming that I don't love you as much?"

"You don't love me in the same way. It has nothing to do with degree. There's something—you save out," you groped. "Maybe I envy that. It's like a reserve tank or something. You walk out of here, and this other source kicks in. You putter around Europe, or Malaysia, until it finally runs low and you come home."

Yet in truth what you had described was closer to my pre-Franklin self. I was once an efficient little unit, like one of those travel toothbrushes that folds into a box. I know I tend to over-romanticize those times, though in the early days especially I had a fire under me. I was a kid, really. I'd initially gotten the idea for Wing and a Prayer halfway through my own first

trip to Europe, for which I'd brought way too little cash. This notion of a
bohemian travel guide gave me a sense of purpose in what was otherwise
disintegrating into one long cup of coffee, and from then on I went everywhere with a tattered notebook, recording rates for single rooms, whether
they had hot water or the staff spoke any English or the toilets backed up.

It's easy to forget, now that AWAP has attracted so much competition, but in the mid-sixties globe-trotters were pretty much at the mercy
of *The Blue Guide*, whose target audience was middle-aged and middle class.
In 1966, when the first edition of *Western Europe on a Wing and a Prayer* went
into a second printing almost overnight, I realized that I was onto something. I like to portray myself as shrewd, but we both know I was lucky. I
couldn't have anticipated the backpacking craze, and I wasn't enough of an
amateur demographer to have taken deliberate advantage of all those restless baby boomers coming of age at once, all on Daddy's dime in an era of
prosperity, but all optimistic about how far a few hundred dollars would
take them in Italy and desperate for advice on how to make a trip Dad
never wanted them to take in the first place last as long as possible. I
mostly reasoned that the next explorer after me would be scared, the way
I was scared, and nervous of being taken, the way I was sometimes taken,
and if I was willing to get the food poisoning first I could make sure that
at least our novice wayfarer didn't stay up heaving on that first electric
night overseas. I don't mean that I was benevolent, only that I wrote the
guide that I wished I'd been able to use myself.

You're rolling your eyes. This lore is shopworn, and maybe it's inevitable that the very things that first attract you to someone are the same
things with which you later grow irritated. Bear with me.

You know that I was always horrified by the prospect of turning out
like my mother. Funny, Giles and I only learned the term "agoraphobic"
in our thirties, and I've always been perplexed by its strict definition,
which I've looked up more than once: "fear of open or public spaces."
Not, from what I could tell, an apt description of her complaint. My
mother wasn't afraid of football stadiums, she was afraid to leave the
house, and I got the impression she was just as panicked by enclosed
spaces as by open ones, so long as the enclosed space did not happen to be
137 Enderby Avenue in Racine, Wisconsin. But there doesn't seem to be a

word for that (Enderbyphilia?), and at least when I refer to my mother as agoraphobic, people seem to understand that she orders in.

Jesus that's ironic, I've heard more times than I can count. *With all the places you've been?* Other people savor the symmetry of apparent opposites.

But let me be candid. I *am* much like my mother. Maybe it's because as a child I was always running errands for which I was too young and that therefore daunted me; I was sent out to locate new gaskets for the kitchen sink when I was eight years old. In pushing me to be her emissary while I was still so small, my mother managed to reproduce in me the same disproportionate anguish about minor interactions with the outside world that she herself felt at thirty-two.

I can't recall a single trip abroad that, up against it, I have truly wanted to take, that I haven't in some way dreaded and wanted desperately to get out of. I was repeatedly forced out the door by a conspiracy of previous commitments: the ticket purchased, the taxi ordered, a host of reservations confirmed, and just to box myself in a little further I would always have talked up the journey to friends, before florid farewells. Even on the plane, I'd have been blissfully content for the wide-body to penetrate the stratosphere for all eternity. Landing was agony, finding my first night's bed was agony, though the respite itself—my ad hoc replication of Enderby Avenue—was glorious. At length, I got hooked on this sequence of accelerating terrors culminating in a vertiginous plunge to my adoptive mattress. My whole life I have been making myself do things. I never went to Madrid, Franklin, out of appetite for paella, and every one of those research trips you imagined I used to slip the surly bonds of our domestic tranquillity was really a gauntlet I'd thrown down and compelled myself to pick up. If I was ever glad to have gone, I was never glad to go.

But over the years the aversion grew milder, and surmounting a mere annoyance is not so rich. Once I habituated to rising to my own challenge—to proving repeatedly that I was independent, competent, mobile, and grown-up—gradually the fear inverted: The one thing I dreaded more than another trip to Malaysia was staying home.

So I wasn't only afraid of becoming my mother, but *a* mother. I was afraid of being the steadfast, stationary anchor who provides a jumping-off place for another young adventurer whose travels I might envy and whose future is still unmoored and unmapped. I was afraid of being that archetypal figure in the doorway—frowzy, a little plump—who waves good-bye and blows kisses as a backpack is stashed in the trunk; who dabs her eyes with an apron ruffle in the fumes of departing exhaust; who turns forlornly to twist the latch and wash the too-few dishes by the sink as the silence in the room presses down like a dropped ceiling. More than of leaving, I had developed a horror of being left. How often I had done that to you, stranded you with the baguette crusts of our farewell dinner and swept off to my waiting taxi. I don't believe I ever told you how sorry I was for putting you through all those little deaths of serial desertion, or commended you on constraining expression of your quite justifiable sense of abandonment to the occasional quip.

Franklin, I was *absolutely terrified of having a child.* Before I got pregnant, my visions of child rearing—reading stories about cabooses with smiley faces at bedtime, feeding glop into slack mouths—all seemed like pictures of someone else. I dreaded confrontation with what could prove a closed, stony nature, my own selfishness and lack of generosity, the thick, tarry powers of my own resentment. However intrigued by a "turn of the page," I was mortified by the prospect of becoming hopelessly trapped in someone else's story. And I believe that this terror is precisely what must have snagged me, the way a ledge will tempt one to jump off. The very insurmountability of the task, its very unattractiveness, was in the end what attracted me to it.

Eva

Dear Franklin,

I've settled myself down in a little coffee shop in Chatham, which is why this is handwritten; then, you were always able to decipher my spidery scrawl on postcards, since I gave you a terrible lot of practice. The couple at the next table is having a knockdown drag-out over the application process for absentee ballots in Seminole County—the kind of minutiae that seems to consume the whole country right now, since everyone around me has turned into a procedural pedant. All the same, I bask in their heatedness as before a woodstove. My own apathy is bone chilling.

The Bagel Café is a homey establishment, and I don't think the waitress will mind if I nurse a cup of coffee by my legal pad. Chatham, too, is homey, authentic—with the kind of Middle America quaintness that more well-to-do towns like Stockbridge and Lenox spend a great deal of money to feign. Its railroad station still receives trains. The commercial main drag sports the traditional lineup of secondhand bookstores (full of those Loren Estleman novels you devoured), bakeries with burnt-edged bran muffins, charity consignment shops, a cinema whose marquee says "theatre" on the parochial presumption that British spelling is more sophisticated, and a liquor store that, along with Taylor magnums for the locals, stocks some surprisingly pricey California zinfandels for out-of-towners. Manhattan residents with second homes keep this disheveled hamlet alive now that most local industries have closed—these summer folk and, of course, the new correctional facility on the outskirts of town.

I was thinking about you on the drive up, if that doesn't go without saying. By way of counterpoint, I was trying to picture the kind of man I assumed I'd end up with before we met. The vision was doubtless a composite of the on-the-road boyfriends you always rode me about. Some of my romantic blow-ins were sweet, though whenever a woman describes a man as *sweet*, the dalliance is doomed.

If that assortment of cameo companions in Arles or Tel Aviv was anything to go by (sorry—"the losers"), I was destined to settle down with a stringy cerebral type whose skittering metabolism burns chickpea concoctions at a ferocious rate. Sharp elbows, prominent Adam's apple, narrow wrists. A strict vegetarian. An anguished sort who reads Nietzsche and wears spectacles, alienated from his time and contemptuous of the automobile. An avid cyclist and hill walker. Professional marginalia—perhaps a potter, with a love of hardwoods and herb gardens, whose aspirations to an unpretentious life of physical toil and lingering sunsets on a porch are somewhat belied by the steely, repressed rage with which he pitches disappointing vases into an oil drum. A weakness for weed; brooding. An understated but ruthless sense of humor; a dry, distant laugh. Back massages. Recycling. Sitar music and a flirtation with Buddhism that is mercifully behind him. Vitamins and cribbage, water filters and French films. A pacifist with three guitars but no TV, and unpleasant associations with team sports from a picked-on childhood. A hint of vulnerability in the receding hairline at the temples; a soft, dark ponytail whisping down the spine. A sallow, olive complexion, almost sickly. Tender, whispering sex. Curious carved wooden talisman thonged around the neck that he will neither explain nor take off, even in the bath. Diaries that I mustn't read, pasted up with sick squib clippings that illustrate what a terrible world we live in. ("Grisly Find: Police found assorted bits of a man's body, including a pair of hands and two legs, in six luggage lockers in Tokyo's central railway station. After inspecting all 2,500 coin lockers, police found a pair of buttocks in a black plastic garbage bag.") A cynic about mainstream politics with an unabating ironic detachment from popular culture. And most of all? With fluent if prettily accented English, a *foreigner*.

We would live in the countryside—in Portugal, or a little village in Central America—where a farm up the road sells raw milk, fresh-churned sweet butter, and fat, seedy pumpkins. Our stone cottage would writhe with creepers, its window boxes blushing red geraniums, and we would bake chewy ryes and carrot brownies for our rustic neighbors. An overeducated man, my fantasy partner would still root about the soil of our idyll for the seeds of his own discontent. And surrounded by natural bounty, grow spitefully ascetic.

Are you chuckling yet? Because then along came you. A big, broad meat eater with brash blond hair and ruddy skin that burns at the beach. A bundle of appetites. A full, boisterous guffaw; a man who tells knock-knock jokes. Hot dogs—not even East 86th Street bratwurst, but mealy, greasy pig guts of that terrifying pink. Baseball. Gimme caps. Puns and blockbuster movies, raw tap water and six-packs. A fearless, trusting consumer who only reads labels to make sure there are plenty of additives. A fan of the open road with a passion for his pickup who thinks bicycles are for nerds. Fucks hard and talks dirty; a private though unapologetic taste for porn. Mysteries, thrillers, and science fiction; a subscription to *National Geographic*. Barbecues on the Fourth of July and intentions, in the fullness of time, to take up *golf*. Delights in crappy snack foods of every description: Burgles. Curlies. Cheesies. Squigglies—you're laughing, but I don't eat them—anything that looks less like food than packing material and at least six degrees of separation from the farm. Bruce Springsteen, the early albums, cranked up high with the truck window down and your hair flying. Sings along, off-key—how is it possible that I should be endeared by such a tin ear? Beach Boys. Elvis—never lost your roots, did you, loved plain old rock and roll. Bombast. Though not impossibly stodgy; I remember, you took a shine to Pearl Jam, which was exactly when Kevin went off them . . . (sorry). It just had to be noisy; you hadn't any time for my Elgar, my Leo Kottke, though you made an exception for Aaron Copeland. You wiped your eyes brusquely at Tanglewood, as if to clear gnats, hoping I didn't notice that "Quiet City" made you cry. And ordinary, obvious pleasures: the Bronx Zoo and the Botanical Gardens, the Coney Island roller coaster, the Staten Island ferry, the Empire State Building. You were the only New Yorker I'd ever met who'd actually taken the ferry to the Statue of Liberty. You dragged me along once, and we were the only tourists on the boat who spoke English. Representational art—Edward Hopper. And my lord, Franklin, a *Republican*. A belief in a strong defense but otherwise small government and low taxes. Physically, too, you were such a surprise—yourself a strong defense. There were times you worried that I thought you too heavy, I made so much of your size, though you weighed in at a pretty standard 165, 170, always battling those five pounds' worth of cheddar widgets that would settle over your belt. But to me you were *enormous.* So sturdy and solid, so wide, so thick, none of that delicate wristy business of my imaginings. Built like an oak tree, against which I could pitch my pillow and read; mornings, I could curl into the crook of your branches. How lucky we are, when we're spared what we think we want! How weary I might have grown of all those silly pots and fussy diets, and how I detest the whine of sitar music!

But the biggest surprise of all was that I married an *American.* Not just any American either, a man who happened to be American. No, you were American by choice as well as by birth. You were, in fact, a patriot. I had never met one before. Rubes, yes. Blind, untraveled, ignorant people who thought the United States was the whole world, so to say anything against it was like decrying the universe, or air. Instead, you had been a few places—Mexico, one disastrous trip to Italy with a woman whose cornucopia of allergies included tomatoes—and had decided that you liked your own country. No, that you *loved* your own country, its smoothness and efficiency, its practicality, its broad, unpretentious accents and emphasis on honesty. I would say—I did say—that you were enamored of an archaic version of the U.S., either an America that was long past or that never was; that you were enamored of an idea. And you would say—did say—that part of what America was was an idea, and that was more than most countries could claim, which were mostly scrappy pasts and circumscriptions on a map. It was a fine, it was a beautiful idea, too, you said, and you pointed out—I granted you this—that a nation that aimed to preserve above all the ability of its citizens to do pretty much whatever they wanted was exactly the sort of place that should have captivated the likes of me. But it hasn't worked out that way, I'd object, and you'd counter, better than anywhere else, and we would be off.

It is true that I grew disenchanted. But I would still like to thank you for introducing me to my own country. Wasn't that how we met? We'd decided at AWAP to run those advertisements in *Mother Jones* and *Rolling Stone,* and when I was vague about the photos we wanted, Young & Rubicam had you stop in. You showed up at my office in a flannel shirt and dusty jeans, a beguiling impertinence. I tried so hard to be professional, because your shoulders were distracting. France, I supposed. The Rhone Valley. And then I dithered over the expense—sending you over, putting you up. You laughed. Don't be ridiculous, you dismissed. I can find you the Rhone Valley in Pennsylvania. Which indeed you did.

Hitherto, I had always regarded the United States as a place to leave. After you brazenly asked me out—an executive with whom you had a business relationship—you goaded me to admit that had I been born elsewhere, the U.S. of A. was perhaps the first country I would make a beeline to visit: whatever else I might think of it, the place that called the shots and pulled the strings, that made the movies and sold the Coca-Cola and shipped *Star Trek* all the way to Java; the center of the action, a country that you needed a relationship with even if that relationship was hostile; a country that demanded if not acceptance at least rejection—anything but neglect. The country in every other country's face, that would visit you whether you liked it or not almost anywhere on the planet. Okay, okay, I protested. *Okay.* I would visit.

So I visited. In those early days, remember your recurrent astonishment? That I had never been to a baseball game. Or to Yellowstone. Or the Grand Canyon. I sneered at them, but I had never eaten a McDonald's hot apple pie. (I confess: I liked it.) Someday, you observed, there would be no McDonald's. Just because there are lots of them doesn't mean that the hot apple pies aren't excellent or that it isn't a privilege to live in a time when you can buy them for 99 cents. That was one of your favorite themes: that profusion, replication, popularity wasn't necessarily devaluing, and that time itself made all things rare. You loved to savor the present tense and were more conscious than anyone I have ever met that its every constituent is fleeting.

And that was your perspective on your country as well: that it was not forever. That of course it was an empire, though that was nothing to be ashamed of. History is made of empires, and the United States was by far and away the greatest, richest, and fairest empire that had ever dominated the earth. Inevitably, it would fall. Empires always did. But we were lucky, you said. We got to participate in the most fascinating social experiment ever attempted. Sure it was imperfect, you would add, with the same hastiness with which I observed before Kevin was born that of course some children "had problems." But you said that if the U.S. were to fall or founder during your lifetime, collapse economically, be overrun by an aggressor, or corrupt from within into something vicious, you would weep.

I believe you would. But I sometimes considered during those days you were carting me off to the Smithsonian, needling me to recite the presidents in order, grilling me on the causes of the Haymarket Riots, that I wasn't visiting the country, quite. I was visiting *your* country. The one you had made for yourself, the way a child constructs a log cabin out of Popsicle sticks. It was a lovely reproduction, too. Even now, when I glimpse snippets of the Preamble to the Constitution, *We, the people* . . . , the hair raises on the back of my neck. Because I hear your voice. The Declaration of Independence, *We hold these truths*—your voice.

Irony. I have thought about you and irony. It always got your back up when my friends from Europe would come through and dismiss our countrymen as "having no sense of irony." Yet (ironically) in the latter twentieth century, irony was huge in the U.S., painfully so. In fact, I was sick of it, though I didn't realize that until we met. Coming into the eighties, everything was "retro," and there was an undercurrent of snideness, a distancing in all those fifties diners with chrome stools and oversized root-beer floats. Irony means at once having and not having. Irony involves a prissy dabbling, a disavowal. We had friends whose apartments were completely tricked out in sardonic kitsch—pickaninny dolls, framed advertisements for Kellogg's cornflakes from the twenties ("Look at the bowlfuls go!")—who owned nothing that wasn't a joke.

You wouldn't live that way. Oh, to have "no sense of irony" was supposedly to not know what it was—to be a moron—to have no sense of humor. And you knew what it was. You laughed, a little, at the lamp-bearing cast-iron black jockey that Belmont picked up for their hearth, to be polite. You got the joke. You just didn't think it was that funny, really, and in your own life you wanted objects that were truly beautiful and not just a laugh. Such a bright man, you were sincere by design and not merely by nature, *American* by personal fiat, and you would embrace all that was good in that. Is it called naïveté when you're naive on purpose? You would go on picnics. You would take conventional vacations to national monuments. You would sing *O'er the la-and of the free!* at the top of your tuneless voice at Mets games, and never with a smirk. The United States, you claimed, was on the existential cutting edge. It was a country whose prosperity was without precedence, where virtually everyone had enough to eat; a country that strove for justice and offered up nearly every entertainment and sport, every religion, ethnicity, occupation, and political affiliation to be had, with a wild wealth of landscapes, of flora and fauna and weather. If it was not possible to have a fine, rich, sumptuous life in this country, with a beautiful wife and a healthy, growing boy, then it was not possible anywhere. And even now, I believe that you may be right. But that it may not be possible anywhere.

9 P.M. (BACK HOME)

The waitress was tolerant, but the Bagel Café was closing. And print out may be impersonal, but it's easier on the eye. For that matter, I worry that throughout that handwritten passage you've been skimming, reading ahead. I worry that the instant you spotted "Chatham" up top you could think of nothing else, and that you for once couldn't care less about my feelings for the United States. *Chatham. I go to Chatham?*

I do. I go at every opportunity. Fortunately, these journeys every two weeks up to Claverack Juvenile Correctional Facility are aimed at such a restrictive window of visiting hours that I am not free to consider going an hour later or another day. I leave at exactly 11:30 because it is the first Saturday of the month and I must arrive immediately after the second lunch slot at 2:00. I do not indulge myself in reflection over how much I dread going to see him, or, more improbably, look forward to it. I just go.

You're astonished. You shouldn't be. He's my son, too, and a mother should visit her child in prison. I have no end of failings as a mother, but I have always followed the rules. If anything, following the letter of the unwritten parental law was one of my failings. That came out in the trial—the civil suit. I was appalled by how upstanding I looked on paper. Vince Mancini, Mary's lawyer, accused me in court of visiting my son so dutifully in detention during his own trial only because I anticipated being sued for parental negligence. I was acting a part, he claimed, going through the motions. Of course, the trouble with jurisprudence is that it cannot accommodate subtleties. Mancini was onto something. There may indeed be an element of theater in these visits. But they continue when no one is watching, because if I am trying to prove that I am a good mother, I am proving this, dismally, as it happens, to myself.

Kevin himself has been surprised by my dogged appearances, which is not to say, in the beginning at least, pleased. Back in 1999, at sixteen, he was still at that age when to be seen with your mother was embarrassing; how bittersweetly these truisms about teenagers persist through the most adult of troubles. And in those first few visits he seemed to regard my very presence as an accusation, so before I said a single word he'd get angry. It didn't seem sensible that *he* should be the one mad at *me*.

But in the same vein, when a car nearly sideswipes me in a crosswalk, I've noticed that the driver is frequently furious—shouting, gesticulating, cursing—at me, whom he nearly ran over and who had the undisputed right of way. This is a dynamic particular to encounters with male drivers, who seem to grow all the more indignant the more completely they are in the wrong. I think the emotional reasoning, if you can call it that, is transitive: You make me feel bad; feeling bad makes me mad; ergo, you make me mad. If I'd had the presence back then to seize on the first part of that proof, I might have glimpsed in Kevin's instantaneous dudgeon a glimmer of hope. But at the time, his fury simply mystified me. It seemed so unfair. Women tend more toward chagrin, and not only in traffic. So I blamed me, and he blamed me. I felt ganged up on.

Hence, when he was first incarcerated we didn't have conversations as such. Simply being in front of him made me limp. He sapped me even of the energy to cry, which anyway would not have been very productive. After five minutes, I might ask him, my voice hoarse, about the food. He would gawk at me incredulously, as if under the circumstances the inquiry were as inane as it actually was. Or I'd ask, "Are they treating you all right?" although I wasn't sure what that meant or even whether I *wanted* his minders to treat him "all right." He'd slur that *sure they kiss me beddy-bye every night.* It didn't take long for me to run out of pro forma Mommy questions, for which I think we were both relieved.

If it took little time to get past my posing as the loyal mother who's only concerned that sonny is eating his vegetables, we are still contending with Kevin's more impenetrable pose as the sociopath who is beyond reach. The trouble is, while my role as a mother who stands by her son no matter what is ultimately demeaning—it is mindless, irrational, blind, and sappy, hence a part I might gratefully shed—Kevin gets too much sustenance from his own cliché to let it go quietly. He still seems intent on demonstrating to me that he may have been a subjugant in my house who had to clean his plate, but now he's a celebrity who's been on the cover of *Newsweek*, whose fricative appellation, *Kevin Khatchadourian*—or "KK" to the tabloids, like Kenneth Kaunda in Zambia—has tsked chidingly off every major network news anchor's tongue. He's even had a hand in setting the national agenda, sparking new calls for corporal punishment, juvenile death sentences, and the V-chip. In lockup, he would have me know that he is no tinhorn delinquent, but a notorious fiend of whom his less accomplished fellow juveniles are in awe.

Once in those early days (after he'd grown more talkative), I asked him: "How do they regard you, the other boys? Do they . . . are they critical? Of what you did?" This was as close as I could come to asking, do they trip you in hallways or hawk in your soup. At first, you see, I was hesitant, deferential. He frightened me, physically frightened me, and I was desperate not to set him off. There were prison guards nearby, of course, but there had been security personnel in his high school, police in Gladstone, and what good had they been? I never feel protected any more.

Kevin honked, that hard, joyless laugh forced through his nose. And said something like, "Are you kidding? They fucking worship me, Mumsey. There's not a juve in this joint who hasn't taken out fifty dickheads in his *peer group* before breakfast—in his head. I'm the only one with the stones to do it in real life." Whenever Kevin cites "real life," it is with the excessive firmness with which fundamentalists reference heaven or hell. It's as if he's trying to talk himself into something.

I had only his word, of course, that far from being shunned Kevin had achieved a status of mythic proportions among hoods who had merely hijacked cars or knifed rival drug dealers. But I have come to believe he must have once garnered some prestige, since, in his oblique fashion, just this afternoon he allowed that it had begun to ebb.

He said, "Tell you what, I'm fucking tired of telling that same fucking story"—from which I could infer that, rather, his fellow inmates were tired of hearing it. Over a year and a half is a long time for teenagers, and Kevin is already yesterday's news. He's getting old enough to appreciate, too, that one of the differences between a "perp," as they say in cop shows, and your average newspaper reader is that onlookers are allowed the luxury of getting "fucking tired of the same fucking story" and are free to move on. Culprits are stuck in what must be a tyrannical rehearsal of the same old tale. Kevin will be climbing the stairs to the aerobic-conditioning alcove of the Gladstone High gym for the rest of his life.

So he is resentful, and I don't blame him for being bored with his own atrocity already, or for envying others their capacity to abandon it. Today, he went on to grouse about some "pipsqueak" new arrival at Claverack who was only thirteen. Kevin added for my benefit, "His cock's the size of a Tootsie Roll. The little ones, you know?" Kevin wiggled his pinkie. "Three for a quarter." With relish, Kevin explained the boy's claim to fame: An elderly couple in an adjacent apartment had complained about how loudly he played his CDs of the Monkees at three in the morning. The next weekend, the couple's daughter discovered her parents in their bed, slit from crotch to throat.

"That's appalling," I said. "I can't believe anyone still listens to the Monkees."

I earned a begrudging snort. He went on to explain that the police have never found the entrails, which is the detail on which the media, not to mention the boy's overnight Claverack fan club, has seized.

"Your friend's precocious," I said. "The missing entrails—didn't you teach me that to get noticed in this business you have to add a twist?"

You may be horrified, Franklin, but it has taken me the better part of two years to get this far with him, and our black, straight-faced banter passes for progress. But Kevin is still not comfortable with my gameliness. I usurp his lines. And I had made him jealous.

"I don't think he's so smart," said Kevin aloofly. "Probably just looked down at those guts and thought, *Cool! Free sausages!*"

Kevin shot me a furtive glance. My impassivity was clearly a disappointment.

"Everyone around here thinks that twerp's so tough," Kevin resumed. "All like, 'Man, you can play, like, "Sound of Music" loud's you want, I ain't sayin' *nuttin.*'" His *African-American* accent has become quite accomplished and has made inroads into his own. "But I'm not impressed. He's just a kid. Too little to know what he was doing."

"And you weren't?" I asked sharply.

Kevin folded his arms and looked satisfied; I had gone back to playing Mother. "I knew exactly what I was doing." He leaned onto his elbows. "*And I'd do it again.*"

"I can see why," I said primly, gesturing to the windowless room whose walls were paneled in vermilion and chartreuse; I have no idea why they decorate prisons like Romper Room. "It's worked out so well for you."

"Just swapped one shithole for another." He waved his right hand with two extended fingers in a manner that betrayed he's taken up smoking. "Worked out swell."

Subject closed, as usual. Still I made a note of the fact that this thirteen-year-old parvenu's stealing the Claverack limelight aggrieved our son. It seems that you and I needn't have worried about his dearth of ambition.

As for my parting with him today, I had thought to leave it out. But it is just what I would like to withhold from you that I may need most to include.

The guard with a mud-spatter of facial moles had called time; for once we had used up the full hour without spending most of it staring at the clock. We were standing on either side of the table, and I was about to mumble some filler line like "I'll see you in two weeks," when I realized Kevin had been staring straight at me, whereas his every other glance had been sidelong. That stopped me, unnerved me, and made me wonder why I had ever wanted him to look me in the eye.

Once I was no longer fussing with my coat, he said, "You may be fooling the neighbors and the guards and Jesus and your gaga mother with these goody-goody visits of yours, but you're not fooling me. Keep it up if you want a gold star. But don't be dragging your ass back here on my account." Then he added, "Because I hate you."

I know that children say that all the time, in fits: *I hate you, I hate you!* eyes squeezed with tears. But Kevin is approaching eighteen, and his delivery was flat.

I had some idea of what I was supposed to say back: *Now, I know you don't mean that,* when I knew that he did. Or, *I love you anyway, young man, like it or not.* But I had an inkling that it was following just these pat scripts that had helped to land me in a garish overheated room that smelled like a bus toilet on an otherwise lovely, unusually clement December afternoon. So I said instead, in the same informational tone, "I often hate you, too, Kevin," and turned heel.

So you can see why I needed a pick-me-up coffee. It was an effort to resist the bar.

Driving home, I was reflecting that however much I might wish to eschew a country whose citizens, when encouraged to do "pretty much what they want," eviscerate the elderly, it made perfect sense that I would marry another American. I had better reason than most to find foreigners passé, having penetrated their exoticism to the chopped liver they are to one another. Besides, by the time I was thirty-three I was tired, suffering the cumulative exhaustion of standing all day that you only register when you sit down. I was forever myself a foreigner, feverishly rehearsing phrase-book Italian for "basket of bread." Even in England, I had to remember to say "pavement" instead of "sidewalk." Conscious that I was an ambassador of sorts, I would defy a daily barrage of hostile preconceptions, taking care not to be arrogant, pushy, ignorant, presumptuous, crass, or loud in public.

But if I had arrogated to myself the whole planet as my personal backyard, this very effrontery marked me as hopelessly American, as did the fanciful notion that I could remake myself into a tropical internationalist hybrid from the horribly specific origins of Racine, Wisconsin. Even the carelessness with which I abandoned my native land was classically of a piece with our nosy, restless, aggressive people, who all (save you) complacently assume that America is a permanent fixture. Europeans are better clued. They know about the liveness, the contemporariness of history, its immediate rapacities, and will often rush back to tend their own perishable gardens to make sure that Denmark, say, is still there. But to those of us for whom "invasion" is exclusively associated with outer space, our country is an unassailable bedrock that will wait indefinitely intact for our return. Indeed, I had explained my peripatetics more than once to foreigners as facilitated by my perception that "the United States doesn't need me."

It's embarrassing to pick your life partner according to what television shows he watched as a child, but in a way that's exactly what I did. I wanted to describe some wiry, ineffectual little man as a "Barney Fife" without having to tortuously append that Barney was a character in a warm, rarely exported serial called *The Andy Griffith Show*, in which an incompetent deputy was always getting into trouble by dint of his own hubris. I wanted to be able to hum the theme song to *The Honeymooners* and have you chime in with, "How sweet it is!" And I wanted to be able to say "That came out of left field" and not kick myself that baseball images didn't necessarily scan abroad. I wanted to stop having to pretend I was a cultural freak with no customs of my own, to have a house that itself had rules about shoes to which its visitors must conform. You restored to me the concept of home.

Home is precisely what Kevin has taken from me. My neighbors now regard me with the same suspicion they reserve for illegal immigrants. They grope for words and speak to me with exaggerated deliberation, as if to a woman for whom English is a second language. And since I have been exiled to this rarefied class, the mother of one of those "Columbine boys," I, too, grope for words, not sure how to translate my off-world thoughts into the language of two-for-the-price-of-one sales and parking tickets. Kevin has turned me into a foreigner again, in my own country. And maybe this helps to explain these biweekly Saturday visits, because it is only at Claverack Correctional that I need not translate my alien argot into the language of the suburban mundane. It is only at Claverack Correctional that we can make allusions without explanations, that we can take as understood a shared cultural past.

Eva

Dear Franklin,

I'm the one at Travel R Us who volunteers to stay late and finish up, but most of the Christmas flights are booked, and this afternoon we were all encouraged as a "treat" to knock off early, it being Friday. Beginning another desolate marathon in this duplex at barely 5 P.M. makes me close to hysterical.

Propped before the tube, poking at chicken, filling in the easy answers in the *Times* crossword, I often have a nagging sensation of waiting for something. I don't mean that classic business of waiting for your life to begin, like some chump on the starting line who hasn't heard the gun. No, it's waiting for something in particular, for a knock on the door, and the sensation can grow quite insistent. Tonight it's returned in force. Half an ear cocked, something in me, all night, every night, is waiting for you to come home.

Which inevitably puts me in mind of that seminal May evening in 1982, when my expectation that you would walk into the kitchen anytime now was less unreasonable. You were location scouting in the pine barrens of southern New Jersey for a Ford advertisement and were due home about 7:00 P.M. I'd recently returned from a monthlong trip to update *Greece on a Wing and a Prayer*, and when you hadn't shown up by 8:00, I reminded myself that my own plane had been six hours late, which had ruined your plans to sweep me from JFK to the Union Square Café.

Still, by 9:00 I was getting edgy, not to mention hungry. I chewed distractedly on a chunk of pistachio halvah from Athens. On an ethnic roll, I'd made a pan of moussaka, with which I planned to convince you that, nestled against ground lamb with loads of cinnamon, you did like eggplant after all.

By 9:30, the custard topping had started to brown and crust around the edges, even though I'd turned the oven down to 250°. I took out the pan. Balanced on the fulcrum between anger and anguish, I indulged a fit of pique, banging the drawer when I went for the aluminum foil, grumbling about having fried up all those circles of eggplant, and now it was turning into a *big, dry, charred mess!* I yanked my Greek salad out of the fridge and furiously pitted the calamatas, but then left it to wilt on the counter and the balance tipped. I couldn't be mad anymore. I was petrified. I checked that both phones were on the hook. I confirmed that the elevator was working, though you could always take the stairs. Ten minutes later, I checked the phones again.

This is why people smoke, I thought.

When the phone did ring at around 10:20, I pounced. At my mother's voice, my heart sank. I told her tersely that you were over three hours late, and I mustn't tie up the line. She was sympathetic, a rare sentiment from my mother, who then tended to regard my life as one long accusation, as if the sole reason I ventured to yet another country was to rub her nose in the fact that for one more day she had not left her porch. I should have remembered that she, too, had been through this very experience at twenty-three, and not for hours but for weeks, until a slim envelope flipped through her front door slot from the War Department. Instead I was cruelly rude, and hung up.

Ten-forty. Southern New Jersey wasn't perilous—timber and farmland, not like Newark. But there were cars like primed missiles, and drivers whose stupidity was murderous. *Why didn't you call?*

That was before the advent of mobile phones, so I'm not blaming you. And I realize this experience is common as dirt: Your husband, your wife, your child is late, terribly late, and then they come home after all and there's an explanation. For the most part, these brushes against a parallel universe in which they never do come home—for which there is an explanation, but one that will divide your whole life into before and after—vanish without a trace. The hours that had elongated into lifetimes suddenly collapse like a fan. So even though the salty terror in my gums tasted familiar, I couldn't recall a specific instance when I had paced our loft before, head swimming with cataclysms: an aneurysm, an aggrieved postal worker with an automatic in Burger King.

By 11:00, I was making vows.

I gulped a glass of sauvignon blanc; it tasted like pickle juice. This was wine without you. The moussaka, its dry, dead hulk: This was food without you. Our loft, rich with the international booty of baskets and carvings, took on the tacky, cluttered aspect of an import outlet: This was our home without you. Objects had never seemed so inert, so pugnaciously incompensatory. Your remnants mocked me: the jump rope limp on its hook; the dirty socks, stiff, caricatured deflations of your size eleven feet.

Oh, Franklin, of course I knew that a child can't substitute for a husband, because I had seen my brother stooped from the pressure to be the "little man of the house"; I had seen the way it tortured him that Mother was always searching his face for resemblances to that ageless photo on the mantle. It wasn't fair. Giles couldn't even remember our father, who died when he was three and who had long since transformed from a flesh-and-blood Dad who dribbled soup on his tie into a tall, dark icon looming over the fireplace in his spotless army air corps uniform, an immaculate emblem of all that the boy was not. To this day Giles carries himself with a diffidence. When in the spring of 1999 he forced himself to visit me and there was nothing to say or do, he flushed with speechless resentment, because I was reviving in him the same sense of inadequacy that had permeated his childhood. Even more has he resented the public attention refracted off our son. Kevin and *Thursday* have routed him from his rabbit hole, and he's furious with me for the exposure. His sole ambition is obscurity, because Giles associates any scrutiny with being found wanting.

Still I kicked myself that you and I had made love the night before and one more evening I had absently slipped that rubber hat around my cervix. What could I do with your jump rope, your dirty socks? Wasn't there only one respectable memento of a man worth keeping, the kind that draws Valentines and learns to spell *Mississippi?* No offspring could replace you. But if I ever had to miss you, miss you forever, I wanted to have someone to miss you alongside, who would know you if only as a chasm in his life, as you were a chasm in mine.

When the phone rang again at nearly midnight, I hung back. It was late enough to be a reluctant emissary of a hospital, the police. I let it ring a second time, my hand on the receiver, warming the plastic like a magic lantern that might grant one last wish. My mother claims that in 1945 she left the envelope on the table for hours, brewing herself cup after cup of black, acid tea and letting them grow cold. Already pregnant with me from his last home leave, she took frequent trips to the toilet, closing the bathroom door and keeping the light off, as if hiding out. Haltingly, she had described to me an almost gladiatorial afternoon: facing down an adversary bigger and more ferocious than she, and knowing that she would lose.

You sounded exhausted, your voice so insubstantial that for one ugly moment I mistook it for my mother's. You apologized for the worry. The pickup had broken down in the middle of nowhere. You'd walked twelve miles to find a phone.

There was no point in talking at length, but it was agony to end the call. When we said good-bye, my eyes welled in shame that I had ever declared, "I love you!" in that peck-at-the-door spirit that makes such a travesty of passion.

I was spared. In the hour it took a taxi to drive you to Manhattan, I was allowed the luxury of slipping back to my old world of worrying about casseroles, of seducing you into eggplant and nagging you to do the laundry. It was the same world in which I could put off the possibility of our having a child another night, because we had reservations, and there were many more nights.

But I refused to relax right away, to collapse into the casual heedlessness that makes everyday life possible, and without which we would all batten ourselves into our living rooms for eternity like my mother. In fact, for a few hours I had probably been treated to a taste of my mother's whole postwar life, since what she lacks may not be courage so much as a necessary self-deceit. Her people slaughtered by Turks, her husband plucked from the sky by devious little yellow people, my mother sees chaos biting at her doorstep, while the rest of us inhabit a fabricated playscape whose benevolence is a collective delusion. In 1999, when I entered my mother's universe for good—a place where anything could happen and often did—toward what Giles and I had always regarded as her neurosis I grew much kinder.

You would indeed come home—this once. But when I put the phone down, it registered with a whispered click: There could yet come a day when you did not.

Thus instead of going slack and infinite, time still felt frantically short. When you walked in you were so tired you could hardly speak. I let you skip dinner, but I would not let you sleep. I have experienced my share of burning sexual desire, and I can assure you that this was an urgency of another order. I wanted to arrange a backup, for you and for us, like slipping a carbon in my IBM Selectric. I wanted to make sure that if anything happened to either of us there would be something left beside socks. Just that night I wanted a baby stuffed in every cranny like money in jars, like hidden bottles of vodka for weak-willed alcoholics.

"I didn't put in my diaphragm," I mumbled when we were through.

You stirred. "Is it dangerous?"

"It's very dangerous," I said. Indeed, just about any stranger could have turned up nine months later. We might as well have left the door unlocked.

The next morning, you said while we dressed, "Last night—you didn't just forget?" I shook my head, pleased with myself. "Are you sure about this?"

"Franklin, we're never going to be sure. We have no idea what it's like to have a kid. And there's only one way to find out."

You reached under my arms and lifted me overhead, and I recognized your lit-up expression from when you'd played "airplane" with Brian's daughters. "Fantastic!"

I had sounded so confident, but when you brought me in for a landing I started to panic. Complacency has a way of restoring itself of its own accord, and I'd already stopped worrying whether you would live through the week. *What had I done?* When later that month I got my period, I told you I was disappointed. That was my first lie, and it was a whopper.

During the following six weeks you applied yourself nightly. You liked having a job to do and bedded me with the same boisterous if-you're-going-to-do-anything-do-it-right with which you had knocked up our bookshelves. Myself, I wasn't so sure about this yeomanlike fucking. I had always fancied the frivolousness of sex, and I liked it down and dirty. The fact that even the Armenian Orthodox Church would now look on with hearty approval could put me right out of the mood.

Meanwhile, I came to regard my body in a new light. For the first time I apprehended the little mounds on my chest as teats for the suckling of young, and their physical resemblance to udders on cows or the swinging distensions on lactating hounds was suddenly unavoidable. Funny how even women forget what breasts are for.

The cleft between my legs transformed as well. It lost a certain outrageousness, an obscenity, or achieved an obscenity of a different sort. The flaps seemed to open not to a narrow, snug dead end, but to something yawning. The passageway itself became a route to somewhere else, a real place, and not merely to a darkness in my mind. The twist of flesh in front took on a devious aspect, its inclusion overtly ulterior, a tempter, a sweetener for doing the species' heavy lifting, like the lollipops I once got at the dentist.

Lo, everything that made me pretty was intrinsic to motherhood, and my very desire that men find me attractive was the contrivance of a body designed to expel its own replacement. I don't want to pretend that I'm the first woman to discover the birds and the bees. But all this was new to *me*. And frankly, I wasn't so sure about it. I felt expendable, throw-away, swallowed by a big biological project that I didn't initiate or choose, that produced me but would also chew me up and spit me out. I felt used.

I'm sure you remember those fights about booze. According to you, I shouldn't have been drinking at all. I balked. As soon as I discovered I was pregnant—*I* was pregnant, I didn't go in for this *we* stuff—I'd go cold turkey. But conception could take years, during which I was not prepared to killjoy my every evening with glasses of milk. Multiple generations of women had tippled cheerfully through their pregnancies and what, did they all give birth to retards?

You sulked. You went quiet if I poured myself a second glass of wine, and your disapproving glances despoiled the pleasure (as they were meant to). Sullenly, you'd grumble that in my place *you'd* stop drinking, and yes, for years if necessary, about which I had no doubt. I would let parenthood influence our behavior; you would have parenthood dictate our behavior. If that seems a subtle distinction, it is night and day.

I was deprived that clichéd cinematic tip-off of heaving over the toilet, but it doesn't appear to be in moviemakers' interests to accept that some women don't get morning sickness. Although you offered to accompany me with my urine sample, I dissuaded you: "It's not as if I'm getting tested for cancer or something." I remember the remark. Much like what they say in jest, it's telling what people claim something is *not*.

At the gynecologist's, I delivered my marinated artichoke jar, a brisk-ness covering the intrinsic embarrassment of handing off smelly effluents to strangers, and waited in the office. Dr. Rhinestein—a cold young woman for her profession, with an aloof, clinical temperament that would have suited her better for pharmaceutical trials with rats—swept in ten minutes later and leaned over her desk to jot. "It's positive," she said crisply.

When she looked up, she did a double take. "Are you all right? You've turned white."

I did feel strangely cold.

"Eva, I thought you were *trying* to get pregnant. This should be good news." She said this severely, with reproach. I got the impression that if I wasn't going to be happy about it, she would take my baby and give it to someone who'd got their mind right—who would hop up and down like a game-show contestant who'd won the car.

"Drop your head between your legs." It seems I had begun to weave.

Once I had forced myself to sit up, if only because she seemed so bored, Dr. Rhinestein went through a long list of what I couldn't do, what I couldn't eat and drink, when I *would*—never mind my plans to update "WEEWAP," as the office now called our Western European edition, thanks to you—return for my next appointment. This was my introduc-tion to the way in which, crossing the threshold of motherhood, suddenly you become social property, the animate equivalent of a public park. That coy expression "you're eating *for two* now, dear," is all by way of goading that your very dinner is no longer a private affair; indeed, as *the land of the free* has grown increasingly coercive, the inference seems to run that "you're eating for *us* now," for 200-some million meddlers, any one of whose pre-rogative it is to object should you ever be in the mood for a jelly donut and not a full meal with whole grains and leafy vegetables that covers all five major food groups. The right to boss pregnant women around was surely on its way into the Constitution.

Dr. Rhinestein itemized recommended brands of vitamins and lec-tured on the dangers of continuing to play squash.

I had the afternoon to assemble myself into the glowing mother-to-be. Instinctively, I chose a plain cotton sundress more pert than sexy, then gathered the ingredients for a meal that was aggressively nutritious (the sautéed sea trout would be unbreaded, the salad would sport sprouts). In the meantime, I tried on different approaches to a shopworn scene: coy, delayed; bemused, artificially offhand; gushing—*oh, darling!* None of them seemed to suit. As I whisked about the loft twisting fresh candles into holders, I made a brave attempt at humming but could only think of show tunes from big-budget musicals like *Hello, Dolly!*

I hate musicals.

Ordinarily, the finishing touch on a festive occasion was choosing the wine. I stared dolefully at our ample rack, bound to gather dust. Some celebration.

When the elevator clanked at our floor, I kept my back turned and arranged my face. With one glance at the tortured collection of conflicting twitches we make when we "arrange" our faces, you spared me the announcement. "You're pregnant."

I shrugged. "Looks that way."

You kissed me, chastely, no tongue. "So when you found out—how'd you feel?"

"A bit faint, actually."

Delicately, you touched my hair. "Welcome to your new life."

Since my mother was as terrified of alcohol as she was of the next street over, a glass of wine had never lost for me its tantalizing quality of the illicit. Although I didn't think I had *a problem,* a long draught of rich red at day's end had long been emblematic to me of adulthood, that vaunted American Holy Grail of liberty. But I was beginning to intuit that full-blown maturity was not so very different from childhood. Both states in their extreme were all about following the rules.

So I poured myself a flute of cranberry juice and toasted, brightly. *"La chaim!"*

Funny how you dig yourself into a hole by the teaspoon—the smallest of compromises, the little roundings off or slight recastings of one emotion as another that is a tad nicer or more flattering. I did not care so much about being deprived of a glass of wine per se. But like that legendary journey that begins with a single step, I had already embarked upon my first resentment.

A petty one, but most resentments are. And one that for its smallness I felt obliged to repress. For that matter, that is the nature of *resentment*, the objection we cannot express. It is silence more than the complaint itself that makes the emotion so toxic, like poisons the body won't pee away. Hence, hard as I tried to be a grown-up about my cranberry juice, chosen carefully for its resemblance to a young Beaujolais, deep down inside I was a brat. While you came up with names (for boys), I wracked my brain for what in all this—the diapers, the sleepless nights, the rides to soccer prac- tice—I was meant to be looking forward to.

Eager to participate, you had volunteered to give up booze for my pregnancy, though our baby would be no more bouncing should you forgo your predinner microbrew. So you began festively knocking back cranberry juice to beat the band. You seemed to relish the opportunity to prove how little drinking meant to you. I was annoyed.

Then, you were always captivated by self-sacrifice. However ad- mirable, your eagerness to give your life over to another person may have been due in some measure to the fact that when your life was wholly in your lap you didn't know what to do with it. Self-sacrifice was an easy way out. I know that sounds unkind. But I do believe that this desperation of yours—to rid yourself of yourself, if that is not too abstract—burdened our son hugely.

You remember that evening? We should have had so much to talk about, but we were awkward, halting. We were no longer Eva and Franklin, but Mommy and Daddy; this was our first meal as a *family*, a word and a concept about which I had always been uneasy. And I was short-tempered, discarding all the names you came up with, Steve and George and Mark, as "way too ordinary," and you were hurt.

I couldn't talk to you. I felt pent up, clogged. I wanted to say: Franklin, I'm not sure this is a good idea. You know in your third trimester they won't even let you onto a plane? And I hate this whole rec- titudinous *thing*, the keeping to a *good* diet and setting a *good* example and finding a *good* school . . .

It was too late. We were supposed to be celebrating and I was sup- posed to be elated.

Frantic to recreate the longing for a "backup" that had got me into this, I roused the memory of the night you were stranded in the pine barrens—*barren*, had that set me off? But that May evening's rash decision had been an illusion. I had made up my mind all right, but long before, back when I fell so hard and irrevocably for your guileless American smile, your heartbreaking faith in picnics. However weary I might have grown with writing up new countries, over time it is inevitable that food, drink, color, and trees—the very state of being alive is no longer fresh. If its shine had tarnished, this was still a life I loved, and one into which children didn't readily fit. The single thing I loved more was Franklin Plaskett. You coveted so little; there was only one big-ticket item you wanted that was in my power to provide. How could I have denied you the light in your face when you lifted Brian's squealing little girls?

With no bottle over which to linger, we went to bed on the early side. You were nervous about whether we were "supposed" to have sex, if it would hurt the baby, and I grew a little exasperated. I was already victimized, like some princess, by an organism the size of a pea. Me, I really wanted to have sex for the first time in weeks, since we could finally fuck because we wanted to get laid and not to do our bit for the race. You acquiesced. But you were depressingly tender.

Though I expected that my ambivalence would evanesce, this conflicted sensation grew only sharper, and therefore more secret. At last I should come clean. I think the ambivalence didn't go away because it wasn't what it seemed. It is not true that I was "ambivalent" about motherhood. You wanted to have a child. On balance, I did not. Added together, that seemed like ambivalence, but though we were a superlative couple, we were not the same person. I never did get you to like eggplant.

Eva

Dear Franklin,

I know I wrote only yesterday, but I now depend on this correspondence to debrief from Chatham. Kevin was in a particularly combative humor. Right off the bat he charged, "You never wanted to have me, did you?"

Before being impounded like a pet that bites, Kevin wasn't given to asking me about myself, and I actually took the question as promising. Oh, he reached for it in dull restiveness, pacing his cage, but there's something to be said for being bored *out of your mind.* He must have previously recognized that I had a life, in order to go about ruining it with such a sense of purpose. But now he had further appreciated that I had volition: I'd chosen to have a child and had harbored other aspirations that his arrival might have thwarted. This intuition was at such odds with the therapists' diagnosis of "empathic deficiency" that I felt he deserved an honest reply.

"I thought I did," I said. "And your father, he wanted you—desperately."

I looked away; Kevin's expression of sleepy sarcasm was immediate. Perhaps I shouldn't have cited, of all things, your desperation. Me, I loved your longing; I had personally profited from your insatiable loneliness. But children must find such hunger disquieting, and Kevin would routinely translate disquiet into contempt.

"You *thought you did,*" he said. "You changed your mind."

"I thought I needed a change," I said. "But no one needs a change for the worse."

Kevin looked victorious. For years he has tempted me to be nasty. I remained factual. Presenting emotions as facts—which they are—affords a fragile defense.

"Motherhood was harder than I'd expected," I explained. "I'd been used to airports, sea views, museums. Suddenly I was stuck in the same few rooms, with Lego."

"But I went out of my way," he said with a smile that lifted lifelessly as if by hooks, "to keep you entertained."

"I'd anticipated mopping up vomit. Baking Christmas cookies. I couldn't have expected—." Kevin's look dared me. "I couldn't have expected that simply *forming an attachment* to you," I phrased as diplomatically as I knew how, "would be so much work. I thought—." I took a breath. "I thought that part came for free."

"Free!" he jeered. "Waking up every morning isn't free."

"Not any more," I conceded dolefully. Kevin's and my experience of day-to-day life has converged. Time hangs off me like molting skin.

"Ever occur to you," he said slyly, "maybe *I* didn't want to have *you?*"

"You wouldn't have liked any other couple better. Whatever they did for a living, you'd think it was stupid."

"Cheapskate travel guides? Scouting another banked turn for a Jeep Cherokee ad? Gotta admit, that's *especially* stupid."

"See?" I exploded. "Honestly, Kevin—would *you* want you? If there is any justice, you'll wake up one day with *yourself* next to your bed in a crib!"

Rather than recoil or lash out, he went slack. This aspect of his, it's more common to the elderly than to children: the eyes glaze and drop, the musculature goes sloppy. It's an apathy so absolute that it's like a hole you might fall in.

You think I was mean to him, and that's why he withdrew. I don't think so. I think he wants me to be mean to him the way other people pinch themselves to make sure they're awake, and if anything he slackened in disappointment that here I was finally pitching a few halfheartedly injurious remarks and he felt nothing. Besides, I expect it was the image of "waking up with yourself" that did it, since that's just what he does do, and why his every morning feels so costly. Franklin, I have never met anyone—and you do *meet* your own children—who found his existence more of a burden or indignity. If you have any notion that I've brutalized our boy into *low self-esteem*, think again. I saw that same sullen expression in his eyes when he was one year old. If anything, he thinks very well of himself, especially since becoming such a celebrity. There is an enormous difference between disliking yourself and simply not wanting to be here.

In parting, I threw him a bone. "I did fight very hard to give you my last name."

"Yeah, well, saved you trouble. The old *K-h-a* . . . ?" he slurred. "Thanks to me, now everybody in the country knows how to spell it."

Did you know that Americans stare at pregnant women? In the low birth-rate First World, gestation is a novelty, and in the days of T&A on every newsstand, real *pornography*—conjuring intrusively intimate visions of spread hams, incontinent seepage, that eely umbilical slither. Casting my own eye down Fifth Avenue as my belly swelled, I would register with incredulity: Every one of these people came from a woman's cunt. In my head, I used the crudest word I could, to bring home the point. Like the purpose of breasts, it's one of those glaring facts we tend to suppress.

Still, I once turned heads with a short skirt, and the flickered glances from strangers in shops began to get on my nerves. Along with the fascination, even enchantment on their faces, I also spotted the incidental shiver of revulsion.

You think that's too strong. I don't. Ever notice how many films portray pregnancy as infestation, as colonization by stealth? *Rosemary's Baby* was just the beginning. In *Alien,* a foul extraterrestrial claws its way out of John Hurt's belly. In *Mimic,* a woman gives birth to a two-foot maggot. Later, the *X-Files* turned bug-eyed aliens bursting gorily from human midsections into a running theme. In horror and sci-fi, the host is consumed or rent, reduced to husk or residue so that some nightmare creature may survive its shell.

I'm sorry, but I didn't make these movies up, and any woman whose teeth have rotted, whose bones have thinned, whose skin has stretched, knows the humbling price of a nine-month freeloader. Those nature films of female salmon battling upstream to lay their eggs only to disintegrate—eyes filming, scales dropping—made me mad. The whole time I was pregnant with Kevin I was battling the idea of Kevin, the notion that I had demoted myself from driver to vehicle, from householder to house.

Physically, the experience was easier than I expected. The greatest affront of the first trimester was a watery thickening that easily passed as a weakness for Mars bars. My face filled out, beveling my androgynously angular features into the softer contours of a girl. My face was younger but, I thought, dumber looking.

I don't know what took me so long to notice that you were simply assuming that our baby would take your surname, and even on the Christian name we weren't like-minded. You'd propose *Leonard* or *Peter*. When I countered with *Engin* or *Garabet*—or *Selim*, after my paternal grandfather—you assumed the same tolerant expression I wore when Brian's girls showed me their Cabbage Patch Kids. Finally you said, "You cannot possibly be proposing that I name my son *Garabet Plaskett.*"

"Nnoo," I said. "*Garabet Khatchadourian*. Has more of a ring."

"It has the ring of a kid who's not related to me."

"Funny, that's exactly how *Peter Plaskett* sounds to me."

We were at the Beach House, that charming little bar around the corner on Beach Street, no longer extant I'm afraid, and rather wasted on my orange juice straight up, though they did serve a mean bowl of chili.

You drummed your fingers. "Can we at least nix *Plaskett-Khatchadourian?* Because once the hyphenated start marrying each other, kids'll be going by whole phone books. And since somebody's gotta lose, it simplest to stick with tradition."

"According to *tradition*, women couldn't own property until, in some states, the 1970s. *Traditionally* in the Middle East we walk around in a black sack and *traditionally* in Africa we get our clitorises carved out like a hunk of gristle—"

You stuffed my mouth with cornbread. "Enough of the lecture, babe. We're not talking about female circumcision but our kid's last name."

"Men have always gotten to name children after themselves, while not doing *any of the work.*" Cornbread crumbs were sailing from my mouth. "Time to turn the tables."

"Why turn them on me? Jesus, you'd think American men were pussy-whipped enough. You're the one who complains they're all quiche-eating faggots who go to crying workshops."

I folded my arms and brought out the heavy artillery. "My father was born in Dier-ez-Zor concentration camp. The camps were riddled with disease and the Armenians had hardly any food or even water—it's amazing the baby survived, because his three brothers didn't. His father, Selim, was shot. Two-thirds of my mother's extended family, the Serafians, was so neatly obliterated that not even their stories have survived. I'm sorry to pull rank. But Anglo-Saxons are hardly an endangered species. My forebears were systematically exterminated, and no one ever even talks about it, Franklin!"

"A *million* and a half people!" you chimed in, gesticulating wildly. "Do you *realize* it was what the Young Turks did to the Armenians in 1915 that gave *Hitler* the *idea* for the *Holocaust*?"

I glared.

"Eva, your brother's got two kids. There are a million Armenians in the U.S. alone. Nobody's about to disappear."

"But you care about your last name just because it's yours. I care about mine—well, it seems more important."

"My parents would have a cow. They'd think I was denying them. Or that I was under your thumb. They'd think I was an asshole."

"I should get varicose veins for a *Plaskett*? It's a gross name!"

You looked stung. "You never said you didn't like my name."

"That wide *A*, it's kind of blaring and crass—"

"Crass!"

"It's just so awfully *American*. It reminds me of fat nasal tourists in Nice whose kids all want ice cream. Who shout, *Honey, look at that 'Pla-a-as-kett'* when it's French and the word's really pronounced *plah-skay*."

"It's not *Plah-skay*, you anti-American prig! It's Plaskett, a small but old and respectable Scottish family, and a name I'd be proud to hand on to my kids! Now I know why you didn't take it when we got married. You hated my name!"

"I'm sorry! Obviously I love your name in a way, if only because it's *your* name—"

"Tell you what," you proposed; in this country, the injured party enjoyed a big advantage. "If it's a boy, it's a Plaskett. A girl, and you can have your *Khatchadourian*."

I pushed the bread basket aside and jabbed your chest. "So a girl doesn't matter to you. If you were Iranian, she'd be kept home from school. If you were Indian, she'd be sold to a stranger for a cow. If you were Chinese, she'd be starved to death and buried in the backyard—"

You raised your hands. "If it's a *girl* it's a Plaskett, then! But on one condition: None of this *Gara-souvlaki* stuff for a boy's first name. Something *American*. Deal?"

It was a deal. And in hindsight we made the right decision. In 1996, fourteen-year-old Barry Loukaitis killed a teacher and two students while taking a whole class hostage in Moses Lake, Washington. A year later, thirteen-year-old Tronneal Mangum shot dead a boy at his middle school who owed him $40. The next month, sixteen-year-old Evan Ramsey killed a student and his principal and wounded two others in Bethel, Alaska. That fall, sixteen-year-old Luke Woodham murdered his mother and two students, wounding seven, in Pearl, Mississippi. Two months later, fourteen-year-old Michael Carneal shot dead three students and wounded five in Paducah, Kentucky. The next spring in 1998, thirteen-year-old Mitchell Johnson and eleven-year-old Andrew Golden opened fire on their high school, killing one teacher and four students, wounding ten, in Jonesboro, Arkansas. A month after that, fourteen-year-old Andrew Wurst killed a teacher and wounded three students in Edinboro, Pennsylvania. The following month in Springfield, Oregon, fifteen-year-old Kip Kinkel massacred both his parents, proceeding to kill two more students and wounding twenty-five. In 1999, and a mere ten days after a certain *Thursday*, eighteen-year-old Eric Harris and seventeen-year-old Dylan Klebold planted bombs in their Littleton, Colorado, high school and went on a shooting rampage that killed one teacher and twelve students, while wounding twenty-three, after which they shot themselves. So young Kevin—your choice—has turned out as American as a Smith and Wesson.

As for his surname, our son has done more to keep the name *Khatchadourian* alive than anyone else in my family.

Like so many of our neighbors who latched onto tragedy to stand out from the crowd—slavery, incest, a suicide—I had exaggerated the ethnic chip on my shoulder for effect. I've learned since that tragedy is not to be hoarded. Only the untouched, the well-fed and contented, could possibly covet suffering like a designer jacket. I'd readily donate my story to the Salvation Army so that some other frump in need of color could wear it away.

The name? I think I just wanted to make the baby mine. I couldn't shake the sensation of having been appropriated. Even when I got the sonogram and Dr. Rhinestein drew her finger around a shifting mass on the monitor, I thought, *Who is that?* Though right under my skin, swimming in another world, the form seemed far away. And did a fetus have feelings? I had no way of anticipating that I would still be asking that question about Kevin when he was fifteen.

I confess that when Dr. Rhinestein pointed out the blip between the legs, my heart sank. Although according to our "deal" I was now bearing a Khatchadourian, just getting my name on the title deeds wasn't going to annex the kid for his mother. And if I enjoyed the company of men—I liked their down-to-earth quality, I was prone to mistake aggression for honesty, and I disdained daintiness—I wasn't at all sure about *boys*.

When I was eight or nine, and once more sent on some errand by my mother to fetch something grown-up and complicated, I'd been set upon by a group of boys not much older than myself. Oh, I wasn't raped; they wrenched up my dress and pulled down my panties, threw a few dirt clods and ran away. Still, I was frightened. Older, I continued to give wide berth to eleven-year-olds in parks—pointed into bushes with their flies down, leering over their shoulders and sniggering. Even before I had one myself, I was well and truly frightened by boys. And nowadays, well, I suppose I'm frightened by just about everybody.

For all our squinting at the two sexes to blur them into duplicates, few hearts race when passing gaggles of giggling schoolgirls. But any woman who passes a clump of testosterone-drunk punks without picking up the pace, without avoiding the eye contact that might connote challenge or invitation, without sighing inwardly with relief by the following block, is a *zoological* fool. A boy is a dangerous animal.

Is it different for men? I never asked. Perhaps you can see through them, to their private anguish about whether it's normal to have a curved penis, the transparent way they show off for one another (though that's just what I'm afraid of). Certainly the news that you'd be harboring one of these holy terrors in your own home so delighted you that you had to cover your enthusiasm a bit. And the sex of our child made you feel that much more that the baby was yours, yours, *yours*.

Honestly, Franklin, your proprietary attitude was grating. If I ever cut it close crossing the street, you weren't concerned for my personal safety but were outraged at my irresponsibility. These "risks" I took—and I regarded as going about my regular life—seemed in your mind to exhibit a cavalier attitude toward one of your personal belongings. Every time I walked out the door, I swear you glowered a little, as if I were bearing away one of your prized possessions without asking.

You wouldn't even let me *dance*, Franklin! Really, there was one afternoon that my subtle but unrelenting anxiety had mercifully lifted. I put on our Talking Heads' *Speaking in Tongues* and began buoyantly herky-jerkying around our underfurnished loft. The album was still on the first song, "Burning Down the House," and I'd barely worked up a sweat when the elevator clanked and in you marched. When you lifted the needle preemptorily, you scratched a groove, so that forever after the song would skip and keep repeating, *Baby what did you expect* and never make it to *Gonna burst into fla-ame* without my depressing the cartridge gently with a forefinger.

"Hey!" I said. "What was that about?"

"What the fuck do you think you're doing?"

"For once I was having a good time. Is that illegal?"

You grabbed my upper arm. "Are you *trying* to have a miscarriage? Or do you just get a kick out of tempting fate?"

I wrestled free. "Last time I read, pregnancy wasn't a prison sentence."

"Leaping around, throwing yourself all over the furniture—"

"Oh, get out, Franklin. Not that long ago women worked in the fields right up until giving birth and then squatted between rows of vegetables. In the olden days, kids really did come from the cabbage patch—"

"In the *olden days* infant and maternal mortality were sky high!"

"What do you care about maternal mortality? So long as they scoop the kid out of my lifeless body while its heart is still beating you'll be happy as a clam."

"That's a hideous thing to say."

"I'm in the mood to be hideous," I said blackly, plopping onto the couch. "Though before Papa Doc came home, I was in a great mood."

"Two more months. Is it that big a sacrifice to take it easy for the well-being of a whole other person?"

Boy, was I already sick of having the *well-being of a whole other person* held over my head. "*My* well-being, apparently, now counts for beans."

"There's no reason you can't listen to music—although at a volume that doesn't have John thumping his ceiling downstairs." You replaced the needle at the beginning of the A side, turning it down so low that David Byrne sounded like Minnie Mouse. "But like a normal pregnant woman, you can sit there and *tap your foot.*"

"I don't know about that," I said. "All the vibration—it might travel up to Little Lord Fauntleroy and trouble his beauty sleep. And aren't we supposed to be listening to Mozart? Maybe Talking Heads isn't in The Book. Maybe by playing 'Psycho Killer' we're feeding him Bad Thoughts. Better look it up."

You were the one powering through all those parental how-tos, about breathing and teething and weaning, while I read a history of Portugal.

"Stop feeling sorry for yourself, Eva. I thought the whole idea of becoming parents was to grow up."

"If I'd realized that's what it meant to you, affecting some phony, killjoy adulthood, I'd have reconsidered the whole business."

"Don't you *ever say that,*" you said, your face beet-red. "It's too late for second thoughts. *Never, ever* tell me that you regret our own kid."

That's when I started to cry. When I had shared with you my most sordid sexual fantasies, in such disturbing violation of heterosexual norms that, without the assist of your own disgraceful mental smut shared in return, I'm too embarrassed to mention them here—since when was there anything that one of us was *never, ever* to say?

Baby what did you expect—Baby what did you expect—

The track had started to skip.

Eva

Dear Franklin,

Well, I had no desire to linger at the agency today. The staff has gone from good-hearted jousting to all-out war. Observing the showdowns in our small office without taking sides has lent these scenes the slightly comic, unaffecting quality of television with the sound off.

I'm a little at a loss as to how "Florida" has become a race issue, except in the way that sooner or later everything becomes a race issue in this country—sooner, as a rule. So the three other Democrats here have been throwing terms like "Jim Crow" at the two beleaguered Republicans, who huddle together in the back room and speak in low tones that the rest construe as the conspiratorial mutter of shared bigotry. Funny; before the election none of these people displayed the least interest in what was generally agreed to be a dreary contest.

Anyway, today some Supreme Court decision was due, and the radio was on all day. The staff's recriminations flew so fast and furious that more than one customer, abandoned at the counter, simply walked out. At length I did the same. Whereas the two conservatives tend to argue nakedly for *their side*, the liberals are always weighing in on behalf of truth, justice, or humanity. Though once a staunch Democrat, I long ago gave up on defending humanity. It's beyond me on most days to defend myself.

Then, while I do hope this correspondence hasn't degenerated into shrill self-justification, I worry equally that I may seem to be laying the groundwork for claiming that Kevin is all my fault. I do indulge that sometimes, too, gulping down blame with a powerful thirst. But I did say *indulge*. There's a self-aggrandizement in these wallowing mea culpas, a vanity. Blame confers an awesome power. And it's simplifying, not only to onlookers and victims but to culprits most of all. It imposes order on slag. Blame conveys clear lessons in which others may take comfort: *if only she hadn't*—, and by implication makes tragedy avoidable. There may even be a fragile peace to be found in the assumption of total responsibility, and I see that calm in Kevin on occasion. It is an aspect that his keepers confuse with remorselessness.

But for me this greedy gorging on fault never works. I am never able to get the full story inside me. It's larger than I am. It has damaged too many people, aunts and cousins and best friends whom I will never know and would not recognize if we met. I cannot at once contain the suffering of so many family dinners with one empty chair. I haven't anguished that the photo on the piano is forever tainted because that was the snapshot given to the newspapers or because sibling portraits on either side continue to mark occasions of greater maturity—college graduations, weddings—while the static high school yearbook photo loses color in the sun. I haven't been privy to the month-by-month deterioration of marriages once robust; I haven't sniffed the sickly sweet waft of gin off the breath of a formerly industrious realtor at advancingly earlier hours of the afternoon. I haven't felt the weight of all those cartons dragged into a van after a neighborhood lush with oaks, bubbling with smooth-rocked creeks, and alive with the laughter of other people's healthy children has suddenly become intolerable overnight. It seems as if for me to feel guilty in any meaningful way, I should have to suspend all these losses in my head. Yet like those car games in which you recite, *I'm going on a trip, and I'm going to take an ambling aardvark, a babbling baby, a capering caterpillar . . .* , I always blank on an element or two before the end of the alphabet. I start to juggle Mary's unnaturally beautiful daughter, the Fergusons' short-sighted computer whiz kid, the Corbitts' gangling redhead who was always overacting in school plays, and then I throw in that uncannily gracious English teacher Dana Rocco and the balls fall on the floor.

Of course, just because I can't manage to swallow all the blame doesn't mean that others won't heap it on me anyway, and I'd have been glad to provide a useful receptacle if I thought the heaping did them any good: I always come back to Mary Woolford, whose experience of injustice had hitherto run to a particularly inconvenient one-way street. I suppose I'd call her spoiled; she did stir up rather an excessive fuss when Laura didn't make the track team, even though her daughter, however lovely, was physically languid and not the least athletic. But it may not be fair to call it a character flaw that someone's life has always gone well with minimal impedance. Moreover, she was a restive woman, and like my Democratic coworkers given to indignation by nature. Previous to *Thursday*, she had been accustomed to venting this quantity, which I presume would otherwise build up in her at combustive levels, on campaigns to have the town council put in a pedestrian crossing or to ban homeless shelters from Gladstone; consequently, the denial of funds for such a crossing or the arrival of hairy riffraff on the outskirts of town had previously constituted her version of catastrophe. I'm not sure how such people manage to get their heads around proper disaster after having repeatedly exercised the full powers of their consternation on traffic.

So I can see how a woman who'd long slept restlessly on peas might have difficulty lying on an anvil. Nevertheless, it's a pity that she couldn't remain within the still, serene well of sheer incomprehension. Oh, I realize you can't stay bewildered—the need to understand or at least to pretend you do is too great—but I myself have found wide white mystification a place in my mind that is blessedly quiet. And I fear that Mary's alternative outrage, her evangelical fever to bring the guilty to book, is a clamorous place that creates the illusion of a journey, a goal to be achieved, only so long as that goal remains out of reach. Honestly, I had to fight the impulse at the civil trial to take her aside and charge gently, "You can't imagine that you'll feel better if you win, do you?" In fact, I became convinced that she would find more consolation in having what proved a surprisingly slight parental negligence case dismissed, because then she'd be able to nurture this theoretical alternative universe in which she had successfully unloaded her agony onto a callous, indifferent mother who deserved it. Somehow Mary seemed confused as to what the problem was. The problem was not who was punished for what. The problem was that her daughter was dead. Although I couldn't have been more sympathetic, it was not subject to unloading onto anyone else.

Besides, I might be more kindly disposed to this ultra-secular notion that whenever bad things happen someone must be held accountable if a curious little halo of blamelessness did not seem to surround those very people who perceive themselves as bordered on every side by agents of wickedness. That is, it seems to be the same folks who are inclined to sue builders who did not perfectly protect them from the depredations of an earthquake who will be the first to claim that their son failed his math test because of attention deficit disorder, and not because he spent the night before at a video arcade instead of studying complex fractions. Further, if underlying this huffy relationship to cataclysm—the hallmark of the American middle class—were a powerful conviction that bad things simply shouldn't happen, period, I might find the naïveté disarming. But the core conviction of these incensed sorts—who greedily rubberneck interstate pileups—seems rather that bad things shouldn't happen to *them*. Lastly, though you know I've never been especially religious after having all that Orthodox guff forced on me as a child (though luckily by the time I was eleven, my mother could no longer brave the church a whole four blocks away and held halfhearted "services" at home), I still wonder at a race grown so anthrocentric that all events from volcanoes to global temperature shift have become matters for which its individual members are answerable. The species itself is an act, for lack of a better word, of God. Personally, I would argue that the births of single dangerous children are acts of God as well, but therein lay our court case.

Harvey thought from the start that I should settle. You remember Harvey Landsdown; you thought he was self-important. He is, but he told such marvelous stories. Now he goes to other people's dinner parties and tells stories about me.

Harvey did rattle me a bit, since he's a get-to-the-point type. In his office, I stumbled and digressed; he messed with papers, implying that I was wasting his time or my money—same thing. We were at odds on our understanding of what constitutes truth. He wanted gist. Me, I think you only get at gist by assembling all the tiny inconclusive anecdotes that would fall flat at a dinner table and that seem irrelevant until you collect them in a pile. Maybe that's what I'm attempting here, Franklin, because though I tried to answer his questions directly, whenever I made simple, exculpatory statements like, "Of course I love my son," I felt that I was lying and that any judge or jury would be able to tell.

Harvey didn't care. He's one of those attorneys who think of the law as a game, not as a morality play. I'm told that's the kind you want. Harvey is fond of declaiming that being in the right never won anyone's case, and he even left me with the unfocused sense that having justice on your side is a faint disadvantage.

Of course, I was not at all sure that justice was on my side, and Harvey found my hand-wringing tedious. He commanded me to stop dithering about how it looked, accepting a reputation as a Bad Mother, and he clearly couldn't have cared less about whether I really was a bad mother. (And Franklin, I was. I was terrible at it. I wonder if you can ever forgive me.) His reasoning was straightforward economics, and I gather this is how many suits are decided. He advised that we could probably pay off the parents out of court for a great deal less than a sentimental jury might award. Crucially, there was no guarantee that we'd be compensated for court costs even if we won. So that means, I sorted out slowly, that in this country where you're "innocent until proven guilty" someone can accuse me of whatever he wants and I could be out hundreds of thousands even if I prove the accusation groundless? Welcome to the U.S. of A., he said gaily. I miss you to rail to. Harvey wasn't interested in my exasperation. He found these legal ironies amusing, because it was not his company started from a single discount plane ticket that was on the line.

Looking back, Harvey was absolutely right—about the money, that is. And I have reflected since on what drove me to make Mary take her case against me to trial in defiance of sound legal counsel. I must have been angry. If I had done anything wrong, it seemed to me that I had already been punished roundly. No court could have sentenced me to anything worse than this arid life in my poky duplex, with my chicken breast and cabbage, my tremulous halogen bulbs, my robotic biweekly visits to Chatham—or perhaps even worse, to nearly sixteen years of living with a son who, as he asserted, did not want me as a mother and who gave me almost daily good reason to not want him as a son. All the same, I really ought to have worked out for myself that if a jury's damning verdict would never assuage Mary's grief, a more kindly judgment would never temper my own sense of complicity, either. I'm sad to say that I must have been motivated in some not inconsiderable part by a desperation to be publicly exonerated.

Alas, it was not public exoneration that I truly craved, which may be why I sit here night after night and try to record every incriminating detail. Look at this sorry specimen: As a mature, happily married woman of nearly thirty-seven, she is informed of her first pregnancy and almost faints in horror, a response she disguises from her delighted husband with a pert gingham sundress. Blessed with the miracle of new life, she chooses to dwell instead on a forgone glass of wine and the veins in her legs. She throws herself about her living room to the tune of tawdry popular music with no thought of her unborn child. At a time that she ought best to be learning in her very gut the true meaning of *ours*, she chooses instead to fret about whether the forthcoming baby is *hers*. Even beyond the point at which she should have more than learned her lesson, she is still banging on about a movie in which human birth is confused with the expulsion of an oversized maggot. And she's a hypocrite who's impossible to please: After admitting that flitting about the globe is not the magical mystery tour she once pretended it was—that these superficial peripatetics have in fact become trying and monotonous—the moment this gadding about is imperiled by the needs of someone else, she starts swooning over the halcyon life she once led when jotting down whether Yorkshire youth hostels provide kitchen facilities. Worst of all, before her hapless son has even managed to survive the inhospitable climate of her clenched, reluctant womb, she has committed what you yourself, Franklin, deemed the officially unspeakable: She has capriciously changed her mind, as if children are merely little outfits you can try on back home and—after turning critically before the mirror to conclude, no, sorry, it's a pity but this really just doesn't quite *suit*—cart back to the store.

I recognize that the portrait I'm painting here is not *attractive*, and for that matter I can't remember the last time I felt attractive, to myself or anyone else. In fact, years before I got pregnant myself I met a young woman at the White Horse in the Village with whom I'd gone to college in Green Bay. Though we hadn't spoken since then, she had recently given birth to her own first child, and I needed only to say hi for her to begin spewing her despair. Compact, with unusually broad shoulders and close curly black hair, Rita was an attractive woman—in the physical sense. With no solicitation on my part she regaled me with the irreproachable state of her physique before she conceived. Apparently she'd been using the Nautilus every day, and her definition had never been so sharp, her fat-to-muscle ratio was unreal, her aerobic conditioning topping the charts.

Then pregnancy, well it was *terrible!* The Nautilus just didn't *feel good* any more and she'd had to stop——. Now, now, she was a *mess*, she could hardly do a *sit-up*, much less three sets of proper crunches, she was starting from scratch or *worse*——! This woman was fuming, Franklin; she clearly muttered about her abdominal muscles when she seethed down the street. Yet at no point did she mention the name of her child, its sex, its age, or its father. I remember stepping back, excusing myself to the bar, and slipping away without telling Rita good-bye. What had most mortified me, what I had to flee, was that she sounded not only unfeeling and narcissistic but *just like me.*

I'm no longer sure whether I rued our first child before he was even born. It's hard for me to reconstruct that period without contaminating the memories with the outsized regret of later years, a regret that bursts the constraints of time and gushes into the period when Kevin wasn't there yet to wish away. But the last thing I've wanted is to whitewash my own part in this terrible story. That said, I'm determined to accept due responsibility for every wayward thought, every petulance, every selfish moment, not in order to gather all the blame to myself but to admit *this* is my fault and *that* is my fault but *there, there,* precisely *there* is where I draw a line and on the other side, *that, that,* Franklin, *that* is *not.*

Yet to draw that line I fear I must advance to its very edge.

By the last month, the pregnancy was almost fun. I was so ungainly that the condition had a goofy novelty, and for a woman who had always been so conscientiously trim there was a relief to be found in becoming a cow. How the other half lives, if you will—more than half, I gather, as of 1998, the first year in which more people in the U.S. were officially fat than not.

Kevin was two weeks late. Looking back, I am superstitiously convinced that he was foot-dragging even in the womb—that he was hiding. Perhaps I was not the only party to this experiment who had reservations.

Why were you never tortured with our foreboding? I had to discourage you from buying so many bunnies and buggies and Huggy Snuggy afghans before the birth. What if, I noted, something goes wrong? Couldn't you be setting yourself up for a fall? You pished that to plan on disaster was to court it. (Hence, in contemplating a darker twin of the dazzlingly hale and happy boy you were counting on, I allowed the changeling into the world.) I was the over-thirty-five mother keen on getting the fetus tested for Downs; you were adamantly opposed. All they can give you is a percentage chance, you argued. Are you going to tell me that if it's one in 500 you'll go ahead, but one in fifty and it's flush and start again? Of course not, I said. One in ten, then. One in three. What's the cutoff? Why force yourself to make that kind of choice?

Your arguments were convincing, though I wonder if behind them didn't lurk a poorly thought out romance with the handicapped child: one of those clumsy but sweet-tempered emissaries of God who teaches his parents that there's so much more to life than smarts, a guileless soul who is smothered in the same hair-tousling affection lavished on a family pet. Thirsty to quaff whatever funky genetic cocktail our DNA served up, you must have flirted with the prospect of all those bonus points for self-sacrifice: Your patience when it takes our darling dunderhead six months of daily lessons to tie his shoes proves superhuman. Unstinting and fiercely protective, you discover in yourself a seemingly bottomless well of generosity on which your I'm-leaving-for-Guyana-tomorrow wife never draws, and at length you abandon location scouting, the better to devote yourself full-time to our five-foot-something three-year-old. The neighbors all extol your make-the-best-of-it resignation to the hand Life has dealt, the roll-with-the-punches maturity with which you face what others in our race and class would find a crippling body blow. You were just desperate to throw yourself into this parenting business, weren't you? To plunge from a cliff, to pitch yourself on a pyre. Was our life together that unbearable to you, that bleak?

I never told you, but I got the test behind your back. The optimism of its result (about one in 100) allowed me to once more elude the enormity of our differences. Me, I was picky. My approach to parenthood was conditional, and the conditions were strict. I did not want to mother an imbecile or a paraplegic; whenever I saw fatigued women wheeling their stick-limbed progeny with muscular dystrophy for water therapy at Nyack Hospital, my heart didn't melt, it sank. Indeed, an honest list of all that I did not want to nurture, from the garden-variety moron to the grotesquely overweight, might run damningly to a second page. In retrospect, however, my mistake was not that I got the test in secret but that I found reassurance in its result. Dr. Rhinestein did not test for malice, for spiteful indifference, or for congenital meanness. If they could, I wonder how many fish we might throw back.

As for the birth itself, I had always played up a macho attitude toward pain that merely betrayed that I'd never suffered from a debilitating illness, broken a single bone, or emerged from a four-car pileup. Honestly, Franklin, I don't know where I got this idea of myself as so tough. I was the Mary Woolford of the physical world. My concept of pain derived from stubbed toes, skinned elbows, and menstrual cramps. I knew what it was like to feel a little achy after the first day of a squash season; I had no idea what it was like to lose a hand to industrial machinery or to have a leg run over by the Seventh Avenue IRT. Nevertheless, how eagerly we buy into one another's mythologies, no matter how farfetched. You accepted my blasé response to cut fingers in the kitchen—a transparent bid for your admiration, my dear—as sufficient evidence that I would force a form the size of a standing rib roast through an orifice that had previously accommodated nothing larger than a bratwurst with equal stoicism. It simply went without saying that I would shun anesthetics.

I cannot for the life of me understand what we were trying to prove. For your part, maybe that I was the heroic larger-than-life that you wanted to have married. For my part, I may have got sucked into that little competition between women about childbirth. Even Brian's demure wife Louise announced that she had managed a twenty-six-hour labor with Kiley while soothed only by "raspberry leaf tea," a treasured family factoid that she repeated on three separate occasions. It was encounters of this variety that swelled the ranks of the natural childbirth course I took at the New School, though I wager that many of those students who talked this "I want to know what it feels like" game broke down and begged for an epidural at the first contraction.

Not me. I wasn't brave, but I was stubborn and prideful. Sheer obstinacy is far more durable than courage, though it's not as pretty.

So the first time my insides twisted as if rung like a wet sheet, my eyes bulged slightly, the lids widening in surprise; my lips compressed. I impressed you with my calm. I meant to. We were lunching at the Beach

House again, and I decided against finishing my chili. In a show of returning equanimity, you dispatched a piece of cornbread before retreating to
the rest room for a foot-high stack of freshly banded paper towels; my water had broken, gallons of it, or so it seemed, and I had drenched the
bench. You paid the bill and even remembered to leave a tip before leading
me by the hand back to our loft, checking your watch. We were not going
to embarrass ourselves by turning up at Beth Israel hours before my cervix
had begun to dilate.

Later that afternoon, as you drove me across Canal Street in your
baby-blue pickup, you mumbled that everything would be all right,
though you had no way of knowing. At admissions, I was struck by the
commonplace character of my condition; the nurse yawned, fortifying my
resolve that I would prove an exemplary patient. I would astound Dr.
Rhinestein with my gruff practicality. I knew this was a natural process,
and I was not going to make a fuss. So when another contraction doubled
me as if I had just been caught unawares by a right hook, I merely exhaled
a little *hoof*.

It was all a ridiculous and perfectly pointless act. There was no reason
to try to amaze Dr. Rhinestein, whom I did not especially like. If I intended to do you proud, you were getting a son out of the bargain, sufficient payoff to put up with a little screaming and rudeness. It might even
have done you good to recognize that the woman you married was an ordinary mortal who adored comfort and hated suffering and so would opt
sanely for anesthetic. Instead I made feeble jokes on my stretcher in the
corridor, and I held your hand. That was the hand that you told me afterward I very nearly broke.

Oh, Franklin, there is no use pretending now. It was awful. I may be
capable of toughness in respect to certain kinds of pain, but if so, my for-
titude dwells in my calves or forearms but not between my legs. This was
not a part of my body that I had ever associated with endurance, with
anything so odious as exercise. And as the hours dragged on, I began to
suspect that I was just too old for this, that I was too inelastic approaching forty to stretch to this new life. Dr. Rhinestein said, primly, that I was
small, as if to indicate an inadequacy, and after about fifteen hours, she
despaired sternly, *Eva! You really must make an effort.* So much for earning her
amazement.

There were times after about twenty-four hours that a few tears would leak down my temples, and I hastily wiped them away, not wanting you to see. More than once I was offered an epidural, and my determination to forgo its deliverance acquired a demented aspect. I seized on this refusal, as if passing this little test were the point, and not passing an infant son. So long as I declined the needle, I was winning.

In the end it was the threat of a cesarean that did it; Dr. Rhinestein made no bones about the fact that she had other patients back at her office and that she was disgusted by my lackluster performance. I had an abnormal horror of being sliced open. I didn't want the scar; like Rita, I'm ashamed to say, I feared for my stomach muscles; and the procedure was too reminiscent of all those horror films.

So I *made an effort*, at which point I had to recognize that I'd been resisting the birth. Whenever the enormous mass approached that tiny canal, I'd been sucking it back. Because it hurt. It hurt a *whole lot*. In that New School course, they drummed into you that the pain was *good*, you were supposed to *go with it*, push *into the pain*, and only on my back did I contemplate what retarded advice this was. Pain, *good*? I was overcome with contempt. In fact, I never told you this before, but the emotion on which I fastened in order to push beyond a critical threshold was *loathing*. I despised being spread out like some farm exhibit with strangers gawking between my canted knees. I detested Dr. Rhinestein's pointed, ratlike little face and her brisk, censorious manner. I hated myself for ever having agreed to this humiliating theater, when I was *fine* before and right at this moment I could have been in *France*. I repudiated all my female friends, who used to share their reservations about supply-side economics or at least halfheartedly ask after my last trip abroad, yet for months now had only nattered about stretch marks and remedies for constipation or gaily brandished horror stories about terminal preeclampsia and autistic offspring who would do nothing but rock back and forth all day and bite their hands. Your eternally hopeful, encouraging expression made me *sick*. All very easy for you to want to be a *Daddy*, to buy into all that stuffed-bunny schlock, when I was the one who had to blow up like a sow, I was the one who had to turn into a goody-two-shoes teetotaler sucking down vitamins, I was the one who had to watch her breasts get puffy and bloated and sore when they used to be so neat and close, and I was the one who would be ripped to ribbons ramming a watermelon through a passage the size of a garden hose. I did, I hated you and your little coos and mumbles, I wished you'd stop patting my brow with that damp washcloth as if it made the slightest bit of difference, and I think I knew I was hurting your hand. And yes, I even hated the baby—which so far had not brought me hope for the future and *story* and content and "a turn of the page" but unwieldiness and embarrassment and a rumbling subterranean tremor quaking through the very ocean floor of who I thought I was.

But pushing past that threshold I met such a red blaze of agony that I could no longer afford the expenditure of loathing. I screamed, and I didn't care. I'd have done anything in that instant to get it to stop: hocked my company, sold our child into slavery, committed my soul to hell. "Please—," I gasped, "give me—that epidural!"

Dr. Rhinestein chided, "It's too late for that now, Eva, if you couldn't take it you should have said so earlier. The baby is crowning. For pity's sake don't let up *now*."

And suddenly it was over. Later we'd joke about how long I held out and how I begged for relief only once it was withdrawn, but at the time it wasn't funny. In the very instant of his birth, I associated Kevin with my own limitations—with not only suffering, but defeat.

Eva

Dear Franklin,

When I walked into work this morning I could tell immediately from a malignant Democratic sullenness that "Florida" was over. The sense of letdown in both camps feels postpartum.

But if my coworkers of both stripes are disappointed that such an invigorating affray is finished, I feel a measure more disconsolate still, banished even from their shared, binding sense of loss. Multiplied by many times, this loneliness of mine must approximate my mother's experience of the end of the war, for my birthday of August 15 coincides with VJ-Day, when Hirohito broadcast his surrender to the Japanese. Apparently the nurses were so ecstatic that it was hard to get them to attend to the timing of her contractions. Listening to champagne corks pop down the hall, she must have felt so dolefully left out. Many of the nurses' husbands would be coming home, but my father would not. If the rest of the country had won the war, the Khatchadourians of Racine, Wisconsin, had lost.

Later she must have felt similarly at odds with the sentiments embalmed by the commercial greeting card company for which she went to work (anything but Johnson Wax). How eerie, boxing other people's Happy Anniversary tributes and having no need to slip one in her purse when the date came around in her own home. I'm of two minds as to whether I should be glad that the job gave her the idea of starting her own handcrafted greeting-card business, which allowed her to withdraw to Enderby Avenue in perpetuity. But I will say that the "On the Birth of Your First Baby" card that she made up especially for me—layered with bled tissue in blues and greens—well, it was lovely.

In fact, when my head cleared in Beth Israel, I remembered my mother and felt ungrateful. My father had been unable to hold her hand as you held mine. Yet, offered the clasp of a living husband, I crushed it.

Still, we all know that women in labor can grow abusive, so I'm tempted to admit to having gotten a little hostile in the thick of things, and to leave my confession at that. After all, I was immediately abashed and kissed you. This was before the days when doctors slid a newborn right onto the mother's breast, gore and all, and we had a few minutes while they tied the cord and cleaned him up. I was excited, stroking and squeezing your arm, nestling my forehead into the soft inside of your elbow. I had never held our child.

But I cannot let myself off the hook so lightly.

Up until April 11, 1983, I had flattered myself that I was an exceptional person. But since Kevin's birth I have come to suppose that we are all profoundly normative. (For that matter, thinking of one's self as exceptional is probably more the rule than not.) We have explicit expectations of ourselves in specific situations—beyond expectations; they are requirements. Some of these are small: If we are given a surprise party, we will be delighted. Others are sizable: If a parent dies, we will be grief-stricken. But perhaps in tandem with these expectations is the private fear that we will fail convention in the crunch. That we will receive the fateful phone call and our mother is dead and we feel nothing. I wonder if this quiet, unutterable little fear is even keener than the fear of the bad news itself: that we will discover ourselves to be monstrous. If it does not seem too shocking, for the duration of our marriage I lived with one terror: that if something happened to you it would break me. But there was always an odd shadow, an underfear, if you will, that it would not—that I would swing off blithely that afternoon to play squash.

The fact that this *underfear* rarely becomes overweening proceeds from a crude trust. You have to keep faith that if the unthinkable does come to pass, despair will come crashing in of its own accord; that grief, for example, is not an experience you need summon or a skill you need practice, and the same goes for prescriptive joy.

Thus even tragedy can be accompanied by a trace of relief. The discovery that heartbreak is indeed heartbreaking consoles us about our humanity (though considering what people get up to, that's a queer word to equate with compassion, or even with emotional competence). By way of a ready example, take yesterday, Franklin. I was driving to work on Route 9W when a Fiesta turned right, cutting off a bicycle on the shoulder. The passenger door made a pretzel of the bike's front wheel, flipping the cyclist over the roof. He landed in a position that was subtly impossible, as if sketched by an unpromising art student. I'd already driven by, but in my rearview mirror, three other cars behind me pulled onto the shoulder to help.

It seems perverse to find solace in such misfortune. Yet presumably none of the drivers who descended to ring emergency services knew this cyclist personally or had any vested interest in his fate. Still, they cared enough to inconvenience themselves potentially to the point of having to testify in court. On my own account, the drama left me physically shaken—my hands trembled on the wheel, my mouth dropped and went dry. But I had acquitted myself well. I still blanch at the agony of strangers.

Yet I do know what it's like to get off-script. Surprise party? Funny I should have cited that. The week I was to turn ten I sensed something was up. There were whispers, a closet I was directed to avoid. If that weren't enough wink-and-nod, Giles crooned, "You're going to be surprised!" The second week of August I knew what signal day was approaching, and by the time it came around I was bursting.

Early afternoon of my birthday, I was ordered to the backyard.

"Surprise!" When I was invited back in, I discovered that five of my friends had been sneaked in the front while I'd been trying to peek through the drawn kitchen curtains. In our bunted living room, they surrounded a card table spread with a paper lace cloth and set with colorful paper plates, beside which my mother had placed matching seating cards inscribed with the fluid calligraphy of her professional work. There were also store-bought party favors: miniature bamboo umbrellas, noisemakers that tongued and honked. The cake, too, was from a bakery, and she had dyed the lemonade a vivid pink to make it seem more festive.

Doubtless my mother saw my face fall. Children are so lousy at covering up. At the party, I was desultory, laconic. I opened and closed my umbrella and rapidly tired of it, which was odd; I had powerfully envied other girls who had gone to parties to which I hadn't been invited and returned to school with precisely these pink-and-blue parasols. Yet somehow it was revealed to me that they came in packets of ten in a plastic bag and could be purchased even by the likes of us, and that devalued the favors more than I could say. Two of the guests I did not much like; parents never get it right about your friends. The cake was sealed in fondant icing like a plastic puck, and flavorlessly sweet; my mother's baking was better. There were more presents than usual, but all I remember of them is that each was unaccountably disappointing. And I was visited by a prescient taste of adulthood, an unbracketed "No Exit" sensation, which rarely plagues children: that we were sitting in a room and there was nothing to say or do. The minute it was over, the floor messy with crumbs and wrapping, I cried.

I must sound spoiled, but I wasn't spoiled. Little had been made of my birthdays in the past. Looking back, I feel simply despicable, too. My mother had gone to so much trouble. Her business didn't make much money for the longest time; she would labor over one card for over an hour and then sell it for a quarter, a price at which her customers would still squawk. In terms of our family's midget economy, the outlay had been considerable. She must have been bewildered; if she were a different sort of parent, she'd have spanked my ungrateful behind. Whatever had I contemplated that in comparison made my surprise party such a letdown?

Nothing. Or nothing in particular, nothing that I could form concretely in my head. That was the problem. I had been awaiting something large and amorphous, a vast big thing so marvelous that I could not even imagine it. The party she threw was all too imaginable. For that matter, had she brought in a brass band and magicians I'd have still been crestfallen. There was no extravagance that would not have fallen short, because it would be finite and fixed, one thing and not another. It would be only what it was.

The point is, I don't know what exactly I'd foreseen would happen to me when Kevin was first hoisted to my breast. I hadn't foreseen anything *exactly*. I wanted what I could not imagine. I wanted to be transformed; I wanted to be transported. I wanted a door to open and a whole new vista to expand before me that I had never known was out there. I wanted nothing short of revelation, and revelation by its nature cannot be anticipated; it promises that to which we are not yet privy. But if I extracted one lesson from my tenth birthday party, it was that expectations are dangerous when they are both high and unformed.

I may have misrepresented myself here. Of course I had misgivings. But my expectations of motherhood *were* high, or I wouldn't have agreed to go through with it. I'd attended hungrily to accounts from friends: *You have no idea what it's like until you have one of your own.* Whenever I allowed that I was less than enamored of infants and small children, I was assured: *I felt the same way! Couldn't stand other people's kids! But it's different—it's totally different—when they're yours.* I loved that, the prospect of *another country*, a strange land in which insolent miscreants were miraculously alchemized into, as you had said yourself, an answer to the "Big Question." Indeed, I may even have misrepresented my feelings about foreign countries. Yes, I was suffering travel fatigue, and yes, I did always fight a hereditary dread before hopping a plane. But setting foot in Namibia, or Hong Kong, even Luxembourg for the first time made me high as a kite.

What I hadn't realized, Brian had confided, *is that you fall in love with your own children. You don't just love them. You fall in love. And that moment, when you lay eyes on them for the first time—it's indescribable.* I do wish he had described it anyway. I do wish he had given it a try.

Dr. Rhinestein dangled the infant over my breast and rested the tiny creature down with—I was glad to see her evidence it at last—painstaking gentleness. Kevin was damp, and blood creased his neck, the crooks of his limbs. I put my hands diffidently around him. The expression on his twisted face was disgruntled. His body was inert; I could only interpret his lassitude as a lack of enthusiasm. Sucking is one of our few innate instincts, but with his mouth right at my enlarged brown nipple, his head lolled away in distaste.

Though I'd been warned that I wouldn't lactate on demand like a cafeteria milk dispenser, I kept trying; he kept resisting; he liked the other nipple no better. And all the while I was waiting. My breath shallow, I was waiting. And I kept waiting. *But everybody says—*, I thought. And then, distinctly: *Beware of what "everybody says."*

Franklin, I felt—absent. I kept scrabbling around in myself for this new *indescribable* emotion, like stirring a crowded silverware drawer for the potato peeler, but no matter how I rattled around, no matter what I moved out of the way, it wasn't there. The potato peeler is *always* in the drawer after all. It's under the spatula, it's slipped into the fold of the food-processor guarantee—

"He's beautiful," I mumbled; I had reached for a line from TV.

"Can I?" you asked shyly.

I offered the baby up. Whereas newborn Kevin had squirmed miserably on my breast, he rested an arm around your neck, as if having found his real protector. When I looked at your face, eyes closed, cheek pressed against our infant son, I recognized, if this does not sound too flippant: There's the potato peeler. It seemed so unfair. You were clearly choked up, filled to the back of your throat with a wonderment that defied expression. It was like watching you lick an ice cream cone that you refused to share.

I sat up, and you returned him reluctantly, at which point Kevin began to squall. Holding the baby, who still refused to suckle, I was revisited by that now-what sensation of my tenth birthday party: Here we were, in a room, and there seemed nothing to say or do. Minutes wore on, Kevin would yowl, rest limply, and jerk irritably from time to time; I felt the first stirrings of what, appallingly, I can only call boredom.

Oh, please don't. I know what you'd say. I was exhausted. I'd had a thirty-seven-hour labor and it was ridiculous to think I'd be capable of feeling anything but weary and numb. And it had been absurd to imagine fireworks; a baby is a baby. You'd goad me to remember that nutty little story I told you about the first time I ever went overseas for my junior year abroad at Green Bay, and I stepped onto the airstrip in Madrid to be obscurely disheartened that Spain, too, had trees. *Of course Spain has trees!* you jeered. I was embarrassed; of course I knew, in a way, it had trees, but with the sky and the ground and the people walking around—well, it just didn't seem that different. Later you referenced that anecdote to illustrate that my expectations were always preposterously outsized; that my very ravenousness for the exotic was self-destructive, because as soon as I seized upon the otherworldly, it joined this world and didn't count.

Besides, you would cajole, parenthood isn't something that happens in an instant. The fact of a baby—when so recently there was none—is so disconcerting that I probably just hadn't made the whole thing real to myself yet. I was dazed. That's it, I was dazed. I wasn't heartless or defective. Besides, sometimes when you're watching yourself too hard, scrutinizing your own feelings, they flee, they elude capture. I was self-conscious, and I was trying too hard. I had worked myself up into a kind of emotional paralysis. Didn't I just observe that these spontaneous outpourings of high passion are matters of faith? So my belief had flickered; I had allowed the *underfear* temporarily to get the best of me. I just needed to relax and let nature take its course. And for God's sake, to get some rest. I know you'd say all these things, because I said them to myself. And they didn't make a dent—in my sense that the whole thing was going wrong from the start, that I was not following the program, that I had dismally failed us and our newborn baby. That I was, frankly, a freak.

While they stitched up the tearing, you offered to take Kevin again, and I knew I should protest. I didn't. At being relieved of him, my gratitude was soul-destroying. If you want to know the truth, I was angry. I was frightened, I was ashamed of myself, but I also felt cheated. I wanted my surprise party. I thought, if a woman can't rely on herself to rise to an occasion like this, then she can't count on anything; from this point onward the world was on its ear. Prostrate, with my legs agape, I made a vow: that while I might have learned to expose my "private" parts for all the world to see, I would never reveal to anyone on earth that childbirth had left me unmoved. You had your unspeakable—"Never, ever tell me that you regret our own kid"; now I had mine. Reminiscing in company about this moment later, I would reach for that word, *indescribable*. Brian was a splendid father. I would borrow my good friend's tenderness for the day.

Eva·

Dear Franklin,

Tonight was our office Christmas party, which isn't easy to pull off with six people fresh from one another's throats. We have little in common, but in general I am glad for their companionship—not so much for heart-to-hearts over a sandwich as for quotidian exchanges about package deals in the Bahamas. (I'm sometimes so grateful for the busywork of flights to book that I could weep.) Likewise, the simple adjacency of warm bodies supplies the deepest of animal comfort.

The manager was kind to take me into her employ. *Thursday* having wounded so many people in this area, Wanda did worry at first that folks might start to avoid her premises just to keep from thinking about it. Yet to be fair to our neighbors, it is often an exceptionally heartfelt-sounding season's greetings that tips me off that a customer recognizes who I am. It's the staff whom I've disappointed. They must have hoped that rubbing up against a celebrity of sorts would confer distinction on themselves and that I would furnish stirringly disturbing stories for my coworkers to dine out on. But the association is too tangential, and I doubt their friends are impressed. Most of my tales are ordinary. There is only one story they want to hear, really, and that one they knew backward and forward before I came on board.

A wide-hipped divorcée with a braying laugh, Wanda herself may have hoped that we would become fast friends. By the end of our first lunch, she had confided that her ex-husband got an erection watching her pee, that she had just had a hemorrhoid "tied off," and that, until a near-miss with a Saks security guard at thirty-six, she'd been a compulsive shoplifter. I returned with the disclosure that after six months in my toy duplex I had finally gotten myself to buy curtains. You can see how she might have been a little put out that I'd got Manhattan while she got beads.

So tonight Wanda cornered me by the fax machine. She didn't want to pry, but had I sought out "help"? I knew what she meant, of course. The entire student body of Gladstone High School was offered free counseling by the school board, and even some of this year's intake, not even enrolled in 1999, has claimed to be traumatized and plunged to the couch. I didn't want to seem hostile and so say honestly that I couldn't see how the mere iteration of my troubles to a stranger would lessen them one iota, and that surely counseling was the logical refuge of those whose problems were ephemeral fancies and not matters of historical fact. So I demurred that my experience with the mental health profession had been rather sour, kindly omitting that the failures of my son's psychiatric care had made headlines coast to coast. Moreover, it didn't seem wise to confide that thus far I had found my only "help" in writing to you, Franklin. For somehow I feel certain that these letters are not on the list of prescribed therapies, since you are at the very heart of what I need to "get past" so that I might experience "closure." And what a terrible prospect is that.

Even back in 1983, I was bewildered why a standardized psychiatric label like *postnatal depression* was supposed to be consoling. Our compatriots seem to put much stock in slapping a tag on their ailments. Presumably a complaint common enough to have a name implies that you are not alone and dangles options like Internet chat rooms and community support groups for rhapsodic communal bellyaching. This compulsion to bandwagon has even infiltrated American small talk. I can't remember the last time anyone told me that he "took a long time to wake up." Instead I'm informed that he's *not a morning person.* All those fellow travelers who require killer cups of coffee on waking must provide one's disinclination to hop out of bed for a ten-mile run some extra clout.

I might have achieved a renewed appreciation for my own normative propensities, including a not unreasonable expectation that when bearing a child I will actually feel something, even something nice. But I hadn't changed that much. I'd never found solace in being just like everybody else. And though Dr. Rhinestein offered up *postnatal depression* like a present, as if simply being told that you are unhappy is supposed to cheer you up, I did not pay professionals to be plied with the obvious, with the merely descriptive. The term was less diagnostic than tautological: I was depressed after Kevin's birth because I was depressed after Kevin's birth. Thanks.

Yet she also suggested that because Kevin's disinterest in my breast had persisted, I might be suffering feelings of rejection. I colored. It embarrassed me that I might take the opaque predilections of such a tiny, half-formed creature to heart.

Of course she was right. At first I thought I was doing something wrong, not guiding his mouth. But no; I would place the nipple between his lips, where else could it go? He had sucked a time or two, but turned away, the bluish milk running down his chin. He'd cough, and, perhaps I imagined it, he even seemed to gag. When I went for an emergency appointment, Dr. Rhinestein informed me flatly that "sometimes this happens." My lord, Franklin, what you discover *sometimes happens* when you become a parent! I was distraught. In her office, I was surrounded by leaflets about building your baby's immune system. And I tried everything. I didn't drink. I eliminated dairy products. At tremendous sacrifice, I gave up onions, garlic, and chilies. I eliminated meat and fish. I installed a gluten-free regime, which left me with little more than a bowl of rice and an undressed salad.

In the end I was starving, while Kevin continued to feed in his lackluster way on a bottle of microwaved formula that he would only accept from you. He wouldn't even take my milk from a bottle, writhing from it without a sip. He could smell it. He could smell me. Yet he didn't test positive for an allergy, at least in the medical sense. Meanwhile, my once diminutive breasts were taut, sore, and leaking. Rhinestein was adamant that I not let my milk dry up, since occasionally this aversion—that was the word she used, Franklin, *aversion*—would abate. It was so awkward and painful that I never did quite get the hang of the expressing pump, though it was sweet of you to go out and buy that hospital-grade Medela. I'm afraid I came to hate it, a chill plastic substitute for a warm suckling infant. I was aching to give him the very milk of human kindness, and he did not want it, or he did not want it from me.

I shouldn't have taken it personally, but how could I not? It wasn't mother's milk he didn't want, it was Mother. In fact, I became convinced that our little bundle of joy had found me out. Infants have great intuition, because intuition's about all they've got. I felt certain that he could detect a telltale stiffening in my arms when I picked him up. I was confident that he could infer from a subtly exasperated quality in my voice when I burbled and cooed that burbling and cooing did not come naturally to me and that his precocious ear could isolate in that endless stream of placating blather an insidious, compulsive sarcasm. Moreover, since I had read—sorry, you had read—that it was important to smile at infants to try to elicit a smile in response, I smiled and smiled, I smiled until my face hurt, but when my face did hurt I was sure he could tell. Every time I forced myself to smile, he clearly knew that I didn't feel like smiling, because he never smiled back. He hadn't seen many smiles in his lifetime but he had seen yours, enough to recognize that in comparison there was something wrong with Mother's. It curled up falsely; it evaporated with revelatory rapidity when I turned from his crib. Is that where Kevin got it? In prison, that marionette smile, as if pulled up by strings.

I know you doubt me on this, but I did try very hard to form a passionate attachment to my son. But I had never experienced my feeling for you, for example, as an exercise that I was obliged to rehearse like scales on the piano. The harder I *tried*, the more aware I became that my very effort was an abomination. Surely all this tenderness that in the end I simply aped should have come knocking at the door uninvited. Hence it was not just Kevin who depressed me, or the fact that your own affections were increasingly diverted; I depressed me. I was guilty of emotional malfeasance.

But Kevin depressed me as well, and I do mean *Kevin* and not *the baby*. From the very beginning that child was particular to me, whereas you often asked How's *the kid?* or How's *my boy?* or W *here's the baby?* To me he was never "the baby." He was a singular, unusually cunning individual who had arrived to stay with us and just happened to be very small. For you he was "our son"—or, once you started to give up on me, "my son." There was a persistently generic character to your adoration that I'm certain he sensed.

Before you get your back up, I don't mean that as a criticism. It must be this overarching commitment to what is really an abstraction, to one's children right or wrong, that can be even more fierce than the commitment to them as explicit, difficult people, and that can consequently keep you devoted to them when as individuals they disappoint. On my part it was this broad covenant with children-in-theory that I may have failed to make and to which I was unable to resort when Kevin finally tested my maternal ties to a perfect mathematical limit on *Thursday*. I didn't vote for parties, but for candidates. My opinions were as ecumenical as my larder, then still chock full of salsa verde from Mexico City, anchovies from Barcelona, lime leaves from Bangkok. I had no problem with abortion but abhorred capital punishment, which I suppose meant that I embraced the sanctity of life only in grown-ups. My environmental habits were capricious; I'd place a brick in our toilet tank, but after submitting to dozens of spit-in-the-air showers with derisory European water pressure, I would bask under a deluge of scalding water for half an hour. My closet wafted with Indian saris, Ghanaian wraparounds, and Vietnamese *au dais*. My vocabulary was peppered with imports—*gemütlich, scusa, hugge, mzungu*. I so mixed and matched the planet that you sometimes worried I had no commitments to anything or anywhere, though you were wrong; my commitments were simply far-flung and obscenely specific.

By the same token, I could not love *a* child; I would have to love this one. I was connected to the world by a multitude of threads, you by a few sturdy guide ropes. It was the same with patriotism: You loved the *idea* of the United States so much more powerfully than the country itself, and it was thanks to your embrace of the American aspiration that you could overlook the fact that your fellow Yankee parents were lining up overnight outside FAO Schwartz with thermoses of chowder to buy a limited release of Nintendo. In the particular dwells the tawdry. In the conceptual dwells the grand, the transcendent, the everlasting. Earthly countries and single malignant little boys can go to hell; the idea of countries and the idea of sons triumph for eternity. Although neither of us ever went to church, I came to conclude that you were a naturally religious person.

In the end, mastitis put an end to my desperate search for whatever foodstuff was putting Kevin off my milk. Poor nutrition may have made me susceptible. That and fumbling to get Kevin to take the breast, which could have lacerated the nipples enough to transmit infection from his mouth. Inimical to my sustenance, he could still introduce me to corruption, as if already at year zero the more worldly party of our pair.

Since the first sign of mastitis is fatigue, it's little wonder that the early symptoms went unobserved. He'd worn me out for weeks. I bet you still don't believe me about his fits of pique, though a rage that lasts for six to eight hours seems less a fit than a natural state, from which the tranquil respites you witnessed were bizarre departures. Our son had *fits of peace*. And this may sound completely mad, but the consistency with which Kevin shrieked with precocious force of will the whole time he and I were alone, and then with the abruptness of switching off a heavy-metal radio station desisted the moment you came home—well, it seemed deliberate. The silence still ringing for me, you'd bend over our slumbering angel who unbeknownst to you was just beginning to sleep off his Olympian exertions of the day. Though I'd never have wished on you my own pulsing headaches, I couldn't bear the subtle distrust that was building between us when your experience of our son did not square with mine. I have sometimes entertained the retroactive delusion that even in his crib Kevin was learning to divide and conquer, scheming to present such contrasting temperaments that we were bound to be set at odds. Kevin's features were unusually sharp for a baby, while my own still displayed that rounded Marlo Thomas credulity, as if he had leeched my very shrewdness in utero.

Childless, I'd perceived baby crying as a pretty undifferentiated affair. It was loud; it was not so loud. But in motherhood I developed an ear. There's the wail of inarticulate need, what is effectively a child's first groping after language, for sounds that mean *wet* or *food* or *pin*. There's the shriek of terror—that no one is here and that there may never be anyone here again. There's that lassitudinous *wah-wah*, not unlike the call to mosque in the Middle East or improvisational song; this is creative crying, fun crying, from babies who, while not especially unhappy, have failed to register that we like to constrain weeping to conditions of distress. Perhaps saddest of all is the muted, habitual mewl of a baby who may be perfectly miserable but who, whether through neglect or prescience, no longer anticipates reprieve—who in infancy has already become reconciled to the idea that to live is to suffer.

Oh, I imagine there are as many reasons that newborn babies cry as that grown ones do, but Kevin practiced none of these standard lachrymal modes. Sure, after you got home he'd sometimes fuss a little like a *normal* baby that he wanted feeding or changing, and you'd take care of it and he'd stop; and then you'd look at me like, see? and I'd want to slug you.

With me, once you left, Kevin was not to be bought off with anything so petty and transitory as milk or dry diapers. If fear of abandonment contributed to a decibel level that rivaled an industrial buzz saw, his loneliness displayed an awesome existential purity; it wasn't about to be allayed by the hover of that haggard cow with her nauseating waft of white fluid. And I discerned no plaintive cry of appeal, no keen of despair, no gurgle of nameless dread. Rather, he hurled his voice like a weapon, howls smashing the walls of our loft like a baseball bat bashing a bus shelter. In concert, his fists sparred with the mobile over his crib, he kick-boxed his blanket, and there were times I stepped back after patting and stroking and changing and marveled at the sheer athleticism of the performance. It was unmistakable: Driving this remarkable combustion engine was the distilled and infinitely renewable fuel of *outrage.*

About what? you might well ask.

He was dry, he was fed, he had slept. I would have tried blanket on, blanket off; he was neither hot nor cold. He'd been burped, and I have a gut instinct that he didn't have colic; Kevin's was not a cry of pain but of wrath. He had toys dangling overhead, rubber blocks in his bed. His mother had taken six months off from work to spend every day by his side, and I picked him up so often that my arms ached; you could not say he lacked for attention. As the papers would be so fond of observing sixteen years later, Kevin had everything.

I have theorized that you can locate most people on a spectrum of the crudest sort and that it may be their position on this scale with which their every other attribute correlates: exactly how much they like being here, just being alive. I think Kevin hated it. I think Kevin was off the scale, he hated being here so much. He may even have retained some trace spiritual memory from before conception, and glorious nullity was far more what he missed than my womb. Kevin seemed incensed that no one had ever consulted him about turning up in a crib with time going on and on, when nothing whatsoever interested him in that crib. He was the least curious little boy I've ever encountered, with a few exceptions to that rule that I shudder to contemplate.

One afternoon I started to feel draggier than usual, at times a bit lightheaded. For days I'd been unable to keep warm, and it was late May;

outside, New Yorkers were in shorts. Kevin had pulled off a virtuosic recital. Huddled on the couch in a blanket, I reflected crankily on the fact that you'd stacked up more work than ever. Fair enough, as a free-lancer you didn't want your long-term clients to find an alternative scout, whereas my own company could be trusted to underlings and wouldn't just go away. But somehow this meant that I was stuck all day with hell in a handbasket while you tooled merrily off in your baby-blue pickup to window-shop for fields with the right-colored cows. I sus-pected that if our situation were reversed—you headed a thriving com-pany while I was a lone freelance location scout—Eva would be ex-pected to drop the scouting altogether like a hot brick.

When the elevator clanked and shuddered, I was just noticing that a small patch under my right breast had turned bright red, tender, and strangely stiff, mirroring the much larger such patch on the left. You opened the lattice gate and went straight to the crib. I was glad you were turning into such an attentive father, but of the two other inhabitants of our loft it was only your wife who appreciated the meaning of the word *hello*.

"*Please* don't wake him up," I whispered. "He's only been down twenty minutes and he's outdone himself today. I doubt he ever goes to sleep. He passes out."

"Well, has he been fed?" Deaf to my imprecations, you had laid him on your shoulder and were poking at his conked-out face. He looked de-ceptively content. Dreams of oblivion, perhaps.

"Yes, Franklin," I said with immoderate control. "After *four or five hours* of listening to little Kevin bring the house down, I thought of that. — Why are you using the stove?"

"Microwaving kills nutrients." Over lunch at McDonald's, you read baby books.

"It isn't so simple as figuring out what he wants and can't ask for. Most of the time he has no idea what he wants." I caught it: Your eyes flicked to-ward the ceiling like, oh-brother-not-this-again. "*You think I'm exaggerating.*"

"I didn't say that."

"You think he's 'crabby.' He's 'fussy' sometimes, because he's hungry—"

"Listen, Eva, I'm sure he gets a little ill-tempered—"

"See? A *little ill-tempered.*" I waddled to the kitchen in my blanket. "You don't believe me!" I had broken out in a cold sweat and must either have been flushed or pale. Walking hurt the soles of my feet and sent pains shivering down my left arm.

"I believe you're being straight up about your *perception* of how hard it is. But what did you expect, a walk in the park?"

"Not a carefree stroll, but this is like being *mugged* in the park!"

"Look, he's my son, too. I see him, too, every day. Sometimes he cries a little. So what. I'd worry if he didn't."

Apparently my testimony was tainted. I would have to bring in other witnesses. "You realize that John, downstairs, is threatening to move out?"

"John's a fag, and they don't like babies. This whole country's anti-child, I'm only just starting to notice." The severity wasn't like you, except that for once you were talking about the real country and not the star-spangled Valhalla in your head. "See?" Kevin had roused on your shoulder, then took the bottle peaceably without opening his eyes. "I'm sorry, but most of the time he seems pretty good-natured to me."

"He's not *good-natured* right now, he's exhausted! And so am I. I know I'm run down, but I don't feel right. Dizzy. Chills. I wonder if I'm running a fever."

"Well, that's a shame," you said formally. "Get some rest, then. I'll make dinner."

I stared. This coldness was so unlike you! I was supposed to belittle my own infirmities, you to make a to-do over them. Forcing you to go through the motions of your old solicitation, I took the bottle and plastered your hand to my forehead.

"Touch warm," you said, withdrawing the hand right away.

I'm afraid that I couldn't stand up anymore, and my skin hurt wherever the blanket touched it. So I staggered back to the couch, as if reeling from my revelation: You were angry at me. Fatherhood hadn't disappointed you; I had. You thought you'd married a trooper. Instead your wife was proving a whiner, the very peevish sort she decried amid America's malcontented overfed, for whom a commonplace travail like missing a FedEx delivery three times in a row and having to go to the depot constitutes intolerable "stress," the stuff of costly therapies and pharmaceutical redress. Even for Kevin's refusal to take my breast you held me dimly accountable. I had denied you the maternal tableau, that luscious Sunday-morning loll amid the sheets with buttered toast: son suckling, wife aglow, breasts spilling their bounty over the pillow, until you are forced out of bed for the camera.

Here I thought that I'd brilliantly disguised my true feelings about motherhood thus far, to the point of dereliction; so much lying in marriage is merely a matter of keeping quiet. I had refrained from throwing that self-evident diagnosis of *postnatal depression* down on our coffee table like a trophy but had kept this formal accreditation to myself. Meanwhile, I'd brought home loads of editing work but had only got through a few pages; I was eating badly and sleeping badly and showering at most every three days; I saw no one and rarely got out because Kevin's rages, in public, were not socially acceptable; and daily, I faced a purple churn of insatiable fury while rehearsing to myself with dull incomprehension, *I'm supposed to love this.*

"If you're having trouble coping, we don't lack for resources." You towered over my couch with your son, like one of those mighty peasant icons of dedication to family and motherland in Soviet murals. "We could hire a girl."

"Oh, I forgot to tell you," I mumbled. "I had a conference call with the office. We're researching demand for an African edition. AFRIWAP. Thought it had a ring."

"I did not mean," you stooped, your voice deep and hot in my ear, "that someone else could raise our son while you go python-hunting in the Belgian Congo."

"Zaire," I said.

"We're in this together, Eva."

"Then *why do you always take his side?*"

"He's only seven weeks old! He's not big enough to have a side!"

I wrenched myself to a stand. You may have mistaken me for tearful, but my eyes were watering of their own accord. When I lumbered into the bathroom, it was less to get the thermometer than to underscore the fact that you had failed to fetch it for me. When I returned with the tube poking from my mouth, was I imagining it, or were your eyes once more rolling toward the ceiling?

I scrutinized the mercury under a lamp. "Here—you read it. Everything's a bit blurry."

Absently you held the tube to the light. "Eva, you screwed it up. You must have put it near the bulb or something." You shook the mercury down, poked the end in my mouth, and left to change Kevin's diaper.

I shuffled to the changing table and made my offering. You checked the reading and stabbed me with a black glance. "It's not funny, Eva."

"What are you talking about?" This time they were tears.

"Heating the thermometer. It's a shitty joke."

"I'm not heating the thermometer. I just put the bulb under my tongue—"

"Crap, Eva, it reads practically 104°."

"Oh."

You looked at me. You looked at Kevin, for once torn between loyalties. Hastily you scooped him from the table, then bedded him with such perfunctoriness that he forgot his strict theatrical schedule and cranked up his daytime I-hate-the-whole-world shriek. With that manliness I'd always adored, you ignored him.

"I'm so sorry!" In one swoop you lifted me off the floor and swept me back to the couch. "You're really sick. We've got to call Rhinestein, get you to a hospital—"

I was sleepy, fading. But I do remember thinking that it had taken too much. Wondering if I would have a cool cloth on my forehead, ice water and three aspirin at my side, and Dr. Rhinestein on the telephone if the thermometer had read only 101°.

Eva

DECEMBER 21, 2000

Dear Franklin,

I'm a bit rattled, since the phone just rang and I have no idea how this Jack Marlin person got my unlisted number. He claimed to be a documentary maker from NBC. I suppose the droll working title of his project, "Extracurricular Activities," sounds authentic enough, and at least he was quick to distance himself from "Anguish at Gladstone High," that hasty Fox show that Giles informed me was mostly on-camera weeping and prayer services. Still I asked Marlin why he imagined that I would want to participate in one more sensationalist postmortem of the day my life as I understood it came to an end, and he said I might want to tell "my side of the story."

"What side would that be?" I was on record as assuming the opposition when Kevin was seven weeks old.

"For example, wasn't your son the victim of sexual abuse?" Marlin plied.

"A *victim*? Are we talking about the same boy?"

"What about this Prozac business?" The sympathetic purr could only have been put on. "That was his defense at the trial, and it was pretty well supported."

"That was his lawyer's idea," I said faintly.

"Just generally—maybe you think Kevin was misunderstood?"

I'm sorry Franklin, I know I should have hung up, but I speak to so few people outside the office . . . . What did I say? Something like, "I'm afraid I understand my son all too well." And I said, "For that matter, Kevin must be one of the best-understood young men in the country. Actions speak louder than words, don't they? Seems to me he got across his personal *worldview* better than most. Seems to me that you should be interviewing children who are a great deal less accomplished at self-expression."

"What do you think he was trying to say?" asked Marlin, excited at having snagged a real live specimen of what has become a remote parental elite, whose members are strangely uneager for their fifteen minutes on TV.

I'm sure the call was recorded, and I should have watched my tongue. Instead I blurted, "Whatever his *message* was, Mr. Marlin, it was clearly disagreeable. Why on earth would you like to provide him one more forum for propounding it?"

When my caller launched into some nonsense about insight into disturbed boys being vital so that next time "we can see it coming," I cut him off.

"I saw it coming for nearly sixteen years, Mr. Marlin," I snapped. "A fat lot of good that did." And I hung up.

I know he was only doing his job, but I don't like his job. I'm sick of newshounds snuffling at my door like dogs that smell meat. I am tired of being made a meal of.

I was gratified when Dr. Rhinestein, having lectured that it was practically unheard of, was forced to concede that I had indeed contracted mastitis in both breasts. Those five days in Beth Israel on an antibiotic drip were painful, but I was coming to treasure physical pain as a form of suffering I understood, in contrast to the baffling despair of new motherhood. The relief of simple quiet was immense.

Still in the grip of your breadwinning fever and perhaps—admit it— reluctant to put our son's "good-natured" temperament to the test, you took this opportunity to hire a nanny. Or should I say two nannies, since by the time I came home the first one had quit.

Not that you were volunteering this information. In the pickup as you were driving me home you simply began nattering about the marvelous Siobhan, and I had to stop you. "I thought her name was Carlotta."

"Oh, *her*. You know, a lot of these girls are immigrants who plan to go AWOL when their visa turns into a pumpkin. They don't really care about kids."

Whenever the pickup hit a bump, my breasts flamed. I wasn't looking forward to the excruciating process of expressing milk on arrival, which

I'd been dictated to do religiously every four hours for the sake of the mastitis, even if only to pour the milk down the drain. "I take it Carlotta didn't work out."

"I told her up front he was a *baby*. A pooping, farting, burping—"

"—Screaming—"

"—*Baby*. She seemed to have expected, like, a self-cleaning oven or something."

"So you sacked her."

"Not exactly. But Siobhan is a saint. From Northern Ireland, of all places. Maybe folks used to being bombed and shit can keep a little whimpering in perspective."

"You mean Carlotta quit. After only a few days. Because Kevin was— what's the term of art? *Cranky*."

"After one day, if you can believe it. And when I call at lunchtime to make sure everything's all right, she has the gall to insist I cut my workday short and relieve her of my son. I was tempted not to pay her a dime, but I didn't want us blacklisted with her agency." (Prophetic. We were black-listed by her agency two years later.)

Siobhan *was* a saint. A bit homely at first glance, with unruly black curls and that deathly white Irish skin, she had one of those doll-baby bodies that didn't narrow at the joints, but merely crimped a bit; though she was slim enough, the columnar limbs and waistless torso gave the impression of thickness. Yet I grew to regard her as prettier with time because she was so good-hearted. True, I was apprehensive when she mentioned at our introduction that she was a member of that Alpha Course Christian sect. I conceived of such people as mindless fanatics and dreaded being subjected to daily testimonials. A prejudice, and one Siobhan did not substantiate; she rarely raised the subject again. Maybe this offbeat religious route was her bid to opt out of the Catholic-Protestant folderol back in County Antrim, of which she never spoke, and from which she had further insulated herself with the Atlantic Ocean as if for good measure.

You teased me that I took such a shine to Siobhan just because she was a *Wing and a Prayer* fan, for she'd used AWAP when traveling the Continent. Unsure what God would "call" her to do, she said she couldn't imagine a more delightful occupation than professional globetrotting, stirring my nostalgia for a life already growing distant. She ignited the same pride that I hoped Kevin would some day kindle, when he got old enough to appreciate his parents' accomplishments. I'd already indulged the odd fantasy whereby Kevin would pore over my old photographs, asking breathlessly, *Where's this? What's that? You've been to AFRICA? Wow!* But Siobhan's admiration proved cruelly misleading. Kevin did *pour over* a box of my photographs once—with kerosene.

After a second round of antibiotics, the mastitis cleared up. Resigned that Kevin was on formula for keeps, I allowed my breasts to engorge and dry up, and with Siobhan holding down the fort was at length able to return to AWAP that fall. What a relief, to dress well, to move briskly, to speak in low, adult tones, to tell someone what to do and to have them do it. While I took fresh relish in what had previously grown workaday, I also chided myself for having imputed to a tiny bundle of confusion such malign motives as an intent to drive a wedge between you and me. I'd been unwell. It had been harder to adapt to our new life than I'd expected. Recuperating some of my old energy and discovering with pleasure that I had agitated myself back down to my former figure, I assumed that the worst was over and made a mental note that the next time one of my friends bore a first child I would fall all over myself to sympathize.

Often I'd invite Siobhan to linger with me for a cup of coffee when I came home, and the enjoyment I took in conversing with a woman roughly half my age may have been less the delight of leaping generations than the more standard one of talking to anybody. I was confiding in Siobhan because I was not confiding in my husband.

"You must have wanted Kevin something fierce," said Siobhan on one such occasion. "Seeing the sights, meeting amazing people—and paid for the pleasure, if you can credit it! I can't imagine giving that up."

"I haven't given it up," I said. "After a year or so, I'll resume business as usual."

Siobhan stirred her coffee. "Is that what Franklin expects?"

"It's what he ought to expect."

"But he mentioned, like," she was not comfortable with tattling, "that your running off for months at a go, like—that it was over."

"For a while there, I was a little burned out. Always running out of fresh underwear; all those French train strikes. It's possible I gave the wrong impression."

"Oh, aye," she said sorrowfully. I doubt that she was trying to make trouble, though she saw it coming. "He must have been lonely, when you'd go away. And now if you take your trips again, he'd be the only one to mind wee Kevin when I'm not here. Of course, in America, don't some da's stay home, and the ma's go to work?"

"There are Americans and Americans. Franklin's not the type."

"But you run a whole company. Sure you could afford . . . "

"Only in the financial sense. It's hard enough when a man's wife is profiled in *Fortune* magazine and he's only location-scouted the advertisement on the facing page."

"Franklin said you used to be on the road five months a year."

"Obviously," I said heavily, "I'll have to cut back."

"You know, you may find that Kevin's a wee bit tricky, like. He's a—an uneasy baby. Sometimes they grow out of it." She hazarded starkly, "Sometimes they don't."

You thought that Siobhan was devoted to our son, but I read her loyalty as more to you and me. She rarely spoke of Kevin in other than a logistical sense. A new set of bottles had been sterilized; our disposable "nappies" were running low. For such a passionate girl this mechanical approach seemed unlike her. (Though she did observe once, "He has like, beady eyes, so he does!" She laughed nervously and qualified, "I mean—intense." "Yes, they're unnerving, aren't they," I rejoined, as neutrally as I knew how.) But she adored the two of us. She was entranced with the freedom of our dual self-employment, and, despite the evangelical romance with "family values," was clearly disconcerted that we would willfully impair this giddy liberty with the ball and chain of an infant. And maybe we gave her hope for her future. We were middle-aged, but we listened to The Cars and Joe Jackson; if she didn't approve of bad language, she may still have been broadly heartened that a codger nearing forty could decry a dubious baby manual as *horseshit*. In turn, we paid her well and accommodated her church obligations. I gave her the odd present, like a silk scarf from Thailand, which she gushed over so much that I was embarrassed. She thought you devastatingly handsome, admiring the sturdiness of your figure and the disarming flop of your flaxen hair. I wonder if she didn't "fancy" you a tad.

Having every reason to assume that Siobhan was contented in our employ, I was puzzled to note as the months advanced that she began to look curiously drawn. I know the Irish don't age well, but even for her thin-skinned race she was much too young to develop those hard worry lines across her forehead. She could be testy when I returned from the office, snapping when I had simply expressed surprise that we were low again on baby food, "Och, it doesn't all go in his mouth, you know!" She immediately apologized, and grew fleetingly tearful but wouldn't explain. She became more difficult to entice into a debriefing cup of coffee, as if anxious to be quit of our loft, and I was nonplussed by her reaction when I proposed that she move in. You remember that I offered to wall off that ill-used catchall corner, and to install a separate bath. What I had in mind would have been far more capacious than the cubbyhole she shared in the East Village with a loose, boozing, godless waitress she didn't much like. I wouldn't have cut her salary, either, so she'd have saved buckets on rent. Yet at the prospect of becoming a live-in nanny, she recoiled. When she protested that she could never break her lease on that Avenue C hovel, it sounded like, well, *horseshit*.

And then she started calling in sick. Just once or twice a month at first, but at length she was phoning in with a sore throat or an upset stomach at least once a week. She looked wretched enough; she couldn't have been eating well, because those doll-baby curves had given way to a stick-figure frailty, and when the Irish pale, they look exhumed. So I was hesitant to accuse her of faking. Deferentially I inquired if she had boyfriend problems, if there was trouble with her family in Carickfergus, or if she was pining for Northern Ireland. "Pining for *Northern Ireland*," she repeated wryly. "You're having me on." That moment of humor served to highlight that her jokes had grown rare.

These impromptu vacations of hers put me to great inconvenience, since according to the now-established logic of your tenuous freelance employment versus my fatuous security as CEO, I was the one to stay home. Not only would I have to reschedule meetings or conduct them awkwardly in conference calls, but a whole extra day spent with our precious little ward tipped a precarious equilibrium in me; by nightfall on a day I had not been girded for Kevin's unrelenting horror at his own existence, I was, as our nanny would say, *mental*. It was through the insufferable addition of that extra day a week that Siobhan and I came, tacitly at first, to understand each other.

Clearly, God's children are meant to savor His glorious gifts without petulance, for Siobhan's uncanny forbearance could only have issued from catechism. No amount of wheedling would elicit whatever was driving her abed every Friday. So if only to give her permission, I complained myself.

"I have no regrets about my travels," I began one early evening as she prepared to go, "but it's a shame I met Franklin so late. Four years just the two of us wasn't nearly enough time to get tired of him! I think it must be nice if you meet your partner in your twenties, with long enough as a childless couple to, I don't know, get a little bored even. Then in your thirties you're ready for a change, and a baby is welcome."

Siobhan looked at me sharply, and though I expected censure in her gaze I caught only a sudden alertness. "Of course, you don't mean Kevin isn't welcome."

I knew the moment mandated hurried reassurances, but I couldn't furnish them. This would happen to me sporadically in the coming years: I would do and say what I was supposed to week upon week without fail until abruptly I hit a wall. I would open my mouth and *That's a really pretty drawing, Kevin* or *If we tear the flowers out of the ground they'll die, and you don't want them to die, do you?* or *Yes, we're so awfully proud of our son, Mr. Cartland* would simply not come out.

"Siobhan," I said reluctantly. "I've been a little disappointed."

"I know I've been poorly, Eva—"

"Not in you." I considered that she may have understood me perfectly well and had misinterpreted me on purpose. I shouldn't have burdened this young girl with my secrets, but I felt strangely impelled. "All the bawling and the nasty plastic toys . . . I'm not sure quite what I had in mind, but it wasn't this."

"Sure you might have a touch of postpartum—"

"Whatever you call it, I don't feel joyful. And Kevin doesn't seem joyful either."

"He's a baby!"

"He's over a year and a half. You know how people are always cooing, *He's such a happy child!* Well, in that instance there are unhappy children. And nothing I do makes the slightest bit of difference."

She kept fiddling with her daypack, nestling the last of her few possessions into its cavity with undue concentration. She always brought a book to read for Kevin's naps, and I finally noticed that she'd been stuffing the exact same volume in that daypack for months. I'd have understood if it was a Bible, but it was only an inspirational text—slim, the cover now badly stained—and she had once described herself as an avid reader.

"Siobhan, I'm useless with babies. I've never had much rapport with small children, but I'd hoped . . . Well, that motherhood would reveal another side of myself." I met one of her darting glances. "It hasn't."

She squirmed. "Ever talk to Franklin, about how you're feeling?"

I laughed with one *ha.* "Then we'd have to *do* something about it. Like what?"

"Don't you figure the first couple of years is the tough bit? That it gets easier?"

I licked my lips. "I realize this doesn't sound very nice. But I keep waiting for the emotional payoff."

"But only by giving do you get anything back."

She shamed me, but then I thought about it. "I give him my every weekend, my every evening. I've even given him my husband, who has no interest in talking about anything but our son, or in doing anything together besides wheeling a stroller up and down the Battery Park promenade. In return, Kevin smites me with the evil eye, and can't bear for me to hold him. Can't bear much of anything, as far as I can tell."

This kind of talk was making Siobhan edgy; it was domestic heresy. But something seemed to cave in her, and she couldn't keep up the cheerleading. So instead of forecasting what delights were in store for me once Kevin became a little person in his own right, she said gloomily, "Aye, I know what you mean."

"Tell me, does Kevin—respond to you?"

"*Respond?*" The sardonicism was new. "You could say that."

"When you're with him during the day, does he laugh? Gurgle contentedly? *Sleep?*" I realized that I had refrained from asking her as much for all these months, and that in so doing I'd been taking advantage of her ungrudging nature.

"He pulls my hair," she said quietly.

"But all babies—they don't know—"

"He pulls it very hard indeed. He's old enough now and I think he knows it hurts. And Eva, that lovely silk muffler from Bangkok. It's in shreds."

Ch-plang! Ch-plang! Kevin was awake. He was banging a rattle onto that metal xylophone you came home with (alas), and was not showing musical promise.

"When he's alone with me," I said over the racket. "Franklin calls it *cranky*—"

"He throws all his toys out of the playpen, and then he screams, and he will not stop screaming until they are all back, and then he throws them out again. *Flings* them."

P-p-plang-k-chang-CHANG! PLANK! P-P-P-plankpankplankplank! There was a violent clatter, from which I construed that Kevin had kicked the instrument from between the slats of his crib.

"It's desperate!" Siobhan despaired. "He does the same thing in his highchair, with Cheerios, porridge, cream crackers ... With all his food on the floor like, I haven't a baldy where he gets the energy!"

"You mean," I touched her hand, "you don't know where *you* get the energy."

Mwah ... Mmwah ... Mmmmwhawhah ... He started like a lawnmower. Siobhan and I looked each other in the eye. *Mwah-eee! EEEeee! EEEEEEEE! EEahEEEEEEEE!* Neither of us arose from our chair.

"Of course," said Siobhan hopefully, "I guess it's different when it's yours."

"Yup," I said. "Totally different."

EEahEEEEEahEEEE! EEahEEEEEahEEEE! EEahEEEEEahEEEE!

"I used to want a big family," she said, turning away. "Now I'm not so sure."

"If I were you," I said, "I'd think twice."

Kevin filled the silence between us as I fought a rising panic. I had to say something to forestall what was coming next, but I couldn't think of any comment to pass that wouldn't further justify what I wished fervidly to prevent.

"Eva," she began. "I'm knackered. I don't think Kevin likes me. I've prayed until I'm blue—for patience, for love, for strength. I thought God was testing me—"

"When Jesus said *Suffer the little children*," I said dryly, "I don't think nannying is what he had in mind."

"I hate to think I've failed Him! Or you, Eva! Still, do you think there's any chance—do you think you could use me at Wing and a Prayer? Those guidebooks, you said loads of them's researched by university students and that. Could you—could you please, please send me to Europe, or Asia? I'd do a brilliant job, I promise!"

I sagged. "You mean you want to quit."

"You and Franklin been dead decent, you must think me terrible ungrateful. Still, when you lot move to the suburbs you'd have to find someone else anyway, right? 'Cause I came over here bound and determined to live in New York City."

"I am, too! Who says we're moving to the burbs?"

"Franklin, of course."

"We're not moving to any suburbs," I said firmly.

She shrugged. She had already withdrawn so from our little unit that she regarded this miscommunication as none of her affair.

"Would you like more money?" I offered pathetically; my full-time residence in this country was beginning to take its toll.

"The pay's great, Eva. I can't do it anymore, just. Every morning I wake up . . . ."

I knew exactly how she woke feeling. And I couldn't do it to her any longer. I think I'm a bad mother, and you always thought so, too. But deep inside me lurks the rare maternal bone. Siobhan was at her limit. Though it ran wildly counter to our interests, her earthly salvation was within my power to grant.

"We're updating NETHERWAP," I said morosely; I had an awful premonition that Siobhan's resignation would be effective right away.

"Would you like that? Rating hostels in Amsterdam? The rijsttafels are delicious."

Siobhan forgot herself and threw her arms around me. "Would you like for me to try and quiet him?" she offered. "Maybe his nappy——"

"I doubt that; it's too rational. No, you've put in a full day. And take the rest of the week off. You're shattered." I was already sweetening her up, to get her to stick around until we found a replacement. Fat chance.

"One last thing," said Siobhan, tucking my note with the name of NETHERWAP's editor into her pack. "Wee'uns vary, of course. But Kevin should really be talking by now. A few words anyway. Maybe you should ask your doctor. Or talk to him more."

I promised, then saw her to the elevator, shooting a rueful glance at the crib. "You know, it is different when it's yours. You can't go home." Indeed, my yearning to *go home* had grown recurrent, but was most intense when I was already there.

We exchanged wan smiles, and she waved behind the gate. I watched from the front window as she ran down Hudson Street, away from our loft and *wee Kevin* as fast as her unshapely legs could carry her.

I returned to our son's marathon and looked down at his writhing dudgeon. I was not going to pick him up. No one was there to make me and I didn't want to. I would not, as Siobhan had suggested, check his diaper, nor would I warm a bottle of milk. I would let him cry and cry. Resting both elbows on the crib rail, I cradled my chin on intertwined fingers. Kevin was crouched on all fours in one of the positions that the New School commended for birthing: primed for exertion. Most tots cry with their eyes shut, but Kevin's were slit open. When our gazes locked, I felt we were finally communicating. His pupils were still almost black, and I could see them flintily register that for once Mother was not going to get in a flap about whatever might be the matter.

"Siobhan thinks I should talk to you," I said archly over the din. "Who else is going to, since you drove her off? That's right, you screamed and puked her out the door. What's your problem, you little shit? Proud of yourself, for ruining Mummy's life?" I was careful to use the insipid falsetto the experts commend. "You've got Daddy snowed, but Mummy's got your number. You're a little shit, aren't you?"

Kevin hoisted to a stand without missing a yowl. Clutching the bars, he screamed at me from just a few inches away, and my ears hurt. So scrunched up, his face looked like an old man's, and it was screwed into the I'm-gonna-get-you expression of a convict who's already started digging a tunnel with a nail file. On a purely zoo-keeping level, my proximity was hazardous; Siobhan hadn't been kidding about the hair.

"Mummy was happy before widdle Kevin came awong, you know that, don't you? And now Mummy wakes up every day and wishes she were in France. Mummy's life sucks now, doesn't Mummy's life suck? Do you know there are some days that Mummy would rather be dead? Rather than listen to you screech for one more minute there are some days that Mummy would jump off the Brooklyn Bridge—"

I turned, and blanched. I may never have seen quite that stony look on your face.

"They understand speech long before they learn to talk," you said, pushing past me to pick him up. "I don't understand how you can stand there and watch him cry."

"Franklin, ease up, I was only kidding around!" I shot a parting private glare at Kevin. It was thanks to his caterwauling that I hadn't heard the elevator gate. "I'm blowing off a little steam, okay? Siobhan quit. Hear that? Siobhan quit."

"Yeah, I heard you. Too bad. We'll get someone else."

"It turns out that all along she's regarded this job as a modern rewrite of the Book of Job—Look, I'll change him."

You wrenched him away. "You can steer clear until you get your mind right. Or jump off a bridge. Whichever comes first."

I trailed after you. "Say, what's this about *moving to the suburbs*? Since when?"

"Since—I quote—*the little shit* is getting mobile. That elevator is a death trap."

"We can gate off the elevator!"

"He needs a *yard*." Sanctimoniously, you balled the wet diaper in the pail. "Where we can toss a baseball, fill a pool."

The awful revelation dawned that we were dealing with your childhood—an idealization of your childhood—that could prove, like your fantasy United States, an awesome cudgel. There's no more doomed a struggle than a battle with the imaginary.

"But I love New York!" I sounded like a bumper sticker.

"It's dirty and swimming in diseases, and a kid's immune system isn't fully developed until he's seven years old. And we could stand to move into a good school district."

"This city has the best private schools in the country."

"New York private schools are snobbish and cutthroat. Kids in this town start worrying about getting into Harvard at the age of six."

"What about the tiny matter that your wife doesn't want to leave this city?"

"You had twenty years to do whatever you wanted. I did, too. Besides, you said you yearned to spend our money on something worthwhile. Now's your chance. We should buy a house. With land and a tire swing."

"My mother never made a single major decision based on what was good for *me*."

"Your mother has locked herself in a closet for forty years. Your mother is insane. Your mother is hardly the parent to look to as a role model."

"I mean that when I was a kid, parents called the shots. Now I'm a parent, kids call the shots. So we get fucked coming and going. I can't believe this." I flounced onto the couch. "I want to go to Africa, and you want to go to *New Jersey*."

"What's this about Africa? Why do you keep bringing it up?"

"We're going ahead with AFRIWAP. *The Lonely Planet* and *The Rough Guide* are starting to squeeze us badly in Europe."

"What does this edition have to do with you?"

"The continent is huge. Someone has to do a preliminary canvass of countries."

"Someone *other than you*. You still don't get it, do you? Maybe it was a mistake for you to think of motherhood as 'another country.' This is no overseas holiday. It's serious—"

"*We're talking about human lives, Jim!*"

You didn't even smile. "How would you feel if he lost a hand reaching through that elevator gate? If he got asthma from all this crap in the air? If some loser kidnapped him from your grocery cart?"

"The truth is, *you* want a house," I charged. "*You* want a yard. You have this dorky Norman Rockwell vision of Daddydom, and *you* want to coach Little League."

"Got that right." You straightened victoriously at the changing table, Kevin in his blazing fresh Pampers on your hip. "And there are two of us, and one of you."

It was a ratio I was destined to confront repeatedly.

Eva

Dear Franklin,

I agreed to visit my mother for Christmas, so I'm writing from Racine. At the last minute—when he found out I was coming—Giles decided that his family would spend the holiday with his in-laws instead. I could choose to feel injured, and I do miss my brother if only as someone with whom to mock my mother, but she's getting so frail now at seventy-eight that our patronizing despair on her behalf seems unfair. Besides, I understand. Around Giles and his kids, I never mention Kevin, Mary's lawsuit; a little traitorously, I never even mention you. But through benign discussion of the snow, whether to put pine nuts in the *sarma*, I still personify a horror that, in defiance of my mother's locked doors and sealed windows, has gotten inside.

Giles resents my having co-opted the role of family tragic figure. He only moved as far as Milwaukee, and the child at closer hand is always chopped liver, while for decades I made a living from being as far away from Racine as I could get. Like De Beers restricting the supply of diamonds, I made myself scarce, a cheap gambit in Giles's view for artificially manufacturing the precious. Now I have stooped even lower, using my son to corner the market on pity. Having kept his head below the parapet working for Budweiser, he's in grudging awe of anyone who's been in the newspaper. I keep trying to find some way of telling him that this is the kind of dime-store fame that the most unremarkable parent could win in the sixty seconds it takes an automatic assault rifle to fire a hundred bullets. I don't feel special.

You know, there's a peculiar smell in this house that I used to find rank. Remember how I used to insist that the air was thin? My mother rarely opens a door, much less airs the place out, and I was convinced that the distinctive headache that always hit me on arrival was the beginnings of carbon dioxide poisoning. But now the close, clinging admixture of stale lamb grease, dust, and mildew sharpened with the medicinal reek of her colored inks comforts me somehow.

For years I wrote off my mother as having no grasp of my life, but after *Thursday* I came to terms with the fact that I'd made no effort to understand hers. She and I had been distant for decades not because she was agoraphobic but because I'd been remote and unsparing. Needing kindness myself, I am kinder now, and we get on amazingly well. During my traveling days, I must have seemed uppity and superior, and my new desperation for safety has restored my status as a proper child. For my part, I have come to recognize—since any world is by definition self-enclosed and, to its inhabitants, all there is—that geography is relative. To my intrepid mother, the living room could be Eastern Europe, my old bedroom Cameroon.

Of course, the Internet is the best and worst thing that ever happened to her, and she is now able to order anything from support hose to grape leaves over the Web. Consequently, the multitude of errands I used to run for her whenever I was home is already dispatched, and I feel a little useless. I suppose it's good that technology has granted her independence— if that's what it's called.

My mother, by the way, doesn't avoid talking about Kevin at all. This morning as we opened our few presents beside her spindly tree (ordered on-line), she noted that Kevin rarely misbehaved in the traditional sense, which always made her suspicious. All children misbehave, she said. You were better off when they did so in plain view. And she recalled our visit when Kevin was about ten—old enough to know better, she said. She'd just finished a stack of twenty-five one-of-a-kind Christmas cards commissioned by some wealthy Johnson Wax exec. While we were preparing *khurabia* with powdered sugar in the kitchen, he systematically snipped the cards into ragged paper snowflakes. (You said—a mantra—he was "just trying to help.") *That boy had something missing*, she pronounced, in the past tense, as if he were dead. She was trying to make me feel better, though I worried that what Kevin was missing was a mother like mine.

In fact, I trace the flowering of my present filial grace to a gasping phone call the night of *Thursday* itself. To whom else was I to turn but my mother? The primitiveness of the tie was sobering. For the life of me, I can't remember a single time that Kevin—distraught over a scraped knee, a falling-out with a playmate—has called me.

I could tell from her collected, formal greeting, *Hello, Sonya Khatchadourian speaking,* that she hadn't seen the evening news.

Mother? was all I could manage—plaintive, grade-school. The ensuing heavy breathing must have sounded like a crank call. I felt suddenly protective. If she lived in mortal dread of a trip to Walgreens, how would she confront the vastly more appreciable terror of a murderous grandson? For pity's sake, I thought, she's seventy-six, and she already lives through a mail slot. After this, she'll never pull the covers off her head.

But Armenians have a talent for sorrow. You know, she wasn't even *surprised?* She was somber but remained composed, and for once, even at her advanced age, she acted and sounded like a real parent. I could depend on her, she assured me, an assertion that hitherto would have made me scoff. It was almost as if all that dread of hers finally redeemed itself; as if on some level she was relieved that her whole batten-down-the-hatches gestalt hadn't proved baseless. After all, she'd been here before, where the rest of the world's tragedy lapped at her shore. She may have hardly left the house, but of everyone in our family, she most profoundly appreciated how the careless way adjacent people live their lives can threaten all you hold dear. Most of her extended family had been slaughtered, her very husband picked off by Japanese like skeet; Kevin's rampage fit right in. Indeed, the occasion seemed to liberate something in her, not only love but bravery, if they are not in many respects the same thing. Mindful that the police were bound to expect me to remain on hand, I declined her invitation to Racine. Gravely, my shut-in mother *offered to fly to me.*

It was shortly after Siobhan jumped ship (she never did come back, and I had to post her last paycheck to AmEx in Amsterdam) that Kevin stopped screaming. Stopped cold. Maybe, his nanny dispatched, he felt his mission accomplished. Maybe he'd finally concluded that these high-decibel workouts did not reprieve him from the remorseless progress of life-in-a-room and so were not worth the energy. Or maybe he was hatching some new gambit now that Mother had grown inured to his wailing, as one does in the latter stages of a neglected car alarm.

While I was hardly complaining, Kevin's silence had an oppressive quality. First off, it was truly silence—total, closed-mouth, cleansed of the coos and soft cries that most children emit when exploring the infinitely fascinating three square feet of their nylon net playpen. Second, it was inert. Although he was now able to walk—which, like every skill to come, he learned in private—there didn't appear to be anywhere he especially wanted to go. So he would sit, in the playpen or on the floor, for hours, his unlit eyes stirring with an unfocused disaffection. I couldn't understand why he didn't at least comb up a little aimless fluff from our Armenian rugs, even if he refused to loop colored rings on their plastic spike or crank the noisemaker on his Busy Box. I would surround him with toys (there was hardly a day you didn't come home with a new one), and he would stare at them or kick one away. He did not play.

You'd remember that period largely as the time we were fighting about whether to move and whether I would take that long trip to Africa. But I mostly remember staying home on those draggy days after we'd once again lost a nanny, and mysteriously they did not pass any faster than the ones during which Kevin bellowed.

Previous to motherhood I had imagined having a small child at elbow as something like owning a bright, companionable dog, but our son exerted a much denser presence than any pet. Every moment, I was hugely aware he was there. Though his new phlegmatism made it easier to edit copy at home, I felt watched and grew restive. I'd roll balls to Kevin's feet, and once I did entice him into rolling it back. Excited, ridiculously so, I rolled it back; he rolled it back. But once I rolled it between his legs a third time, that was that. With a listless glance, he left the ball at his knee. I did begin to think, Franklin, that he was smart. In sixty seconds, he got it: Were we to pursue this "game," the ball would continue to roll back and forth along the same trajectory, an exercise that was overtly pointless. I was never able to engage him in it again.

This impenetrable flatness of his, combined with a reticence extending well past the point that all your manuals forecast first attempts at speech, compelled me to consult our pediatrician. Dr. Foulke was reassuring, ready with the conventional parental sop that "normal" developmental behavior embraced a range of idiosyncratic stalls and leaps, though he did subject our son to a battery of simple tests. I'd expressed concern that Kevin's unresponsiveness was due to a hearing deficit; whenever I called his name, he turned with such an in-his-own-good-time deadpan that it was impossible to tell whether he had heard me. Yet though he was not necessarily *interested* in anything I said, his ears worked fine, and my theory that the volume of his infantile screaming had damaged his vocal chords was not borne out by medical science. I even voiced a worry that Kevin's withdrawn quality might indicate early signs of autism, but apparently he did not display the telltale rocking and repetitive behavior of such unfortunates trapped in their own world; if Kevin was trapped, it was in the same world as yours and mine. In fact, the most I wrested from Dr. Foulke was his musing that Kevin "was a floppy little boy, wasn't he?" in reference to a certain physical slackness. The doctor would lift our son's arm, let go, and the arm would drop like a wet noodle.

So insistent was I that Foulke pin a disability to our son, stamp a name-brand American syndrome on Kevin's forehead, that the pediatrician must have thought me one of those neurotic mothers who craved distinction for her child but who in our civilization's latter-day degeneracy could only conceive of the exceptional in terms of deficiency or affliction. And honestly, I did want him to find something wrong with Kevin. I yearned for our son to have some small disadvantage or flaw to kindle my sympathy. I was not made of stone, and whenever I espied a little boy with a piebald cheek or webbed fingers waiting patiently in the outer office, my heart went out to him, and I quivered to consider what tortures he would suffer at recess. I wanted to at least feel sorry for Kevin, which seemed a start. Did I truly wish our son to have webbed fingers? Well, yes, Franklin. If that's what it took.

He was underweight, in consequence of which he never had those rounded, blunt features of the roly-poly toddler that can make even homely children adorable for that photogenic window between two and three. Instead his face had that ferret-like sharpness from his earliest years. If nothing else, I'd have liked to have been able to gaze later at photographs of a pudgy heartbreaker and wonder what went wrong. Instead, the snaps I have (and you took stacks) all document a sobersided wariness and disturbing self-possession. The narrow olive face is instantly familiar:

recessed eyes, sheer straight nose with a wide bridge and slight hook, thin lips set in an obscure determination. Those pictures are recognizable not only for their resemblance to the class photograph that appeared in all the papers but for their resemblance to me.

But I wanted him to look like you. His whole geometry was based on the triangle and yours on the square, and there is something cunning and insinuating about acute angles, stable and trustworthy about the perpendicular. I didn't expect to have a little Franklin Plaskett clone running around the house, but I wanted to glance at my son's profile and apprehend with a flash of lambent joy that he had your strong tall forehead— rather than one that shelved sharply over eyes that might begin as strikingly deep-set but were destined with age to look sunken. (I should know.) I was gratified that his appearance was noticeably Armenian, but I had hoped that your robust Anglo optimism would quicken the sluggish, grudge-bearing blood of my Ottoman heritage, brightening his sallow skin with ruddy hints of football games in fall, highlighting his sullen black hair with glints of Fourth of July fireworks. Moreover, the furtiveness of his gaze and the secrecy of his silence seemed to confront me with a miniature version of my own dissembling. He was watching me and I was watching me, and under this dual scrutiny I felt doubly self-conscious and false. If I found our son's visage too shrewd and contained, the same shifty mask of opacity stared back at me when I brushed my teeth.

I was averse to plunking Kevin in front of the television. I hated children's programming; the animation was hyperactive, the educational shows boppy, insincere, and condescending. But he seemed so understimulated. So one afternoon when I had burned out on bubbling, *It's time for our juice!* I switched on the after-school cartoons.

"I don like dat."

I reeled away from the beans I was tailing for dinner, certain from the lifeless monotonic delivery that this line had not escaped from the A-Team. I rushed to turn the TV down low and stooped to our son. "What did you say?"

He repeated levelly, "I don like dat."

With more urgency than I may ever have applied to this foundering relationship, I took one of his shoulders in each hand. "Kevin? *What do you like?*"

It was a question that he was not prepared to answer and that to this day at the age of seventeen he is still unable to answer to his own satisfaction, much less to mine. So I returned to what he *didn't like*, a subject that would soon prove inexhaustible.

"Sweetheart? What is it you want to stop?"

He batted a hand against the television tube. "I don like dat. Turn id ov."

I stood up and marveled. Oh, I turned the cartoon off all right, thinking *Christ, I have a toddler with good taste.* As if myself the child, I was impelled to experiment with my riveting new toy, to poke at its buttons and see what lit up.

"Kevin, do you want a cookie?"

"I hate cookies."

"Kevin, will you talk to Daddy when he comes home?"

"Not if I don leew wike it."

"Kevin, can you say 'Mommy'?"

I'd been queasy about what I wanted our son to call me. *Mommy* sounded babyish, *Ma* rube-ish, *Mum* servile. *Mama* was the stuff of battery-operated doll babies, *Mom* rang earnest and gee-whiz, *Mother* seemed formal for 1986. Looking back, I wonder if I did not like being called any of the popular names for mother because I did not like—well, because I was still ill at ease with being one. Little matter, since the predictable answer was, "No."

When you came home, Kevin refused to repeat his loquacious performance, but I recited it word for word. You were ecstatic. "Complete sentences, right off the bat! I've read that what seem like late bloomers can be incredibly bright. They're perfectionists. They don't want to try it out on you until they've got it right."

I nursed a competing theory: that, having secretly been able to talk for years, he had enjoyed eavesdropping on the unwitting; that he was a spy. And I attended less to his grammar than to what he said. I know this kind of assertion always gets up your nose, but I did sometimes consider that, between us, I was the more interested in Kevin. (In my mind's eye, I can see you going apoplectic.) I mean, interested in Kevin as Kevin really was, not Kevin as Your Son, who had continually to battle against the formidable fantasy paragon in your head, with whom he was in far more ferocious competition than he ever was with Celia. For example, that evening I remarked, "I've been waiting ages to find out what's going on behind those piercing little eyes."

You shrugged. "Snakes and snails and puppy dog tails."

See? Kevin was (and remains) a mystery to me. You had that insouciant boy-thing going and blithely assumed that you had been there yourself and there was nothing to find out. And you and I may have differed on so profound a level as the nature of human character. You regarded a child as a partial creature, a simpler form of life, which evolved into the complexity of adulthood in open view. But from the instant he was laid on my breast I perceived Kevin Khatchadourian as pre-extant, with a vast, fluctuating interior life whose subtlety and intensity would if anything diminish with age. Most of all, he seemed hidden from me, while your experience was one of sunny, leisurely access.

Anyway, for several weeks he would talk to me during the day, and when you came home he clammed up. At the clank of the elevator, he'd shoot me a complicitous glance: Let's put one over on Daddy. I may have found a guilty pleasure in the exclusivity of my son's discourse, thanks to which I was apprised that he *did not like* rice pudding with or without cinnamon and he *did not like* Dr. Seuss books and he *did not like* the nursery rhymes put to music that I checked out from the library. Kevin had a specialized vocabulary; he had genius for N-words.

The sole memory I retain of any proper childhood glee during this era was at his third birthday party, when I was busy pouring cranberry juice in his sippy cup, and you were tying ribbons on packages that you would only have to untie for him minutes later. You had brought home a three-tiered marble layer cake from Vinierro's on First Avenue that was decorated with a custom butter-cream baseball theme and had placed it proudly on the table in front of his booster chair. In the two minutes our backs were turned, Kevin displayed much the same gift that he'd exhibited earlier that week by methodically pulling all the stuffing through a small hole in what we thought was his favorite rabbit. My attention was drawn by a dry chuckle that I could only characterize as a nascent snicker. Kevin's hands were those of a plasterer. And his expression was rapturous.

Such a young birthday boy, not yet fully comprehending the concept of birthdays, had no reason to grasp the concept of *slices*. You laughed, and after you'd gone to so much trouble I was glad you could take the mishap as comedy. But as I cleaned his hands with a damp cloth, my chortle was muted. Kevin's technique of plunging both hands mid-cake and spreading its whole body apart in a single surgical motion was uneasily reminiscent of those scenes in medical shows when the patient is "coding" and some doctor yells, "Crack 'em!" Gorier programs toward the end of the millennium left little to the imagination: The ribcage is riven with an electric hacksaw, the ribs pulled back, and then our handsome ER doc plunges into a red sea. Kevin hadn't simply played with that cake. He had ripped its heart out.

In the end, of course, we finalized the inevitable swap: I would license you to find us a house across the Hudson; you would license me to take my reconnaissance trip to Africa. My deal was pretty raw, but then desperate people will often opt for short-term relief in exchange for long-term losses. So I sold my birthright for a bowl of soup.

I don't mean that I regret that African sojourn, though in terms of texture it was badly timed. Motherhood had dragged me down to what we generally think of as the lower matters: eating and shitting. And that's ultimately what Africa is about. This may be ultimately what every country is about, but I have always appreciated efforts to disguise that fact, and I might have been better off traveling to more decorative nations, where the bathrooms have roseate soaps and the meals at least come with a garnish of radicchio. Brian had commended children as a marvelous antidote for jadedness; he said that you get to re-appreciate the world through their awestruck eyes and everything that you were once tired of suddenly looks vibrant and new. Well, the cure-all had sounded terrific, better than a facelift or a prescription for Valium. But I am disheartened to report that whenever I saw the world through Kevin's eyes, it tended to appear unusually dreary. Through Kevin's eyes the whole world looked like Africa, people milling and scrounging and squatting and lying down to die.

Yet amid all that squalor I still couldn't locate a safari company that could properly be considered budget; most charged hundreds of dollars per day. Likewise, the lodging divided off in a way that eliminated my target market: It was either luxurious and pricey, or filthy and too cut-rate. A variety of Italian and Indian restaurants were a good value, but authentic African eateries served mostly unseasoned goat. Transport was appalling, the train lines prone to simply stop, the aircraft decrepit, the pilots fresh from Bananarama Flight School, the driving kamikaze, the buses bursting with cackling passengers three times over capacity and aflap with chickens.

I know I sound finicky. I had been to the continent once in my twenties and had been entranced. Africa had seemed truly *elsewhere.* Yet in the interim, the wildlife population had plummeted, the human one burgeoned; the intervening rise in misery was exponential. This time appraising the territory with a professional eye, I discounted whole countries as out of the question. Uganda was still picking corpses from the mouths of crocodiles discarded by Amin and Obote; Liberia was ruled by that murderous idiot, Samuel Doe; even in those days, Hutus and Tutsis were hacking each other to pieces in Burundi. Zaire was in the grip of Mobutu Sese Seko, while Mengistu continued to ransack Ethiopia and Renamo ran amok in Mozambique. If I listed South Africa, I risked having the entire series boycotted in the States. As for the bits that were left, you may have accused me of being *unnurturing,* but I was reluctant to take responsibility for callow young Westerners trooping off to these perilous parts armed only with a distinctive sky-blue volume of *Wing and a Prayer.* I was bound to read about robberies in Tsavo that left three dead in a ditch for 2,000 shillings, a camera, and a guidebook and feel certain it was all my fault. As Kevin would later illustrate, I attract liability, real or imagined.

So I began to conclude that the marketing people's heads were up their backsides. They had researched the demand, but not the supply. I did not have faith that even our intrepid army of college students and my thoroughgoing staff could put together a solitary volume that would protect its users from making the grossest of missteps for which they could pay so dearly that a continent full of bargains would still seem overpriced. For once I did feel motherly—toward customers like Siobhan, and the last place I'd want pastily complected, there's-good-in-all-of-us Siobhan to end up was in a scorching, pitiless Nairobi slum. AFRIWAP was a nonstarter.

But my greatest disappointment was in myself. While relinquishing the idea of AFRIWAP might have freed me to gallivant about the continent without taking notes, I'd grown dependent on research for a sense of purpose on the road. Released from an itinerary dictated by conveniently tabbed chapters, I felt aimless. Africa is a lousy place to wonder incessantly what you are doing there, though there is something about its careless, fetid, desperate cities that presses the question.

I could not shut you and Kevin from my mind. That I missed you fiercely served as an aching reminder that I had been missing you since Kevin was born. Away, I felt not emancipated but remiss, sheepish that unless you'd finally solved the nanny problem you'd have to cart him with you in the pickup to scout. Everywhere I went, I felt laden, as if slogging the potholed streets of Lagos with five-pound leg weights: I had started something back in New York, it was not finished by any means, I was shirking, and what's more, what I had started was going badly. That much I faced; that much my isolation was good for. After all, the one thing you cannot escape in Africa is children.

In the latter legs of the three-month trip, which you'll recall I cut short, I made resolutions. One too many sojourns —this one launched less in a spirit of exploration than simply to make a point, to prove that my life had *not* changed, that I was still young, still curious, still free—was only proving beyond doubt that my life had indeed changed, that at forty-one I was not remotely young, that I had truly sated a certain glib curiosity about other countries, and that there was a variety of liberty of which I could no longer avail myself without sinking the one tiny island of permanence, of durable meaning and lasting desire, that I had managed to annex in this vast, arbitrary sea of international indifference.

Camping in Harare's airport lounge on gritty linoleum because there were no seats and the plane was eight hours late, the whole 737 having been appropriated by some government minister's wife who wanted to go shopping in Paris, I seemed to have unaccountably lost my old serene certainty that inconvenience (if not outright disaster) was the springboard for nearly every proper adventure abroad. I was no longer persuaded by that old saw planted in every AWAP intro that the worst thing that can happen to any trip is for everything to go smoothly. Instead, like any standard Western tourist, I was impatient for air-conditioning and disgruntled that the only available drinks were Fanta orange, which I did not like. With the concessions' refrigeration broken down, they were boiling.

That sweaty, protracted delay allowed me to contemplate that so far my commitment to motherhood had been toe-in-the-water. In a funny way, I resolved, I had to remake that arduous decision of 1982 and jump into parenthood with both feet. I had to get pregnant with Kevin all over again. Like his birth, raising our son could be a transporting experience, but only if I stopped fighting it. As I was at pains to teach Kevin for years thereafter (to little effect), rarely is the object of your attentions innately dull or compelling. Nothing is interesting if you are not interested. In vain, I had been waiting for Kevin to prove out, to demonstrate as I stood arms folded that he was worthy of my ardor. That was too much to demand of a little boy, who would only be as lovable to me as I allowed him to be. It was past time that I at least met Kevin halfway.

Flying into Kennedy, I was bursting with determination, optimism, and goodwill. But in retrospect, I do feel obliged to observe that I was at my most passionate about our son when he was not there.

Merry Christmas,
Eva

Dear Franklin,

Having asked gently beforehand if I was up to it, tonight my mother had a little holiday hen party here, and I think she regretted her timing. As it happened, yesterday in Wakefield, Massachusetts, a very large, unhappy man—a software engineer named Michael McDermott, who the whole nation now knows is a science fiction fan, much as most men off the street are familiar with our son's predilection for undersized clothing—walked into Edgewater Technology with a shotgun, an automatic, and a pistol and murdered seven of his coworkers. I gather Mr. McDermott was upset—and here I am, conversant with details of his financial life, down to the fact that his six-year-old car was on the verge of repossession—that his employers had garnished his wages for back taxes.

I couldn't help but think of your parents, since they don't live far from Wakefield. Your father was always concerned that his top-of-the-line appliances have a fine sense of proportion, a preoccupation that surely extends to behavioral ratios like grievance to redress. Your parents must imagine that the world of the physically preposterous, which doesn't respect *materials*, is closing in on them.

Having long since given up on the painful charade of inviting Sonya Khatchadourian for soirees in return and suffering the kind of fanciful excuses she always supplied me for why she could not attend opening night of my school play, these old birds had sampled my mother's *lahmajoon* and sesame-topped *ziloogs* many times before and were disinclined to dwell on the finger food. Instead, with some diffidence, given the guest of honor, they were all dying to talk about Michael McDermott. One dowager commented sorrowfully that she could see how a young man might feel rejected with a nickname like "Mucko." My crusty Aunt Aleen muttered that her own ongoing fight with the IRS—a $17 disputed underpayment in 1991 had over the years ballooned from interest and late fees to over $1,300—might soon move her to firearms herself. But they all subtly deferred to me, the resident expert with insight into the twitchy mind.

I was finally forced to remind these women firmly that this friendless, overweight loner and I had never met. It seemed to register all at once that no one in this country specialized in plain old murder these days, any more than a lawyer would study plain old Law. There was Workplace Massacre, and there were School Shootings, quite another field of concentration altogether, and I sensed a collective embarrassment in the room, as if they'd all rung the Sales Department when they should have asked for Customer Relations. Since it's still too dangerous to bring up "Florida" in company without being sure that everyone is on-side, someone prudently changed the subject back to the *lahmajoon*.

Anyway, who says crime doesn't pay? I doubt the IRS will ever see a dime of Mucko's money now, and the forty-two-year-old tax cheat is bound to cost Uncle Sam a far prettier penny in prosecution costs than the IRS would ever have squeezed from his paycheck.

That's the way I think now, of course, since the price of justice is no longer an abstract matter in my own life but a hard-nosed tally of dollars and cents. And I do often have little flashbacks of that trial—the civil trial. The criminal one is almost a blank.

"Ms. Khatchadourian," I will hear Harvey begin stentoriously on his re-direct. "The prosecution has made much of the fact that you ran a company in Manhattan while leaving your son to the care of strangers, and that when he turned four you were away in Africa."

"At the time I was unaware that having a life was illegal."

"But after your return from this trip you hired someone else to oversee the day-to-day business of your firm, in order to be a better mother to your child?"

"That's right."

"Didn't you take over as his primary caregiver? In fact, aside from occasional baby-sitters, didn't you cease to bring in outside help altogether?"

"Frankly, we gave up on hiring a nanny because we couldn't find any-one to put up with Kevin for more than a few weeks."

Harvey looked sour. His client was self-destructive. I imagined that this quality made me special, but my lawyer's fatigued expression sug-gested that I was a set type.

"But you were concerned that he needed continuity, and that's why you terminated this revolving door of young girls. You no longer went into the office nine-to-five."

"Yes."

"Ms. Khatchadourian, you loved your work, correct? It gave you great personal satisfaction. So this decision was a considerable sacrifice, all for the sake of your child?"

"The sacrifice was enormous," I said. "It was also futile."

"No further questions, your honor." We had rehearsed *enormous*, period; he shot me a glare.

Was I, back in 1987, already planning my defense? Though my open-ended leave from AWAP was on a grand, over-compensatory scale, it was cosmetic. I thought it *looked good*. I'd never conceived of myself as someone who dwelled upon what other people thought, but hoarders of guilty se-crets are inevitably consumed with appearances.

Hence, when you two met my plane at Kennedy I stooped to hug Kevin first. He was still in that disconcerting rag-doll phase, "floppy"; he didn't hug back. But the strength and duration of my own embrace pa-raded my born-again conversion in Harare. "I've missed you so much!" I said. "Mommy's got two surprises, sweetheart! I brought you a present. But I'm also going to promise that Mommy's never, ever going away for this long again!"

Kevin just got floppier. I stood up and arranged his willful shocks of hair, embarrassed. I was playing my part, but onlookers might have de-duced from my child's unnatural lassitude that I kept him handcuffed to the water heater in the basement.

I kissed you. Although I'd thought children liked to see their parents be affectionate with one another, Kevin stamped impatiently and mooed, dragging at your hand. Maybe I was mistaken. I never saw my mother kiss my father. I wish I had.

You cut the kiss short and mumbled, "It may take a while, Eva. For kids this age, three months is a lifetime. They get mad. They think you're never coming back."

I was about to josh that Kevin seemed more put out that I *had* come back, but I caught myself; one of our first sacrifices to family life was lightness of heart. "What's this *uherr, uherr!* thing?" I asked as Kevin continued to tug at you and moo.

"Cheese doodles," you said brightly. "The latest must-have. Okay, buster! Let's go find you a bag of glow-in-the-dark petrochemicals, kiddo!" And you tottered off down the terminal in tow, leaving me to wheel my luggage.

In the pickup, I had to remove several viscous doodles from the passenger seat, in various stages of dissolve. Kevin's dietary enthusiasm did not extend to eating the snacks; he sucked them, leeching off their neon coating and imbuing them with enough saliva to melt.

"Most kids like sugar?" you explained zestfully. "Ours likes salt." Apparently a sodium fetish was superior to a sweet tooth in every way.

"The Japanese think they're opposites," I said, slipping my gooey collection out the window. Though there was a shallow back seat, Kevin's child seat was fastened between us, and I was sorry that I couldn't, as I used to, place a hand on your thigh.

"Mommer farted," said Kevin, now halving the difference between *Mommy* and *Mother*. (It was cute. It must have been.) "It stinks."

"That's not the kind of thing you have to announce, Kevin," I said tightly. I'd had that mashed beans and banana side dish at the Norfolk before catching the plane.

"How about Junior's?" you proposed. "It's on the way, and they're kid-friendly."

It wasn't like you to fail to consider that I'd been in transit from Nairobi for fifteen hours, so I might be a little tired, bloated from the flight, overfed with airline Danishes and cheddar packets, and less than in the mood for a loud, camp, brightly lit hash house whose sole redeeming feature was cheesecake. I'd privately hoped that you'd have found a sitter and met my plane alone, to sweep me off to a quiet drink where I could bashfully reveal my turned maternal leaf. In other words, I wanted to get away from Kevin the better to confide to you how very much more time I planned to spend with him.

"Fine," I said faintly. "Kevin, either eat those cheese thingies or I'll put them away. Don't crumble them all over the truck."

"Kids are messy, Eva!" you said merrily. "Loosen up!"

Kevin shot me a crafty orange smile and fisted a doodle into my lap.

At the restaurant, Kevin scorned the booster seat as for babies. Since clearly parenthood turns you overnight into an insufferable prig, I lectured, "ALL right, Kevin. But remember: You only get to sit like an adult if you *act* like one."

"NYEE nyee, nyeh nyeh. Nyeh nyeh-*nyee*-nyeh: Nyeh *nyeh*-nyeh nyeh-nyeh nyeh-nyeh nyeh *nyeh*-nyeh nyeh-nyeh *nyee* nyeh nyeh." With waltzing mockery, he had captured my stern cadence and preachy inflection with such perfect pitch that he might have a future singing covers as a lounge singer.

"Cut it out, Kevin." I tried to sound offhand.

"Nye-nye *nyee*, nye nye!"

I turned to you. "How long has *this* been going on?"

"Nyeh nyeh nyeh NYEE nyeh nyeh-nyeh nyeh?"

"A month? It's a phase. He'll grow out of it."

"Nyeh nyeh? Nyeh-nyeh nyeee. Nyeh nyeh nyeh-nyeh-nyeh."

"I can't wait," I said, increasingly loath to let anything out of my mouth, lest it come parroting back to me in *nyeh-nyeh*-speak.

You wanted to order Kevin onion rings, and I objected that he must have been eating salty crap all afternoon. "Look," you said. "Like you, I'm grateful when he eats anything. Maybe he's craving some trace element, like iodine. Trust nature, I say."

"Translation: You like eaty-whizzes and curly-munchies, too, and you've been bonding over snack food. Order him a hamburger patty. He needs some protein."

When our waitress read back our order, Kevin *nye-nye*-ed throughout; "NYEE-nyeh nyeh-nyeh, nyeh nyeh-nyeh nyeh-nyeh-nyeeeh" apparently translates "garden salad, house dressing on the side."

"What a cute little boy," she said, glancing with desperation at the wall clock.

When his patty came, Kevin retrieved the tall, faceted saltcellar with huge pour-holes and covered the beef with salt until it looked like Mount Kilimanjaro after a recent snow. Disgusted, I reached over with a table knife to scrape it off, but you held my arm. "Why can't you let anything with this little guy be fun, or funny?" you chided quietly. "The salt thing is a phase too, and he'll grow out of it too, and later we'll tell him about it when he's older and it'll make him feel he had plenty of quirky personality even when he was a little kid. It's life. It's good life."

"I doubt Kevin's going to have a hard time finding quirks." Although the sense of maternal mission that had powered me through my last fortnight was fast abating, I had made myself a promise, Kevin a promise on arrival, implicitly you one as well. I took a breath. "Franklin, I made a major decision while I was gone."

With the classic timing of dining out, our waitress arrived with my salad and your cheesecake. Her feet gritted on the lino. Kevin had emptied the saltcellar onto the floor.

"That lady has poop on her face." Kevin was pointing at the birthmark on our waitress's left cheek, three inches across and roughly the shape of Angola. She'd slathered beige concealer over the big brown blotch, but most of the makeup had worn off. Like most disguises, the cover-up was worse than honest flaw, a lesson I had yet to register on my own account. Before I could stop him, Kevin asked her directly, "Why don't you clean your face? It's poopy."

I apologized profusely to the girl, who couldn't have been much more than eighteen and had no doubt suffered from that blemish her whole life. She managed a dismal smile and promised to bring my dressing.

I wheeled to our son. "You knew that spot wasn't 'poop,' didn't you?"

"Nyeh NYEE nyeh nyeh nyeh-nyeh *nyee*, nyeh-nyeh nyeh?" Kevin skulked in the booth, his eyes at half-mast and glittering. He'd placed his fingers on the table and his nose against its rim, but I could tell from that telltale sparky squint that below the table lurked a grin: wide, tight-lipped, and strangely forced.

"Kevin, you know that hurt her feelings, didn't you?" I said. "How would you like it if I told you your face was 'poopy'?"

"Eva, kids don't understand that grown-ups can be touchy about their looks."

"Are you sure they don't understand that? You read this somewhere?"

"Can we not ruin our first afternoon out together?" you implored. "Why do you always have to think the worst of him?"

"Where did that come from?" I asked, looking perplexed. "It sounds more as if *you* always think the worst of *me*."

Innocent mystification would remain my tack for the next three years. Meantime, the mood had gone all wrong for my announcement, so I got it over with as unceremoniously as I could. I'm afraid my intentions came out as defiant: Stick that in your pipe and smoke it, if you think I'm such a rotten mother.

"Wow," you said. "Are you sure? That's a big step."

"I remembered what you said about Kevin and talking, that maybe he didn't for so long because he wanted to do it right. Well, I'm a perfectionist, too. And I'm not doing AWAP *or* motherhood right. At the office, I'm continually taking days off with no warning, and publications get behind schedule. Meanwhile, Kevin wakes up and has no idea who's taking care of him today, his mother or some hopeless hireling who'll hightail it by the end of the week. I'm thinking mostly until Kevin is in primary school. Hey, it might even be good for W&P. Bring in a new perspective, fresh ideas. The series may be overly dominated by my voice."

"*You*," shock-horror, "domineering?"

"*NYEEEEEEE?* Nyeh-nyeh *nyeeeeh* nyeh?"

"Kevin, stop it! That's enough. Let Mommer and Daddy talk—"

"NYEH-nyeh, NYEEEE nyeh—! Nyeh nyeh-NYEEH—!"

"I mean it, Kevin, quit the *nyeh-nyeh* or we're leaving."

"Nyeh NYEE nyeh, nyeh nyeh, nyeh nyeh *nyeh-nyeh* nyeh nyeh *NYEE-nyeh!*"

I don't know why I threatened him with departure, lacking any evidence that he wanted to stay. This was my first taste of what would become a chronic conundrum: how to punish a boy with an almost Zen-like indifference to whatever you might deny him.

"Eva, you're just making everything worse—"

"How do you propose to get him to shut up?"

"Nyeh nyeh NYEEE nyeh-*nyeeh* nyeh nyeh-nyeh nyeh nyeeeeeee-nyeeeeeeee?"

I slapped him. It wasn't very hard. He looked happy.

"Where'd you learn that trick?" you asked darkly. And it was a trick: This was the first sentence of mealtime conversation that did not get translated into *nyeh-nyeh.*

"Franklin, he was getting louder. People were starting to look over."

Now Kevin started to wail. His tears were a bit late, in my view. I wasn't moved. I left him to it.

"They're looking over because you hit him," you said sotto voce, lifting our son and cuddling him into your lap as his weeping escalated to a shriek. "It's not done anymore, Eva. Not here. I think they've passed a law or something. Or they might as well have. It's considered assault."

"I smack my own kid, and I get arrested?"

"There's a consensus—that violence is no way to get your point across. Which it sure as heck isn't. I don't want you to do that again, Eva. *Ever.*"

So: I slap Kevin. You slap me. I got the picture.

"Can we please get out of here?" I proposed coldly. Kevin was winding down to lurching sobs, but he could easily milk the decrescendo another good ten minutes. Christ, it was practically a love pat. What a little performer.

You signaled for the bill. "This is hardly the context in which I wanted to make *my* announcement," you said, wiping Kevin's nose with a napkin. "But I have some news, too. I bought us a house."

I did a double take. "You *bought* us a house. You didn't find one for me to look at. It's a done deal."

"If I didn't pounce it was going to be snapped up by somebody else. Besides, you weren't interested. I thought you'd be pleased, glad it's over."

"Well. There's only so pleased I'm going to get over something that wasn't my idea in the first place."

"That's it, isn't it? You can't get behind anything that isn't your own pet project. If you didn't personally cook up SUBURBAWAP then you're all disaffected. Good luck doing all that delegating at the office. It doesn't come naturally."

You left a generous tip. The extra three bucks, I inferred, was to cover those *poopy face* cracks. Your motions were mechanical. I could see you were hurt. You'd searched far and wide for this house, you'd been looking forward to delivering your big news, and you must have been excited about the property or you wouldn't have bought it.

"I'm sorry," I whispered as we walked out, and other patrons peered furtively at our party. "I'm just tired. I *am* pleased. I can't wait to see it."

"Nyeh *nyeh*-nyeh. Nyeh-nyeh nyeh. Nyeh *nyeh* nyeh . . . "

I thought, *Everyone in this restaurant is relieved we're leaving.* I thought, *I've become one of those people I used to feel sorry for.* I thought, *And I still feel sorry for them, too.*

More than ever.

Eva

Dear Franklin,

Call it a New Year's resolution, since for years I've been busting to tell you: I hated that house. On sight. It never grew on me, either. Every morning I woke to its glib surfaces, its smart design features, its sleek horizontal contours, and actively hated it.

I grant that the Nyack area, woodsy and right on the Hudson, was a good choice. You had kindly opted for Rockland County in New York rather than somewhere in New Jersey, a state in which I'm sure there are many lovely places to live but that had a *sound* to it that would have slain me. Nyack itself was racially integrated and, to meet the eye, down-market, with the same slight dishevelment of Chatham—though unlike Chatham, its shabby, unassuming quality was an illusion, since pretty much all the new arrivals for decades had been stinking rich. Main Street eternally backed up with Audis and BMWs, its overpriced fajita joints and wine bars bursting, its dumpy outlying two-bedroom clapboards listing for 700 grand, Nyack's one pretension was its lack of pretension. In contrast to Gladstone itself, I'm afraid, a relatively new bedroom community to the north, whose tiny town center—with fake gas street lamps, split-rail fencing, and commercial enterprises like "Ye Olde Sandwich Shoppe"—epitomized what the British call "twee."

In fact, my heart sank when you first plowed the pickup proudly up the long, pompous drive off Palisades Parade. You'd told me nothing about the property, the better to "surprise" me. Well. I was surprised. A flat-roofed, single-storied expanse of glass and sandy brick, at a glance it resembled the headquarters of some slick, do-gooding conflict-resolution outfit with more money than it knew what to do with, where they'd give "peace prizes" to Mary Robinson and Nelson Mandela.

Had we never discussed what I envisioned? You must have had some idea. My fantasy house would be old, Victorian. If it had to be big it would be high, three stories and an attic, full of nooks and crannies whose original purpose had grown obsolete—slave quarters and tackle rooms, root cellars and smokehouses, dumbwaiters and widow's walks. A house that was falling to bits, that dripped history as it dropped slates, that cried out for fiddly Saturday repairs to its rickety balustrade, while the fragrant waft of pies cooling on counters drifted upstairs. I'd furnish it with secondhand sofas whose floral upholstery was faded and frayed, garage-sale drapes with tasseled tiebacks, ornate mahogany sideboards with speckled looking glass. Beside the porch swing, struggling geraniums would spindle out of an old tin milking pail. No one would frame our ragged quilts or auction them off as rare early American patterns worth thousands; we'd throw them on the bed and wear them out. Like wool gathering lint, the house would seem to accumulate junk of its own accord: a bicycle with worn brake shoes and a flat tire; straight-backs whose dowel rods need regluing; an old corner cabinet of good wood but painted a hideous bright blue, which I keep saying I'm going to strip down and never do.

I won't go on, because you know *exactly* what I'm talking about. I know they're hard to heat, I know they're drafty. I know the septic tank would leak, the electric bills run high. I know you'd anguish that the old well in the backyard was a dangerous draw for neighborhood urchins, for I can picture this home so vividly in my mind that I can walk across its overgrown yard with my eyes closed and fall in that well myself.

Curling out of the truck onto the semicircular concrete turnaround in front of our new abode, I thought, *abode*, isn't that the word. My ideal home was cozy and closed the world out; looking out onto the Hudson (admittedly, the view was smashing), these wide plate glass windows advertised an eternal open house. Pink pebble-fill with flagstone paths skirted its splay like one big welcome mat. The facade and central walkway were lined with stunted shrubs. No black walnut trees, no uncultivated riot of goldenrod and moss, but *shrubs*. Surrounding them? A lawn. Not even the sweet cool sort, whose fine bright shoots tempt a laze with lemonade and bees, but that springy, scratchy kind, like those green abrasive scrub pads for washing dishes.

You flung open the entrance. The foyer dribbled into a living room the size of a basketball court, and then up a couple of low stairs and there was the dining "room," partially segmented from the kitchen with a divider to pass food through—some concoction with *sun-dried tomatoes*, no doubt. I had yet to lay eyes on one door. I panicked, thinking, *There's nowhere to hide.*

"Tell me this isn't dramatic," you said.

I said honestly, "I'm dumbstruck."

I'd have thought that a small child, let loose in a vast, unfurnished expanse of glossy wooden floors blazing in insipid sunshine would go dashing about, sliding down halls in socks, giggling and rampaging, utterly unfazed by the antiseptic wasteland—*wasteland*, Franklin—into which he had been dropped. Instead, Kevin slackened on your hand into dead weight and had to be urged to "go explore." He plodded to the middle of the living room and sat. I'd suffered more than a few moments of alienation from my son, but just then—his eyes Little Orphan Annie O's and dulled over like wax buildup, hands plopping on the floorboards like fish on a dock—I couldn't have felt more akin.

"You've got to see the master bedroom," you said, grabbing my hand. "The skylights are spectacular."

"Skylights!" I said brightly.

All the angles in our massive bedroom were askew, its ceiling slanted. The effect was jangled, and the evident distrust of standard parallels and perpendiculars, like the whole building's uneasiness with the concept of rooms, felt insecure.

"Something else, huh?"

"Something else!" At some indeterminate point in the nineties, expanses of teak would become passé. We weren't there yet, but I had a premonition of the juncture.

You demonstrated our built-in teak laundry hamper, cleverly doubling as a bench, a cushion of smiley-face yellow strapped to its lid. You rolled back the doors of the closet on their gliding wheelies. The moving parts of the house were all silent, its surfaces smooth. The closet doors had no handles. None of the woodwork had fixtures. Drawers had gentle indents. The kitchen cabinets pushed open and shut with a click. Franklin, the whole house was on Zoloft.

You led me out the glass sliding doors to the deck. I thought, I have a *deck.* I will never shout, "I'm on the porch!" but "I'm on the *deck.*" I told myself it was only a word. Still, the platform cried out for barbecues with neighbors I did not much like. The swordfish steaks would be raw one minute, overcooked the next, and I would care.

Darling, I know I sound ungrateful. You'd searched very hard, taking on the job of finding us a home with all the seriousness of location scouting for Gillette. I'm better familiar with the real estate scarcity in the area now, so I trust that every other available property you looked at was plain hideous. Which this place was not. The builders had spared no expense. (Woe to those who *spare no expense.* I should know, since these are the travelers who scorn AWAP for holidays in "foreign" countries so comfortable that they qualify as near death experiences.) The woods were precious—if in more than one sense—the taps gold-plated. The previous owners had commissioned it to their own exacting specifications. You had bought us some other family's Dream Home.

I could see it. Our industrious couple works their way up from shoddy rentals to a series of nothing-special split-levels, until at last: an inheritance, a market upswing, a promotion. Finally they can afford to construct from the ground up *the house of their heart's desire.* The couple pores over blueprints, weighing where to hide every closet, how to segue gracefully between the living area and the den ("With a DOOR!" I want to scream, but it is too late for my stodgy advice). All those innovative angles look so dynamic on paper. Even shrubs are rather adorable a quarter of an inch high.

But I have a theory about Dream Homes. Not for nothing does "folly" mean both *foolhardy mistake* and *costly ornamental building.* Because I've never seen a Dream Home that works. Like ours, some of them *almost* work, though unqualified disasters are equally common. Part of the problem is that regardless of how much money you lavish on oak baseboards, an unhistoried house is invariably cheap in another dimension. Otherwise, the trouble seems rooted in the nature of beauty itself, a surprisingly elusive quality and rarely one you can buy outright. It flees in the face of too much effort. It rewards casualness, and most of all it deigns to arrive by whim, by *accident*. On my travels, I became a devotee of found art: a shaft of light on a dilapidated 1914 gun factory, an abandoned billboard whose layers have worn into a beguiling pentimento collage of Coca-Cola, Chevrolet, and Burma Shave, cut-rate pensions whose faded cushions perfectly match, in that unplanned way, the fluttering sun-blanched curtains.

Confoundingly then, this Gladstone Xanadu, beam by beam, would have materialized into a soul-destroying disappointment. Had the builders cut corners, an arrogant architect taken liberties with those painstaking plans? No, no. Down to the torturously blank kitchen cabinets, the visionary designs had been followed to the letter. That mausoleum on Palisades Parade came out precisely as its creators intended, and *that's* what made it so depressing.

To be fair, the gap between most people's capacity to conjure beauty from scratch and to merely recognize it when they see it is the width of the Atlantic Ocean. So all evidence to the contrary, the original owners may have had pretty good taste; more's the pity if they did. Certainly the fact that those two built a horror show was no proof against my theory that they knew very well that they'd constructed a horror show, too. I was further convinced that neither husband nor wife ever let on to the other what a downer this vapid atrocity turned out to be, that they each braved out the pretense that it was the house of their prayers, while at the same time separately scheming, from the day they moved in, to get out.

You said yourself the place was only three years old. *Three years old?* It would have taken that long to build! Who goes to that much trouble only to leave? Maybe Mr. Homeowner was transferred to Cincinnati, though in that case he accepted the job. What else would drive him out that clunky front door besides revulsion for his own creation? Who could live day after day with the deficiency of his own imagination made solid as brick?

"Why is it," I asked as you led me around the sculpted backyard, "that the folks who built this place sold it so soon? After constructing a house that's clearly so—ambitious?"

"I got the impression they were sort of, going in different directions."

"Getting a divorce."

"Well, it's not as if that makes the property cursed or something."

I looked at you with curiosity. "I didn't say it did."

"If houses passed that sort of thing along," you blustered, "there wouldn't be a shack in the country safe for a happy marriage."

Cursed? You obviously intuited that, sensible as the suburban recourse seemed on its face—big parks, fresh air, good schools—we had drifted alarmingly astray. Yet what strikes me now is not your foreboding, but your capacity to ignore it.

As for me, I had no premonitions. I was simply bewildered how I had landed, after Latvia and Equatorial Guinea, in Gladstone, New York. As if standing in the surf at Far Rockaway during a tide of raw sewage, I could barely keep my balance as our new acquisition exuded wave after wave of stark physical ugliness. *Why couldn't you see it?*

Maybe because you've always had a proclivity for *rounding up*. In restaurants, if 15 percent came to $17, you'd tip with a twenty. Should we have spent a tiresome evening with new acquaintances, I'd write them off; you'd want to give them a second chance. When that Italian girl I barely knew, Marina, turned up at the loft for two nights and then your watch disappeared, I was fuming; you grew only the more convinced that you must have left it at the gym. Lunch with Brian and Louise ought to have been fun? It was fun. You seemed to be able to squint and blur off the rough edges. As you gave me the grand tour of our new property, your camp counselor hard sell contrasted with a soulful look in your eyes, a pleading to play along. You talked nonstop, as if strung out on speed, and a lacing of hysteria fatally betrayed your own suspicion that 12 Palisades Parade was no formidable architectural exploit but an ostentatious flop. Still, through a complex combination of optimism and longing and bravado, you would *round it up*. While a cruder name for this process is *lying*, one could make a case that delusion is a variant of generosity. After all, you practiced *rounding up* on Kevin from the day he was born.

Me, I'm a stickler. I prefer my photographs in focus. At the risk of tautology, I like people only as much as I like them. I lead an emotional life of such arithmetic precision, carried to two or three digits after the decimal, that I am even willing to allow for degrees of agreeableness in my own son. In other words, Franklin: I leave the $17.

I hope I persuaded you that I thought the house was lovely. It was the first big decision you'd ever made independently on our behalf, and I wasn't about to pee all over it just because the prospect of living there made me want to slit my wrists. Privately I concluded that the explanation wasn't so much your different aesthetic, or lack of one; it's just that you were very suggestible. I hadn't been there, whispering in your ear about dumbwaiters. In my absence, you reverted to the taste of your parents.

Or an updated version of same. Palisades Parade was trying lethally to be "with it"; the house your parents built in Gloucester, Mass., was a traditional New England saltbox. But the spare-no-expense workmanship, the innocent faith in Niceness, was unmistakable.

My enjoyment of your father's motto, "Materials are everything," was not entirely at his expense. Up to a point, I saw the value of people who made things, and to the highest standard: Herb and Gladys built their own house, smoked their own salmon, brewed their own beer. But I had never met two people who existed so exclusively in three dimensions. The only times I saw your father excited were over a curly maple mantle or a creamy-headed stout, and I think it was over static physical perfection that he exalted; sitting before the fire, drinking the beer, were afterthoughts. Your mother cooked with the precision of a chemist, and we ate well on visits. Her meringue-topped raspberry pies that might have been clipped out of magazines, though again I would have the strong impression that it was pie-as-object that was the goal, and eating the pie, gouging into her creation, was a kind of vandalism. (How telling that your cadaverously thin mother is a marvelous cook but has no appetite.) If the assembly-line production of goods sounds mechanical, it felt mechanical. I was always a little relieved to get out of your parents' house, and they were so kind to me, if materially kind, that I felt churlish.

Still, everything in their house was buffed to a high, flat shine, so much reflection to protect the fact that there was nothing underneath. They didn't read; there were a few books, a set of encyclopedias (the wine-colored spines warmed up the den), but the only well-leafed volumes were instruction manuals, do-it-yourself how-to's, cookbooks, and a haggard set of *The Way Things Work*, volumes one and two. They had no comprehension why anyone would seek out a film with an unhappy ending or buy a painting that wasn't pretty. They owned a top-shelf stereo with speakers worth $1,000 apiece, but only a handful of easy-listening and best-of CDs: *Opera Stoppers; Classical Greatest Hits.* That sounds lazy, but I think it was more helpless: They didn't know what music was for.

You could say that about all of life, with your family: They don't know what it's for. They're big on life's mechanics; they know how to get its cogs to interlock, but they suspect that they're building a widget for its own sake, like one of those coffee-table knickknacks whose silver metal balls click fruitlessly back and forth until friction tires them. Your father was profoundly dissatisfied when their house was finished, not because there was anything wrong with it, but because there wasn't. Its high-pressure shower head and hermetic glass stall were impeccably installed, and just as he trooped out for a generic who-cares selection of best-of CDs to feed his magisterial stereo, I could easily envision your father running out to roll in the dirt to provide that shower a daily raison d'être. For that matter, their house is so neat, glossy, and pristine, so fitted out with gizmos that knead and julienne, that defrost and slice your bagels, that it doesn't seem to need its occupants. In fact, its puking, shitting, coffee-sloshing tenants are the only blights of untidiness in an otherwise immaculate, self-sustaining biosphere.

We've talked about all this on visits of course—exhaustively, since, overfed and forty minutes from the nearest cinema, we'd resort to dissecting your parents for entertainment. The point is, when Kevin—*Thursday*—well, they weren't prepared. They hadn't bought the right machine, like their German-made raspberry de-seeder, that would process this turn of events and make sense of it. What Kevin did wasn't rational. It didn't make a motor run more quietly, a pulley more efficient; it didn't brew beer or smoke salmon. It did not compute; it was *physically idiotic.*

The irony is, though your parents always deplored his absence of Protestant industry, those two have more in common with Kevin than anyone I know. If they don't know what life is for, what to do with it, Kevin doesn't, either; interestingly, both your parents and your firstborn abhor *leisure time.* Your son always attacked this antipathy head-on, which involves a certain bravery if you think about it; he was never one to deceive himself that, by merely filling it, he was putting his time to productive use. Oh, no—you'll remember he would sit by the hour stewing and glowering and doing nothing but reviling every second of every minute of his Saturday afternoon.

For your parents, of course, the prospect of being unoccupied is frightening. They don't have the character, like Kevin, to face the void. Your father was forever puttering, greasing the machinery of daily life, although the additional convenience, once he was finished, burdened him with only more odious *leisure time*. What's more, by installing a water softener or a garden irrigation system he had no idea whatsoever what it was he was trying to improve. Hard water had offered the happy prospect of regular, industrious de-lime-scaling of the drain board by the kitchen sink, and he rather liked sprinkling the garden by hand. The difference is that your father would wittingly install the water softener for no good reason and Kevin would not. Pointlessness has never bothered your father. Life is a collection of cells and electrical pulses to him, it *is* material, which is why *materials are everything*. And this prosaic vision contents him— or it did. So herein lies the contrast: Kevin, too, suspects that materials are everything. He just doesn't happen to care about materials.

I'll never forget the first time I visited your parents after *Thursday*. I confess I'd put it off, and that was weak. I'm sure it would have been colossally difficult even if you'd been able to come with me, but of course *irretrievable breakdown* prevented that. Alone, without the cartilage of their son, I was presented with the stark fact that we were no longer organically joined, and I think they both felt the same disconnect. When your mother opened the door, her face turned ashen, but when she asked me to come in she might have been politely ushering in a salesman for Hoover uprights.

To call your mother stiff would be unjust, but she is a great one for social form. She likes to know what to do now and what comes next. That's why she's such a fan of elaborate meals. She finds repose in set courses, the soup before the fish, and she doesn't resist, as I would have done, the numbing way in which preparing, serving, and cleaning up after three meals a day can stitch up a cook's time from morning to night. She does not, as I do, struggle against convention as a constraint; she is a hazily well-meaning but unimaginative person, and she is grateful for rules. Alas, there doesn't appear to be recorded—yet—an etiquette for afternoon tea with your former daughter-in-law after your grandson has committed mass murder.

She seated me in the formal sitting room instead of the den, which was a mistake; the rigidity of the high-backed wing chairs only served to emphasize that by contrast The Rules were in free fall. The colors of the velveteen, sea green and dusty rose, were at such variance with the glistening, livid subtext of my visit as to seem musty or faintly nauseous; these were the colors of mold. Your mother fled to the kitchen. I was about to cry after her not to bother because I really couldn't eat a thing when I realized that to deny her this one busywork delay for which she was so thankful would be cruel. I even forced myself to eat one of her Gruyère twists later, though it made me a little sick.

Gladys is such a nervous, high-strung woman that her brittleness—and I don't mean she couldn't be warm or kind—her bodily brittleness had kept her looking much the same. True, the lines in her forehead had rippled into an expression of permanent perplexity; her eyes darted every which way even more frenetically than usual, and there was, especially when she wasn't aware I was watching, a quality of lostness in her face that reminded me what she must have looked like as a little girl. The overall effect was of a woman who was stricken, but the contributing elements of this effect were so subtle that a camera might not have captured it on film.

When your father came up from the basement (I could hear his tread on the stairs, and fought dread; though seventy-five, he'd always been a vigorous man, and the steps were too slow and heavy), the change wasn't subtle at all. His cotton work clothes sloughed off him in great drooping folds. It had only been six weeks, a period during which I was shocked that it was possible to lose so much weight. All the flesh in his weathered face had dropped: the lower eyelids sagged to expose a red rim; his cheeks slung loose like a bloodhound's. I felt guilty, infected by Mary Woolford's consuming conviction that someone must be to blame. Then, that was your father's conviction as well. He is not a vengeful person, but a retired electronics machine-toolmaker (too perfect, that he'd made machines that made machines) took matters of corporate responsibility and better business practices with the utmost seriousness. Kevin had proven defective, and I was the manufacturer.

Rattling my fluted teacup in its gilt saucer, I felt clumsy. I asked your father how his garden was doing. He looked confused, as if he'd forgotten he had a garden. "The blueberry bushes," he remembered mournfully, "are just beginning to bear." The word *bear* hung in the air. Bushes maybe, but your father had not begun to bear anything.

"And the peas? You've always grown such lovely sugar snaps."

He blinked. The chimes struck four. He never explained about the peas, and there was a horrible nakedness in our silence. We had exposed that all those other times I'd asked I hadn't cared about his peas, and that all those other times he'd answered he hadn't cared about telling me.

I lowered my eyes. I apologized for not visiting sooner. They didn't make any noises about that's all right we understand. They didn't make *any* noises, like *say* something, so I just kept talking.

I said that I had wanted to go to all the funerals if I was welcome. Your parents didn't look baffled at the non sequitur; we had been effectively talking about *Thursday* from the moment your mother opened the door. I said that I hadn't wanted to be insensitive, so I rang the parents beforehand; a couple of them had simply hung up. Others implored me to stay away; my presence would be *indecent*, said Mary Woolford.

Then I told them about Thelma Corbitt—you remember, her son Denny was the lanky red-haired boy, the budding thespian—who was so gracious that I was abashed. I hazarded to your mother that tragedy seems to bring out all varieties of unexpected qualities in people. I said it was as if some folks (I was thinking of Mary) got dunked in plastic, vacuum-sealed like backpacking dinners, and could do nothing but sweat in their private hell. And others seemed to have just the opposite problem, as if disaster had dipped them in acid instead, stripping off the outside layer of skin that once protected them from the slings and arrows of other people's outrageous fortunes. For these sorts, just walking down the street in the wake of every stranger's ill wind became an agony, an aching slog through this man's fresh divorce and that woman's terminal throat cancer. They were in hell, too, but it was everybody's hell, this big, shoreless, sloshing sea of toxic waste.

I doubt I put it as fancily as that, but I did say that Thelma Corbitt was the kind of woman whose private suffering had become a conduit for other people's. And I didn't regale your parents with the whole phone call of course, but the full conversation did come flooding back to me: Thelma immediately admiring the "courage" it must have taken for me to pick up the phone, inviting me right away to Denny's funeral, but only if it wasn't too painful for me to go. I allowed to Thelma that it might help me to express my own sorrow for her son's passing, and for once I realized that I wasn't simply going through the motions, saying what I was supposed to. Apropos of not much, Thelma explained that Denny had been named after the chain restaurant where she and her husband had their first date. I almost stopped her from going on because it seemed easier for me to know as little as possible about her boy, but she clearly believed that we would both be better off if I knew just who my son had murdered. She said Denny had been rehearsing for the school's spring play, Woody Allen's *Don't Drink the Water,* and she'd been helping him with his lines. "He had us in stitches," she offered. I said that I'd seen him in *Streetcar* the year before and that (stretching the truth) he'd been terrific. She seemed so pleased, if only that her boy wasn't just a statistic to me, a name in the newspaper, or a torture. Then she said she wondered whether I didn't have it harder than any of them. I backed off. I said, that couldn't be fair; after all, at least I still had my son, and the next thing she said impressed me. She said, "Do you? Do you really?" I didn't answer that, but thanked her for her kindness, and then we both got lost in such a tumble of mutual gratitude—an almost impersonal gratitude, that everyone in the world wasn't simply horrid—that we both began to cry.

So, as I told your parents, I went to Denny's funeral. I sat in the back. I wore black, though in funerals these days that is old-fashioned. And then in the receiving line to convey my condolences, I offered Thelma my hand and said, "I'm so sorry for my loss." That's what I said, a miscue, a gaffe, but I thought it would be worse to correct myself—"*your* loss, I mean." To your parents, I was blithering. They stared.

Finally I took refuge in logistics. The legal system is itself a machine, and I could describe its workings, as your father had once explained to me, with poetic lucidity, the workings of a catalytic converter. I said that Kevin had been arraigned and was being held without bail, and I was hopeful that the terminology, so familiar from TV, would comfort; it failed to. (How vital, the hard glass interface of that screen. Viewers don't want those shows spilling willy-nilly into their homes, any more than they want other people's sewage to overflow from their toilets.) I said I'd hired the best lawyer I could find—meaning, of course, the most expensive. I thought your father would approve; he himself always bought top-shelf. I was mistaken.

He intruded dully, "What for?"

I had never heard him ask that question of anything in his life. I admired the leap. You and I had always pilloried them behind their backs as being spiritually arid.

"I'm not sure, though it seemed expected . . . To get Kevin off as lightly as possible, I guess." I frowned.

"Is that what you want?" asked your mother.

"No . . . What I *want* is to turn back the clock. What I *want* is to never have been born myself, if that's what it took. I can't have what I want."

"But would you like to see him punished?" your father pressed. Mind, he didn't sound wrathful; he hadn't the energy.

I'm afraid I laughed. Just a dejected *huh!* Still, it wasn't appropriate. "I'm sorry," I explained. "But good luck to them. I tried for the better part of sixteen years to punish Kevin. Nothing I took away mattered to him in the first place. What's the New York state juvenile justice system going to do? Send him to his room? I tried that. He didn't have much use for anything outside his room, or in it; what's the difference? And they're hardly going to shame him. You can only subject people to anguish who have a conscience. You can only punish people who have hopes to frustrate or attachments to sever; who worry what you think of them. You can really only punish people who are already a little bit good."

"He could at least be kept from hurting anyone else," your father submitted.

A defective product is recalled, and withdrawn from the market. I said defiantly, "Well, there is a campaign on, to try him as an adult and give him the death penalty."

"How do you feel about that?" asked your mother. Good grief, your parents had asked me if Wing and a Prayer would ever go public; they had asked if I thought those steam gadgets pressed trousers as well as ironing. They had never asked what I *felt*.

"Kevin is no adult. But will he be any different when he is one?" (They may be technically different specialties, but Workplace Massacre is really just School Shooting Grows Up.) "Honestly, there are some days," I looked balefully out their bay window, "I wish they would give him the death penalty. Get it all over with. But that might be letting myself off the hook."

"Surely you don't blame yourself, my dear!" your mother chimed, though with a nervousness; if I did, she didn't want to hear about it.

"I never *liked* him very much, Gladys." I met her eyes squarely, mother-to-mother. "I realize it's commonplace for parents to say to their child sternly, 'I love you, but I don't always *like* you.' But what kind of love is that? It seems to me that comes down to, 'I'm not oblivious to you—that is, you can still hurt my feelings—but I can't stand having you around.' Who wants to be *loved* like that? Given a choice, I might skip the deep blood tie and settle for being liked. I wonder if I wouldn't have been more moved if my own mother had taken me in her arms and said, 'I *like* you.' I wonder if just enjoying your kid's company isn't more important."

I had embarrassed them. Moreover, I'd done precisely what Harvey had already warned me against. Later they were both deposed, and snippets of this deadly little speech would be quoted back verbatim. I don't think your parents had it in for me, but they were honest New Englanders, and I'd given them no reason to protect me. I guess I didn't want them to.

When I rustled with leave-taking motions, setting down my stone-cold tea, the two of them looked relieved yet frantic, locking eyes. They must have recognized that these cozy teatime chats of ours would prove limited in number, and maybe late at night, unable to sleep, they'd think of questions they might have asked. They were cordial, of course, inviting me to visit any time. Your mother assured me that, despite everything, they still considered me *part of the family*. Their inclusivity seemed less kind than it might have six weeks before. At that time, the prospect of being enveloped into any *family* had all the appeal of getting stuck in an elevator between floors.

"One last thing." Your father touched my arm at the door, and once again asked the kind of question he'd evaded most of his life. "Do you understand *why*?"

I fear my response will only have helped to cure him of such inquiries, for the answers are often so unsatisfying.

Happy New Year, my dear,
Eva

Dear Franklin,

The Electoral College just certified a Republican president, and you must be pleased. But despite your pose as a sexist, flag-waving retrograde, in fatherhood you were a good little liberal, as fastidious about corporal punishment and nonviolent toys as the times demanded. I'm not making fun, only wondering if you, too, go back over those precautions and ponder where we went wrong.

My own review of Kevin's upbringing was assisted by trained legal minds. "Ms. Khatchadourian," Harvey grilled me on the stand, "did you have a rule in your household that children were not allowed to play with toy guns?"

"For what it's worth, yes."

"And you monitored television and video viewing?"

"We tried to keep Kevin away from anything too violent or sexually explicit, especially when he was little. Unfortunately, that meant my husband couldn't watch most of his own favorite programs. And we did have to allow one exception."

"What was that?" Annoyance again; this wasn't planned.

"The History Channel." A titter; I was playing to the peanut gallery.

"The point is," Harvey continued through his teeth, "you made every effort to ensure that your son was not surrounded by coarsening influences, did you not?"

"In my home," I said. "That *is* six acres out of a planet. And even there, I was unprotected from Kevin's coarsening influence on me."

Harvey stopped to breathe. I sensed an alternative-medicine professional had taught him some technique. "In other words, you couldn't control what Kevin played with or watched when he went to other children's homes?"

"Frankly, other children rarely asked Kevin over more than once."

The judge intervened, "Ms. Khatchadourian, please just answer the question."

"Oh, I suppose," I complied lackadaisically; I was getting bored.

"What about the Internet?" Harvey proceeded. "Was your son given free rein to access whatever web sites he liked, including, say, violent or pornographic ones?"

"Oh, we did the whole parental-controls schmear, but Kevin cracked it in a day." I flicked the air dismissively. Harvey had warned me against giving the slightest indication that I didn't take the proceedings seriously, and this case did bring out my perverse streak. But my larger trouble was paying attention. Back at the defense table, my lids would droop, my head list. If only to wake myself up, I added the kind of gratuitous commentary that the judge—a prudish, sharp woman who reminded me of Dr. Rhinestein—had cautioned against.

"You see," I proceeded, "by the time he was eleven or twelve, this was all too late. The no-gun rules, the computer codes . . . Children live in the same world we do. To kid ourselves that we can shelter them from it isn't just naive, it's a vanity. We want to be able to tell ourselves what good parents we are, that we're *doing our best*. If I had it all to do over again, I'd have let Kevin play with whatever he wanted; he liked little enough. And I'd have ditched the TV rules, the G-rated videos. They only made us look foolish. They underscored our powerlessness, and they provoked his contempt."

Although allowed a soliloquy in judicial terms, in my head I'd cut it short. I no longer suffer the constraints of jurisprudential impatience, so allow me to elaborate.

What drew Kevin's contempt was not, as I had seemed to imply, our patent incapacity to protect him from the Big Bad World. No, to Kevin it was the substance and not the ineffectuality of our taboos that was a joke. Sex? Oh, he used it, when he discovered that I was afraid of it, or afraid of it in him, but otherwise? It was a bore. Don't take offense, for you and I did find great pleasure in one another, but sex *is* a bore. Like the Tool Box toys that Kevin spurned as a toddler, the round peg goes in the round hole. The secret is that there is no secret. In fact, plain fucking at his high school was so prevalent, and so quotidian, that I doubt it excited him much. Alternative round holes furnish a transient novelty whose illusoriness he would have seen right through.

As for violence, the secret is more of a cheap trick.

You remember, once we gave up on the rating system to see a few decent films, watching a video of *Braveheart* as, dare I say it, a *family*? In the final torture scene, Mel Gibson is stretched on a rack, all four limbs tied to the corners of the compass. Each time his English captors pulled the ropes tauter, the sisal groaned, and so did I. When the executioner thrust his barbed knife into Mel's bowel and ripped upward, I squeezed my palms to my temples and whinnied. But when I peeked through the crook of my arm at Kevin, his glance at the screen was blasé. The sour half cock of his mouth was his customary expression at rest. He wasn't precisely doing the *Times* crossword, but he was absently blacking in all the white squares with a felt-tip.

Cinematic carve-ups are only hard to handle if on some level you believe that these tortures are being done to you. In fact, it's ironic that these spectacles have such a wicked reputation among Bible thumpers, since gruesome special effects rely for their impact on their audience's positively Christian compulsion to walk in their neighbors' shoes. But Kevin had discovered the secret: not merely that it wasn't real, but that *it wasn't him*. Over the years I observed Kevin watching decapitations, disembowelments, dismemberments, flayings, impalements, deoculations, and crucifixions, and I never saw him flinch. Because he'd mastered the trick. If you decline to identify, slice-and-dice is no more discomfiting than watching your mother prepare beef stroganoff. So what had we tried to protect him from, exactly? The practicalities of violence are rudimentary geometry, its laws those of grammar; like the grade-school definition of a preposition, violence is anything an airplane can do to a cloud. Our son had a better than average mastery of geometry and grammar both. There was little in *Braveheart*—or *Reservoir Dogs*, or *Chucky II*—that Kevin could not have invented for himself.

In the end, that's what Kevin has never forgiven us. He may not resent that we tried to impose a curtain between himself and the adult terrors lurking behind it. But he does powerfully resent that we led him down the garden path—that we enticed him with the prospect of the exotic.

(Hadn't I myself nourished the fantasy that I would eventually land in a country that was somewhere *else?*) When we shrouded our grown-up mysteries for which Kevin was too young, we implicitly promised him that when the time came, the curtain would pull back to reveal—what? Like the ambiguous emotional universe that I imagined awaited me on the other side of childbirth, it's doubtful that Kevin had formed a vivid picture of whatever we had withheld from him. But the one thing he could not have imagined is that we were withholding *nothing.* That there was *nothing* on the other side of our silly rules, *nothing.*

The truth is, the vanity of protective parents that I cited to the court goes beyond look-at-us-we're-such-responsible-guardians. Our prohibitions also bulwark our self-importance. They fortify the construct that we adults are all initiates. By conceit, we have earned access to an unwritten Talmud whose soul-shattering content we are sworn to conceal from "innocents" for their own good. By pandering to this myth of the naïf, we service our own legend. Presumably we have looked *the horror* in the face, like staring into the naked eye of the sun, blistering into turbulent, corrupted creatures, enigmas even to ourselves. Gross with revelation, we would turn back the clock if we could, but there is no unknowing of this awful canon, no return to the blissfully insipid world of childhood, no choice but to shoulder this weighty black sagacity, whose finest purpose is to shelter our air-headed midgets from a glimpse of the abyss. The sacrifice is flatteringly tragic.

The last thing we want to admit is that the forbidden fruit on which we have been gnawing since reaching the magic age of twenty-one is the same mealy Golden Delicious that we stuff into our children's lunch boxes. The last thing we want to admit is that the bickering of the playground perfectly presages the machinations of the boardroom, that our social hierarchies are merely an extension of who got picked first for the kickball team, and that grown-ups still get divided into bullies and fatties and crybabies. What's a kid to find out? Presumably we lord over them an exclusive deed to sex, but this pretense flies so fantastically in the face of fact that it must result from some conspiratorial group amnesia. To this day, some of my most intense sexual memories date back to before I was ten, as I have confided to you under the sheets in better days. No, they have sex, too. In truth, we are bigger, greedier versions of the same eating, shitting, rutting ruck, hell-bent on disguising from somebody, if only from a three-year-old, that pretty much all we do is eat and shit and rut. *The secret is there is no secret.* That is what we really wish to keep from our kids, and its suppression is the true collusion of adulthood, the pact we make, the Talmud we protect.

Sure, by the time he was fourteen we had given up on trying to control the videos he watched, the hours he kept, what little he read. But watching those stupid films and logging onto those stupid web sites, swigging that stupid hooch and sucking those stupid butts and fucking those stupid schoolgirls, Kevin must have felt so fiercely cheated. And on *Thursday*? I bet he still felt cheated.

Meantime, I could tell from Harvey's expression of forbearance that he had regarded my mini-lecture as more destructive self-indulgence. Our case—his case, really—was pearled around the proposition that I had been a normal mother with normal maternal affections who had taken normal precautions to ensure that she raised a normal child. Whether we were the victims of bad luck or bad genes or bad culture was a matter for shamans or biologists or anthropologists to divine, but not the courts. Harvey was intent on evoking every parent's latent fear that it was possible to do absolutely everything right and still turn on the news to a nightmare from which there is no waking. It was a damned sound approach in retrospect, and now that it's been a year or so, I feel a little sheepish about being so cantankerous at the time.

Still, like that depersonalizing rubber stamp of *postnatal depression,* our there-but-for-the-grace-of-God defense put me right off. I felt driven to distinguish myself from all those normal-normal mommies, if only as an exceptionally crummy one, and even at the potential price tag of $6.5 million (the plaintiffs had researched what W&P was worth). I had already lost everything, Franklin, everything but the company that is, the continuing possession of which, under the circumstances, struck me as crass. It is true that since then I have sometimes felt wistful about my corporate offspring, now fostered by strangers, but at the time I didn't care. I didn't care if I lost the case so long as in the process I was at least kept awake, I didn't care if I lost all my money, and I was positively praying to be forced to sell our eyesore house. *I didn't care about anything.* And there's a freedom in apathy, a wild, dizzying liberation on which you can almost get drunk. You can do anything. Ask Kevin.

As usual, I'd conducted my own cross for opposing counsel (they loved me; they'd have liked to call me as a witness for their side), so I was asked to step down. I paused halfway off the stand. "I'm sorry, your honor, I just remembered something."

"You wish to amend your testimony, for the record?"

"We did let Kevin have one gun." (Harvey sighed.) "A squirt gun, when he was four. My husband loved squirt guns as a boy, so we made an exception."

It was an exception to a rule I thought inane to begin with. Keep them away from replicas and kids will aim a stick at you, and I see no developmental distinction between wielding formed plastic that goes *rat-a-tat-tat* on battery power versus pointing a piece of wood and shouting "bang-bang-bang!" At least Kevin liked his squirt gun, since he discovered that it was annoying.

All through the move from Tribeca, he'd soaked the flies of our movers and then accused them of having "peed their pants." I thought the accusation pretty rich from a little boy still refusing to pick up on our coy hints about learning to "go potty like Mommer and Daddy" some two years after most kids were flushing to beat the band. He was wearing the wooden mask I'd brought him from Kenya, with scraggy, electrified looking sisal hair, tiny eyeholes surrounded by huge blank whites, and fierce three-inch teeth made from bird bones. Enormous on his scrawny body, it gave him the appearance of a voodoo doll in diapers. I don't know what I was thinking when I bought it. That boy hardly needed a mask when his naked face was already impenetrable, and the gift's expression of raw retributive rage gave me the creeps.

Schlepping boxes with a wet, itchy crotch couldn't have been a picnic. They were nice guys, too, uncomplaining and careful, so as soon as I noticed their faces begin to twitch I told Kevin to cut it out. At which point he swiveled his mask in my direction to confirm that I was watching, and water-cannoned the wiry black mover in the butt.

"Kevin, I told you to stop it. Don't squirt these nice men who are only trying to help us one more time, and *I mean it.*" Naturally I only managed to imply that the first time I hadn't meant it. An intelligent child takes the calculus of this-time-I'm-serious-so-last-time-I-wasn't to its limit and concludes that all his mother's warnings are horseshit.

So we walk through our paces. Squish-squish-squish. *Kevin, stop that this instant.* Squish-squish-squish. *Kevin, I'm not going to tell you again.* And then (squish-squish-squish) the inevitable: *Kevin, if you squirt anybody one more time I'm taking the squirt gun away,* which earned me, "NYEH-nyeh? Nyeh nyeh nyeh NYEE-nyeh-nyeh-nyeh *nyeh* nyeh nyeee, nyeh NYE-nye nye NYE-nye nye-NYEEEEEEE."

Franklin, what good were those parenting books of yours? Next thing I know you're stooping beside our son and borrowing his dratted toy. I hear muffled giggling and something about *Mommer* and then *you* are squirting *me.*

"Franklin, that's not cute. I told him to quit. You're not helping."

"NYEH-nyeh? Nye *nyeeh nyeeh.* Nyeh *nyeh*-nyeh nyeh *nyeh.* Nyeh *nyeeh nyeeh*-nyeh!" Incredibly, this *nyeh-nyeh* minced from you, after which you shot me between the eyes. Kevin honked (you know, to this day he still hasn't learned how to laugh). When you gave the gun back, he drowned my face in a cascade.

I snatched the gun.

"Aw!" you cried. "Eva, moving's such a pain in the behind!" (*Behind,* that was the way we talked now.) "Can't we have a little fun?"

I had the squirt gun now, so one easy exit was to turn a tonal corner: to squirt you gleefully on the nose, and we could have this rambunctious family riot whereby you wrest the gun away and toss the squirt gun to Kevin . . . . And we'd laugh and fall all over each other and we might even remember it years later, that mythic squirt-gun fight the day we moved to Gladstone. And then one of us would return the toy to Kevin and he'd go back to soaking the movers and I wouldn't have a leg to stand on to get him to quit because I'd been squirting people too. Alternatively, I could do the killjoy thing, which I did, and put the gun in my purse, which I did.

"The movers peed their pants," you told Kevin, "but Mommer pooped the party."

Of course I'd heard other parents talk about the unfair good-cop/bad-cop divide, how the good cop was always the kid's favorite while the bad cop did all the heavy lifting and I thought, what a fucking cliché, how did this happen to me? I'm not even *interested* in this stuff.

Kevin's voodoo alter ego marked the gun's location in my purse. Most boys would have started to cry. Instead he turned his bird-bone grimace mutely to his mother. From preschool, Kevin was a plotter. He knew how to bide his time.

Since a child's feelings are bruisable, his privileges few, his chattel paltry even when his parents are well-to-do, I'd been given to understand that punishing one's own child was terribly painful. Yet in truth, when I commandeered Kevin's squirt gun, I felt a gush of savage joy. As we followed the moving van to Gladstone in the pickup, the continuing possession of Kevin's beloved toy engorged me with such pleasure that I withdrew it from my purse, forefinger on the trigger, riding shotgun. Strapped between us in the front seat, Kevin lifted his gaze from my lap to the dashboard with theatrical unconcern. Kevin's bearing was taciturn, his body slack, but the mask gave him away: Inside he was raging. He hated me with all his being, and I was happy as a clam.

I think he sensed my pleasure and resolved to deprive me of it in the future. He was already intuiting that attachment—if only to a squirt gun—made him vulnerable. Since whatever he wanted was also something I might deny him, the least desire was a liability. As if in tribute to this epiphany, he pitched the mask on the pickup floor, kicked it absently with his tennis shoe, and broke a few teeth. I don't imagine he was such a precocious boy—such a monster—that he had conquered his every earthly appetite by the age of four and a half. He still wanted his squirt gun back. But indifference would ultimately commend itself as a devastating weapon.

When we drove up, the house looked even more hideous than I'd remembered, and I wondered how I would make it through the night without starting to cry. I hopped out of the cab. Kevin could now unstrap himself, and he scorned assistance. He stood on the running board so that I couldn't shut the door.

"Give me my gun back now." This was no wear-Mom-down whine, but an ultimatum. I wouldn't be given a second chance.

"You were a jerk, Kevin," I said breezily, lifting him to the ground by his underarms. "No toys for jerks." I thought, hey, I could come to enjoy being a parent. This is fun.

The squirt gun leaked, so I didn't want to stash it back in my purse. As the movers began to unload, Kevin followed me to the kitchen. I hoisted myself onto the counter and slid his squirt gun with my fingertips on top of the cupboards.

I was busy directing what went where and may not have returned to the kitchen for twenty minutes.

"Hold it right there, mister," I said. "*Freeze.*"

Kevin had shoved one box next to a pile of two to create a stairway to the counter, onto which one of the movers had slid a box of dishes, making another step. But he had waited for the sound of my footsteps before climbing the cabinet shelves themselves. (In Kevin's book, unwitnessed disobedience is wasteful.) By the time I arrived, his tennis shoes were perched three shelves up. His left hand was gripping the top of the wavering cupboard door, while his right hand hovered two inches from his squirt gun. I needn't have shouted *Freeze!* He was already posing as if for someone to snap a picture.

"Franklin!" I bellowed urgently. "Come here, please! Right away!" I wasn't tall enough to lift him to the floor. As I stood below to catch him if he slipped, Kevin and I locked eyes. His pupils stirred with what might have been pride, or glee, or pity. My God, I thought. He's only four, and he's already winning.

"Hey, there, buster!" You laughed and lifted him down, though not before he'd snatched the gun. Franklin, you had such beautiful arms. "Little young to learn to fly!"

"Kevin's been very, very bad!" I sputtered. "Now we're going to have to take that gun away for a very, very, very long time!"

"Aw, he's earned it, haven't you, kiddo? Man, that climb took guts. Real little monkey, aren't you?"

A shadow crossed his face. He may have thought you were talking down to him, but if so the condescension suited his purposes. "I'm the little monkey," he said, deadpan. He strode out of the room, squirt gun swinging at his side with the arrogant nonchalance I associated with airplane hijackers.

"You just humiliated me."

"Eva, moving's hard enough on us, but for kids it's traumatic. Cut him some slack. Listen, I've got some bad news about that rocker of yours . . . "

For our new home's christening dinner the next night we bought steaks, and I wore my favorite caftan, a white-on-white brocade from Tel Aviv. That same evening Kevin learned to fill his squirt gun with concord grape juice. You thought it was funny.

That house resisted me every bit as much as I resisted it. Nothing fit. There were so few right angles that a simple chest of drawers slid into a corner always left an awkward triangle of unfilled space. My furniture, too, was beat-up, though in the Tribeca loft that battered handmade toy box, the tuneless baby grand, the comfortably slumping couch whose pillows leaked chicken feathers hit just the right offbeat note. Suddenly, in our slick new home the funk turned to junk. I felt sorry for those pieces, much as I'd pity unsophisticated but good-hearted high school buddies from Racine at a party milling with hip, sharp-tongued New Yorkers like Eileen and Belmont.

It was the same with the kitchenware: Cluttering sleek green marble counters, my 1940s mixer went from quaint to grungy. Later, you came home with a bullet-shaped KichenAid, and I took the ancient mixer to the Salvation Army as if at gunpoint. When I unpacked my dented pots and pans, their heavy-gauge aluminum encrusted, their crumbling handles duct-taped together, it looked as if some homeless person had nested in a household whose jet-set tenants were in Rio. The pans went, too; you found a matching set at Macy's in fashionable red enamel. I'd never noticed how scummy that old cookware had become, though I'd kind of liked not noticing.

In all, I may have been borderline rich, but I'd never owned much, and aside from the silk hangings from Southeast Asia, a few carvings from West Africa, and the Armenian rugs from my uncle, we dispensed with most of the detritus of my old Tribeca life in frighteningly short order. Even the internationalia assumed an inauthentic aura, as if it hailed from an upmarket import outlet. Since our aesthetic reinvention coincided with my sabbatical from AWAP, I felt as if I were evaporating.

That's why the project in the study was so important to me. I realize that for you that incident epitomizes my intolerance, my rigidity, my refusal to make allowances for children. But that's not what it means to me.

For my study, I chose the one room in that house that didn't have any trees growing through it, had only one skylight, and was *almost* rectangular—no doubt designed near the last, when thankfully our Dream Home couple was running out of bright ideas. Most people would consider papering fine wood an abomination, but we were swimming in teak, and I had an idea that might make me feel, in one room at least, at home: I would plaster the study with maps. I owned boxes and boxes: city maps of Oporto or Barcelona, with all the hostels and pensions I planned to list in IBERIWAP circled in red; Geographical Survey maps of the Rhone Valley with the lazy squiggle of my train journey highlighted in yellow; whole continents jagged with ambitious airline itineraries in ruled ballpoint.

As you know, I've always had a passion for maps. I've sometimes supposed that, in the face of an imminent nuclear attack or invading army, the folks with all the power won't be the white supremacists with guns or the Mormons with canned sardines, but the cartographically clued who know that this road leads to the mountains. Hence the very first thing I do on arrival in a new place is locate a map, and that is only when I couldn't get to Rand McNally in midtown before hopping the plane. Without one, I feel easily victimized and at sea. As soon I have my map, I gain better command of a town than most of its residents, many of whom are totally lost outside a restrictive orbit of the patisserie, charcuterie, and Luisa's house. I've long taken pride in my powers of navigation, for I'm better than the average bear at translating from two dimensions to three, and I've learned to use rivers, railroads, and the sun to find my bearings. (I'm sorry, but what else can I boast about now? I'm getting old, and I look it. I work for a travel agency, and my son is a killer.)

So I associated maps with mastery and may have hoped that, through the literal sense of direction they had always provided, I might figuratively orient myself in this alien life as a full-time suburban mother. I craved some physical emblem of my earlier self if only to remind me that I had deserted that life by choice and might return to it at will. I nursed some distant hope that as he got older, Kevin might grow curious, point to Majorca in the corner, and ask what it was like there. I was proud of my life, and while I told myself that through an accomplished mother Kevin might find pride in himself, I probably just wanted him to be proud of me. I still had no idea what a tall order for any parent that could turn out to be.

Physically, the project was fiddly. The maps were all different sizes, and I had to design a pattern that was not symmetrical or systematic but still made a pleasing patchwork, with a balance of colors and a judicious mix of town centers and continents. I had to learn how to work with wallpaper paste, which was messy, and the older, tattier maps had to be ironed; paper readily browns. With so much else to attend to in a new house and constant hands-on consultation with Louis Role, my new managing editor at AWAP, I was papering my study over the course of several months.

That's what I mean by biding his time. He followed the papering of that study and knew how much trouble it was; he had personally helped to make it more trouble, by tracking wallpaper paste all over the house. He may not have understood the countries the maps signified, but he did understand that they signified something to me.

When I brushed on the last rectangle by the window, a topographical map of Norway stitched with fjords, I climbed down the ladder and surveyed the results with a twirl. It was gorgeous! Dynamic, quirky, lavishly sentimental. Interstitial train ticket stubs, museum floor plans, and hotel receipts gave the collage an additionally personal touch. I had forced one patch of this blank, witless house to mean something. I put on Joe Jackson's *Big World*, lidded the paste, furled the canvas covering my six-foot rolltop desk, rattled it open, and unpacked my last box, arranging my stand of antique cartridge pens and bottles of red and black ink, the Scotch tape, stapler, and tchotchkes for fidgeting—the miniature Swiss cowbell, the terra-cotta penitent from Spain.

Meanwhile I was burbling to Kevin, something all very Virginia Woolf like, "Everyone needs a room of their own. You know how you have your room? Well, this is Mommer's room. And everyone likes to make their room special. Mommer's been lots of different places, and all these maps remind me of the trips I've taken. You'll see, you may want to make your room special some day, and I'll help you if you want—"

"What do you mean *special*," he said, hugging one elbow. In his drooping free hand drizzled his squirt gun, whose leakage had worsened. Although he was still slight for his age, I'd rarely met anyone who took up more meta-physical space. A sulking gravity never let you forget he was there, and if he said little, he was always watching.

"So it looks like your personality."

"What personality."

I felt sure I'd explained the word before. I was continually feeding him vocabulary, or who was Shakespeare; educational chatter filled the void. I had a feeling he wished I'd shut up. There seemed no end to the information that he did not want.

"Like your squirt gun, that's part of your personality." I refrained from adding, like the way you ruined my favorite caftan, that's part of your personality. Or the way you're still shitting in diapers coming up on five years old, *that's* part of your personality, too. "Anyway, Kevin, you're being stubborn. I think you know what I mean."

"I have to put junk on the walls." He sounded put-upon.

"Unless you'd rather not."

"I'd *rather not.*"

"Great, we've found one more thing you don't want to do," I said. "You don't like to go to the park and you don't like to listen to music and you don't like to eat and you don't like to play with Lego. I bet you couldn't think of one more thing you don't like if you tried."

"All these squiggy squares of paper," he supplied promptly. "They're dumb." After Idonlikedat, *dumb* was his favorite word.

"That's the thing about your own room, Kevin. It's nobody else's business. I don't care if you think my maps are dumb. I like them." I remember raising an umbrella of defiance: He wouldn't rain on this parade. My study looked terrific, it was all mine, I would sit at my desk and play grown-up, and I could not wait to screw on my crowning touch, a bolt on its door. Yes, I'd commissioned a local carpenter and had added a *door.*

But Kevin wouldn't let the matter drop. There was something he wanted to tell me. "I don't get it. It was all gucky. And it took forever. Now everything looks dumb. What difference does it make. Why'd you bother." He stamped his foot. "It's *dumb!*"

Kevin had skipped the *why* phase that usually hits around three, at which point he was barely talking. Although the *why* phase may seem like an insatiable desire to comprehend cause and effect, I'd eavesdropped

enough at playgrounds (It's time to go make dinner, cookie! *Why?* Because
we're going to get hungry! *Why?* Because our bodies are telling us to eat!
Why?) to know better. Three-year-olds aren't interested in the chemistry of
digestion; they've simply hit on the magic word that always provokes a response. *But Kevin had a real why phase.* He thought my wallpaper an incom-
prehensible waste of time, as just about everything adults did also struck
him as absurd. It didn't simply perplex him but enraged him, and so far
Kevin's *why* phase has proved not a passing developmental stage but a permanent condition.

I knelt. I looked into his stormy, pinched-up face and placed a hand
on his shoulder. "Because I love my new study. I love the maps. I love
them."

I could have been speaking Urdu. "They're dumb," he said stonily. I
stood up. I dropped my hand. The phone was ringing.

The separate line for my study wasn't installed yet, so I left to grab
the phone in the kitchen. It was Louis, with another crisis regarding JAP-
WAP, whose resolution took a fair amount of time. I *did* call to Kevin to
come out where I could see him, more than once. But I still had a business
to oversee, and have you any notion how fatiguing it is to keep an eye on a
small child every single moment of every single day? I'm tremendously
sympathetic with the sort of diligent mother who turns her back for an
eye blink—who leaves a child in the bath to answer the door and sign for
a package, to scurry back only to discover that her little girl has hit her
head on the faucet and drowned in two inches of water. Two inches. Does
anyone ever give the woman credit for the twenty-four-hours-minus-three-
minutes a day that she has watched that child like a hawk? For the
months, the *years'* worth of don't-put-that-in-your-mouth-sweeties, of
whoops!-we-almost-fell-downs? Oh, no. We prosecute these people, we
call it "criminal parental negligence" and drag them to court through the
snot and salty tears of their own grief. Because only the three minutes
count, those three miserable minutes that were just enough.

I finally got off the phone. Down the hall, Kevin had discovered the
pleasures of a room with a door: The study's was shut. "Hey, kid," I called,
turning the knob, "when you're this quiet you make me nervous—"

My wallpaper was spidery with red and black ink. The more ab-
sorbent papers had started to blotch. The ceiling, too, since I'd papered

that as well; craning on the ladder had been murder on my back. Drips from overhead were staining one of my uncle's most valuable Armenian carpets, our wedding present. The room was so whipped and wet that it looked as if a fire alarm had gone off and triggered a sprinkling system, only the nozzles had flung not water but motor oil, cherry Hawaiian punch, and mulberry sorbet.

From the transitional squirts of a sickly purple I might later conclude that he had used up the bottle of black India ink first before moving on to the crimson, but Kevin left nothing to my deduction: He was still draining the last of the red ink into the barrel of his squirt gun. Just as he'd posed in the process of retrieving the gun from the top of our kitchen cabinet, he seemed to have saved this last tablespoon for my arrival. He was standing on my study chair, bent in concentration; he did not even look up. The filling hole was small, and though he was pouring intently, my burnished oak desk was awash in spatter. His hands were drenched.

"Now," he announced quietly, "it's *special*."

I snatched the gun, flung it on the floor, and stamped it to bits. I was wearing pretty yellow Italian pumps. The ink ruined my shoes.

Eva

Dear Franklin,

Yes, second Saturday of the month, and I'm debriefing in the Bagel Café again. I'm haunted by the image of that guard with the mud-spatter of facial moles, who looked at me today with his routine mixture of sorrow and distaste. I feel much the same way about his face. The moles are large and puffy, like feeding ticks, mottled and gelatinous, widening toadstool-like from a narrower base so that some of them have started to droop. I've wondered if he obsesses over his lesions, doing overtime at Claverack to save for their removal, or has developed a perverse fondness for them. People seem able to get used to anything, and it is a short step from adaptation to attachment.

In fact, I read recently that a neural operation has been developed that can virtually cure some Parkinson's patients. So successful is the surgery that it has moved more than one of its beneficiaries to kill themselves. Yes, you read correctly: to kill themselves. No more trembling, no more spastic arm swings in restaurants that knock over the wine. But also, no more aching sympathy from doe-eyed strangers, no more spontaneous outpourings of tenderness from psychotically forgiving spouses. The recovered get depressed, reclusive. They can't handle it: being just like everybody else.

Between ourselves, I've started to worry that in some backhanded way I've become attached to the disfigurement of my own life. These days it is solely through notoriety that I understand who I am and what part I play in the dramas of others. I'm the mother of "one of those Columbine kids" (and how it grieves Kevin that Littleton has won the generic tag over Gladstone). Nothing I do or say will ever outweigh that fact, and it is tempting to stop fighting and give over. That must explain why some mothers of my ilk have abandoned any attempt to recoup the lives they led before, as marketing directors or architects, and have gone on the lecture circuit or spearheaded the Million Mom March instead. Perhaps this is what Siobhan meant by being "called."

Indeed, I've developed a healthy respect for fact itself, its awesome dominance over rendition. No interpretation I slather over events in this appeal to you has a chance of overwhelming the sheer actuality of *Thursday*, and maybe it was the miracle of fact itself that Kevin discovered that afternoon. I can comment until I'm blue, but what happened simply sits there, triumphing like three dimensions over two. No matter how much enamel those vandals threw at our windowpanes, the house remained a house, and *Thursday* has the same immutable feel about it, like an object I can paint but whose physical enormity will persist in shape, regardless of hue.

Franklin, I'm afraid I caught myself *giving over* in the Claverack visitors' waiting room today. And by the way, I'd be the last to complain about the facilities overall. Newly constructed to supply a burgeoning market sector, the institution is not yet overcrowded. Its roofs don't leak, its toilets flush; *Juvenile Detention on a Wing and a Prayer* (JUVIEWAP) would give the joint an enthusiastic listing. Claverack's classrooms may provide a better meat-and-potatoes education than trendy suburban high schools whose curricula are padded with courses in Inuit Literature and Sexual Harassment Awareness Training. But aside from the incongruous Romper Room primary colors of the visiting area, Claverack is aesthetically harsh—laying bare, once you take away the frippery of life, how terrifyingly little is left. Cinder-block walls a stark white, the pea-green linoleum unpatterned, the visitors' waiting room is cruelly lacking in distractions—a harmless travel poster for Belize, a single copy of *Glamour*—as if to deliberately quash self-deceit. It is a room that does not wish to be confused with anything so anodyne as an airline ticket-purchasing office or a dental waiting room. That lone poster for AIDS prevention doesn't qualify as decor, but as an accusation.

Today a slight, serene black woman sat next to me, a generation younger but doubtless a mother. I kept shooting fascinated glances at her hair, plaited in a complex spiral that disappeared into infinity at the crown, my admiration fighting a prissy middle-class foreboding about how long the braids went unwashed. Her restful resignation was characteristic of the black relatives who frequent that room; I've made a study of it.

White mothers of delinquents, a statistically rarer breed, tend to jitter, or if they are still, they are ramrod rigid, jaws clenched, heads held stiffly as if fixed in place for a CAT-scan. Should low-enough attendance allow, white moms always assume a chair with at least two empty plastic seats on either side. They often bring newspapers. They discourage conversation. The implication is bald: Something has violated the space-time continuum. They do not belong here. I often detect a Mary Woolford brand of outrage, as if these mothers are looking fiercely around the room for someone to sue. Alternatively, I will get a sharp reading of this-cannot-be-happening—an incredulity so belligerent that it can generate a holographic presence in the waiting room of an ongoing parallel universe in which Johnny or Billy came home at the same time he always did after school that day, another ordinary afternoon on which he had his milk and Ho-Hos and did his homework. We white folks cling to such an abiding sense of entitlement that when things go amiss, we cannot let go of this torturously sunny, idiotically cheerful doppelgänger of a world that we deserve in which life is swell.

By contrast, black mothers will sit next to one another, even if the room is practically empty. They may not always talk, but there is an assumption of fellowship in their proximity, an esprit de corps reminiscent of a book club whose members are all plowing through the same arduously long classic. They never seem angry, or resentful, or surprised to find themselves here. They sit in the same universe in which they've always sat. And black people seem to have a much more sophisticated grasp of the nature of events in time. Parallel universes are science fiction, and Johnny—or Jamille—didn't come home that afternoon, did he? End of story.

All the same, there's a tacit understanding among the whole of our circle that you do not fish for details about the misconduct that landed your seatmate's young man here. Although the transgression in question is in many cases the family's most public manifestation, in that room we collude in the seemly view that the stuff of the *Times* Metro Section, the *Post* front page, is a private affair. Oh, a few mothers from time to time will bend a neighbor's ear about how Tyrone never stole that Discman or he was only holding a kilo for a friend, but then the other mothers catch one another's' eyes with bent smiles and pretty soon little Miss We Gonna Appeal This Injustice puts a lid on it. (Kevin informs me that inside, no one claims to be innocent. Instead they confabulate heinous crimes for which they were never caught. "If half these jerk-offs were telling the truth," he slurred wearily last month, "most of the country would be dead." In fact, Kevin has more than once claimed *Thursday* and newbies haven't believed him: "And I'm Sidney *Poitier*, dude." Apparently he dragged one such skeptic to the library by the hair to confirm his credentials in an old copy of *Newsweek*.)

So I was struck by this young woman's repose. Rather than clean her nails or cull old receipts from her pocketbook, she sat upright, hands at rest in her lap. She stared straight ahead, reading the AIDS awareness poster for perhaps the hundredth time. I hope this doesn't sound racist— these days I never know what will give offense—but black people seem terribly good at waiting, as if they inherited the gene for patience along with the one for sickle-cell. I noticed that in Africa as well: dozens of Africans sitting or standing by the side of the road, waiting for the bus or, even harder, waiting for nothing in particular, and they never appeared restive or annoyed. They didn't pull grass and chew the tender ends with their front teeth; they didn't draw aimless pictures with the toes of their plastic sandals in the dry red clay. They were still, and present. The capacity is existential, that ability to just *be*, with a profundity that I have seen elude some very well educated people.

At one point she crossed to the candy machine in the corner. The exact-change light must have been on, because she returned and asked if I had change of a dollar. I fell over myself checking every coat pocket, every cranny of my purse, so that by the time I scrounged the coins together she may have wished she'd never asked. I contend with strangers so infrequently now—I still prefer booking flights in the back room at Travel R Us—that during small transactions I panic. Maybe I was desperate to have a positive effect on someone else's life, if only by providing the means to a Mars Bar. At least this awkward exchange broke the ice, and, to pay me back for what I made seem so much trouble, she spoke when she resumed her seat.

"I ought to bring him fruit, I guess." She glanced apologetically at the M&M's in her lap. "But Lord, you know he'd never eat it."

We shared a sympathetic look, mutually marveling that kids who commit grown-up crimes still have their little-boy sweet tooth.

"My son claims Claverack food is 'hog slop,'" I volunteered.

"Oh, my Marlon do nothing but complain, too. Say it ain't 'fit for human consumption.' And you hear they bake saltpeter in the bread rolls?" (This rusty summer-camp rumor is surely sourced in adolescent vanity: that a teenager's lavish libidinous urges are so seditious as to demand dampening by underhanded means.)

"No, 'hog slop' was all I could get out of him," I said. "But Kevin's never been interested in food. When he was little I was afraid he would starve, until I figured out that he would eat as long as I wasn't watching. He didn't like to be seen needing it—as if hunger were a sign of weakness. So I'd leave a sandwich where he was sure to find it, and walk away. It was like feeding a dog. From around the corner I'd see him cram it in his mouth in two or three bites, looking around, making sure nobody saw. He caught me peeking once, and spat it out. He took the half-chewed bread and cheddar and mashed it onto the plate glass door. It stuck. I left it there for the longest time. I'm not sure why."

My companion's eyes, previously alert, had filmed. She had no reason to be interested in my son's dietary proclivities and now looked as if she regretted having started a conversation. I'm sorry, Franklin—it's just that I go for days barely speaking, and then if I do start to talk it spews in a stream, like vomit.

"At any rate," I continued with a bit more calculation, "I've warned Kevin that once he's transferred to an adult facility the food is bound to be far worse."

The woman's eyes narrowed. "Your boy don't get out at eighteen? Ain't that a shame." Skirting the waiting room's taboo subject, she meant: He must have done something bad.

"New York is pretty lenient with juveniles under sixteen," I said. "But even in this state, kids have to do a five-year minimum for murder—especially when it's seven high school students and an English teacher." I added as her face rearranged, "Oh, and a cafeteria worker. Maybe Kevin has stronger feelings about food than I thought."

She whispered, "*KK*."

I could hear the reels in her head rewinding, as she grasped frantically after everything I'd said to which she'd only half listened. *Now* she had reason to be interested in my son's secretive appetite—and in his "musical" preference for tuneless cacophony randomly generated by computer, in the ingenious little game he used to play composing school essays entirely with three-letter words. What I had just done, it was a kind of party trick. Suddenly she was at a loss for what to say, not because I bored her, but because she was bashful. If she could scavenge a hasty bushel of bruised and mealy details from my conversational drop-fruit, she would present it to her sister over the phone the next day like a Christmas basket.

"None other," I said. "Funny how 'KK' used to mean 'Krispy Kreme.'"

"That must be . . . " She faltered. I was reminded of the time I got a free upgrade to first class, where I sat right next to Sean Connery. Tongue-tied, I couldn't think of a thing to say besides, "You're Sean Connery," of which presumably he was aware.

"That must be a m-mighty cross to bear," she stammered.

"Yes," I said. I was no longer driven to get her attention; I had it. I could control the upchuck of chatter that had embarrassed me minutes before. I experienced a seated sensation, literalized in an improbable physical comfort in my form-fitted orange chair. Any obligation to express interest in the plight of this young woman's own son seemed to vanish. Now I was the serene party, and the one to be courted. I felt almost queenly.

"Your boy," she scrambled. "He holding up okay?"

"Oh, Kevin loves it here."

"How come? Marlon curse this place up one side, down the other."

"Kevin has few interests," I said, giving our son the benefit of the doubt that he had any. "He's never known what to do with himself. After-school hours and weekends hung off him in big drooping folds like an oversized car coat. Bingo, his day is agreeably regimented from breakfast to lights-out. And now he lives in a world where being pissed off all day long is totally normal. I think he even feels a sense of community," I allowed. "Maybe not with the other inmates themselves. But their prevailing humors—disgust, hostility, derision—are like old friends."

Other visitors were clearly eavesdropping, since they flicked averted eyes at our chairs with the swift, voracious motion of a lizard's tongue. I might have lowered my voice, but I was enjoying the audience.

"He look back on what he done, he feel any, you know—"

"Remorse?" I provided dryly. "What could he conceivably regret? Now he's *somebody*, isn't he? And he's *found himself*, as they said in my day.

Now he doesn't have to worry about whether he's a freak or a geek, a grind or a jock or a nerd. He doesn't have to worry if he's gay. He's a murderer. It's marvelously unambiguous. And best of all," I took a breath, "he got away from me."

"Sounds like there's a silver lining, then." She held herself at an inch or two greater distance than women in earnest conversation are wont, eyeing me at an angle that departed from a straight line by about thirty degrees. These subtle removals seemed almost scientific: I was a specimen. "Like, you get away from him, too."

I gestured helplessly at the waiting room. "Not quite."

Glancing at her Swatch, she displayed a growing awareness that in what could prove a once-in-a-lifetime opportunity, she had to work in the one question she had always wanted to ask *KK*'s actual mother before it was too late. I knew what was coming: "You ever figure what it was drove him to—you ever figure out *why*?"

It's what they all want to ask—my brother, your parents, my co-workers, the documentary makers, Kevin's psychiatric consult, the gladstone_carnage.com web-page designers, though interestingly never my own mother. After I steeled myself to accept Thelma Corbitt's gracious invitation for coffee the week after her son's funeral (though she never asked aloud, and she spent most of our session reading me his poems and showing me what seemed like hundreds of snapshots of Denny in school plays), it came off her in pulses, it clutched at my dress: a craving for comprehension that verged on hysteria. Like all those parents, she'd been wracked by the apprehension that the entire gory mess whose sticky pieces we would both be picking up for the rest of our lives was *unnecessary*. Quite. *Thursday* was an elective, like printmaking, or Spanish. But this incessant badgering, this pleading refrain of *why, why, why*—it's so grossly unfair. Why, after all I have borne, am I held accountable for ordering their chaos? Isn't it enough that I suffer the brunt of the facts without shouldering this unreasonable responsibility for what they mean? That young woman at Claverack meant no harm I'm sure, but her all-too-familiar question made me bitter.

"I expect it's my fault," I said defiantly. "I wasn't a very good mother—cold, judgmental, selfish. Though you can't say I haven't paid the price."

"Well, then," she drawled, closing up that two inches and swiveling her gaze thirty degrees to look me in the eye. "You can blame your mother, and she can blame hers. Leastways sooner or later it's the fault of somebody who's dead."

Stolid in my guilt, clutching it like a girl with a stuffed bunny, I failed to follow.

"Greenleaf?" shouted the guard. My companion tucked the candy into her pocketbook, then rose. I could see her calculating that she had just enough time to slip in one more quick question-and-answer or to deliver a parting thought. With Sean Connery, that's always the quandary, isn't it: to siphon information, or to pour. Somehow it impressed me that she chose the latter.

"It's always the mother's fault, ain't it?" she said softly, collecting her coat. "That boy turn out bad cause his mama a drunk, or a she a junkie. She let him run wild, she don't teach him right from wrong. She never home when he back from school. Nobody ever say his daddy a drunk, or his daddy not home after school. And nobody ever say they some kids just damned mean. Don't you believe that old guff. Don't you let them saddle you with all that killing."

"*Loretta Greenleaf!*"

"It hard to be a momma. Nobody ever pass a law say 'fore you get pregnant you gotta be perfect. I'm sure you try the best you could. You here, in this dump, on a nice Saturday afternoon? You still trying. Now you take care of yourself, honey. And you don't be talking any more a that nonsense."

Loretta Greenleaf held my hand and squeezed it. My eyes sprang hot. I squeezed her hand back, so hard and so long that she must have feared I might never let go.

Oh, dear, the coffee is cold.

Eva

(9 P.M.)

Now returned to my duplex, I'm ashamed of myself. I needn't have identified myself as Kevin's mother. Loretta Greenleaf and I might have simply talked about the Claverack food service: *Who says saltpeter suppresses sex drive?* or even, *What the hell is "saltpeter," anyway?*

I was about to write, "I don't know what got into me," but I'm afraid I do, Franklin. I was thirsty for companionship, and I felt her engagement with this garrulous white lady waning. I had the power to rivet her if I wished, and I reached for it.

Of course, in the immediate aftermath of *Thursday* I wanted nothing more than to crawl down a sewage drain and pull the lid. I longed for unobtrusiveness, like my brother, or oblivion, if that is not simply a synonym for wishing you were dead. The last thing in the world I was worried about was my sense of distinction. But the resilience of the spirit is appalling. As I said, I get hungry now, and for more than chicken. What I wouldn't give to go back to the days that I sat beside strangers and made a memorable impression because I had founded a successful company or had traveled extensively in Laos. I wax nostalgic for the time that Siobhan clapped her hands and exclaimed admiringly that she'd used *Wing and a Prayer* on her trips to the Continent. That is the eminence that I chose for myself. But we are all resourceful, and we use what falls to hand. Stripped of company, wealth, and handsome husband, I stoop to my one surefire shortcut to being *somebody*.

Mother of the ignoble Kevin Khatchadourian is who I am now, an identity that amounts to one more of our son's little victories. AWAP and our marriage have been demoted to footnotes, only interesting insofar as they illuminate my role as the mother of the kid everybody loves to hate. On the most private level, this filial mugging of who I once was to myself may be what I most resent. For the first half of my life, I was my own creation. From a dour, closeted childhood, I had molded a vibrant, expansive adult who commanded a smattering of a dozen languages and could pioneer through the unfamiliar streets of any foreign town. This notion that you are your own work of art is an American one, as you would hasten to point out. Now my perspective is European: I am a bundle of other people's histories, a creature of circumstance. It is Kevin who has taken on this aggressive, optimistic Yankee task of making himself up.

I may be hounded by that *why* question, but I wonder how hard I've really tried to answer it. I'm not sure that I want to understand Kevin, to find a well within myself so inky that from its depths what he did makes sense. Yet little by little, led kicking and screaming, I grasp the rationality of *Thursday*. Mark David Chapman now gets the fan mail that John Lennon can't; Richard Ramirez, the "Night Stalker," may have destroyed a dozen women's chances for connubial happiness but still receives numerous offers of marriage in prison himself. In a country that doesn't discriminate between fame and infamy, the latter presents itself as plainly more achievable. Hence I am no longer amazed by the frequency of public rampages with loaded automatics but by the fact that every ambitious citizen in America is not atop a shopping center looped with refills of ammunition. What Kevin did *Thursday* and what I did in Claverack's waiting room today depart only in scale. Yearning to feel *special*, I was determined to capture someone's attention, even if I had to use the murder of nine people to get it.

It's no mystery why Kevin is at home at Claverack. If in high school he was disaffected, he had too much competition; scores of other boys battled for the role of surly punk slumped in the back of the class. Now he has carved himself a niche.

And he has colleagues, in Littleton, Jonesboro, Springfield. As in most disciplines, rivalry vies with a more collegial sense of common purpose. Like many a luminary, he is severe with his contemporaries, calling them to rigorous standards: He derides blubberers like Paducah's Michael Carneal who recant, who sully the purity of their gesture with a craven regret. He admires style—for instance, Evan Ramsey's crack as he took aim at his math class in Bethyl, Alaska, "This sure beats algebra, doesn't it?" He appreciates capable planning: Carneal inserted gun-range earplugs before aiming his .22 Luger; Barry Loukaitis in Moses Lake had his mother take him shopping in seven different stores until he found just the right long black coat under which to hide his .30-caliber hunting rifle. Kevin has a refined sense of irony, too, treasuring the fact that the teacher Loukaitis shot had only recently written on the report card of this A-student, "A pleasure to have in the class." Like any professional, he has contempt for the kind of rank incompetence featured by John Sirola, the fourteen-year-old in Redlands, California, who blasted his principal in the face in 1995, only to trip when fleeing the scene and shoot himself dead. And in the way of most established experts, Kevin is suspicious of parvenus trying to elbow their way

into his specialty with the slightest of qualifications—witness his resentment of that thirteen-year-old eviscerater. He is difficult to impress.

Much as John Updike dismisses Tom Wolfe as a hack, Kevin reserves a
particular disdain for Luke Woodham, "the cracker" from Pearl, Mississippi. He approves of ideological focus but scorns pompous moralizing,
as well as any School Shooting aspirant who can't keep his own counsel—
and apparently before taking out his nominal once-girlfriend with a .30-
.30 caliber shotgun, Woodham couldn't stop himself from passing a note
to a friend in class that read (and you should hear your son's puling rendition): "I killed because people like me are mistreated every day. I did this
to show society push us and we will push back." Kevin decried Woodham's
sniveling while mucus drizzled onto his orange jumpsuit on *Prime Time Live*
as *totally uncool*: "I'm my own person! I'm not a tyrant. I'm not evil and I
have a heart and I have feelings!" Woodham has admitted to warming up
by clubbing his dog, Sparky, wrapping the pooch in a plastic bag, torching
him with lighter fluid, and listening to him whimper before tossing him in
a pond, and after studious consideration Kevin has concluded that animal
torture is clichéd. Lastly, he is especially condemnatory of the way this
whiny creature tried to worm out responsibility by blaming a satanic cult.
The story itself showed panache, but Kevin regards a refusal to stand by
one's own handiwork as not only undignified but as a betrayal of the tribe.

I know you, my dear, and you're impatient. Never mind the preliminaries, you want to hear about the visit itself—what his mood's like, how
he's looking, what he said. All right, then. But by imputation, you asked
for it.

He looks well enough. Though there is still a tinge too much blue in
his complexion, fine veins at his temples convey a promising hint of vulnerability. If he has hacked his hair in uneven shocks, I take that as repre-
sentation of healthy concern with his appearance. The perpetual half cock
on the right corner of his mouth is starting to carve a permanent single
quote into the cheek, remaining behind when he switches to a pursed-
mouth scowl. There's no close quote on the left, and the asymmetry is disconcerting.

No more of those ubiquitous orange jumpsuits these days at Claverack. So Kevin is free to persist in the perplexing style of dress he developed
at fourteen, arguably crafted in counterpoint to the prevailing fashion in

clothing that's oversized—the jib of Harlem toughs, boxers catching sun, sauntering through moving traffic as the waistband of jeans that could rig a small sailboat shimmy toward their knees. But if Kevin's alternative look is pointed, I can only make wild guesses at what it means.

When he first trotted out this fashion in eighth grade, I assumed that the T-shirts biting into his armpits and pleating across his chest were old favorites he was reluctant to let go, and I went out of my way to find duplicates in a larger size. He never touched them. Now I understand that the dungarees whose zipper would not quite close were carefully selected. Likewise the windbreakers whose arms rode up the wrist, the ties that dangled three inches above the belt for when we forced him to look "nice," the shirts that gaped between popping buttons.

I will say, the tiny-clothes thing did get a lot across. At first glance, he looked poverty-stricken, and I stopped myself more than once from commenting that "people will think" we don't earn enough to buy our growing boy new jeans; adolescents are so greedy for signals that their parents are consumed with social status. Besides, a closer inspection revealed that his shrunken getup was designer labeled, lending the pretense at hard luck a parodic wink. The suggestion of a wash load churned at an errantly high temperature connoted a comic ineptitude, and the binding of a child-sized jacket across the shoulders would sometimes pull his arms goofily out from his sides like a baboon's. (That's as close as he's come to fitting the mold of a conventional cutup; no one I've spoken to about our son has ever mentioned finding him funny.) The way the hems of his jeans stopped shy of his socks made a hayseedy impression, consonant with his fondness for playing dumb. There was more than a suggestion of Peter Pan about the style—a refusal to grow up—though I'm confused why he would cling so to being a kid when throughout his childhood he seemed so lost in it, knocking around in those years much the way I was rattling around our enormous house.

Claverack's experimental policy of allowing inmates to wear street clothes has allowed Kevin to reiterate his fashion statement inside. While New York's corner boys flapping in outsized gear look like toddlers from a distance, Kevin's shrunken mode of dress has the opposite effect of making him look bigger—more adult, bursting. One of his psych consultants has accused me of finding the style unnerving for its aggressive sexuality: Kevin's crotch cuts revealingly into his testicles, and the painted-on T-shirts make his nipples protrude. Perhaps; certainly the tight sleeve hems, the taut collars, and the yanked-in waistbands strap his body in cords and remind me of bondage.

He looks uncomfortable, and in this respect the garb is apt. Kevin *is* uncomfortable; the tiny clothing replicates the same constriction that he feels in his own skin. Reading his suffocating attire as equivalent to a penitential hair shirt might seem a stretch, but the waistbands chafe, the collars score his neck. Discomfort begets discomfort in others, of course, and that, too, must be part of the plan. I often find that when I'm with him I pull at my own clothes, discreetly prizing a seam from between my buttocks or releasing an extra button on my blouse.

Eyeing laconic interchanges at adjoining tables, I've detected that some of his fellow inmates have started to mimic Kevin's eccentric dress sense. I gather that T-shirts in unusually small sizes have become prized possessions, and Kevin himself has mentioned smugly that runts are being robbed of their clothes. He may hold imitators up to ridicule, but he does seem gratified at having initiated his very own fad. Were he commensurately concerned with originality two years ago, the seven students he used for target practice would be preparing applications to the college of their choice by now.

Anyway, today? He lounged into the visiting room wearing what must have been one of the runts' sweatpants, since I didn't recognize them as ones I'd bought. The little plaid button-down he wore on top was only secured by the middle two buttons, exposing his midriff. Now even his tennis shoes are too small, and he crushes their heels under his feet. He might not like to hear me say it, but he's graceful. There's a languor to his motions, as to the way he talks. And he always has that skew, too; he walks sideways, like a crab. Leading with his left hip gives him the subtle sidle of a supermodel on a catwalk. If he realized I saw traces of effeminacy in him, I doubt he'd be offended. He prizes ambiguity; he loves to keep you guessing.

"What a surprise," he said smoothly, pulling out the chair; its back legs had lost their plastic feet and the raw aluminum shrieked across the cement, a fingernail-on-the-blackboard sound that Kevin drew out. He slid his elbow across the table, resting his temple on his fist, assuming that characteristic tilt, sardonic with his whole body. I've tried to stop myself, but whenever he sits in front of me I rear back.

I do get irked that I'm always the one who has to come up with something to talk about. He's old enough to carry a conversation. And since he has imprisoned me in my life every bit as much as he's imprisoned himself in his, we suffer an equal poverty of fresh subject matter. Often we run through the same script: "How are you?" I ask with brutal simplicity. "You want me to say *fine*?" "I want you to say something," I throw back. "You're the one came to see me," he reminds me. And he can and will sit it out, the whole hour. As for which of us has the greater tolerance for nullity, there's no contest. He used to spend whole Saturdays propped theatrically in front of the Weather Channel.

So today I skipped even a perfunctory *how's tricks*, on the theory that folks who shun small talk are still dependent on its easing transitions but have learned to make other people do all the work. And I was still agitated by my exchange with Loretta Greenleaf. Maybe having tempted his own mother into boasting about her connection to his filthy atrocity would afford him some satisfaction. But apparently my messianic impulse to take responsibility for *Thursday* onto myself reads to Kevin as a form of stealing.

"All right," I said, no-nonsense. "I need to know. Do you blame me? It's all right to say so, if that's what you think. Is that what you tell your psych consults, or they tell you? It all traces back to your mother."

He snapped, "*Why should you get all the credit?*"

The conversation that I had expected to consume our whole hour was now over in ninety seconds. We sat.

"Do you remember your early childhood very well, Kevin?" I had read somewhere that people with painful childhoods will often draw a blank.

"What's to remember?"

"Well, for example you wore diapers until you were six."

"What about it." If I had some idea of embarrassing him, I was misguided.

"It must have been unpleasant."

"For you."

"For you as well."

"Why?" he asked mildly. "It was warm."

"Not for long."

"Didn't sit in it for long. You were a good mumsey."

"Didn't other kindergartners make fun of you? I worried at the time."

"Oh, I bet you couldn't sleep."

"I worried," I said staunchly.

He shrugged with one shoulder. "Why should they? I was getting away with something and they weren't."

"I was just wondering if, at this late date, you could shed some light on why the delay. Your father gave enough demonstrations."

"*Kevvy-wevvy!*" he cooed, falsetto. "*Honey sweetie! Look at Daddykins! See how he pee-pees in the pooper-dooper? Wouldn't you like that, too, Kevvy-woopsie? Wouldn't it be fun to be just like Dadda-boo, piddle your peenie-weenie over the toiley-woiley?* I was just hoisting you on your own retard."

I was interested that he had allowed himself to be verbally clever; he's generally careful not to let on that he's got a brain. "All right," I said. "You wouldn't use the toilet for yourself, and you and I—you wouldn't do it for me. But why not for your father?"

"*You're a big boy, now!*" Kevin minced. "*You're my big boy! You're my little man!* Christ. What an asshole."

I stood up. "Don't you *ever* say that. Don't you *ever, ever* say that. Not once, not ever, not one more time!"

"Or what," he said softly, eyes dancing.

I sat back down. I shouldn't let him get to me like that. I usually don't. Still any dig at you—.

Oh, maybe I should count myself lucky that he doesn't press this button more often. Then, lately he is always pressing it, in a way. That is, for most of his childhood his narrow, angular features taunted me with my own reflection. But in the last year his face has started to fill out, and as it widens I begin to recognize your broader bones. While it's true that I once searched Kevin's face hungrily for resemblance to his father, now I keep fighting this nutty impression that he's doing it on purpose, to make me suffer. I don't want to see the resemblance. I don't want to spot the same mannerisms, that signature downward flap of a hand when you dismissed something as insignificant, like the trifling matter of neighbor after neighbor refusing to let their kids play with your son. Seeing your strong chin wrenched in a pugnacious jut, your wide artless smile bent to a crafty grin, is like beholding my husband possessed.

"So what would you have done?" I said. "With a little boy who insisted on messing his pants until he was old enough for first grade?"

Kevin leaned further onto his elbow, his bicep flat on the table. "Know what they do with cats, don't you. They do it in the house, and you shove their faces into their own shit. They don't like it. They use the box." He sat back, satisfied.

"That's not that far from what I did, is it?" I said heavily. "Do you remember? What you drove me to? How I finally got you to use the bathroom?"

He traced a faint white scar on his forearm near the elbow with a note of tender possessiveness, as if stroking a pet worm. "Sure." There was a different quality to this affirmation; I felt he truly remembered, whereas these other recollections were post hoc.

"I was proud of you," he purred.

"You were proud of yourself," I said. "As usual."

"Hey," he said, leaning forward. "Most honest thing you ever done."

I stirred, collecting my bag. I may have craved his admiration once, but not for that; for anything but that.

"Hold on," he said. "I answered your question. Got one for you."

This was new. "All right," I said. "Shoot."

"Those maps," he said.

"What about them," I said.

"Why'd you keep them on the walls?"

It's only because I refused to tear those spattered maps from the study for years, or to allow you to paint over them as you were so anxious to, that Kevin "remembers" the incident at all. He was, as you observed repeatedly at the time, awfully young.

"I kept them up for my sanity," I said. "I needed to see something you'd done to me, to reach out and touch it. To prove that your malice wasn't all in my head."

"Yeah," he said, tickling the scar on his arm again. "Know what you mean."

I promise to explain, Franklin, but right now I just can't.

Eva

Dear Franklin,

I'm sorry to have left you dangling, and I've been dreading an explanation ever since. In fact, driving to work this morning, I had another trial flashback. Technically, I committed perjury. I just didn't think I owed that beady-eyed judge (a congenital disorder I'd never seen before, inordinately small pupils, provided her the dazed, insensate look of a cartoon character who's just been hit over the head with a frying pan) what for a decade I'd kept from my own husband.

"Ms. Khatchadourian, did you or your husband ever hit your son?" Mary's attorney leaned threateningly into the witness stand.

"Violence only teaches a child that physical force is an acceptable method of getting your way," I recited.

"The court can only agree, Ms. Khatchadourian, but it's very important that we clarify in no uncertain terms for the record: Did you or your husband ever physically abuse Kevin while he was in your care?"

"Certainly not," I said firmly, and then muttered again for good measure, "certainly not." I rued the repetition. There's something dodgy about any assertion one feels obliged to make twice.

As I left the stand, my foot caught on a floorboard nail, pulling the black rubber heel off my pump. I limped back to my chair, reflecting, better a broken shoe than a long wooden nose.

But keeping secrets is a discipline. I never used to think of myself as a good liar, but after having had some practice I had adopted the prevaricator's credo that one doesn't so much fabricate a lie as marry it. A successful lie cannot be brought into this world and capriciously abandoned; like any committed relationship, it must be maintained, and with far more devotion than the truth, which carries on being carelessly true without any help. By contrast, my lie needed me as much as I needed it, and so demanded the constancy of wedlock: Till death do us part.

I realize that Kevin's diapers embarrassed you, even if they confoundingly failed to embarrass the boy himself. We were already using the extra-large; much longer and we'd have to start mail-ordering the kind for medical incontinence. However many tolerant parenting manuals you'd devoured, you fostered an old-fashioned masculinity that I found surprisingly attractive. You didn't want your son to be a sissy, to present an easy target for teasing peers, or to cling to a talisman of infancy quite so publicly glaring, since the bulge under his pants was unmistakable. "Jesus," you'd grumble once Kevin was in bed, "why couldn't he just suck his thumb?"

Yet you yourself had engaged in an ongoing childhood battle with your fastidious mother over flushing, because the toilet had overflowed once, and every time you pushed the handle thereafter you were terrified that lumps of excrement might begin disgorging endlessly onto the bathroom floor, like a scatological version of *The Sorcerer's Apprentice*. And I had agreed that it was tragic how kids can tie themselves into neurotic knots over pee and poop, and what a waste of angst it all was, so I went along with this new theory about letting toddlers choose to potty train when they were "ready." Nevertheless, we were both getting desperate. You started drilling me about whether he saw me using the toilet during the day (we weren't sure if he should or shouldn't) or whether I might have said anything to frighten him away from this throne of civilized life, in comparison to which amenities like *please* and *thank you* were dispensable as doilies. You accused me by turns of making too much of the matter, and too little.

It was impossible that I made too little of it, since this one developmental stage that our son seemed to have skipped was tyrannizing my life. You will recall that it was only thanks to the new educational ethos of pathological neutrality (there's-no-such-thing-as-worse-or-better-but-only-different) as well as paralytic fear of suit (in horror of which Americans are increasingly reluctant to do anything from giving drowning victims mouth-to-mouth to firing slack-jawed incompetents from their employ) that Kevin wasn't turned away from that pricey Nyack kindergarten until he, well, got his shit together. All the same, the teacher was not about to change a five-year-old boy, claiming that she'd be laying herself open to charges of sexual abuse. (In fact, when I quietly informed Carol Fabricant of Kevin's little eccentricity, she looked at me askance and announced witheringly that this kind of *nonconforming behavior* was sometimes a *cry for help*. She didn't spell it out, but for the next week I lived in fear of a knock on the door and a flashing blue light in our windows.) So no sooner had I dropped him off at Love-'n'-Learn at 9 A.M. and driven back home than I was obliged to return around 11:30 A.M. with my now rather careworn diaper bag.

If he was dry, I'd engage in a bit of pretextual hair tousling and ask to see what he was drawing, though with enough of his "artwork" stuck on the fridge, I'd already have a pretty good idea. (While the other children had graduated to fat-headed stick figures and landscapes with a little strip of blue sky at the top, Kevin was still scrawling formless, jagged scrabble in black and purple crayon.) Yet all too often a midday reprieve meant return to a ringing phone: Miss Fabricant, informing me that Kevin was now drenched and the other kids were complaining because he smelled. Would I please—? I could hardly say no. Thus after picking him up at 2 P.M., I'd have made four trips to Love-'n'-Learn in a day. So much for having plenty of time to myself once Kevin started school, as well as for the fantasy I had improbably kept alive that I might soon be able to resume the directorship of AWAP.

Were Kevin a pliant, eager boy who happened to have this one unpleasant problem, she might have felt sorry for him. But Miss Fabricant's relationship with our son was not thriving for other reasons.

We may have made a mistake in sending him to a Montessori kindergarten, whose philosophy of human nature was, at the least, optimistic. Its supervised but unstructured education—kids were placed in a "stimulating" environment, with play stations including alphabet blocks, counting beads, and pea plants—presumed that children were inborn autodidacts. Yet in my experience, when left to their own devices people will get up to one of two things: nothing much, and no good.

An initial report of Kevin's "progress" that November mentioned that he was "somewhat undersocialized" and "may need assistance with initiating behaviors." Miss Fabricant was loath to criticize her charges, so it was pulling teeth to get her to translate that Kevin had spent his first two months sitting slack on a stool in the middle of the room, gazing dully at his puttering classmates. I knew that look, a precociously geriatric, glaucous-eyed glare sparked only by a sporadic glint of scornful incredulity. When pressed to play with the other boys and girls, he replied that whatever they were doing was "dumb," speaking with the effortful weariness that in junior high school would convince his history teacher that he was drunk. However she persuaded him to craft those dark, furious drawings I will never know.

For me, these crayon mangles were a constant strain to admire. I rapidly ran out of compliments (*That has so much energy, Kevin!*) and imaginative interpretations (*Is that a storm, honey? Or maybe a picture of the hair and soap we pull out of a bathtub drain!*). Hard-pressed to keep cooing over his exciting choice of colors when he drew exclusively in black, brown, and violet, I couldn't help but suggest timidly that abstract expressionism having hit such a dead-end in the fifties, maybe he should try approximating a bird or a tree. But for Miss Fabricant, Kevin's clogged-drain still lifes were proof positive that the Montessori method could work wonders with a doorstop.

Nonetheless, even Kevin, who has such a gift for it, can sustain stasis for only so long without doing something to make life a little interesting, as he demonstrated so conclusively on *Thursday*. By the school year's end Miss Fabricant must have waxed nostalgic for the days when Kevin Khatchadourian did absolutely nothing.

Maybe it goes without saying that the pea plants died, as did the sprouting avocado that replaced them, while at the same time I noticed idly that I was missing a bottle of bleach. There were mysteries: Subsequent to a particular day in January, the moment I led Kevin by the hand into the classroom, a little girl with Shirley Temple curls began to cry, and her wailing worsened until at some point in February she never came back. Another boy, aggressive and rambunctious in September, one of those biffy sorts always boxing your leg and pushing other kids in the sandbox, suddenly became silent and inward, developing at once a severe case of asthma and an inexplicable terror of the coat closet, within five feet of which he would begin to wheeze. What did that have to do with Kevin? I couldn't say; perhaps nothing. And some of the incidents were pretty harmless, like the time little Jason stuck his feet in his bright red galoshes, only to find them filled with squares of apple-spice cake leftover from snack time. Child's play—if *real* child's play—we'd agree.

What most aggrieved Miss Fabricant, of course, was the fact that one after the other of her other charges started to regress in the potty department. She and I had concurred hopefully at the start of the year that Kevin might be inspired by the example of his peers on bathroom breaks, but I fear that quite the opposite took place, and by the time he graduated there was not just one six-year-old in diapers, but three or four.

I was more unsettled by a couple of passing incidents.

One morning some delicate slip of a thing nicknamed Muffet brought a tea set for show-and-tell. It wasn't any ordinary tea set, but an ornate, many-cupped affair whose elements each fit into the formfitted cubbies of a velvet-lined mahogany box. Her mother later huffed that it was a family heirloom that Muffet was only allowed to bring out on special occasions. No doubt the set should never have been taken to a kindergarten, but the little girl was proud of the many matching pieces and had learned to handle them with care, painstakingly laying out the cups in their saucers with china spoons before a dozen of her classmates as they sat at their knee-high tables. After she'd poured a round of "tea" (the ubiquitous pineapple-grapefruit juice), Kevin hoisted his cup by its tiny handle in a salutary toast—and dropped it on the floor.

In rapid succession all eleven of his fellow tea-sippers followed suit. Before Miss Fabricant could get hold of the situation, the saucers and spoons quickly suffered the same tinkling fate, in consequence of which when Muffet's mother retrieved her sobbing daughter that afternoon, nothing remained of the treasured tea set but the pot.

If I had ever nursed the hope that my son might turn out to display leadership qualities, this is not what I had in mind. Yet when I made a remark to this effect, Miss Fabricant was in no mood for drollery. I felt that in general her early twenties exhilaration at molding all those receptive little moppets into multiculturally aware, environmentally responsible vegetarians driven to rectify inequities in the Third World was beginning to fray around the edges. This was her first year of flaking poster paint from her eyebrows, going to sleep at night with the salty taste of paste in her

gums, and exiling so many children at a shot for a "time-out" that there
was no longer any activity to take a time out from. After all, she had announced at our introduction in September that she "simply *loves* children,"
a declaration of which I am eternally dubious. From young women like
Miss Fabricant, with a blunt snub of a nose like a Charlotte potato and
hips like Idahos, the infeasible assertion seems to decode, "I want to get
married." Myself, after having not *a* child but this particular one, I
couldn't see how anyone could claim to *love children* in the generic any more
that anyone could credibly claim to *love people* in a sufficiently sweeping
sense as to embrace Pol Pot, Don Rickles, and an upstairs neighbor who
does 2,000 jumping jacks at three in the morning.

After relating her terrible tale in a breathless stage whisper, she clearly
expected me to leap to cover the cost of the tea set. Financially of course I
could afford to, whatever it was worth, but I could not afford the attendant
assumption of total blame. Face it, Franklin, you'd have had a fit. You were
touchy about your son's being singled out, or as you would say, *persecuted*.
Technically he had only broken the one setting, and covering one-twelfth
of the loss was the most compensation you would countenance. I also offered to speak to Kevin about "respecting the property of others," though
Miss Fabricant was underwhelmed by this assurance. Maybe she intuited
that these set lectures of mine had begun to lilt with the swinging, mocking cadence of the *one-potato, two-potato* rhymes to which girls skip rope.

"That wasn't very nice, Kevin," I said in the car. "Breaking Muffet's
teacup." I've no idea why we parents persist in believing that our kids yearn
to be thought of as *nice*, since when we ourselves commend acquaintances
as *very nice* we usually mean they're dull.

"She has a stupid name."

"That doesn't mean she deserves—"

"It slipped," he said lamely.

"That's not what Miss Fabricant said."

"How would she know." He yawned.

"How would *you* feel, kiddo, if you had something that you cared
about more than anything, and you brought it to show to the class, and
then someone smashed it?"

"Like what?" he asked, innocence tinged with self-congratulation.

I reached casually in my head for an example of a possession that Kevin especially cherished, and it wasn't there. Searching harder, I felt the same rising dismay of patting down all my pockets after discovering that the one in which I always kept my wallet was empty. It was unnatural. In my own rather underfurnished childhood, I was a fetishistic custodian of the lowliest keepsake, from a three-legged windup donkey named Cloppity to a rinsed-out four-pack of food-coloring bottles.

It's not as if Kevin didn't have things in abundance, since you showered him with toys. I'd feel unkind in pointing out that he ignored these Junior Game Boys and Tonka dump trucks across the board, save that your very excess seemed to signal an awareness that none of your previous gifts had taken. Maybe your generosity backfired, by lining his playroom in what must have seemed a kind of plastic dirt; and maybe he could tell that commercial presents were easy for us, being rich, and so, however expensive, cheap.

But I had spent weeks at a time crafting homespun, personalized playthings that should hypothetically have meant *something*. I made sure Kevin watched me, too, so that he knew them for labors of love. The most curiosity he ever exhibited was to ask irritably why I didn't just *buy* a storybook. Otherwise, once my hand-drawn children's book was sandwiched between painted pressboard covers, drilled and hole-punched and bound with bright yarn, he looked vacantly out the window as I read it aloud. I admit that the story line was hackneyed, about a little boy who loses his beloved dog, Snippy, and becomes distraught and looks everywhere and of course in the end Snippy shows up—I probably borrowed it from *Lassie*. I've never pretended to be a gifted creative writer, and the watercolors bled; I was suffering from the delusion that it's the thought that counts. But no matter how many references to the little boy's dark hair and deep brown eyes I planted, I couldn't get him to identify with the boy in the story who pines for his lost puppy. (Remember when you wanted to buy Kevin a dog? I begged you not to. I was glad you never forced me to explain, since I never explained it to myself. I just know that whenever I envisioned our bouncing black lab, or trusting Irish setter, I was filled with horror.) The only interest he displayed in the book was when I left him alone with it to get dinner, only to find that he'd scribbled Magic Marker on every page—an early *interactive edition*, it seems. Later he drowned the stuffed-sock, button-eyed Teddy, aptly as it happens, in Bear Lake; he fed several pieces of my black-and-white wooden jigsaw of a zebra down the driveway's drain.

I clutched at ancient history. "Remember your squirt gun?"

He shrugged.

"Remember when Mommer lost her temper, and stamped on it, and it broke?" I had got into the queer habit of referring to myself in the third person; I may have already begun to dissociate, and "Mommer" was now my virtuous alter ego, a pleasingly plump maternal icon with floury hands and a fire surging in a pot-bellied stove who solved disputes between neighborhood urchins with spellbinding fables and hot Toll House cookies. Meantime, Kevin had dropped *Mommer* altogether, thereby demoting the neologism to my own rather silly name for myself. In the car, I was disquieted to realize that he had ceased to call me anything at all. That seemed impossible, but your children generally use your name when they want something, if only attention, and Kevin was loath to beseech me for so much as a turned head. "You didn't like that, did you?"

"I didn't care," said Kevin.

My hands slithered down the wheel from ten-and-two to a desultory seven-and-five. His memory was accurate. Since according to you in defacing my maps he had *only been trying to help*, you replaced the squirt gun, which he tossed into his slag heap of a toy box and never touched. The squirt gun had served its purpose. Indeed, I'd had a spooky presentiment when I finished grinding the barrel into the floor that since he *had* been attached to it, he was glad to see it go.

When I told you about the tea set, you were about to brush it off, but I shot you a warning glance; we had talked about the need for presenting a united front. "Hey, Kev," you said lightly. "I know teacups are for girls and sort of prissy, but don't break 'em, okay? It's *uncool*. Now how about some Frisbee? We've just got time to work on that bank shot of yours before dinner."

"Sure, Dad!" I remember watching Kevin streak off to the closet to fetch the Frisbee and puzzling. Hands fisted, elbows flying, he looked for all the world like a regular, rambunctious kid, exhilarated at playing in the yard with his father. Except that it was *too* much like a regular kid; almost studied. Even that *Sure, Dad!* had a rehearsed, *nyeh-nyeh* ring to it that I couldn't put my finger on. I had the same queasy feeling on weekends when Kevin would pipe up—yes, *pipe up*—"Gosh, Dad, it's Saturday! Can we go see another *battlefield?*" You'd be so enchanted that I couldn't bring myself to raise the possibility that he was pulling your leg. Likewise, I watched out the dining room window and could not believe, somehow, that Kevin was quite that inept at throwing a Frisbee after all this time. He still tossed the disc on its side, hooking the rim on his middle finger, and curled it ten yards from your feet. You were patient, but I worried that your very patience tempted Kevin to try it.

Oh, I don't remember all the incidents that year aside from the fact that there were several, which you tagged with the umbrella dismissal, "Eva, every boy pulls a few pigtails." I spared you a number of accounts, because for me to report any of our son's misbehavior seemed like *telling on him*. I ended up reflecting badly not on him but on myself. If I were his sister I could see it, but could a mother be a tattletale? Apparently.

However, the sight I beheld in—I think it was March, well, I'm not sure why it unnerved me quite so much, but I couldn't keep it to myself. I had gone to pick up Kevin at the usual time, and no one seemed to know where he was. Miss Fabricant's expression grew pinched, though by this point, were Kevin abducted by the murderous pedophiles we were then led to believe lurked behind every bush, I'd suspect her of having hired them. The missing child being our son, it took a while before one of us thought to check the bathrooms, hardly his bolt-hole of choice.

"Here he is!" sang his teacher at the door to the Girls' Room. And then she gasped.

I doubt your recollection of these rusty stories is all that sharp, so allow me to refresh your memory. There was a slight, dark-haired kindergartner named Violetta whom I must have mentioned earlier that school year, since she touched me so. She was quiet, withdrawn; she would hide in Miss Fabricant's skirts, and it took me ages to coax her to tell me her name. Quite pretty, really, but you had to look at her carefully to discern that, which most people didn't. They couldn't get past the eczema.

It was dreadful. She was covered in it, these massive scaly patches, red and flaking and sometimes cracked, where it scabbed. All down her arms and spindly legs, and worst of all across her face. The crinkling texture

was reptilian. I'd heard that skin conditions were associated with emotional disorders; maybe I was myself susceptible to faddish presupposi-
tions, since I couldn't help wondering if Violetta was being mistreated in
some way or if her parents were undergoing a fractious divorce. In any
case, every time I laid eyes on her something caved in me, and I fought the
impulse to gather her in my arms. I'd never have wished vast angry blem-
ishes on our son per se, but this was just the sort of heartbreaking affliction for which I had hankered at Dr. Foulke's: some temporary misfortune
that would heal but that would meantime stir in me when faced with my
own boy the same bottomless pool of sympathy that rippled whenever
Violetta—a stranger's child—shuffled bashfully into view.

I've only had one outbreak of eczema, on my shin, just a taste but
enough to know that it itches like fury. I'd overheard her mother urging
the girl murmurously not to scratch and assumed that the tube of cream
that Violetta always carried, clutched shamefully in the pocket of her
jumper, was an anti-itch ointment, since if it was a curative it was snake
oil; I'd never seen Violetta's eczema do anything but get worse. But those
antipruritics are only so effective, and her self-control was impressive.
She'd trace a fingernail tantalizingly over her arm, and then grasp the offending hand with the other, as if putting it on a leash.

Anyway, when Miss Fabricant gasped, I joined her in the doorway.
Kevin's back was to us, and he was whispering. When I pushed the door
open a little more, he stopped and stepped back. Facing us before the
washbasins was Violetta. Her face was lifted in what I can only describe as
an expression of bliss. Her eyes were closed, her arms crossed sepulchrally
with each hand at the opposite shoulder, her body listing in a kind of
swoon. I'm sure we'd have neither begrudged this benighted little girl the
ecstasy she so deserved, except for the fact that she was covered with blood.

I don't mean to be melodramatic. It soon became clear after Miss
Fabricant shrieked and pushed Kevin aside for paper towels that Violetta's
abrasions weren't as bad as they looked. I restrained her hands from raking
her upper arms while her teacher dabbed moistened towels on her limbs
and face, desperately trying to clean her up a bit before her mother arrived. I attempted to dust the dandruff of white flecks from her navy
jumper, but the flakes of skin stuck to the flannel like Velcro. There clearly

wasn't time to scrub the splotches of blood from the lacy rim of her anklets and the gathers of her white puffed sleeves. Most of the lacerations were shallow, but they were all over her body, and Miss Fabricant would no sooner daub a patch of eczema—flamed from sullen mauve to incandescent magenta—than it would bead again, and trickle.

Listen: I don't want to have this argument again. I fully accept that Kevin may never have touched her. As far as I could tell she had clawed herself open without any help. It itched and she'd given in, and I dare say that finally scraping her fingernails into that hideous red crust must have felt delicious. I even sensed a trace of vengefulness in the extent of the damage, or perhaps a misguided medical conviction that with sufficiently surgical application she might exfoliate the scaly bane of her existence once and for all.

Still, I've never forgotten my glimpse of her face when we found her, for it bespoke not only plain enjoyment but a release that was wilder, more primitive, almost pagan. She *knew* it would hurt later and she *knew* she was only making her skin condition worse and she *knew* her mother would be beside herself, and it was this very apprehension with which her expression was suffused, and which gave it, even in a girl of five, a hint of obscenity. She would sacrifice herself to this one glorious gorging, consequences be damned. Why, it was the very grotesquerie of the consequences—the bleeding, the stinging, the hair-tear back home, the unsightly black scabs in the weeks to come—that seemed to lie at the heart of her pleasure.

That night you were furious.

"*So* a little girl scratched herself. What has that to do with my son?"

"He was there! This poor girl, flaying herself alive, and he did *nothing*."

"He's not her minder, Eva, he's one of the kids!"

"He could have called someone, couldn't he? Before it went so far?"

"*Maybe*, but he's not even six until next month. You can't expect him to be that resourceful or even to recognize what's 'too far' when all she's doing is scratching. None of which remotely explains why you let Kevin squish around the house, all afternoon from the looks of him, plastered in shit!" A rare slip. You forgot to say *poop*.

"It's thanks to *Kevin* that Kevin's diapers stink because it's thanks to *Kevin* that he wears diapers at all." Bathed by his outraged father, Kevin was in his room, but I was aware of the fact that my voice carried. "Franklin, I'm at my wit's end! I bought all those there's-nothing-dirty-about-poo how-to books and now he thinks they're stupid because they're written for two-year-olds. We're supposed to wait until he's *interested*, but he's not, Franklin! Why should he be when Mother will always clean it up? How long are we going to let this go on, until he's in college?"

"Okay, I accept we're in a positive reinforcement loop. It gets him attention—"

"We're not in a loop but a *war*, Franklin. And our troops are decimated. We're short on ammunition. Our borders are overrun."

"Can we get something straight? Is this your new potty-training theory, let him slum around in his own crap and get it all over our white sofa? This is instructional? Or is it punishment? Because somehow this latest therapy of yours seems all mixed up with your lunatic indignation that some other kid got an itch."

"*He enticed her.*"

"Oh, for Pete's sake."

"She'd been very, very good about leaving that eczema alone. Suddenly we find her in the bathroom with her new little friend, and he's hovering over her and urging her on. . . . My God, Franklin, you should have seen her! She reminded me of that old scare story that circulated in the sixties about how some guy on acid clawed all the skin off his arms because he thought he was infested with bugs."

"Does it occur to you that if the scene was all that terrible then maybe Kevin's a little traumatized himself? That maybe he needs some comfort and reassurance and someone to talk to about it, and not to be banished to his own personal sewer? Jesus, they take kids into foster care for less."

"I should be so lucky," I muttered.

"Eva!"

"I was joking!"

"What is *wrong* with you?" you despaired.

"He wasn't 'traumatized,' he was smug. Riding home, his eyes were sparkling. I haven't seen him that pleased with himself since he eviscerated his birthday cake."

You plopped onto an end of our impractical white couch, head in hands; I couldn't join you, because the other end was still smeared brown. "I'm pretty much at the end of my rope, too, Eva." You massaged your temples. "But not because of Kevin."

"Is that a threat?—"

"It's not a threat—"

"What are you talking about!—"

"Eva, please calm down. I'm never going to break up our family." There was a time you'd have said instead, *I'll never leave you.* Your more rectitudinous declaration had a solidity about it, where pledges of everlasting devotion to a lover are notoriously frail. So I wondered why your bedrock commitment to *our family* made me sad.

"I dress him," I said. "I feed him when he lets me, I ferry him everywhere. I bake his kindergarten snacks. I'm at his beck from morning to night. I change his diapers six times a day, and all I hear about is the one afternoon that he so disturbed me, even frightened me, that I couldn't bear to come near him. I wasn't exactly trying to punish him. But in that bathroom, he seemed so, ah—" I discarded three or four adjectives as too inflammatory, then finally gave up. "Changing him was too intimate."

"Listen to yourself. Because I have no idea what kid you're talking about. We have a happy, healthy boy. And I'm beginning to think he's unusually bright." (I stopped myself from interjecting, *That's what I'm afraid of.*) "If he sometimes keeps to himself, that's because he's thoughtful, reflective. Otherwise, he plays with me, he hugs me good night, I read him stories. When it's just me and him, he tells me everything—"

"Meaning, he tells you what?"

You raised your palms. "What he's been drawing, what they had for snack—"

"And you think that's *telling you everything.*"

"Are you out of your mind? He's five years old, Eva, what else is there to tell?"

"For starters? What happened last year, in that after-preschool play group. One after another, every mother took her kids out. Oh, there was always some excuse—Jordan keeps catching colds, Tiffany is uncomfortable being the youngest. Until it's down to just me and Lorna's kids, and she mumbles something about it not being much of a group anymore and calls it quits. A few weeks later I stop by Lorna's unannounced to drop off a Christmas present? All the old play group is reassembled in her living room. She was embarrassed and we didn't address it, but since Kevin *tells you everything* why not get him to explain what might drive all those mothers to sneak off and reconvene in secret, all to exclude our 'happy, healthy' son."

"I wouldn't ask him because that's an ugly story that would hurt his feelings. And I don't see the mystery—gossip and cliquishness and small-town fallings out. Typical of stay-at-home mothers with time on their hands."

"I'm one of those *stay-at-home* mothers, at considerable sacrifice I'd re-mind you, and the last thing we have is time on our hands."

"So he was blackballed! Why doesn't that make you angry at them? Why assume it was something our son did, and not some neurotic hen with a bug up her ass?"

"Because I'm all too well aware that Kevin doesn't *tell me everything*. Oh, and you could also ask him why not one baby-sitter will come back a sec-ond night."

"I don't need to. Most teenagers around here get an allowance of $100 a week. *Only* 12 bucks an hour isn't very tempting."

"Then at least you could get your sweet, confiding little boy to tell you *just exactly what he said to Violetta.*"

It's not as if we fought all the time. To the contrary, though, it's the fights I remember; funny how the nature of a normal day is the first memory to fade. I'm not one of those sorts, either, who thrives on turmoil—more's the pity, as it turns out. Still, I may have been glad to scratch the dry sur-face of our day-to-day peaceableness the way Violetta had clawed the sere crust on her limbs, anything to get something bright and liquid flowing again, out in the open and slippery between our fingers. That said, I feared what lay beneath. I feared that at bottom I hated my life and hated being a mother and even in moments hated being your wife, since you had done this to me, turned my days into an unending stream of shit and piss and cookies that Kevin didn't even like.

Meanwhile, no amount of shouting was resolving the diaper crisis. In a rare inversion of our roles, you were apt to regard the problem as all very internally complicated, and I thought it was simple: We wanted him to use the toilet, so he wouldn't. Since we weren't about to stop wanting him to use the toilet, I was at a loss.

You doubtless found my usage of the word *war* preposterous. But in corralling Kevin to the changing table—now small for the purpose; his legs dangled over its raised flap—I was often reminded of those scrappy guerrilla conflicts in which underequipped, ragtag rebel forces manage to inflict surprisingly serious losses on powerful armies of state. Lacking the vast if unwieldy arsenal of the establishment, the rebels fall back on cunning. Their attacks, while often slight, are frequent, and sustained aggravation can be more demoralizing over time than a few high-casualty spectaculars. At such an ordnance disadvantage, guerrillas use whatever lies at hand, sometimes finding in the material of the everyday a devastating dual purpose. I gather that you can make bombs, for example, out of methanating manure. For his part, Kevin, too, ran a seat-of-the-pants operation, and Kevin, too, had learned to form a weapon from shit.

Oh, he submitted to being changed placidly enough. He seemed to bask in the ritual and may have inferred from my growing briskness a gratifying embarrassment, for swabbing his tight little testicles when he was nearly six was beginning to feel risqué.

If Kevin enjoyed our trysts, I did not. I have never been persuaded that even an infant's effluents smell precisely "sweet"; a kindergartner's feces benefit from no such reputation. Kevin's had grown firmer and stickier, and the nursery now exuded the sour fug of subway tunnels colonized by the homeless. I felt sheepish about the mounds of nonbiodegradable Pampers we contributed to the local landfill. Worst of all, some days Kevin seemed deliberately to hold his intestines in check for a second strike. If no Leonardo of the crayon world, he had a virtuoso's command of his sphincter.

Mind, I'm setting the table here, but hardly excusing what happened that July. I don't expect you to be anything but horrified. I'm not even asking your forgiveness; it's late for that. But I badly need your understanding.

Kevin graduated from kindergarten in June, and we were stuck with one another all summer. (Listen, I got on Kevin's nerves as much as he got on mine.) Despite Miss Fabricant's modest successes with Drano illustrations, the Montessori method was not working wonders in our home. Kevin had still not learned to play. Left to entertain himself, he would sit like a lump on the floor with a moody detachment that turned the atmosphere of the whole house oppressive. So I tried to involve him in projects, assembling yarn and buttons and glue and scraps of colorful fabric in the playroom for making sock puppets. I'd join him on the carpet and have a cracking good time myself, really, except in the end I would have made a nibbling rabbit with a red felt mouth and big floppy blue ears and drinking-straw whiskers, and Kevin's arm would sport a plain knee-high dipped in paste. I didn't expect our child to necessarily be a crafts wunderkind, but he could at least have made an effort.

I also tried to give him a jump on first grade by tutoring him on the basics. "Let's work on our numbers!" I'd propose.

"What for."

"So when you get to school you'll be better than anyone else at arithmetic."

"What good is arithmetic."

"Well, you remember yesterday, and Mommer paid the bills? You have to be able to add and subtract to pay bills, and know how much money you have left."

"You used a calculator."

"Well, you have to know arithmetic to be sure the calculator is right."

"Why would you use it at all if it doesn't always work."

"It always works," I begrudge.

"So you don't need arithmetic."

"To use a calculator," I say, flustered, "you still have to know what a five looks like, all right? Now, let's practice our counting. What comes after three?"

"Seven," says Kevin.

We would proceed in this fashion, until once after one more random exchange ("What comes before nine?" "Fifty-three.") he looked me lifelessly in the eye and droned in a fast-forward monotone, "Onetwothreefourfivesixseveneightnineteneleventwelve . . . ," pausing two or three times for a breath but otherwise making it flawlessly to a hundred. "Now can we quit?" I certainly felt the fool.

I roused no more enthusiasm for literacy. "Don't tell me," I'd cut him off after raising the prospect of reading time. "*What for. What good is it.* Well, I'll tell you. Sometimes you're going to be bored and there's nothing to do except you can always read a book. Even on the train or at a bus stop."

"What if the book is boring."

"Then you find a different one. There are more books in the world than you'll ever have time to read, so you'll never run out."

"What if they're all boring."

"I don't think that would be possible, Kevin," I'd say crisply.

"I think it's possible," he'd differ.

"Besides, when you grow up you'll need a job, and then you'll have to be able to read and write really well or no one will want to hire you." Privately, of course, I reflected that if this were true most of the country would be unemployed.

"Dad doesn't write. He drives around and takes pictures."

"There are other jobs—"

"What if I don't want a job."

"Then you'd have to go on *welfare*. The government would give you just a little money so you don't starve, but not enough to do anything fun."

"What if I don't want to do anything."

"I bet you will. If you make your own money, you can go to movies and restaurants and even different countries, like Mommer used to." At *used to*, I winced.

"I think I want to go on welfare." It was the kind of line I'd heard other parents repeat with a chortle at dinner parties, and I struggled to find it adorable.

I don't know how those home-schooling families pull it off. Kevin never seemed to be paying any attention, as if listening were an indignity. Yet somehow, behind my back, he picked up what he needed to know. He learned the way he ate—furtively, on the sly, shoveling information like a fisted cheese sandwich when no one was watching. He hated to admit he didn't know something already, and his blanket playing-dumb routine was cunningly crafted to cover any genuine gaps in his education. In Kevin's mind, pretend-ignorance wasn't shameful, and I was never able to discriminate between his feigned stupidity and the real thing. Hence if at the dinner table I decried Robin Williams's role in *Dead Poets Society* as *trite*, I felt obliged to explain to Kevin that the word meant "like what lots of people have done already." But he'd receive this definition with a precocious *uh-duh*. Had he learned the word *trite* at three, when he was faking not being able to talk at all? You tell me.

In any event, after belligerently botching his alphabet for weeks ("What comes after R?" *Elemenno*), he interrupted one of my diatribes—about how he couldn't just sit there and expect learning to pour into his ear all by itself—by singing the alphabet song impeccably start to finish, albeit with an aggressive tunelessness that even for the tin-eared was improbable and tinged with a minor key that made this bouncy children's pneumonic sound like kaddish. I suppose they'd taught it at Love-'n'-Learn, not that Kevin had let on. When he finished mockingly, *Now I've said my ABCs, tell me what you think of me*, I snapped furiously, "I think you're a wicked little boy who enjoys wasting his mother's time!" and he smiled, extravagantly, with both sides of his mouth.

He wasn't precisely disobedient, which is one detail that the Sunday magazine exposés often got wrong. Indeed, he could follow the letter of his assignments with chilling precision. After the obligatory period of aping incompetence—crippled, unclosed P's wilting below the line as if they'd been shot—he sat down on command and wrote perfectly within the lines of his exercise book, "Look, Sally, look. Go. Go. Go. Run. Run. Run. Run, Sally, Run." I have no way of explaining why it was rather awful, except that he exposed to me the insidious nihilism of the grade-school primer. Even the way he formed those letters made me uneasy. They had no character. I mean, he didn't really develop *handwriting* as we understand it, connotatively the personal stamp on standardized script. From the point he admitted he knew how, his printing unerringly replicated the examples in his textbook, with no extra tails or squiggles; his T's were crossed and I's dotted, and never before had the bloated interior of B's and O's and D's seemed to contain so much empty space.

My point is that, however technically biddable, he was exasperating to teach. You could savor his remarkable progress when you came home, but I was never treated to those *Eureka!* moments of sudden breakthrough that reward an adult's hours of patient coaxing and mind-numbing repetition. It is no more satisfying to teach a child who refuses to learn in plain view than it is to feed one by leaving a plate behind in the kitchen. He was clearly denying me satisfaction on purpose. He was determined that I should feel useless and unneeded. Though I may not have been as convinced as you were that our son was a genius, he was—well, I suppose he still is, if such things can be said of a boy who clings to an act of such crowning idiocy—very bright. But my day-to-day experience as his tutor was that of instructing an *exceptional child* only in the euphemistic tradition that seems to concoct an ever more dishonest name for *moron* every year. I would drill what-is-two-plus-three *over* and *over* and *over*, until once when he staunchly, maliciously refused to say *five* one more time I sat him down, scrawled,

12,387
6,945
138,964
3,987,234

scored a line under it and said, "There! Add that up then! And multiply it by 25 while you're at it, since you think you're so smart!"

I missed you during the day, as I missed my old life when I was too busy to miss you during the day. Here I had become quite well versed in Portuguese history down to the order of the monarchy and how many Jews were murdered during the Inquisition, and now I was reciting the alphabet. Not the Cyrillic alphabet, nor the Hebrew one, the *alphabet*. Even if Kevin had proved an ardent pupil, for me the regime would doubtless have felt like a demotion of the precipitous sort commonly constrained to dreams: Suddenly I'm sitting in the back of the class, taking a test with a broken pencil and no pants. Nonetheless, I might have abided this humbling role if it weren't for the additional humiliation of living, for over six years now, up to my elbows in shit.

Okay—out with it.

There came an afternoon in July that, per tradition, Kevin had soiled his diapers once and been cleaned up with the whole diaper cream and talcum routine, only to complete the evacuation of his bowels twenty minutes later.

Or so I assumed. But this time he outdid himself. This was the same afternoon that, after I had insisted he write a sentence that was meaningful about his life and not one more tauntingly inert line about Sally, he wrote in his exercise book, "In kendergarden evrybody says my mother looks rilly old." I'd turned beet-red, and that was when I sniffed another telltale waft. After I'd just changed him *twice*. He was sitting cross-legged on the floor, and I lifted him to a stand by the waist, pulling his Pampers open to make sure. I lost it. "How do you *do* it?" I shouted. "You hardly *eat* anything, where does it *come* from?"

A rush of heat rippled up through my body, and I barely noticed that Kevin was now dangling with his feet off the carpet. He seemed to weigh nothing, as if that tight, dense little body stocked with such inexhaustible quantities of shit was packed instead with Styrofoam peanuts. There's no other way to say this. I threw him halfway across the nursery. He landed with a dull clang against the edge of the stainless steel changing table. His head at a quizzical tilt, as if he were finally *interested* in something, he slid, in seeming slow motion, to the floor.

Eva

Dear Franklin,

So now you know.

I had rash hopes when I first rushed over to him that he was all right—he looked unmarked—until I rolled him over to reveal the arm he fell on. His forearm must have struck the edge of the changing table when for the first time, as you once remarked in jest, our son had learned to fly. It was bleeding and a little crooked and bulging in the middle with something white poking out and I felt sick. *I'm sorry, I'm sorry, I'm so sorry!* I whispered. Yet however weak with remorse, I was still intoxicated from a moment that may put the lie to my preening incomprehension of *Thursday.* On its far side, I was aghast. But the very center of the moment was bliss. Hurtling our little boy I-didn't-care-where-besides-away, I had heedlessly given over, like Violetta, to clawing a chronic, torturous itch.

Before you condemn me utterly, I beg you to understand just how hard I'd been trying to be a good mother. But trying to be a good mother may be as distant from being a good mother as trying to have a good time is from truly having one. Distrusting my every impulse from the instant he was laid on my breast, I'd followed a devout regime of hugging my little boy an average of three times a day, admiring something he did or said at least twice, and reciting *I love you, kiddo* or *You know that your Daddy and I love you very much* with the predictable uniformity of liturgical professions of faith. But too strictly observed, most sacraments grow hollow. Moreover, for six solid years I'd put my every utterance on the five-second delay of call-in radio shows, just to make sure I didn't broadcast anything obscene, slanderous, or contrary to company policy. The vigilance came at a cost. It made me remote, halting, and awkward.

When hoisting Kevin's body in that fluid adrenal lift, for once I'd felt graceful, because at last there was an unmediated confluence between what

I felt and what I did. It isn't very nice to admit, but domestic violence has its uses. So raw and unleashed, it tears away the veil of civilization that comes between us as much as it makes life possible. A poor substitute for the sort of passion we like to extol perhaps, but real love shares more in common with hatred and rage than it does with geniality or politeness. For two seconds I'd felt whole, and like Kevin Khatchadourian's real mother. I felt close to him. I felt like myself—my true, unexpurgated self—and I felt we were finally communicating.

As I swept a shock of hair from his moist forehead, the muscles of Kevin's face worked furiously; his eyes screwed up and his mouth grimaced into a near-smile. Even when I ran to fetch that morning's *New York Times* and slipped it under his arm he did not cry. Holding the paper under the arm—I still remember the headline by his elbow, "More Autonomy for Baltics Stirs Discomfort in Moscow"—I helped him to his feet, asking if anything else hurt and he shook his head. I started to pick him up, another shake; he would walk. Together we shuffled to the phone. It's possible that he wiped away the odd tear when I wasn't looking, but Kevin would no more suffer in plain view than he would learn to count.

Our local pediatrician Dr. Goldblatt met us at Nyack Hospital's tiny, crushingly intimate emergency room, where I felt certain that everyone could tell what I'd done. The notice for the "New York Sheriff's Victim Hotline" beside the registration window seemed posted specially for my son. I talked too much and said too little; I babbled to the admissions nurse about what had happened but not how. Meantime Kevin's unnatural self-control had mutated into the bearing of a martinet; he stood straight with his chin lifted, and turned at right angles. Having assumed responsibility for supporting his arm with the newspaper, he allowed Dr. Goldblatt to hold his shoulder as he marched down the hall but shook off my hand. When he entered the orthopedic surgeon's examining room, he about-faced in the doorway to announce briskly, "I can see the doctor by myself."

"Don't you want me to keep you company, in case it hurts?"

"You can wait out there," he commanded, the muscles rippling in his clenched jaw the only indication that it hurt already.

"That's quite a little man you've got there, Eva," said Dr. Goldblatt. "Sounds like you got your orders." To my horror, he closed the door.

I did, I really did want to be there for Kevin. I was desperate to reestablish that I was a parent he could trust, not a monster who would hurl him about the room at a moment's notice like a vengeful apparition from *Poltergeist*. But, yes, I was also in dread that Kevin would tell the surgeon or Benjamin Goldblatt what I'd done. They have laws about these things. I could be arrested; my case could be written up in the *Rockland County Times* in an appalled sidebar. I could, as I had so tastelessly joked that I would welcome, have Kevin taken away from me for real. At a minimum I might have to submit to mortifying monthly visits from some disapproving social worker sent to check my son for bruises. However much I deserved rebuke, I still preferred the slow burn of private self-excoriation to the hot lash of public reproof.

So as I stared glaze-eyed into the glassed-in case preserving gushy letters to the nursing staff from satisfied customers, I scrambled for soft-core rewrites. *Oh, doctor, you know how boys exaggerate. Throw him? He was running headlong down the hall, and when I walked out of the bedroom I bumped into him, by accident . . . Then he, ah, of course he fell, hard, against—against the lamp stand . . . !* I sickened myself, and every whitewash I concocted sounded preposterous. I had plenty of time to stew in my own juices on one of those hard, sea-green metal chairs in the waiting room, too; a nurse informed me that our son had to undergo surgery to have his "bone ends cleansed," a procedure I was more than happy to have remain opaque.

But when Kevin emerged three hours later with his blindingly white cast, Dr. Goldblatt patted our son on the back and admired what a brave young man I had raised, while the orthopedic surgeon impersonally detailed the nature of the break, the dangers of infection, the importance of keeping the cast dry, and the date Kevin should return for follow-up care. Both doctors were kind enough to omit mention of the fact that the staff had been obliged to change our son's dirty diapers; Kevin no longer smelled. My head bobbed dumbly up and down until I stole a quick glance at Kevin, who met my eyes with the clear, sparkling gaze of perfect complicity.

I owed him one. He knew I owed him one. And I would owe him one for a very long time.

Driving back home, I chattered (*What Mommer did was very, very wrong, and she is so, so sorry*—though this distancing device of the third person must have cast my regrets in a dubious light, as if I were already blaming the incident on my imaginary friend). Kevin said nothing. His expression aloof, almost haughty, the fingers of his plastered right arm tucked Napoleonically in his shirt, he sat upright in the front seat and surveyed the flashes of the Tappan Zee Bridge through the side window, for all the world like a triumphant general, wounded nobly in battle, now basking in the cheers of the crowd.

I enjoyed no such equipoise. I might have escaped the police and social services, but I was condemned to run one more gauntlet. Whether up against the wall I might have contrived some cock-and-bull about *bumping into* Kevin for Dr. Goldblatt, I could not imagine locking eyes and flinging patent nonsense at you.

"Hi! Where were you guys?" you shouted when we walked into the kitchen. Your back was turned as you finished slathering peanut butter on a Ritz cracker.

My heart was thumping, and I still had no idea what I was going to say. So far, I had never wittingly done anything that would imperil our marriage—or our *family*—but I was sure that if anything would push us to the brink, this was it.

"—Jesus, Kev!" you exclaimed with a mouth covered in crumbs, swallowing hard without having chewed. "What the heck happened to *you*?"

You brushed your hands hastily and plunged to your knees before Kevin. My skin prickled all over, as if someone had just switched on the voltage and I were an electric fence. I had that distinctive presentiment of I-have-one-more-second-or-two-after-which-nothing-will-ever-be-the-same-again, the same limp apprehension of spotting an oncoming car in your lane when it's too late to turn the wheel.

But headlong collision was averted at the last minute. Already accustomed to trusting your son's version of events over your wife's, you had gone straight to Kevin. This once you were mistaken. Had you asked me, I promise—or at least I like to think—that, with bowed head, I'd have told you the truth.

"I broke my arm."

"I can see that. How'd that happen?"

"I fell."

"Where'd you fall?"

"I had poopy pants. Mommer went to get more wipes. I fell off the changing table. On—onto my Tonka dump truck. Mommer took me to Doctor Goldbutt."

He was good. He was very, very good; you may not appreciate how good. He was smooth—the story was ready. None of the details were inconsistent or gratuitous; he had spurned the extravagant fantasies with which most children his age would camouflage a spilled drink or broken mirror. He had learned what all skilled liars register if they're ever to make a career of it: Always appropriate as much of the truth as possible. A well-constructed lie is assembled largely from the alphabet blocks of fact, which will as easily make a pyramid as a platform. He did have poopy pants. He remembered, correctly, that the second time I changed him that afternoon I had finished the open box of Wet Wipes. He had, more or less, fallen off the changing table. His Tonka dump truck was indeed—I checked later that night—on the nursery floor at the time. Furthermore, I marveled at his having intuited that simply falling three feet onto the floor would probably not be enough to break his arm; he would need to land haplessly on some hard metal object. And however short, his tale was laced with elegant touches: Using *Mommer* when he had eschewed the cutesy sobriquet for months lent his story a cuddly, affectionate cast that fantastically belied the real story; *Doctor Goldbutt* was playfully scatological, setting you at ease—your *happy, healthy boy* was already back to normal. Perhaps most impressive of all, he did not, as he had at the emergency room, allow himself the one collusive glance in my direction that might have given the game away.

"Gosh," you exclaimed. "That must have hurt!"

"The orthopedist says that for an open fracture," I said, "—it broke the skin—it was pretty clean, and should mend well." Now Kevin and I did look at each other, just long enough to seal the pact. I had ransomed my soul to a six-year-old.

"Are you going to let me sign your cast?" you asked. "That's a tradition, you know. Your friends and family all sign their names and wish you to get well soon."

"Sure, Dad! But first I got to go to the bathroom." He sauntered off, his free hand swinging.

"Did I hear that right?" you asked quietly.

"Guess so." Rigid for hours—fear is an isometric exercise—I was exhausted, and for once the last thing on my mind was our son's toilet training.

You put an arm around my shoulders. "Man, that must have given you a scare."

"It was all my fault," I said, squirming.

"No mother can watch a kid every second."

I wished you wouldn't be so understanding. "Yes, but I should have—"

"Sh-sh!" You raised a forefinger, and a delicate trickling emitted from the hall bathroom: music to the parental ear. "What do you think did the trick, just the shock?" you whispered. "Or maybe he's scared of landing back on that changing table."

I shrugged. Despite appearances, I did not believe that by flying into a rage at yet another soiled diaper I had terrorized our boy into using the toilet. Oh, it had everything to do with our set-to in the nursery, all right. *I was being rewarded.*

"This calls for celebration. I'm going to go in and congratulate that guy—"

I put a hand on your arm. "Don't push your luck. Let him do it quietly, don't make a big deal out of it. Kevin prefers his reversals off-camera."

That said, I knew better than to read pee-pee in the potty as admission of defeat. He had won the larger battle; acceding to the toilet was the kind of trifling concession that a magnanimous if condescending victor can afford to toss a vanquished adversary. Our six-year-old had successfully tempted me into violating my own rules of engagement. I had committed a war crime—for which, barring my son's clement silence, my very husband would extradite me to The Hague.

When Kevin returned from the bathroom tugging up his pants with one hand, I proposed that we have big bowl of popcorn for dinner, adding obsequiously, *with lots and lots of salt!* Drinking in the music of the normal life that I had minutes before kissed good-bye—your clamorous banging of pots, the clarion clang of our stainless steel bowl, the merry rattle of kernels—I'd a foreboding that this crawling-on-my-belly-like-a-reptile mode could endure almost indefinitely so long as Kevin kept his mouth shut.

Why didn't he blab? By all appearances, he was protecting his mother. All right. I'll allow for that. Nevertheless, a balance-sheet calculation may have entered in. Before a distant expiry date, a secret accrues interest by dint of having been kept; compounded by lying, *Know how I really broke my arm, Dad?* might have even more explosive impact in a month's time. Too, so long as he retained the principle of his windfall in his account, he could continue to take out loans against it, whereas blowing his wad all at once would plunge his assets back to a six-year-old's allowance of $5 a week.

Further, after all my sanctimonious singsong lectures *(How would you feel . . . ?)*, I had provided him with a rare opportunity to annex the moral high ground—whose elevation would afford a few novel views, even if this was not, at length, a territory destined to suit his preferences in real estate. Mr. Divide-and-Conquer may also have intuited that secrets bind and separate in strict accordance with who's in on them. My chatter to you about Kevin's needing to opt for baths over showers to keep the cast dry was artificially bright and stilted; when I asked Kevin whether he wanted parmesan on the popcorn, the question was rich with appeal, terror, and slavish gratitude.

For in one respect I was touched, and remain so: I think he had experienced a closeness to me that he was reluctant to let go. Not only were we in this cover-up together, but during the very assault we were concealing, Kevin too may have felt whole, yanked to life by the awesome sisal strength of the umbilical tie. For once I'd known myself for his mother. So he may have known himself also, sailing amazedly across the nursery like Peter Pan, for my son.

The remainder of that summer defied all my narrative instincts. Had I been scripting a TV movie about a violent harridan who flew into fits of blind dudgeon during which she was endowed with superhuman strength, I'd have had her young boy tiptoeing around the house, shooting her tremulous grins, offering up desperate gestures of appeasement, and just in general shuffling, cowering, and yes-massa-ing about the place, anything to keep from taking impromptu trips across whole rooms of their home without his feet ever touching the floor.

So much for the movies. *I* tiptoed. *My* grins quivered. *I* shuffled and cowered as if auditioning for a minstrel show.

Because let's talk about power. In the domestic polity, myth dictates that parents are endowed with a disproportionate amount of it. I'm not so sure. Children? They can break our hearts, for a start. They can shame us, they can bankrupt us, and I can personally attest that they can make us wish we were never born. What can we do? Keep them from going to the movies. But how? With what do we back up our prohibitions if the kid heads belligerently for the door? The crude truth is that parents are like governments: We maintain our authority through the threat, overt or implicit, of physical force. A kid does what we say—not to put too fine a point on it—because we can break his arm.

Yet Kevin's white cast became a blazing emblem, not of what I could do to him, but of what I could not. In resorting to the ultimate power, I had robbed myself of it. Since I could not be trusted to use force in moderation, I was stuck with an impotent arsenal, useless overkill, like a stockpile of nuclear weapons. He knew full well that I would never lay a hand on him again.

So in case you worry that in 1989 I became a convert to Neanderthal brutality, all that wholeness and realness and immediacy that I discovered in using Kevin for a shot put evaporated in a New York minute. I remember feeling physically shorter. My posture deteriorated. My voice went wispy. To Kevin, I couched my every request as an optional suggestion: *Honey, would you like to get in the car? You wouldn't mind terribly if we went to the store? Maybe it would be a good idea if you didn't pick the crust from the middle of Mommer's freshly baked pie.* As for the lessons he found such an insult, I returned to the Montessori method.

At first, he put me through a variety of paces, as if training a performing bear. He would demand something time-consuming for his lunch, like homemade pizza, and after I'd spent the morning kneading dough and simmering sauce he'd pick two pieces of pepperoni off his slices and then fold the remains into a glutinous baseball to pitch to the sink. Then he tired of Mother-as-plaything as quickly as he did of his other toys, which I guess made me lucky.

In fact, as I foisted on the boy the very salt-laden cheesies and whizzies previously meted out in one-ounce rations, my solicitation soon got on his nerves. I had a tendency to hover, and Kevin would shoot me the kind of daggers you fire at a stranger who sits next to you on a train when the car is practically empty. I was proving an unworthy adversary, and any further victories over a guardian already reduced to such a cringing, submissive condition were bound to feel cheap.

Although it was tricky with a sling, he now took baths on his own, and if I stooped to wrap him in a fresh towel, he shied, then swaddled himself. In fact, on the heels of having docilely submitted to diaper changing and testicle swabbing, he developed a stern modesty, and by August, I was banished from the bathroom. He dressed in private. Aside from that remarkable two weeks during which he got so sick when he was ten, he would not allow me to see him naked again until the age of fourteen—at which point I'd gladly have forfeited the privilege.

As for my incontinent outpouring of tenderness, it was tainted with apology, and Kevin was having none of it. When I kissed his forehead, he wiped it off. When I combed his hair, he batted me away and rumpled his locks. When I hugged him, he objected coldly that I was hurting his arm. And when I averred, "I love you, kiddo"—no longer recited with the solemnity of the Apostle's Creed but rather with the feverish, mindless supplication of a Hail Mary—he'd assume a caustic expression from which that permanent left-hand cock of his mouth was enduringly to emerge. One day when I avowed yet again *I love you, kiddo*, Kevin shot back, *Nyeh NYEE nyeh, nyeh-nyeeeeh!* and I gave it a rest.

He clearly believed that he had found me out. He had glimpsed behind the curtain, and no amount of cooing and snack food would erase a vision at least as indelible as a first encounter with parental sex. Yet what surprised me was how much this revelation of his mother's true colors— her viciousness, her violence—seemed to please him. If he had my number, it was one that intrigued him far more than the twos and threes of our dreary arithmetic drills before his "accident," and he side-eyed his mother with a brand new—I wouldn't call it quite respect—*interest.* Yes.

As for you and me, until that summer I'd become accustomed to concealing things from you, but mostly thought crimes—my atrocious blankness at Kevin's birth, my aversion to our house. While to some extent we all shelter one another from the cacophony of horrors in our heads, even these intangible unsaids made me mournful. But it was one thing to keep my own counsel about the dread that had descended on me whenever it was time to fetch our son from kindergarten, quite another to neglect to tell you that, oh, by the way, I broke his arm. However wicked, thoughts didn't seem to take up space in my body, while keeping a three-dimensional secret was like having swallowed a cannonball.

You seemed so far away. I'd gaze at you as you undressed at night with a spectral nostalgia, half expecting that when I crossed to brush my teeth you'd step through my body as easily as through moonlight. Watching you in the backyard teaching Kevin to cup a baseball in a catcher's mitt with his good right hand—though in truth he seemed more gifted with pizza—I'd press my palm against a sun-warmed windowpane as if against a spiritual barrier, stabbed by the same vertiginous well-wishing and aching sense of exclusion that would have tortured me had I been dead. Even when I put my hand on your chest, I couldn't seem to quite touch you, as if every time you shed your clothes there were, like Bartholomew's hats, another L. L. Bean work shirt underneath.

Meantime, you and I never went out just the two of us anymore—to catch *Crimes and Misdemeanors*, grab a bite at the River Club in Nyack, much less to indulge ourselves at the Union Square Café in the city. It's true that we had trouble with sitters, but you acquiesced to our housebound nights readily enough, prizing the light summer evenings for coaching Kevin on fourth downs, three-pointer field goals, and the infield-fly rule. Your blindness to the fact that Kevin displayed neither interest nor aptitude in any of these sports nagged me a bit, but I was mostly disappointed that you didn't ever covet the same *quality time* with your wife.

There's no purpose to talking around it. I was jealous. And I was lonely.

It was toward the end of August when our next-door neighbor leaned on our doorbell with censorious insistence. I heard you answer it from the kitchen.

"You tell your kid it's not funny!" Roger Corley exclaimed.

"Whoa, slow down, Rog!" said you. "Criticize anybody's sense of humor, gotta tell the joke first." Despite your jocular cadence, you did not invite him in, and when I peered out to the foyer I noticed that you had only opened the door halfway.

"Trent just rode his bike down that big hill on Palisades Parade, lost control, and landed in the bushes! He's knocked up pretty bad!"

I'd tried to stay on amicable terms with the Corleys, whose son was a year or two older than Kevin. Though Moira Corley's initial enthusiasm for arranging play dates had waned without explanation, she'd once displayed a gracious interest in my Armenian background, and I'd stopped by only the day before to give her a loaf of freshly baked *katah*—do you ever miss it?—that slightly sweet, obscenely buttery layered bread my mother taught me to make. Being on congenial terms with your neighbors was one of the few appeals of suburban life, and I feared that your narrowing our front door was beginning to appear unfriendly.

"Roger," I said behind you, wiping my hands on a dish towel, "why don't you come in and talk about it? You seem upset."

When we all repaired to the living room, I noted that Roger's getup was a little unfortunate; he had too big a gut for Lycra cycling shorts, and in those bike shoes he walked pigeon-toed. You retreated behind an armchair, keeping it between you and Roger like a military fortification. "I'm awful sorry to hear about Trent's accident," you said. "Maybe it's a good opportunity to go through the fundamentals of bike safety."

"He *knows* the fundamentals," said Roger. "Like, you never leave the quick-release on one of your wheels flipped *open*."

"Is that what you think happened?" I asked.

"Trent said the front wheel started wobbling. We checked the bike, and the release wasn't only flipped over; it'd been turned a few times to loosen the fork. Doesn't take Sherlock Holmes to conclude that *Kevin* was the culprit!"

"Now wait just one minute!" you said. "That's one hell of a—"

"Trent rode that bike yesterday morning, no problem. Nobody's been by since but you, Eva, along with your son. And I want to thank you for that bread you sent over," he added, lowering the volume. "It was real good, and we appreciated your thoughtfulness. But we don't appreciate Kevin's tinkering with Trent's bike. Going a little faster, or around traffic, my kid could've been killed."

"You're making a lot of assumptions here," you growled. "That release could have been tripped in Trent's accident."

"No way. I'm a cyclist myself, and I've had my share of spills. The release never flips all the way over—much less turns around by itself to loosen the spring."

"Even if Kevin did do it," I said (you shot me a black look), "maybe he doesn't know what the lever is for. That leaving it open is dangerous."

"That's one theory," Roger grunted. "That your son's a dummy. But that's not the way Trent describes him."

"Look," you said. "Maybe Trent had been playing with that release, and he doesn't want to take the rap. That doesn't mean my son has to take it instead. Now, if you'll excuse us, we've got some work to do around the yard."

After Roger left, I had a sinking feeling that the Irish soda bread Moira had promised to bake me in return would never materialize.

"Boy, I sometimes think you're right," you said, pacing. "A kid can't skin his knee anymore without it having to be somebody else's fault. Country's completely lost touch with the concept of *accident*. When Kevin broke his arm, did I give you a hard time? Did it have to be somebody's *fault*? No. Shit happens."

"Do you want to talk to Kevin about Trent's bike?" I said. "Or should I?"

"What for? I can't see he's done anything."

I said under my breath. "You never do."

"And you always do," you said levelly.

A standard exchange—not even exceptionally acrimonious—so I'm not sure why it flipped something in me, like Trent Corley's quick-release. Maybe because it *was* standard now, and once it hadn't been. I closed my eyes, cupping the back of the armchair that had walled off Roger Corley's outlandish accusations. Honestly, I'd no idea what I was going to say until I said it.

"Franklin, I want to have another child."

I opened my eyes and blinked. I had surprised myself. It may have been my first experience of spontaneity in six or seven years.

You wheeled. Your response was spontaneous, too. "You *cannot* be serious."

The time didn't seem right for reminding you that you deplored John McEnroe as a poor sport. "I'd like us to start trying to get me pregnant right away."

It was the oddest thing. I felt perfectly certain, and not in the fierce, clutching spirit that might have betrayed a crazy whim or frantic grab at a pat marital nostrum. I felt self-possessed and simple. This was the very unreserved resolve for which I had prayed during our protracted debate over parenthood, and whose absence had led us down tortuously abstract avenues like "turning the page" and "answering the Big Question." I'd never been so sure of anything in my life, so much so that I was disconcerted why you seemed to think there was anything to talk about.

"Eva, forget it. You're forty-four. You'd have a three-headed toad or something."

"Lots of women these days have children in their forties."

"Get out of here! I thought that now Kevin's going to be in school full-time you were planning to go back to AWAP! What about all those big plans to move into Eastern Europe post-glasnost? Get in early, beat *The Lonely Planet?*"

"I've considered going back to AWAP. I may still go back. But I can work for the rest of my life. As you just observed with so much sensitivity, there's only one thing I can do for a short while longer."

"I can't believe this. You're serious! You're seriously—serious!"

"*I'd like to get pregnant* makes a crummy gag, Franklin. Wouldn't you like Kevin to have someone to play with?" Truthfully, I wanted someone to play with, too.

"They're called *classmates.* And two siblings always hate each other."

"Only if they're close together. She'd be younger than Kevin by at least seven years."

"She, is it?" The pronoun made you bristle.

I shrugged my eyebrows. "Hypothetically."

"This is all because you want a *girl?* To dress in little outfits? Eva, this isn't like you."

"No, wanting to dress a girl in *little outfits* isn't like me. So there was no call for you to say that. Look, I can see your having reservations, but I don't understand why the prospect of my getting pregnant again seems to be making you so angry."

"Isn't it obvious?"

"Anything but. I thought you've enjoyed being a parent."

"*I* have, yes! Eva, what gives you the idea that even if you do have this fantasy daughter everything's going to be different?"

"I don't understand," I maintained, having learned the merits of playing dumb from my son. "Why in the world would I want everything to be different?"

"What could possess you, after it's gone the way it's gone, to want to do it again?"

"It's gone what way?" I asked neutrally.

You took a quick look out the window to make sure Kevin was still patting the tether ball to spiral first one way around the pole, then the other; he liked the monotony.

"You never want him to come with us, do you? You always want to find somebody to dump him with so we can waltz off by ourselves, like what you obviously consider the good old days."

"I don't remember saying any such thing," I said stonily.

"You don't have to. I can tell you're disappointed every time I suggest we do something so that Kevin can come, too."

"That must explain why you and I have spent countless long, boozy evenings in expensive restaurants, while our son languishes with strangers."

"See? You resent it. And what about this summer? You wanted to go to Peru. Okay, I was game. But I assumed we'd take a vacation as a family. So I start supposing how far a six-year-old can hike in a day, and you should have seen your face, Eva. It fell like a lead balloon. Soon as Peru would involve Kevin, too, you lose interest. Well, I'm sorry. But I for one didn't have a kid in order to get away from him as often as possible."

I was leery of where this was headed. I'd known that eventually we would need to discuss all that had been left unsaid, but I wasn't ready. I needed ballast. I needed supporting evidence, which would take me a minimum of nine months to gather.

"I'm with him all day," I said. "It makes sense that I'd be more anxious than you for a break—"

"And I never cease to hear about what a terrible sacrifice you've been making."

"I'm sorry that it means so little to you."

"It's not important it mean something to me. It should mean something to him."

"Franklin, I don't understand where—"

"And that's typical isn't it? You stay home *for him* to *impress me*. He just never enters in, does he?"

"*Where* is all this coming from? I only wanted to tell you that I'd like us to have another baby, and for you to be happy about it, or at least start getting used to the idea."

"You pick on him," you said. With another cautionary glance at the tether-ball court up the hill, you had an air of just getting started. "You blame him for everything that goes wrong around this house. *And* at his kindergarten. You've complained about the poor kid at every stage of the game. First he cries too much, then he's too quiet. He develops his own little language, and it's annoying. He doesn't play right—meaning the way *you* did. He doesn't treat the toys you make him like museum pieces. He doesn't pat *you* on the back every time he learns to spell a new word, and since the whole neighborhood isn't clamoring to sign his dance card, you're determined to paint him as a pariah. He develops one, yes, serious psychological problem having to do with his toilet training—it's not that unusual, Eva, but it can be very painful for the kid—and you insist on interpreting it as some mean-spirited, personal contest between you and him. I'm relieved he seems to be over it, but with your attitude I'm not surprised it lasted a long time. I do what I can to make up for your—and I'm very sorry if this hurts your feelings, but I don't know what else to call it—your coldness. But there's no substitute for a mother's love, and I am damned if I am going to let you freeze out another kid of mine."

I was stunned. "Franklin—"

"This discussion is *over*. I didn't enjoy saying all that, and I still hope things can get better. I know you think you make an effort—well, maybe you do make what for you is an effort—but so far it's not enough. Let's all keep trying. —Hey, sport!" You swooped Kevin up as he sauntered in from the deck, raising him over your head as if posing for a Father's Day ad. "At the end of your tether?"

When you set him down, he said, "I wrapped the ball around 843 times."

"That's terrific! I bet next time you'll be able to do it 844 times!"

You were trying to make an awkward transition after an argument that left me feeling run over by a truck, but I can't say I care for the Hollywood gaga that's expected of modern parents. Kevin's own expression flickered with a suggestion of oh-brother.

"If I try really hard," he said, deadpan. "Isn't it great to have a goal?"

"Kevin." I called him over and stooped. "I'm afraid your friend Trent has had an accident. It's not too bad, and he'll be all right. But maybe you and I could make him a get-well card—like the one Grandma Sonya made you when you hurt your arm."

"Yeah, well," he said, moving away. "He thinks he's so cool with that bike."

The AC must have been turned too high; I stood up and rubbed my arms. I didn't remember mentioning anything about a bicycle.

Eva

Dear Franklin,

For some reason I imagine it will reassure you that I still get the *Times*. But I seem to have misplaced the grid I once imposed on it to determine what parts were worth reading. Famines and Hollywood divorces appear equally vital and equally trifling. Arbitrarily, I either devour the paper soup to nuts, or I toss it smooth and cool on the stack by the door. How right I was, in those days; how easily the United States can get on without me.

For the last two weeks I've tossed them unread, for if memory serves, the earnest pomp of presidential inaugurations left me cold even when I had clear enthusiasms and aversions. Capriciously, this morning I read everything, including an article about American workers' excessive over-time—and perhaps it *is* interesting, though I couldn't say, that the Land of the Free prefers work to play. I read about a young electrical lineman who would soon have been married, and who in his eagerness to salt away funds for his family-to-be had slept only five hours in two and a half days. He had been climbing up and down poles for twenty-four hours straight:

> Taking a break for breakfast on Sunday morning, he got yet another call.
>
> At about noon, he climbed a 30-foot pole, hooked on his safety straps and reached for a 7,200-volt cable without first putting on his insulating gloves. There was a flash, and Mr. Churchill was hanging mo-tionless by his straps. His father, arriving before the ladder-truck did and thinking his son might still be alive, stood at the foot of the pole for more than an hour begging for somebody to bring his boy down.

I have no strong feelings about overtime; I'm acquainted with no electrical linemen. I only know that this image—of a father pleading with onlookers themselves as powerless as he, while his hardworking son creaked in the breeze like a hanged man—made me cry. Fathers and sons? Grief and misspent diligence? There are connections. But I also wept for that young man's real father.

You see, it was drilled into me since I could talk that 1.5 million of my people were slaughtered by Turks; my own father was killed in a war against the worst of ourselves, and in the very month I was born, we were driven to use the worst of ourselves to defeat it. Since *Thursday* was the slimy garnish on this feast of snakes, I wouldn't be surprised to find myself hard of heart. Instead, I'm easily moved, even mawkish. Maybe my expectations of my fellows have been reduced to so base a level that the smallest kindness overwhelms me for being, like *Thursday* itself, so unnecessary. Holocausts do not amaze me. Rapes and child slavery do not amaze me. And Franklin, I know you feel otherwise, but Kevin does not amaze me. I am amazed when I drop a glove in the street and a teenager runs two blocks to return it. I am amazed when a checkout girl flashes me a wide smile with my change, though my own face had been a mask of expedience. Lost wallets posted to their owners, strangers who furnish meticulous directions, neighbors who water each other's houseplants—these things amaze me. Celia amazed me.

As you instructed, I never raised the matter again. And I took no relish in deceiving you. But the eerie certainty that descended in August never lifted, and you'd left me no choice.

Kevin's cast had been removed two weeks earlier, but it was as of Trent Corley's bike accident that I stopped feeling guilty. Just like that. There was no equivalence between what I had done and what I would do—it was totally irrational—but still I seemed to have arrived at the perfect antidote or penance. I would put myself to the test. I was not at all sure that I would pass a second sitting.

You did notice I'd become "a horny little beastie," and you seemed glad of a desire that, though we never alluded to the abatement outright, had sadly ebbed. With one or the other of us yawning theatrically before bed "a little beat," we had slid from having sex almost nightly to the American average of once a week. My rekindled passion was no contrivance. I did want you, more urgently than in years, and the more we made love the more insatiable I felt during the day, unable to sit still, rubbing my inside thigh with a pencil at my desk. I, too, was glad of evidence that we had not yet sunk irretrievably into the mechanical bedtime rut that drives so many spouses to the arms of strangers at lunch.

For ever since we'd had a little boy sleeping down the hall, you'd so turned down the volume in bed that I had often to interrupt, "What? . . . Sorry?" Talking dirty by semaphore was too much effort, and at length we'd both withdrawn to private sexual Imax. Unembellished by your im-provisations—and you had a gift for depravity; what a shame to let such talent lie fallow—my own fantasies had come to bore me, and I'd given over to floating pictures instead, rarely erotic in any literal sense, and al-ways dominated by a certain texture and hue. But over time the visions had grown corrosive, like close-ups of a scab or geological illustrations of dried magma. Other nights I'd been afflicted by flashes of filthy diapers and taut, undescended testicles, so you can understand why I might have contributed to reducing our schedule to once a week. Perhaps worst of all, the vibrant scarlets and ceruleans that once permeated my head when we made love in our childless days had gradually muddied and lost their lus-ter, until the miasma on the inside of my eyelids churned with the furious pitch and umber of the drawings on our refrigerator door.

Once I started leaving my diaphragm in its sky-blue case, the vista in my mind during sex went light. Where my visual perimeters had once closed in, now I saw great distances, as if gazing from Mt. Ararat or skim-ming the Pacific in a glider. I peered down long hallways that shimmered endlessly to the vanishing point, their marble parquet blazing, sunlight pouring in windows from either side. Everything I envisioned was bright: wedding dresses, cloudscapes, fields of edelweiss. Please don't laugh at me—I know what I'm describing sounds like a tampon commercial. But it was beautiful. I felt, at last, transported. My mind opened up, where be-fore my head had seemed to be spelunking into an ever narrower, more dimly lit hole. These wide-screen projections weren't mushy soft-focus, either, but sharp and vivid and I remembered them when we were through. I slept like a baby. Rather, like *some* babies, as I was soon to discover.

I was obviously not at my most fertile, and it did take a year. But when I finally missed a period the following fall, I started to sing. Not show tunes this time, but the Armenian folk songs with which my mother had serenaded Giles and me when she tucked us in for the night—like "Soode

Soode" ("It's a lie, it's a lie, it's a lie, everything's a lie; in this world, every-thing's a lie!"). When I discovered that I'd forgotten some of the words, I called her and asked if she might write them out. She was delighted to oblige, since as far as Mother knew, I was still the willful little girl who decried her Armenian lessons as burdensome extra homework, and she in-scribed my favorites—Komitas Vardapet's "Kele Kele," "Kujn Ara," and "Gna Gna"—inside greeting cards pen-and-inked with mountain village scenes and patterns from Armenian carpets.

Kevin noticed my transformation, and while he mightn't have savored his mother groveling about the house like a worm, he was no better pleased when she burst her cocoon as a butterfly. He hung back sullenly and carped, "You sing out of tune" or commanded, reciting a line he had picked up from his multiethnic primary school, "Why don't you speak *English.*" I told him lightly that Armenian folk songs were *polyphonic*, and when he pretended to understand, I asked if he knew what that meant. "It means stupid," he said. I volunteered to teach him a song or two, reminding him, "You're Armenian, too, you know," but he differed. "I'm *American*," he asserted, using the derisive tone of stating the obvious, like "I'm a person" and not an aardvark.

Something was up. Mommer wasn't slumping and shuffling and talk-ing in a peewee voice anymore, yet even pre-broken-arm Mommer had not made a reappearance: the brisk, rather formal woman who marched through the paces of motherhood like a soldier on parade. No, this Mom-mer purled about her duties like a bubbling brook, and any number of stones hurled at her eddies sank with a harmless rattle to her bed. Apprised that her son thought all his second-grade classmates were "retards" and everything they studied he "knew already," this Mommer didn't remon-strate that he would *soon find out he didn't know everything;* she didn't abjure him not to say *retard.* She just laughed.

Although an alarmist by nature, I didn't even get bent out of shape about the escalating threats issuing from the State Department over Iraq's invasion of Kuwait. "You're usually so dramatic about these things," you remarked in November. "Aren't you *worried?*" No, I wasn't worried. About anything.

It was after I'd missed my third cycle that Kevin started accusing me of getting fat. He'd poke at my stomach and jeer, "You're *giant!*" Com-monly vain about my figure, I concurred cheerfully, "That's right, Mom-mer's a big pig."

"You know, you may have gained just a bit around the waist," you remarked finally one night in December. "Maybe we should take it easy on the spuds, huh? Could stand to drop a couple pounds myself."

"Mmm," I hummed, and I practically had to put my fist in my mouth to keep from laughing. "I don't mind a little extra weight. All the better for throwing it around."

"Jesus, what's this, *maturity*? Usually if I suggest you've gained an ounce you go ape-shit!" You brushed your teeth, then joined me in bed. You picked up your mystery but only drummed the cover, sidling your other hand to a swollen breast. "Maybe you're right," you murmured. "A little more Eva is pretty sexy." Slipping the book to the floor, you turned toward me and lifted an eyebrow. "Is it in?"

"Mmm," I hummed again, with an affirmative cast.

"Your nipples are big," you observed, nuzzling. "Time for your period? Seems like it's been a while."

Your head stilled between my breasts. You pulled back. You looked me in the eye with the soberest of expressions. And then you turned white.

My heart sank. I could tell that it would be worse than I'd led myself to believe.

"When were you planning to tell me?" you asked stonily.

"Soon. Weeks ago, really. It just never seemed the right time."

"I can see why it wouldn't," you said. "You expecting to palm this off as some kind of accident?"

"No. It wasn't an accident."

"I thought we discussed this."

"That's what we didn't do, discuss it. You went on a tirade. You wouldn't listen."

"So you just go ahead and—a fait accompli—just—like some kind of mugging. As if it has nothing to do with me."

"It has everything to do with you. But I was right and you were wrong." I faced you squarely. As you would say, there were two of us and one of you.

"This is the most presumptuous . . . arrogant thing you've ever done."

"Yes. I guess it is."

"Now that it *no longer matters* what I think, you going to explain what this is about? I'm listening." You didn't look as if you were listening.

"I have to find something out."

"What's that? How far you can push me before I push back?"

"About—," I decided not to apologize for the word, "about my soul."

"Is there anyone else in your universe?"

I bowed my head. "I'd like there to be."

"What about Kevin?"

"What about him."

"It's going to be hard for him."

"I read somewhere that other children have brothers and sisters."

"Don't be snide, Eva. He's used to undivided attention."

"Another way of saying he's spoiled. Or could get that way. This is the best thing that could possibly happen to that boy."

"Little bird tells me that's not the way he's going to look at it."

I took a moment to reflect that in five minutes we were already dwelling on our son. "Maybe it will be good for you, too. For us."

"It's an agony aunt standard. Stupidest thing you can ever do to cement a shaky marriage is to have a baby."

"Is our marriage shaky?"

"You just shook it," you fired back, and turned away from me on your side.

I switched off the light and slid down on the pillow. We weren't touching. I started to cry. Feeling your arms around me was such a relief that I cried harder still.

"Hey," you said. "Did you really think—? Did you wait so long to tell me so it would be too late? Did you really think I'd ask you to do that? With our own kid?"

"Of course not," I snuffled.

But when I'd calmed down you grew sterner. "Look, I'll come around to this if only because I have to. But you're forty-five, Eva. Promise me you'll get that test."

There was a purpose to "that test" only if we were prepared to act on a discouraging outcome. With *our own kid*. Little wonder that I put off telling you for as long as possible.

I didn't get the test. Oh, I told you I did, and the new gynecologist I found—who was lovely—offered, but unlike Dr. Rhinestein, she did not seem to regard all pregnant women as public property and didn't unduly press the point. She did say that she hoped I was prepared to love and care for whoever—she meant, whatever—came out. I said that I didn't think I was romantic about the rewards of raising a disabled child. But I was probably too strict about what—and whom—I chose to love. So I wanted to trust. For once, I said. To have blind faith in—I chose not to say *life* or *fate* or *God*—myself.

There was never any doubt that our second child was mine. Accordingly, you exhibited none of the proprietary bossiness that tyrannized my pregnancy with Kevin. I carried my own groceries. I drew no scowls over a glass of red wine, which I continued to pour myself in small, sensible amounts. I actually stepped up my exercise regime, including running and calisthenics and even a little squash. Our understanding was no less clear for being tacit: What I did with this lump was my business. I liked it that way.

Kevin had already sensed the presence of perfidy. He hung back from me more than ever, glaring from corners, sipping at a glass of juice as if tasting for arsenic, and poking so warily at anything I left him to eat, often dissecting it into its constituent parts spread equidistant around his plate; he might have been searching for shards of glass. He was secretive about his homework, which he protected like a prisoner encrypting his correspondence with details of savage abuse at the hands of his captors that he would smuggle to Amnesty International.

Someone had to tell him, and soon; I was starting to show. So I suggested that we take this opportunity to explain generally about sex. You were reluctant. Just say you're pregnant, you suggested. He doesn't have to know how it got there. He's only seven. Shouldn't we preserve his innocence a little longer? It's a pretty backward definition of innocence, I objected, that equates sexual ignorance with freedom from sin. And underestimating your kid's sexual intelligence is the oldest mistake in the book.

Indeed. I had barely introduced the subject while making dinner when Kevin interrupted impatiently, "Is this about fucking?"

It was true: They didn't make second-graders the way they used to. "Better to call it *sex*, Kevin. That other word is going to offend some people."

"It's what everybody else calls it."

"Do you know what it means?"

Rolling his eyes, Kevin recited, "The boy puts his peepee in the girl's doodoo."

I went through the stilted nonsense about "seeds" and "eggs" that had persuaded me as a child that making love was something between planting potatoes and raising chickens. Kevin was no more than tolerant.

"I knew all that."

"What a surprise," I muttered. "Do you have any questions?"

"No."

"Not any? Because you can always ask me or Dad anything about boys and girls, or sex, or your own body that you don't understand."

"I thought you were going to tell me something *new*," he said darkly, and left the room.

I felt strangely ashamed. I'd raised his expectations, then dashed them. When you asked how the talk had gone I said okay, I guess; and you asked if he'd seemed frightened or uncomfortable or confused, and I said actually he seemed *unimpressed*. You laughed, while I said dolefully, what's ever going to impress him if that doesn't?

Yet phase two of the Facts of Life was bound to be the more difficult installment.

"Kevin," I began the following evening. "Remember what we talked about last night? Sex? Well, Mommer and Daddy do that sometimes, too."

"What for."

"For one thing, so you could keep us company. But it might be nice for you to have some company, too. Haven't you ever wished you had someone right around the house to play with?"

"No."

I stooped to the play table where Kevin was systematically snapping each crayon of his Crayola 64 set into pieces. "Well, you *are* going to have some company. A little baby brother or sister. And you might find out that you like it."

He glared at me ,a long, sulky beat, though he didn't look especially surprised. "What if I don't like it."

"Then you'll get used to it."

"Just cause you get used to something doesn't mean you like it." He added, snapping the magenta, "You're used to me."

"Yes!" I said. "And in a few months we'll all get used to someone new!"

As a crayon piece gets shorter it's more difficult to break, and Kevin's fingers were now straining against one such obdurate stump. "You're going to be sorry."

Finally, it broke.

I tried to draw you into a discussion about names, but you were indifferent; by then the Gulf War had started, and it was impossible to distract you from CNN. When Kevin slumped alongside you in the den, I noted that the boy stuff of generals and fighter pilots didn't captivate him any more than the ABC song, though he did show a precocious appreciation for the nature of a "nuclar bomb." Impatient with the slow pace of made-for-TV combat, he grumbled, "I don't see why Cune Power bothers with all that little junk, Dad. Nuke 'em. That'd teach the Raqis who's boss." You thought it was adorable.

In the spirit of fair play, I reminded you of our old pact, offering to christen our second child a Plaskett. Don't be ridiculous, you dismissed, not taking your eyes off an incoming Patriot missile. Two kids, different last names? People would think one was adopted. As for Christian names, you were equally apathetic. Whatever you want, Eva, you said with a flap of your hand, is fine with me.

So for a boy I proposed *Frank*. For a girl, I deliberately rejected *Karru* or *Sophia* from my mother's vanquished clan and reached for the vanquished in yours.

The death of your Aunt Celia, your mother's childless younger sister, had hit you hard when you were twelve. A frequent visitor, zany Aunt Celia had a playful taste for the occult; she gave you a magic eight ball that told fortunes and led you and your sister in darkened séances, the more delicious for your parents' disapproval. I'd seen her picture, and she'd been heartbreakingly not-quite-pretty, with a wide mouth and thin lips but piercing, clairvoyant eyes, at once brave and a little frightened. Like me, she was adventurous, and she died young and unmarried after climbing Mt. Washington with a dashing young climber for whom she had high hopes, succumbing to hypothermia after their party was hit by a freak snowstorm. But you shrugged off the tribute with irritation, as if

I were seeking to ensnare you by your Aunt Celia's own supernatural means.

My second confinement felt vastly less restrictive than the first, and with Kevin in second grade, I could involve myself more fully in AWAP. Yet *with child* I also felt less lonely, and when I spoke aloud with you scouting and Kevin in school, I did not feel that I was talking to myself.

Of course, the second time around is always easier. I knew enough to opt for anesthesia, though when the time came, Celia would prove so tiny that I probably could have managed without. I also knew better than to expect a blinding Vulcan mind-meld at her birth. A baby is a baby, each miraculous in its way, but to demand transformation on the instant of delivery was to place too great a burden on a small confused bundle and an exhausted middle-aged mother both. All the same, when she begged to arrive two weeks early on June 14, I couldn't resist inferring an eagerness on her part, as I had once inferred a corresponding reluctance from Kevin's foot-dragging fortnight's delay.

Do babies have feelings, even at zero hour? From my modest study of two, I believe they do. They don't have names for feelings yet, and without separating labels probably experience emotion in a goulash that easily accommodates opposites; I am likely to pin myself to feeling *anxious*, while an infant might have no trouble feeling simultaneously apprehensive and relaxed. Still, on the birth of both my children, I could immediately discern a dominant emotional tone, like the top note of a chord or the foreground color of a canvas. In Kevin, the note was the shrill high pitch of a rape whistle, the color was a pulsing, aortal red, and the feeling was fury. The shriek and pump of all that rage was unsustainable, so as he grew older the note would descend to the uninflected blare of a leaned-on car horn; the paint in his foreground would gradually thicken, its hue coagulating to the sluggish black-purple of liver, and his prevailing emotion would subside from fitful wrath to steady, unabating resentment.

Yet when Celia slid to hand, she may have been visually beet-faced and bloody, but her aural color was light blue. I was overcome by the same clear-skied azure that had visited me when we made love. She didn't cry when she was born, and if she emitted a figurative sound it was the quiet, meandering tune of a rambler far from home who is enjoying the walk and doesn't think anyone is listening. As for the ascendant emotion that exuded from this blind creature—her hands not grasping at the air but wandering, wondering at it, her mouth, once led to the nipple, suckling right away—it was *gratitude*.

I'm not sure if you could tell the difference instantly, though once Celia was fed, tied off, swabbed, and handed over to her father, you did return her rather quickly. Maybe you were still irked at my presumption, and maybe your new daughter's perfection dismayed you further, as living evidence that my deception had been righteous. In any case, the years ahead would later confirm my initial intuition: that you could tell the difference, and that the difference made you angry. I imagine you bristling with a similar resistance if, after living for years in our fatally middlebrow Dream Home, you walked into the Victorian one with the porch swing, dumbwaiter, and mahogany balustrade and learned it was for sale. You'd wish you'd never seen it, and something in you would hate it a bit. On tramping back into our hackneyed cathedral of teak, the scales would fall from your eyes, and you'd see only a slag heap of pretensions, your brave capacity for *rounding up* crippled for life.

That's my only explanation for your coolness, since you seemed so leery of picking her up and anxious to avoid looking at her with those long soulful gazes during which Brian claimed that a parent *falls in love*. I think she frightened you. I think you regarded your attraction to your daughter as a betrayal.

The birth went so smoothly that I only spent the one night, and you brought Kevin with you to retrieve us from Nyack Hospital. I was nervous, having every appreciation for how infuriating it must be for a firstborn child to contemplate the invasion of his patch by a speechless weakling. But when Kevin trailed into the hospital room behind you, he hardly leaped onto the bed to smother my suckling daughter with a pillow. Wearing an "I'm the Big Brother" T-shirt with a smiley face in the O—its fresh squared creases and price tag in the neck betokening your purchase of a last-minute prop from the lobby's gift shop—he slouched around the foot, sauntered to the other side, dragged a zinnia from your bedside bouquet, and set about denuding the flower of petals. Perhaps the safest outcome was that Celia should simply bore him.

"Kevin," I said. "Would you like to meet your sister?"

"Why should I *meet* it," he said wearily. "It's coming home with us, isn't it. That means I'll *meet* it every day."

"So you should at least know her name, shouldn't you?" I gently pulled the baby away from the breast in which Kevin himself had once shown such resolute disinterest, though she'd just started feeding. In that event, most infants would squall, but from the start Celia took deprivation as her due, receiving whatever trifle she was offered with wide-eyed abashment. I tugged up the sheet and held out the baby for inspection.

"This is Celia, Kevin. I know she's not a lot of fun yet, but when she gets a little bigger I bet she'll be your best friend." I wondered if he knew what one was. He'd yet to bring a classmate home from school.

"You mean she'll tag along after me and stuff. I've seen it. It's a pain."

You clapped your hands on Kevin's shoulders from behind and rocked him in a pally motion. Kevin's face twitched. "Yeah, well that's all part of being a big brother!" you said. "I should know, because I had a little sister, too. They never leave you alone! You want to play with trucks, and they're always pestering you to play with doll babies!"

"I played with trucks," I objected, shooting you a look; we would have to talk about this retrograde sex-role crap when we got home. It was a shame that, born back-to-back, you and your sister Valerie—a prissy girl grown officious woman, consumed by the cut of her drapes, and on our brief visits to Philadelphia determined to organize "outings" to historical homes—were never very close. "There's no telling what Celia will like to do, any more than you can tell if Kevin may like to play with dolls."

"In a pig's eye!" you cried fraternally.

"Teenage Mutant Ninja Turtles? Spiderman? Action figures are *dolls.*"

"Great, Eva," you muttered. "Give the little guy a complex."

Meantime, Kevin had sidled closer to the bed and dipped his hand into the glass of water on the bedside table. Eyeing the baby askance, he held his wet hand over her face and let drops of water drip, drip onto her face. Celia twisted, disconcerted, but the baptism didn't seem to be upsetting her, though I would later learn to regard the fact that my daughter hadn't complained or cried out as meaningless. His face stirring with a rare if clinical curiosity, Kevin wet his hand again and spattered his sister's nose and mouth. I wasn't sure what to do. Kevin's christening reminded me of fairy tales in which an aggrieved relative arrives to curse the princess in her crib. Yet he wasn't really hurting her, and I didn't want to taint this introduction with a reprimand. So when he dipped his hand a third time,

I resettled myself on the pillow and, dabbing her face with the sheet, discreetly withdrew the baby out of his reach.

"Hey, Kev!" You rubbed your hands. "Your mother has to get dressed, so let's go find something *really greasy* and *really salty* in those machines down the hall!"

When we left the hospital together, you said I must be shot after being up and down all night with a newborn and volunteered to baby-sit while I got some sleep.

"No, it's the oddest thing," I whispered. "I did get up a couple of times for feeding, but I had to set an alarm. Franklin—she doesn't cry."

"Huh. Well, don't expect that to last."

"You never know—they're all different."

"Babies ought to cry," you said vigorously. "Kid just lolls in bed and sleeps all day, you're raising a doormat."

When we came home, I noticed that the framed photo of me in my late twenties that we kept on the little table in the foyer was missing, and I asked you if you'd moved it. You said no, shrugging, and I declined to pursue the matter, assuming it would turn up. It didn't. I was a little perturbed; I no longer looked nearly that pretty, and these verifications that we were once lineless and lovely do grow precious. The shot had been snapped on an Amsterdam houseboat with whose captain I had a brief, uncomplicated affair. I treasured the expression he'd captured—expansive, relaxed, warm; it fixed a simple glorying in all that I then required of life: light on water, bright white wine, a handsome man. The portrait had softened the severity that marked most of my pictures, with that shelved brow of mine, my deep-set eyes in shadow. The houseboat captain had mailed me the photo, and I didn't have the negative. Oh, well. Presumably, while I was in the hospital Kevin had snatched the print to poke pins in.

Anyway, I was in no mood to get exercised over one silly snapshot. In fact, though I fear that my martial metaphor may seem provocative, when I carried Celia over our threshold I had the exhilarating impression of having reset our troop strengths at a healthy par. Little could I know that, as a military ally, a trusting young girl is worse than nothing, an open left flank.

Eva

Dear Franklin,

You know, I was just thinking that I might have been able to handle every-thing—*Thursday*, the trials, even our separation—if only I'd been allowed to keep Celia. Nevertheless (and this may surprise you), I like picturing her with you, imagining the two of you together. I'm glad if, at last, you may be getting to know one another better. You were a good father to her—I don't mean to criticize—but you were always so sensitive about slighting Kevin that you may have overdone it, the reassurance that you were still on his side. You kept her a little at arm's length. And as she got older, she got so pretty, didn't she? In a tentative, bashful way, with that fine gold hair flut-tering forever in her face. I think you resented it, on Kevin's behalf—how other people found her so enchanting, whereas with Kevin they tended to be wary and so overly hearty or false and sometimes visibly relieved when we showed up at their house and hadn't brought him along. It wasn't fair, you thought. I suppose, in that big universal way, it wasn't.

Maybe my love for Celia was too easy. Maybe in my own terms she was a kind of cheating, since my whole life I had striven to surmount difficulty, to overcome terrors. Celia was plainly lovable. I can't recall anyone who didn't find her sweet, though I wonder if she stuck in the mind. Neighbors rarely liked Kevin, even if they were too polite to say so outright, but they remem-bered him. Both our families copped attitudes. Your sister Valerie was always edgy about leaving Kevin unattended anywhere in her fastidiously decorated house and, just to check up on him, kept bringing our son sandwiches he didn't want; whenever he picked up a candy dish or fiddled with the tassel of a tieback, she'd jump up and take it away. Well before Kevin's deficiencies be-came national news, whenever Giles asked after our son my brother seemed to be fishing for mean little stories to confirm a private prejudice. Kevin was hard to like, much less to love, but in this way he should have been perfectly fashioned for the likes of his mother. Kevin was hard to love in the same manner that it was hard to eat well in Moscow, find a cheap place to stay in London, or locate a commercial Laundromat in Bangkok. But I had moved back to the United States, grown soft. As I would sometimes cave to expedience and order takeout curries with a side of naan instead of simmering chicken in turmeric for hours on my stove, I chose the easy comfort of a compliant, ready-made child rather than break down the stringy fibers of a tough kid with long low heat. I had been rising to challenges for most of my life. I was tired, and, latterly, flabby; in a spiritual sense, I was out of shape.

But it is only natural for the current of emotion to follow the path of least resistance. To my amazement, when I put Celia down she slept; I guess we were indeed raising "a doormat." Whereas Kevin had screeched with every conceivable need met, Celia would submit to all manner of material deprivations with barely a mewl or stir, and she could pickle for hours in a wet diaper unless I remembered to check. She never wept out of hunger yet always took the breast, so I was obliged to feed her according to a fixed schedule. I may have been the first mother in history to despair that her baby didn't cry enough.

Kevin's disconsolate infancy had segued to wholesale boredom; Celia was entranced by the least bauble. Every bit as delighted with a scrap of colored tissue paper as with that expensive mother-of-pearl mobile over her crib, she displayed an indiscriminate fascination with the tactile universe that would have driven your Madison Avenue masters to distraction. Ironically for a girl so easy to please, it would grow difficult to buy her presents because she was so infatuated with the toys she had. As she got older she formed such passionate loyalties to tattered stuffed animals that the gift of plush, fresh-furred creatures seemed to throw her into turmoil—as if, like her second-time father, she feared that to enlarge her little family was to imperil previous, more primitive commitments. The newer animals were only allowed in her bedtime embrace once they had proved themselves by losing an ear or had joined the fallible, mortal world with a baptismal stain of strained broccoli. Once she could speak, she confided to me that she was careful to play with each member of the menagerie every day, lest one feel neglected or jealous. Her favorite, most fiercely defended toys were the ones that (thanks to Kevin) were broken.

It's possible that she was too much of a girl-girl for you, and her feminine diffidence and delicacy were foreign to me as well. You might have preferred a boisterous, fearless tomboy who made you proud by conquering the summits of jungle gyms, arm-wrestling boys, and declaring to visitors that she planned to be an astronaut—a rough-and-tumble hellion who sauntered about the house in cowboy chaps covered in motor oil. I might have enjoyed that kind of girl, too, but that was not the daughter we got.

Instead, Celia loved to don lacy frocks and dab on the lipstick I rarely wore. But her girlishness wasn't limited to captivation with jewelry on my dresser, to wobbles in my high-heeled shoes. It expressed itself in a larger weakness, dependency, and trust. She had so many lovely qualities, but she didn't have guts. She was full of terrors, and not only of the dark, but of the vacuum cleaner, the basement, and the drain. Eager to please, she began to use the potty well before the age of two but into kindergarten was still mortified by venturing into the bathroom by herself. She watched me open and throw out a moldy Columbo container once and for weeks thereafter would not come near the refrigerator, nor touch any substance, like vanilla pudding or even white poster paint, that resembled yogurt. Like many children, she was supersensitive to texture; though tolerant of mud, she reviled what she called "drydirt," pronounced as one word: fine silty soil, dust on linoleum, even plain flour. The first time I taught her to roll a pie crust, she stood stricken in the middle of the kitchen with her floured hands held out from her side, fingers spread, eyes popped wide. Celia always expressed horror in silence.

As for food, it took me a while to discern what turned out to be fierce aversions. Loath to seem choosy, she would force herself to choke down whatever she was offered, unless I attended to her indrawn shoulders and stifled little gags. She was revulsed by anything with "lumps" (tapioca, pumpernickel with raisins), "slime" (okra, tomatoes, sauces thickened with cornstarch), or "skin" (a rubbery bottom on Jell-O, the cooled brown surface on hot cocoa, even an unpeeled peach). While I was relieved to have a child with tastes at all—I might have fashioned Kevin's meals from colored wax—quaking before these comestibles, she grew so pale and moist that the food might have been poised to eat her. For Celia, her whole surround was animate, and each tapioca lump had a dense, nauseating little soul.

I know it was frustrating, always having to remember to leave the hall light on or getting up in the middle of the night to accompany her to the toilet. More than once you accused me of coddling her, since to indulge a fear was to feed it. But what was I to do on discovering a four-year-old trembling in the hall at 3 A.M., chilled in her nightie and clutching between her legs, but beg her to always, always wake one of us up if she needed to pee? Besides, Celia was frightened of so many different things that it's possible she was, in her own terms, courageous. Of what a variety of dreadful textures or murky corners might she have been terrified and quietly faced down by herself?

But I drew the line when you despaired that Celia was "clingy." It's an ugly word, isn't it, that describes the honey of the heart as a sticky, pestersome substance that won't brush off. And to whatever degree clinginess is not simply a mean appellation for the most precious thing on earth, it involves an unacceptably incessant demand for attention, approbation, ardor in return. But Celia beseeched us for nothing. She didn't nag us to come see what she'd built in the playroom or paw and tug at us while we tried to read. Whenever I hugged her unbidden, she returned my embrace with a thankful ferocity that implied unworthiness. After I went back to working at AWAP, she never complained at my absence, though her face would turn ashen with grief when I dropped her at preschool and would light like Christmas when I came home.

Celia was not *clingy*. She was simply affectionate. She did sometimes wrap her arms around my leg in the kitchen, press her cheek to my knee, and exclaim with amazement, "You're my friend!" Yet whatever difficulty you may have had with her arrival, you were never so hard a man as to find such demonstrations anything but touching. Indeed, confirmation that we were her *friends* seemed to entrance her far more than broad, rather abstract protestations of parental love. Although I know you thought Kevin the far smarter of the two, Kevin entered this world utterly stymied by what it was for and what to do with it, where Celia arrived with unshakable certainty about what she wanted and what made life worth living: that goo that wouldn't brush off. Surely that constitutes intelligence of a kind.

All right, she didn't do well in school. But that's because she tried too hard. She became so caught up in wanting to get things right, so seized by the prospect of failing her parents and teachers, that she couldn't get down to the task itself. At least she didn't hold everything they tried to teach her in contempt.

I tried to drill into her: You just memorize that the capital of Florida is Tallahassee, period. As great a believer in mystery as her namesake, Celia couldn't imagine it was that simple, that there wasn't a magic trick, and she doubted herself, so that taking the state capitals test she would immediately question "Tallahassee" for the very reason that it popped into her head. Kevin never had any trouble with mystery. He ascribed to the whole world the same terrifying plainness, and the question was never whether he was able to learn something, but whether to bother. Celia's faith, as emphatic in relation to others as it was deficient in relation to herself, assured her that no one would ever insist that she study the manifestly useless. Kevin's cynicism equally assured him that a malign, sadistic pedagogy would pitch him nothing but chaff.

I don't mean that Celia couldn't exasperate me as well. Like Kevin, she was impossible to punish, though there was rarely reason to punish her aside for something that, as it turned out, she didn't actually do. Still, she took the least admonition to heart, so that any remonstrance was like killing a fly with a sledgehammer. At the least suggestion that she had disappointed us, she was inconsolable, pouring out apologies before she was quite sure what we'd like her to regret. A single sharp word would send her into a tailspin, and I admit it would have been a relief once in a while to be able to bark out, "Celia, I told you to set the table!" (she was rarely disobedient, but she was absent-minded) and not have my daughter melt into a time-consuming puddle of remorse.

But my primary exasperation was otherwise. Judiciously applied, fear is a useful tool of self-protection. While the drain would hardly leap out and bite her, Celia was sufficiently replete with dread to have plenty left over for dangers that could. There was one thing in our house of which she might have been justifiably afraid, and she adored him.

On this point I'm brooking no argument, and I intend to take ruthless advantage of the fact that this is my account, to whose perspective you have no choice but to submit. I don't pretend to know the whole story, because I don't think that's a story that you or I will ever fully know. I remember uneasily from my own childhood that on Enderby Avenue, where the alliance between my brother and me was far more fickle, Giles and I conducted the main of our lives below our mother's line of sight. One of us might run to her to argue our side (frowned upon as cheating), but for the most part our collusions, battles, and mutually inflicted tortures took place, if not out of view, in code. So total was my own immersion in the world of other short people that my memories before about the age of twelve are largely depopulated of adults. Maybe it was different for you and Valerie, since you didn't like each other much. But many, perhaps most siblings share a private universe tropical with benevolence, betrayal, vendetta, reconciliation, and the use and abuse of power of which their parents know practically nothing.

Still, I wasn't blind, and a measure of parental innocence is stark disinterest. If I walked into a playroom to find my daughter curled on her side, ankles tied with knee socks, hands bound behind her back with her hair ribbon, mouth duct-taped shut, and my son nowhere in evidence, I could work out for myself what her whimpered explanation of "playing kidnapping" amounted to. I might not have been privy to the Masonic passwords of my children's secretive sect, but I did know my daughter well enough to be confident that, despite her claims to the contrary, she would never hold the head of her favorite plastic horsey over the flame of the stove. And if she was alarmingly compliant about forcing down foodstuffs I hadn't realized she couldn't abide, she was not an outright masochist. Thus when I discovered her strapped into her booster chair at the dining table covered in vomit, I could reasonably assume that the bowl before her of mayonnaise, strawberry jam, Thai curry paste, Vaseline petroleum jelly, and *lumps* of balled up bread had not followed a recipe of her personal concoction.

You would assert, of course—since you did at the time—that older siblings traditionally torment younger ones, and Kevin's petty persecution remained within the range of the *perfectly normal*. You might now object that I can only find incidents of typical childhood cruelty in any way forbidding with benefit of hindsight. Meanwhile, millions of children survive families rife with roughhouse bullying, often profitably the wiser about the Darwinian pecking orders they will negotiate as adults. Many of these onetime tyrants develop into sensitive husbands who remember anniversaries, while their onetime victims grow into confident young women with high-flying careers and aggressive views on a woman's right to choose. Yet my present position offers few enough perquisites, and I *do* have the benefit of hindsight, Franklin, if *benefit* is the word.

As I shuttled to Chatham last weekend, I considered that I might also benefit from our shy, fragile daughter's example of Christian forgiveness. But Celia's baffling incapacity to hold a grudge from age zip seems to suggest that the ability to forgive is a gift of temperament, not necessarily a trick for old dogs. Besides, on my own account, I am not sure what "forgiving" Kevin entails. Surely it doesn't involve sweeping *Thursday* artificially under the carpet or ceasing to hold him accountable, which couldn't be in his larger moral interests. I can't imagine that I'm supposed to *get over it*, like hopping a low stone wall; if *Thursday* was a barrier of some kind, it was made of razor wire, which I did not bound over but thrash through, leaving me in flayed pieces and on the other side of something only in a temporal sense. I can't pretend he didn't do it, I can't pretend I don't wish he hadn't, and if I have abandoned that felicitous parallel universe to which my white confederates in Claverack's waiting room are prone to cling, the relinquishment of my private if-only derives more from a depleted imagination than any healthy reconcilement that what's done is done. Honestly, when Carol Reeves formally "forgave" our son on CNN for murdering her boy, Jeffrey, who was already precocious enough at the classical guitar to be courted by Juilliard, I had no idea what she talking about. Had she built a box around Kevin in her head, knowing that only rage dwelled there; was our son now simply a place her mind refused to go? At best, I reasoned that she had successfully depersonalized him into a regrettable natural phenomenon that had descended on her family like a hurricane or opened a maw in their living room like an earthquake, concluding that there was nothing to be gained from railing at the likes of weather or tectonic plate shifts. Then, there is nothing to be gained by railing in virtually every circumstance, and that doesn't stop most of us.

Celia, though. I can't imagine that Celia successfully boxed up or demoted to cloudburst the day that Kevin, with the delicacy of a budding entomologist, removed a nest of bagworms from our white oak in the backyard and left them to hatch in her backpack. Subsequently, she reached for her spelling book in her first-grade class, withdrawing it covered in striped caterpillars—the kind that Kevin squished to green goo on our deck—several of which crawled onto her hand and up her rigored arm. Unfortunately, Celia wasn't given to screaming, which might have brought rescue more quickly. Instead I gather she seized up—breath whiffing, nostrils flaring, pupils dilating to saucers—and her teacher kept explaining the "hard C" in *candy* on the blackboard. Finally, the girls in adjacent desks began to shriek, and pandemonium ensued.

Yet however fresh the memory of those bagworms, the recollection simply didn't feature two weeks later when Kevin offered her a "ride" on his back as he climbed the white oak, and she clasped his neck. No doubt she was surprised when Kevin urged her off to perch tremulously on an upper branch, after which he climbed calmly to the ground. In fact, when she puled, "Kewin? Kewin, I can gedown!" she must have sincerely believed that, even after abandoning her twenty feet high and waltzing inside for a sandwich, he would return to help her out of the tree. Is that forgiveness? Like Charlie-Brown taking one more running lunge at Lucy's football, no matter how many stuffed animals he eviscerated and Tinkertoy cathedrals he felled, Celia never lost faith that deep down inside her big brother was a nice guy.

You can call it innocence or you can call it gullibility, but Celia made the most common mistake of the good-hearted: She assumed that everyone else was just like her. Evidence to the contrary found nowhere to lodge, like a book on chaos theory in a library that didn't have a physics section. Meanwhile, she never told tales, and without a testimonial it was often impossible to pin her misfortunes on her brother. As a consequence, from the moment his sister was born, Kevin Khatchadourian, figuratively at least, got away with murder.

I confess that during Celia's early years, Kevin receded for me, taking two giant steps backward like Simon Says. Small children are absorbing, and he had meanwhile assumed a militant independence. And you were so good about taking him to ball games and museums in your spare time that I may have handed him off a bit. That put me in your debt, which is why I feel especially awkward about observing what, from those two giant steps away, became only more striking.

Franklin, our son was developing the personality equivalent of the black-and-white cookie. It started back in kindergarten if not before, but it kept getting worse. Exasperatingly, we're all pretty much restricted to learning what people are like with the permanent confound of our own presence, which is why those chance glimpses of someone you love just walking down the street can seem so precious. So you'll just have to take my word for it—I know you won't—that when you weren't home, Kevin was sour, secretive, and sarcastic. Not just once in a while, on a bad day. Every day was a bad day. This laconic, supercilious, unforthcoming persona of his did seem real. Maybe it wasn't the only thing that was real, but it didn't come across as completely confected.

In contrast to—Franklin, I feel so lousy about this, as if I'm trying to take something away from you that you cherish—Kevin's behavior around you. When you walked in, his face changed. His eyebrows shot up, his head cocked, and he put on a closed-mouth smile high up on his chin, his lips meeting at his upper gum. Altogether, his features assumed the permanent expression of startled happiness that you see on aging starlets who have had too much plastic surgery. *Hi Dad!* he'd cry. *How was work today, Dad? Did you take any pictures of some real cool stuff? Any more cows, Dad? Any more fields or big buildings or really loaded-people's houses?* You'd light into an enthusiastic description of the sections of roadway you'd shot, and he'd enthuse, *Gosh, that's great! Another car ad! I'm gonna tell everybody at school that my dad takes pictures for Oldsmobile!* One night you brought home a copy of the new *Atlantic Monthly*, flipping proudly to the Colgate advertisement that sponsored our very own pink-marbled master bath. *Gee, Dad!* Kevin exclaimed. *Since our bathroom is in a toothpaste ad, does that make us famous?* "Just a little famous," you allowed, and I swear I remember wising off, "To be really famous in this country, you've got to kill somebody."

Oh, you were by no means uniquely credulous; Kevin pulled the wool over his teachers' eyes for years. I still have, thanks to you, stacks of his schoolwork. An amateur student of American history, you were the family chronicler, the photographer, the scrapbook paster, while I was more apt to regard experience itself as my souvenir. So I'm not quite sure what possessed me to rescue, from among the Stairmasters and egg slicers I abandoned en masse when I moved, the file folders of Kevin's essays.

Did I save the files just for your tight, slanted cursive, "First Grade"? For once, I think not. I have been through two trials, if what preceded them is not to be considered a third, and I have learned to think in terms of evidence. Why, I've become so accustomed to abdicating ownership of my life to other people—to journalists, judges, web-site writers; to the parents of dead children and to Kevin himself—that even now I'm reluctant to fold or deface my son's essays lest it constitute actionable tampering.

Anyway, it's a Sunday afternoon, and I have been forcing myself to read a few. (Do you realize that I could sell these? I don't mean for spare change, either. Apparently this is just the kind of ephemera that gets auctioned on eBay for thousands, along with the passably competent landscapes of Adolph Hitler.) Their innocent physical manifestation is disarming: the fat, characterless printing, the fragile yellowed paper. How prosaic, I thought at first; I'll learn nothing but that, like a good boy, he did his homework. But as I read on, I grew more compelled, drawn in with the nervous fascination that leads one to poke and squeeze at an emerging cyst or a burrowing ingrown hair.

I've concluded that Kevin was prone to snow his schoolmasters less with that scrubbed-behind-the-ears Partridge-family buoyancy with which he greeted your return from work than with an eerie lack of affect. Kevin's papers always follow the assignment excessively to the letter; he adds nothing, and whenever they are marked down, it is usually for being too short. There is nothing wrong with them. They are factually correct. Their spelling is accurate. On those rare occasions his teachers jot vague notes about how he might "take a more personal approach to the material," they are unable to pinpoint anything in his essays that is precisely lacking:

> Abraham Lincoln was president. Abraham Lincoln had a beard. Abraham Lincoln freed the African-American slaves. In school we study great African-American Americans for a whole month. There are many great African-American Americans. Last year we studied the same African-American Americans during African-American History Month. Next year we will study the same African-American Americans during African-American History Month. Abraham Lincoln was shot.

If you don't mind my weighing in on Kevin's side for once, you and his teachers thought all through primary school that he needed help on his organizational skills, but I've decided that his organizational skills were razor sharp. From first grade on, those assignments demonstrate an intuitive appreciation for the arbitrary, for the numbing powers of repetition, and for the absurdist possibilities of the non sequitur. More, his robotic declaratives do not indicate a failure to master the niceties of prose style; they *are* his prose style, refined with all the fastidiousness that attended H. L. Mencken's. Uneasy intimations to us at parent-teacher conferences that Kevin "didn't seem to put his heart into his schoolwork" to the contrary, Kevin *did* put his heart into his work, his heart and soul. Check out this fourth-grade rendition of the assignment, "Meet My Mother":

> My mother goes somewhere else. My mother sleeps in a different bed. My mother eats different food. My mother comes home. My mother sleeps at home. My mother eats at home.
>
> My mother tells other people to go somewhere else. Other people sleep in a different bed. Other people eat different food. Other people come home. Other people sleep at home. Other people eat at home. My mother is rich.

I know what you're thinking, or I know what you thought then. That it was Kevin's surly, remote pose with me that was fake, while with you he could relax and be his sprightly, chipper self. That the pervasive stiltedness of his written work revealed a commonplace gap between his thoughts and his powers of expression. I'm willing to grant that his closed condescension toward me was an artifice, even if its *biding-time* quality, tracing back to my appropriation of his squirt gun, felt true. But neither the Beaver Cleaver nor the windup schoolboy straight man was any less bogus. Kevin was a shell game in which all three cups were empty.

I just glanced over what I've written so far and realized that I was being awfully summary about a solid seven years of our lives together; moreover, that the abundance of that summary concerned Celia. I'm ashamed of this, I really am, but while I can remember how we spent every one of Celia's birthdays during those years, my memories of Kevin from the age of eight to about fourteen tend to blur.

Oh, a few bits and pieces stick out, especially my disastrous attempt to impart the enthusiasms of my professional life by taking you and thirteen-year old Kevin (you'll recall that Celia, too young, stayed with my mother) to Vietnam. I deliberately chose that country because it's a place that to any American, at least of our generation, inescapably means something, saving it from the dissociated Just Somewhere Else and Who Cares feeling that foreign countries so easily induce when you visit them for the first time, and to which Kevin would naturally fall prey. Too, Vietnam had only recently opened up to tourism, so I couldn't resist the opportunity on my own account. But I grant that this sense of connectedness, of guilty intimacy with rice paddies and wizened old women in conical straw hats, would pertain mostly to you and me. I'd marched on Washington in my twenties, while you had actually begged the Draft Board, if to no avail, not to reject you because of flat feet; with Saigon already fallen three years before, we had some bracing knockdown drag-outs over the war when we met. Kevin had no such associations, so maybe despite my intentions to the contrary, I had indeed dragged him to Just Somewhere Else and Who Cares. Nonetheless, I'll never forget my stinging humiliation when our son—if nothing else, ever a quick study—sauntered through the sea of scooters in Hanoi telling the "gooks" to get out of the way.

However, one other memory rises eidetically above the blur, and it is not, Franklin, one more mean, slanderous example of how our son was heartless from birth.

I refer to that two weeks when he got so sick. He was ten. For a while, Dr. Goldblatt worried that it was meningitis, though an excruciating spinal tap only proved that it wasn't. Despite his poor appetite, Kevin was generally a healthy boy, and this was my only experience of our son laid so low for so long.

When he first started coming down with it, I noticed that the spirit in which he turned up his nose at my meals was no longer sneering; he'd look at his plate and slump, as if in defeat. In fact, since he was accustomed—like his mother—to battling his own impulses as much as outside forces, he struggled to stuff down one of my lamb *sarma* before giving up. He didn't lurk in shadows or march martinet-style down the hall but began to wander, sagging against furniture. The rigid set of his face went limp and lost that smirking sideways skew. Eventually I found him curled helplessly on my study's ink-stained Armenian carpet, and I was astonished that when I helped him up and lifted him to bed that he offered no resistance. Franklin, he *put his arms around my neck.*

In his bedroom, he let me undress him, and when I solicited which pajamas he wanted to wear, rather than roll his eyes and say *I don't care*, he thought for a moment and then whispered in a small voice, "The space-man ones. I like the monkey in the rocket." This was the first I'd heard that he *liked* a single garment in his possession, and when I discovered this was the one pair in the laundry hamper, I was distraught, shaking them out and hurrying back to promise that the next day I would wash them to be nice and fresh. I expected, "Don't *bother*," but instead got—another first—"Thanks." When I tucked him in, he huddled gladly with the blanket to his chin, and when I slipped the thermometer between his flushed lips—his face had a bright febrile blotch—he suckled the glass with gentle rhythmic contractions, as if finally, at the age of ten, having learned to nurse. His fever was high for a child—over 101°—and when I stroked his forehead with a moist washcloth, he hummed.

I cannot say whether we are less ourselves when we are sick, or more. But I did find that remarkable two-week period a revelation. When I sat on the edge of his bed, Kevin would nestle his crown against my thigh; once I became convinced that it wouldn't be pushing my luck, I pulled his head onto my lap and he clutched my sweater. A couple of times when he threw up he didn't make it to the toilet; yet when I cleaned up the mess and told him not to worry, he exhibited none of the self-satisfied complacency of his diaper-changing phase but whimpered that he was sorry and seemed, despite my re-assurances, ashamed. I know that we all transform one way or another when we're ill, but Kevin wasn't just cranky or tired, he was a completely different person. And that's how I achieved an appreciation for how much energy and commitment it must have taken him the rest of the time to generate this other boy (or boys). Even you had conceded that Kevin was "a little antago-nistic" toward his sister, but when our two-year-old tiptoed into his bedroom, he let her pet his head with damp little pats. When she offered him her get-well drawings, he didn't dismiss them as dumb or take advantage of feeling bad to tell her, as was well within his rights, to leave him alone, instead exert-ing himself to say weakly, "That's a nice picture, Celie. Why don't you draw me another one?" I had thought that dominant emotional tone of his, so ex-travagant from birth, was immutable. Call it rage or resentment, it was only a matter of degree. But underneath the levels of fury, I was astonished to dis-cover, lay a carpet of despair. He wasn't mad. He was sad.

The other thing that amazed me was his curious aversion to your company. You may not remember, since after he'd rebuffed you once or twice—imploring when you popped in that he'd like to go to sleep or laying your present of rare collectible comics silently, wearily on the floor—you were injured enough to withdraw. Maybe he felt unable to muster the *Gee, Dad* boisterousness of your Saturday afternoon Frisbee tosses, but in that instance he clearly regarded this rah-rah boy mode as compulsory with his father. I comforted you that children always prefer their mothers when they're sick, but you were still a little jealous. Kevin was breaking the rules, ruining the balance. Celia was mine, and Kevin was yours. You and Kevin were *close*, he would *confide in you*, and *lean on you* in times of trouble. But I think that was the very reason he recoiled: your insistence, your crowding, your wanting, your cajoling, chummy Daddishness. It was too much. He didn't have the energy—not to give you the intimacy you demanded, but to resist it. Kevin made himself up for you, and there must have been, in the very lavishness of his fabrication, a deep and aching desire to please. But do you ever consider how disappointed he must have been when you accepted the decoy as the real thing?

The second industry he could no longer afford was the manufacture of apathy—though you'd think that apathy would come naturally in a state of malaise. Instead, little islands of shy desire began to emerge like bumps of sun-warmed dry land in a cold receding sea. Once he was holding down food, I asked what he'd like to eat, and he confessed that he liked my clam chowder, going so far as to assert that he preferred the milk-based to the tomato. He even requested a toasted slice of *katah*, whereas he had previously gone out of his way to disdain anything Armenian. He confessed to a fancy for one of Celia's ragged stuffed animals (the gorilla), which she donated solemnly to his pillow as if her humble primate had been selected for a rare honor—as indeed it had been. When I asked him what I should read to him on the long afternoons—I had taken time off from AWAP, of course—he was a bit at a loss, but I think that was only because when either of us had read stories before he had refused to listen. So just on a hunch—it seemed an appealing tale for a boy—I picked *Robin Hood and His Merry Men*.

He loved it. He implored me to read *Robin Hood* over and over, until he must have committed whole passages to heart. To this day I will never know whether this particular tale took so because I read it at some perfect chemical point—where he was strong enough to pay attention but still too weak to generate a force field of indifference—or whether there was something about the nature of this one story that captured his imagination. Like many children foisted into the headlong march of civilization when it was already well down the road, he may have found comfort in the trappings of a world whose workings he could understand; horse-drawn carts and bows and arrows are pleasantly fathomable to the ten-year-old. Perhaps he liked stealing from the rich and giving to the poor because he had an instinctive appreciation for the anti-hero. (Or, as you quipped at the time, maybe he was just a budding tax-and-spend Democrat.)

If I will never forget those two weeks, as indelible was the morning that he felt well enough to get out of bed, informing me that he would dress himself and would I please leave the room. I obliged, trying to hide my disappointment, and when I returned later to ask what he'd like for lunch, maybe clam chowder again, he jerked his head in annoyance. "Whatever," he said, his generation's watchword. A grilled cheese sandwich?— "I don't give a *rat's ass*," he said—a phrase that, whatever they say about kids growing up fast these days, still took me aback from a child of ten. I withdrew, though not before noticing that the set of his mouth was once more askew. I told myself I should be pleased; he was better. *Better?* Well, not to me.

Yet his fever had never burned quite high enough to sear the seeds of a tiny, nascent *interest* to ash. I caught him the following week, reading *Robin Hood* to himself. Later, I helped you two buy his first bow-and-arrow set at the sporting goods store at the mall and construct the archery range at the crest of our sloping backyard, praying all the while that this little bloom of rapture in our firstborn would endure the length of the project. I was all for it.

Eva

Dear Franklin,

When I saw Kevin today his left cheek was bruised, his lower lip swollen; his knuckles were scabbed. I asked if he was all right and he said he cut himself shaving. Maybe the lamest remarks pass for drollery when you're locked up. It gave him palpable pleasure to deny me access to his travails inside, and who am I to interfere with his few enjoyments; I didn't press the matter. Afterward, I might have complained to the prison authorities about their failure to protect our son, but considering what Kevin has himself inflicted on his peers, objection to a few scrapes in return seemed worse than petulant.

I dropped any further preliminaries. I'm increasingly indifferent to setting him at ease on my visits when his own efforts are aimed solely at my discomfiture.

"It's been preying on me," I said right off. "I can almost understand going on some indiscriminate frenzy, venting your frustrations on whomever happens to be in the way. Like that quiet, unassuming Hawaiian a year or two ago, who just flipped—"

"Bryan Uyesugi," Kevin provided. "He kept fish."

"Seven coworkers?"

Kevin patted his hands in mock applause. "Two thousand fish. And it was Xerox. He was a copy-machine repairman. Nine-millimeter Glock."

"I'm so pleased," I said, "that this experience has afforded you an expertise."

"He lived on 'Easy Street,'" Kevin noted. "It was a dead-end."

"My point is, Uyooghi—"

"Yoo-SOO-ghee," Kevin corrected.

"It clearly didn't matter who those employees were—"

"Guy was a member of the Hawaiian Carp Association. Maybe he thought that meant he was supposed to complain."

Kevin was showing off; I waited to make sure the little recital was over.

"But your get-together in the gym," I resumed, "was By Invitation Only."

"All my *colleagues* aren't indiscriminate. Take Michael McDermott, last December. Wakefield, Mass., Edgewater Tech—AK, .12-gauge shotgun. Specific targets. Accountants. Anybody had to do with docking his paycheck 2,000 bucks—"

"I don't want to talk about Michael McDermott, Kevin—"

"He was fat."

"—*Or* about Eric·Harris and Dylan Klebold—"

"Morons. Give mass murderers a bad name."

I told you, Franklin, he's obsessed with those Columbine kids, who upstaged him only twelve days later with six more fatalities; I'm sure I brought them up just to rile him.

"At least Harris and Klebold had the courtesy to save the taxpayer a bundle and make a quick exit," I observed coolly.

"Weenies just trying to inflate their casualty figures."

"Why didn't you?"

He didn't seem to take offense. "Why make it easy for everybody."

"Everybody like me."

"You included," he said smoothly. "Sure."

"But why Dana Rocco and not another teacher, why those particular kids? What made them so special?"

"Uh, *dub*," said Kevin. "I didn't like them."

"You don't like anybody," I pointed out. "What, did they beat you at kickball? Or do you just not like Thursdays?"

In the context of Kevin's new specialty, my oblique reference to Brenda Spencer qualified as a classical allusion. Brenda killed two adults and wounded nine students in her San Carlos, California, high school only because, as the Boomtown Rats' hit single subsequently attested, "I Don't Like Mondays." The fact that this seminal atrocity dates back to 1979 distinguishes the sixteen-year-old as ahead of her time. My nod to his puerile pantheon earned me what in other children would have been a smile.

"It must have been quite a project," I said, "trimming the list."

"Massive," he agreed affably. "Started out like, fifty, sixty serious contenders. Ambitious," he said, then shook his head. "But impractical."

"All right, we have forty-five more minutes," I said. "Why Denny Corbitt?"

"—The ham!" he said, as if checking his grocery list before checkout.

"You remember the name of a copy-machine repairman in Hawaii, but you're not too sure about the names of the people you murdered."

"Uyesugi actually did something. Corbitt, if I remember right, just sat all google-eyed against the wall as if waiting for his director to block the scene."

"My point is, so Denny was a ham. So what?"

"See that dork do Stanley in *Streetcar*? I could do a better Southern accent *underwater*."

"What part are you playing? The surliness, the swagger. Where'd it come from? Brad Pitt? You know, you've picked up a bit of a Southern accent yourself. It isn't very good, either."

His fellow inmates are abundantly black, and his locution has begun to warp accordingly. He's always spoken with a peculiar slowness, that effortfulness, as if he had to hoist the words from his mouth with a shovel, so the slack-jawed urban-ghetto economy of dropped consonants and verbs is naturally infectious. Still, I was pleased with myself; I seemed to have annoyed him.

"I'm not playing a part. I am the part," he said hotly. "Brad Pitt should play *me*."

(So he'd heard; a movie was already in development at Miramax.)

"Don't be ridiculous," I said. "Brad Pitt's way too old to play some pipsqueak high school sophomore. Even if he were the right age, no audience would buy that a guy who looks that street-smart would do anything so moronic. I've read they're having trouble casting, you know. Nobody in Hollywood will touch your filthy little part with a barge pole."

"Just as long as it isn't DiCaprio," Kevin grumbled. "He's a twit."

"Back to business." I sat back. "What was your problem with Ziggy Randolph? You could hardly accuse him of failing your exalted artistic standards, like Denny. Word was that he had a professional future in ballet."

"What had a *professional future*," said Kevin, "was his butthole."

"He got an overwhelming reception when he gave that speech, explaining he was gay and proud of it at assembly. You couldn't bear that, could you? The whole student body cooing how *courageous* he was."

"And how do you like that," Kevin marveled. "Standing ovation for taking it up the ass."

"But I really haven't been able to figure why Greer Ulanov," I said. "The fuzzy-headed girl, short, with prominent teeth."

"Buck teeth," he corrected. "Like a horse."

"You generally had it in for the lookers."

"Anything to get her to shut up about her 'vast right-wing conspiracy.'"

"Ah, she was the one," I clued. "The petition." (I don't know if you remember, but an indignant petition to New York congressmen circulated Gladstone High School when Clinton was impeached.)

"Admit it, *Mumsey*, having a crush on the president is totally low-rent."

"*I* think," I hazarded, "you don't like people who have crushes of any sort."

"More theories? 'Cause *I* think," he returned, "you need to get a life."

"I had one. You took it."

We faced off. "Now you're my life," I added. "All that's left."

"That," he said, "is pathetic."

"But wasn't that the plan? Just you and me, getting to know one another at last."

"More *theories*! Aren't I fascinating."

"Soweto Washington." I had a long list to get through, and I had to keep the program moving. "He's going to walk again, I've read. Are you disappointed?"

"Why should I care?"

"Why did you ever care? Enough to try to kill him?"

"Didn't try to kill him," Kevin maintained staunchly.

"Oh, I see. You left him with holes in both thighs and that's all on purpose. Heaven forbid that Mr. Perfect Psychopath should miss."

Kevin raised his hands. "Hey, hey! I made mistakes! Letting that little movie nerd off scot-free was the last thing I had in mind."

"Joshua Lukronsky," I remembered, though we were getting ahead of ourselves. "Did you hear that your friend Joshua's been brought on board the Miramax film, as a script consultant? They want to be historically accurate. For a "movie nerd," it's a dream come true."

Kevin's eyes screwed up. He doesn't like it when tangential characters collect on his cachet. He was equally resentful when Leonard Pugh posted his web page, KK's_best_friend.com, which has garnered thousands of hits and purports to expose our son's darkest secrets for the price of a double-click. *Best friend my ass!* Kevin snarled when the site went up. *Lenny was closer to a pet hamster.*

"If it makes you feel better," I added sourly, "Soweto's basketball career is no longer a *slam-dunk.*"

"Yeah, well as a matter of fact that does make me feel better. Last thing the world needs is one more darkie who wants to play hoops in the NBA. Talk about stale."

"Talk about stale! Another high school rampage?"

Kevin cleaned his nails. "I prefer to think of it as *tradition.*"

"The media assumed you picked on Soweto because he was black."

"That makes sense," Kevin snorted. "Nine kids locked in that gym. Only one of them's of the *Negro* persuasion, and bingo, it's a 'hate crime.'"

"Oh, it was a hate crime, all right," I said quietly.

Kevin half smiled. "Totally."

"They said the same thing about Miguel Espinoza. That you went for him because he was Latino."

"Superopic? I leave out *communities of color,* they'd say I discriminated."

"But the real reason was he was such an academic bright spark, isn't it? Skipped a grade. All those dizzyingly high scores on state achievement tests and the PSAT."

"Whenever he talk to you, turn out he just trying to use 'echelon' in a sentence."

"But you know what 'echelon' means. You know all kinds of big words. That's why you thought it was such a hoot to write whole essays with words three letters long."

"Fine. So it's not like I was *jealous.* Which, if I'm getting the drift of this *bor-ing* third degree, is what you're getting at."

I took a moment; you know, Kevin *did* look bored. Documentary makers like Jack Marlin, criminologists dashing off best-sellers, the principals and teachers and reverends interviewed on the news; your parents, Thelma Corbitt, Loretta Greenleaf—all these people obsessing over *why KK did it*, with the notable exception of our son. It was one more subject in which Kevin was simply not interested: himself.

"The cafeteria worker," I raised. "He doesn't fit the pattern." (I always feel sheepish that I can't remember his name.) "He wasn't on the list, was he?"

"Collateral damage," said Kevin sleepily.

"*And*," I said, determined to say something to get him to look alive, "I know your secret about Laura Woolford. She was pretty, wasn't she?"

"Saved her trouble," Kevin slurred. "First sign of a wrinkle and she'd a killed herself anyway."

"Very, very pretty."

"Yep. Bet that girl's mirror was all wore out."

"*And you were sweet on her.*"

If I'd any remaining doubt, Kevin's theatrical guffaw cleared it right up. He doesn't often, but he rent me then, just a little. Adolescents are so obvious. "Give me credit," he sneered, "for better taste. That Barbie doll was all accessories."

"It embarrassed you, didn't it?" I prodded. "The eyeliner, the Calvin Klein, the designer haircuts. The nylons and opalescent pumps. Not icy, misanthropic *KK's* style."

"She wasn't all that hot-looking when I was finished."

"It's the oldest story in the book," I goaded. "*After confiding darkly to friends that, 'If I can't have her, then no one else is going to . . . ,' Charlie Schmoe opened fire . . .* 'Is that what this whole sorry mess was meant to cover? Another pimply teen smitten with the unattainable prom queen goes berserk?"

"In your dreams," said Kevin. "You wanna turn this into a Harlequin romance, that's your midget imagination, not mine."

"Luke Woodham was lovesick, wasn't he? In Pearl? You know, 'The Whiner.'"

"He only went out with Christy Menefee *three times*, and they'd been busted up for a year!"

"*Laura rebuffed you, didn't she?*"

"I never came within a mile of that cunt. And as for that fat Woodham fuck, you know his *mother* came with him on every date? No wonder he reamed her with a butcher knife."

"What happened? Did you finally work yourself up into cornering her against a locker during lunch? Did she slap you? Laugh in your face?"

"That the story you wanna tell yourself," he said, scratching his exposed midriff, "I can't stop you."

"Tell other people, too. I was approached by a documentary filmmaker not long ago. Terribly anxious to hear 'my side.' Maybe I should call him back. I could explain to him how it was unrequited love all along. My son was head-over-heels for this smashing little number who wouldn't give him the time of day. After all, how did Laura go down? Kevin may have made a hash of the rest of that crowd, but he shot her *straight through the heart*, our own cupid of Gladstone High. All those other poor wretches were just camouflage, just—what did he call it? *Collateral damage.*"

Kevin leaned forward and lowered his voice confidentially. "How much did you care what girls I did and didn't like before I whacked a couple? How much did you care about anything that went on in my head until it got out?"

I'm afraid that at that point I lost it a bit. "*You want me to feel sorry for you?*" I said in a voice that carried; the mole guard looked over. "Well, first I'll feel sorry for Thelma Corbitt, and Mary Woolford. For the Fergusons and the Randolphs, for the Ulanovs and the Espinozas. I'll let my heart break over a teacher who bent over backward to get inside your precious head, over a basketball player who can barely walk, and even a cafeteria worker I've never met, and *then* we'll see if there's any pity left over for you. There just might be, but it's the scraps of my table you're due, and for scraps you should count yourself lucky."

"Nyeh *nyeh* nyeh nyeh *nyeh* nyeh-nyeh *nyeh*-nyeh!"

Then he laughed. Oh, Franklin. Whenever I let fly he seems so satisfied.

I admit, I tried to make him mad today. I was determined to make him feel small, not the deep dark impenetrable conundrum of Our Contemporary Society, but the butt of a joke, *hoisted on his own retard*. Because every time Kevin takes another bow as Evil Incarnate, he swells a little larger. Each slander slewed in his direction—*nihilistic, morally destitute, depraved, degenerate,* or *debased*—bulks his scrawny frame better than my cheese sandwiches ever did. No wonder he's broadening out. He eats the world's hearty denunciations for breakfast. Well, I don't want him to feel unfathomable, a big beefed-up allegory of generational disaffection; I don't want to allow him to cloak the sordid particulars of his tacky, crappy, gimcrack, derivative stunt with the grand mantle of Rudderless Youth Today. I want him to feel like one more miserable, all-too-understandable snippet of a plain dumb kid. I want him to feel witless and sniveling and inconsequential, and the last thing in the world I want to betray is how much of my day, every day, I spend trying to figure out what makes that boy tick.

My needling about his being stuck on Laura was merely an educated guess. Although any suggestion that his grandiose atrocity derived from a tawdry little broken heart was certain to offend, I'm not honestly sure how much Kevin's crush on Laura Woolford had anything to do with *Thursday*. For all I know, he was trying to impress her.

But I have made a study of those victims, whether or not he cares to examine the list himself. At first glance, it was a disparate group, so motley that their names might have been drawn from a hat: a basketball player, a studious Hispanic, a film buff, a classical guitarist, an emotive thespian, a computer hacker, a gay ballet student, a homely political activist, a vain teen beauty, a part-time cafeteria worker, and a devoted English teacher. Slice of life; an arbitrary assemblage of eleven characters scooped willy-nilly from the fifty or so whom our son didn't happen to like.

But Kevin's displeasure is not the only thing that his victims had in common. Okay, throw out the cafeteria worker, clearly there by mistake; Kevin has a neat mind, and he'd prefer a tidy group of ten. Otherwise, every one of them *enjoyed* something. Never mind whether this passion was pursued with any flash; whatever his parents claim, I gather Soweto Washington hadn't a chance at going pro; Denny was (forgive me, Thelma) an atrocious actor, and Greer Ulanov's petitioning New York congressmen who were going to vote with Clinton anyway was a waste of time. No one is willing to admit as much now, but Joshua Lukronsky's obsession with movies was apparently annoying to many more students than just our son; he was forever quoting whole sequences of dialogue from Quentin Tarantino scripts and staging tiresome contests at lunch, when the rest of the table preferred to negotiate trades of roast beef sandwiches for slices of pound cake, over who could name ten Robert DeNiro films in chronological order. Be that as it may, Joshua did love movies, and even his outright irksomeness didn't keep Kevin from coveting the infatuation itself. It didn't seem to matter infatuation with what. Soweto Washington loved sport and at least the illusion of a future with the Knicks; Miguel Espinoza, learning (at any rate, Harvard); Jeff Reeves, Telemann; Denny Corbitt, Tennessee Williams; Mouse Ferguson, the Pentium III processor; Ziggy Randolph, *West Side Story*, not to mention other men; Laura Woolford loved herself; and Dana Rocco—the ultimate unforgivable—loved Kevin.

I realize that Kevin doesn't experience his aversions as envy. To Kevin, all ten of his victims were supremely ridiculous. They each got excited over trifles, and their enthusiasms were comical. But like my wallpaper of maps, impenetrable passions have never made Kevin laugh. From early childhood, they have enraged him.

Sure, most children have a taste for spoliation. Tearing things apart is easier than making them; however exacting his preparations for *Thursday*, they couldn't have been nearly as demanding as it would have been to befriend those people instead. So annihilation is a kind of laziness. But it still provides the satisfactions of agency: I wreck, therefore I am. Besides, for most people, construction is tight, concentrated, bunchy, whereas vandalism offers release; you have to be quite an artist to give positive expression to abandon. And there's an ownership to destruction, an intimacy; an appropriation. In this way, Kevin has clutched Denny Corbitt and Laura Woolford to his breast, inhaled their hearts and hobbies whole. Destruction may be motivated by nothing more complicated than acquisitiveness, a kind of ham-handed, misguided greed.

I watched Kevin despoil other people's pleasures for most of his life. I can't count the number of times I picked up the word *favorite* during some hot-under-the-collar maternal diatribe—the red galoshes stuffed with snack cake in kindergarten were Jason's *favorite* footwear. Kevin could easily have overheard that the white caftan he squirted with concord grape juice was my *favorite* floor-length dress. For that matter, each walking adolescent bull's-eye in that gym was some teacher's *favorite* student.

He seems to especially revile enjoyments I can only call innocent. For example, he habitually beelined for anyone who was poised to snap a photograph and walked deliberately in front of the lens. I began to dread our trips to national monuments, if only on behalf of the Japanese and all their wasted film. Why, across the globe are scattered dozens of collectible snaps, blurred head shots of the notorious *KK* in profile.

Further illustrations are countless; I'll cite only one in detail.

When Kevin had just turned fourteen, I was approached at his middle school's PTA meeting to chaperone the eighth-grade spring dance. I remember being a little surprised that Kevin intended to go, since he boycotted most organized school activities. (In retrospect, maybe the draw was Laura Woolford, whose shimmering crotch-high frock for the occasion must have set Mary back hundreds.) This end-of-the-year bash was the highlight of the school's social calendar, and most of his classmates would have been anticipating admission to this exclusively senior rite of passage since the sixth grade. The idea was to give these kids practice at being Real Teenagers and to let them swagger around as kings of the hill before entering the adjoining high school as hacked-on peon freshmen at the bottom of the pecking order.

Anyway, I said I'd do it, not especially looking forward to confiscating pints of Southern Comfort; I treasured the memory of my own hot, surreptitious hits from hip flasks behind the stage curtains of William Horlick High School in Racine. I was never keen on getting stuck with the role of Big Killjoy Meanie and wondered if I might not look quietly the other way so long as the kids were discreet and didn't get sloppy drunk.

Of course I was naive, and Southern Comfort was the least of the administration's worries. At our preparatory meeting the week before, the first thing they taught chaperones was how to recognize a crack vial. Graver still, the faculty was still anguished over a couple of national incidents at the start of the calendar year. Kids graduating from eighth grade may be *only* fourteen, but Tronneal Mangum had been *only* thirteen when that January in West Palm Beach, he shot and killed another classmate in front of his middle school because the boy owed him $40. Only three weeks later in Bethel, Alaska (it's embarrassing, Franklin, but I remember all this stuff because when conversation flags at Claverack, Kevin often reverts to reciting his favorite bedtime stories), Evan Ramsey had got hold of his family's .12-gauge shotgun, murdered a popular school athlete at his desk, shot up the school, and then systematically stalked and blew away his high school principal—in my day, a word whose spelling we were taught to distinguish from *principle* by the mnemonic, "The principal is your PAL."

Statistically, of course, in a country with 50 million schoolkids, the killings were insignificant, and I remember going home after that meeting and complaining to you about the faculty's overreaction. They'd moaned about the fact that there wasn't enough left in the budget to purchase metal detectors, while training a whole cadre of chaperones on how to frisk every kid on the way in. And I indulged myself in a bit of liberal indignation (that always revulsed you).

"Of course, for ages *black* kids and *Hispanic* kids have been shooting each other in shithole junior high schools in Detroit," I opined over a late dinner that night, "and that's all very by-the-by. A few *white* kids, *middle-class* kids, protected, private-telephone-line, own-their-own-TV *suburban* kids go ballistic, and suddenly it's a national emergency. Besides, Franklin, you should have seen those parents and teachers eat it up." My stuffed chicken breast was getting cold. "You've never seen so much self-importance, and when I made a joke once they all turned to me with this *it's not funny* expression, like airport security when you make a crack about a bomb. They all love the idea of being on the front line, doing something ooh-ooh dangerous instead of chaperoning a *sock hop*, for God's sake, being in the national spotlight so they can participate in the usual politics of hysteria. I swear on some level they're all jealous, because Moses Lake and Palm Beach and Bethel have had one, what's wrong with Gladstone, why can't we have one, too. Like they're all secretly hoping that as long as Junior or Baby Jane sneaks off without a scratch wouldn't it be keen if the eighth-grade dance turned into a melee and we could all get on TV before the whole tacky number becomes passé. . . ."

I'm making myself a little sick here, but I'm afraid I did spout this sort of thing, and yes, Kevin was probably listening. But I doubt there was a household in the United States that didn't talk about those shootings one way or another. Decry the "politics of hysteria" as I might, they hit a nerve.

I'm sure that this dance has emerged in such high relief in my mind because of where it took place. After all, it's a small memory; whether to the disappointment of those parents or not, the event passed without a hitch, and as for the one student who probably remembers the evening as a calamity, I never even knew her name.

The gym. It was in that gym.

Because the middle school and high school had been built on the same campus, they often shared facilities. Fine facilities they were, too, for it was partly this *good school* that had drawn you to buy us a house nearby. Since, to your despair, Kevin shunned school sports, we'd never attended his middle school's basketball games, so this glorified baby-sitting job remains my sole experience of that structure from the inside. Freestanding, it was cavernous, more than two stories high, slick and expensive—I think it even converted to an ice hockey rink. (How wasteful that the Nyack School Board has, last I read, decided to tear the whole thing down; students are apparently dodging PE courses by claiming that the gym is haunted.) That night, the arena made quite a booming echo chamber for the DJ. Any sports equipment had been cleared off, and though my expectation of balloons and bunting was clearly a hangover from my own dance debut doing the twist in 1961, they had hung a mirror ball.

I may have been a rotten mother—just shut up, it's true—but I wasn't so deplorable as to hang around my fourteen-year-old son at his school dance. So I positioned myself on the opposite side of the gym, enjoying a good view of his sideways slump against the cinder-block wall. I was curious; I'd rarely seen him in the context of his larger social milieu. The only student beside him was the unshakable Leonard Pugh, with his weaselly hee-hee face, and even at 100 yards exuding that greasy toadying quality, a sniggering obsequiousness that always seemed of a piece with his faint odor of day-old fish. Lenny had recently pierced his nose, and the area around the stud had got infected—one nostril was bright red and half again as large as the other; its smear of antibiotic cream caught the light. Something about that kid always put me in mind of brown smudges in underpants.

Kevin had recently conceived his tiny-clothes fashion, which (typically) Lenny had aped. Kevin's black jeans might have fit him when he was eleven. The legs reached mid-calf, exposing dark hairs sprouting on his shins; the crotch, whose zipper would not quite close, well sponsored his equipment. Lenny's ocherous cotton slacks would have looked nearly as hideous had they fit. They were both wearing stretched Fruit of the Loom white T-shirts, leaving the usual three inches of bare midriff.

Perhaps it was my imagination, but whenever schoolmates passed by, they seemed to give those two wide berth. I might have been alarmed that our son appeared to be the object of avoidance—and I was, rather, though his classmates didn't snicker at Kevin as if he were a social reject. If anything, had the other students been laughing, they stopped. In fact, when crossing in front of that pair, other students ceased to talk altogether and only resumed their chatter once well out of the duo's earshot. The girls held themselves unnaturally erect, as if holding their breath. Instead of squinting at the tiny-clothes brigade askance, even football types trained their eyes straight ahead, only darting an edgy backward glance at Kevin and his *pet hamster* once a safe stone's throw away. Meanwhile, as eighth-graders hung back from the dance floor and flowered the walls of the gym, the space on either side of our son and his sidekick remained deserted for a good ten feet. Not one of his classmates nodded, smiled, or ventured so much as an innocuous how's tricks, as if hesitant to risk—what?

I'd anticipated that the music would make me feel old—by groups I'd never heard of, whose pounding appeal would elude the decrepit. But when the sound system cranked up, I was startled to recognize, between selections of timeless bubblegum, some of the same "artists," as we pretentiously called them then, to which you and I would have flopped about in our twenties: The Stones, Credence, The Who; Hendrix, Joplin, and The Band; Franklin, Pink Floyd! With little to do with myself and repelled by the sweet red punch (which cried out for a slug of vodka), I wondered if the fact that Kevin's peers were still nodding along with Crosby, Stills, Nash, & Young, The Grateful Dead, and even The Beatles made our own era especially distinguished, or his especially destitute. When "Stairway to Heaven" came on—that old warhorse!—I had to stifle a laugh.

I never expected that Kevin would dance; that would be *dumb*, and in some respects that boy hadn't changed since he was four. The rest of the group's reluctance to break in the dance floor was pro forma; we were the same way, no one wanting to be first, to draw excessive and inevitably less than kind attention to themselves. In my day, we'd all dare one another interminably, nip at Dutch courage behind the curtains, and finally shuffle from the walls in concert once our safety-in-numbers quorum had reached at least ten. So I was impressed when, the midcourt populated by no more than whirling polka dots from the mirror ball, one lone soul took the floor. She didn't assume a shadowy corner, either, but the center.

With pale, translucent skin, the girl not only had blond hair but blond lashes and eyebrows, whose tentative definition made her features look washed-out. There was also a weakness in her chin—small and skisloped—and it was mostly due to this one less than classical feature that she'd never be considered pretty (by how little we're undone). The other problem was her clothes. Most girls at the dance had played it safe with jeans, and the few dresses I'd spotted were either black leather or sleek, spangled, and smashing, like Laura Woolford's. But this fourteen-year-old—for shorthand, let's call her Alice—was wearing a dress that came almost to her knees and tied in the back with a bow. It was a tan plaid. It had puffed sleeves. She had a ribbon in her hair and patent leather on her feet. She'd clearly been clad by a mother afflicted with some woefully generic notion of what a young girl wore to "a party," never mind the year.

Even I recognized at once that Alice was *uncool*—a word whose improbable currency from our generation to the next testifies to the timelessness of the concept. What is cool changes; that there is such a thing as cool is immutable. And in our heyday, anyway, the average nerd got a little credit for acting mortified and apologetic, staring at his shoes. But I'm afraid this poor chinless waif didn't have enough social intelligence to rue her puffed-sleeve, tan-plaid, tie-bowed party dress. When her mother brought it home, she doubtless threw her arms around the woman in moronic gratitude.

It was "Stairway to Heaven" that had enticed her to strut her stuff. Yet however we may all keep a warm place in our hearts for that old Led Zeppelin standard, it's terribly slow and I personally remembered the tune as undanceable. Not that this stopped Alice. She extended her arms and lunged in ever-widening circles with her eyes closed. She was clearly transported, oblivious to the fact that enthusiastic turns exposed her panties. As she got caught up in the thrall of bass guitar, her moves lost any semblance of rock-and-roll boogie and wobbled between unschooled ballet and Sufi dancing.

In case I've sounded mean, I was really rather enchanted. Our little Isadora Duncan understudy was so uninhibited, so exuberant! I may even have envied her a little. Wistfully I remembered jigging around our Tribeca loft to Talking Heads when pregnant with Kevin, and it saddened me that I no longer did that. And though she was a good eight years older than Celia, something about this girl as she flounced and pirouetted from one end of the gym to the other reminded me of our daughter. An unlikely exhibitionist, she seemed to have taken to the floor simply because this was one of her *favorite* songs—that word again—and because the empty space made it easier to rush around the floor in a swoon. She probably emoted about her own living room to the same song and saw no reason not to dance in exactly the same flamboyant manner merely because 200 malicious adolescents were leering on the sidelines.

It always seems interminable, but "Stairway to Heaven" *was* almost over; he might have held off two more minutes. But no. I felt a peculiar stab of fear as Kevin peeled languidly off the cinder block and sauntered in an unerring straight line toward Alice, tracking her like a Patriot missile homing in on a Scud. Then he stopped, right under the mirror ball, having correctly calculated that Alice's next pirouette would land her left ear exactly in line with his mouth. There. Contact. He leaned, just a little, and whispered.

I would never pretend to know what he said. But the image has informed all my subsequent mental reconstructions of *Thursday*. Alice froze. Her face infused with all the self-consciousness of which it had a moment before been so conspicuously absent. Her eyes darted left and right, unable to find a single resting place that afforded respite. Suddenly all too well aware of her audience, she seemed to register the obligations of the folly she'd begun; the song wasn't quite finished, and she was compelled to keep up appearances by bobbing to a few more bars. For the next forty seconds or so, she floundered back and forth in a macabre slow-motion death dance, like Faye Dunaway at the end of *Bonnie and Clyde*.

The DJ having aptly segued to Jefferson Airplane's "White Rabbit," she clutched her tan-plaid skirt and bunched it between her legs. Hobbling toward a dark corner, Alice pressed her elbows tightly to her waist, as each hand fought for cover under the other. I sensed that, in some sickening fashion, over the course of the previous minute she had just grown up. Now she knew that her dress was geeky, that her chin was weak. That her mother had betrayed her. That she was *uncool*; that she would never be pretty. And most of all, she had learned to never, ever take to an empty dance floor—possibly any dance floor—for the rest of her life.

I wasn't there, on *Thursday*. But two years before, I was witness to its harbinger in that same gym, when a lone graduate of Gladstone Middle School was assassinated.

Eva

Dear Franklin,

My colleague Ricky approached me at the end of the workday today, and his proposal was the closest he's ever come to acknowledging the unmentionable: He invited me to attend his church. I was embarrassed, and thanked him, but said vaguely, "I don't think so"; he didn't let it go and asked why. What was I supposed to say, "Because it's a load of crap"? I always feel a little condescending toward religious people, as they feel condescending toward me. So I said, I wish I could, that I could believe, and sometimes I try very hard to believe, but nothing about my last few years suggests that an entity with any kindness is watching over me. Ricky's comeback about *mysterious ways* left neither of us very impressed. Mysterious, I said. Now you can say that again.

I've often returned to the remark you made in Riverside Park before we became parents, "At least a kid is an answer to the Big Question." It perturbed me at the time that your life was posing this Big Question with such persistence. Our childless period must have had its shortfalls, but I recall charging in the same conversation that maybe we were "too happy," a distinctly more agreeable excess than a surfeit of harrowing emptiness. Maybe I'm shallow, but you were enough for me. I loved scanning for your face outside Customs after those long trips that were so much harder on you than on me, and sleeping late the next morning in a hot, pectoral cocoon. It was enough. But our twosome was not, it seems, enough for you. While that may make you, between us, the more spiritually advanced, it hurt my feelings.

Yet if there's no reason to live without a child, how could there be with one? To answer one life with a successive life is simply to transfer the onus of purpose to the next generation; the displacement amounts to a cowardly and potentially infinite delay. Your children's answer, presumably, will be to procreate as well, and in doing so to distract themselves, to foist their own aimlessness onto their offspring.

I raise this matter because I think that you did expect Kevin to answer your Big Question, and that he could sense that fantastic expectation from an early age. How? Small things. The aggressive heartiness in your voice, under which gasped a shy desperation. The ferocity of your embraces, which he may have found smothering. The resolve with which you cleared your decks every weekend to put yourself at his disposal, for I suspect that children want their parents to be busy; they don't want to have to fill your schedule with their paltry needs. Children want to be assured that there are other things to do, important things; more important, on occasion, than they are.

I'm not commending neglect. But he was only a little boy, and he alone was supposed to answer a Big Question that had his grown father stymied. What a burden to place on the newly arrived! What's worse, children, like adults, vary drastically in what I can only call their religious appetites. Celia was more like me: a hug, a crayon, and a cookie, and she was sated. Though Kevin seemed to want practically nothing, I now realize that he was spiritually ravenous.

Both of us were lapsed, so it made sense to raise our kids as neither Armenian Orthodox nor Presbyterian. Although I'm reluctant to inveigh that Youth Today just need to crack the Old Testament, it sobers me that, thanks to us, Kevin may never have seen the inside of a church. The fact that you and I were brought up with something to walk away from may have advantaged us, for we knew what lay behind us, and what we were not. So I wonder if Kevin, too, would have been better off had we spewed a lot of incense-waving hooey that he could have coughed back in our faces—those extravagant fancies about virgin births and commandments on mountaintops that really stick in a kid's throat. I'm being impractical; I doubt we could have faked a faith for the children's sake, and they'd have known we were posing. Nevertheless, repudiation of self-evident dross like travel guides and Oldsmobile ads must be so unsatisfying.

It was Kevin's starvation that his teachers—with the exception of Dana Rocco—never detected, preferring to diagnose our little underachiever as one more fashionable victim of attention deficit disorder. They were determined to find something mechanically wrong with him, because broken machines can be fixed. It was easier to minister to passive incapacity than to tackle the more frightening matter of fierce, crackling disinterest. Clearly Kevin's powers of attention were substantial—witness his painstaking preparations for *Thursday* or his presently impeccable command of the malevolents' Roll of Honor, right down to the population of Uyesugi's pet fish. He left assignments unfinished not because he couldn't finish them, but because he could.

This voracity of his may go some distance toward explaining his cruelty, which among other things must be an inept attempt at taking part. Having never seen the point—of anything—he must feel so brutally left out. The Spice Girls are *dumb*, Sony Playstations are *dumb*, *The Titanic* is *dumb*, mall cruising is *dumb*, and how could we disagree? Likewise, taking photos of the Cloisters is *dumb*, and dancing to "Stairway to Heaven" in the latter 1990s is *dumb*. As Kevin approached the age of sixteen, these convictions grew violent.

He didn't want to have to answer your Big Question, Franklin. He wanted an answer from you. The glorified loitering that passes for a fruitful existence appeared so inane to Kevin from his very crib that his claim last Saturday that he was doing Laura Woolford "a favor" on *Thursday* may have been genuine.

But me, I'm superficial. Even once the shine was off travel, I could probably have sampled those same old foreign foods and that same old foreign weather for the rest of my life, just so long as I flew into your arms at Kennedy when I came home. I didn't want much else. It is Kevin who has posed my Big Question. Before he came along, I'd been much too busy attending to a flourishing business and a marvelous marriage to bother about what it all amounted to. Only once I was stuck with a bored child in an ugly house for days on end did I ask myself what was the point.

And since *Thursday*? He took away my easy answer, my cheating, slipshod shorthand for what life is for.

We last left Kevin at the age of fourteen, and I'm getting anxious. I may have dwelt so on his early years to stave off rehashing the more recent incidents that set you and me so agonizingly against one another. Doubtless we both dread wading back through events whose only redeeming feature is that they are over. But they are not over. Not for me.

During the first semester of Kevin's ninth-grade year in 1997, there were two more School Shootings: in Pearl, Mississippi, and Paducah, Kentucky, both small towns I had never heard of, both now permanently marked in the American vocabulary as synonyms for adolescent rampage. The fact that Luke Woodham in Pearl not only shot ten kids, three fatally, but killed his mother—stabbing her seven times and crushing her jaw with an aluminum baseball bat—may have given me an extra private pause. (Indeed, I remarked when the reports first started pouring in, "Look, all they do is go on and on about how he shot those kids. And then, oh, by the way, he also murdered his mom. *By the way?* It's obvious that the whole thing had to do with his mother." This, in due course, was an observation that would qualify in legal terms as *admission against interest.*) Still, I'm not so pretentious as to impute to myself during that period a sense of deep personal foreboding, as if I perceived these repeated tragedies on the news as an inexorable countdown to our own family's misfortune. Not at all. Like all news, I regarded it as having nothing to do with me. Yet like it or not, I had morphed from maverick globetrotter to one more white, well-off suburban mother, and I couldn't help but be unnerved by deadly flights of lunacy from fledglings of my own kind. Gangland killings in Detroit or L.A. happened on another planet; Pearl and Paducah happened on mine.

I did feel a concentrated dislike for those boys, who couldn't submit to the odd faithless girlfriend, needling classmate, or dose of working-single-parent distraction—who couldn't serve their miserable time in their miserable public schools the way the rest of us did—without carving their dime-a-dozen problems ineluctably into the lives of other families. It was the same petty vanity that drove these boys' marginally saner contemporaries to scrape their dreary little names into national monuments. And the self-pity! That nearsighted Woodham creature apparently passed a note to one of his friends before staging a tantrum with his father's deer rifle: "Throughout my life I was ridiculed. Always beaten, always hated. Can you, society, blame me for what I do?" And I thought, *Yes, you little shit! In a heartbeat!*

Michael Carneal in Paducah was a similar type—overweight, teased, wallowing in his tiny suffering like trying to take a bath in a puddle. But he'd never been a discipline problem in the past; the worst he'd ever been caught at theretofore was watching the Playboy video channel. Carneal distinguished himself by opening fire on, of all things, a prayer group. He managed to kill three students and wound five, but judging from the cheek-turning memorial services and merciful banners in classroom windows—one of which embraced photos not only of his victims but of Carneal himself with a heart—the born-again got theirs back by forgiving him to death.

The October night that news of Pearl came in, I exploded as you and I watched the *Jim Lehrer Newshour.* "Jesus, some kid calls him a *fag* or pushes him in the hallway, and suddenly it's *ooh, ooh, I'm gonna shoot up the school, I'm gonna crack from all this terrible pressure!* Since when did they make American kids so soft?"

"Yeah, you gotta ask yourself," you agreed, "whatever happened to heading out to the playground to duke it out?"

"Might get their hands dirty." I appealed to our son as he glided through on the way to the kitchen; he'd been eavesdropping, which as a rule he preferred to participating in family conversations. "Kevin, don't boys at your school ever settle their differences with an old-fashioned fistfight?"

Kevin stopped to regard me; he always had to weigh up whether anything I asked him was worthy of reply. "Choice of weapons," he said at last, "is half the fight."

"What's that supposed to mean?"

"Woodham's weak, flabby, unpopular. Fistfight's low percentage. A doughboy's got way better odds with a 30 millimeter. Smart call."

"Not that smart," I said hotly. "He's sixteen. That's the cutoff in most states for being tried as an adult. They'll throw away the key." (Indeed, Luke Woodham would be given three life sentences, and 140 extra years for good measure.)

"So?" said Kevin with a distant smile. "Guy's life is already over. Had more fun while it lasted than most of us ever will. Good for him."

"Cool it, Eva," you intervened as I sputtered. "Your son's pulling your leg."

For most of his life, Kevin's troubles, too, remained on a minor scale. He was bright but hated school; he had few friends, and the one we knew was smarmy; there were all those ambiguous incidents, from Violetta to let-us-call-her-Alice, that set off alarm bells at a volume only I seemed able to hear. Yet character expresses itself with remarkable uniformity, be it on a battlefield or in the supermarket. To me, everything about Kevin was of a piece. Lest my theories about his existential disposition seem too high-falutin, let's reduce the unifying glue to one word: *spite*. Consequently, when two Orangetown policemen showed up at our door on that night in December 1997 with Kevin and the unsavory Leonard Pugh in tow, you were shocked, while I regarded this constabulary visit as overdue.

"What can I do for you, officers?" I overheard.

"Mr. Khadourian?"

"Plaskett," you corrected, not for the first time. "But I am Kevin's father."

Having been helping Celia with her homework, I crept up to hover behind you in the foyer, buzzing from voyeuristic excitement.

"We had a motorist phone in a complaint, and I'm afraid we found your son and his friend here, on that pedestrian overpass over 9W? We had to run these two down, but it seemed pretty obvious that they were the kids throwing detritus onto the roadway."

"Onto the cars?" you asked, "or just empty lanes?"

"Wouldn't be much sport in *empty lanes*," snarled the second officer.

"It was mostly water babies, Dad!" said Kevin behind the police. I know his voice was changing, but whenever he spoke to you, Franklin, it skipped up an octave.

"Wasn't water balloons this motorist called in about," said the second, chunkier cop, who sounded the more worked up. "It was *rocks*. And we checked the highway on either side of the overpass—littered with chunks of brick."

I nudged in urgently. "Was anyone hurt?"

"Thankfully, there were no direct hits," said the first officer. "Which makes these boys real, real lucky."

"I don't know about lucky," Lenny sniveled, "when you get nabbed by the cops."

"Gotta have luck to push it, kid," said the policeman with the hotter head. "Ron, I still say we should—"

"Look, Mr. Plastic," the first cop overrode. "We've run your son through the computer, and his record's clean. Far as I can tell, he comes from a good family." (*Good*, of course, meaning rich.) "So we're going to let this young man off with a warning. But we take this sort of thing real serious—"

"Hell," the second cop interrupted, "a few years back, some creep tossed a quarter in front of a woman doing seventy-five? Shattered the windscreen and drove right into her head!"

Ron shot his partner a glance that would get them the more quickly to Dunkin' Donuts. "Hope you give this young man a good talking to."

"And how," I said.

"I expect he'd no idea what kind of risk he was taking," you said.

"Yeah," said Cop No. 2 sourly. "That's the whole attraction of throwing bricks from an overpass. It seems so harmless."

"I appreciate your leniency, sir," Kevin recited to the primary. "I've sure learned my lesson, sir. It won't happen again, sir."

Policemen must get this *sir* stuff a lot; they didn't look bowled over. "The *leniency* won't happen again, friend," said the second cop, "that is for damned sure."

Kevin turned to the hothead, meeting the man's eyes with a glitter in his own; they seemed to share an understanding. Though picked up by the police for (as far as I knew) the first time in his life, he was unruffled. "And I appreciate the lift home. I've always wanted to ride in a police car—*sir.*"

"Pleasure's all mine," the cop replied jauntily, as if smacking gum. "But my money says that's not your last spin in a black-and-white—*friend.*"

After a bit more fawning gratitude from both of us, they were on their way, and as they left the porch, I heard Lenny whining, "We almost outran you guys you know, 'cause you guys are like, totally out of shape . . . !"

You had seemed so sedate and courteous through this exchange that when you wheeled from the door I was surprised to observe that your face was livid and lit with rage. You grabbed our son by the upper arm and shouted, "You could have caused a pileup, a fucking catastrophe!"

Flushed with a morbid satisfaction, I stepped back to leave you to it. *Cursing*, no less! Granted, had one of those bricks indeed smashed someone's windshield I'd readily have forgone this petty jubilation for the full-blown anguish at which I would later get so much practice. But spared calamity, I was free to muse with the singsong of the playground, *You're gonna get in trou-ble.* Because I'd been so exasperated! The unending string of misadventures that trailed in Kevin's wake never seemed, as far as you were concerned, to have anything to do with him. Finally, a tattletale besides me—the police, whom Mr. Reagan Republican had no choice but to trust—had caught our persecuted innocent red-handed, and I was going to enjoy this. Moreover, I was glad for you too to experience the bizarre helplessness of being this supposedly omnipotent parent and being completely flummoxed by how to impose a punishment that has the slightest deterrent effect. I wanted you to apprehend for yourself the lameness of sending a fourteen-year-old for a "time-out," the hackneyed predictability of "grounding" when, besides, there was never anywhere that he wanted to go, and the horror of realizing that, if he did launch out to his archery range in defiance of your prohibition on practicing the sole activity that he seemed to enjoy, you would have to decide whether to physically tackle him to the lawn. Welcome to my life, Franklin, I thought. *Have fun.*

Celia wasn't used to seeing you manhandle her brother, and she'd started to wail. I hustled her from the foyer back to her homework at the dining table, soothing that the policemen were our friends and just wanted to make sure we were safe, while you rustled our stoic son down the hall to his room.

In such an excitable state, I had difficulty concentrating as I coaxed Celia back to her primer about farm animals. The yelling subsided surprisingly soon; you sure didn't burn out that fast when you were mad at me. Presumably you'd switched to the somber disappointment that for many children is more devastating than a lost temper, though I'd tried stern gravity ad nauseam with our firstborn, and this was one more impotence I was glad for you to sample. Why, it was all I could do to stop myself from creeping down the hall and listening at the crack of the door.

When you emerged at last, you closed Kevin's door behind you with ministerial solemnity, and your expression as you entered the dining area was curiously at peace. I reasoned that getting all that shame and disgust out of your system must have been cleansing, and when you motioned me over to the kitchen, I assumed that you were going to explain what kind of punishment you'd levied so that we could exact it as a team. I hoped that you'd come up with some novel, readily enforceable penalty that would get to our son in a place—I'd never found it—where it hurt. I doubted he was now remorseful about the brick-throwing itself, but maybe you had convinced him that outright juvenile delinquency was a tactical error.

"Listen," you whispered. "The whole caper was Lenny's idea, and Kevin went along because Lenny was only proposing water babies at first. He thought the balloons would just make a splash—and you know how kids think that kind of thing is funny. I told him even a little balloon exploding might have startled a driver and been dangerous, and he says he realizes that now."

"What," I said. "What—about—the bricks."

"Well—they ran out of water babies. So Kevin says that before he knew it, Lenny had pitched a stone—maybe it was a piece of brick—when a car was coming. Kevin says he immediately told Lenny not to do that, since somebody could get hurt."

"Yeah," I said thickly. "That sure sounds like Kevin."

"I guess Lenny managed to get a few more bits of brick over the side before Kevin leaned on him hard enough that he cut it out. That must have been when somebody with a mobile called the cops. Apparently they were still up there, you know, just hanging out, when the police pulled up on the shoulder. It was spectacularly dumb—he admits that, too—but for a kid who's never had trouble with the law before those blinking blue lights must be pretty scary, and without thinking—"

"Kevin's a very bright boy, you always say." Everything that came out of my mouth was heavy and slurred. "I sense he's done plenty of *thinking.*"

"Mommy—?"

"Sweetheart," I said, "go back and do your homework, okay? Daddy's telling Mommy a really good story, and Mommy can hardly wait to hear how it ends."

"Anyway," you resumed, "they ran. Didn't get very far, since he realized that running was crazy, and he grabbed Lenny's jacket to put the brakes on. And here's the thing: It seems our friend Lenny Pugh already has something on his record—the old sugar-in-the-gas-tank trick, or some such. Lenny had been told that if he was caught at anything else they'd press charges. Kev reckoned that with his own clean record, they'd probably let him off with a warning. So Kevin told the cops that *he* was the ringleader, and he was the only one who threw rocks. I have to say, once the whole thing was on the table, I felt kind of sheepish for laying into him like that."

I looked up at you with dumbstruck admiration. "Did you apologize?"

"Sure." You shrugged. "Any parent's got to admit when he's made a mistake."

I groped my way to a chair at the kitchen table; I had to sit down. You poured yourself a glass of apple juice, while I declined one (what was wrong with you that you couldn't tell I needed a *stiff drink*?). You pulled up a chair yourself, leaning forward chummily as if this whole *misunderstanding* was going to make us an even more closely knit, supportive, remember-that-daft-business-about-the-overpass family.

"I'll tell you," you said, and took a gulp of juice, "we just had this terrific conversation, all about the complexities of loyalty, you know? When to stick by your friends, where to draw the line when they're doing something you think is out of bounds, how much you should personally sacrifice for a buddy. Because I warned him, he could have miscalculated by taking the fall. He could have been booked. I admired the gesture, but I told him, I said I wasn't exactly sure that Lenny Pugh was worth it."

"Boy," I said. "No holds barred."

Your head whipped around. "Was that sarcastic?"

Okay, if you weren't going to attend to a medical emergency, I would pour a glass of wine myself. I resumed my seat and finished off half of it in two slugs. "That was a very detailed story. So you won't mind my clarifying a few things."

"Shoot."

"Lenny," I began. "Lenny is a worm. Lenny's actually kind of stupid. It took me a while to figure out what the appeal is—for Kevin, I mean. Then I got it: That's the appeal. That he's a stupid, pliant, self-abasing worm."

"Hold on, I don't like him much either, but *self-abasing*—?"

"Did I tell you that I caught them out back, and Lenny had his pants down?"

"Eva, you should know about pubescent boys. It may make you uncomfortable, but sometimes they're going to experiment—"

"Kevin didn't have his pants down. Kevin was fully clothed."

"Well, what's that supposed to mean?"

"That Lenny isn't his *friend*, Franklin! Lenny is his slave! Lenny does anything Kevin tells him to, the more degrading the better! So the prospect of that miserable, sniggering, brownnosing dirtbird having an idea to do anything—much less being the 'ringleader' of some nasty, dangerous prank, dragging poor virtuous Kevin unwillingly along—well, it's perfectly preposterous!"

"Would you keep it down? And I don't think you need another glass of wine."

"You're right. What I really need is a fifth of gin, but Merlot will have to do."

"Look. He may have made a dubious call, and he and I discussed that. But taking the rap still took guts, and I'm pretty damned proud—"

"*Bricks*," I interrupted. "They're heavy. They're big. Builders don't store bricks on pedestrian overpasses. How did they get there?"

"Piece of brick. I said piece."

"Yes," my shoulders slumped, "I'm sure that's what Kevin said, too."

"He's our son, Eva. That should mean having a little faith."

"But the police said—" I left the thought dangling, having lost my enthusiasm for this project. I felt like a dogged attorney who knows that the sympathy of the jury is already lost but who still has to do the job.

"Most parents," you said, "apply themselves to *understanding* their kids, and not to picking apart every little—"

"*I am trying to understand him.*" My ferocity must have carried; on the other side of the partition, Celia started to whimper. "I wish you would!"

"That's right, go tend to Celia," you muttered as I got up to leave. "Go dry Celia's eyes and pat Celia's pretty gold hair and do Celia's homework for her, since God forbid she should learn to do one miserable assignment by herself. Our son was just picked up by the cops for something he didn't do, and he's pretty shaken up, but never mind, because Celia needs her milk and cookies."

"That's right," I returned. "Because one of our children is spelling farm animals, while another of our children is pitching bricks at oncoming headlights. It's about time you learned to tell the difference."

I was really angry about that night, and I wasted most of my subsequent workday at AWAP mumbling to myself about how I could have married a *complete fool*. I'm sorry. And this was despicable of me, but I never told you what I stumbled across late that afternoon. Maybe I was just embarrassed, or too proud.

So beside myself with fury and frustration that I was getting nothing done, I took the CEO's prerogative of cutting out early. When I got back and relieved Celia's baby-sitter Robert, I heard voices down the hall. It seems that the *stupid, pliant, self-abasing worm* didn't even have the good sense to make himself scarce for a few days after showing up at our door with the police, because I recognized the nasal, querulous pule emitting from Kevin's nightmarishly tidy bedroom. Unusually, the door was ajar; but then I wasn't expected home for another two hours. When I headed toward the bathroom I wasn't exactly eavesdropping, but—oh, I guess I was eavesdropping. The urge to listen at that door had been upon me the night before and had lingered.

"Hey, you see that cop's fat butt hanging out his pants?" Lenny was reminiscing. "Working man's smile grinning ear-to-ear! I bet if that guy'd taken a dump while he was running, it would've cleared his belt!"

Kevin did not seem to be joining in with Lenny's cackle. "Yeah, well," he said. "Lucky for you I got *Mr. Plastic* off my back. But you should have heard the scene in here, Pugh. Straight out of *Dawson's Creek*. Fucking nauseating. Thought I'd bust into tears before a commercial break from our sponsors."

"Hey, I hear you! Like, with those cops dude, you were so smooth dude, I thought that fat fuck was going to take you to some little room and kick the shit out of you, 'cause you were driving him like, fucking insane! *Sir, I really must terribly protest, sir, that it was me—* "

"It was *I*, you grammatical retard. And just remember, chump, you owe me one."

"Sure, bro. I owe you big-time. You took the heat like some superhero, like—like you was Jesus!"

"I'm serious, pal. This one's gonna cost you," said Kevin. "'Cause your low-rent stunt could do my reputation some serious damage. I got standards. Everybody knows I got standards. I saved your ass this time, but don't expect a sequel, like, 'Ass-Save II.' I don't like associating myself with this shit. *Rocks over an overpass.* It's fucking trite, man. It's got no class at all, it's fucking *trite.*"

Eva

Dear Franklin,

You've put it together: I felt ashamed of my false accusations, and that's the real reason I decided to ask Kevin on that mother-son outing, just the two of us. You thought it was a weird idea, and, when you commended so heartily that Kevin and I should do that sort of thing more often, I knew you didn't like it—especially once you added that barb about how we'd better avoid any pedestrian overpasses, "Since, you know, Kev would have an uncontrollable urge to throw whole Barcaloungers onto the road."

I was nervous about approaching him but pushed myself, thinking, there's no point in moaning about how your adolescent never talks to you if you never talk to him. And I reasoned that the trip to Vietnam the summer before last had backfired for being overkill, three solid weeks of close familial quarters when at thirteen no kid can bear to be seen with his parents, even by communists. Surely one day at a time would be easier to take. Besides, I had forced my own enthusiasm for travel down his throat, instead of making an effort to do what he wanted to do—whatever that was.

My dithering beforehand over how to pop the question made me feel like a bashful schoolgirl gearing up to invite our son to a rock concert. When I finally cornered him—or myself, really—in the kitchen, I went with the sensation, saying, "By the way, I'd like to ask you out on a date."

Kevin looked mistrustful. "What for."

"Just to do something together. For fun."

"Like, do what."

This was the part that made me nervous. Thinking of something "fun" to do with our son was like trying to think of a really great trip to take with your pet rock. He hated sports and was indifferent to most movies; food was chaff, and nature an annoyance, merely the agent of heat or cold or flies. So I shrugged. "Maybe do a little Christmas shopping. Take you to dinner?" Then I pulled out my ace in the hole, playing perfectly to Kevin's absurdist strong suit. "And play a round or two of *miniature golf.*"

He cracked that sour half smile, and I'd secured a companion for Saturday. I worried about what to wear.

In a switch-off reminiscent of *The Prince and the Pauper,* I would assume the role of Kevin's caring, engaged parent, while you would become Celia's protector for the day. "Gosh," you quipped lightly, "going have to come up with something to do that doesn't terrify her. Guess that rules out vacuuming."

To say that I wanted, truly desired, to spend all afternoon and evening with my prickly fourteen-year-old son would be a stretch, but I did powerfully desire to desire it—if that makes any sense. Knowing how time went slack around that boy, I had scheduled our day: miniature golf, shopping on Main Street in Nyack, and then I would treat him to a nice dinner out. The fact he didn't care about Christmas presents or fine dining seemed no reason to skip the lesson that this is simply what people do. As for our sporting escapade, no one is meant to care about miniature golf, which must be why it felt so apt.

Kevin reported for duty in the foyer with an expression of glum forbearance, like a convict being hauled off to serve his sentence (though in that very circumstance not two years later, his face would instead appear cool and cocky). His ridiculous child-sized Izod knit was the loud orange of prison jumpsuits—not, as I would have much opportunity to establish, a very becoming color on him—and with the tight shirt pulling his shoulders back, he might have been handcuffed. His low-slung khaki slacks from seventh grade were at fashion's cutting edge: Extending to mid-calf, they presaged the renaissance of pedal pushers.

We climbed into my new metallic double-yellow VW Luna. "You know, in my day," I chattered, "these VW bugs were everywhere. Rattletrap and usually beaten up, full of destitute longhairs smoking dope and blasting Three Dog Night on tinny eight-tracks. I think they cost something like $2,500. Now this reissue is ten times that; it still fits two adults and a cat, but it's a luxury automobile. I don't know what that is—ironic, funny."

Silence. At last, laboriously: "It means you'll spend twenty-five grand to kid yourself you're still nineteen, and still not get any trunk space."

"Well, I guess I do tire of all this retro-boomer stuff," I said. "The film remakes of *The Brady Bunch* and *The Flintstones*. But the first time I saw it, I fell in love with this design. The Luna doesn't copy the original, it *alludes* to the original. And the old Beetle was poky. The Luna is still a little bump on the road, but it's a surprisingly beautiful car."

"Yeah," said Kevin. "You've said all that before."

I colored. It was true. I had.

I pulled into that funky little course in Sparkhill called "9W Golf" and finally noticed that Kevin hadn't worn a jacket. It was chilly, too, and overcast. "Why didn't you wear a *coat?*" I exploded. "You just can't get uncomfortable enough, can you?"

"Uncomfortable?" he said. "With my own mother?"

I slammed the door, but with that German engineering it only made a muffled *clump*.

Heaven knows what I'd been thinking. Miniature golf being fundamentally ludicrous, maybe I'd hoped that it would lend our afternoon a leavening element of whimsy. Or maybe I'd hoped instead for some emotional inversion, whereby because everything that meant something to me meant nothing to Kevin, something that meant nothing to me might mean something to Kevin. In any case, it was wrongheaded. We paid the attendant and marched to the first hole—a bathtub sprouting dead weeds, guarded by a plaster giraffe that looked like a pony with a wrung neck. In fact, all the course's models were gimcrack and careless, lending the place an ambiance of, as Kevin would say, who-gives-a-rat's-ass. The traffic on 9W was loud and relentless, and meanwhile, stiff goose bumps rose on Kevin's arms. He was freezing and I was making him do this anyway, because I had this wonky notion of having a mother-son "outing" and we would, goddamn it, have *fun*.

Naturally, anybody could roll a golf ball between the claw feet of that bathtub, since the feet were a yard apart. But once the course grew harder—under the missile, over to the lighthouse, down the suspension bridge, around the milk churns, through the doors of the model Sparkhill-Palisades Fire Department—Kevin set aside the studied ineptitude of curling a Frisbee on its side in the backyard, displaying instead the striking hand-eye coordination that his archery instructor had remarked upon more than once. But somehow the very fact that he was so good at this made it all the more pointless, and I couldn't help but be reminded of our first "game" when he was two, rolling the ball back and forth on the floor exactly three times. For my part, the rank silliness of this exercise had become so glaring that I grew apathetic and muffed the holes. We said nothing, and the course took very little time to complete, if only by the clock; I glanced constantly at my watch. This is what it's like to be Kevin, I thought. The leaden passage of minute by minute: This is what it's like to be Kevin all the time.

At the end Kevin posed with his club like a dapper gentleman, still silent but with a *now-what?* look, as if to say, okay, I did what you wanted and I hope you're satisfied.

"Well," I said grimly. "You won."

I insisted on driving home to get his jacket, though reappearing back at the house so soon embarrassed me—you looked bemused—and going up through Nyack to Gladstone and back to Nyack to shop introduced yet more awkwardness. Nevertheless, now that Kevin had made a hash of my one playful, offbeat idea for our afternoon—having turned it into a mechanical, bone-chilling farce—he seemed more contented. Once we parked (way down Broadway, because the mid-December traffic was bumper-to-bumper and we were lucky to find the space we got), to my astonishment he volunteered a thought.

"I don't get why you celebrate *Christ*mas when you aren't a *Christ*ian." He pronounced the *Christ* with a long *I* to emphasize the Jesus bit.

"Well," I said, "it's true that your father and I don't believe that some young man who was good at sound bites 2,000 years ago was the son of God. But it's nice to have holidays, isn't it? To make part of the year a little different, something to look forward to. I learned studying anthropology at Green Bay is that it's important to observe cultural rituals."

"Just so long as they're totally empty," said Kevin breezily.

"You think we're hypocrites."

"Your word, not mine." He glided past the Runcible Spoon around the corner to Main Street, turning the heads of some older high school girls loitering across the way by the Long Island Drum Center. Frankly I don't think his smoky Armenian looks drew their attention so much as the languid elegance of his manner, at such odds with his preposterous clothes: He moved levelly on the same plane, as if rolling on casters. Then, those fine exposed hipbones couldn't have hurt.

"So," Kevin summed up, weaving through pedestrians, "you want to keep the presents and the high-test eggnog, but chuck the prayers and the boring Christmas Eve service. To cash in on the good stuff without having to pay for it with the shit."

"You could say that," I agreed cautiously. "In a broad sense I've tried to do that all my life."

"Okay, long as you can get away with it," he said cryptically. "Not sure it's always possible." And he let the subject go.

Conversation once again ceased to flow, so when one of them almost ran me over, I supposed aloud that maybe we could buy Celia one of those superthin aluminum Razor scooters that had abruptly become so popular.

Kevin said, "You know, couple years ago, you give a kid some geeky *scooter* for Christmas and he'd have bawled his eyes out."

I lunged at the chance to be collegial. "You're right, that's one of the things that's wrong with this country, it's so faddish. It was the same with in-line skates, right? Overnight, a must-have. Still——" I bit my lip, watching yet another boy whiz past on one of those narrow silver frames. "I wouldn't want Celia to feel left out."

"Mumsey. Get real. Ceil would be scared shitless. You'd have to hold her little hand everywhere she went or you'd have to *carry* her, scooter and all. You ready? 'Cause count me out."

Okay. We didn't get the scooter.

In fact, we didn't buy anything. Kevin made me so self-conscious that everything I considered seemed to damn me. I looked at the scarves and hats through his eyes and they suddenly seemed stupid or unnecessary. We had scarves. We had hats. Why bother.

Though I was sorry to lose our parking space, I was glad of the chance to act the proper mother for once and announced sternly that we would now go back to the house, where he would dress for dinner in *normal-sized clothes*—although his airy response, "Whatever you say," made me more aware of the limits to my authority than of its force. As we passed back in front of the Runcible Spoon on the way to the car, a corpulent woman was sitting alone at a table by the window, and her hot fudge sundae was built on that lavish American scale that Europeans both envy and disparage.

"Whenever I see fat people, they're eating," I ruminated safely out of the diner's earshot. "Don't give me this it's glands or genes or a slow metabolism rubbish. It's food. They're fat because they eat the wrong food, too much of it, and all the time."

The usual lack of pickup, not even *mm-hmm*, or *true*. Finally, a block later: "You know, you can be kind of harsh."

I was taken aback and stopped walking. "You're one to talk."

"Yeah. I am. Wonder where I got it."

Driving home, then, every time I came up with something to say—about pushy SUV drivers (or, as I preferred to playfully misspeak, *SRO* drivers), garish Nyack Christmas lights—I realized it was whittling, and I'd swallow the remark. I was apparently one of those types who, should she follow that edict about *if you can't say something nice*, would say nothing at all. Our raw silence in my Luna supplied a foretaste of the long periods of dead air that would pass in Claverack.

Back home, you and Celia had been working on homemade tree ornaments all afternoon, and you'd helped her to weave tinsel in her hair. You were in the kitchen arranging frozen fish sticks on a tray when I bustled from the bedroom and asked you to fasten the top button of my hot-pink silk dress. "Wow," you said, "you're not looking very maternal."

"I'd like to create a sense of occasion," I said. "I thought you liked this dress."

"I do. Still," you mumbled, buttoning, "That slit up the thigh is cut pretty high. You don't want to make him uneasy."

"I'm making someone uneasy, obviously."

I left to find some earrings and to splash on a little Opium, then returned to the kitchen to discover that Kevin had not, for once, merely followed the letter of my law, for I'd half expected to find him decked out in a "normal-sized" bunny suit. He was standing at the sink with his back to me, but even so I could see that his lush black rayon slacks rested gently on his narrow hips and fell to his cordovans with a slight break. I hadn't bought him that white shirt; with its full sleeves and graceful drape, it may have been fencing garb.

I was touched, I really was, and I was about to exclaim about what a handsome figure he cut when he didn't wear clothes designed for an eight-year-old when he turned around. In his hands was the carcass of a whole cold chicken. Or it had been whole, before he clawed off both breasts and a leg, the drumstick of which he was still devouring.

I probably turned white. "I'm about to take you to dinner. Why are you eating the better part of a roast chicken before we go?"

Kevin wiped a little grease off the corner of his mouth with the heel of his hand, ill-concealing a smirk. "I was hungry." A rare enough admission that it could only be a ruse. "You know—growing boy?"

"Put that away *right now* and get your coat."

So naturally once we were seated in Hudson House our *growing boy* had grown enough for the day, and he allowed that his appetite had waned. I would break bread with my son only in the most literal sense, for he refused to order an entrée or even an appetizer, preferring to tear at the basket of hard rolls. Though he ripped the sourdough into ever smaller pieces, I don't think he ate any.

Defiantly, I ordered the mesclun salad, pigeon-breast appetizer, salmon, and a whole bottle of sauvignon blanc that I sensed I would finish.

"So," I began, battling discomfiture as I picked at greens under Kevin's ascetic eye; we were in a restaurant, why should I feel apologetic about eating? "How's school going?"

"It's going," he said. "Can't ask for more than that."

"I can ask for a few more details."

"You want my course schedule?"

"*No.*" I badly did not want to get annoyed. "Like, what's your favorite subject this semester?" I remembered too late that for Kevin the word *favorite* attached exclusively to the enthusiasms of others that he liked to despoil.

"You imply I like any."

"Well," I thrashed, having difficulty stabbing a forkful of arugula small enough that it wouldn't smear honey-mustard dressing on my chin. "Have you thought about joining any after-school clubs?"

He looked at me with the same incredulity that would later meet my inquiries about the cafeteria menus at Claverack. Maybe the fact that he wouldn't deign to answer this question at all made me lucky.

"What about your, ah, teachers? Are any of them, you know, especially—"

"And what *bands* are you listening to these days?" he said earnestly. "Next you can wheedle about whether there isn't some cute little cunt in the front row that's got me itchy. That way you can segue into how it's all up to me of course, but before balling the chick in the hallway I might decide to *wait* until I'm *ready*. Right around dessert you can ask about *druuugs*. Careful, like, 'cause you don't want to scare me into lying my head off, so you have to say how you *experimented* but that doesn't mean I should *experiment too*. Finally, once you've sucked up that whole bottle you can go gooey-eyed and say how great it is to spend *quality time* together and you can shift out of your chair and put an arm around my shoulder and give it a little *squeeze*."

"All right, Mr. Snide." I abandoned my lettuce. "What do *you* want to talk about?"

"This was your idea. I never said I wanted to talk about a fucking thing."

We squared off over my pigeon breast and red-currant confit, and I began to saw. Kevin had a way of turning pleasures into hard work. As for the turn he took after three or four minutes' silence, I can only conclude that he took pity on me. Later in Claverack he would never be the one to blink first, but after all, in Hudson House he was only fourteen.

"Okay, I've got a *topic*," he proposed slyly, picking up a carmine crayon from the restaurant's complimentary glass of Crayolas, grown ubiquitous as scooters. "You're always griping about this country and wishing you were in Malaysia or something. What's your problem with the place. Really. American *materialism*?"

Much like Kevin when I proposed this date, I suspected a trap, but I had an entrée and two-thirds of a bottle to go, and I didn't want to spend it drawing tic-tac-toes on the disposable tablecloth. "No, I don't think that's it," I answered sincerely. "After all, as your grandfather would say—"

"*Materials are everything*. So what's your beef?"

This is sure to dumbfound you, but in that moment I couldn't think of one thing wrong with the United States. I'm often stymied in this vein when some stranger on a plane, making conversation when I put down my book, asks what other novels I've enjoyed: I draw such a perfect blank that my seatmate might infer that the paperback stuffed in the magazine pocket is the first fiction I've read in my life. My leery outlook on the United States was precious to me—even if, thanks to you, I had learned to give the country grudging credit for at least being a spirited, improvisational sort of place that, despite its veneer of conformity, cultivated an impressive profusion of outright lunatics. Abruptly incapable of citing a single feature of this country that drove me around the bend, I felt the bottom fall out for a second and worried that maybe I hadn't kept the U.S. at arm's length from sophisticated cosmopolitanism, but rather from petty prejudice.

Nevertheless, on airplanes it eventually comes to me that I adore Paul Bowles's *The Sheltering Sky*. Then I remember V. S. Naipaul's *A Bend in the River*, which always reminds me of Paul Theroux's delightful *Girls at Play*, and I'm away, restored to literacy again.

"It's ugly," I submitted.

"What? The amber waves of grain?"

"The fast-food taka-taka. All that plastic. And it's spread all around the country like potato blight."

"You said you like the Chrysler Building."

"It's old. Most modern American architecture is horrendous."

"So this country's a dump. Why's anywhere else any better."

"You've hardly been anywhere else."

"Vietnam was a shithole. That lake in Hanoi stank."

"But didn't you think the people were gorgeous? Even just physically gorgeous."

"You took me to Asia for chink pussy? I could of booked one of those package holidays on the Web."

"Having fun?" I asked dryly.

"I've had better." He shot a ball of bread into the basket. "'Sides. The guys all looked like girls to me."

"But I thought it was refreshing," I insisted, "along that lake—even if it does smell—the way the Vietnamese pay entrepreneurs with bathroom scales a few dong to weigh themselves, in the hopes that they've *gained* a few pounds. It's biologically sane."

"Put those gooks around a bottomless vat of French fries for long enough and they'll pork out wider than they are tall, just like mall rats in New Jersey. You think only Americans are greedy? I don't pay attention in European History too good, but I don't think so."

Served the salmon for which I now had little appetite, I drummed my fingers. With the backdrop of the wallwide seascape at Hudson House, in that flashy white shirt with its billowing sleeves, raised collar, and a V-neck cut to the sternum, Kevin could have passed for Errol Flynn in *Captain Blood.*

"The accent," I said. "I hate it."

"It's your accent, too," he said. "Even if you do say *tomahto.*"

"You think that's pretentious."

"Don't *you?*"

I laughed, a little. "Okay. It's pretentious."

Something was loosening up, and I thought, my, maybe this "outing" wasn't a bad idea after all. Maybe we're getting somewhere. I began to throw myself into the conversation in earnest. "Look, one of the things about this country I really can't stand? It's the lack of accountability. Everything wrong with an American's life is somebody else's fault. All these smokers raking in millions of dollars in damages from tobacco companies, when, what, they've known the risks for *forty years.* Can't quit? Stick it to Philip Morris. Next thing you know, fat people will be suing fast-food companies because they've eaten too many Big Macs!" I paused, catching myself. "I realize you've heard this before."

Kevin was winding me up, of course, like a toy. He had the same intent, mischievous expression I'd seen recently on a boy making his model race car hurtle off the rocks in Tallman Park by remote control. "Once or twice," he allowed, repressing a smile.

"Power walkers," I said.

"What about them."

"They drive me insane." Of course, he'd heard this, too. But he hadn't heard this, because until then I hadn't quite put it together: "People around here can't just *go for a walk*, they have to be getting with some kind of program. And you know, this may be at the heart of it, *what's my beef.* All those intangibles of life, the really good but really elusive stuff that makes life worth living—Americans seem to believe they can all be obtained by joining a group, or signing up to a subscription, or going on a special diet, or undergoing aroma therapy. It's not just that Americans think they can buy everything; they think that if you follow the instructions on the label, the product has to work. Then when the product doesn't work and they're still unhappy even though the right to happiness is enshrined in the Constitution, they sue the bejesus out of each other."

"What do you mean, *intangibles*," said Kevin.

"*Whatever*, as your friends would say. Love—joy—insight." (To Kevin, I could as well have been talking about little green men on the moon.) "But you can't order them on the Internet or learn them in a course at the New School or look them up in a How-To. It's not that easy, or maybe it is easy . . . so easy that trying, following the directions, gets in the way . . . I don't know."

Kevin was doodling furiously on the tablecloth with his crayon. "Anything else?"

"Of course there's anything else," I said, feeling the momentum that gets rolling in those plane chats when I finally get access to the library in my head, remembering *Madame Bovary*, and *Jude the Obscure*, and *A Passage to India*. "Americans are fat, inarticulate, and ignorant. They're demanding, imperious, and spoiled. They're self-righteous and superior about their precious democracy, and condescending toward other nationalities because they think they've got it right—never mind that half the adult population doesn't vote. And they're boastful, too. Believe it or not, in Europe it isn't considered acceptable to foist on new acquaintances right off the bat that you went to Harvard and you own a big house and what it cost and which celebrities come to dinner. And Americans never pick up, either, that in some places it's considered crass to share your taste for anal sex with someone at a cocktail party you've known for five minutes—since the whole concept of privacy here has fallen by the wayside. That's because Americans are trusting to a fault, innocent in a way that makes you stupid. Worst of all, they have no idea that the rest of the world can't stand them."

I was talking too loudly for such a small establishment and such abrasive sentiments, but I was strangely exhilarated. This was the first time that I'd been able to really talk to my son, and I hoped that we'd crossed the Rubicon. At last I was able to confide things that I well and truly believed, and not just lecture—please don't pick the Corleys' prize-winning roses.

Granted, I'd begun in a childishly inept way, asking *how's school*, while he was the one who'd conducted our talk like a competent adult, drawing out his companion. But as a consequence I was proud of him. I was just fashioning a remark along these lines, when Kevin, who had been scribbling intently on the tablecloth with that crayon, finished whatever he was drawing, looked up, and nodded at the scrawl.

"Wow," he said. "That's a whole lot of adjectives."

Attention deficit disorder in a pig's eye. Kevin was an able student when he bothered, and he hadn't been doodling; he'd been taking notes.

"Let's see," he said, and proceeded to check off successive elements of his list with his red crayon. "*Spoiled.* You're rich. I'm not too sure what you think you're doing without, but I bet you could afford it. *Imperious.* Pretty good description of that speech just now; if I was you, I wouldn't order dessert, 'cause you can bet the waiter's gonna hawk a loogie in your raspberry sauce. *Inarticulate?* Lemme see . . . " He searched the tablecloth, and read aloud, "*It's not that easy, or maybe it is easy, I don't know.* I don't call that Shakespeare myself. Also, seems to me I'm sitting across from the lady who goes on these long rants about 'reality TV' when she's never watched a single show. And that—one of your favorite words, Mumsey—is *ignorant.* Next: *boasting.* What was all that these-dumb-fucks-suck-dead-moose-dick-and-I'm-so-much-cooler-than-them if it wasn't showing off? Like somebody who *thinks she's got it right* and nobody else does. *Trusting . . . with no idea other people can't stand them.*" He underscored this one and then looked me in the eye with naked dislike. "Well. Far as I can tell, about the only thing that keeps you and the other dumb-ass *Americans* from being peas in a pod is you're not *fat.* And just because you're skinny you act *self-righteous—condescending—*and *superior.* Maybe I'd rather have a big cow of a mother who at least didn't think she was better than everybody else in the fucking country."

I paid the bill. We wouldn't conduct another mother-son outing until Claverack.

Discouraged from getting her the scooter, I went to considerable trouble to locate a "small-eared elephant shrew" as a Christmas present for Celia. When we'd visited the Small Mammals exhibit in the Bronx Zoo, she'd been enchanted by this incongruous little fellow, who looked as if an elephant crossed with a kangaroo had interbred with several generations of mice. The importation was probably illegal—if not outright endangered, this tiny creature from southern Africa was identified at the zoo as "threatened, due to habitat loss"—which didn't help my case when you grew impatient with the time it took to find one. At length we struck a deal. You'd look the other way as I located a pet shop that specialized in "unusual" animals on the Internet, I the other way as you bought Kevin that crossbow.

I never told you what Celia's present cost, and I don't think I'll tell you now, either. Suffice it to say that once in a while it was nice to be wealthy. The short-eared elephant shrew—inaptly named; neither elephant nor shrew, it has flanged, cupped ears that are proportionately enormous—was, bar none, the most successful present I've ever given. Celia would have been bowled over by a roll of Lifesavers, but even our agreeable daughter expressed degrees of exhilaration, and when she unwrapped the big glass cage her eyes bulged. Then she flew into my arms with a torrent of thanks. She kept getting up from Christmas dinner to check that the cage was warm enough or to feed him a raw cranberry. I was already worried. Animals don't always flourish in alien climates, and giving such a perishable present to a sensitive child was probably rash.

Then, I may have purchased "Snuffles," as Celia christened him, as much for myself as for her, if only because his delicate, wide-eyed vulnerability reminded me so of Celia herself. With long, downy fur reminiscent of our daughter's fine hair, this five-ounce fluff ball looked as if, with one good puff, he would scatter to the winds like a dandelion. Balanced on haunches that narrowed to slender stilts, Snuffles looked precarious when upright. His signature snout, trumpet-shaped and prehensile, routed about the dirt-lined cage, both touching and comic. The animal didn't run so much as hop, and his bounding within the confines of his hemmed-in world exuded the cheerful make-the-best-of-it optimism with which Celia would soon face her own limitations. Although elephant shrews are not strictly vegetarian—they eat worms and insects—massive brown eyes gave Snuffles an awed, frightened appearance, anything but predatory. Constitutionally, Snuffles, like Celia, was quarry.

Appreciating that her pet mustn't be overhandled, she would poke a nervous finger through the cage door to stroke the tips of his tawny fur. When she had friends over to play, she kept her bedroom door shut while she decoyed playmates to more durable toys. Maybe that means she's learning, I prayed, about other people. (Celia was popular partly for being indiscriminate, since she brought home the playmates that other children despised—like that spoiled, strident creature Tia, whose mother had the gall to advise me quietly that it was "really better if Tia is allowed to win board games." Celia deduced as much without being told, as she asked me pensively after her bossy companion had left, "Is it okay to cheat to lose?") Contemplating our daughter as she defended Snuffles, I searched for a firmness, a resolve in her expression that might indicate an incipient capacity to defend herself.

Yet unwillingly, I considered the possibility that, while lovely to my own eye, Celia was fetching in a way that outsiders might be apt to overlook. She was only six, but I already feared that she would never be beautiful—that she was unlikely to carry herself with that much authority. She had your mouth, too wide for her small head; her lips were thin and bloodless. Her tremulous countenance encouraged a carefulness around her that was wearing. That hair, so silken and wispy, was destined to grow lank, its gold to give way to a dingier blond by her teens. Besides, isn't true beauty a tad enigmatic? And Celia was too artless to imply concealment. She had an available face, and there is something implicitly uninteresting about the look of a person who will tell you whatever you want to know. Why, already I could see it: She would grow into the kind of adolescent who conceives a doomed crush on the president of the student council, who doesn't know she's alive. Celia would always give herself away cheaply. Later, she would move in— too young—with an older man who would abuse her generous nature, who would leave her for a more buxom woman who knows how to dress. But at least she would always come home to us for Christmas, and had she opportunity, she would make a far finer mother than I ever was.

Kevin shunned Snuffles, its very name an indignity to a teenage boy. He was more than willing to catch spiders or crickets and dangle the live morsels into the cage—standard boy-stuff and the perfect job for him, since Celia was too squeamish. But the cool, deadpan teasing was merciless. You couldn't have forgotten the night I served quail, and he convinced her that the scrawny carcass on her plate was you-know-who.

I know, Snuffles was just a pet, an expensive pet, and some kind of unhappy ending was inevitable. I should have thought of that before I gave her the little beast, though surely to avoid attachments for fear of loss is to avoid life. I had hoped he'd last longer, but that wouldn't have made it any easier for Celia when calamity hit.

That night in February 1998 is the only instance I can remember of Celia's dissembling. She kept darting around the house, crawling on the floor, picking up the couch skirting and peering under the sofa, but when I asked her what she was looking for she chirped, "Nothing!" She continued scuffling around on all fours past her bedtime, refusing to explain the game she was playing, but begging to play it longer. Finally, enough was enough, and I hauled her off to bed as she struggled. It wasn't like her to be such a brat.

"How's Snuffles?" I asked, trying to distract her when I turned on the light.

Her body stiffened, and she didn't look at the cage when I bounced her onto the mattress. After a pause, she whispered, "He's fine."

"I can't see him from here," I said. "Is he hiding?"

"He's hiding," she said, in an even smaller voice.

"Why don't you go find him for me?"

"He's *hiding*," she said again, still not looking at the cage.

The elephant shrew did sometimes sleep in a corner or under a branch, but when I searched the cage myself, I couldn't spot any tufts. "You didn't let *Kevin* play with Snuffles, did you?" I asked sharply, in the same tone of voice I might have asked, *You didn't put Snuffles in a blender, did you?*

"It's all my fault!" she gasped, and began to sob. "I th-thought I closed the cage door, but I guess I d-d-d-didn't! 'Cause when I came in after supper it was open and he was gone! I've looked everywhere!" *Shsh, now there, we'll find him*, I cooed, but she would not be quieted. "I'm stupid! Kevin says so and he's right. I'm stupid! Stupid, stupid, stupid!" She hit herself so hard on the temple with her balled up fist that I had to grab her wrist.

I was hopeful that her crying jag would burn itself out, but a little girl's grief has astonishing staying power, and the strength of her self-loathing tempted me to make false promises. I assured her that Snuffles could not have got very far and that he would *definitely* be right back in his cozy cage by morning. Grasping at my perfidious straw, Celia shuddered and lay still.

I don't think we gave up until about 3 A.M.—and thanks, again, for your help. You had another scouting job the next day, and we would both miss sleep. I can't think of a cranny we didn't check; you moved the dryer, I combed the trash. Mumbling good-naturedly, "Where is that bad boy?" you pulled all the books out of the lower shelves while I steeled myself to check for hair in the disposal.

"I don't want to make this worse with an I-told-you-so," you said when we both collapsed in the living room with dust balls in our hair. "And I did think it was cute. But that's a rare, delicate animal, and she's in first grade."

"But she's been so conscientious. Never out of water, careful about overfeeding. Then to just, leave the door open?"

"She is absent-minded, Eva."

"True. I suppose I could order another one . . . "

"Fugeddaboutit. One lesson in mortality is enough for the year."

"You think maybe he got outside?"

"In which case he's already frozen to death," you said cheerfully.

"Thanks."

"Better than *dogs*. . . . "

That was the story I put together for Celia the next day: that Snuffles had gone to play outdoors, where he was much happier with lots of nice fresh air, and where he'd make lots of animal friends. Hey, why not turn it to my advantage? Celia would believe anything.

All things being equal, I'd expect to recollect our daughter's ashen mope of the following week, but not ordinary housekeeping chores. But under the circumstances, I have good reason to recall that the kids' bathroom sink backed up that weekend. Janis wouldn't be in until Monday, and I'd never spurned a little upkeep of my own home now and again. So I smote the clog with a few glugs of Liquid-Plumr, poured in one cup of cold water, and left it to sit, according to the directions. Then I put the Liquid-Plumr away. Did you seriously imagine that after all this time I would change my story? *I put it away.*

Eva

Dear Franklin,

My God, there's been another one. I should have known on Monday afternoon when all my coworkers suddenly started to avoid me.

Standard issue. In a suburb outside San Diego, fifteen-year-old Charles "Andy" Williams—a scrawny, unassuming-looking white kid with thin lips and matted hair like well-trod carpet—brought a .22 to Santana High School in his backpack. He hid out in the boys' bathroom, where he shot two, proceeding to the hallway to fire at anything that moved. Two students were killed, thirteen injured. Once he had retreated to the bathroom again, the police found him cowering on the floor with the gun to his head. He whimpered incongruously, "It's only me"; they arrested the boy without a struggle. It almost goes without saying by now that he'd just broken up with his girlfriend—who was twelve.

Curiously, on the news Monday night, some of his fellow students characterized the shooter, as usual, as "picked on," persecuted as a "freak, a dork, and a loser." Yet a whole other set of kids attested that Andy had plenty of friends, wouldn't remotely qualify as unpopular or especially ragged on, and was to the contrary "well-liked." These latter descriptions must have confused our audience, since when Jim Lehrer revisited the story tonight for another inquiry into *why, why, why,* all depictions along the lines of "well-liked" had been expunged. If Andy Williams hadn't been "bullied," he failed to support the now fashionable revenge-of-the-nerds interpretation of these incidents, which were now meant to teach us not stricter gun control but concern for the agonies of the underage outcast.

Accordingly, while "Andy" Williams is now nearly as famous as his crooner counterpart, I doubt there's a news consumer in the country who could tell you the name of either of the two students he shot dead—teenagers who never did anything wrong outside of heading to the bathroom on a morning that their more fortunate classmates resolved to hold their bladders through Geometry: Brian Zuckor and Randy Gordon. Exercising what I can only regard as a civic duty, I have committed their names to heart.

I've heard parents throughout my life allude to horrifying incidents in which something happened to their children: a full-immersion baptism by a boiling pot of turkey stew or the retrieval of a wayward cat via an open third-story window. Prior to 1998, I had casually assumed that I knew what they were talking about—or what they avoided talking about, since there's often a private fence around such stories, full access to which, like intensive care units, only immediate family is allowed. I'd always respected those fences. Other people's personal disasters of any sort are exclusionary, and I'd be grateful for that Don't Enter sign, behind which I might shelter a secret offensive relief that my own loved ones were safe. Still I imagined that I knew roughly what lay on the other side. Be it a daughter or a grandfather, anguish is anguish. Well, I apologize for my presumption. I had no idea.

When you're the parent, no matter what the accident, no matter how far away you were at the time and how seemingly powerless to avert it, a child's misfortune feels like your fault. You're all your kids have, and their own conviction that you will protect them is contagious. So in case you expect, Franklin, that I'm simply setting about one more time to deny culpability, to the contrary. Broadly, it still feels like my fault, and broadly, it felt like my fault at the time.

At the very least, I wish I'd stuck to my guns on our child-care arrangements. We'd hired Robert, that seismology student from Lamont-Doherty Earth Observatory, to pick up Celia from school and stick around the house until one of us got home, and that's the way the rules should have stayed. Against all odds, we managed to keep Robert, too— though he threatened to quit—once we assured him that Kevin was now old enough to look after himself and he need only look after Celia. But you were on this responsibility kick. Kevin was fourteen, as old as many sitters in our neighborhood. If Kevin was to become trustworthy, he had first to be trusted; sure, it sounded good. So you told our child-minder that as long as Kevin had returned from ninth grade and had been apprised that he was now to keep an eye on Celia, Robert could go. That solved the problem that kept cropping up, that you would get stuck in traffic and I would work a bit late, and (however well-compensated for his time) Robert would get stranded, chafing, on Palisades Parade when he had research at Lamont to which he needed to return.

When I try to remember that Monday, my mind shies, like ducking a hurtling tether ball. Then the memory curves centrifugally back around again, so that when I stand back up it hits me in the head.

I was once more working a little late. The new arrangement with Robert made me feel less guilty for putting in an extra hour, and AWAP's preeminence in the budget-travel niche had started to slide. We had so much more competition than when I started out—*The Lonely Planet* and *The Rough Guide* had sprung up; meanwhile, with the whole country aslosh in cash from a buoyant stock market, demand for the really dirt-cheap travel in which we specialized had dropped. So against my better judgment, I was working up a proposal for a whole new series, *Wing and a Prayer for Boomers*—whose target audience would be flush with Internet start-up stock, probably overweight, nostalgic about their first seat-of-the-pants trip to Europe with a beat-up copy of *W&P* in the sixties, convinced they were still college students if not in fact then in spirit, accustomed to $30 cabernets but, by conceit, still adventurous, that is, eager for comfort so long as that's not what it was called and by all means in horror of resorting to the stodgy *Blue Guide* like their parents—when the phone rang.

You said to drive carefully. You said that she was already in the hospital and there was nothing I could do now. You said that her life was not endangered. You said that more than once. All this was true. Then you said that she was going to be "all right," which was not true, though for most messengers of dismal tidings the urge to issue this groundless reassurance seems to be irresistible.

I had no choice but to drive carefully, because the traffic on the George Washington Bridge was barely moving. When at last I laid eyes on your collapsed expression in the waiting room, I realized that you loved her after all, which I castigated myself for ever having doubted. Kevin wasn't with you, to my relief, because I might have clawed his eyes out.

Your embrace had rarely offered so little solace. I kept hugging you harder to get something out of it, like squeezing an empty bottle of hand lotion until it wheezes.

She was already in surgery, you explained. While I'd driven in, you'd run Kevin home, because there was nothing to do but wait, and there was no point making this harder on her brother than it was already. But I wondered if you hadn't whisked him from the waiting room to safeguard him from me.

We sat in those same sea-green metal chairs where I had agonized over what Kevin would tell the doctors when I broke his arm. Maybe, I supposed miserably, for the last eight years he'd been *biding his time.* I said, "I don't understand what happened." I was quiet; I didn't shout.

You said, "I thought I told you. Over the phone."

"But it doesn't make sense." Anything but contentious, my tone was simply baffled. "Why would she—what would she be doing with that stuff?"

"Kids." You shrugged. "Playing. I guess."

"But," I said. "She'll, ah—." My mind kept blanking out. I had to reconstruct what I'd wanted to say all over again, repeating the conversation to myself, where we were, what came next. . . . Bathroom. Yes.

"She'll go to the bathroom by herself now," I resumed. "But she doesn't like it in there. She never has. She wouldn't *play* in there." An incipient insistence in my voice must have sounded dangerous; we would shrink back from the ledge. Celia was still in surgery. We wouldn't fight, and you would hold my hand.

It seemed hours later that the doctor emerged. You'd called home on your cell phone, twice, out of my earshot as if sparing me something; you'd bought me coffee from the machine along the wall, and it was now topped with crinkled skin. When a nurse pointed us out to the surgeon, I suddenly understood why some people worship their doctors, and why doctors are prone to feel godlike. But with one look at his face, I could see that he wasn't feeling very godlike.

"I'm sorry," he said. "We really tried. But there was too much damage. I'm afraid we couldn't save the eye."

We were encouraged to go home. Celia was heavily sedated, and she would remain so for some time. Not long enough, I thought. So we stumbled from the waiting room. At least, you pointed out numbly, he says the other eye is probably okay. Just that morning I'd taken for granted the fact that our daughter had two.

Out in the parking lot, it was cold; in my flight from the office, I'd left my coat. We had two cars to drive home, which made me feel colder. I sensed we were at a junction of sorts and feared that if we each launched off in separate vehicular universes we would end up in the same place only in the most banal, geographical sense. You must have felt the same need to confirm that we were, as my staff had lately taken to saying five times a day, *on the same page*, because you invited me into your truck for a few minutes to debrief and get warm.

I missed your old baby-blue pickup, which I associated with our courtship, powering along the turnpike with the windows down and sound system pounding, like a living Bruce Springsteen lyric. And the pickup was more you, old-you anyway: classic, down-home, honest. Pure, even. Edward Hopper would never have painted the bulky 4x4 with which you replaced it. Reared up unnaturally above wide, oversized tires, the body had the blunted, bulging contours of an inflatable dinghy. Its bullying fenders and puffed-up posture reminded me of those poor little lizards whose only weapon is display, and the truck's overdrawn, cartoon manliness had prompted me to quip in better days, "If you check under the chassis, Franklin, I bet you'll find a tiny dick." At least you'd laughed.

The heating worked well; too well, since once we'd idled for a few minutes the cab got stuffy. It was bigger than the Ford, but your baby-blue had never felt this claustrophobic with just the two of us.

Finally, you knocked your head back on the padded headrest and stared at the ceiling. "I can't believe you left it out."

Stunned, I didn't respond.

"I thought about not saying that," you proceeded. "But if I swallowed it, I'd be not saying it, and not saying it, for weeks, and that seemed worse."

I licked my lips. I had begun to tremble. "I didn't leave it out."

You dropped your head, then sighed. "Eva. Don't make me do this. You used that Liquid-Plumr on Saturday. I remember because you went on about how the kids' drain smelled weird or something, and then later that afternoon you warned us not to run any water in that sink for the next hour because you'd put drain cleaner in it."

"I put it away," I said. "Back in that *high* cabinet with the child-lock on it, which Celia couldn't even reach with a chair!"

"Then *how did it get out?*"

"Good question," I said icily.

"Look, I realize that you're usually very careful with caustic substances and lock that shit up automatically. But people aren't machines—"

"I *remember* putting it away, Franklin."

"Do you *remember* putting your shoes on this morning, do you *remember* closing the door behind you when you left the house? How many times have we been in the car, and we've had to go back inside and make sure that the stove isn't on? When turning it off is presumably second nature?"

"But the stove is never on, is it? It's almost a rule of life, a, what, some kind of fortune-cookie aphorism: The Stove Is Never On."

"I'll tell you when it's on, Eva: the *one time* that you don't bother to double-check. And *that* is when the fucking house burns down."

"Why are we having this inane conversation? With our daughter in the hospital?"

"I want you to admit it. I'm not saying I won't forgive you. I know you must feel terrible. But part of getting through this has to be facing up—"

"Janis came this morning, maybe *she* left it out." In truth, I never thought for a moment that Janis had been so sloppy, but I was desperate to keep at bay the picture that began to form in my head when I entertained a more credible suspect.

"Janis had no need for drain cleaner. All the drains were clear."

"All right," I said, steeling myself. "Then ask *Kevin* how that bottle got left out."

"I knew we'd get around to this. First it's oh, what a mystery, then it's the housekeeper's fault, who's left? And, what a surprise, that Eva—who never does anything wrong herself—should finger her own son!"

"He was supposed to be taking care of her. *You* said he was old enough—"

"Yes, it was on his watch. But she was in the bathroom, he says the door was closed, and we've hardly encouraged our fourteen-year-old boy to bust in on his sister in the john."

"Franklin, this story doesn't add up. Never mind for now why it was out, all right? Forget that. But why would Celia pour drain cleaner in her *own eye?*"

"I haven't a clue! Maybe because kids are not only dumb but creative and the combination is death. Why else would we keep that shit locked up? What's important is Kevin did everything he should have. He says when she started to scream he came running, and when he found out what it was he ran water over her face and rinsed her eye the best he could, and *then* he called an ambulance, *even* before he called me on the cell—which was *just* right, the order was *just* right, he was a *star.*"

"He didn't call me," I said.

"Well," you said. "I wonder why."

"The damage—" I took a breath. "It's bad, isn't it. It had to have been very, very bad—." I had started to cry, but I made myself stop, because I had to get this out. "If she's lost the eye, and surgeons are better at this kind of thing than they used to be, then it was—. It was a mess. It takes, ah. It takes a while." I stopped again, listening to the *wah* from the heat vents. The air had grown dry, my saliva sticky. "It takes a while for that stuff to work. That's why the label tells you to—to let it sit."

Compulsively, I had pressed my fingertips against my own eyes, padding the papery lids, guarding the smooth, tender roll of the balls.

"What are you saying? Because it's bad enough to accuse him of neglect—"

"The doctor said there'd be scarring! That she was burned, all across that side of her face! Time, it would have taken time! Maybe he did wash it out, but *when?* When he was *finished?*"

You grabbed each of my arms, raised them on either side of my head, and looked me in the eye. "Finished with what? His homework? His archery practice?"

"Finished," I groaned, "with *Celia.*"

"Don't you ever say that again! Not to anyone! Not even to me!"

"Think about it!" I wrenched my arms free with a twist. "Celia, douse herself with acid? Celia's afraid of everything! And she's six, she's not *two.* I know you don't think she's very smart, but she's not retarded! She knows not to touch the stove, and she doesn't eat bleach. Meanwhile, Kevin can reach that cabinet, and Kevin can work child-locks in his sleep. He's not her *savior*. He did it! Oh, Franklin, he did it—"

"I'm ashamed of you, *ashamed*," you said at my back as I curled against the door. "Demonizing your own kid just because you can't admit to your own carelessness. It's worse than craven. It's sick. Here you're flailing around making *outrageous* accusations, and as usual you have no proof. That doctor—did he say anything about Kevin's story not squaring with her injuries? No. No, he didn't. Only his mother can detect a cover-up of some unspeakable evil because she's such a medical expert, such an expert on corrosive chemicals because she's occasionally cleaned house."

As ever, you couldn't keep shouting at me while I was crying. "Look," you implored. "You don't know what you're saying because you're upset. You're not yourself. This is hard, and it's going to keep being hard, because you're going to have to look at it. She's going to be in pain, and it's going to look nasty for a while. The only thing that's going to make it easier is if you confront your part in this. Celia—even *Celia*, with that elephant shrew—admits it's her fault. She left the cage open! And that's part of it, what hurts, that not only did something sad happen but if she'd done something differently it wouldn't have happened. She takes responsibility, and she's only six! *Why can't you?*"

"I wish I could take responsibility," I whispered, fogging the side window. "I'd say, 'Oh, I could kill myself for leaving that drain cleaner where she could find it!' Don't you see how much easier that would be? *Why* would I be so upset? If it were my fault, *only* my fault? In that case, it wouldn't be frightening. Franklin, this is serious, it's not just a little girl scratching her eczema anymore. I don't how he got this way but he's a horror, and he *hates her*—"

"That's enough!" Your announcement had a liturgical finality, deep and booming like the ringing *Amen* in a benedictory prayer. "I don't often lay down the law. But Kevin's been through an incredible trauma. His sister will never be the same. He kept his head in a crisis, and I want him to be proud of that. Still, he was the one baby-sitting, and he's inevitably going to worry that it was all his fault. So you are going to promise me, right now, that you'll do everything in your power to assure him that it *wasn't*."

I pulled the handle of the door and opened it a few inches. I thought, I have to get out of here, I have to get away.

"Don't go, not yet," you said, holding my arm. "I want you to promise."

"Promise to keep my mouth shut or to believe his feeble story? I might add, another one."

"I can't make you believe in your own son. Though I've sure as fuck tried."

On one point you were right: I didn't have any proof. Only Celia's face. Hadn't I been right. She'd never be beautiful, would she.

I climbed from the truck and faced you through the open door. The chill wind whipping my hair, I stood at attention, reminded of brittle military truces struck between mistrustful generals in the middle of barren battlefields.

"All right," I said. "We'll call it an accident. You can even tell him, 'I'm afraid your mother forgot to put the Liquid-Plumr away on Saturday.' After all, he knew I unclogged that drain. But in return you promise me: that we will never again leave Kevin alone with Celia. Not for five minutes."

"Fine. I bet Kevin's none too keen for more baby-sitting jobs right now anyway."

I said I'd see you at home; a civil farewell was an effort.

"Eva!" you called at my back, and I turned. "You know I'm not usually big on shrinks. But maybe you should talk to somebody. I think you need help. That's not an accusation. It's just—you're right on one score. This is getting serious. I'm afraid it's beyond me."

Indeed it was.

The following couple of weeks were eerily quiet around the house, with Celia still recovering in the hospital. You and I spoke little. I'd ask what you'd like for dinner; you'd say you didn't care. In relation to Celia, we largely addressed logistics—when each of us would visit. Although it seemed sensible for us to go separately so that she'd have companionship for more of the day, the truth was that neither of us was anxious to share your overheated 4x4 once more. Back home, we could discuss the particulars of her condition, and though the particulars were distressing—an infection subsequent to her *enucleation*, a vocabulary lesson I could have skipped, had further damaged the optic nerve and ruled out a transplant—

facts fed the conversational maw. Shopping for an oculist for her follow-up, I seized on a doctor named Krikor Sahatjian on the Upper East Side. Armenians look out for each other, I assured you. He'll give us special attention. "So would Dr. Kevorkian," you grunted, well aware that the godfather of assisted suicide was one Armenian my conservative community was reluctant to claim. Still, I was grateful for an exchange that almost qualified as banter, in conspicuous short supply.

I remember being on my best behavior, never raising my voice, never objecting when you barely touched a meal that I'd have gone to great trouble to fix. Cooking, I tried not to make too much noise, muffling the clang of a knocked pot. In respect to Celia's uncannily sunny disposition in Nyack Hospital, I swallowed many an admiring remark for seeming somehow indecorous, as if her improbable good nature were an affront to lesser mortals who quite reasonably wail from pain and grow irascible during convalescence. In our household, my praise of our daughter always seemed to get confused with bragging on my own account. Throughout, I made a concerted effort to *act normal*, which, along with *trying* to have fun and *trying* to be a good mother, we can now add to our list of projects that are inherently doomed.

That remark you made about my "needing help" proved disquieting. I had replayed the memory of putting that Liquid-Plumr away so many times that the tape was worn and I couldn't quite trust it. I would review my suspicions and sometimes they didn't . . . well, nothing would seem clear-cut. *Did* I put that bottle away? *Was* the injury too severe for the story the way Kevin told it? Could I point to a single shred of solid evidence that would hold up in court? I didn't want to "talk to somebody," but I'd have given my eye teeth to be able to talk to you.

It was only a couple of days after the *accident* when you convened our roundtable of three. We'd just had dinner, loosely speaking; Kevin had shoveled his food directly from the stove. Humoring you, he assumed his rueful, sideways slouch at the dining table. Having been unwillingly summoned to this convocation as well, I felt like a kid myself, once more forced at age nine to formally apologize to Mr. Wintergreen for pilfering drops from the walnut tree in his front yard. Sneaking a glance at Kevin, I wanted to say, *Wipe that smirk off your face, this isn't a joke; your sister's in the hospital.* I wanted to say, *Go put on a T-shirt that isn't five sizes too small for you, just being in the same room with that getup makes me itch.* But I couldn't. In the culture of our family, such commonplace parental admonitions, from me anyway, were impermissible.

"In case you're nervous, Kev," you began (though he didn't look nervous to me), "this isn't an inquisition. We mostly want to tell you how much you impressed us with your quick thinking. Who knows, if you hadn't called those medics in right away, it could have been even worse." (*How?* I thought. Though I suppose she could've taken a bath in it.) "And your mother has something she wants to tell you."

"I wanted to thank you," I began, avoiding Kevin's eye, "for getting your sister to the hospital."

"Tell him what you told me," you prompted. "Remember, you said you were concerned, that he might feel, you know . . . "

This part was easy. I looked at him straight on. "I thought you probably felt responsible."

Unflinching, he squinted back, and I confronted my own wide-bridged nose, my narrow jaw, my shelved brow and dusky complexion. I was looking in the mirror, yet I had no idea what my own reflection was thinking. "Why's that?"

"Because you were *supposed* to be taking care of her!"

"But you wanted to remind him," you said, "that we'd never expected him to watch her every single minute, and accidents happen, and so it *wasn't* his fault. What you told me. You know. In the truck."

It was exactly like apologizing to Mr. Wintergreen. When I was nine, I'd wanted to blurt, *Most of those stupid walnuts were wormy or rotten, you old coot,* but instead I'd promised to harvest a full peck of his crummy nuts and return them fully shelled.

"We don't want you to blame yourself." My tone duplicated Kevin's own, when he'd spoken to the police—*sir* this, *sir* that. "I'm the one at fault. I should never have left the Liquid-Plumr out of the cabinet."

Kevin shrugged. "Never said I blamed myself." He stood up. "I be excused?"

"One more thing," you said. "Your sister's going to need your help."

"Why?" he said, ranging into the kitchen. "Only one eye, wasn't it. Not like she needs a guide dog or a white stick."

"Yes," I said. "*Lucky her.*"

"She'll need your support," you said. "She's going to have to wear a patch—"

"Cool," he said. He came back with the bag of lychees from the refrigerator. It was February; they were in season.

"She'll be fitted with a glass eye down the line," you said, "but we'd appreciate your sticking up for her if neighborhood kids tease her—"

"Like how?" he said, carefully pulling the rough salmon-colored husk off the fruit, exposing the pinkish-white flesh. *"Celia does not look like a geek?"* When the pale translucent orb was peeled, he popped it in his mouth, sucked, and pulled it back out.

"Well, however you—"

"I mean, *Dad.*" Methodically, he splayed the lychee open, parting the slippery flesh from the smooth brown seed. "Not sure you remember too good, being a kid." He angled the mangle into his mouth. "Ceil's just gonna have to suck it up."

I could feel you internally beaming. Here was your teenager trotting out his archetypal teenagery toughness, behind which he hid his confused, conflicted feelings about his sister's tragic accident. It was an act, Franklin, a candy-coated savagery for your consumption. He was plenty confused and conflicted, but if you looked into his pupils they were thick and sticky as a tar pit. This teenage angst of his, it wasn't *cute.*

"Hey, Mister Plastic," Kevin offered. "Want one?" You demurred.

"I didn't know you liked lychees," I said tightly once he'd started on a second one.

"Yeah, well," he said, stripping the fruit bare and rolling the pulpy globe around the table with one forefinger. It was the ghostly, milky color of a cataract.

"It's just, they're very delicate," I said, fretting.

He tore into the lychee with his front teeth. "Yeah, whadda you call it." He slurped. *"An acquired taste."*

He was clearly planning to go through the whole bag. I rushed from the room, and he laughed.

On the days that I took the early afternoon visiting hours, I worked from home; Kevin's school bus would often drop him off at the same time as I returned from the hospital. The first time I passed him as he sauntered

languidly across Palisades Parade, I pulled over in my Luna and offered
him a ride up our steep drive. You'd think that just being alone with your
own son in a car was a pretty ordinary affair, especially for two minutes.
But Kevin and I rarely put ourselves in such stifling proximity, and I remember babbling associatively all the way up. The street was lined with
several other vehicles waiting to rescue children from having to walk as
much as ten feet on their own steam, and I remarked on the fact that every
single car was an *SRO*. It was out of my mouth before I remembered that
Kevin hated my teasing malapropism for SUV—one more pretend-gaffe
to service the myth that I didn't really live here.

"You know, those things are a metaphor for this whole country," I
went on. I had been put on notice that this sort of talk drove my son insane, but maybe that's why I pursued it, much as I would later bring up
Dylan Klebold and Eric Harris in Claverack just to goad him. "They sit
up on the road higher and mightier than anyone else, and they have more
power than anyone knows what to do with. Even the profile they cut—
they always remind me of fat shoppers, waddling down the mall in square-
cut Bermuda shorts and giant padded sneakers, stuffing their faces with
cinnamon buns."

"Yeah, well, ever ride in one?" (I admitted I hadn't.) "So what do you
know?"

"I know they piggy up too much of the road, guzzle gas, sometimes
roll over—"

"Why do you care if they roll over? You hate these people anyway."

"I don't hate—"

"*Single-room occupancy!*" Shaking his head, he slammed the VW door behind him. The next time I offered him a lift up the hill, he waved me off.

There was even something strangely unbearable about those couple of
hours he and I sometimes shared the house before your 4x4 plowed into
the garage. You'd think it would be easy enough, in that vast splay of teak,
but no matter where each of us settled I never lost an awareness of his
presence, nor he, I suspect, of mine. Lacking you and Celia as a buffer, just
the two of us in the same residence felt—the word *naked* comes to mind.
We barely spoke. If he headed for his room, I didn't ask about his homework; if Lenny stopped by, I didn't ask what they were doing; and if Kevin

left the house, I didn't ask where he was headed. I told myself that a parent should respect an adolescent's privacy, but I also knew that I was a coward.

This sensation of nakedness was assisted by the real thing. I know that fourteen-year-old boys are brimming with hormones, all that. I know that masturbation is a normal, vital relief, a harmless and enjoyable pastime that shouldn't be slandered as a vice. But I also thought that for teenagers—let's be serious, for everyone—this entertainment is covert. We all do it (or I used to—yes, once in a while, Franklin, what did you think?), we all know we all do it, but it isn't customary to say, "Honey, could you keep an eye on the spaghetti sauce, because I'm going to go masturbate."

It had to happen more than once for me to finally mention it, because after our set-to in the hospital parking lot I had blown my tattling allowance for several months.

"He leaves the bathroom door open," I reported reluctantly in our bedroom late one night, at which point you began to brush the hairs from your electric shaver intently. "And you can see the toilet from the hallway."

"So he forgets to close the door." You were clipped.

"He doesn't forget. He waits until I go to the kitchen to fix a cup of coffee, so I'll see him on my way back to my study. It's very deliberate. And he's, ah—loud."

"At his age, I probably jerked off three times a day."

"In front of your mother?"

"Around the corner, behind the door. I thought I kept it secret, but I'm sure she knew."

"Behind the door," I noted. "The door. It's important." My, that shaver was really clogged with stubble tonight. "Knowing I can see—I think it excites him."

"Well, no matter how *healthy* you try to be about it, everybody's a little weird in this department."

"You're not, um—getting it. I know he's going to do it, I don't have a problem with his doing it, but I'd rather not be included. It's inappropriate." That word took heavy duty during this era. The Monica Lewinsky scandal had broken the month before, and President Clinton would later put a napkin over the specifics by deeming their relations *inappropriate*.

"So why don't you say something?" You got tired of intercession, I suppose.

"What if Celia were masturbating in front of you? Would you talk to her about it or prefer that I did?"

"So what do you want me to say?" you asked wearily.

"That he's making me uncomfortable."

"That's a new one."

I flounced onto the bed and grabbed a book I'd be unable to read. "Just tell him to keep the goddamned door shut."

I shouldn't have bothered. Yes, you reported that you'd done as you were told. I pictured you poking your head into his room and saying something jovial and collusive about "growing a little hair on the palm," a dated expression he probably didn't get, and then I bet you tossed off, super-casual, "Just remember it's private, okay sport?" and said good-night. But even if you instead had a long, earnest, stern discussion, you'd have tipped him off that he'd gotten to me, and with Kevin that's always a mistake.

So the very next afternoon after your "talk," I'm heading to the study with my cup of coffee and I can hear a telltale grunting down the hall. I'm praying that he's gotten the message and there will at least be a thin but blessed wooden barrier between me and my son's budding manhood. I think: Aside from closets, there are only about four, five doors in the whole bloody house, and we should really be getting our money's worth out of them. But as I advance another step or two the noise level belies this most minimal attempt at propriety.

I press my warm coffee cup between my eyes to soothe a nascent headache. I've been married for nineteen years and I know how men work and there's no reason to be afraid of a glorified spigot. But subjected to the urgent little moans down the hall, I'm ten years old again, sent on errands across town for my shut-in mother, having to cut through the park, eyes trained straight ahead while older boys snicker in the bushes with their flies down. I feel stalked, in my own house, nervous, hounded, and mocked, and I don't mind telling you I'm pretty pissed off about it.

So I dare myself, the way I always got home in the old days, when I would discipline myself not to run and so give chase. I march rather than tiptoe down the hall, heels hitting the floorboards, clop-clop. I get to the kids' bathroom, door agape, and there is our firstborn in all his pubescent splendor, down to a rash of fiery pimples on his backside. Feet planted wide and back arched, he has pivoted his stance at an angle to the toilet so that I can see his handiwork—purple and gleaming with what I first assume is K-Y jelly, but which the silver wrapper on the floor suggests is my Land O'Lakes unsalted butter—and this is my introduction to the fact that my son has now grown fine, uncommonly straight pubic hair. Though most males conduct this exercise with their eyes closed, Kevin has cracked his open, the better to shoot his mother a sly, sleepy glance over the shoulder. In return, I glare squarely at his cock—doubtless what I should have done in the park instead of averting my gaze, since the appendage is so unimpressive when confronted head-on that it makes you wonder what all the fuss is about. I reach in and pull the door shut, hard.

The hallway rings with a dry chuckle. I clip back to the kitchen. I've spilled coffee on my skirt.

So. I know you must have wondered. Why didn't I simply walk out? Nothing stopped me from grabbing Celia while she still had one eye left and hightailing it back to Tribeca. I could have left you with your son and that horrible house, a matched set. After all, I had all the money.

I'm not sure you'll believe me, but it never occurred to me to leave. I may have spent long enough in your orbit to have absorbed your ferocious conviction that a happy family cannot be a mere myth or that even if it is, better to die trying for the fine if unattainable than sulking in passive, cynical resignation that hell is other people you're related to. I hated the prospect of defeat; if in bearing Kevin to begin with I picked up my own gauntlet, bearing Kevin on a daily basis involved rising to a greater challenge still. And there may have been a practical side to my tenacity as well. He was about to turn fifteen. He had never spoken of college—had never spoken of his adult future at all; never having expressed the slightest interest in a trade or profession, for all I knew he was sticking to his five-year-old vow to go on welfare. But theoretically our son was out of the house in about three years. Thereafter, it would just be you, me, and Celia, and then we would see about that happy family of yours. Those three years are almost over now, and if they have proved the longest of my life, I had no way of anticipating that at the time. Lastly, and this may strike you as simplistic, I loved you. I loved you, Franklin. I still do.

Nevertheless, I did feel under siege. My daughter had been half blinded, my husband doubted my sanity, and my son was flouting his butter-greased penis in my face. Abetting the sensation of assault from all sides, Mary Woolford chose this of all times to make her first indignant visit to our house—and the last, come to think of it, since the next time we'd meet would be in court.

She was still whippet slim then, her dark hair jet to the roots so I'd never have known it was dyed; the way it was pinned up was a tad severe. Even to make this neighborly call she was dressed to the nines in a Chanel suit, a demure jeweled spray on her lapel twinkling with respectability. Who'd have guessed that a scant three years later she'd be shambling the Nyack Grand Union in a streaked outfit that needed pressing and vandalizing raw eggs in the child seat of another woman's cart.

She introduced herself curtly, and, despite the chill, declined an invitation inside. "My daughter, Laura, is a lovely girl," she said. "A mother would naturally think so, but I believe her attractiveness is also apparent to others. With two important exceptions: Laura herself, and that young man of yours."

I wanted to reassure the woman that by and large, my surly son failed to see the attractiveness of anyone, but I sensed that we were still in the preamble. This sounds unkind considering that my son would, in just over a year, murder this woman's daughter, but I'm afraid I took an immediate dislike to Mary Woolford. She moved jaggedly, her eyes shifting this way and that, as if roiling from some constant inner turmoil. Yet some people coddle their own afflictions the way others spoil small pedigreed dogs with cans of pâté. Mary struck me straight off as one of this sort, for whom my private shorthand was Looking for a Problem—rather a waste of detective powers I always thought, since in my experience most proper problems come looking for you.

"For the last year or so," Mary continued, "Laura has suffered under the misapprehension that she is overweight. I'm sure you've read about the condition. She skips meals, she buries her breakfast in the trash, and lies about having eaten at a friend's. Laxative abuse, diet pills—suffice it to say that it's all very frightening. Last September she got so frail that she was hospitalized with an intravenous drip, which she would tear out if not watched round the clock. Are you getting the picture?"

I mumbled something feebly commiserating. I would normally lend a sympathetic ear to such stories, though just then I couldn't help thinking that my daughter was in the hospital, too, and not—I was fiercely convinced—because she done anything stupid to herself. Besides, I'd heard too many Karen Carpenter tales at Gladstone PTA meetings, and they often took the form of boasts. The prestigious diagnosis of anorexia seemed much coveted not only by the students but by their mothers, who would compete over whose daughter ate less. No wonder the poor girls were a mess.

"We had been making progress," Mary continued. "For the last few months she's submitted to her modest portions at family meals, which she is compelled to attend. She's finally gained a little weight back—as your son Kevin was *more than eager to point out.*"

I sighed. In comparison to our visitor, I must have looked haggard. What I wouldn't have looked is surprised, and my failure to gasp oh-my-goodness-me-what-has-that-boy-done seemed to inflame her.

"Last night I caught my beautiful daughter vomiting her dinner! I got her to admit, too, that she's been making herself upchuck for the last week. *Why?* One of the boys at school keeps telling her she's *fat!* Barely 100 pounds and she's tormented for being a 'porker'! Now, it wasn't easy to get his name out of her, and she begged me not to come here tonight. But I for one believe it's time we parents start accepting responsibility for our children's destructive behavior. My husband and I are doing everything we can to keep Laura from hurting herself. So you and your husband might please keep your son from hurting her, too!"

My head bobbed like one of those dogs in car windows. "Ho-ow?" I drawled. It's possible she thought I was drunk.

"I don't care how—!"

"Do you want us to *talk to him?*" I had to tighten the corners of my mouth to keep them from curling into an incredulous smirk all too reminiscent of Kevin himself.

"I should think so!"

"Tell him to be *sensitive to the feelings of others* and to *remember the Golden Rule?*" I was leaning on the door jamb with something close to a leer, and Mary stepped back in alarm. "Or maybe my husband could have a *man-to-man chat,* and teach our son that a *real man* isn't cruel and aggressive, but a *real man* is gentle and compassionate?"

I had to stop for a second to keep from laughing. I suddenly pictured you jaunting into the kitchen to report, *Well, honey, it was all a big misunderstanding! Kevin says that poor skin-and-bones Laura Woolford simply heard wrong! He didn't call her "fat," he called her "fab"! And he didn't say she was a "porker"—he said she told a joke that was a "corker"!* A grin must have leaked out despite me, because Mary turned purple and exploded, "I cannot for the life of me understand why you seem to think this is funny!"

"Ms. Woolford, do you have any boys?"

"Laura is our only child," she said reverently.

"Then I'll refer you back to old schoolyard rhymes as to just what *little boys are made of.* I'd like to help you out, but practically? If Franklin and I say anything to Kevin, the consequences for your daughter at school will be even worse. Maybe it's better you teach Laura—what do the kids say? To *suck it up.*"

I would pay for this bout of realism later, though I could hardly have known then that my hard-bitten counsel would be trotted out in Mary's testimony at the civil trial two years hence—with a few acid embellishments for good measure.

"Well, thank you for nothing!"

Watching Mary harumph down the flagstones, I reflected on the fact that you, Kevin's teachers, and now this Mary Woolford woman were regaling me that as a mother I must *accept responsibility.* Fair enough. But if I was so all-fired responsible, why did I still feel so helpless?

Celia came home at the beginning of March. Kevin had never been to visit her once; protective, I'd never encouraged him. You'd issued the odd invitation to come along, but backed off in deference to his trauma. He never even asked how she was doing, you know. Anyone listening in wouldn't have thought he had a sister.

I had only made modest headway in accommodating myself to her new appearance. The burns spattered on her cheek and streaked across her temple, though starting to heal, were still crusty, and I begged her not to pick at them lest she make the scarring even worse. She was good about it, and I thought of Violetta. Hitherto out of touch with monocular fashions, I'd expected her eye patch to be black, and Shirley Temple flashbacks of *The Good Ship Lollipop* may have comforted me with anodyne visions of my little blond pirate. I think I'd have preferred a black one, too, so that I might have run out to buy her a three-cornered hat and made some pathetic attempt at turning this macabre nightmare into a fancy-dress game to distract her.

Instead, the flesh color of those stick-on 3M Opticlude patches turned the left-hand side of her face blank. Swelling on the left side obliterated any defining structures like her cheekbone. It was as if her face wasn't quite three-dimensional anymore, but rather like a postcard, with a picture on one side and clean white paper on the other. I could catch a glimpse of her right-hand profile, and for a moment my cheerful moppet was unchanged; with a glimpse of the left, she was erased.

This now-you-see-me, now-you-don't quality to her countenance gave expression to my painful new awareness that children were a perishable consumer good. Though I don't think I had ever taken her for granted, once she came home I pretty much gave up on whatever effort I had ever made to disguise my preference for one child over the other. She could never bring herself to leave my side any longer, and I allowed her to shadow me softly around the house and join me on errands. I'm sure you were right that we shouldn't have let her slip any further behind in school and that the sooner she got used to her disability in public the better, but I still took some time off from AWAP and kept her home for two more weeks. Meanwhile, she lost some of the skills she had mastered, for instance, tying her tennis shoes, and I'd have to go back to tying them for her and start the lesson from scratch.

I watched her around Kevin like a hawk. I admit that she did not act afraid of him. And he went right back to issuing her a plenitude of bored orders; ever since she'd gotten old enough to run and fetch, he'd treated her like a pet with a limited range of tricks. But even in response to some small, harmless request like to grab him a cracker or toss him the TV remote, I thought I now detected in his sister a momentary hesitation, a little freeze, like a hard swallow. And though she had once begged to carry his quiver and felt honored to help him prize his arrows from the target out back, the first time he casually suggested that she resume these duties, I put my foot down: I knew he was careful, but Celia had only one eye left and she was not to go near that archery range. I had expected Celia to whimper. She was always desperate to prove of use to him and had loved to watch her brother stand Hiawatha-tall and release those arrows unerringly into the bull's-eye. Instead she shot me a glance that looked grateful, and her hairline glistened from a light sweat.

I was surprised when he invited her out to play Frisbee—play with his sister, now that was a first—and even a little impressed. So I told her it was all right so long as she wore her safety glasses; my relationship to her good eye now was hysterical. But when a few minutes later I looked out the window, he was *playing with* his sister only in the sense that one plays with the Frisbee itself. Celia's depth perception was still very poor, and she kept grabbing for the Frisbee before it had reached her, missing, and then it would hit her in the chest. Very funny.

Of course, the hardest part at first was addressing that hole in Celia's head, which had to be swabbed frequently with baby shampoo and a moistened Q-Tip. While Dr. Sahatjian assured us that the secretions would subside once the prosthesis was fitted and the healing complete, at first the cavity oozed that yellowish discharge continually, and sometimes in the morning I'd have to soak the area with a wet Kleenex because the lid would have crusted shut in her sleep. The lid itself sagged—*sulcus*, her oculist called it—and was also puffy, especially since it had been damaged by the acid and had been partially reconstructed with a small flap of skin from Celia's inner thigh. (Apparently eyelid augmentation has developed into a fine art because of high demand in Japan for anglification of Occidental features, which in better days I'd have found a horrifying testimony to the powers of Western advertising.) The swelling and slight purpling made her look like one of those battered children in posters that encourage you to turn in your neighbors to the police. With one eyelid depressed and her other eye open, she seemed to be winking hugely, as if we shared a lurid secret.

I'd told Sahatjian that I wasn't sure I could bring myself to clean that hollow daily; he assured me that I'd get used to it. He was right in the long run, but I fought a swell of nausea when I first lifted the lid myself with my thumb. If it wasn't quite as harrowing as I'd feared, it was disturbing on a subtler level. No one was home. The effect recalled those almond-eyed Modiglianis whose absence of pupils give the figures a hypnotic mildness and tranquillity, though a dolorousness as well, and a hint of stupidity. The cavity went from pink at the rim to a merciful black toward the back, but when I got her under the light to administer her antibiotic drops, I could see that incongruous plastic conformer, which kept the socket from collapsing; I might have been staring into a doll.

I know you resented my fawning over her so much, and that you felt bad for resenting it. In compensation, you were firmly affectionate with Celia, drawing her into your lap, reading her stories. Me, I recognized too well the mark of deliberateness about these efforts—so this was *trying to be a good father*—but I doubt that it looked to Kevin like anything other than surfaces would suggest. Clearly his little sister's injury had won her only more doting—more *Do you need an extra blanket, honey?* more *Would you like another piece of cake?* more *Why don't we let Celia stay up, Franklin, it's an animal show.* Checking out the tableau in the living room as Celia fell asleep in the crook of your arm and Kevin glared at "My Granny Had My Boyfriend's Baby" on Jerry Springer, I thought, *Didn't our little stratagem backfire.*

In case you're wondering, I did not ply Celia unduly for details about that afternoon in the bathroom. I was every bit as shy of discussing the matter as she was; neither of us had any desire to relive that day. Yet out of a sense of parental obligation—I didn't want her to think the subject taboo, in case its exploration would prove therapeutic—I did ask her just once, casually, "When you got hurt? What happened?"

"Kevin—." She pawed at the lid with the back of her wrist; it itched, but lest she dislodge the conformer she had learned to always rub toward her nose. "I got something in my eye. Kevin helped me wash it out."

That's all she ever said.

Eva

Dear Franklin,

It looks as if that Andy Williams thing sparked off a rash of copycat crimes. But then, they're all copycat crimes, don't you agree?

There were four more School Shootings that spring of 1998. I remember clearly when news came in of the first one, because that was the same day Dr. Sahatjian did the drawings for Celia's prosthesis and then took a mold of her socket. Celia was entranced when he painstakingly painted the iris of her good eye by hand; I was surprised that it wasn't scanned by computer, but still limned with fine brushes in watercolors. Iris-painting is apparently quite an art, since every eye is as unique as a fingerprint, and even the whites of our eyes have a distinctive color, their fine red veins a personal skein. It was certainly the only element of this agonizing process that could have passed for charming.

As for the mold making, we'd been assured that it wouldn't be painful, though she might experience "discomfort," a term beloved of the medical profession that seems to be a synonym for agony that isn't yours. Though the stuffing of her socket with white putty was indisputably unpleasant, she merely mewled a little; she never really cried. Celia's bravery was peculiarly disproportionate. She was a stoic little trooper when she lost an eye. She still screamed bloody murder if she spotted mildew on the shower curtain.

As his assistant restored the conformer and applied a fresh eye patch, I asked Krikor Sahatjian idly what drew him to this niche occupation. He volunteered that at age twelve, when taking a shortcut through a neighbor's yard, he had climbed over a spiked fence; he slipped, and the tip of an arrow-shaped iron rod . . . . Leaving the rest mercifully to my imagination, he said, "I was so fascinated by the process of making my own prosthesis that I decided I'd found my calling." Incredulous, I looked again at his soulful brown eyes, reminiscent of Omar Sharif's. "You're surprised," he said amiably. "I hadn't noticed," I admitted. "You'll find that's common," he said. "Once the prosthesis is in, many people will never know that Celia is monocular. And there are ways of covering it up—moving your head instead of your eyes to look at someone. I'll teach her, when she's ready." I was grateful. For the first time her *enucleation* didn't seem like the end of the world, and I even wondered if the distinction the disability conferred, and the strength it could summon, might help Celia grow into herself.

When Celia and I returned from the Upper East Side, you'd gotten home before us and were settled in the den with Kevin in front of one of those Nick at Night back-to-back binges of *Happy Days*. I commented in the doorway, "Ah, the 1950s that never were. I keep waiting for somebody to tell Ron Howard about Sputnik, McCarthyism, and the arms race." I added ruefully, "Though I see you two are *bonding*."

In those days, I always lavished a laden irony on trendy American buzz phrases, as if picking them up with rubber gloves. In kind, I had explained to Kevin's English teacher that the misuse of the word *literally* was "one of my issues" with an exaggerated wink-and-nod that must only have perplexed the woman. I'd always thought of American culture as a spectator sport, on which I could pass judgment from the elevated bleachers of my internationalism. But these days I join in aping beer advertisements when my workmates at Travel R Us cry in unison, *Whass uuuuup?*, I use *impact* as a transitive verb, and I omit prissy quotation marks. Real culture you don't observe but embody. I live here. As I would soon discover in spades, there is no opt-out clause.

Our son, however, could read all the above and more into my disdainful pronunciation of *bonding*. "Is there anything, or anybody," he asked, looking me in the eye, "you don't feel superior to?"

"I've been candid with you about my problems with this country," I said stiffly, leaving little doubt that this candor was the source of regret, and making perhaps my sole allusion since to our disastrous dinner at Hudson House. "But I don't know what gives you the idea that I feel 'superior.'"

"Ever notice you never talk about Americans as 'we'?" he said. "It's always 'they.' Like you'd talk about the Chinese or something."

"I've spent a large amount of my adulthood out of the country, and I probably—"

"Yeah, yeah, yeah." Kevin broke eye contact and stared back at the screen. "I just want to know what makes you think you're so *special.*"

"Eva, grab a seat and join the fun!" you said. "This is the one where Richie's forced to blind-date the boss's daughter, so he gets Potsie—"

"Meaning you've seen it twenty times," I chided affectionately, thankful for your rescue. "How many *Happy Days* has it been in a row now, three or four?"

"This is the first one! Five more to go!"

"Before I forget, Franklin—I got Dr. Sahatjian to agree to glass." Petting Celia's fine blond hair as she hung on my leg, I refrained from citing glass-what. It had fallen to me earlier that afternoon to disabuse our daughter of the expectation that her new eye would be able to see.

"E-va," you sang, not in the mood for a fight. "Polymer is state of the a-art."

"So is this German Cryolite."

"Fewer infec-tions, less chance of brea-kage—"

"*Polymer*'s just a fancy name for plastic. I hate plastic." I closed the argument, *"Materials are everything."*

"Look at that," you pointed out to Kevin. "Richie sleazes out of the date, and it turns out she's a hottie."

I didn't want to poop your party, but the mission from which I'd just returned was pretty grim, and I couldn't immediately start munching your visual junk food. "Franklin, it's almost seven. Can we please watch the news?"

"Bor-ing," you cried.

"Not lately it isn't." Monica-gate was still breaking in prurient slow motion. "Lately it's X-rated. Kevin?" I turned politely to our son. "Would you mind very much if, after this episode is over, we switched to the news?"

Kevin was slumped in the easy chair, eyes at half-mast. "Whatever."

You sang along with the signature tune, Monday, Tuesday, happy days . . . ! as I knelt to pick white putty from Celia's hairline. At the hour, I switched to Jim Lehrer. It was the lead story. For once our president would have to keep his fly zipped to make way for two unpleasant little boys in his home state, the older of whom was all of thirteen, the younger only eleven.

I groaned, flopping onto the leather couch. "Not another one."

Outside Westside Middle School in Jonesboro, Arkansas, Mitchell Johnson and Andrew Golden had lain in wait, huddled in the bushes in camouflage outfits after setting off the school's fire alarm. As students and teachers exited the building, the two opened fire with a Ruger .44-caliber rifle and a 30.06 hunting rifle, killing four girls and one teacher, and injuring eleven other students. Himself wounded, if only by romantic disappointment, the older boy had apparently warned a friend the day before with cinematic swashbuckling, "I got some killin' to do," while little Andrew Golden had sworn to a confidant that he was planning to shoot "all the girls who'd ever broken up with him." A single boy was injured; the other fifteen victims were female.

"Fucking idiots," I growled.

"Yo, Eva!" you abjured. "Watch the mouth."

"More drowning in self-pity!" I said. *"Oh, no, my girlfriend doesn't love me any more, I'm gonna go kill five people!"*

"What about all that Armenian shit?" asked Kevin, cutting his eyes toward me flintily. *"Oh, no, like, a million years ago the Turks were big meanies and now nobody cares!* That's not self-pity?"

"I'd hardly put genocide on a par with being jilted," I snapped.

"Nyeh *nyeh*-nyeh nyeh NYEH-nyeh-nyeh nyeh-nyeh *nyeh* nyeh nyeh-nyeh NYEE-nyeeh!" Kevin mocked under his breath. "Jesus, give it a rest."

"—And what's this about wanting to kill *all the girls who'd ever broken up with him?*" I jeered.

"Could you *shut up?*" said Kevin.

"Kevin!" you scolded.

"Well, I'm *trying* to follow this, and she *said* she wanted to watch the news." Kevin often spoke of his mother as I spoke of Americans. We both preferred the third person.

"But the brat's eleven years old!" I hated people who talked over the news, too, but I couldn't contain myself. "How many girlfriends can that be?"

"On average?" said our resident expert. "About twenty."

"Why," I said, "how many have *you* had?"

"Ze-ro." Kevin was now so slumped as to be nearly supine, and his voice had a gravelly creakiness that he would soon employ all the time. "Hump 'em and dump 'em."

"Whoa, Casanova!" you said. "This is what we get for telling a kid the facts of life at seven."

"Mommy, who are Humpum and Dumpum? Are they like Tweedle-dum and Tweedledee?"

"Celia, sweetheart," I said to our six-year-old, whose sexual education did not seem so urgent. "Wouldn't you like to go play in the playroom? We're watching the news, and it's not much fun for you."

"Twenty-seven bullets, sixteen hits," Kevin calculated appreciatively. "Moving targets, too. You know, for little kids that's a decent percentage."

"No, I want to stay with you!" said Celia. "You're my friennnd!"

"But I want a picture, Celia. You haven't drawn me a picture all day!"

"Oh-kay." She lingered, fisting her skirt.

"Here, first give me a hug, then." I drew her to me, and she threw her arms about me. I wouldn't have thought a six-year-old could squeeze so hard, and it was painful to have to pry her fingers from my clothing when she wouldn't let go. Once she had shuffled out of the room, after pausing in the archway and waving with a cupped hand, I caught you rolling your eyes at Kevin.

In the meantime, a reporter on screen was interviewing Andrew Golden's grandfather, from whom some of the kids' stockpile of weapons had been stolen, including three high-powered rifles, four pistols, and a trove of ammunition. "It's a terrible tragedy," he said unsteadily. "We've lost. They've lost. Everybody's lives are ruined."

"You can say that again," I said. "I mean, what was ever going to happen but they'd be nabbed and nailed and put away for eternity? What were they thinking?"

"They weren't thinking," you said.

"You kidding?" said Kevin. "This stuff takes planning. 'Course they were thinking. Probably never thought harder in their whole crummy lives." From their first occurrence, Kevin owned these incidents, and whenever the subject arose he assumed an air of authority that got on my nerves.

"They weren't thinking about what comes next," I said. "They may have thought out their stupid attack, but not the next five minutes—much less the next fifty years."

"Wouldn't be so sure," said Kevin, reaching for a handful of nacho tortilla chips with glow-in-the-dark cheese. "You weren't listening—as usual—cause Celie had to have her huggy-wuggies. They're under fourteen. According to the law in Arkansas, Batman and Robin there'll be back in the Batmobile by eighteen."

"That's outrageous!"

"Records sealed, too. Bet everybody in Jonesboro's really lookin' forward to it."

"But you can't seriously imagine that they took a trip to the law library beforehand and checked out the statute books."

"Mm," Kevin hummed noncommittally. "How do you know? Anyway, maybe it's dumb to think about the future all the time. Put off the present long enough and it, like, never happens, know what I'm sayin'?"

"They have lower sentences for juveniles for good reason," you said. "Those kids had no idea what they were doing."

"You don't think so," said Kevin caustically. (If he was offended by my ridicule of adolescent angst, our son may have been more affronted by your compassion.)

"No eleven-year-old has any real grasp of death," you said. "He doesn't have any real concept of other people—that they feel pain, even that they exist. And his own adult future isn't real to him, either. Makes it that much easier to throw it away."

"Maybe his future is real to him," said Kevin. "Maybe that's the problem."

"Come on, Kev," you said. "All the kids in these shootings have been middle class, not guys from some urban sewer. Those boys were looking at a life with a mortgage and a car and a job in management, with yearly holidays to Bali or something."

"Yeah," Kevin purred. "Like I said."

"You know what?" I said. "Who cares. Who cares whether shooting people is or isn't real to them, and who cares about their painful bust-ups with girlfriends that don't even have tits yet. Who cares. The problem is guns. Guns, Franklin. If guns weren't kicking around these people's houses like broom handles, none of these—"

"Oh God, here we go again," you said.

"You heard Jim Lehrer say that in Arkansas it isn't even illegal for minors to possess firearms?"

"They stole them—"

"They were there to steal. And both boys owned rifles of their own. It's absurd. No guns, and those two creeps go kick a cat, or—*your* idea of how to solve differences—go punch their ex-girlfriends in the face. Bloody nose; everybody goes home. These shootings are so inane that I'd think you'd be grateful to find some little turd of a lesson in them."

"Okay, I can see restricting automatic weapons," you said, getting that preachy sound that for me was the bane of parenthood. "But guns are here to stay. They're a big part of this country, target shooting and hunting, not to mention self-defense—." You stopped because I had obviously stopped listening.

"The answer, if there is one, is the *parents*," you resumed, now ranging the room and raising your voice above the TV, from which Monica Lewinsky's big fat lovelorn face was once more ogling. "You can bet your bottom dollar those boys had no one to turn to. No one they could really pour their hearts out to, who they could trust. When you love your kids, and you're there for them, and you take them on trips, like to museums and battlefields, and make time for them, you have faith in them and express an interest in what they think? *That's* when this kind of plunging off the deep end doesn't happen. And if you don't believe me, *ask Kevin.*"

But for once Kevin wore his derision on his sleeve. "Yeah, *Dad!* It makes a real big difference to me that I can tell you and Mumsey anything, especially when I'm under all this *peer pressure* and junk! You always ask what *video games* I'm playing or what my *homework* is, and I always know I can turn to you in *times of need!*"

"Yeah, well, if you couldn't turn to us, buster," you grumbled, "you wouldn't think it was so damned funny."

Celia had just crept back to the den's archway, where she hung back, fluttering a piece of paper. I had to motion her inside. She'd always seemed undefended, but this cringing, Tiny Tim meekness of hers was new, and I hoped it was only a phase. After resealing the edges of her Opticlude bandage, I pulled her into my lap to admire her picture. It was discouraging. Dr. Sahatjian's white coat was drawn so large that his head was off the page; the self-portrait of Celia herself rose only to the oculist's knee. Although her drawings were usually light, deft, and meticulous, in the place where her left eye should have been, she's crayoned a formless scribble that violated the outline of her cheek.

Meanwhile, you were asking, "Seriously, Kev—do any of the students at your school ever seem unstable? Does anyone ever talk about guns, or play violent games or like violent movies? Do you think something like this could happen at your school? And are there at least counselors there, professionals kids can talk to if they're unhappy?"

Broadly, you probably did want answers to these questions, but their caring-Dad intensity came across as self-serving. Kevin cased you before he replied. Kids have a well-tuned radar to detect the difference between an adult who's interested and an adult who's keen to seem interested. All those times I stooped to Kevin after kindergarten and asked him what he did that day—even as a five-year-old he could tell that I didn't care.

"All the kids at my school are unstable, Dad," he said. "They play nothing but violent computer games and watch nothing but violent movies. You only go to a counselor to get out of class, and everything you tell her is a crock. Anything else?"

"I'm sorry, Franklin," I said, lifting Celia to sit beside me, "but I don't see how a few more heart-to-hearts are going to put the brakes on what is clearly becoming some kind of fad. It's spreading just like *Teletubbies*, only instead of having to have a rubber doll with a TV in its belly, every teenager has to shoot up his school. This year's must-have accessories: a *Star Wars* cell phone and a *Lion King* semiautomatic. Oh, and some accompanying sob story about being picked on, or ditched by a pretty face."

"Show a little empathy," you said. "These are disturbed boys. They need help."

"They're also *imitative* boys. Think they didn't hear about Moses Lake and West Palm Beach? About Bethel, Pearl, and Paducah? Kids pick up things on TV, they listen to their parents talking. Mark my words, every well-armed temper tantrum that goes down only increases the likelihood of more. This whole country's lost, everybody copies everybody else, and everybody wants to be famous. In the long term, the only hope is that these shootings get so ordinary that they're not news anymore. Ten kids get shot in some Des Moines primary school and it's reported on page six. Eventually any fad gets to be uncool, and thank God at some point hip thirteen-year-olds just won't want to be *seen* with a Mark-10 in second period. Until then, Kevin, I'd keep a sharp eye on any of your classmates who start feeling sorry for themselves in camouflage gear."

As I reconstruct this tirade of mine, I can't help but observe its implicit lesson: that if School Shootings would inevitably grow hackneyed, ambitious adolescents with a taste for the headlines had best make their bids while the going was good.

Just over a month later in Edinboro, Pennsylvania, fourteen-year-old Andrew Wurst promised one day to make his eighth-grade graduation dance "memorable," and indeed, the next day he did. On the patio of Nick's Place at 10 P.M., where 240 middle-schoolers were dancing to "My Heart Will Go On" from the film *Titanic,* Wurst shot a forty-eight-year-old teacher fatally in the head with his father's .25-caliber handgun. Inside, he fired several more shots, wounding two boys and grazing a female teacher. Fleeing out the back, he was apprehended by the owner of Nick's Place, who was carrying a shotgun and convinced the fugitive to back down in the face of superior firepower. As journalists were eager to observe for a welcome note of drollery, the theme of the dance was "I've Had the Time of My Life."

Each of these incidents was distinguished by whatever sorry lessons could be squeezed from it. Wurst's nickname was "Satan," which resonated with the commotion over Luke Woodham in Pearl having been involved in a demonic cult. Wurst was a fan of an androgynous heavy-metal vocalist called Marilyn Manson, a man who jumped about on stage in poorly applied eyeliner, so this singer who was only trying to make an honest buck out of teenage bad taste was deplored in the media for a spell. Myself, I was sheepish about having been so derisive regarding the precautions taken at Kevin's own eighth-grade dance the previous year. As for the shooter's motivation, it sounded amorphous. "He hated his life," said a friend. "He hated the world. He hated school. The only thing that would make him happy was when a girl he liked would talk to him"—exchanges that we're forced to conclude were infrequent.

Maybe School Shootings were already growing passé, because the story of eighteen-year-old Jacob Davis in Fayetteville, Tennessee, in mid-May pretty much got lost in the shuffle. Davis had already won a college scholarship and had never been in trouble. A friend remarked to reporters later, "He didn't hardly ever even talk. But I guess that's the ones that will get you—the quiet ones." Outside his high school three days before they were both to graduate, Davis approached another senior who was dating his ex-girlfriend and shot the boy thrice with a .22-caliber rifle. It seems the breakup had hit him hard.

I may have been impatient with lovesick teen melodrama, but as killers go Davis was a gentleman. He left a note behind in his car assuring his parents and his former girlfriend how much he loved them. Once the deed was done, he put down his gun, sat down next to it, and put his head in his hands. He stayed just like that until the police arrived, at which time the papers reported that he "surrendered without incident." This time, anomalously, I was touched. I could see it: Davis knew he had done something stupid, and he had known it was stupid beforehand. For these two facts to be concurrently true would present him with the great human puzzler for the rest of his four-walled life.

Meanwhile, out in Springfield, Oregon, young Kipland Kinkel had digested the lesson that wasting a single classmate was no longer a sure route to immortality. Just three days after Jacob Davis broke his beloved parents' hearts, this scrawny, weasel-faced fifteen-year-old upped the ante. Around 8 A.M. as his classmates at Thurston High finished up their breakfast, Kinkel walked calmly into the school cafeteria bearing a .22-caliber handgun, a 9-millimeter Glock, and a .22-caliber semiautomatic rifle under a trench coat. Deploying the most efficacious weapon first, he sprayed the room with rifle fire, shattering windows and sending students diving for cover. Nineteen in the cafeteria were shot but survived, while four additional students were injured in the panic to get out of the building. One student was killed outright, a second would die in the hospital, and a third would have died as well, had Kipland's semiautomatic not run out of ammunition. Pressed to a boy's temple, the rifle went *click, click, click.*

As Kinkel scrambled to insert a second clip, sixteen-year-old Jake Ryker—a member of the school wrestling team who'd been shot in the chest—lunged at the killer. Kinkel pulled a pistol from his trench coat. Ryker grabbed the gun and wrenched it away, taking another bullet in the hand. Ryker's younger brother jumped on the shooter, then helped wrestle him to the ground. As other students piled on top, Kinkel shouted, "Shoot me, shoot me now!" Under the circumstances, I'm rather surprised they didn't.

Oh, and *by the way:* Once in custody, Kinkel advised the police to check his home address—a lovely two-story house in an affluent subdivision lush with tall firs and rhododendrons—where they discovered a middle-aged man and woman shot dead. For at least a day or two there was much evasion in the press about who these two people might be exactly, until Kinkel's grandmother identified the bodies. I'm a little disconcerted as to just who the police imagined might be living in Kinkel's home besides his parents.

Now, as they go, this story was rich, its moral agreeably clear. Little Kipland had bristled with "warning signs" that hadn't been taken with sufficient seriousness. In middle school, he'd been voted "Most Likely to Start World War III." He had recently given a class presentation on how to construct a bomb. In the main, he was predisposed to vent violent inclinations through the most innocuous of schoolwork. "If the assignment was to write about what you might do in a garden," said one student, "Kipland would write about mowing down the gardeners." Though in an eerie coincidence Kip Kinkel's initials were also "KK," he was so universally disliked by his schoolmates that even after his performance in the cafeteria they refused to give him a nickname. Most damningly of all, the very day before the shooting he had been arrested for possession of a stolen firearm, only to be released into his parents' custody. So the word went out: Dangerous students give themselves away. They can be spotted, ergo, they can be stopped.

Kevin's school had been acting on this assumption for most of that school year, though news of every new shooting jacked up the paranoia another notch. Gladstone High had taken on a battened-down, military atmosphere, except the McCarthyite presumption ran that the enemy was within. Teachers had been provided lists of deviant behaviors to look out for, and in school assemblies students were coached to report the most casually threatening remark to the administration, even if it "seemed like" a joke. Essays were combed for an unhealthy interest in Hitler and Nazism, which made teaching courses in twentieth-century European History rather tricky. Likewise, there was a supersensitivity to the satanic, so that a senior named Robert Bellamy, who was known by the handle "Bobby Beelzebub," was hauled before the principal to explain—and change—his sobriquet. An oppressive literalism reigned, so that when some excitable sophomore screamed, "I'm gonna kill you!" to a volleyball teammate who dropped the ball, she was slammed into the guidance counselor's office and expelled for the rest of the week. Yet there was no safe haven in the metaphoric, either. When a devout Baptist in Kevin's English class wrote in a poem, "My heart is a bullet, and God is my marksman," his teacher went straight to the principal, refusing to teach her class again until the boy was transferred. Even Celia's primary school grew fatally po-faced: A boy in her first-grade class was kicked out for three days because he had pointed a chicken drumstick at the teacher and said, "Pow, pow, pow!"

It was the same all over the country, if the embarrassing little squibs in *New York Times* sidebars were anything to go by. In Harrisburg, Pennsylvania, a fourteen-year-old girl was strip searched—*strip searched*, Franklin—and suspended when, in a class discussion about School Shootings, she said she could see how kids who'd been teased might eventually snap. In Ponchatoula, Louisiana, a twelve-year-old boy was locked up in juvenile detention for an entire two weeks because his warning to his fellow fifth-graders in the cafeteria line that he'd "get them" if they didn't leave him enough potatoes was construed as a "terrorist threat." On a two-page web site, Buffythevampireslayer.com, an Indiana student posited a theory that must have crossed many a high-schooler's mind from time to time that his teachers were devil worshipers; unsatisfied with his mere suspension, his teachers filed a federal lawsuit charging both the boy and his mother with defamation and infliction of emotional distress. A thirteen-year-old was suspended for two weeks because on a field trip to Albuquerque's Atomic Museum, he had piped, "Are they going to teach us how to build a bomb?" while another boy got the third degree from a school administrator just for carrying his chemistry

textbook. Nationwide, kids were expelled for wearing trench coats like Kipland Kinkel, or just for wearing black. And my personal favorite was a nine-
year-old's suspension after a class project about diversity and Asian culture,
during which he wrote the fortune cookie message, "You will die an honor-
able death."

Although Kevin was ordinarily tight-lipped about goings-on at his
school, he went out of his way to deliver us tidbits of this escalating hysteria. The reportage had the intended effect: You were more afraid *for* him;
I was more afraid *of* him. He enjoyed the sensation of seeming dangerous,
yet clearly regarded the school's precautions as farcical. "They keep this
up," he remarked once, and on this point he was astute, "they just gonna
give kids *ideas*."

It was an evening near graduation, a falling off the edge of childhood
that for seniors always has a hint of the apocalyptic, and so might have
made the faculty antsy even without Kip Kinkel's help. After his usual dinner—a brutish nosh before the open refrigerator—Kevin cooled back in
the den's easy chair and delivered the latest installment: The entire student
body had just been subjected to a "lockdown" in their classrooms for four
periods straight while the police searched every locker and prowled the
hallways with sniffer-dogs.

"What were they looking for, drugs?" I asked.

Kevin said lightly, "Or *poems*."

"It's this Jonesboro-Springfield nonsense," you said. "They were obviously looking for guns."

"What really slays me," said Kevin, stretching out and spewing his
words like cigarette smoke, "—if you'll *excuse* the expression—is they sent
a memo on the search procedure to the teachers? That loser drama teacher,
Pagorski, left it on her desk, and Lenny saw it—I was impressed; didn't
know he could read. Anyway, word got around. Whole school knew this
was coming. Kid with an AK in his locker had plenty of time to reconsider his piss-poor hiding place."

I asked, "Kevin, didn't any of your classmates object to this?"

"Few of the girls did, after a while," he said airily. "Nobody could
take a leak, see. Fact," Kevin achieved a wheezy little laugh, "that donkey-
face Ulanov wet herself."

"Did anything make the administration especially alarmed? Or was it just, oh it's Wednesday, why don't we play with sniffer-dogs?"

"Probably an anonymous tip. They run a telephone hotline now, so you can rat out your friends. For a quarter, I could get out of Environmental Science any day of the week."

"An anonymous tip from whom?" I asked.

"*Hello-o.* If I told you who it was, then it wouldn't be anonymous, would it?"

"Well after all that bother, did they even find anything?"

"Sure they did," Kevin purled. "Shitload of overdue library books. Some old French fries that were starting to stink. One really juicy, evil poem had them going for while, till it turned out to be Big Black lyrics: *This is Jordan, we do what we like* . . . —Oh, and one more thing. A list."

"What kind of list?"

"A hit list. Not 'My Favorite Songs,' but the other kind. You know, with THEY ALL DESERVE TO DIE scrawled at the top, big as life."

"Jesus!" You sat up. "These days, that's not funny."

"Noooo, they didn't think it was funny."

"I hope they're planning to give this kid a good talking-to," you said.

"Oooh, I think they'll do better than a *talking-to.*"

"Well, who was it?" I asked. "Where did they find it?"

"In his locker. Funniest thing, too. Last guy you'd expect. Superspic."

"Kev," you said sharply. "I've warned you about that kind of language."

"'Scuse me. I mean *Señor Espinoza.* Guess he's just bustin' with *ethnic hostility* and *pent-up resentment* on behalf of *the Latino people.*"

"Hold on," I said. "Didn't he win some big academic prize last year?"

"Can't say as I recall," said Kevin blithely. "But that three-week suspension is going to nasty up his record something terrible. *Ain't* that a shame? Geez, and you think you know people."

"If everyone knew this search was coming," I said, "why wouldn't this Espinoza boy clear such an incriminating list from his locker beforehand?"

"Dunno," said Kevin. "Guess he's an amateur."

I drummed my fingers on the coffee table. "These lockers. The kind I grew up with had slits in the top. Aeration vents. Do yours?"

"Sure," he said, heading from the room. "So the French fries keep better."

They suspended the valedictorian-in-waiting; they made Greer Ulanov pee her pants. They punished the poets, the hotheaded sportsmen, the morbidly dressed. Anyone with a jazzy nickname, an extravagant imagination, or the less than lavish social portfolio that might mark a student as an "outcast" became suspect. As far as I could tell, it was War on Weirdos.

But I identified with weirdos. In my own adolescence, I had strong, stormy Armenian features and so wasn't considered pretty. I had a funny name. My brother was a quiet, dour nobody who'd scored me no social points as a predecessor. I had a shut-in mother who would never drive me anywhere or attend school functions, if her insistence on continuing to manufacture excuses was rather sweet; and I was a dreamer who fantasized endlessly about escape, not only from Racine but the entire United States. Dreamers don't watch their backs. Were I a student at Gladstone High in 1998, I'd surely have written some shocking fantasy in sophomore English about putting my forlorn family out of its misery by blowing the sarcophagus of 112 Enderby Avenue to kingdom come, or in a civics project on "diversity" the gruesome detail in which I recounted the Armenian genocide would betray an *unhealthy* fascination with violence. Alternatively, I'd express an inadvisable sympathy with poor Jacob Davis sitting beside his gun with his head in his hands, or I'd tactlessly decry a Latin test as *murderous*—one way or another, I'd be out on my ear.

Kevin, though. Kevin wasn't weird. Not so's you notice. He did brandish the tiny-clothes thing, but he didn't wear all black, and he didn't skulk in a trench coat; "tiny clothes" were not on the official photocopied list of "warning signs." His grades were straight Bs, and no one seemed to find this astonishing but me. I thought, this is a bright kid, grade inflation is rife, you'd think he'd make an A by *accident*. But no, Kevin applied his intelligence to keeping his head below the parapet. I think he overdid it, too. That is, his essays were so boring, so lifeless, and so monotonous as to border on deranged. You'd think someone would have noticed that those choppy, stultifying sentences ("Paul Revere rode a horse. He said that the British were coming. He said, 'The British are coming. The British are coming.'") were sticking two fingers up his teacher's butt. But it was only when he wrote a paper contrived to repeatedly use the words *snigger*, *niggardly*, and *Nigeria* for his Black History teacher that he pushed his luck.

Socially, Kevin camouflaged himself with just enough "friends" so as not to appear, alarmingly, a loner. They were all mediocrities—exceptional mediocrities, if there is such a thing—or outright cretins like Lenny Pugh. They all pursued this minimalist approach to education, and they didn't get into trouble. They may well have led a whole secret life behind this gray scrim of bovine obedience, but the one thing that didn't raise a red flag at his high school was being suspiciously drab. The mask was perfect.

Did Kevin take drugs? I've never been sure. You agonized enough about how to approach the subject, whether to pursue the rectitudinous course and denounce all pharmaceuticals as the sure route to insanity and the gutter or to play the reformed hell-raiser and vaunt a long list of substances that you once devoured like candy until you learned the hard way that they could rot your teeth. (The truth—that we hadn't cleaned out the medicine cabinet, but we'd both tried a variety of recreational drugs, and not only in the sixties but up to a year before he was born; that better living through chemistry had driven neither of us to an asylum or even to an emergency room; and that these gleeful carnival rides on the mental midway were far more the source of nostalgia than remorse—was *unacceptable*.) Each path had pitfalls. The former doomed you as a fuddy-duddy who'd no notion what he was talking about; the latter reeked of hypocrisy. I recall you finally charted some middle way and admitted to smoking dope, told him for the sake of consistency that it was okay if he wanted to "try it," but to not get caught, and to please, please not tell anyone that you'd been anything but condemnatory about narcotics of any kind. Me, I bit my lip. Privately I believed that downing a few capsules of ecstasy could be the best thing that ever happened to that boy.

As for sex, the accuracy of that "hump 'em and dump 'em" boast is up for grabs. If I've claimed, of us two, to "know" Kevin the better, that is only to say that I know him for being opaque. I know that I don't know him. It's possible he's still a virgin; I'm only sure of one thing. That is, if he has had sex, it's been grim—short, pumping; shirt on. (For that matter, he could have been sodomizing Lenny Pugh. It's uncannily easy to picture.) Hence Kevin may even have heeded your stern caution that if he ever felt ready for sex he should always use a condom, if only because a slimy rubber sheath bulging with milky come would have made his vacuous encounters that much more delectably sordid. I reason that nothing about a blindness to beauty necessitates a blindness to ugliness, for which Kevin long ago developed a taste. Presumably there are as many fine shades of the gross as the gorgeous, so that a mind full of blight wouldn't preclude a certain refinement.

There was one more matter at the end of Kevin's ninth-grade school year that I never bothered you about, but I'll mention it in passing for the sake of being thorough.

I'm sure you would remember that in early June, AWAP's computers were contaminated with a computer virus. Our technical staff traced it to an e-mail titled, cleverly, "WARNING: Deadly new virus in circulation." No one seemed to trouble with hard-copy dumps or those chintzy little floppies anymore, so that since the virus also infected our backup drive, the results were disastrous. With file after file, access was denied, it didn't exist, or it came up on screen all squares, squiggles, and tildes. Four different editions were put back for at least six months, encouraging scores of our most devoted bookstores, including the chains, to put in bountiful orders for *The Rough Guide* and *The Lonely Planet* when *Wing and a Prayer* couldn't satisfy the brisk summer market with up-to-date listings. (We didn't make any friends, either, when the virus sent itself to every e-mail address on our marketing list.) We never fully recouped the trade we lost that season, so the fact that I was forced to sell the company in 2000 for less than half its valuation two years earlier traces in some measure to this contagion. For me, it substantially contributed to 1998's zeitgeist of siege.

I did not tell you about its source out of shame. I should never have been snooping, you'd say. I should have minded every parenting manual's edict to respect the inviolability of a child's bedroom. If I suffered dire consequences, I had made my own bed. It's the oldest switcheroo in the book, and a favorite of the faithless the world over: When folks discover something incriminating by poking around where they're not supposed to, you immediately flip the issue to the snooping itself, to distract from what they found.

I'm not sure what led me to go in there. I'd stayed home from AWAP to take Celia in for another oculist appointment, to check on her adaptation to the prosthesis. There was little enough in Kevin's room to attract curiosity, though it may have been this very quality—its mysterious blankness—that I found so magnetic. When I creaked open the door I felt powerfully that I wasn't meant to be there. Kevin was in school, you were scouting, Celia was poring over homework that should have taken her ten minutes and would therefore take her a good two hours, so the chances of my being discovered were slim. Still, my heart raced and my breath was bated. This is silly, I told myself. I'm in my own house, and if improbably interrupted I can claim to be checking for dirty dishes.

Fat chance, in that room. It was immaculate; you teased Kevin about being a "granny," he was such a neatnik. The bed was made with boot-camp precision. We'd offered him a bedspread of racing cars or Dungeons and Dragons; he'd been quite firm on preferring plain beige. The walls were unadorned; no posters of Oasis or the Spice Girls, no leering Marilyn Manson. The shelves lay largely bare: a few textbooks, a single copy of *Robin Hood*; the many books we gave him for Christmas and birthdays simply disappeared. He had his own TV and stereo system, but about the only "music" I'd heard him play was some kind of Philip Glass-like CD that sequenced computer-generated phrases according to a set mathematical equation; it had no form, no peaks or valleys, and approximated the white noise that he would also tune in on the television when he was not watching the Weather Channel. Again, the CDs we'd given him when trying to sort out what he "liked" were nowhere in evidence. Though you could get delightful screen savers of leaping dolphins or zooming space-ships, the one on his Gateway merely pointillated random dots.

Was this what it looked like inside his head? Or was the room, too, a kind of screen saver? Just add a seascape above the bed, and it looked like an unoccupied unit at a Quality Inn. Not a photograph at his bedside, nor keepsake on his bureau—the surfaces were slick and absent. How much I'd have preferred to walk into a hellhole jangling with heavy-metal, lurid with *Playboy* centerfolds, fetid from muddy sweats, and crusty with year-old tuna sandwiches. That was the kind of no-go teen lair that I understood, where I might discover safe, accessible secrets like a worn Durex packet under the socks or a baggie of cannabis stuffed in the toe of a smelly sneaker. By contrast, the secrets of this room were all about what I would not find, like some trace of my son. Looking around, I thought uneasily, *He could be anyone.*

But as for its conceit that there was nothing to hide, I wasn't buying. So when I spotted a stack of floppies on the shelf above the computer, I shuttled through them. Inscribed with characterless perfect printing, their titles were obscure: "Nostradamus," "I Love You," "D4-X." Feeling wicked, I picked one of them out, put the rest back the way I found them, and slipped out the door.

In my study, I inserted the floppy in my computer. I didn't recognize the suffixes on the A drive, but they weren't regular word-processing files, which disappointed me. In hoping to find a private journal or diary, I may have been less eager to discover the precise content of his inmost thoughts than to confirm that at least he *had* inmost thoughts. Not about to give up easily, I went into the Explorer program and loaded one of the files; perplexingly, Microsoft Outlook Express came up on screen, at which point Celia called from the dining table that she needed help. I was gone for about fifteen minutes.

When I returned, the computer was blank. It had shut itself off, which it had never done without being told. Disconcerted, I turned it on again but got nothing but error messages, even when I took the disk from the drive.

You're way ahead of me. I carted the thing into work the next day so that my technical people might sort it out, only to discover the entire office milling about. It wasn't exactly pandemonium, more like the atmosphere of a party that had run out of drink. Editors were chatting aimlessly in one another's cubicles. No one was working. They couldn't. There wasn't a terminal functioning. Later I was almost relieved when George informed me that my PC's hard drive was so corrupted that I might as well buy a new one. Perhaps with the infectious object destroyed, no one would ever know that the virus had been forwarded by AWAP's own executive director.

Furious at Kevin for keeping the modern equivalent of a pet scorpion, I held onto the disk as evidence for several days rather than discreetly sliding it back on his shelf. But once I simmered down, I had to admit that Kevin hadn't personally wiped out my company's files, and the debacle was my fault. So one evening I knocked on his door, was granted admission, and closed it behind me. He was sitting at the desk. The screen saver was blipping in its desultory fashion, dot here, dot there.

"I wanted to ask you," I said, tapping his floppy. "What's this?"

"A virus," he said brightly. "You didn't load it in, did you?"

"Of course not," I said hastily, discovering that lying to a child feels much the same as lying to a parent; my cheeks prickled as they had when I assured my mother after losing my cherry at seventeen that I'd spent the night with a girlfriend she'd never heard of. Mother knew better; Kevin did, too. "I mean," I revised mournfully, "only once."

"Only takes once."

We both knew that it would have been ridiculous for me to have sneaked into his room and stolen a disk, with which I subsequently ruined my computer and paralyzed my office, only to come storming in to accuse him of industrial sabotage. So the interchange proceeded with an evenness.

"Why do you have it?" I asked respectfully.

"I keep a collection."

"Isn't that a peculiar thing to collect?"

"I don't like stamps."

Just then I had a presentiment of what he might have said had you burst in determined to find out *why the heck* he had a stack of computer viruses above his desk: *Well, after we watched* Silence of the Lambs, *I decided I wanted to be an FBI agent! And you know how they have this whole task-force that, like, tracks down hackers who spread those terrible computer viruses? So I'm studying them and everything, 'cause I've read it's a really big problem for the new economy and globalization and even for our country's defense . . . !* That Kevin skipped such a performance—he collected computer viruses, end of story, so what?—left me feeling strangely flattered.

So I asked bashfully. "How many do you have?"

"Twenty-three."

"Are they—difficult to find?"

He looked at me gamely, with that old sense of indecision, but on some whim he decided to experiment with talking to his mother. "They're hard to *capture alive*," he said. "They get away, and they bite. You have to know how to handle them. You know—like a doctor. Who studies diseases in a lab but doesn't want to get sick himself."

"You mean, you have to keep them from infecting your own machine."

"Yeah. Mouse Ferguson's been teaching me the ropes."

"Since you collect them. Maybe you can explain to me—why do people make them? I don't get it. They don't achieve anything. What's the appeal?"

"I don't get," he said, "what you don't get."

"I understand hacking into AT&T to get free phone calls or stealing encrypted credit card numbers to run up a bill at The Gap. But this sort of computer crime—nobody benefits. What's the point?"

"That is the point."

"I'm still lost," I said.

"Viruses—they're kind of elegant, you know? Almost—pure. Kind of like—charity work, you know? It's *selfless*."

"But it's not that different from creating AIDS."

"Maybe somebody did," he said affably. "'Cause otherwise? You type on your computer and go home and the refrigerator comes on and another computer spits out your paycheck and you sleep and you enter more shit on your computer . . . Might as well be dead."

"So it's this—. Almost to, what, know you're alive. To show other people they don't control you. To prove you can do something, even if it could get you arrested."

"Yeah, pretty much," he said appreciatively. In his eyes, I had exceeded myself.

"Ah," I said, and handed him his disk back. "Well, thanks for explaining."

As I turned to go, he said, "You're computer's fucked, isn't it."

"Yes, it's fucked," I said ruefully. "I guess I deserved it."

"You know, if there's anybody you don't like?" he offered. "And you got their e-mail address? Just lemme know."

I laughed. "Okay, I'll be sure to do that. Though, some days? The people I don't like come to quite a list."

"Better warn them you got friends in low places," he said.

So this is *bonding!* I marveled, and closed the door.

Eva

MARCH 16, 2001

Dear Franklin,

Well, it's another Friday night on which I gird myself for a visit to Chatham tomorrow morning. The halogen bulbs are trembling again, flickering like my stoic resolve to be a good soldier and live out what's left of my life for the sake of some unnamable duty. I've sat here for over an hour, wondering what keeps me going, and more specifically just what it is I want from you. I guess it goes without saying that I want you back; the volume of this correspondence—though it's more of a *respondence*, isn't it?—attests heavily to that. But what else? Do I want you to forgive me? And if so, for what exactly?

After all, I was uneasy with the unsolicited tide of forgiveness that washed over the shipwreck of our family in the wake of *Thursday*. In addition to mail promising either to beat his brains out or to bear his babies, Kevin has received dozens of letters offering to share his pain, apologizing for society's having failed to recognize his spiritual distress and granting him blanket moral amnesty for what he has yet to regret. Amused, he's read choice selections aloud to me in the visiting room.

Surely it makes a travesty of the exercise to forgive the unrepentant, and I speak for myself as well. I, too, have received a torrent of mail (my e-mail and postal address were billboarded on both partnersnprayer.org and beliefnet.com without my consent; apparently at any one time, thousands of Americans have been praying for my salvation), much of it invoking a God in whom I was less disposed to believe than ever, while sweepingly acquitting my shortcomings as a mother. I can only assume that these well-meaning people felt moved by my plight. Yet it bothered me that nearly all this deliverance was bestowed by strangers, which made it seem cheap, and an undercurrent of preening betrayed that conspicuous clemency has become the religious version of driving a flashy car. By contrast, my brother

Giles's staunch incapacity to pardon us for the unwelcome attentions that our wayward son has visited upon his own family is a grudge I treasure, if only for its frankness. Thus I was of half a mind to mark the envelopes "Return to sender," like Pocket Fishermans and Gensu knives I hadn't ordered. In the early months, still asthmatic with grief, I was more in the mood for the bracing open air of the pariah than for the close, stifling confines of Christian charity. And the vengefulness of my hate mail was meat-red and raw, whereas the kindness of condolences was pastel and processed, like commercial baby food; after reading a few pages from the merciful, I'd feel as if I'd just crawled from a vat of liquefied squash. I wanted to shake these people and scream, *Forgive us! Do you know what he did?*

But in retrospect it may grate on me most that this big dumb absolution latterly in vogue is doled out so selectively. Weak characters of an everyday sort—bigots, sexists, and panty fetishists—need not apply. "KK" the murderer harvests sheaves of pitying pen pals; an addled drama teacher too desperate to be liked is blackballed for the rest of her life. From which you may correctly construe that I'm not so bothered by the caprices of all America's compassion as I am by yours. You bent over backward to be understanding about killers like Luke Woodham in Pearl and little Mitchell and Andrew in Jonesboro. So why had you no sympathy to spare for Vicki Pagorski?

The first semester of Kevin's sophomore year in 1998 was dominated by that scandal. Rumors had circulated for weeks, but we weren't in the loop, so the first we heard about it was when the administration sent that letter around to all Ms. Pagorski's drama students. I'd been surprised that Kevin elected to take a drama course. He tended to shy from the limelight in those days, lest scrutiny blow his Regular Kid cover. On the other hand, as his room suggested, *he could be anybody*, so he may have been interested in acting for years.

"Franklin, you should take a look at this," I said one November evening while you were grumbling over the *Times* that Clinton was a "lying sack of shit." I handed you the letter. "I don't know what to make of it."

As you adjusted your reading glasses, I had one of those juddering update moments when I realized that your hair had now passed decisively from blond to gray. "Seems to me," you determined, "this lady's got a taste for tenderloin."

"Well, you have to infer that," I said. "But if someone's made an accusation, this letter's not defending her. *If your son or daughter has reported anything irregular or inappropriate . . . Please speak to your child . . .* They're digging for more dirt!"

"They have to protect themselves. —KEV! Come into the den for a sec!"

Kevin sauntered across the dining area in tiny dove-gray sweats, their elastic ankles bunched under his knees.

"Kev, this is a little awkward," you said, "and you haven't done anything wrong. Not a thing. But this drama teacher, Ms.—Pagorski. Do you like her?"

Kevin slumped against the archway. "Okay, I guess. She's a little . . . "

"A little what?"

Kevin looked elaborately in all directions. "Hinky."

"Hinky how?" I asked.

He studied his unlaced sneakers, glancing up through his eyelashes. "She like, wears funny clothes and stuff. Not like a teacher. Tight jeans, and sometimes her blouse—" He twisted, and scratched an ankle with his foot. "Like, the buttons at the top, they're not . . . See, she gets all excited when she's directing a scene, and then . . . It's sort of embarrassing."

"Does she wear a bra?" you asked bluntly.

Kevin averted his face, suppressing a grin. "Not always."

"So she dresses casually, and sometimes—provocatively," I said. "Anything else?"

"Well, it's not a big deal or anything, but she does use a lot of dirty words, you know? Like, it's okay, but from a teacher and everything, well, like I said, it's hinky."

"Dirty like *damn* and *hell?*" you prodded. "Or harder core?"

Kevin raised his shoulders helplessly. "Yeah, like—sorry, Mumsey—"

"Oh, skip it, Kevin," I said impatiently; his discomfiture seemed rather overdone. "I'm a grown-up."

"Like *fuck*," he said, meeting my eyes. "She says, like, *That was a fucking good performance*, or she'll direct some guy, *Look at her like you really want to fuck her, like you want to fuck her till she squeals like a pig.*"

"Little out there, Eva," you said, eyebrows raised.

"What does she look like?" I said.

"She's got big, uh," he mimed honeydews, "and a really wide," this time he couldn't contain the grin, "like, a huge butt. She's old and everything. Sort of a hag, basically."

"Is she a good teacher?" I said.

"She's sure into it anyway."

"Into it how?" you said.

"She's always trying to get us to stay after school and practice our scenes with her. Most teachers just want to go home, you know? Not Pagorski. She can't get enough."

"Some teachers," I said sharply, "are very passionate about their work."

"That's what she is," said Kevin. "Real, real *passionate*."

"Sounds like she's a little bohemian," you said, "or a bit of a loon. That's all right. But other things aren't all right. So we need to know. Has she ever touched you. In a flirtatious way. Or—below the waist. In any way that made you uncomfortable."

The squirming became extravagant, and he scratched his bare midriff as if it didn't really itch. "Depends on what you mean by *uncomfortable*, I guess."

You looked alarmed. "Son, it's just us here. But this is a big deal, all right? We have to know if anything—happened."

"Look," he said bashfully. "No offense, Mumsey, but would you mind? I'd rather talk to Dad in private."

Frankly, I minded very much. If I was going to be asked to trust this story, I wanted to hear it myself. But there was nothing for it but to excuse myself to the kitchen and fret.

Fifteen minutes later, you were steamed. I poured you a glass of wine, but you couldn't sit down. "Tell you what, Eva, this woman went beyond the pale," you murmured urgently, and gave me the lowdown.

"Are you going to report this?"

"Bet your life I'm going to report this. That teacher should be fired. Hell, she should be arrested. He's underage."

"Do you—do you want to go in together?" I'd been about to ask instead, *Do you believe him?* but I didn't bother.

I left turning state's evidence to you, while I volunteered to meet Dana Rocco, Kevin's English teacher, for a routine parent-teacher conference.

Whisking out of Ms. Rocco's classroom at 4 P.M., Mary Woolford passed me in the hallway with barely a nod; her daughter was no academic bright spark, and she looked, if this was not merely a permanent condition, put out. When I entered, Ms. Rocco had that having-just-taken-a-deep-breath expression, as if drawing on inner resources. But she recovered readily enough, and her handclasp was warm.

"I've been looking forward to meeting you," she said, firm rather than gushy. "Your son's quite an enigma to me, and I've been hoping you could help me crack the code."

"I'm afraid I rely on his teachers to explain the mystery to *me*," I said with a wan smile, assuming the hot seat by her desk.

"Though I doubt they've been enlightening."

"Kevin turns in his homework. He isn't a truant. He doesn't, as far as anyone knows, take knives to school. That's all his teachers have ever cared to know."

"I'm afraid that most teachers here have nearly 100 students—"

"I'm sorry, I didn't mean to be critical. You're spread so thin that I'm impressed you've even learned his name."

"Oh, I noticed Kevin right away—." She seemed about to say more, and stopped. She placed a pencil eraser on her bottom lip. A slim, attractive woman in her mid-forties, she had decisive features that tended to set in an implacable expression, her mouth faintly pressed. Yet if she exuded an air of restraint, her reserve did not seem natural but learned, perhaps by expensive trial and error.

It wasn't an easy time to be a schoolteacher, if it ever had been. Squeezed by the state for higher standards and by parents for higher grades, under the magnifying glass for any ethnic insensitivity or sexual impropriety, torn by the rote demands of proliferating standardized tests and student cries for creative expression, teachers were both blamed for everything that went wrong with kids and turned to for their every salvation. This dual role of scapegoat and savior was downright messianic, but even in 1998 shekels Jesus was probably paid better.

"What's his game?" Ms. Rocco resumed, bouncing the eraser on her desk.

"Pardon?"

"What do you think that boy's up to? He tries to hide it, but he's smart. Quite the savage social satirist, too. Has he always done these tongue-in-cheek papers, or are these deadpan parodies something new?"

"He's had a keen sense of the absurd since he was a toddler."

"Those three-letter-word essays are tours de force. Tell me, is there anything he doesn't find ridiculous?"

"Archery," I said miserably. "I have no idea why he doesn't get tired of it."

"What do you think he likes about it?"

I frowned. "Something about that arrow—the focus—its purposiveness, or sense of direction. Maybe he envies it. There's a ferocity about Kevin at target practice. Otherwise, he can seem rather aimless."

"Ms. Khatchadourian, I don't want to put you on the spot. But has anything happened in your family that I should know about? I was hoping you could help explain why your son seems so *angry*."

"That's odd. Most of his teachers have described Kevin as placid, even lethargic."

"It's a front," she said confidently.

"I do think of him as a little rebellious—"

"And he rebels by doing everything he's supposed to. It's very clever. But I look in his eyes, and he's raging. Why?"

"Well, he wasn't too happy when his sister was born . . . But that was over seven years ago, and he wasn't too happy before she was born, either." My delivery had grown morose. "We're pretty well off—you know, we have a big house . . . " I introduced an air of embarrassment. "We try not to spoil him, but he lacks for nothing. Kevin's father adores him, almost— too much. His sister did have an—accident last winter in which Kevin was—involved, but he didn't seem very bothered by it. Not bothered enough, in fact. Otherwise, I can't tell you any terrible trauma he's been through or deprivation he's suffered. We lead the good life, don't we?"

"Maybe that's what he's angry about."

"Why would affluence make him mad?"

"Maybe he's mad that this is as good as it gets. Your big house. His good school. I think it's very difficult for kids these days, in a way. The country's very prosperity has become a burden, a dead end. Everything works, doesn't it? At least if you're white and middle class. So it must often seem to young people that they're not needed. In a sense, it's as if there's nothing more to do."

"Except tear it apart."

"Yes. And you see the same cycles in history. It's not only children."

"You know, I've tried to tell my kids about the hardships of life in countries like Bangladesh or Sierra Leone. But it's not their hardship, and I can't exactly tuck them in on a bed of nails every night so they'll appreciate the miracle of comfort."

"You said your husband 'adores' Kevin. How do you get along with him?"

I folded my arms. "He's a teenager."

Wisely, she dropped the subject. "Your son is anything but a hopeless case. That's what I most wanted to tell you. He's sharp as a tack. Some of his papers—did you read the one on the SUV? It was worthy of Swift. And I've noticed that he asks challenging questions merely to catch me out—to humiliate me in front of the class. In fact, he knows the answer beforehand. So I've been playing along. I call on him, and he asks what *logomachy* means. I gladly admit I don't know, and bingo, he's learned a new word—because he had to find it in the dictionary to ask the question. It's a game we play. He spurns learning through regular channels. But if you get at him through the back door, your young man has spark."

I was jealous. "Generally when I knock at the door, it's locked."

"Please don't despair. I assume that with you, just as in school, he's inaccessible and sarcastic. As you said, he's a teenager. But he's also inhaling information at a ferocious rate, if only because he's determined that nobody get the better of him."

I glanced at my watch; I'd run overtime. "These high school massacres," I said offhandedly, collecting my purse. "Do you worry that something like that could happen here?"

"Of course it could happen here. Among a big enough group of people, of any age, somebody's going to have a screw loose. But honestly, my turning violent poetry into the office only makes my students mad. In fact, it should make them mad. Madder, even. So many kids take all this censorship, these locker searches—"

"Flagrantly illegal," I noted.

"—Flagrantly illegal searches." She nodded. "Well, so many of them take it lying down like sheep. They're told it's for 'their own protection,' and for the most part they just—buy it. When I was their age we'd have staged sit-ins and marched around with placards—." She stopped herself again. "*I* think it's good for them to get their hostilities out on paper. It's harmless, and a release valve. But that's become a minority view. At least these horrible incidents are still very rare. I wouldn't lose any sleep over it."

"And, uh—," I stood, "the rumors about Vicki Pagorski. Think there's anything to them?"

Ms. Rocco's eyes clouded. "I don't think that's been established."

"I mean, off the record. Is it credible. Assuming you know her."

"Vicki is a friend of mine, so I don't feel impartial—." She once more put that eraser on her chin. "This has been a painful time for her." That was all she would say.

Ms. Rocco saw me to the door. "I want you to give Kevin a message for me," she said with a smile. "You tell him I'm *onto him.*"

I'd often nursed the same conviction, but I'd never have asserted it in such a cheerful tone of voice.

Anxious to avert legal action, the Nyack School Board held a closed disciplinary hearing at Gladstone High, to which only the parents of four of Vicki Pagorski's students were invited. Trying to keep the event casual, they put the meeting in a regular classroom. Still the room sizzled with a sense of occasion, and the other three mothers had dressed up. (I realized I'd made terribly classist assumptions about Lenny Pugh's parents, whom we'd never met, when I found myself scanning for overweight trailer-park trash in loud polyester to no avail. I later discerned that he was the banker-type in chalk-stripe, she the stunning, intelligent-looking redhead in understated gear that was clearly designer label, because it didn't show any buttons. So we all have our crosses to bear.) The school board and that beefy principal, Donald Bevons, had assumed a set of folding chairs along one wall, and they were all scowling with rectitude, while we parents were stuck in those infantilizing school desks. Four other folding chairs were arranged on one side of the teacher's desk at the front, where there sat two nervous-looking boys I didn't know, along with Kevin and Lenny Pugh, who kept leaning over toward Kevin and whispering behind his hand. On the other side of the desk was seated, I could only assume, Vicki Pagorski.

So much for the powers of adolescent description. She was hardly a hag; I doubt she was even thirty. I would never have depicted her breasts as large or her keister as wide, for she had the agreeably solid figure of a woman who ate her Wheaties. Attractive? Hard to say. With that snub nose and freckles, she had a lost, girlish, innocent look that some men like. The drab dun suit was doubtless donned for the event; her friend Dana Rocco would have counseled against tight jeans and a low-cut shirt. But it's too bad she hadn't done anything about her hair, which was thick and kinky; it frizzed from her head in all directions and suggested a ditzy, frazzled state of mind. The glasses, too, were unfortunate: The round oversized frames gave her a pop-eyed appearance, inducing the impression of dumb shock. Hands twisting in her lap, knees locked tightly together under the straight wool skirt, she reminded me a bit of let-us-call-her-Alice at that eighth-grade dance immediately after Kevin whispered I-didn't-want-to-know.

When the chairman of the school board, Alan Strickland, called the little group to order, the room was already unpleasantly quiet. Strickland said that they hoped to clear up these allegations one way or the other without landing this business in court. He talked about how seriously the board took this sort of thing and blathered on about teaching and trust. He emphasized that he didn't want anything we said that evening leaving this room until the board decided what action to take, if any; the stenographer was taking notes for internal purposes only. Belying the rhetoric of informal chitchat, he explained that Miss Pagorski had declined to ask her attorney to be present. And then he asked Kevin to have a seat in the chair placed in front of the teacher's desk and to just tell us in his own words what happened that afternoon in October in Miss Pagorski's classroom.

Kevin, too, recognized the importance of costuming, and for once was wearing plain slacks and a button-down of the customary size. On command, he assumed the shuffling, averted-eye squirm that he'd practiced in the archway of our den. "You mean, like, that time she asked me to stay after school, right?"

"I never asked him to stay after school," Pagorski blurted. Her voice was shaky but surprisingly forceful.

"You'll get your chance, Miss Pagorski," said Strickland. "For now we're going to hear Kevin's side of things, all right?" He clearly wanted this hearing to proceed calmly and civilly, and I thought, *good luck*.

"I don't know," said Kevin, ducking and weaving his head. "It just got kinda *intimate*, you know? I wasn't gonna say anything or anything, but then my dad started asking questions and I like, told him."

"Told him about what?" Strickland asked gently.

"You know—what I told Mr. Bevons about, too, before." Kevin sandwiched his hands between his thighs and looked at the floor.

"Kevin, I realize this is difficult for you, but we're going to need details. Your teacher's career is on the line."

Kevin looked to you. "Dad, do I have to?"

"Afraid so, Kev," you said.

"Well, Miss Pagorski's always been nice to me, Mr. Strickland. *Real* nice. Always asking did I need help choosing a scene or could she read the other part so I could memorize mine . . . And I've never thought I was all that good, but she'd say I was a great actor and she loved my 'dramatic face' and my 'tight build' and with my looks I could be in the movies. I don't know about that. Still, I sure wouldn't want to get her in trouble."

"You leave that to us, Kevin, and just tell us what happened."

"See, she'd asked me several times if I could stay after school so she could coach me on my delivery, but before I'd always said I couldn't. Actually, I could, most days, I mean, I didn't have anything I had to do or anything, but I just didn't—I felt funny about it. I don't know why, it just felt kinda weird when she'd pull me over to her desk after class and, like, pick off little pieces of lint on my shirt that I wasn't sure were really there. Or she'd take the flap of my belt and tuck it back in the loop?"

"Since when has Kevin ever worn a *belt*?" I whispered. You shushed me quiet.

"—But this one time she was real insistent, almost like I had to, like it was part of class work or something. I didn't want to go—I told you, I don't know why exactly, I just didn't—but it seemed like this time I didn't have any choice."

Most of this was addressed to the linoleum, but Kevin would shoot quick glances at Strickland from time to time, and Strickland would nod reassuringly.

"So I waited around till 4 o'clock, since she said she had stuff to do right after the bell, and by then there wasn't hardly anybody around anymore. I walked into her classroom, and I thought it was kinda strange that she'd changed clothes since our fourth-period class. I mean, just the shirt, but now it was one of those stretchy T's that are scooped low and it was clingy enough I could see her—you know."

"Her what?"

"Her . . . nipples," said Kevin. "So I said, 'You want me to go though my monologue?' and she got up and closed the door. And she locked it. She said, "We need a little privacy, don't we?" I said, actually, I didn't mind the air. Then I asked should I start at the top, and she said, 'First we've got to work on that posture of yours.' She said I've got to learn to speak from the diaphragm, right *here*, and she put her hand on my chest and she left it there. Then she said, and you've got to stand up real straight, and she put her other hand on my lower back and pressed and sort of smoothed around. I sure did stand up straight. I remember holding my breath, like. Since I was nervous. Then I started my monologue from *Equus*—actually, I'd wanted to do Shakespeare, you know? That *to be or not to be* thing. I thought it was kinda cool."

"In your own good time, son. But what happened next?"

"I think she interrupted me after only two or three lines. She said, 'You have to remember that this play is all about *sex*.' She said, 'When he blinds those horses, it's an *erotic act*.' And then she started asking if I've ever seen horses, big horses up close, not the like, geldings, but stallions, and had I ever noticed what a big— I'm sorry, do you want me to say what she really said, or should I just, you know, summarize?"

"It would be better if you used her exact words, as well as you can remember."

"Okay, you asked for it." Kevin inhaled. "She wanted to know if I'd ever seen a horse's *cock*. How big it was. And all this time I'm feeling kinda—funny. Like, restless. And she put her hand on my, uh. Fly. Of my jeans. And I was pretty embarrassed, because with all that talk, I'd got . . . a little worked up."

"You mean you had an erection," said Strickland sternly.

"Look, do I have to go on?" Kevin appealed.

"If you can, it would be better if you finished the story."

Kevin glanced at the ceiling and crossed his legs tightly, tapping the toe of his right sneaker in an agitated, irregular rhythm against the toe of the left. "So I said, 'Miss Pagorski maybe we should work on this scene some other time, 'cause I've got to go soon.' I wasn't sure whether to say anything about her hand, so I just kept saying that maybe we should *stop*, that I wanted to *stop*, that I should *go* now. 'Cause it didn't seem right, and, you know, I like her, but not like *that*. She could be my mother or something."

"Let's be clear here," said Strickland. "Legally, it's only so important, because you're a minor. But on top of the fact that you're only fifteen, these were *unwanted advances*, is this correct?"

"Well, yeah. She's ugly."

Pagorski flinched. It was the brief, floppy little jerk you get when you keep shooting a small animal with a high-caliber pistol and it's already dead.

"So did she stop?" asked Strickland.

"No, sir. She started rubbing up and down through my jeans, all the while saying, 'Jesus' . . . Saying, and I really apologize Mr. Strickland but you asked me . . . She said every time she saw a horse's cock she 'wanted to suck it.' And that's when I—"

"Ejaculated."

Kevin dropping his head to look at his lap. "Yeah. It was kind of a mess. I just ran out. I skipped class a couple of times after that, but then I came back and tried to act as if nothing happened since I didn't want to wreck my grade-point average."

"How?" I murmured under my breath. "By getting *another* B?" You shot me a glare.

"I know this hasn't been easy for you, and we want to thank you, Kevin, for being so forthcoming. You can take a seat now."

"Could I go sit with my parents?" he implored.

"Why don't you sit over there with the other boys for now, because we might need to ask you a few more questions. I'm sure your parents are very proud of you."

Kevin hove back to his original perch, curling with a tinge of shame—
nice touch. Meanwhile, the classroom was pin-drop silent, as parents met
one another's eyes and shook their heads. It was a bravura performance. I
cannot pretend that I was not impressed.

But then I looked to Vicki Pagorski. Early in Kevin's testimony she'd
emitted the odd repressed squeal, or she'd dropped her mouth open. But
by the time it was over she was beyond histrionics, and this was a drama
teacher. She was drooped so bonelessly in her folding chair that I feared
she would fall off, while the frizz of her hair evanesced into the air as if
her whole head were in a state of dissolve.

Strickland turned to the drama teacher's chair, though he kept his distance. "Now, Miss Pagorski. It's your contention that this encounter never
happened?"

"That's—." She had to clear her throat. "That's right."

"Do you have any idea why Kevin would tell such a story if it wasn't
true?"

"No, I don't. I can't understand it. Kevin's class is an unusually tal-
ented group, and I thought we'd been having a lot of fun. I've given him
plenty of individual attention—"

"It's the individual attention he seems to have a problem with."

"I give all my students individual attention!"

"Oh, Miss Pagorski, let's hope not," Strickland said sorrowfully. Our
small audience chuckled. "Now, you claim you *didn't* invite Kevin to stay
after school?"

"Not separately. I told the whole class that if they want to use my
classroom to practice their scenes after school, I'd make it available."

"So you *did* invite Kevin to stay after school, then." As Pagorski sputtered, Strickland proceeded, "Have you ever admired Kevin's looks?"

"I may have said something about his having very striking features,
yes. I try to instill confidence in my students—"

"How about this 'speaking from the diaphragm.' Did you say that?"

"Well, yes—"

"And have you put your hand on his chest, to indicate where the
diaphragm is?"

"Maybe, but I *never* touched him on—"

"Or on his lower back, when 'improving' his posture?"

"Possibly. He has a tendency to slump, and it ruins his—"

"What about the selection from *Equus*? Did Kevin choose this passage?"

"I recommended it."

"Why not something from *Our Town*, or Neil Simon, a little less racy?"

"I try to find plays that students can relate to, about things that are important to them—"

"Things like sex."

"Well, yes, among other things, of course—." She was getting flustered.

"Did you describe the content of this play as 'erotic'?"

"Maybe, probably, yes! I thought that drama about adolescent sexuality and its confusions would naturally appeal—"

"Miss Pagorski, are *you* interested in adolescent sexuality?"

"Well, who isn't?" she cried. Someone should have given the poor woman a shovel, so intent was she on digging her own grave. "But *Equus* isn't steamy and explicit, it's all symbolism—"

"Symbolism you were eager to explain. And did you talk about horses to Kevin?"

"Of course, the play—"

"Did you talk about stallions, Miss Pagorski."

"Well, we did discuss what made them such common symbols of virility—"

"And what *does* make them 'virile'?"

"Well, they're muscular and very beautiful and powerful, sleek—"

"Just like teenage boys," Strickland noted sardonically. "Did you ever draw attention to a horse's penis. To its size?"

"Maybe; how could you ignore it? But I never said—"

"Some people can't ignore it, apparently."

"You don't understand! These are young people and they're easily bored. I have to do something to get them excited!"

Strickland just let that one sit there for a beat. "Yes, well," he said. "You seem to have succeeded there."

Deathly pale, Pagorski turned to our son. "What did I ever do to you?"

"That's just what we're trying to find out," Strickland intervened. "But we've got more testimony to get through, and you'll have opportunity to respond. Leonard Pugh?"

Lenny murmured to Kevin before sauntering to the center chair. Surely at any moment one of the boys would start writhing in agony because *Goody Pagorski* was smiting them with evil spirits.

"Now Leonard, you, too, met with your drama teacher after school?"

"Yeah, she seemed real hot to have a *conference*," said Lenny, with his poo-making smile. His nose stud was infected again, the left nostril red and puffy. He'd recently gotten a fade, which was neo-Nazi short with the letter Z shaved into one side. When I'd asked him what the Z stood for, he'd said, *Whatever*, which I'd been forced to point out began with a W.

"Can you tell us what happened?"

"It was just like Kevin said. I thought we was just gonna practice and shit. And I come in the room and she like, shuts the door? She's wearing this really short skirt, you know, you can almost see her cheeks." Lenny mugged a bit.

"And did you practice your work for class?" asked Strickland, though coaching proved quite unnecessary. More, detail proved Lenny's strong suit.

"We sure practiced something!" said Lenny. "She said, 'I've been watching you in the back row, when I'm sitting at my desk? And some afternoons I get so wet I have to do myself in class!'"

Strickland looked a little queasy. "Did Miss Pagorski do anything that you thought was inappropriate?"

"Well then she like, sits on the edge of her desk? With her legs spread wide open. So I go up to the desk, and I can see *she's not wearing panties*. It's like, this, wide open beaver, you know? All red and hairy, and it's just, you know, *dripping*—"

"Leonard, let's just get the facts—." Strickland was massaging his forehead. Meanwhile, chalk-stripe was twisting his tie; the redhead had her face in her hands.

"So she says, 'You want some? 'Cause I look at that bulge in your pants, and I can't keep my hands off my pussy—'"

"Could you please watch your language—!" said Strickland, making desperate slashing motions at the stenographer.

"—So if you don't do me right now, I'm gonna shove this eraser in my hole and bring myself off!'"

"Leonard, that's enough—"

"Girls around here are pretty tight with it, so I wasn't about to pass on free pussy. So I did her, right on the desk, and you shoulda heard her begging to let her suck it—"

"Leonard, take your seat right now."

Well, wasn't it awkward. Lenny shambled back to his chair, and Strickland announced that the board had heard enough for one night, and he thanked everyone for coming. He repeated his admonition that we not spread rumors until a decision had been made. We would be notified if any action would be taken on this case.

After the three of us had climbed into your 4x4 in silence, you finally said to Kevin, "You know, that friend of yours made you look like a liar."

"Moron," Kevin grumbled. "I should never have told him about what happened with Pagorski. He copies me in everything. I guess I just needed to tell somebody."

"Why didn't you come straight to me?" you asked.

"It was gross!" he said, bunched in the back seat. "That whole thing back there was totally embarrassing. I should never have told anybody. You shouldn'ta made me do that."

"On the *contrary*." You twisted around the headrest. "Kevin, if you have a teacher whose behavior is out of bounds, I want to know about it, and I want the school to know about it. You have nothing to be ashamed of. Except possibly your choice of friends. Lenny is something of a fabulist. Little distance might be in order there, sport."

"Yeah," said Kevin. "Like to *China*."

I don't think I said a word the whole drive back. When we got home I left it to you to thank Robert for getting Celia, amazingly, to go to sleep without a forty-five-minute tucking-in from her mother. I was reluctant to open my mouth even a little bit, much as one might hesitate to put even a very small hole in an inflated balloon.

"Kev, Triskets?" you offered when Robert had left. "Sodium City, man."

"Nah. I'm going to my room. I'll come out when I can show my face again. Like in about fifty years." He moped off. Unlike the stagy melancholy of the weeks to come, he seemed truly glum. He seemed to be suffering the lingering sense of injustice that would attend a tennis player who had valiantly distinguished himself in a game of doubles but whose partner had muffed it, so they lost the match.

You busied yourself putting stray dishes in the washer. Every piece of silverware seemed to make an extraordinary amount of noise.

"Glass of wine?"

I shook my head. You looked over sharply; I would always have a glass or two before bed, and it had been a stressful evening. But it would turn to vinegar on my tongue. And I still couldn't open my mouth. I knew we had been here before. Yet I finally apprehended that we couldn't keep visiting this place—or rather, these places; that is, we could not indefinitely oc-cupy parallel universes of such diametrical characters without eventually inhabiting different places in the most down to earth, literal sense.

That's all it took, my turning down a glass of wine, which you inter-preted as hostile. In defiance of our set roles—I was the family booze hound—you grabbed yourself a beer.

"It didn't seem *advisable*," you began after a vengeful swig, "to *apologize* to that Pagorski woman after the hearing. That could help the defense if this ends up in court."

"It won't end up in court," I said. "We won't press charges."

"Well, I'd prefer not to put Kevin through that myself. But if the school board allows that perv to keep teaching—"

"This cannot continue."

Even I was not quite sure what I meant, though I felt it forcefully. You waited for me to elucidate.

"It's gone too far," I said.

"What's gone too far, Eva? Cut to the chase."

I licked my lips. "It used to have mostly to do with us. My wall of maps. Then later, it was little things—eczema. But it's bigger now—Celia's eye; a teacher's career. I can't keep looking the other way. Not even for you."

"If that lady's career is on the line, she has only herself to blame."

"I think we should consider sending him to boarding school. Some-where strict, old-fashioned. I never thought I'd say this, but maybe even a military academy."

"Whoa! Our son has been sexually abused, and your answer is to ban-ish him to boot camp? Jesus, if some creep were interfering with *Celia* you'd be down at the police station right now, filling out forms! You'd be on the phone to the *New York Times* and ten victim-support groups, and never mind a school in Annapolis—you'd never let her leave your lap!"

"That's because if Celia said someone had messed with her, the situation would be far more grave than she let on. Celia is more likely to let some dirty old geez finger her for years because she doesn't want to get the nice man in trouble."

"I know what's behind this: typical double standard. A girl gets pawed at and it's ooh terrible put the sicko away. But a woman paws all over a boy and it's gosh, lucky kid, gets his first taste, bet he really enjoyed it! Well, just because a boy responds—from physical reflex—doesn't mean it can't be a degrading, humiliating violation!"

"Professionally," I said, pressing an index finger patiently to my forehead, "I may have been fortunate, but I've never thought of myself as all that bright. Kevin came by his intelligence from somewhere. So you must have at least considered the possibility that this whole thing was a sadistic frame-job."

"Just because Lenny Pugh's horning in on the show was bogus—"

"Lenny didn't 'horn in,' he just didn't learn his lines. He's lazy, and a lousy drama student, apparently. But Kevin clearly put the other boys up to it."

"*Balls—!*"

"He didn't have to call her 'ugly.'" I shuddered, remembering. "That was twisting the knife."

"Some nympho seduces our own son, and the only person you care about—"

"He made one mistake, did you notice? He said she locked the door. Then he claimed he 'ran out' after she *had her way with him.* Those doors don't even lock, you know, from the inside. I checked."

"Big deal she didn't literally lock it! He obviously felt trapped. More to the point, why in God's name would Kevin make that story up?"

"I can't say." I shrugged. "But this certainly fits."

"With what?"

"With a wicked and dangerous little boy."

You looked at me clinically. "Now, what I can't figure is whether you're trying to hurt me, or hurt him, or if this is some confused self-torture."

"This evening's witch trial was excruciating enough. We can knock out *self-torture.*"

"Witches are mythical. Pedophiles are real as sin. One look at that loon and you could tell she was unstable."

"She's a type," I said. "She wants them to like her. She courts their favor by breaking the rules, by choosing racy plays and saying *fuck* in class. She may even like the idea of their ogling her a bit, but not at this price. And there's nothing illegal about being pathetic."

"He didn't say she spread her legs and begged like Lenny Pugh, did he? No, she got a little carried away and crossed a line. He even kept his pants on. I could see it happening. That's what convinced me. He wouldn't make that part up about *through his jeans*."

"Interesting," I said. "That's exactly how I knew he was lying."

"Lost me."

"Through his jeans. It was calculated authenticity. The believability was *crafted*."

"Let's get this straight. You don't believe his story because it's too believable."

"That's right," I agreed evenly. "He may be scheming and malicious, but his English teacher is right. He's *sharp as a tack*."

"Did he seem as if he wanted to testify?"

"Of course not. He's a genius."

Then it happened. When you collapsed into the chair opposite, you did not come to a dead halt only because I had made up my mind and you could no more dislodge my conviction that Kevin was a Machiavellian miscreant than I could dislodge yours that he was a misunderstood choirboy. It was worse than that. Bigger. Your face sagged much as a short time later I would see your father's droop as he emerged from his basement stairwell—as if all your features had been artificially held up by tacks that had suddenly fallen out. Why, at that moment you and your father would have appeared nearly the same age.

Franklin, I'd never appreciated how much energy you expended to maintain the fiction that we were a broadly happy family whose trifling, transient problems just made life more interesting. Maybe every family has one member whose appointed job is to fabricate this attractive packaging. In any event, you had abruptly resigned. In one form or another, we had visited this conversation countless times, with the habitual loyalty that sends other couples to the same holiday home every summer. But at some point such couples must look about their painfully familiar cottage and admit to each other, *Next year we'll have to try somewhere else.*

You pressed your fingers into your eye sockets. "I thought we could make it until the kids were out of the house." Your voice was gray. "I even thought that if we made it that far, maybe . . . But that's ten years from now, and it's too many days. I can take the years, Eva. But not the days."

I had never so fully and consciously wished that I had never borne our son. In that instant I might even have forgone Celia, whose absence a childless woman in her fifties would not have known well enough to rue. From a young age there was only one thing I had always wanted, along with getting out of Racine, Wisconsin. And that was a good man who loved me and would stay true. Anything else was ancillary, a bonus, like frequent-flier miles. I could have lived without children. I couldn't live without you.

But I would have to. I had created my own Other Woman who happened to be a boy. I'd seen this in-house cuckolding in other families, and it's odd that I'd failed to spot it in ours. Brian and Louise had split ten years before (all that wholesomeness had been a little meat-and-potatoes for him, too; at a party for his fifteenth wedding anniversary, a jar of pickled walnuts smashed on the floor, and he got caught fucking his mistress in the walk-in pantry), and of course Brian was far more upset about separation from those two blond moppets than about leaving Louise. There shouldn't be any problem loving both, but for some reason certain men choose; like good mutual-fund managers minimizing risk while maximizing portfolio yield, they take everything they once invested in their wives and sink it into children instead. What is it? Do they seem safer, because they need you? Because you can never become their ex-father, as I might become your ex-wife? You never quite trusted me, Franklin. I took too many airplanes in the formative years, and it never entirely registered that I always bought a round-trip.

"What do you want to do?" I asked. I felt light-headed.

"Last out the school year, if we can. Make arrangements over the summer.

"At least custody is a no-brainer, isn't it?" you added sourly. "And doesn't that say it all."

At the time, of course, we had no way of knowing that you would keep Celia, too.

"Is it——?" I didn't want to sound pitiful. "You've decided."

"There's nothing left to decide, Eva," you said limply. "It's already happened."

Had I imagined this scene—and I had not, for to picture such things is to invite them—I'd have expected to stay up until dawn draining a bottle, agonizing over what went wrong. But I sensed that if anything we would turn in early. Like toasters and sub-compacts, one only tinkers with the mechanics of a marriage in the interests of getting it up and running, again; there's not much point in poking around to see where the wires have disconnected prior to throwing the contraption away. What's more, though I'd have expected to cry, I found myself all dried up; with the house overheated, my nostrils were tight and smarting, my lips cracked. You were right, it had already happened, and I may have been in mourning for our marriage for a decade. Now I understood how the mates of long senile spouses felt when, after dogged, debilitating visits to a nursing home, what is functionally dead succumbs to death in fact. A culminatory shudder of grief; a thrill of guilty relief. For the first time since I could remember, I relaxed. My shoulders dropped a good two inches. I sat into my chair. I sat. I may have never sat so completely. All I was doing was sitting.

Thus it took a supreme effort to lift my eyes and turn my head when a flicker of motion in the mouth of the hallway distracted from the perfect stasis of our still life. Kevin took a deliberate step into the light. One glance confirmed that he'd been eavesdropping. He looked different. Those sordid afternoons with the bathroom door open notwithstanding, this was the first time in years I had seen him naked. Oh, he was still wearing the normal-sized clothes from the hearing. But he'd lost the sideways skew; he stood up straight. The sarcastic wrench of his mouth dropped; his features were at rest. I thought, he really is "striking," as his drama teacher purportedly remarked. He looked older. But what most amazed me were his eyes. Ordinarily, they glazed with the glaucous film of unwashed apples—flat and unfocused, bored and belligerent, they shut me out. Sure, they glittered with occasional mischief, like the closed metal doors of a smelting furnace around which a little red rim would sometimes smolder, from which stray flames would lick. But as he stepped into the kitchen, the furnace doors swung wide to bare the jets.

"I need a drink of water," he announced, somehow managing to hiss without pronouncing any S's, and strode to the sink.

"Kev," you said. "Don't take anything you might have overheard to heart. It's easy to misunderstand when you hear something out of context."

"Why would I not know the context?" He took a single swallow from his glass. "I am the context." He put the glass on the counter, and left.

I'm certain of it: That moment, that hard swallow, is when he decided.

A week later, we received another letter from the school board. Already relieved of her classes when the accusations were first made, Vicki Pagorski would be permanently removed to administrative duties and never allowed direct supervision of students again. Yet in the absence of any evidence beyond the boys' word against hers, she was not to be discharged. We both found the decision cowardly, though for different reasons. It seemed to me that she was either guilty or she was not, and there was no justification for taking an innocent from an occupation that she clearly adored. You were outraged that she was not to be fired and that none of the other parents planned to sue.

After slumping around the house as pointedly as one can go about an exercise that is essentially rounded, Kevin confided in you that he had grown depressed. You said you could see why. Stunned by the injustice of the school board's slap on the wrist, Kevin felt humiliated, so of course he was depressed. Equally you fretted that he had intuited an impending divorce that we both wanted to put off making official until we had to.

He wanted to go on Prozac. From my random sampling, a good half of his student body was on one antidepressant or another, though he did request *Prozac* in particular. I've always been leery of legal restoratives, and I did worry about the drug's reputation for flattening; the vision of our son even more dulled to the world boggled the mind. But so rarely out of the States those days, I, too, had acculturated myself to the notion that in a country with more money, greater freedom, bigger houses, better schools, finer health care, and more unfettered opportunity than anywhere else on earth, of course an abundance of its population would be out of their minds with sorrow. So I went along with it, and the psychiatrist we sought seemed as happy to hand out fistfuls of pharmaceuticals as our dentist to issue free lollipops.

Most children are mortified by the prospect of their parents' divorce, and I don't deny that the conversation he overheard from the hallway sent Kevin into a tailspin. Nevertheless, I was disconcerted. That boy had been trying to split us up for fifteen years. Why wasn't he satisfied? And if I really was such a horror, why wouldn't he gladly jettison his awful mother? In retrospect, I can only assume that it was bad enough living with a woman who was cold, suspicious, resentful, accusatory, and aloof. Only one eventuality must have seemed worse, and that was living with you, Franklin. Getting stuck with Dad.

Getting stuck with Dad the Dupe.

Eva

Dear Franklin,

I have a confession to make. For all my ragging on you in these days, I've become shamefully dependent on television. In fact, as long as I'm baring all: One evening last month in the middle of *Frasier*, the tube winked out cold, and I'm afraid that I rather fell apart—banging the set, plugging and unplugging, wiggling knobs. I'm long past weeping over *Thursday* on a daily basis, but I go into a frenzy when I can't find out how Niles takes the news that Daphne's going to marry Donnie.

Anyway, tonight after the usual chicken breast (a bit overcooked), I was flicking through the channels when the screen suddenly filled with our son's face. You'd think I'd be used to it by now, but I'm not. And this wasn't the ninth-grade school photo all the papers ran—out of date, black-and-white, with its acid grin—but Kevin's more robust visage at seventeen. I recognized the interviewer's voice. It was Jack Marlin's documentary.

Marlin had ditched the dry thriller title "Extracurricular Activities" for the punchier "Bad Boy," reminding me of you; *I'll finish off that bad boy in a couple of hours*, you'd say, about an easy scouting job. You applied the expression to just about everything save our son.

To whom Jack Marlin applied it readily enough. Kevin, you see, was the star. Marlin must have gotten Claverack's consent, for interspersed with shots of the tearful aftermath—the piles of flowers outside the gym, the memorial service, Never Again town meetings—was an exclusive interview with *KK* himself. Rattled, I almost switched it off. But after a minute or two, I was riveted. In fact, Kevin's manner was so arresting that at first I could barely attend to what he said. He was interviewed in his dormitory cubicle—like his room, kept in rigid order and unadorned with posters or knickknacks. Tipping his chair on two legs, hooking an elbow around its back, he looked thoroughly in his element. If anything, he seemed larger, full of himself, bursting from his tiny sweats, and I had never seen him so animated and at his ease. He basked under the camera's eye as if under a sunlamp.

Marlin was off-screen, and his questions were deferential, almost tender, as if he didn't want to scare Kevin away. When I tuned in, Marlin was asking delicately whether Kevin still maintained that he was one of the tiny percentage of Prozac patients who had a radical and antipathetic reaction to the drug.

Kevin had learned the importance of sticking by your story by the time he was six. "Well, I definitely started feeling a little weird."

"But according to both the *New England Journal of Medicine* and the *Lancet*, a causal linkage between Prozac and homicidal psychosis is purely speculative. Do you think more research—?"

"Hey," Kevin raised a palm, "I'm no doctor. That defense was my lawyer's idea, and he was doing his job. I said I felt a little weird. But I'm not looking for an excuse here. I don't blame some satanic cult or pissy girlfriend or big bad bully who called me a fag. One of the things I can't stand about this country is lack of *accountability*. Everything Americans do that doesn't work out too great has to be somebody else's fault. Me, I stand by what I done. It wasn't anybody's idea but mine."

"What about that sexual abuse case? Might that have left you feeling bruised?"

"Sure I was *interfered with*. But hell," Kevin added with a confidential leer, "that was *nothing* compared to what happens *here*." (They cut to an interview with Vicki Pagorski, whose denials were apoplectic with methinks-thou-dost-protest-too-much excess. Of course, too feeble an indignation would have seemed equally incriminating, so she couldn't win. And she really ought to do something about that hair.)

"Can we talk a little about your parents, Kevin?" Marlin resumed.

Hands behind head. "Shoot."

"Your father—did you get along, or did you fight?"

"Mister Plastic?" Kevin snorted. "I should be so lucky we'd have a fight. No, it was all cheery chirpy, hot dogs and Cheez Whiz. A total fraud, you know? All like, *Let's go to the Natural History Museum, Kev, they have some really neat-o rocks!* He was into some Little League fantasy, stuck in the 1950s. I'd get this, *I luuuuuuv you, buddy!* stuff, and I'd just look at him like, *Who are you talking to, guy?* What does that mean, your dad 'loves' you and hasn't a [*bleep*]ing clue who you are? What's he love, then? Some kid in *Happy Days.* Not me."

"What about your mother?"

"What about her?" Kevin snapped, though until now he'd been affable, expansive.

"Well, there was that civil suit brought for parental negligence—"

"Totally bogus," said Kevin flatly. "Rank opportunism, frankly. More culture of compensation. Next thing you know, geezers'll be suing the government for getting old and kids'll be taking their mommies to court because they came out ugly. My view runs, life sucks; tough luck. Fact is, the lawyers knew Mumsey had deep pockets, and that Woolford cow can't take bad news on the chin."

Just then the camera angle panned ninety degrees, zooming in on the room's only decoration that I could see taped over his bed. Badly creased from having been folded small enough to fit in a pocket or wallet, it was a photograph of me. Jesus Christ, it was that head-shot on an Amsterdam houseboat, which disappeared when Celia was born. I was sure he'd torn it to pieces.

"But whether or not your mother was legally remiss," Marlin proceeded, "maybe she paid you too little attention—?"

"*Oh, lay off my mother.*" This sharp, menacing voice was alien to me, but it must have been useful inside. "Shrinks here spend all day trying to get me to trash the woman, and I'm getting a little tired of it, if you wanna know the truth."

Marlin regrouped. "Would you describe your relationship as close, then?"

"She's been all over the world, know that? You can hardly name a country where she hasn't got the T-shirt. Started her own company. Go into any bookstore around here, you'll see her series. You know, *Smelly Foreign Dumps on a Wing and a Prayer?* I used to cruise into Barnes and Noble in the mall just to look at all those books. Pretty cool."

"So you don't think there's any way she might have—"

"Look, I could be kind of a creep, okay? And she could be kind of a creep, too, so we're even. Otherwise, it's *private*, okay? Such a thing in this country anymore as *private*, or do I have to tell you the color of my underwear? Next question."

"I guess there's only one question left, Kevin—the big one. Why'd you do it?"

I could tell Kevin had been preparing for this. He inserted a dramatic pause, then slammed the front legs of his plastic chair onto the floor. Elbows on knees, he turned from Marlin to directly address the camera.

"Okay, it's like this. You wake up, you *watch* TV, and you get in the car and you *listen* to the radio. You go to your little job or your little school, but you're not going to hear about that on the 6:00 news, since guess what. *Nothing is really happening.* You *read* the paper, or if you're into that sort of thing you *read* a book, which is just the same as watching only even more boring. You *watch* TV all night, or maybe you go out so you can *watch* a movie, and maybe you'll get a phone call so you can tell your friends what you've been *watching.* And you know, it's got so bad that I've started to notice, the people on TV? *Inside* the TV? Half the time they're *watching TV.* Or if you've got some romance in a movie? What do they do but *go to a movie.* All these people, Marlin," he invited the interviewer in with a nod. "What are they watching?"

After an awkward silence, Marlin filled in, "You tell us, Kevin."

"People like me." He sat back and folded his arms.

Marlin would have been happy with this footage, and he wasn't about to let the show stop now. Kevin was on a roll and had that quality of just getting started. "But people watch other things than killers, Kevin," Marlin prodded.

"Horseshit," said Kevin. "They want to watch something happen, and I've made a study of it: Pretty much the definition of something happening is it's bad. The way I see it, the world is divided into the watchers and the watchees, and there's more and more of the audience and less and less to see. People who actually do anything are a goddamned endangered species."

"On the contrary, Kevin," Marlin observed sorrowfully, "all too many young people like yourself have gone on killing sprees in the last few years."

"Lucky for you, too! You need us! What would you do without me, film a documentary on paint drying? What are all those folks doing," he waved an arm at the camera, "but *watching* me? Don't you think they'd have changed the channel by now if all I'd done is get an A in Geometry? Bloodsuckers! I do their dirty work for them!"

"But the whole point of asking you these questions," Marlin said soothingly, "is so we can all figure out how to keep this sort of Columbine thing from happening again."

At the mention of *Columbine*, Kevin's face soured. "I just wanna go on the record that those two weenies were not pros. Their bombs were duds, and they shot plain old anybody. No standards. My crowd was hand-picked. The videos those morons left behind were totally embarrassing. They copied me, and their whole operation was obviously designed to one-up Gladstone—"

Marlin tried quietly to intrude something like, "Actually, police claim that Klebold and Harris were planning their attack for at least a year," but Kevin plowed on.

"Nothing, not one thing in that circus went according to plan. It was a 100-percent failure from top to bottom. No wonder those miserable twits wasted themselves—and I thought that was chicken. Part of the package is facing the music. Worst of all, they were hopeless geeks. I've read sections of Klebold's whining, snot-nosed journal. Know one of the groups that chump wanted to avenge himself against? *People who think they can predict the weather.* Had no idea what kind of a statement they were making. Oh, and get this—at the end of the Big Day, those two losers were originally planning to *hijack a jet* and *fly it into the World Trade Center.* Give me a break!"

"You, ah, note that your victims were 'handpicked,'" said Marlin, who must have been wondering, *What was that about?* "Why those particular students?"

"They happened to be the people who got on my nerves. I mean, if you were planning a major operation like this, wouldn't *you* go for the priss-pots and faggots and eyesores you couldn't stand? Seems to me that's the main perk of taking the rap. You and your cameramen here leech off my accomplishments, and you get a fancy salary and your name in the credits. Me, I have to do time. Gotta get something out of it."

"I have one more question, Kevin, though I'm afraid you may have answered it already," said Marlin with a tragic note. "Do you feel any remorse? Knowing what you do now, if you could go back to April 8th, 1999, would you kill those people all over again?"

"I'd only do one thing different. I'd put one right between the eyes of that Lukronsky dork, who's been making a mint off his *terrible ordeal* ever since. I read he's now gonna be *acting* in that Miramax flick! Feel sorry for the cast, too. He'll be quoting *Let's get in character* from *Pulp Fiction* and doing his Harvey Keitel imitations and I bet in Hollywood that shit gets old quick. And while we're on that, I wanna complain that Miramax and everybody should be paying me some kind of fee. They're stealing my story, and that story was a lot of work. I don't think it's legal to swipe it for free."

"But it's against the law in this state for criminals to profit from—"

Again, Kevin swung to the camera. "My story is about all I got to my name right now, and that's why I feel robbed. But a story's a whole lot more than most people got. All you people watching out there, you're listening to what I say because I have something you don't: *I got plot.* Bought and paid for. That's what all you people want, and why you're sucking off me. You want my plot. I know how you feel, too, since hey, I used to feel the same way. TV and video games and movies and computer screens . . . On April 8th, 1999, I jumped *into* the screen, I switched to watch*ee.* Ever since, I've known what my life is about. I give good story. It may have been kinda gory, but admit it, *you all loved it.* You *ate it up.* Nuts, I ought to be on some government payroll. Without people like me, the whole country would jump off a bridge, 'cause the only thing on TV is some housewife on *Who Wants to Be a Millionaire?* winning $64,000 for remembering the name of the president's dog."

I turned off the set. I couldn't take any more. I could feel another interview with Thelma Corbitt coming up, bound to include an appeal for the "Love for Kids with Determination" scholarship fund she'd set up in Denny's honor, to which I'd already contributed more than I could afford.

Obviously, this flashy thesis about the passive spectating of modern life was but a twinkle in Kevin's eye two years ago. He has time on his hands at Claverack, and he'd knocked together that fancy motive in much the way older convicts manufacture vanity license plates. Still, I reluctantly have to admit that his post hoc exegesis contained a nugget of truth. Were

NBC to broadcast an unabating string of documentaries on the mating habits of sea otters, viewership would dwindle. Listening to Kevin's diatribe, I was struck despite myself by what a sizable proportion of our species feeds off the depravity of a handful of reprobates, if not to earn a living then to pass the time. It isn't only journalists, either. Think tanks generating mountains of paper over the sovereign disposition of fractious little East Timor. University Conflict Studies departments issuing countless Ph.D.s on ETA terrorists who number no more than 100. Filmmakers generating millions by dramatizing the predations of lone serial killers. And think of it: the courts, police, National Guard—how much of government is the management of the wayward 1 percent? With prison building and warding one of the biggest growth industries in the United States, a sudden popular conversion to civilization across the board could trigger a recession. Since I myself had craved a *turn of the page*, is it really such a stretch to say of *KK* that we need him? Beneath his bathetic disguise, Jack Marlin had sounded grateful. He wasn't interested in the mating habits of sea otters, and he was *grateful*.

Otherwise, Franklin, my reaction to that interview is very confusing. A customary horror mixes with something like—pride. He was lucid, self-assured, engaging. I was touched by that photograph over his bed, and no little chagrined that he hadn't destroyed it after all (I guess I've always assumed the worst). Recognizing snippets of his soliloquy from my own tirades at table, I'm not only mortified, but flattered. And I'm thunderstruck that he has ever ventured into a Barnes and Noble to gaze at my handiwork, for which his "Meet My Mother" essay didn't betray great respect.

But I'm dismayed by his unkind remarks about you, which I hope you don't take to heart. You tried so hard to be an attentive, affectionate father. Yet I did warn you that children are unusually alert to artifice, so it makes sense that it's your very effort that he derides. And you can understand why in relation to you of all people he feels compelled to portray himself as the victim.

I was grilled at length by Mary's lawyers about the "warning signs" that I should have picked up sufficiently in advance to have headed off calamity, but I think most mothers would have found the tangible signals difficult to detect. I did ask about the purpose of the five chain-and-padlock

Kryptonites when they were delivered to our door by FedEx, since Kevin had a bike lock, along with a bike he never rode. Yet his explanation seemed credible: He'd come across a terrific deal on the Internet, and he planned to sell these Kryptonites, which went for about $100 apiece retail, at school for a profit. If he'd never before displayed such entrepreneurial spunk, the aberration only seems glaring now that we know what the locks were for. How he got hold of school stationery I've no idea, and I never ran across it. And while he laid in a generous supply of arrows for his crossbow over a period of months, he never ordered more than half a dozen at a time. He was always ordering arrows, and the stockpile, which he kept outside in the shed, didn't attract my attention.

The one thing that I did notice through the rest of December and the early months of 1999 was that Kevin's *Gee, Dad* routine now extended to *Gee, Mumsey.* I don't know how you put up with it. *Gosh, are we having some of that great Armenian food tonight? Terriff! I sure want to learn more about my ethnic heritage! Lots of guys at school are plain old white-bread, and they're superjealous that I'm a member of a real-live persecuted minority!* Insofar as he had any tastes in food at all, he hated Armenian cuisine, and this disingenuous boppiness hurt my feelings. With me, Kevin's behavior had been hitherto as unadorned as his bedroom—stark, lifeless, sometimes hard and abrasive, but (or so I imagined) uncamouflaged. I preferred that. It was a surprise to discover that my son could come to seem even farther away.

I interpreted his transformation as induced by that conversation in the kitchen that he'd overheard—to which neither you nor I had alluded again, even in private. Our prospective separation loomed as a great smelly elephant in the living room, trumpeting occasionally or leaving behind massive piles of manure for us to trip over.

Yet astonishingly, our marriage blossomed into a second honeymoon, remember? We pulled off that Christmas with unequaled warmth. You secured me a signed copy of Peter Balakian's *Black Dog of Fate,* as well as Michael J. Arlen's *Passage to Ararat,* Armenian classics. In turn, I gave you a copy of *Alistair Cooke's America* and a biography of Ronald Reagan. If we were poking fun at one another, the teasing was tender. We indulged Kevin with some sports clothes that were grotesquely too small, while Celia, typically, was every bit as entranced with the bubble wrap it came in as with her glass-eyed antique doll. We made love more often than we had in years under the implicit guise of for-old-time's-sake.

I was unsure whether you were reconsidering a summer split or were merely impelled by guilt and grief to make the most of what was irrevocably terminal. In any event, there is something relaxing about hitting bottom. If we were about to get a divorce, nothing worse could possibly happen.

Or so we thought.

Eva

Dear Franklin,

I know it's bound to be a touchy subject for you. But I promise, if you hadn't given him that crossbow for Christmas, it would have been the longbow or poison darts. For that matter, Kevin was sufficiently resourceful to have capitalized on the Second Amendment and would have laid hands on the more conventional arsenal of pistols and deer rifles that his more modern-minded colleagues prefer. Frankly, traditional School Shooting instruments would not only have improved his margin of error but would have heightened the likelihood that he could best the competition in fatalities—clearly one of his driving ambitions, since before those Columbine upstarts came along twelve days later, he topped the charts. And you can be sure that he considered this issue at great length. He said himself at fourteen, "Choice of weapons is half the fight." So on the face of it, the archaic selection is peculiar. It handicapped him, or so it would seem.

He may have liked that. Maybe I passed on my own inclination to rise to a challenge, the very impulse that got me pregnant with the boy in the first place. And though he may have enjoyed sticking his mother, who fancied herself so "special," with the insult of cliché—like it or not, little Ms. International Traveler would become one more assembly-line mother of a tacky American type, and he knew how much it pained me that my sassy VW Luna was now every fifth car in the Northeast—he still liked the idea of setting himself apart. Since after Columbine he grumbled in Claverack that "any idiot can fire a shotgun," he must have recognized that being "the crossbow kid" would mark his little prank in the popular imagination. Indeed, by the spring of 1999 the field was crowded, and the once indelibly impressed names of Luke Woodham and Michael Carneal were already beginning to fade.

Moreover, he was certainly showing off. Maybe Jeff Reeves played a mean guitar riff, Soweto Washington could swish his free-throws, and Laura Woolford could get the whole football team to ogle her slim behind as it twitched down the hall, but Kevin Khatchadourian could put an arrow through an apple—or an ear—from fifty meters.

Nevertheless, I'm convinced that his leading motivation was ideological. Not that "I got plot" nonsense he fobbed off on Jack Marlin. Rather, I have in mind the "purity" he admired in the computer virus. Having registered the social compulsion to derive some broad, trenchant lesson from every asinine murder spree, he must have painstakingly parsed the prospective fallout from his own.

His father, at least, was forever dragging him off to some cluttered Native American museum or dreary Revolutionary War battlefield, so that anyone who tried to portray him as the neglected victim of the self-centered two-career marriage would have an uphill battle, and whatever he may have intuited, we were not divorced: no copy there. He wasn't a member of a satanic cult; most of his friends didn't go to church either, so godlessness was unlikely to emerge as a cautionary theme. He wasn't picked on—he had his unsavory friends, and his contemporaries went out of their way to leave him be—so the poor-persecuted-misfit, we-must-do-something-to-stop-bullying-in-schools number wouldn't go very far. Unlike the mental incontinents he held in such contempt, who passed malignant notes in class and made extravagant promises to confidants, he'd kept his mouth shut; he hadn't posted a homicidal web site or written essays about blowing up the school, and the most creative social commentator would be hard-pressed to deploy a satire about sports utility vehicles as one of those unmissable "warning signs" that are now meant to drive vigilant parents and teachers to call confidential hotlines. But best of all, if he accomplished his stunt entirely with a mere crossbow, his mother and all her mush-headed liberal friends wouldn't be able to parade him before Congress as one more poster boy for gun control. In short, his choice of weapon was meant to ensure to the best of his ability that *Thursday* would mean absolutely nothing.

When I got up at the usual 6:30 A.M. on April 8, 1999, I wasn't yet impelled to put that day of the week in italics. I picked out a blouse I rarely wore; you bent to me as I buttoned it in the mirror and said that I might not like to admit it, but I looked good in pink, and you kissed my temple. In those days your smallest kindness was writ large, and I blushed with pleasure. Once again I hoped you might be having second thoughts about separation, although I was reluctant to ask you outright and so risk spoiling the illusion. I made coffee, then roused Celia, helping her to clean and replace her prosthesis. She was still having trouble with discharge, and wiping the yellow crust off the glass and out of her eyelashes and tear duct could take a good ten minutes. Though it is amazing what you get used to, I still felt relieved once the glass eye was in, her watery blue gaze restored.

Aside from the fact that Kevin got up without having to be rousted three times, it began as a normal morning. As ever, I marveled at your appetite, recently revived; you may have been the last WASP in America who still regularly breakfasted on two eggs, bacon, sausage, and toast. I could never manage more than coffee, but I loved the sizzle of smoked pork, the fragrance of browning bread, and the general atmosphere of relish for the day ahead that this ritual fostered. The sheer vigor with which you prepared this feast must have scrubbed your arteries of its consequences.

"Look at you!" I exclaimed when Kevin emerged. I was carefully frying Celia's French toast completely dry, lest a little undercooked egg seem like *slime.* "What happened, were all your size-one clothes in the wash?"

"Some days you just wake up," he said, tucking his billowing white fencing shirt into the same rippling black rayon slacks he had worn to Hudson House, "with a sense of occasion."

In plain view, he packed the five Kryptonite locks and chains into his backpack. I assumed he'd found takers at school.

"Kevin looks really handsome," said Celia shyly.

"Yup, your brother's a heartbreaker," I said. And wouldn't he be.

I sifted a generous dusting of confectioner's sugar over the toast, stooping by Celia's soft blond hair to mumble, "Now don't dawdle, you don't want to be late for school again. You're supposed to eat it, not make friends with it."

I tucked her hair behind her ears and kissed the top of her head, and as I did so Kevin cut a glance toward me as he loaded the backpack with another chain. Though he'd entered the kitchen with a rare energy, now his eyes had gone dead.

"Hey, Kev!" you cried. "I ever show you how this camera works? Good knowledge of photography never hurt anybody; it's sure paid off for me. Get over here, there's time. I don't know what's got into you, but you have forty-five minutes to spare." You pushed your greasy plate out of the way and opened the camera bag at your feet.

Unwillingly, Kevin floated over. He didn't seem in the mood for *Gee-Dadding* this morning. As you went through the lighting and f-stop positions, I felt a pang of recognition. Your own father's awkward version of intimacy was always to explain in far greater detail than anyone cared to hear exactly how some device worked. You didn't share Herbert's conviction that to take apart the clockwork of the universe was to unlock the extent of its mysteries, but you had inherited a resort to mechanics as an emotional crutch.

"This reminds me," you said mid-instruction. "I want to shoot a roll of you at archery practice sometime soon. Capture that steely gaze and steady arm for posterity, how about it? We could do a whole photomontage for the foyer: Braveheart of the Palisades!"

Slapping his shoulder was probably a mistake; he flinched. And for the briefest of moments I appreciated what little access we ever had to what really went on in Kevin's head, since for a second the mask fell, and his face curdled with—well, with revulsion, I'm afraid. To allow even so brief a glimpse of its workings, he must have had other things on his mind.

"Yeah. *Dad*," he said effortfully. "That would be . . . *great*."

Yet I chose this of all mornings to gaze upon our domestic tableau in soft focus. All teenagers hate their parents, I thought, and there was something priceless about the antipathy if you could take it. As the sun caught the fine gold of Celia's hair while she cut her French toast into ridiculously tiny pieces and you embarked on a riff about the dangers of backlighting while Kevin twitched with impatience, I was so heartened by this Norman Rockwell moment that I considered sticking around until the kids had to leave for school, maybe giving Celia a lift myself instead of leaving the run to you. Would that I had given in to the temptation! But children need routine, I decided, and if I didn't get a jump on the morning rush hour, there would be hell to pay on the bridge.

"Shut up!" Kevin barked suddenly at your side. "That's *enough*. Shut up!"

Warily, we all three peered at this unprompted impertinence.

"I don't *care* how your camera works," he continued levelly. "I don't *want* to be a location scout for a bunch of crappy products. I'm *not interested*. I'm not interested in *baseball* or the *founding fathers* or *decisive battles* of the *Civil War*. I hate *museums* and *national monuments* and *picnics*. I don't want to memorize the *Declaration of Independence* in my spare time, or read *de Tocqueville*. I can't stand reruns of *Tora, Tora, Tora!* or documentaries about *Dwight Eisenhower*. I don't want to play *Frisbee* in the backyard or one more game of *Monopoly* with a sniveling, candy-ass, one-eyed midget. I don't give a *fuck* about *stamp collecting* or *rare coins* or pressing *colorful autumn leaves* in encyclopedias. And I've had it up to my eyeballs with *heart-to-heart father-son talks* about aspects of my life that are *none of your business*."

You looked stunned. I met your eyes, then just perceptibly shook my head. It was unusual for me to counsel restraint. But the pressure cooker was very popular among my mother's generation. After an incident now mythic in my family involving *madagh* scraped off the ceiling with a broom, I'd learned at an early age that when that chittering round whistle is blowing off steam, the worst thing you can do is open the pot.

"Okay," you said tightly, fitting your lenses back in the case. "You're on the record."

As abruptly as he had exploded, Kevin folded right back up, once again the complacent, unimaginative tenth-grader preparing for another humdrum day of school. I could see him shutting out your hurt feelings, one more thing in which, I suppose, he was *not interested*. For about five minutes no one said anything, and then we gradually resumed the pretense of an ordinary morning, making no mention of Kevin's outburst the way polite people are meant to pretend they didn't notice the release of a very loud fart. Still the smell lingered, if less of gas than of cordite.

Although by now in a hurry, I had to say good-bye to Celia twice. I stooped and brushed her hair, picked a last bit of crust from her lower lash, reminded her which books she had to take today, and then gave her a big long hug, but after I'd turned to collect my things, I noticed her still standing there where I'd left her looking stricken, hands held stiffly out from her side as if contaminated with *drydirt*. So I hoisted her by the armpits into my arms, though she was nearly eight now and supporting her full weight was hard on my back. She wrapped her legs around my waist, buried her head in my neck, and said, "I'll miss you!" I said I would miss her, too, though I had no idea how much.

Perhaps unnerved by Kevin's unwarranted harangue and in need of safe harbor, your own kiss good-bye was for once not an absent peck on the cheek, but feverish, open-mouthed. (Thank you, Franklin. I have relived that moment so many times now that the memory cells must be pale and broken down, like the denim of much-loved jeans.) As for my earlier uncertainty over whether children enjoy watching their parents kiss, one look at Kevin's face settled the matter. They didn't.

"Kevin, you have that independent study archery for gym today, don't you?" I reminded him, keen to consolidate our normality while bustling into my spring coat. "Don't forget to bring your kit."

"You can count on it."

"Also, you should make up your mind what you want to do for your birthday," I said. "It's only three days away, and sixteen is something of a milestone, don't you think?"

"In some ways," he said noncommittally. "Ever notice how *milestone* turns into *millstone* by changing only one letter?"

"What about Sunday!"

"I might be tied up."

I was frustrated that he always made it so difficult to be nice to him, but I had to go. I didn't kiss Kevin lately—teenagers didn't like it—so I brushed the back of my hand lightly against his forehead, which I was surprised to find damp and cold. "You're a little clammy. Do you feel all right?"

"Never better," said Kevin. I was on my way out the door when he called, "Sure you don't want to say good-bye to Celie *one more time?*"

"Very funny," I said behind me, and closed the door. I thought he was just riding me. In retrospect, he was giving me very sound advice that I really ought to have taken.

I have no idea what it must be like to wake up with such a terrible resolve. Whenever I picture it, I see myself roll over on the pillow muttering, *On second thought, I can't be bothered,* or at the very least, *Screw it, I'll do it tomorrow.* And tomorrow and tomorrow. Granted, the horrors we like to term "unthinkable" are altogether thinkable, and countless kids must fantasize about revenge for the thousand natural shocks that tenth-graders are heir to. It's not the visions or even half-baked plans that set our son apart. It's the staggering capacity to travel from plan to action.

Having racked my brains, the only analogy I've located in my own life is an awful stretch: all those trips to foreign countries that, up against it, I really didn't want to take. I would ease myself through by breaking a seemingly monumental excursion into its smallest constituent parts. Rather than dare myself to spend two months in thief-riddled Morocco, I would dare myself to pick up the phone. That's not so hard. And with a minion on its other end, I would have to say something, so I would order a ticket, taking refuge in the mercifully theoretical nature of airline sched- ules on dates at such marvelous remove that they could never possibly come to pass. Behold, a ticket arrives in the mail: Plan becomes action. I would dare myself to purchase histories of North Africa, and I would later dare myself to pack. The challenges, broken down, were surmount- able. Until, after daring myself into a taxi and down a jetway, it would be too late to turn back. Big deeds are a lot of little deeds one after the other, and that's what Kevin must have cottoned onto—ordering his Kryp- tonites, stealing his stationery, loading those chains into his backpack one by one. Take care of the components, and the sum of their parts unfolds as if by magic.

For my own part that Thursday—still plain old Thursday—I was busy; we were rushing to meet a due date at the printers. But in the odd unoccupied moment, I did reflect on Kevin's peculiar outburst that morn- ing. The diatribe had been signally absent the *likes*, *I means*, *sort of*s, and *I guesses* that commonly peppered his passable imitation of a regulation teenager. Rather than slump at an angle, he had stood upright, speaking from the center of his mouth rather than out one corner. I was certainly distressed that he would hurt his father's feelings with such abandon, but the young man who made these stark, unmediated declarations seemed a very different boy than the one I lived with every day. I found myself hop- ing we would meet again, especially at such a time that this stranger-son's state of mind was more agreeable—an unlikely prospect that to this day I continue to look forward to.

Around 6:15 P.M., there was a commotion outside my office, a conspiratorial huddling by my staff, which I interpreted as a sociable gossip as they knocked off for the day. Just as I was resigning myself to working into the evening on my own, Rose, their elected representative I suppose, knocked tentatively on my door. "Eva," she said gravely. "Your son's at Gladstone High School, isn't he?"

It was already on the Internet.

The details were incomplete: "Fatalities Feared in Gladstone High Shooting." Who and how many students had been shot was unclear. The culprit was unknown. In fact, the news flash was exasperatingly brief. "Security staff" had come upon "a scene of carnage" in the school gym, to which police were now "trying to gain access." I know I was flustered, but it didn't make the slightest bit of sense to me.

I immediately called your mobile, cursing when it was turned off; you did that all too often, treasuring the uninterrupted solitude of your 4x4 as you tooled around New Jersey searching for the right-colored cows. I appreciated that you didn't want to hear from a rep from Kraft or your Madison Avenue minders, but you might have thought to turn it on for me. What's the point of *having* the damned thing? I fretted. I called home but got our machine; it was a lovely spring evening, and doubtless Robert had taken Celia out in the backyard to play. The fact that Kevin didn't pick up made my stomach churn, but I reasoned feverishly that of course he could have slunk off with Lenny Pugh, with whom he had inexplicably patched things up since the Pagorski hearing. Perhaps the trade in slavish disciples was not so brisk that a self-abasing sidekick could be easily replaced.

So I grabbed my coat and resolved to go straight to the school. As I left, my staff was already regarding me with the awe that attends those who have even the most tangential association with the cameo news flash on the America On-Line home page.

As we follow me running down to the garage to my VW , gunning out of midtown only to get stuck on the West Side Highway, let's get one thing straight. I did think Kevin screamed in his crib out of free-floating rage, and not because he needed feeding. I fiercely believed that when he poked fun at our waitress's "poopy face" he knew he would hurt her feelings, and that he defaced the maps on my study walls out of calculated

malice, not misguided creativity. I was still convinced that he systematically seduced Violetta into clawing a layer of skin from the better part of
her body and that he continued to require diapers until he was six years
old not because he was traumatized or confused or slow to develop, but
because he was on a full-time war-footing with his mother. I thought he
destroyed the toys and storybooks I painstakingly fashioned because they
were worth more to him as emblems of his own up-yours ingratitude than
as sentimental playthings, and I was sure that he learned to count and read
in secret deliberately to deprive me of any sense of usefulness as a parent.
My certainty that he was the one who flipped the quick-release on the
front wheel of Trent Corley's bicycle was unwavering. I was under no illusion that a nest of bagworms had dropped into Celia's backpack by itself
or that she had climbed twenty feet up our white oak only to get stranded
on an upper branch all by her lonesome; I believed it was no more her idea
to stir together a lunch of petroleum jelly and Thai curry paste than it was
to play "kidnapping" and "William Tell." I was pretty damned sure that
whatever Kevin whispered in the ear of let-us-call-her-Alice at that eighth-
grade school dance, it wasn't admiration of her dress; and however
Liquid-Plumr got in Celia's left eye, I was dead positive that her brother
had something to do with it beyond his role as her noble savior. I regarded
his jerking off at home with the door wide open as wanton sexual
abuse—of his mother—and not the normal uncontrolled bubbling of
adolescent hormones. Although I may have told Mary that Laura should
suck it up, I found it entirely credible that our son had told her frail, under-
fed daughter that she was fat. It was no mystery to *me* how a hit list turned
up in Miguel Espinoza's locker, and though I took full responsibility for
spreading one to my own company, I couldn't see the hobby of collecting
computer viruses as anything but disturbed and degenerate. I remained
firmly of the view that Vicki Pagorski had been persecuted in a show trial
of Kevin Khatchadourian's personal contrivance. Granted, I'd been mistaken about our son's responsibility for chucking chunks of bricks at oncoming cars on 9W, and until ten days ago I had chalked up the disap-
pearance of a treasured photograph from Amsterdam as yet another
victim of my son's unparalleled spite. So I have, as I said, always believed
the worst. But even my unnatural maternal cynicism had its limits. When

Rose told me there'd been a vicious assault at Kevin's high school and some students were feared dead, I worried for his well-being. Not for an instant did I imagine that our son was the perpetrator.

The testimony of witnesses to an event is notoriously shambolic, especially on its immediate heels. On-scene, misinformation rules. Only after the fact is order imposed on chaos. Hence, with a few keystrokes on-line I can now access numerous versions of our son's actions that day that make crude chronological sense. Few pieces of this tale were available to me when I careened into the school parking lot with the radio on, but years of contemplative reflection spread before me for the leisurely assembly of this hobbyistic jigsaw, much as Kevin himself has years more access to un-derequipped wood shops in which to file, sand, and polish his excuse.

Schools do not necessarily regard their letterhead stationery as the keys to the kingdom, and I doubt it's all locked up. However he acquired it, Kevin had paid enough attention in Dana Rocco's English class to digest that form dictates tone. As you do not use popular slang in an article for the school paper, neither do you indulge nihilistic little games involving three-letter words when printing on letterhead stationery. Hence, the official missive sent to Greer Ulanov, for example—in sufficient advance to allow for Nyack's lacklustre postal service—exhibits the same keen ear for authenticity that Kevin displayed in playing Ron Howard to you and the shy, flustered victim to Alan Strickland:

Dear _____ *Greer* _____ ,

The faculty of Gladstone High School is proud of *all* their students, each of whom contributes his or her own remarkable talents to the community. Yet certain students invariably come to our attention as having distinguished themselves in the arts or having done even more than their share in shaping a dynamic educational environment. We are pleased to reward this unusual excellence at the end of the school year.

In consultation with teachers and staff, I have compiled a list of nine exemplary students who seem most worthy of our new Bright and Shining Promise Award. I am delighted to inform you that you are one of these nine, singled out for your outstanding contributions in ____*politics and civic awareness*____.

In furtherance of this process, we are asking all BSPA winners to assemble in the gym on Thursday, April 8 at 3:30 P.M. It is our hope that you can begin to put together an assembly program for early June in which the BSPA prizes will be awarded. Some demonstration of your exceptional gifts would be appropriate. Those of you in the arts can readily demonstrate your skills; others with more academic talents may have to exercise creativity as to how best to exemplify your accomplishments.

While we have made our decisions based solely on merit, we have tried to arrive at a mix of gender, race, ethnicity, religion, and sexual preference so that the BSPA will suitably reflect our community's diversity.

Lastly, I would implore you all to please keep your selection for this award to yourselves. If I hear of any boasting, the administration may be forced to reconsider your candidacy. We truly wish it were possible to give *every* student a prize for being the very special person that he or she is, and it is very important that you not cause unnecessary jealousy before the award winners are made public.

My heartfelt congratulations.

> Sincerely,
> Donald Bevons
> Principal

Identical notices were sent to eight other students, with the blanks filled in accordingly. Denny Corbitt was commended for acting, Jeff Reeves for classical guitar, Laura Woolford for "personal grooming," Brian "Mouse" Ferguson for computing skills, Ziggy Randolph not only for ballet but for "encouraging tolerance of difference," Miguel Espinoza for academic achievement and "vocabulary skills," Soweto Washington for sports, Joshua Lukronsky for "cinematic studies" and—I fault Kevin here for not being able to control himself—"memorizing whole Quentin Tarantino scripts," though most people are disinclined to regard flattery with suspicion. Dana Rocco was sent a somewhat different letter that requested she chair this Thursday meeting but also advising that she herself had been selected for the Most Beloved Teacher Award and likewise requesting, since all the other teachers are *also* beloved, that she keep her MBTA on the q.t.

If the trap was well set, it was not immune to glitches. Dana Rocco might have mentioned the meeting to Bevons, who would have protested ignorance, and the whole business might have come unraveled. Can we really call Kevin *lucky*? She didn't.

On the evening of April 7, Kevin set his alarm for half an hour earlier than usual and laid out clothing for the morning roomy enough to allow for ease of mobility, choosing that dashing white shirt with billowing fencing-style sleeves in which he might photograph well. Personally, I would have tossed through such a night in anguish, but then I personally would never have contrived this grotesque project in the first place, so I can only assume that if Kevin lost any sleep it was from excitement.

Riding the school bus the following morning he would have been encumbered—those bike locks weighed 6.2 pounds apiece—but Kevin had arranged for this independent-study archery course at the beginning of the semester, interest in the unpopular pastime being too slight for a proper class. Other students had been trained to regard his lugging archery equipment to school as ordinary. No one was sufficiently attuned to the niceties of this dorky sport to be disturbed that Kevin wasn't lugging his standard bow or his longbow but his crossbow, which the administration later bent over backward to deny would ever have been allowed on school grounds. Though the number of arrows in his possession was considerable—he was obliged to cart them in his duffel—no one remarked on the bag; the wide berth that his classmates allowed Kevin in eighth grade had by his sophomore year only broadened.

After stashing his archery materiel, as usual, in the equipment room of the gym, he attended all of his classes. In English, he asked Dana Rocco what *maleficence* means, and she beamed.

His independent-study archery practice was scheduled for the last period of the day, and—his enthusiasm firmly established—PE teachers no longer checked up on him as he fired arrows into a sawdust target. Hence, Kevin had ample time to clear the gym of any apparatuses such as punching bags, horses, or heavy tumbling mats. Conveniently, the bleachers were already up, and to make sure they stayed up, he clipped small combination padlocks around the intersection of two iron supports on both banks, ensuring that they could not fold out. When he was finished there was absolutely nothing in that gym except six blue mats—the thin kind, for sit-ups—arranged in a convivial circle in the middle.

The logistics, for those impressed by such things, were impeccably worked out. The physical education building is a freestanding structure, a good three-minute walk from the main campus. There are five entrances to the central gym itself—from the boys' and girls' locker rooms and the equipment room, as well as from the lobby; a door on the second floor opens onto an alcove, used for the aerobic conditioning machines, that overlooks the gym. Yet not one of these entrances lies on the outside of the building. The gym is unusually high, a full two stories, and there are windows only at the top; you can't see inside from ground level. There were no sporting events scheduled for that afternoon.

The bell rang at 3:00, and by 3:15 the distant clamor of departing students was dying down. The gym itself was deserted, though Kevin must have still padded with trepidation as he glided into the boys' locker room and unlooped his first Kryptonite bike lock from around his shoulder. He's a methodical person in the most ordinary of circumstances, so we can be sure that he had twist-tied the correct key to each bright yellow, plastic-coated padlock. Looping the heavy chain around each handle of the double doors, he pulled the chain taut. After hiking up the chain's protective black nylon sheath, he hooked the sunny yellow padlock into a middle link, clicked the lock shut, twisted the round key from its socket, and slipped it in his pocket. I dare say he tested the doors, which would now only open with a crack between them before they seized. He repeated this exercise in the girls' locker room, then at the gym entrance from the equipment room, exiting from its back door into the weights room.

I now know that these locks were state-of-the-art in bicycle security. The U-shaped portion of the tiny, sturdy padlock is only about two inches high, denying prospective thieves the leverage for a crowbar. The chain itself is forged interlinking at the factory; each link is half an inch thick. Kryptonite chains are famously resistant to heat, since professional cycle thieves have been known to use torches, and the company is sufficiently confident of its technology that if your bicycle is stolen, it guarantees a full refund for the purchase value of the bike. Unlike many competitors' models, the guarantee is even good in New York.

Despite his avowed disinterest in your work, Franklin, Kevin was about to launch Kryptonite's most successful advertising campaign to date.

By 3:20, giggling with self-congratulatory glee, the first BSPA winners were starting to arrive through the main entrance from the lobby, which remained unlocked.

"*Personal hygiene,* my *momma!*" Soweto declared.

"Hey, we're *bright and shining,*" said Laura, tossing her silken brown hair. "Don't we get any chairs?"

Mouse crossed to the equipment room to scrounge some fold-ups, but when he came back reporting the room already locked for the day Greer said, "I don't know, it's kind of neat this way. We can sit cross-legged, like around a campfire."

"Puh-*lease,*" said Laura, whose outfit was—scant. "Cross-legged, in this skirt? And it's Versace, for Chrissake. I don't want to stink it up with sit-up sweat."

"Yo, girl," Soweto nodded at her spindly figure, "that close as you gonna come to *sit-up sweat.*"

Kevin was able to listen in on his prizewinners from the alcove, an inset shelf on the upper level; so long as he remained against the back wall, he couldn't be seen from below. The three stationary bicycles, treadmill, and rowing machine had already been dragged away from the alcove's protective railing. Transferred from the duffel, his stash of some hundred arrows bristled from two fire buckets.

Enticed by the marvelous echo, Denny emoted a few lines from *Don't Drink the Water* at the top of his lungs, while Ziggy, who made a habit of flouncing around school in a leotard and tights to show off his calves, couldn't resist making what Kevin later called "a big queeny entrance," dancing a series of turns in *pointe* position across the length of the gym and finishing with a *grand jeté.* But Laura, who doubtless thought it uncool to ogle fags, only had eyes for Jeff Reeves—though quiet and terminally earnest, a handsome blue-eyed boy with a long blond ponytail with whom a dozen girls were known to be smitten. One of Jeff's salivating fans, according to an interview with a friend recorded by NBC, was Laura Woolford, which more than his mastery of the twelve-string guitar may have explained why he, too, was christened Bright and Shining.

Miguel, who must have told himself he was unpopular for being smart or Latino—anything but for being a little pudgy—promptly plunked himself on one of the blue mats, to burrow with knit-browed seriousness into a battered copy of Alan Bloom's *The Closing of the American Mind*. Beside him, Greer, who made the mistake common to rejects everywhere of assuming that outcasts like each other, was busy trying to engage him in a discussion of NATO's intervention in Kosovo.

Dana Rocco arrived at 3:35. "Come on troops!" she rallied them. "Ziggy, that's all very dramatic, but this isn't ballet practice. Can we get down to business here? This is a happy occasion, but it's still after-hours for me, and I'd like to get home before Letterman."

At this point, the cafeteria worker arrived, carting a tray of cellophaned sandwiches. "Where you want these, ma'am?" he asked Rocco. "We got a order from Mr. Bevons to provide refreshments."

"Wasn't that thoughtful of Don!" she exclaimed.

Well. It was thoughtful of someone. And I have to say, the sandwiches were a nice touch, that little garnish of an authentic school occasion. But Kevin may have been over-egging the pudding a bit, and the gesture would cost him *collateral damage*.

"Ma'am, my shift's over now, you mind if I shoot a few? I just be over at the far end there, won't be no trouble. Don't got no hoop in my neighborhood. I'd be much obliged."

Rocco would have hesitated—the noise would be a distraction—but the cafeteria worker was black.

Kevin must have been kicking himself for having left that basketball off in the corner, but by this time—3:40—he'd have been more distracted by the no-show. Only nine of his ten party guests had reported for duty, along with one gate-crasher. This operation was not organized for latecomers, and as the meeting got underway he must have been frantically concocting a contingency plan to allow for the dilatory performance of Joshua Lukronsky.

"Oh, gr-ooss!" said Laura, passing the platter. "Turkey *roll*. Total waste of calories."

"First off, you guys," Rocco began, "I want to congratulate you all on having been picked for this special award—"

"O-kay!" The lobby doors burst wide. *"Let's get in character!"*

Kevin would never have been quite so happy to see the consummately irritating Joshua Lukronsky. As the circle enlarged to make a place for Josh, Kevin crept out of the alcove and slipped downstairs with another Kryptonite. Although he was as quiet as he could be, the chain did rattle a little, and he may have been grateful for the banging of the cafeteria worker's basketball at that. Back up in the alcove, he slipped his last padlock and chain around the inside bars of the alcove's double doors.

Voilà. Fish in a barrel.

Was he having second thoughts, or simply enjoying himself? Their meeting had proceeded another five minutes by the time Kevin advanced stealthily toward the rail with his loaded crossbow. Though he drew into sight from below, the group was too engrossed in planning their own accolades to look up.

"I could give a speech," Greer proposed. "Like on how the office of special prosecutor should be abolished? Because I think Kenneth Starr is evil incarnate!"

"What about something a little less divisive?" Rocco proposed. "You don't want to alienate Republicans—"

"Wanna *bet*?"

A soft, rushing sound. Just as there is a tiny pause between lightning and thunderclap, there was a single, dense instant of silence between the arrow's *shsh-thunk* through Laura Woolford's Versace blouse and the point at which the other students began to scream.

"Oh, my God!"

"Where'd it come from!"

"She's bleeding all OVER!"

Shsh-thunk. Not yet struggled to his feet, Miguel took one in the gut. *Shsh-thunk.* Jeff was nailed between the shoulder blades as he bent over Laura Woolford. I can only conclude that for those many hours Kevin spent in our backyard, the little black bull's-eye in the middle of all those concentric circles was in his mind's eye a perfect circle of Versace viscose. Struck perfectly through the heart, she was dead.

"He's up there!" Denny pointed.

"Kids, get out! Run!" Rocco ordered, though she needn't have; the unin-jured remainder had already stampeded toward the main exit, where they were giving new meaning to the term *panic bars.* Yet given the position of the alcove, there wasn't one square foot in that gym that couldn't be pene-trated from over its railing, as they were all soon to discover.

"Oh, shit, I should have known!" screamed Joshua with an upward glance, rattling the equipment room door that Mouse had already tried. "It's *Khatchadourian!"*

Shsh-thunk. As he pounded on the main doors calling for help while the arrow stuck in his back quivered, a shaft sank into the nape of Jeff Reeves's neck. As Mouse streaked to the boys' locker room exit and the doors gave just a little and held fast, he took an arrow in the ass; it wouldn't kill him, but as he hobbled to the one last exit on the girls' side, he was surely begin-ning to realize that there was plenty of time for one that did.

Dana Rocco got to the girls' exit at about the same time, weighed down by Laura's body in her arms—a fruitless but valiant effort that would feature prominently in the memorial service. Mouse met Rocco's eyes and shook his head. As his shrieking classmates began to circle from door to door in a churning motion like dough in a mixing bowl, Mouse shouted over the uproar, "The doors are locked! All the doors are locked! Take cover!"

Behind *what?*

The cafeteria worker—less attuned to the School Shooting format than the students, who had been through whole preparatory assemblies and *got into character* right away—had been easing along the walls as if feel-ing for one of those secret passageways in murder mysteries, moving slowly, attracting minimum attention. The cinder block unavailing, he now crouched into a fetal ball, holding the basketball between the archer and his head. Kevin was doubtless annoyed at having allowed any obstacle to remain in the gym however small, and the ineffectual protection just drew fire. *Shsh-phoot.* The ball was skewered.

"Kevin!" cried his English teacher, triangulating Mouse behind her body into the corner farthest from the alcove. "Please stop! Please, please stop!"

"Maleficence," Kevin hissed distinctly from overhead; Joshua said later that it was weird how you could hear this relatively quiet word above the

din. For the duration, it was all that Kevin said. Thereafter, Kevin fixed his staunchest ally on the Gladstone faculty steadily in his sight and put an arrow straight between her eyes.

As she fell, Mouse was exposed in the corner, and though he began to crouch in the shelter of her body, he took another shaft that pierced a lung. That would teach him to share the secrets of computer viruses with mere cyber-dilettantes who were really much more interested in archery.

But Mouse, in Joshua's view, had the right idea; so far, Lukronsky's scrabbling up all the thin blue sit-up mats and trying to fashion some kind of shield wasn't working nearly as well as it would have in the movies, and already two arrows had whizzed within inches of his head. Scooting over to Mouse's corner while Kevin was occupied with reaming Soweto Washington's powerful thighs, Joshua built himself an impromptu lean-to in the corner constructed of the blue foam rubber, Dana Rocco, Laura Woolford, and the groaning, half-conscious body of Mouse Ferguson. It was from this stuffy tent that he observed the denouement, peering from under Laura's armpit as Mouse's breath bubbled. It was hot, suffused with the rank fumes of fearful sweat and another, more disturbing smell that was nauseously cloying.

Giving up on safe haven, Greer Ulanov had marched right up to the wall that dropped from the alcove's railing, standing twenty feet immediately below their malevolent Cupid. She had finally found a bête noir more odious than Kenneth Starr.

"I hate you, you stupid creep!" she screeched. "I hope you fry! I hope they shoot you full of poison and I get to watch you die!" It was a rapid conversion. Only the month before, she'd written an impassioned essay denouncing capital punishment.

Leaning over the railing, Kevin shot straight down, striking Greer through the foot. The arrow went through to the wooden floor, and pinned her where she stood. As she blanched and struggled to pull the arrow from the floor, he pinned her second foot as well. He could afford the fun; he must still have had fifty, sixty arrows in reserve.

By this time, the other injured had all crawled to the far wall, where they flopped like voodoo dolls stuck with pins. Most bunched on the floor, trying to present the smallest targets possible. But Ziggy Randolph, yet unscathed, now strode to the very middle of the gym, where he presented himself with chest blown out, heels together, toes pronated. Dark and fine-featured, he was a striking boy with a commanding presence, though tritely effeminate in manner; I have never been sure if homosexuals' limp-wristed gestures are innate, or studied.

"Khatchadourian!" Ziggy's voice resonated over the sound of sobbing. "Listen to me! You don't have to do this! Just put the bow on the floor, and let's talk. A lot of these guys'll be all right, if we just get some medics right away!"

It's worth inserting a reminder here that after Michael Carneal shot up that prayer group in Paducah, Kentucky, in 1997, a devout Heath High School senior, a preacher's son with the novelistic name Ben Strong was feted from coast to coast for having advanced soothingly on the shooter, urging the boy to put down his weapon and putting himself in mortal danger in the process. In response, according to legend, Carneal dropped the pistol and collapsed. Due to nationwide hunger for heroes in events that were otherwise becoming irredeemable international embarrassments, the story was widely known. Strong was featured in *Time* magazine and interviewed on *Larry King Live*. Ziggy's own familiarity with this parable may have bolstered his courage to confront their assailant, and the unprecedented admiration that had met Ziggy's "coming out" to an assembly earlier that semester would have further enhanced his faith in his persuasive powers of oratory.

"I know you must be really upset about something, okay?" Ziggy continued; most of Kevin's victims were not yet dead, and someone was already feeling sorry for him. "I'm sure you're hurting inside! But this is no way out—"

Unfortunately for Ziggy, the apocryphal nature of Ben Strong's stern, mesmerizing *Michael? Put down the gun!* would not come out until the spring of 2000, when a suit filed by the victims' parents against more than fifty other parties—including parents, teachers, school officials, other teenagers, neighbors, the makers of "Doom" and "Quake" video games, and the film producers of *The Basketball Diaries*—came to trial in circuit court. Under oath, Strong confessed that an initially sloppy rendition of events to his principal had been further embellished by the media and taken on a life of its own. Trapped in a lie, he'd been miserable ever since. Apparently by the time our hero approached, Michael Carneal had already stopped shooting and had collapsed, his surrender unrelated to any eloquent, death-defying appeal. "He just got done," Strong testified, "and he dropped it."

Shsh-thunk. Ziggy staggered backward.

I hope I haven't related this chronology in so dispassionate a fashion that I seem callous. It's just that the facts remain bigger, bolder, and more glistening than any one small grief. I'm simply reiterating a sequence of events strung together by *Newsweek.*

In parroting its copy, however, I do not pretend any remarkable insight into Kevin's state of mind, the one foreign country into which I have been most reluctant to set foot. Descriptions from Joshua and Soweto of our son's expression from overhead depart from the reportage of similar events. Those Columbine children, for example, were manic, eyes glazed, grinning crazily. Kevin, by contrast, was described as "concentrated" and "deadpan." But then, he always looked that way on the archery range, if only on the archery range, come to think of it—as if he became the arrow, and thus discovered in this embodiment the sense of purpose that his phlegmatic daily persona so extravagantly lacked.

Yet I have reflected on the fact that for most of us, there is a hard, impassable barrier between the most imaginatively detailed depravity and its real-life execution. It's the same solid steel wall that inserts itself between a knife and my wrist even when I'm at my most disconsolate. So how was Kevin able to raise that crossbow, point it at Laura's breastbone, and then really, actually, in time and space, squeeze the release? I can only assume that he discovered what I never wish to. That there is no barrier. That like my trips abroad or this ludicrous scheme of bike locks and invitations on school stationery, the very squeezing of that release can be broken down into a series of simple constituent parts. It may be no more miraculous to pull the trigger of a bow or a gun than it is to reach for a glass of water. I fear that crossing into the "unthinkable" turns out to be no more athletic than stepping across the threshold of an ordinary room; and that, if you will, is the trick. The secret. As ever, the secret is that there is no secret. He must almost have wanted to giggle, though that is not his style; those Columbine kids *did* giggle. And once you have found out that there is nothing to stop you—that the barrier, so seemingly uncrossable, is *all in your head*—it must be possible to step back and forth across that threshold again and again, shot after shot, as if an unintimidating pipsqueak has drawn a line across the carpet that you must not pass and you launch tauntingly over it, back and over it, in a mocking little dance.

That said, it is the last bit that harrows me most. I have no metaphors to help us.

If it seems extraordinary that no one responded to the cries for help, the gym is isolated, and the stragglers at the school who later admitted to hearing screams and shouts understandably assumed that an exciting or fractious sporting event was underway. There was no telltale crack of gunfire. And the most obvious explanation for this absence of alarm is that, while it may take a while to tell, the melee couldn't have lasted more than ten minutes. But if Kevin had entered into some sort of altered mental state, it was far more sustained than ten minutes.

Soweto passed out, which probably saved him. As Joshua remained motionless, his fleshy fortress shook from a systematic rain of arrows, some combination of which would finish Mouse Ferguson. Shouts for help or wails of pain further down the wall were silenced with additional shots. He took his time, Franklin—emptying both buckets, until that line of limp casualties bristled like a family of porcupines. But more appalling than this cheap archery practice—his victims could no longer be regarded as moving targets—was its cessation. It's surprisingly difficult to kill people with a crossbow. Kevin knew that. And so he waited. When at last at 5:40 a security guard jingled by to lock up, was dismayed by the Kryptonite, and peeked through the crack of the door to see red, Kevin waited. When the police arrived with those massive but useless cutters (which the chain merely dented) and at length were driven to secure an electric metal saw that shrieked and spit sparks—all of which took time—Kevin put his feet up on the alcove rail and waited. Indeed, the protracted interlude between his last arrow and the SWAT team's final burst through the lobby door at 6:55 was one of those untenanted periods for which I'd advised him at age six that he'd be grateful for a book.

Laura Woolford and Dana Rocco were killed by the trauma of the arrows themselves. Ziggy, Mouse, Denny, Greer, Jeff, Miguel, and the cafeteria worker all bled to death, trickle by drop.

(April 6, 2001—Continued)

When I wheeled out of the car, the lot was already jammed with ambulances and police cars. A bunting of yellow tape marked its perimeter. It was just getting dark, and careworn paramedics were lit in ghoulish admixtures of red and blue. Stretcher after stretcher paraded into the lot—I was aghast; there seemed no end to them. Yet even amid pandemonium, a familiar face will flash brighter than emergency vehicles, and my eyes seized on Kevin in a matter of seconds. It was a classic double take. Although I may have had my problems with our son, I was still relieved that he was alive. But I was denied the luxury of wallowing in my healthy maternal instincts. At a glance, it was obvious that he was not marching but *being marched* down the path from the gym by a brace of policemen, and the only reason he could possibly be holding his hands behind his back rather than swinging them in his conventionally insolent saunter is that he hadn't any choice.

I felt dizzy. For a moment, the lights of the parking lot scattered into meaningless splotches, like the patterns behind the lids when you rub your eyes.

"Ma'am, I'm afraid you'll have to clear the area—." It was one of the officers who appeared at our door after the overpass incident, the heavier, more cynical of the pair. They must meet a plethora of wide-eyed parents whose darling little reprobates issued "from a good family," because he didn't seem to recognize my face.

"You don't understand," I said, adding the most difficult claim of fealty I'd ever made, "*That's my son.*"

His face hardened. This was an expression I would get used to; that, and the melting you-poor-dear-I-don't-know-what-to-say one, which was worse. But I was not inured to it yet, and when I asked him what had happened, I could already tell from the flinty look in his eye that whatever I was now indirectly responsible for, it was bad.

"We've had some casualties, ma'am," was all he was inclined to explain. "Best you came down to the station. Just take 59 to 303, and exit at Orangeberg Road. Entrance on Town Hall Road. That's *assuming* you've never been there before."

"Can I—talk to him?"

"You'll have to see that officer there, ma'am. With the cap?" He has-
tened away.

Making my way toward the police car into whose back seat I'd seen a
policeman shove our son with a hand on the top of his head, I was forced
to run a gamut, explaining with increasing fatigue who I was to a sequence
of officers. I finally understood the New Testament story about St. Peter,
and why he might have been driven to thrice deny association with some
social pariah who'd been set upon by a lynch mob. Repudiation may have
been even more tempting for me than for Peter, since, whatever he might
have styled himself, that boy was no messiah.

I finally battled to the Orangetown black-and-white, whose envelop-
ing inscription on the side, "In partnership with the community," no
longer seemed to include me. Staring at the back window, I couldn't see
through the glass for the blinking reflections. So I cupped my hand over
the window. He wasn't crying or hanging his head. He turned to the window. He had no trouble looking me in the eye.

I had thought to scream, *What have you done?* But the hackneyed excla-
mation would have been self-servingly rhetorical, a flouting of parental
disavowal. I would know the details soon enough. And I could not imagine a conversation that would be anything but ridiculous.

So we stared at each other in silence. Kevin's expression was placid. It
still displayed remnants of resolution, but determination was already sliding to the quiet, self-satisfied complacency of a job well done. His eyes
were strangely clear—unperturbed, almost peaceful—and I recognized
their pellucidity from that morning, though breakfast already seemed ten
years past. This was the stranger-son, the boy who dropped his corny,
shuffling disguise of *I mean* and *I guess* for the plumb carriage and lucidity
of a man with a mission.

He was pleased with himself, I could see that. And that's all I needed
to know.

Yet when I picture his face through that back window now, I remember something else as well. He was searching. He was looking for something in my face. He looked for it very carefully and very hard, and then
he leaned back a little in his seat. Whatever he'd been searching for, he

hadn't found it, and this, too, seemed to satisfy him in some way. He didn't smile. But he might as well have.

Driving to the Orangetown police station, I'm afraid I got enraged with you, Franklin. It wasn't fair, but your mobile was still switched off, and you know how one fixates on these small, logistical matters as a distraction. I wasn't able, yet, to get angry at Kevin, and it seemed safer to vent my frustrations on you, since you hadn't done anything wrong. Hitting that redial button over and over, I railed aloud at the wheel. "Where *are* you? It's almost 7:30! Turn on the fucking phone! For God's sake, of all the nights, why did you have to work late *tonight?* And haven't you listened to the *news?*" But you didn't play the radio, in your truck; you preferred CDs of Springsteen, or Charlie Parker. *"Franklin, you son of a bitch!"* I shouted, my tears still the hot, leaking, stingy ones of fury. "How could make me go through this all by myself?"

I drove past Town Hall Road at first, since that slick, rather garish green-and-white building looks like a chain steakhouse or subscription fitness center from the outside. Aside from its clumsily wrought bronze frieze memorializing four Orangetown officers fallen in the line of duty, the foyer, too, was an expanse of white walls and characterless linoleum where you would expect to find directions to the pool. But the reception room itself was horrifyingly intimate, even more claustrophobically tiny than the emergency room at Nyack Hospital.

I was accorded anything but priority status, though the receptionist did inform me coldly through the window that I could accompany my "minor"—a word that seemed inappropriately reductive—while he was booked. Panicked, I pleaded, "Do I have to?" and she said, "Suit yourself." She directed me to the single black vinyl sofa, to which I was abandoned untended as police officers raced back and forth. I felt both implicated and irrelevant. I didn't want to be there. In case that sounds like a grievous understatement, I mean that I had the novel experience of not wanting to be anywhere else, either. Flat out, I wished I were dead.

For a short time, on the opposite side of my sticky black vinyl couch sat a boy whom I now know to be Joshua Lukronsky. Even had I

been familiar with this student, I doubt I'd have recognized him at that
moment. A small boy, he no longer resembled an adolescent, but a
child closer to Celia's age, for he lacked any of the wisecracking swagger for which he was apparently known at school. His shoulders were
drawn in, his cropped black hair disheveled. Hands shoved inward in
his lap, he kept his wrists bent at the unnaturally severe angle of children in the advanced stages of muscular dystrophy. He sat perfectly
still. He never seemed to blink. Awarded a police minder that my own
role didn't merit—I already had that feeling of being infected, contagious, quarantined—he didn't respond as the uniformed man standing
next to him tried to interest him in a glassed-in case of model police
vehicles. It was quite a charming collection, all metal, some very old—
vans, horse trailers, motorcycles, '49 Fords from Florida, Philadelphia,
L.A. With fatherly tenderness, the officer explained that one car was
very rare, from the days that New York City police cars were green-
and-white—before NYPD blue. Joshua stared blankly straight ahead.
If he knew I was there at all, he did not appear to know who I was, and
I was hardly going to introduce myself. I wondered why this boy had
not been taken to the hospital like the others. There was no way of
telling that none of the blood drenching his clothes belonged to him.

After a few minutes, a large, plump woman flew through the reception
room door, swooping down on Joshua and lifting him in a single motion
into her arms. "Joshua!" she cried. At first limp in her clasp, gradually
those muscular-dystrophy wrists curled around her shoulders. His shirt-
sleeves left red smears on her ivory raincoat. The small face buried in her
ample neck. I was simultaneously moved, and jealous. This was the reunion that I'd been denied. *I love you so much! I'm so, so relieved you're all right!*
Me, I was no longer entirely relieved that our own son was *all right*. From
my glance in that car window, it was his very seeming *all right*ness that had
begun to torment me.

The trio shuffled through the inside door. The officer behind the reception window ignored me. If at wit's end, I was probably grateful for my
little task with the mobile, which I worried like a rosary; dialing gave me
something to do. If only for variety, I switched to trying our home phone
for a while, but I kept getting the machine, and I'd hang up in the middle of
that stilted recording, hating the sound of my own voice. I'd already left

three, four messages, the first controlled, the last weeping—what a tape to come home to. Realizing that we were both running late, Robert had obviously taken Celia to McDonald's; she loved their hot apple pies. Why didn't *he* call me? He had my mobile number! Hadn't *Robert* listened to the news? Oh, I know, McDonald's broadcasts Muzak, and he wouldn't necessarily switch on his car radio for such a short trip. But wouldn't someone mention it while standing on line? How could anyone in Rockland County be talking about anything else?

By the time two officers fetched me into that plain little room to take my statement, I was so distraught that I was less than polite. I probably sounded thick, too; I couldn't see the purpose of contacting our family's lawyer when there didn't appear to be any question that Kevin did it. And this was the first time that anyone had seen fit to give his mother even the sketchiest lowdown on did *what*. The casualty estimates that one officer rattled off matter-of-factly would later prove exaggerated, but back then I'd had no reason to have researched the fact that atrocity figures are almost always inflated when first released. Besides, what is the difference, really, between bearing a son who murders *only* nine people instead of thirteen? And I found their questions obscenely immaterial: how Kevin did in school, what had he been like that morning.

"He was a little testy with my husband! Otherwise, nothing special! What was I supposed to do, my son was rude to his father, so I call the police?"

"Now, calm down Mrs. Kachourian—"

"Khatchadourian!" I insisted. "Can you *please* get my name right?"

Oh, they would.

"Mrs. *Khadourian*, then. Where might your son have gotten that crossbow?"

"It was a Christmas present! Oh, I *told* Franklin it was a mistake, I *told* him. Can I please call my husband again?"

They allowed the call, and after another fruitless redial, I wilted. "I'm so sorry," I whispered. "I'm so sorry, I'm so sorry. I didn't mean to be unkind to you, I don't care about my name, I hate my name. I never want to hear my name again. I'm so sorry—"

"Mrs. Khadarian—" One officer patted my shoulder gingerly. "Maybe we should take a full statement another time."

"It's just, I have a daughter, a little girl, Celia, at home, could you—"

"I understand. Now, I'm afraid Kevin's going to have to stay in custody. Would you like to speak to your son?"

Picturing that smarmy, implacable expression of serenity I met through the police car window, I shuddered, covering my face with my hands. "No. Please, no," I begged, feeling an awful coward. I must have sounded like Celia, imploring weakly not to be forced to bathe when there was still all that dark, sticky horror lurking in the bathtub trap. "Please don't make me. Please don't. I couldn't face him."

"Then maybe it would be best for now if you just went on home."

I stared at him stupidly. I was so ashamed, I honestly believed they were going to keep me in jail.

If only to fill the awkward silence as I just looked at him, he added gently, "Once we get a warrant, we will have to search your house. That'll probably be tomorrow, but don't you worry. Our officers are very respectful. We won't turn the place upside down."

"You can burn that house for all I care," I said. "I hate it. I've always hated it—"

The two looked at each other: *hysterical*. And they ushered me out the door.

Freed—I couldn't believe it—out in the parking lot, I wandered desolately past my car, failing to recognize it the first time down the row; everything in what was already my old life had grown alien. And I was dumbfounded. How could they just let me go? Even at this early juncture I must have begun to feel a deep need to be brought to book, to be called to account. I had to stop myself from pounding on the station door and importuning reception to please let me spend the night in a cell. Surely I belonged there. I was convinced that the only pallet on which I would be able to lie peacefully that night would be a cheap, lumpy mattress with a scratchy institutional sheet, and the only lullaby that could possibly sing me to sleep would be the grit of cordovans on concrete and the distant clink of keys.

Yet once I found the car I became strangely calm. Sedate. Methodical. Like Kevin. Keys. Lights. Seat belt. Windshield wipers on interval, for there was a thin mist. My mind went blank. I ceased talking to myself. I drove home very slowly, braking on yellow, coming to a legally complete halt at the four-way stop, though there was no other traffic. And when I curved up our long drive and noticed that none of the lights were on, I thought nothing of it. I preferred not to.

I parked. Your truck was in the garage. I moved very slowly. I turned off the wipers, and the lights. I locked the car. I put the keys in my Egyptian bag. I paused to think of some other small everyday thing I needed to take care of before walking in the house; I picked a leaf off the windscreen, scooped your jump rope off the garage floor and hung it on its hook.

When I turned on the light in the kitchen, I thought how unlike you it was to have left all those greasy breakfast dishes. The skillet for your sausage was upright in the drainer, but not the one for the French toast, and most of the plates and juice glasses were still on the counter. Sections of the *Times* splayed on the table, though taking the paper out to the stack in the garage every morning was one of your neatnik obsessions. Flicking the next light switch, I could see at a glance that no one was in the dining room, living room, or den; that was the advantage of a house with no doors. Still I walked through every room. Slowly.

"Franklin?" I called. "Celia?" The sound of my own voice unnerved me. It was so small and tinny, and nothing came back.

As I advanced down the hall, I paused at Celia's bedroom and had to force myself to walk in. It was dark. Her bed was empty. The same, in the master bedroom, the bathrooms, out on the deck. Nothing. Nobody. Where were you? Had you gone looking for me? I had a mobile. You knew the number. And why wouldn't you have taken the truck? Was this a game? You were hiding, giggling in a closet with Celia. This of all nights you chose to play a game?

The house was empty. I felt a surging, regressive urge to call my mother.

I walked through it twice. Though I had checked the rooms before, the second time through I felt only deeper trepidation. It was as if there were someone in the house, a stranger, a burglar, and he was just out of view, stalking behind me, ducking under cabinets, clutching a cleaver. Finally, shaking, I returned to the kitchen.

The previous owners must have installed those floodlights in the back in expectation of lavish garden parties. We didn't incline toward garden parties and rarely used the floods, but I was familiar with the switch: just to the left of the pantry, beside the sliding glass doors that opened to our banked backyard. This was where I used to stand and watch you throw a baseball with Kevin, feeling wistful, left out. I felt a little that way at that moment—left out. As if you'd held some family celebration of great sentimental significance, and of all people I hadn't been invited. I must have kept my hand on that switch a good thirty seconds before I flipped it. If I had it to do over again, I'd have waited a few moments more. I would pay good money for every instant in my life without that image in it.

On the crest of the hill, the archery range lit up. Soon I would understand the drollery behind Kevin's lunchtime phone call to Lamont, when he'd apparently told Robert not to bother to pick up Celia from school, since she was "unwell." Backed against the target was Celia—standing at attention, still and trusting, as if eager to play "William Tell."

As I wrenched the door open and flailed up the rise, my haste was irrational. Celia would wait. Her body was affixed to the target by five arrows, which held her torso like stick-pins tacking one of her crimped self-portraits to a class bulletin board. As I stumbled nearer calling her name, she winked at me, grotesquely, with her head knocked back. Though I remembered putting in her prosthesis that morning, it was missing now.

There are things we know with our whole being without ever having to actively think them, at least with that verbal self-conscious prattle that chatters on the surface of our minds. It was like that; I knew what else I would find without having to specify it to myself outright. So when, scrambling up to the archery range, I tripped over something sticking from bushes, I may have sickened, but I wasn't surprised. I recognized the obstacle in an instant. I had bought pairs of chocolate-brown Stove brogans from Banana Republic often enough.

Oh, my beloved. I may need too badly to tell myself a story, but I've felt compelled to weave some thread of connection between the otherwise meaningless dishevelment of that backyard and the finest in the man I married.

With a good twenty minutes remaining before they had to leave for school, you'd let the kids go out to play. In fact, it would have encouraged you that for once the two of them were horsing around together—*bonding*. You dawdled through the *Times*, though it was the *Home* C-section on a

Thursday, which wouldn't entice you. So you started on the breakfast dishes. You heard a scream. I don't doubt that you were out the sliding doors in a flash. From the bottom of the hill, you went for him. You were a robust man, even in your fifties, still skipping rope forty-five minutes a day. It would have taken a lot to stop a man like you in his tracks. And you almost made it, too—a few yards from the crest, with the arrows raining.

So here is my theory: I believe you paused. Outside on the deck, with our daughter pinioned to an archery target with an arrow through her chest, while our firstborn pivoted on his mound and sighted his own father down the shaft of his Christmas crossbow, you simply didn't believe it. There was such a thing as a good life. It was possible to be a good dad, to put in the weekends and the picnics and the bedtime stories, and so to raise a decent, stalwart son. This was America. And you had done everything right. Ergo, this could not be happening.

So for a single, deadly moment this overweening conviction—what you wanted to see—fatally interposed itself. It is possible that your cerebrum even managed to reconfigure the image, to remix the sound track: Celia, pretty make-the-best-of-it Celia, darling look-on-the-bright-side Celia, is once more inured to her disability and tossing her fine gold hair cheerfully into the spring breeze. She isn't screaming, she's laughing. She's *shrieking* with laughter. The only reason Kevin's helpful girl Friday could conceivably be standing right in front of the target is to faithfully collect her brother's spent arrows—ah, Franklin, and wouldn't she. As for your handsome young son, he has been practicing archery for six years. He has been scrupulously instructed by well-compensated professionals, and he is nothing if not safety conscious. He would never point a loaded crossbow at another person's head, least of all at his own father's.

Clearly, the sunlight had played some visual trick. He is merely waving an upraised arm. He must be hoping, without saying as much—he is a teenager, after all—to apologize for lashing out at breakfast with those harsh, ugly repudiations of everything his father has tried to do for him. He *is* interested in how the Canon works, and he hopes you'll explain what "f-stop" means another time. In truth he deeply admires his father's enterprise in having seized upon such a quirky profession, one that allows such creative latitude and independence. It's just awkward for an adolescent boy. They get competitive at this age. They want to take you on. Still the boy feels awful now, for having let fly. The fit of pique was all a lie. He treasures all those trips to Civil War battlefields, if only because war is something that only men can understand with other men, and he's learned one *heck* of a lot from museums. Back in his room some nights, he takes out those autumn leaves you two collected on the grounds of Theodore Roosevelt's ancestral home and pressed inside the *Encyclopedia Britannica* last year. Seeing that the colors are beginning to fade reminds him of the mortality of all things, but especially of his own father, and he cries. *Cries.* You will never see it; he will never tell you. But he doesn't have to. See? The waving? He's waving for you to bring the camera. He's changed his mind, and with another five minutes left before he has to catch the bus, he wants you to take some photographs after all—to start the montage, Braveheart of the Palisades, for the foyer.

This masterful remake may not have lasted more than a second or two before it corrupted, as a frozen frame will blister and crenellate before a hot projection lamp. But it would have lasted just long enough for Kevin to sink his first crippling shaft—perhaps the one I found angled through your throat and protruding from the back of your neck. It must have severed an artery; around your head, under the flood lamps, the grass was black. The three other arrows—stuck in the hollow between your pectorals where I loved to rest my head, fixed fast into the fibrous muscle of your broad rope-skipping calf, and extending from the groin whose pleasures we had so recently rediscovered together—were just-to-be-on-the-safe-side touches, like a few extra stakes around the edges of a well-pitched tent.

All the same, I do wonder just how hard you struggled up that hill, really—wheezing, beginning to choke on your own blood. It wasn't that you didn't care for her, but you may have grasped with a glance that it was too late to save Celia. The fact she was no longer screaming was a bad sign. As for saving yourself, maybe it just wasn't in you. Stark in the glare of the floods, sharpened by the shadow cast by the shaft in your neck, the expression on your face—it was so disappointed.

Eva

Dearest Franklin,

I don't know if you keep up with these things, but about a week ago a Chinese fighter plane ran into an American surveillance craft over the South China Sea. The Chinese pilot was probably drowned, and the crippled American spy plane landed on the Chinese island of Hainan. There seems to be some question as to whose craft hit whose. Anyway, it's become quite a diplomatic showdown, and now China is holding the twenty-four American crew members hostage—for an apology, of all things. I haven't had the energy to follow who is and is not at fault, but I have been intrigued that world peace (or so they say) hangs in the balance over the sole matter of remorse. Previous to my education in such things, I might have found the situation exasperating. Just say you're sorry then, if that will get them back! But nowadays the matter of remorse looms great to me, and it neither surprises nor frustrates me that momentous events might be decided in accordance with it. Besides, so far this Hainan conundrum is relatively simple. It is so much more often the case that an apology brings no one back.

Lately, too, politics seems to have dissolved for me into a swarm of tiny, personal stories. I don't seem to believe in it anymore. There are only people and what happens to them. Even that fracas in Florida—to me it was about a man who wanted to be president since he was a little boy. Who got so close that he could taste it. About a person and his sadness and his desperation to turn back the clock, to count again and again until the news is good at last—about his poignant denial. Similarly, I think less about trade restrictions and future arms sales to Taiwan than I do about those twenty-four young people, in a strange building with strange smells, fed meals that don't resemble the take-out Chinese they grew up with, sleeping badly, imagining the worst—being charged as a spy and rotting in a Chinese prison while diplomats trade acid communiqués that no one lets them read. Young people who thought they were hungry for adventure until they got one.

I am sometimes awed by the same naïveté of my own younger self— disheartened that Spain has trees, despairing that every unexplored frontier turns out to have food and weather. I wanted to go somewhere *else*, I thought. Witlessly, I conceived of myself as harboring an insatiable appetite for the exotic.

Well, Kevin has introduced me to a real foreign country. I can be sure of that, since the definition of the truly foreign locale is one that fosters a piercing and perpetual yearning to go home.

A couple of these small, truly foreign experiences I have held back. Which isn't like me. You remember how I once loved to return from a trip abroad and present you my cultural bric-a-brac, the kind of mundane how-they-do-things-elsewhere discoveries that you only make if you actually go there, like the queer little fact that in Thailand commercial loaves of bread aren't twist-tied at the heel of the loaf, but on the top.

As for the first tidbit I've withheld, I may be guilty of plain condescension. I should give you more credit, since Kevin's escapade screamed premeditation; in another life he might have grown up to do well at, say, staging large professional conferences—anything that's advertised as requiring "strong organizational abilities and problem-solving skills." Hence even you realize that *Thursday* being staged three days before he turned the age of full legal accountability was no coincidence. He may have been virtually sixteen on *Thursday*, but in a statutory sense he was still fifteen, meaning that in New York state a more lenient raft of sentencing guidelines would apply, even if they threw the book at him and tried him as an adult. Kevin is sure to have researched the fact that the law does not, like his father, *round up*.

Still, his lawyer did locate a range of convincing expert witnesses who told alarming medical anecdotes. Typically, downhearted but mild-mannered fifty-something goes on Prozac, experiences an acute personality flip into paranoia and dementia, shoots his whole family and then himself. I wonder, have you ever clutched at the pharmaceutical straw? Our good son was just one of those unfortunate few whose reaction to antide-pressants was adverse, so that instead of lightening his burdens the drug plunged him into darkness? Because I really tried to believe that myself for a while, especially during Kevin's trial.

Though that defense neither got him off completely nor released him into psychiatric care as intended, Kevin's sentence may have been slightly more lenient for the doubt his lawyer raised over his chemical stability. Af-ter the sentencing hearing at which Kevin got seven years, I thanked his lawyer, John Goddard, outside the courthouse. I didn't, in fact, feel very grateful at the time—seven years had never seemed so short—but I did appreciate that John had done his best at a disagreeable job. Scrambling for something of substance to admire, I commended his inventive ap-proach to the case. I said I'd never heard of Prozac's alleged psychotic ef-fect on some patients or I'd never have allowed Kevin to take it.

"Oh, don't thank me, thank Kevin," said John easily. "I'd never heard of the psychosis thing, either. That whole approach was his idea."

"But—he wouldn't have had access to a library, would he?"

"No, not in pretrial detention." He looked at me with real sympathy for a moment. "I hardly needed to lift a finger, frankly. He knew all the ci-tations. Even the names and locations of expert witnesses. That's a bright boy you've got, Eva." But he didn't sound upbeat. He sounded depressed.

As for the second tidbit—regarding how they do things in that faraway land where fifteen-year-olds murder their classmates—I haven't held it back because I thought you couldn't take it. I just didn't want to think about it myself or subject you to it, though until this very afternoon I was living in eternal fear that the episode would repeat itself.

It was perhaps three months after *Thursday*. Kevin had already been tried and sentenced, and I had recently installed those robotic Saturday visits to Chatham in my routine. We had still not learned to talk to one another, and the time dragged. In those days the conceit on his part ran that my visits were an imposition, that he dreaded my arrival and ap-plauded my departure, and that his real family was inside, among his wor-shipful juvenile boosters. When I informed him that Mary Woolford had just filed suit, I was surprised that he didn't seem gratified but only the more disgruntled; as Kevin would later object, *why should I get all the credit?* So I said, that's a fine how do you do, isn't it, after I lose my husband and daughter? To get sued? He grunted something about my feeling sorry for myself.

"Don't *you?*" I said. "Don't you feel sorry for me?"

He shrugged. "Got out of this safe and sound, didn't you? Not a scratch."

"Did I?" I added, "And why was that, anyway?"

"When you're putting on a show, you don't shoot the audience," he said smoothly, rolling something in his right hand.

"You mean leaving me alive was the best revenge." We were already way beyond revenge-for-what.

I couldn't talk about anything more to do with *Thursday* at that point, and I was about to resort to the old are-they-feeding-you-all-right, when my eye was drawn again by the object he kept palming from hand to hand, palpating it rhythmically with his fingers like a string of worry beads. Honestly, I just wanted to change the subject, I didn't care at all about his toy—though if I took his fidgeting as a sign of moral discomfort in the presence of a woman whose family he had slaughtered, I was sadly mistaken.

"What is that?" I asked. "What have you got there?"

With a small, crafty smile, he opened his palm, displaying his talisman with the shy pride of a boy with his prize shooting marble. I stood up so quickly that my chair clattered backward onto the floor. It isn't often that when you look at an object, it looks back.

"Don't you ever pull that out again," I said hoarsely. "If you do, I will never come back here. Not ever. Do you hear me?"

I think he knew that I meant it. Which gave him a powerful amulet to ward off these ostensibly pestilential visits from *Mumsey.* The fact that Celia's glass eye has remained out of my sight since can only mean, I suppose, that, on balance, he's glad I come.

You probably think that I'm just telling more tales, the meaner the better. What a hideous boy we have, I must be saying, to torment his mother with so ghastly a souvenir. No, not this time. It's just that I had to tell you that story in order that you better understand the next one, from this very afternoon.

You surely noticed the date. It's the two-year anniversary. Which also means that in three days, Kevin will be eighteen. For the purposes of voting (which as a convicted felon he will be banned from doing in all but two states) and enlisting in the armed services, that's when he officially becomes a grown-up. But on this one I'm more inclined to side with the judicial system, which tried him as an adult two years ago. To me the day on which we all formally came of age will always be April 8th, 1999.

So I put in a special request to meet with our son this afternoon. Though they routinely turn down appeals to meet with inmates on birthdays, my request was granted. Maybe this is the kind of sentimentality that prison warders appreciate.

When Kevin was issued in, I noticed a change in his demeanor before he said a word. All that snide condescension had fallen away, and I finally appreciated how fatiguing it must be for Kevin to generate this world-weary who-gives-a-fuck the livelong day. Given the epidemic thieving of small-sized sweats and T-shirts, Claverack has given up on its experiment in street clothes, so he was wearing an orange jumpsuit—for once one that wasn't only normal-sized but too big for him, in which he looked dwarfed. Three days from adulthood, Kevin is finally starting to act like a little boy—confused, bereft. His eyes had shed their glaze and tunneled to the back of his head.

"You don't look too happy," I ventured.

"Have I ever?" His tone was wan.

Curious, I asked, "Is something bothering you?" though the rules of our engagement proscribe such a direct and motherly solicitation.

The more extraordinary, he answered me. "I'm almost eighteen, aren't I?" He rubbed his face. "Outta here. I heard they don't waste much time."

"A real prison," I said.

"I don't know. This place is sure real enough for me."

". . . Does the move to Sing Sing make you nervous?"

"*Nervous?*" he asked incredulously. "*Nervous!* Do you know *anything* about those places?" He shook his head in dismay.

I looked at him in wonder. He was shaking. Over the course of the last two years, he has acquired a maze of tiny battle scars across his face, and his nose is no longer quite straight. The effect doesn't make him look tougher, but disarranged. The scars have smudged the once sharp, Armenian cut of his features into a doughier blur. He could have been drawn by an uncertain portraitist who constantly resorts to an eraser.

"I'll still come to visit you," I promised, bracing myself for sarcastic reproof.

"Thanks. I was hoping you would."

Incredulous, I'm afraid I stared. As a test, I brought up the news from March. "You always seem to keep up with these things. So I assume you saw the stories out of San Diego last month? You have two more *colleagues*."

"You mean, Andy, uh—Andy Williams?" Kevin remembered vaguely. "What a sucker. Wanna know the truth, I felt sorry for the chump. He's been had."

"I warned you this fad would grow passé," I said. "Andy Williams didn't make the headlines, did you notice? Dick Cheney's heart problems and that huge storm-that-never-happened both got bigger billing in the *New York Times*. And the second shooting, on its heels—with one fatality, in San Diego, too? That got almost no coverage at all."

"Hell, that guy was *eighteen*." Kevin shook his head. "I mean, really. Don't you think he was a little old for it?"

"You know, I saw you on TV."

"Oh, that." He squirmed with a tinge of embarrassment. "It was filmed a while ago, you know. I was into a—thing."

"Yes, I didn't have a lot of time for the *thing*," I said. "But you were still—you were very articulate. You present yourself very well. Now all you have to come up with is something to say."

He chuckled. "You mean that isn't horseshit."

"You do know what day it is, don't you?" I introduced shyly. "Why they let me come see you on a Monday?"

"Oh, sure. It's my *anniversary*." He is finally turning that sardonicism on himself.

"I just wanted to ask you—," I began, and licked my lips. You're going to think this curious, Franklin, but I had never put this question to him before. I'm not sure why; maybe I didn't want to be insulted with a lot of rubbish like *jumping into the screen*.

"It's been two years," I proceeded. "I miss your father, Kevin. I still talk to him. I even write to him, if you can believe it. I write him letters. And

now they're in a big messy stack on my desk, because I don't know his address. I miss your sister, too—badly. And so many other families are still so sad. I realize that journalists, and therapists, maybe other inmates ask you all the time. But you've never told me. So please, look me in the eye. You killed eleven people. My husband. My daughter. Look me in the eye, and tell me why."

Unlike the day he turned to me through the police car window, pupils glinting, Kevin met my gaze this afternoon with supreme difficulty. His eyes kept shuttering away, making contact in sorties, then flickering back toward the gaily painted cinder-block wall. And at last gave up, staring a little to the side of my face.

"I used to think I knew," he said glumly. "Now I'm not so sure."

Without thinking, I extended my hand across the table and clasped his. He didn't pull away. "Thank you," I said.

Does my gratitude seem odd? In fact, I'd harbored no preconception of what answer I wanted. I certainly had no interest in an explanation that reduced the ineffable enormity of what he had done to a pat sociological aphorism about "alienation" out of *Time* magazine or a cheap psychological construct like "attachment disorder" that his counselors were always retailing at Claverack. So I was astonished to discover that his answer was word-perfect. For Kevin, progress was deconstruction. He would only begin to plumb his own depths by first finding himself unfathomable.

When he did pull his hand back at last, it was to reach into his coverall pocket. "Listen," he said. "I made you something. A—well—sort of a present."

As he withdrew a dark rectangular wooden box about five inches long, I apologized. "I know it's your birthday coming up. I haven't forgotten. I'll bring your present next time."

"Don't bother," he said, polishing the oiled wood with a wad of toilet paper. "It'd just get ripped off in here anyway."

Carefully, he slid the box across the table, keeping two fingers on the top. It wasn't quite rectangular after all, but coffin-shaped, with hinges on one side and tiny brass hooks on the other. He must have made it in shop. The morbid shape seemed typical, of course. The gesture, however, moved me, and the workmanship was surprisingly fine. He'd given me a few

Christmas presents in the olden days, but I always knew you'd bought them, and he'd never given me anything while inside.

"It's very nicely made," I said sincerely. "Is it for jewelry?" I reached for the box, but he kept his fingers on it fast.

"Don't!" he said sharply. "I mean, please. Whatever you do. Don't open it."

Ah. Instinctively, I shrank back. In an earlier incarnation, Kevin might have crafted this very same "present," lined mockingly with pink satin. But he'd have relinquished it blithely—suppressing a grisly little smile as in innocent expectation I unhooked the clasps. Today it was his warning—*don't open it*—that may have constituted the greatest measure of my gift.

"I see," I said. "I thought this was one of your most precious possessions. Why ever would you give it up?" I was flushed, a little shocked, a little horrified really, and my tone was stinging.

"Well, sooner or later some goon was going to swipe it, and it'd get used for some cheap gag—you know, it'd turn up in somebody's soup. Besides. It was like she was, sort of, looking at me all the time. It started to get spooky."

"She is looking at you, Kevin. So is your father. Every day."

Staring at the table, he shoved the box a little farther toward me, then removed his hand. "Anyway, I thought you might take this and, well, maybe you could, you know—"

"Bury it," I finished for him. I felt heavy. It was an enormous request, for along with his dark-stained homemade coffin I was to bury a great deal else.

Gravely, I agreed. When I hugged him good-bye, he clung to me childishly, as he never had in childhood proper. I'm not quite sure, since he muttered it into the upturned collar of my coat, but I like to think that he choked, *"I'm sorry."* Taking the risk that I'd heard correctly, I said distinctly myself, *"I'm sorry, too, Kevin. I'm sorry, too."*

I will never forget sitting in that civil courtroom and hearing the judge with tiny pupils announce primly that the court finds for the defendant. I'd have expected to feel so relieved. But I didn't. Public vindication of my motherhood, I discovered, meant nothing to me. If anything, I was irate.

Supposedly we were all to go home now, and I would feel redeemed. To the contrary, I knew I'd go home and feel hideous, as usual, and desolate, as usual, and dirty, as usual. I'd wanted to be cleansed, but my experience on that bench was much like a typically sweaty, gritty afternoon in a Ghana hotel room: turning on the shower to find that the water main was turned off. This disdainful rusty drip was the only baptism the law would afford me.

The sole aspect of the verdict that gave me the slightest satisfaction was being stuck with my own court costs. Although the judge may not have thought much of Mary Woolford's case, she had clearly taken a personal dislike to me, and plain animosity from key parties (ask Denny Corbitt) can cost you. Throughout the trial I had been aware that I cut an unsympathetic figure. I had disciplined myself never to cry. I'd been loath to use you and Celia for so venal a purpose as ducking liability, and so the fact that my son had not only killed his classmates but my own husband and daughter tended to get lost in the shuffle. Though I know they didn't mean to undermine my defense, that testimony from your parents about my fatally forthcoming visit to Gloucester was disastrous; we don't like mothers who "don't like" their own sons. I don't much like such mothers, either.

I had broken the most primitive of rules, profaned the most sacred of ties. Had I instead protested Kevin's innocence in the face of mountains of hard evidence to the contrary, had I railed against his "tormentors" for having driven him to it, had I insisted that after he started taking Prozac "he was a completely different boy"—well, I guarantee you that Mary Woolford and that defense fund she raised through the Internet would have been forced to pay my court costs to the final dime. Instead, my demeanor was repeatedly described in the papers as "defiant," while my disagreeable characterizations of my own flesh and blood were submitted no-comment, to hang me out to dry. With such an ice queen for a mother, little wonder, observed our local *Journal News*, that KK turned *bad boy*.

Harvey was outraged, of course, and immediately whispered that we should appeal. Paying costs was punitive, he said. He should know; he was the one who would write the bill. But me, I was cheered up. I wanted a verdict that was punitive. I had already depleted all our liquid assets for Kevin's pricey defense and had taken out a second mortgage on Palisades

Parade. So I knew immediately that I would have to sell AWAP, and I would have to sell our awful, empty house. Now *that* was cleansing.

But since then—and throughout writing these letters to you—I have come full circle, making a journey much like Kevin's own. In asking petulantly whether *Thursday* was my fault, I have had to go backward, to deconstruct. It is possible that I am asking the wrong question. In any event, by thrashing between exoneration and excoriation, I have only tired myself out. I don't know. At the end of the day, I have no idea, and that pure, serene ignorance has become, itself, a funny kind of solace. The truth is, if I decided I was innocent, or I decided I was guilty, what difference would it make? If I arrived at the right answer, would you come home?

This is all I know. That on the 11th of April, 1983, unto me a son was born, and I felt nothing. Once again, the truth is always larger than what we make of it. As that infant squirmed on my breast, from which he shrank in such distaste, I spurned him in return—he may have been a fifteenth my size, but it seemed fair at the time. Since that moment we have fought one another with an unrelenting ferocity that I can almost admire. But it must be possible to earn a devotion by testing an antagonism to its very limit, to bring people closer through the very act of pushing them away. Because after three days short of eighteen years, I can finally announce that I am too exhausted and too confused and too lonely to keep fighting, and if only out of desperation or even laziness I love my son. He has five grim years left to serve in an adult penitentiary, and I cannot vouch for what will walk out the other side. But in the meantime, there is a second bedroom in my serviceable apartment. The bedspread is plain. A copy of *Robin Hood* lies on the bookshelf. And the sheets are clean.

Forever your loving wife,
Eva

Reading group questions that have arisen from publication of *We Need to Talk About Kevin* in the USA

Was Kevin just born wicked, or is his cold heart the inevitable consequence of an unaffectionate mother? Does the novel answer this question? And do you think the answer to this classic "nature versus nurture" debate—whether character is formed by one's environment or innate—has to be one or the other?

Do you completely trust Eva's version of events? More than once, she admits that she was mistaken about something she assumed that Kevin did. Is she perhaps exaggerating her son's malignancy to make herself seem less blameworthy, or was she just the only party in this story who foresaw what he was capable of well in advance of *Thursday*?

Do you think that Kevin was guilty of damaging his little sister's eye? If so, what evidence do you find for this assumption? Would it stand up in court?

Franklin always looks on the bright side of parenthood, and interprets whatever Kevin gets up to in the most favorable light possible. Do you find this eagerness to give his own child a break sympathetic? Or is Franklin a fool?

We're often most repelled by other people who share our own flaws. Eva confesses that she never really liked her son. But what are some of the traits that Kevin and his mother have in common?

Why *do* people have children, when kids are expensive and exhausting, and the risks of something going wrong are so high?

While you were reading the novel, did you ever wonder what Franklin was doing, and why he never seemed to write back to Eva?

Eva was sued in civil court for being a negligent parent. Many school shooting incidents have resulted in similar suits. If you were the judge in that case, what ruling would you have handed down? Are there any other parties in this story who seem to you conspicuously remiss?

Does the novel truly explain why high school killings have become a social phenomenon in the United States? And did you want an explanation?

Is Eva a bad mother? Is she too hard on herself, or is she not hard enough?

What do you believe ultimately motivated Kevin to stage *Thursday*?

Fiction
Non-fiction
Literary
Crime

Popular culture
Biography
Illustrated
Music

dare to read at serpentstail.com

Visit serpentstail.com today to browse and buy our books, and for exclusive previews, promotions, interviews with authors and forthcoming events.

| NEWS | cut to the literary chase with all the latest news about our books and authors |

| EVENTS | advance information on forthcoming events, author readings, exhibitions and book festivals |

| EXTRACTS | read first chapters, short stories, bite-sized extracts |

| EXCLUSIVES | pre-publication offers, signed copies, discounted books, competitions |

| BROWSE AND BUY | browse our full catalogue, fill up a basket and proceed to our **fully secure** checkout - our website is your oyster |

FREE POSTAGE & PACKING ON ALL ORDERS ANYWHERE!

---

sign up today and receive our new free full colour catalogue

KT-415-507

INTRODUCTION

WHAT MAKES A LAND BAD?

It's got nothing to do with geography or topography. Rivers don't invade, deserts don't become corrupt and, while terrorists may hide out in a country's mountains and valleys, the land itself has nothing to do with why a Bad Land turns to the dark side. My travels through the Bad Lands took me through staggeringly impressive country from endless desert dunes to snow-capped mountain peaks, from winding rivers to tropical beaches, but always in the background was the nagging realisation that these were countries that had gone wrong and that people, not nature, had made the wrong turns.

So while my travels include a varied assortment of geographic and cultural marvels, it's delving into history and politics, much of it very recent, that illuminates how each country achieved Bad Land status. I could not have asked for a better cast of characters – medal-dripping dictator despots, fatally flawed national heroes, heroically doomed reformers, religious fanatics and Nobel Prize winners all played their part in the Bad Land stories. Genghis Khan, Mother Theresa, Osama bin Laden, Lawrence of Arabia and, of course, George W Bush all make appearances. The obsessive pursuit of power can also lead to some decidedly eccentric behaviour; for some Bad Land rulers, dressing up ranks second only to erecting statues and portraits in their personality cult enthusiasms.

Of course, it's not just the locals. One country's terrorists are another country's freedom fighters, and ill-thought-out measures to discourage terrorists can actually encourage them. We don't even have to fund them directly – although some very respectable countries have done exactly that. For some countries, turning bad may be all their own work, but equally often outside influences from colonial meddling to big power-proxy struggles have played a disproportionate part in a Bad Land's sorry situation.

I've been travelling for a long time. Although I was born in England, I lived in Pakistan until the age of five and did almost all my high-school years in the USA. I've kept on travelling ever since, co-founding Lonely Planet Publications in the early 1970s, writing dozens of travel-related books and maintaining a keen interest in the world's weirder places. 'Where's your favourite place?' I'm often asked, and my honest answer is, 'The departure lounge.'

On the ground, walking the streets, you quickly pick up whether a place is safe or dangerous and often have a far better idea of how well the average person is doing than expert economists can glean from any number of GNP and GDP statistics, or international journalists from meeting with government officials and spokespeople after parachuting into a five-star hotel.

I'm not the only person to feel that way. In an article in the Columbia Journalism Review in 2006, American writer Robert Kaplan commented that 'In the 1990s, when it was particularly hard to get visas to Iran – and much of the information about that country emerged out of seminars in Washington – the best thing to read on the subject was *Iran: A Travel Survival Kit* by David St Vincent, published in the Lonely Planet series.'

INTRODUCTION

How did I choose my Bad Lands?

A country doesn't even need to be a fully fledged Bad Land to have some bad marks on its scorecard. Even nice little Switzerland has its bad side; if an evil dictator from a real Bad Land wants a place to stash his ill-gotten gains, the Swiss are only too happy to provide a secure, anonymous, no-questions-asked bank vault.

The selection criteria were simple enough: how does a country treat its own citizens? Is it involved in terrorism? Is it a threat to other countries? The Axis of Evil was an obvious starting point. Iran, Iraq and North Korea went straight on to my list. Then I added Burma (Myanmar) because it's regularly cited as an appalling example of human rights abuse and its military government has kept a Nobel Prize winner locked up because she had the temerity to win an election. Cuba because the USA has been shouting for regime change there for most of the past 50 years with a conspicuous lack of success. Libya because it's done absolutely everything wrong – oppressed its own citizens, funded and actually organised terrorism, worked on Weapons of Mass Destruction and even invaded a neighbouring state. And got away with it.

Afghanistan joins the list for harbouring the terrorist who can claim to be the biggest single factor in creating the War on Terrorism with which we're all caught up, whether we want to be or not. Saudi Arabia went in as the place that bred lots of terrorists – and, what's worse, rich terrorists – by mismanaging things at home. Finally I threw in Albania, not because it's a Bad Land at all anymore, but simply because it's a fascinating example of a tiny, peculiar little dictatorship that cut itself off from the outside world at considerable cost to its own people.

Finally I ran my Evil Meter™ across the countries. How bad is really bad? The Evil Meter™ decides.

Bad Lands is a tourist account – places to go, places to stay, places to avoid. It is certainly not a Most Dangerous Places. Although I sipped tea in the garden of the British embassy in Kabul while guns rattled outside

09.

the walls, mused on whether Pyongyang was real or a movie set and felt distinctly nervous when my taxi driver found himself in a dead-end alley in Kirkuk in Iraq, but I'm careful, cautious and have a low tolerance for pain. I had an extraordinarily interesting time visiting my nine Bad Lands. Only in Afghanistan and Iraq was I even slightly concerned for my own safety and I always ate well, slept comfortably, stayed healthy and, as a bonus, made some good friends.

It's worth reminding ourselves of Benjamin Franklin's immortal words: 'They that can give up essential liberty to obtain a little temporary safety deserve neither liberty nor safety.' Franklin's words about foolishly trading short-term expediency against the long-term good followed me on my Bad Lands trails, but so did the Persian poet Hafez. I visited his tomb in Iran, but I also remembered his words in another country where he is held in high esteem, Afghanistan:

Although the road may be dangerous and the final destination far out of sight.
There is no route which does not come to an end: do not despair.

AFGHANISTAN

UZBEKISTAN   TAJIKISTAN   CHINA

TURKMENISTAN

○ Faizabad

Balkh ○ ○ Mazar-i
            Sharif   ○ Kunduz

Samangan ○   ○ Salang   Panjshir
               Tunnel ○ Valley

Band-i-Amir ○   Bamiyan ○   ○ Ghorband

Herat   KABUL ☆   ○ Jalalabad
○   Jam
Chisht-e-Sharif ○ ○ Obey   Khyber Pass

○ Ghazni

IRAN

Kandahar ○

PAKISTAN

INDIA

I make a pilgrimage straight to Chicken Street. Back in the 'hippy trail' era of the late 1960s and early 1970s, this was the Kabul epicentre and Sigi's restaurant, with its giant chessboard in the courtyard, was one of the prime attractions. I don't recognise a thing along the reincarnation of this hippy highway, although the shops probably have precisely the same collection of goods – antique weapons, carpets, gemstones and Kashmiri crafts – as they did all those years ago.

'You could probably kit yourself out in authentically mirrored Afghan hippy gear on Chicken Street 2006', I think as I round the corner and pass by the Mustafa Hotel. Maureen and I stayed at the Mustafa back in 1972 and, as soon as the Taliban departed, the family that owned the hotel reopened it, barely skipping a beat. The threesome – two young guys and a chick (in hippy-era speak) – tumbling out of the door and hoisting their backpacks on to their shoulders have scarcely missed a beat either. From the baggy trousers to the billowing kaftans, they're time-warped straight from the Flower Power era.

I cross the road and duck in to the Shah Book Company, the real-life home of Norwegian writer Åsne Seierstad's bestseller *The Bookseller of Kabul*.

I'm back in Afghanistan after a 34-year absence.

This ancient land has always been plundered, invaded and fought over, but even the worst acid-propelled bad trip could not have encompassed the chaos and turmoil since my last visit. Then, the country was enjoying the final months of a long spell of stability, peace and relative progress. A year later, it all started to fall apart. King Mohammed Zahir Shah popped off to Rome on holiday and his cousin Daoud Shah took advantage of his absence to mount a revolution. The king must have thought Rome's title 'The Eternal City' was accurate – his holiday stretched on for 29 years. It was not until 2002, at the age of 87, that he would finally return. During that period Afghanistan suffered almost continuous conflict – the Soviet invasion, civil war, mujaheddin madness, Taliban tyranny, the War on Terror. As I packed my bags for Afghanistan in 2006 a third of the country was 'racked by violent insurgency' according to the UN Secretary-General Kofi Annan, suicide bombings were on the rise, foreign contractors kidnapped, police officers and government officials murdered. The Taliban were resurgent and NATO forces were taking ever more casualties.

There will be little peace and love, and few flowers in our hair this time around.

• • • •

Situated at the crossroads between Asia and the Middle East, Afghanistan has always been a mosaic of ethnic groups and cultures. Travellers have been lured there for years, attracted by adventure and the thrill of the unknown. In 1972 I arrived in a beat-up old English Mini, having driven across Asia from Europe. Today I fly in from Dubai on a Kam Air 737. I'm staying at the guesthouse of Afghan Logistics, a transport, travel and tourism business run by the Jamshady brothers. The six brothers appear to be perfect Afghan entrepreneurs. Dad had bought and sold cars, an activity that produced zero return during the mujaheddin violence or in the subsequent Taliban years.

'The only way to make money was to be in the army or in a mujaheddin force,' recalled Mobin, the eldest brother, 'but when I told my father I wanted to become a soldier he said, "If you want to be a robber or kill people, then go ahead. If that's not what you want then do something else, but be patient, things will change"'.

Mobin had left to work as a car mechanic in Tehran, but then the carpet business rebounded during the Taliban era.

'For a while there was a lot of money in carpets', Muqim, the second brother, recalled. 'We had 80 or 90 people working for us, mainly women and children, and once they'd made the carpets we'd export them via Pakistan.' I had heard rumours that many carpets bearing 'Made in Pakistan' labels were actually Afghan products, the tags simply slapped on them to get around restrictions on exports from the Taliban-controlled nation.

'Then the carpet business collapsed, the Pakistanis stopped it, so I went to Iran', Mobin explained. 'And Muqim used the money I sent back to study English.

'When the Americans arrived, Muqim worked as an interpreter to journalists and NGOs,' he continued, 'and we soon realised that as well as interpreters they also wanted vehicles. So I left Tehran, went to Dubai, bought the first of our Land Cruisers and drove it back across Iran and through Afghanistan to Kabul. I had to grow a beard to get through Kandahar. We started our business under our family name until someone pointed out that Jamshady didn't roll off foreigners' tongues. So we renamed it something much more catchy: Afghan Logistics.'

15.

I'm staying at their office, which also includes a guesthouse and the compound where they keep their assorted cars and four-wheel drives. It's in the Shahr-e Naw area, adjacent to the embassy area, and the streets are surprisingly neat and tidy. Sure they're potholed and often falling apart, but they're also swept clean, even if a lot of the garbage simply goes into the streetside channel known as a jube. Mobin and I set off to look around Kabul, first of all wandering down Chicken Street and Flower Street and then heading off to the bazaar near the river.

There's plenty of mobile coverage, but my phone can't roam on the Afghan networks. I buy a SIM card from Roshan. They have the best TV ads, Mobin tells me, and their coverage is good. Unfortunately my phone doesn't want to know about the Roshan SIM card so we go in search of someone to re-engineer it. Unsuccessfully as it turns out, although a couple of young phone-shop hotshots pull out the appropriate lead to hook my phone up to their computer, surf the net to find the correct protocols to change, and try to download them to my phone. They're clearly cluey young tech-heads even if they can't make it work. This street is wall-to-wall mobile phone shops. Mix in the abundant supply of internet cafés and Kabul seems a long way from some sort of medieval outpost.

'To hell with it', I decide after the third failure and chuck over another $45 for a handset as well.

· · · ·

The next morning Mobin and I fly off west to Herat, perhaps the most beautiful of Afghanistan's ancient cities. The road routes are either downright dangerous (via Kandahar) or difficult and possibly dangerous (via Mazar-i Sharif or straight across the middle from Bamiyan via the Minaret of Jam). The Kam Air flight across the country is superb. It's a crystal-clear day and the mountains, still dusted or even thickly coated with snow, look terrific. Afghanistan is a landlocked country largely bordered by Pakistan in the south and east, China in the far east and

Iran in the west. To the north Afghanistan is bordered by Turkmenistan, Uzbekistan and Tajikstan, all formerly parts of the USSR. The largest of the 'stans', Borat's Kazakhstan, lies further to the north.

Herat has been a settlement for over 2500 years and a centre of Persian art and learning. In more recent times it was the scene of a bloody slaughter that provoked the Russian invasion of Afghanistan. Having extended his cousin's Rome vacation, Daoud Shah, despite his strongman reputation, proved notably ineffective as a ruler and in April 1978 he was killed in a pro-Communist coup, which immediately split into opposing Khalq and Parcham factions. The radical form of Communism the Khalq group tried to impose, and the brutality of their rule, soon had the Afghans up in arms. Less than a year later, in March 1979, Ismail Khan – at that time a captain in the Afghan army, Khan is legendary in modern Herat – mounted a revolt that resulted in the slaughter of Soviet advisers and their families. The Afghan Communist government responded, pulverising the city using Russian-supplied bombers and killing more than 20,000 Heratis, but Khan escaped to the countryside and assembled a rebel army, which was widely supported by the Herat population. It was a portent of the horrors to come. By this time the USSR was trying to rein in the wilder excesses of their Afghan clients and even the Khalq faction had split into opposing groups.

In December 1979 the USSR, exasperated with the chaos developing and fearful that it would spread across the border to their Central Asian republics, arrived in force and the real trouble started. It was an occupation that would last 10 years and cost countless lives.

All the things I remember from the last visit – the Masjid-e-Jami (or Blue Mosque), the four magnificently askew minarets of Baiqari's long-lost madrasah, and the even more dangerously leaning minaret in Gowhar Shad's Musalla Complex – look better than ever. Herat even one-ups my last visit thanks to the Citadel, aka The Ark, which was off-limits back then. Now this ancient fortress is spookily empty and open with amazing views across the city from its collection of towers and lookouts. It's a fine sunset finale to a fine day in Afghanistan's western metropolis.

I've come to Herat mainly because I want to continue on to central Afghanistan to see the Minaret of Jam, and the next morning it's entirely appropriate that I should be heading there in a Toyota Hilux. In the cities the Toyota Corolla is *the* vehicle. Vast numbers of them have turned up in Afghanistan since the Taliban's departure, but once you're outside the cities Afghan roads require a sturdy four-wheel drive. In the immediate aftermath of the American-led invasion in 2001, it quickly became clear that the Hilux was the Taliban transport of choice. Back at headquarters the pricier Toyota Land Cruiser was the top wheels (Osama bin Laden had a fleet of them), but, as one commentator noted, at a local level the country was run by anybody with 'a beard, a gun, a Toyota Hilux and at least a little authority'.

The ubiquitous presence of the Hilux prompted Toyota to deny that it had been supplying them, although Wade Hoyt, a Toyota spokesman in New York, noted that 'it shows that the Taliban are looking for the same qualities as any truck buyer: durability and reliability' (John F Burns, *The New York Times*, 23 November 2001). In Australia a popular Toyota TV ad series, ending with a freeze-frame of the owners jumping for joy beside their wheels, was spoofed with an imitation ad showing a group of gun-toting beards and their burka-clad partners airborne beside a Hilux, which has just emerged unscathed from the best the US Air Force could throw at it. As the supply of Taliban targets began to run low, even a Hilux was worth getting in your bombsights.

Motorcycles have flooded in to post-Taliban Afghanistan in even greater numbers than cars, most of them Chinese clones of popular Japanese brands. Since there are no Chinese motorcycle brands worth coveting, any name seems to be slapped on the two-wheelers as they roll off the assembly lines. As well as real Hondas you could ride a Hond,

Handa or Hondie. Or if you want something geographically appropriate, try a Pamir, Caspian or Great Kabul. And if you simply can't get enough of Toyotas, why not ride a Corolla or a Land Cruiser?

Despite the comforts of my Hilux, the road to Jam is seriously hard work. The first 150 kilometres through Obey and Chisht-e-Sharif are quite feasible even for a regular car. We see plenty of Corollas. Then the road deteriorates and our hardy four-wheel drive starts to come into its own. Occasionally the needle reaches 40 kilometres per hour, but 15 kilometres per hour seems the appropriate average speed. The trip takes 15 hours, but however tough the travel there's always someone doing it even harder. We cruise by a minibus packed with 16 people who've been going two hours longer than us already and the back-seat passengers have a couple of goats across their knees.

There's plenty to see along the way. A wide, flat valley dotted with villages for the first few hours; stops at *chaikhana*, traditional Afghan teahouses, for breakfast and lunch; a long-abandoned caravanserai and a decaying fortress; the beautiful ancient *gombad* (domes) at Chisht-e-Sharif; and finally a series of pretty little villages wedged into corners of canyons and valleys.

It's dark by the time we arrive at the guesthouse directly beneath the great minaret so my first sight of Afghanistan's first World Heritage Site is in the morning. The Statue of Liberty, Eiffel Tower, Taj Mahal and Sydney Opera House get thousands of visitors every day. The Minaret of Jam has to wait until late May for the year's first arrival: I am 2006's first foreign tourist!

Hidden away at the junction of two rivers and beneath towering canyon walls, the minaret is big, beautiful and mysterious. Although it dates back to the late 12th century it's so remote that it wasn't discovered by the outside world until 1943 and not visited and properly described until 1957. Until recently only the Qutb Minar minaret in Delhi stood taller and, apart from its Pisa-like lean, the Minaret of Jam is remarkably well

19.

preserved. Yet why here and for what purpose? If it was a minaret, where was the mosque? And if it was a victory tower, like the Qutb Minar, why build it so far from any habitation? Recent research has indicated that this may have been the site of the lost city of Firuzkoh, destroyed by Genghis Khan when he smashed his way through the region.

We spend a day exploring the area around the minaret, climbing the surrounding hills for views from above, crossing the Hari Rud river on a flying fox to check the view from the other side, and finally climbing the spiral stairway inside the minaret. We lounge back at the top of the stairs admiring the views and sipping tea, which our driver, Abdul Ghani Ahsan, has thoughtfully toted up to the top. Even the climb is something of a mystery. There are two separate stairways, clockwise and anticlockwise, but they disappear below ground level. To get to the stairs you have to clamber through a head-high hole in the side of the minaret. This is clearly something for future archaeologists to investigate. Conveniently, the Lonely Planet Foundation is helping to fund the Minaret of Jam Archaeological Project.

• • • •

We depart at 3am for the long drive back to Herat. I'm beginning to realise there's a curious do-it-yourself nature to *chaikhana* dining. From dawn onwards as we drive through each village, Mobin leans out the window and calls out to passing shops and stallholders, 'Any eggs?' The answer is always no, but clearly it's going to be eggs for breakfast if at all possible. At 7.30am, four hours and 60 kilometres from Jam, we stop at a *chaikhana* and Mobin tells the owner to 'get bread and send a boy down to the village to look for eggs. It doesn't matter what they cost, I'll pay'.

20.

Inside, Mobin immediately spots a pile of potatoes heaped on the floor, demands a knife and sits on the ground to peel them. A frying pan also appears, but the gas cylinder produces so feeble a flame that Mobin heads into the kitchen to produce his fry-up (the eggs have arrived) on a wood fire. There are enough flies in the *chaikhana* to make an outback Aussie feel comfortably at home. Fifteen minutes later we're tucking into fried potatoes, eggs and tomatoes.

The next day it's a total mystery what time the flight back to Kabul leaves. At first there's a rumour it will be at 10am or 11am. Later that stretches to 3pm. We depart for the airport at 1.30pm and sit on the floor of a dusty room full of flies until 2.45pm when somebody turns up and takes over the desk and chair, which are the only furniture in the small building. It appears the only reason we've been here is for a preliminary ticket check, but Mobin is clearly a master of this process and has seated himself right by the desk so that we're straight through. Quite what good that does us is unclear since we now find ourselves sitting outside the same building with more dust, although fewer flies. Getting there first does give us chairs to sit on until 3.30pm when the signal is given to leave this compound and head for the airport terminal. We recruit a young lad to wheelbarrow our bags the couple of hundred metres. He's so small that there's no way he can push the barrow even without our bags in it, so Mobin takes over and tells him to spend the money we pay him on education.

The terminal is grey, gloomy and windowless, and the only aircraft outside is a Spanish Air Force Hercules that soon departs. There is some flying going on, however. Two swallows have attached their nests to the terminal ceiling and frantic chirping from the baby birds announces that a parent has flown in through the terminal entrance or exit door, executed a skilful turn around the whirling ceiling fan, deposited something tasty into an open beak and headed straight out again, whisking through somebody's hair (or turban or burka) if they happen to be standing in the doorway.

At 4.15pm there's a sudden surge for the boarding gate, just a narrow channel fenced in with wire. Perhaps 30 seconds later the dozen or so female passengers appear from some hidden location and are escorted straight out on to the tarmac. Another 30 seconds passes and the Kam

Air flight from Mazar-i Sharif touches down. Now we go through security, which, as in Kabul, is haphazardly hopeless. My nail clippers and a pair of tweezers were confiscated from my wash kit in Kabul, but my Swiss Army knife was overlooked. In fact I'd intended all three items to be in my checked-in bag, except it was never checked in. This time two AA batteries get confiscated and the Swiss Army knife is again overlooked. While it's being overlooked, the batteries roll on to the floor so I quickly pocket them.

At 4.45pm we finally board and any pushing to the front turns out to be pointless because they reverse the queue and board the last guy in the line first. The burkas are already all aboard. I still score a window and, just like the Kabul–Herat flight, the views are terrific. For the first 20 minutes we follow the road to Jam exactly, the trip that had taken us nearly as many hours by car. My GPS tells me we pass just eight kilometres north of the lonely minaret.

Mohammed, sitting next to me, could almost be a poster boy for the new Afghanistan. After 21 years as a refugee in Quetta, Pakistan, moving there as a young child, he returned to Afghanistan just three years ago to work as a techie with Roshan, my mobile phone company. He agrees with me that relations with Pakistan are touchy, but underlines, as so many others have done, that Afghanis owe a huge debt to their neighbour. Pakistan and Iran both took in huge numbers of Afghan refugees fleeing the fighting and hardships of the 1980s and 1990s.

The Soviets occupied Afghanistan for virtually the whole of the 1980s without ever bringing the countryside under effective control. They were opposed by a feral assortment of mujaheddin – 'strugglers' – all armed to a greater or lesser extent by the USA, who saw the Afghan turmoil as an opportunity to weaken the USSR. President Reagan praised the mujaheddin as freedom fighters and even the movie *Rambo III* portrayed them as heroic, but all these wild bunches were equally likely to squabble with each other if they weren't fighting the Russians. When Mikhail

Gorbachev took over in 1985, getting out of Afghanistan was high on his agenda. In February 1989 the last Russian troops withdrew, but the US and its allies lost interest in Afghanistan and did little to help rebuild the war-ravaged country or influence events there. The CIA had fulfilled their intention of 'fighting the Soviets to the last Afghan'; now the place could be forgotten. The USSR continued to support President Najibullah (formerly the head of the secret service, Khad) but without the support of the Soviet forces his pro-Communist government steadily lost ground to the guerrilla forces. Anyone with any sense had long since fled over the borders.

'My education was all in Pakistan', Mohammed explains in flawless English. 'We all have to be thankful for the help they have given us.

'Roshan only started in 2003, but already we have built 500 communications towers and provide coverage in 28 centres. And we have eight lakh subscribers,' he continues, proving his English came courtesy of the subcontinent, where a lakh is 100,000.

The Kam Air 737 seems to have had a previous life in Latin America. I should Mantenga Abrochado el Cinturon, it says on my tray-back, which also tells me that my Chaleco Salvavidas can be found Bajo su Asiento. Where else?

• • • •

Kabul has seen more than its fair share of bloodshed over the years. The huge quantities of arms left with the Kabul government by the Russians and supplied to the mujaheddin by the Americans allowed the opposing groups to inflict severe damage on the city.

Remarkably the Russian departure did not lead to an immediate mujaheddin takeover. The mujaheddin skill at harassing the Soviets did not translate into the ability to mount a campaign against an entrenched force, and Najibullah hung on in Kabul for three years until the Cold War

ended and Ahmad Shah Massoud and Abdul Rashid Dostum's Northern
Alliance, a military-political coalition of various Afghan groups, took
the city in April 1992. The fall of Kabul still did not bring peace.
Gulbuddin Hekmatyar, who for years had been the major recipient of the
American arms aid funnelled through Pakistan to the mujaheddin, had
established himself outside Kabul and 'Rocketing Kabul' became part of
the vocabulary as he rained missiles upon the city. Then in 1994 Dostum
decided to switch sides and join Hekmatyar against his former comrade
Massoud. In that year 10,000 people were killed in Kabul.

Meanwhile in the south, a new group had developed – the Taliban.
A *talib* is a student. Taliban is simply the plural. In late 1994 I remember
first hearing of this 'student army' rising up around Kandahar and
marching on Kabul, determined to defeat the ruthless mujaheddin who
only seemed to stop looting and raping to switch sides and start the whole
process over again.

The Taliban sought to impose a strict interpretation of Islamic Sharia
law and the population faced massive freedom restrictions and human
rights violations. Women were banned from jobs and girls forbidden
to attend schools or universities. Those who resisted were punished.
Communists were systematically eradicated, as was eventually the
majority of the opium production. The Taliban took Kabul in 1996 and
Najibullah, reluctant to escape from the city with Massoud's retreating
forces, was hauled out of the UN compound, beaten, castrated, shot
and hung from a lamppost. The Taliban destroyed dozens of statues and
figures in the city's once-magnificent museum, which had already been
comprehensively looted during the mujaheddin era.

• • • •

By the end of 2000 the Taliban had captured 95 per cent of the
country, aside from the opposition Northern Alliance strongholds in

the northeast, but more crises were developing. A terrible drought was exacerbating already severe food shortages. The Taliban government seemed more concerned about enforcing their religious strictures and continuing their battles with the remaining mujaheddin of the Northern Alliance than grappling with the problem of feeding the Afghan population. That, they seemed to feel, could be left to the UN and other NGOs, while at the same time they made the work of those organisations steadily more difficult.

As the Taliban's international support, apart from Pakistan, shrivelled up completely, the power and influence of the Arab-financed extremists of Al-Qaeda became steadily more significant. Osama bin Laden had been a prominent mujaheddin organiser and financier, funnelling money, arms and Muslim fighters from around the world into Afghanistan.

In January 2001 the UN Security Council tightened the screws on the Taliban and demanded the extradition of Osama bin Laden. Pakistan found itself in the difficult position of agreeing to enforce the UN sanctions and at the same time wanting to look after its Afghan clients. Not all was going well for the Taliban, however. Ahmad Shah Massoud, the charismatic leader of the Northern Alliance, had visited Europe to rally support while Abdul Rashid Dostum had received support from Turkey and had led his Uzbek men against the Taliban. In the west Ismail Khan, the Herat strongman (remember him?), had established a new base with Iranian support. In April the last vestige of moderation within the Taliban ranks disappeared when the deputy leader died of cancer in Karachi. More strictures were placed on humanitarian workers and in May, in a move seemingly modelled on Nazi Germany, Hindus were required to wear yellow badges.

In August UN Secretary-General Kofi Annan pushed for more carrots and sticks to be used on the Taliban while at the same time pointing out that the numbers of Islamic radicals, the majority of them Arabs, in Afghanistan had reached record levels. The summer offensive against the forces of the Northern Alliance included 10,000 non-Afghans in the 25,000-strong Taliban force and it was these non-Afghans who often inflicted the greatest cruelty on the local population, particularly the unfortunate Shiite Hazaras.

By this time Afghans made up the world's largest number of refugees, the drought continued without a break and the UN's World Food Programme was faced with feeding 5.5 million people, against 3.8 million just a year previously. August was also the month when Australia put up the 'no entry' sign for 438 mainly Afghan refugees picked up from a sinking Indonesian boat by the Norwegian container ship Tampa.

In short, by the beginning of September 2001 Afghanistan was an unholy mess, and took another step towards disaster with the assassination of Massoud on 9 September. It's theorised that the suicide killing, using a booby-trapped video camera, was planned and executed by Al-Qaeda, knowing that the September 11 attacks were only hours away and that disposing of the Taliban's number-one opponent would ensure the opposition's support when the inevitable American reaction hit. Now all it took was four aircraft hijacks.

· · · ·

I wake up from a weird dream about staying in somebody's home, inadvertently leaving a door unlocked and getting robbed. In the middle of a discussion about how this happened the burglar alarm suddenly goes off, except it isn't a wailing siren, clanging bell or shrieking scream; it's just a very loud voice repeatedly enunciating: ALARM, ALARM, ALARM. It's so loud I wake up with a start, in time to hear the last 'Allah Akbar' boom out from a nearby minaret in the muezzin's pre-dawn call to prayer. I was getting up soon anyway. This morning Mobin and I are off to the Bamiyan Valley in central Afghanistan, the centre of the Hazarajat, the homeland of the country's Shiite Hazaras.

26.

To my eternal regret we didn't visit Bamiyan back in 1972. My diary reveals that we decided the transport alternatives were either too expensive – 'US$15 round trip' – or too difficult – '12 hours from 3am on the local bus'. Now the giant Buddhas, which looked out over the beautiful valley from their hillside niches, are gone, destroyed by the Taliban. An ancient reclining Buddha image in Ghazni also fell to the Taliban's iconoclastic urges.

In retrospect the destruction of the Bamiyan Buddhas in March 2001 seems like an omen of what was to come in New York six months later. The Taliban leader, Mullah Omar, had promised to protect them. Now he reversed course, an indication it was Osama bin Laden and the Arab fundamentalists who were in control, according to Nancy Hatch Dupree, the American author of *An Historical Guide to Afghanistan*, first published back in 1970 and still the classic guide to the country. 'It was the hardliners' way of saying: "We have won. We call the shots. We don't give a damn"', Dupree explained.

The destruction of the Buddhas seems to me like the perfect example of religious intolerance. 'Our religion is the only correct religion. You're an infidel; we're going to treat your religion with zero respect. Get fucked.' Angry Muslims (anger is something Islam seems to do very well), however, had been working Bamiyan over long before the Taliban arrived on the scene. Faces of Buddha images had been hacked off centuries ago.

Unfortunately Islam is far from the only religion to play these games. Knocking your temple down to build my temple right on top of it seems to be a game most religions like to play. It was certainly a favourite with Christian missionaries in the Pacific. Once they'd stopped those lascivious hip-shaking dances and covered up the grass skirts and bare boobs with nice Mother Hubbard dresses, their favourite activity was flattening Polynesian temples and building a church on top. Christianity has also included bouts of iconoclasm. The 16th-century Reformation in

Europe featured plenty of destruction of 'graven images'.

The route to Bamiyan is not unlike the road from Herat to Jam. A rough and rugged road that took just 6½ hours back in the 1970s (according to Dupree) today takes us 11 hours. There's plenty to see along the way. Villages surrounded by green fields and walled orchards pop up regularly, just like on the Jam route, but there are also regular *kala* (fortified houses) and ancient caravanserais. Dupree's guidebook faithfully notes these ancient markers, but they've since been joined by much more recent Russian tanks looking as if their crew just parked them by the roadside and walked away. Once a tank has stopped it's clearly all but impossible to shift. We stop for lunch at a very busy *chaikhana* in Ghorband. From our seat on the upstairs balcony I can see two tanks abandoned right in the middle of the village.

Next morning I gaze up at the empty Buddha niches looking reproachfully out on the valley, but what a beautiful valley it is and there's plenty of interest apart from the missing Buddhas. Everything around Bamiyan reminds me of somewhere else. The valley itself takes me back to Ladakh, the Tibetan region of north India. There are the same gently folded hills, beautifully shadowed in early and late light, with lines of poplar trees providing a green contrast to the grey-brown earth. Then in the background are the snowy peaks. There's also a touch of Turkey: the caves that dot the hillsides, not just around the niches for the great Buddha images but all around the valley, have a definite flavour of Goreme, the Anatolian area of troglodyte dwellings. When we head out to Band-i-Amir, the recollections turn to Tibet – the rolling, utterly treeless sweep of country, still with mountains on the horizon, but also with that Tibetan habit of diverting off on a totally new road route every now and then.

Overtaking a slow-moving truck is rarely a problem. You just take the other fork when the road divides and a kilometre later the roads rejoin and the truck is behind you. Plus there's an Ethiopian interlude every now and then – Russian tanks from the Soviet era are seen, abandoned by the roadside, just as often as in that African nation.

The Hazara people of the Bamiyan region were among the first to rise up against the Russian invaders and they succeeded in driving the Russians out of the Hazarajat region by 1981. The unfortunate Hazaras have always done it tough. Physically they look quite different to the other Afghan tribes. They're said to be descendants of Genghis Khan's Mongolian followers who remained behind after his destructive invasion from 1220. Furthermore they're the Shiite minority among the country's Sunni Muslims and as a result they've always been looked down upon and discriminated against by the other Afghan groups. Khaled Hosseini's bestseller *The Kite Runner* revolves around the Hazaras' unfortunate position in Afghan society and in particular the mistreatment they suffered at the hands of the Taliban. It was only in September 1998 that the Taliban finally captured Bamiyan, only to lose it again less than a year later. They finally regained it in 2000 and underlined their control by destroying the Buddhas and massacring large numbers of Hazaras, people they looked upon as little better than nonbelievers.

From Bamiyan it's only a couple of hours along a much better road to the beautiful lakes of Band-i-Amir where we're suddenly in the American southwest with soaring pinnacles and plunging canyons, but a surreal southwest because of those otherworldly blue lakes. Writers are keen to announce that no description can ever prepare you for the sheer beauty of these lakes and they're right. Like so many visitors in the past I am awestruck by the incredible blue of the main lake – Band-i-Haibat, the 'Dam of Awe'. The lake has created its own dam over the years with the sulphur deposits now rising to more than 10 metres high and continuing to build up as the water spills over the edge. There's a touch of Australia in the language – in Australian English a dam means not just the device to hold back the water, but also the water behind the dam.

Also awestruck by the lake are François and Arnaud, two French motorcyclists who have arrived overland from Europe intending to continue to Vietnam. It's great to see some tourists rediscovering the country. There's also a small group of Japanese tourists, led by feisty Michiko Suzuki, who has spent three years in the country and complains that the Japanese government, like the Australian one, contends that the whole country is a no-go zone. She's irate about this. 'My name is black in Japan', she contends. She manages to get adventurous tour groups like this together anyway, even if the government doesn't like it. 'The Taiwanese are the only people who come here and aren't worried about it', she continues.

There's much more traffic on the way back to Kabul than there was on the way out. The road seems to be crowded with goats, sheep, donkeys and even camels, quite apart from vehicles. There's a disproportionate number of the standard UN vehicle, the white Toyota Land Cruiser, out and about today and, as always with the UN, travelling way too fast.

'They don't own them', comments Mobin. 'If the drivers owned the vehicles, they wouldn't drive like that.'

A surprising number of the Afghan minibuses and Corollas seem to be driven by 10-year-olds, barely able to see over the steering wheel and looking even younger among their grey-bearded, turbaned passengers.

Coming down the hill from the Shibar Pass, we stop to photograph a particularly nicely situated abandoned tank, its gun barrel blocking part of the road. To my amazement the tank commander suddenly pops his head up from the hatch. Has a left-behind Russian been waiting all these years? More likely it's the donkey herder taking a break from the wind while his scatter of hee-haws graze up the hill.

Just before we reach the sealed Kabul–Mazar road, just north of Charikar, there are a string of car-wash guys, waiting to hose the dust off before you get back on the tarmac for 60 Afs, about US$1.20, plus a good tip. Every car seems to stop for this pre-big-city service.

• • • •

My third and final excursion from Kabul is up to Mazar-i Sharif, the northern centre close to the border with the northern 'stans', which were once part of the USSR. Back in 1972 Maureen and I drove across Afghanistan entering from Iran to Herat, looping south to the current no-go zone of Kandahar, heading north to Kabul and then turning east to cross the Khyber Pass into Pakistan. We never went to Mazar.

Mazar may be peaceful today, but the Taliban takeover of the northern metropolis was a microcosm of the entire country's quarter-century of absurd infighting and treachery. It was a 'bloody drama of betrayals, counter-betrayals and inter-ethnic bloodshed which was astounding even by Afghan standards' according to Ahmed Rashid's seminal book *Taliban*.

In 1997 the Taliban controlled their southern redoubt of Kandahar, the western centre of Herat and the recently captured capital, Kabul. Ahmad Shah Massoud was marginalised, driven back to his final stronghold in the Panjshir Valley. If the Taliban could capture Mazar-i Sharif, they had effective control of the whole country. The capture, however, required the defeat of the ruthless Uzbek leader Abdul Rashid Dostum, the strongest of Afghan strongmen. Dostum had managed to keep Mazar clear of the turmoil that had devastated so much of the country, but he had a weak point – his second-in-command, Malik Pahlawan.

Defeating Dostum was, for the Taliban, simply a matter of bribing Malik to switch sides. It's only about 50 kilometres from Mazar to the Uzbekistan border and Dostum managed to escape, although Ismail Khan, the Herat commander who had been cooperating with Dostum, ended up in the Taliban's hands. Malik quickly found that his deal with the Taliban was really a Taliban takeover, not some joint power-sharing, and within two weeks the whole deal unravelled. Mazar included a substantial Hazara population as well as its Uzbek majority and the Shiia Hazara rose in revolt and slaughtered the Taliban invaders and their Pakistani supporters. Naturally Malik took this opportunity to renege on his recent deal and also went on the attack.

The Taliban survivors fled south only to find that Massoud had taken this opportunity to venture out of the Panjshir Valley to blow up the southern entrance to the Salang Tunnel, which links northern and southern Afghanistan, thus trapping the terrified Taliban forces in the north. Meanwhile the Hazara also rose up from their Bamiyan Valley stronghold and the straightforward capture of Mazar instead turned into a disastrous rout.

Nevertheless a strong Taliban force remained in the north and less than four months later they resumed their attack on Mazar. Of course, this was the signal for Uzbek supporters of Dostum and Malik to start fighting each other as well as the Pashtun Talibans, and at this point Dostum reappeared on the scene from exile in Turkey. Apart from battling with his untrustworthy former supporter Malik, he now found himself fighting to regain the city not from the Taliban, but from the Hazaras, who had established themselves in the city during the chaos.

The Taliban fled south for a second time, taking the opportunity to conduct the occasional massacre of Hazaras as they went, and the Uzbeks added a new definition to the term 'containerisation'. Taliban captives were herded into shipping containers in the desert where, under the fierce summer sun, they died from either asphyxiation or simply roasting to death. It was difficult to tell from their blackened corpses how they had died. Dostum and Khan are both major forces in the Afghanistan government today.

• • • •

It's just over 400 kilometres to Mazar and time-wise a good part of it is getting clear of Kabul. The dusty, potholed back roads to Jam and Bamiyan might be slow, hard going and crowded, but well-kept roads like this one are seriously scary. Drivers regularly pull out to overtake against oncoming traffic, confident that it will pull on to the shoulder to let them through. Sometimes a faster overtaker passes a slower overtaker and on occasions somebody else will simultaneously overtake on the inside, putting four vehicles abreast on a single lane. The signature Afghan overtaking technique is the 'approaching a speed bump' manoeuvre. As one vehicle slows for one of the far-too-frequent speed bumps, another vehicle pulls out but then also has to slow down to a near stop. Since it's quite likely that somebody is trying the same trick in the opposite direction the end result is total gridlock with two other cars also occupying the whole road width. Speed bumps are often made by simply draping a Russian tank track across the road.

Once we're through the Salang Tunnel, the four-kilometre long tunnel built with Russian aid back in the late 1950s and early 1960s, we zip along at 100 kilometres per hour. There's still snow around the tunnel exit on the northern side. We stop beside the Doshakh bridge, where the melting water from the mountains rushes past a meadow lined with a cluster of *chaikhana* set up to cater to the passing traffic. Unhappily the whole site is rapidly submerging under a blizzard of soft-drink cans, plastic bags and other assorted garbage. I don't say anything about it, but Mobin is so annoyed he goes off to lecture the owner of the main *chaikhana*.

Mazar has a single major attraction, the Shrine of Hazrat Ali. Ali is the Prophet Mohammed's son-in-law and a main player in the great split between Shiite and Sunni Muslims. The Shiites believe he is the true successor to the prophet; the Sunnis disagree. Both sides do, generally, agree that Ali is buried in Najaf in Iraq, but somehow an alternative theory developed that he's here in Mazar in Afghanistan. Either way it's an important site, beautiful and peaceful in the evening glow and home to a famous flock of white pigeons.

The Hotel Farhat in Mazar has 'old Soviet character', according to the guidebook. It's also packed full of huge overstuffed furniture and features the sagging carpet-on-top-of-carpet on the stairs, which seems to be a design norm in Afghan hotels with pretensions. My room also has neatly folded sheets on the bed in case I feel like making it, two suitcase-like containers with blankets in case the temperature drops, and an air-con unit, which might prove more useful. Sitting on a chair beside the bed is a big metal box with instrument dials. A cable snakes out of it in one direction and another cable coils all over one side of the room before disappearing, who knows where? Heart monitor? No, it's a voltage stabiliser for the air-con.

We dine in the Bahaar Restaurant, which is liberally decorated with nicely misspelled calendars from the Kefayar Hotel & Weeding Centre. Presumably after the ceremony the couple can get down to some serious maintenance of the vegetable patch. Back at the hotel it's late and quiet. All the guests' shoes are scattered around just inside the entrance to the building.

The next morning we drive to neighbouring Balkh, the region's other big attraction. Today it's just a village, but it was a great Buddhist centre two millennia ago and already dubbed 'the mother of cities' when Islam arrived on the scene. Genghis Khan put an end to that and when Marco Polo stopped by, there were only ruins to impress him. The remains of the city's great mud walls still stretch for 10 kilometres.

The ancient Masjid-e No Gombad once had nine domes, or *gombad*, and is crying out for an archaeological investigation. The intricately moulded stucco columns, which once supported the domes, disappear into the ground for half their height. What lies beneath the surface?

The tomb of Rabi'a Balkhi in the circular park in the centre of modern Balkh is a potent reminder of the hidden half of Afghanistan. Her poetry proves that Afghanistan's women do have a voice and that love can still exist, even in such a male-dominated society. Rabi'a Balkhi fell in love with her slave, was imprisoned here and committed suicide by slashing her wrists, writing her final poem on her prison walls with her own blood. I'm about to stroll to the shade of a tree to check my guidebook's description of this event when Mobin warns me off.

'Don't go that way. There is woman', he says in a tone reminiscent of those old nautical maps with their 'here be monsters' notations at the edges. Two women are indeed sitting under the tree and it reminds me that several times Mobin has taken care to steer me away from approaching too close to the forbidden half of this country.

•   •   •   •

We're off early the next morning, heading south for a small pilgrimage up the Panjshir Valley, Massoud's power base and final retreat. First, though, there's a short side-trip. So many wonderful places in this world meet all our expectations while failing to surprise us. We've had so many previews, seen so many photographs, glimpsed them as backgrounds to so many movies, read about them so many times that there's no unexpected shock. We know what to expect.

Every once in a while we suddenly find ourselves looking at something for which there has been no advance warning. Something that has had no book-cover portraits nor even the odd black-and-white photograph on some museum wall. Something like Takht-e-Rustam, only a few kilometres off the Kabul–Mazar road at Samangan, a Buddhist complex featuring a cave monastery and a rock-cut stupa. It's the stupa that really blows me away. I thought I knew my way around the stupas of Asia, but I have never even seen a photograph of this two-millennium-old rock dome. Here's something too solid for even the Taliban to damage. Clearly it has similarities to the temples of Ajanta and Ellora in India, also cut out of solid rock, or even the cave temples of Petra in Jordan, but the place it really reminds me of is Lalibela in Ethiopia, where you also can stand at surface level and look down at the marvel at your feet.

We pause for lunch again at the beautiful Doshakh bridge collection of *chaikhana*. There's no sign of anything happening about the trash situation. At the other side of the Salang Tunnel we diverge up

35.

the Panjshir Valley to visit the tomb (a grand mausoleum is under construction) of Ahmad Shah Massoud, the 'Hero of Afghanistan', the 'Lion of Panjshir'. Massoud kept the Russians at bay and guarded the only region of Afghanistan not to fall to the Taliban until, just two days before September 11, he was assassinated by Taliban suicide bombers.

Back in Kabul that night we're accompanied at dinner by Mobin's small-screen obsession. It seems Mobin has a number of obsessions, starting with photography. His little digital camera works overtime and he gets good results. In part it may be because people are so enthusiastic about getting photographed. Mobin will haul a farmer out of the field and run him through a hundred poses as if Mobin was a fashion photographer and the hapless labourer was a high-fashion model.

Then there's food: 'We must have vegetables' has been a regular announcement. A bag of salad ingredients rides around in the back of the car and if the *chaikhana* can't provide a suitable salad Mobin will provide it for them, preparing it as well if necessary.

Genghis Khan – aka Jenghiz or Chenghiz in these parts – is a definite obsession. We run into him on a regular basis. Old Genghis was in a particularly destructive mood when he swept through Afghanistan, and Shahr-e-Gholghola, the 'City of Screams' in the Bamiyan Valley, is a pretty good example of his handiwork. The screams came from the city's inhabitants as Genghis slaughtered every man, woman and child. Mobin totes around an Afghan history book (two volumes), which he dips into periodically.

'If I meet him after I die, I will kill him' is a typical Mobin pronouncement about Genghis.

Finally there's Indian soap opera. After two weeks in Afghanistan I'm beginning to suffer from Bollywood overkill. Every hotel lobby or restaurant I step into has a television tuned to India, picking up either Bollywood movies, Bollywood soap operas or Bollywood MTV-style music videos. The music videos feature the usual sashaying around, sultry

36.

looks and sexy moves, but without ever getting too explicit. Anything too raunchy goes fast-forward or out of focus, but the Taliban ban on music and dancing has clearly resulted in a pent-up demand that all of Afghanistan is working overtime to service.

'Nobody wants to watch anything from Pakistan,' Mobin explains, 'but Iran is OK.' The Iranian passion for torch singers may generate lots of cassette sales in the bazaar, but it's not going to work as a video clip. A filmy sari works much better than an all-encompassing chador and when it comes to dancing Bollywood's a clear winner.

'My Mother-in-Law was a Bride' is the Hindi-to-Dari-to-English translation of the soap that has Mobin in thrall. Most of Afghanistan as well it seems, from the number of times I catch the theme tune and see the (rapidly becoming familiar) characters casting anxious/angry/ passionate/perplexed looks at each other. Over dinner at the guesthouse this soap, with the actors' Hindi dubbed in to Dari, was always the focus of attention.

'This programme is perfect for Afghanistan', Muqim explains. 'Exactly the same concerns face people in Kabul', he continues, explaining that the pretty young woman arguing with her husband was complaining that he wasn't making enough money to buy her sufficient jewellery.

'I can't sleep if I don't have a lot of jewellery', she whines.

Once her husband had mooched out she snatches up the phone to complain to her mother as well.

'There's no air-conditioning in the apartment and I have to fix my own breakfast', she wails. 'How can I live like this?'

'Get a life', her mother wisely responds.

'We have four TV networks now', Mobin observes. 'Guess how many we had under the Taliban?

'Zero.'

• • • •

I have a final visit in Kabul – the OMAR (Organisation for Mine Clearance and Afghan Rehabilitation) Land Mine Museum. Most of the operation is indeed devoted to mines and clearing them, but the museum has all sorts of military equipment as well as those most horrific weapons of often very minor destruction. It's a gruesome little collection of warped ingenuity, a bastard marriage of neat design and ugly practicality.

Don't those stylish Italians turn out smart little pressure-sensitive mines, perfectly packaged to take a child's legs off? The Russian mine packing a thousand pieces of rusty iron – 'chopped rod' – around the seven kilos of explosive is nowhere near as elegant, but it's guaranteed to make a real mess of anybody nearby when it goes off. Some of the nastier examples include the 'bounding mines', which, when triggered, jump a metre or so into the air before exploding, high enough to take your legs off at thigh level or a child's head off her neck.

Have I been getting too blasé about this country? Emerging from the hotel in Mazar, Mobin ducks down to look under the wheel arches.

'Checking for bombs?' I inquire.

'I don't know how good the security is at this hotel', he announces. 'I'm pretty sure they're OK, but I tell our drivers they must always check their cars.'

He doesn't mean the water and oil levels.

'If they put a bomb under your car, it will usually be close to the fuel tank.'

Mobin is almost annoyingly protective. He always manages to manoeuvre himself between me and oncoming traffic as we cross roads. Getting across the road always entails a game of chicken with the drivers. There are no pedestrian roads and very few traffic lights. Indeed, were there any traffic lights at all? He isn't happy about my heading out on to the streets alone.

'Relax,' I feel like saying. 'I can look after myself.' I don't say it, though, and it's not a problem. I'm quite happy to go along with being shadowed.

On that final full day in Kabul my tranquil attitude finally gets a wake-up call.

I drop round to the British embassy to talk to a contact there and, after an interesting discussion, lazing back in the warm sunshine on the embassy's patch of grass – sipping tea in a traditionally English fashion – I head back to the separate arrivals building, hand in my visitor pass, retrieve my passport and phone Mobin. The guesthouse is only a kilometre or two away and he said he'd zip round to pick me up as soon as I call.

I can't get through. The lines are congested or there's some sort of problem with the connection. I sit down, wait a few minutes and call again. Still no luck. Five minutes later I'm about to try again when my embassy contact reappears to announce that something is happening out on the streets and the embassy is being locked down. We wander back by the dining area, grab another cup of tea, and retire to the garden again. The British embassy has a lot of guys around with security written all over them, in appearance if not words. The Land Cruisers are armoured and so are some of these guys. Gradually the rumours start to percolate and the very first one is pretty close to the truth: there's been a car accident between a foreigner and an Afghani. Somebody, presumably the Afghani, has been killed and there's trouble.

Soon alternative rumours pop up. It's been a collision between an American army vehicle and one or more cars and when the crowd became threatening the Americans fired into the crowd. Or they didn't and the angry reaction to the accident is simply the resentment already seething from a recent raid in the south, which – choose your standard report – got a lot of Taliban bad guys or got a lot of innocent civilians. Quite possibly both. A sudden burst of gunfire coming from just outside the embassy wall confirms that whatever is happening is more than just a rumour.

By this time the news is coming through on the TV: scenes of Hummers racing by angry rock-hurling crowds, a government office and something else – a restaurant? a hotel? – being attacked, a car on fire.

The angry crowds are moving towards the parliament building in the south of the city. The embassy quarter, where I'm holed up, is in the north, but then the TV reports that they're moving north towards the city centre, looting as they go. A hot new rumour says that the German embassy, virtually next door to us, is under attack. Obviously the American embassy is being threatened, but it appears the military are keeping the protesters well away from that tasty target.

We have lunch and talk some more. None of my embassy contact's afternoon appointments are going to turn up so I don't have to feel guilty about stealing his time. Barbara Stapleton, a European Union representative, is also marooned at the embassy and unable to phone out to find out what's happening. We were both in Cambodia in 1993, at the time of the first post–Pol Pot elections, and we swap tales about that sad but lovely country.

I mention Frank Zappa's definition of what it takes to be a country: 'You can't be a real country unless you have a beer and an airline – it helps if you have a football team, or some nuclear weapons, but at least you need a beer', and we show our age by remembering some classic rock concerts at the old Rainbow Theatre in London. Barbara recalls a Bob Marley concert where the mood turned uglier and uglier as the crowd waited for the reggae master to finally come on stage. And then it turned completely as the audience linked arms for another dose of redemption.

We also talk about the drug situation. The British are about to commit more troops to policing the Taliban-controlled Helmand province, site for much of Afghanistan's huge opium production. The Taliban did clamp down on opium production when they were in power, but that policy was reversed once they were out of power. Not only does the money from opium support the Taliban and spread violence, it also causes huge problems all the way from poppy field to some junkie's veins in New York or London. Naturally some leaks out along the way so Pakistan, the old Russian Central Asian republics and Iran all face increasing problems with drug addiction and all the crime, corruption and carnage it brings. Russian journalist Artyom Borovik pointed out in *The Hidden War*, his fine account of the Soviet war in Afghanistan, that money to support the mujaheddin didn't only come from the CIA; plenty of Western junkies were also doing their unintentional best to support capitalism's war with Communism.

We're told we can stay the night at the embassy if necessary and we both joke that in places like this you should always bring your toothbrush along. Things aren't so friendly out on the streets and when Barbara can finally get a call out it's to hear that the Care International offices, opposite her own, have been attacked and set on fire. A few minutes later her phone rings. It's not her driver, who has been caught on the other side of a police roadblock, but a driver she used to have, simply phoning up to check she's all right.

Reports of what happened have now become fairly clear. A US military convoy crashed into a number of cars, possibly accidentally, possibly due to some sort of mechanical failure. It's irrelevant. In this situation you're guilty, whatever the cause. Some of the final 11 deaths are a direct consequence of the accident; others result from gunfire from the convoy personnel, the Afghan military or the police. That's hardly relevant either. Amusingly, an American embassy spokesman announces that everybody has been moved to a secure location within their heavily fortified building.

Round at the British embassy we're still sitting out in the garden.

Despite the events outside, my embassy contact still thinks there are reasons to be confident about Afghanistan's future. President Karzai has been successful at co-opting the warlords, weaning them away from their fiefdoms and installing them in some important-sounding (and possibly even actually important) role in Kabul. Abdul Rashid Dostum has been lured away from Mazar and Ismail Khan from Herat. Could Khan possibly be persuaded to give up Herat for the title of Minister of Energy?

Turned out he could.

'People worry about simply ignoring the damage these guys did,' muses another of my fellow embassy captives, 'but they were successful warlords not only because they were ruthless, but also because they were good administrators. Afghanistan needs good administrators.'

Finally my phone rings and Mobin announces he's coming round to collect me. I've been trying to call him and Muqim regularly, but without success. I've been at the embassy for six hours.

Ten minutes later we're cruising through quiet although not deserted streets. There are plenty of police and Afghan military, but no coalition personnel, at every junction. We're turned back as we approach the guesthouse, but Mobin nonchalantly cruises down one-way Chicken Street in the wrong direction and we're soon home. Surprisingly, apart from one burnt-out car and a scattering of broken glass at a handful of shops and police boxes or their close brethren, the security boxes, which stand at the entrances to secured compounds, there's no sign of damage. Most shops are shuttered, but the Italian restaurant Popolano, just round the corner from the guesthouse, looks like it's planning to open for business this evening.

Next morning it's pretty clear that everything is unclear. I've watched the local TV (Tolo TV is all over town talking to people) and scanned the websites from CNN to BBC World, the *Guardian* in the UK to the *Age* back in Melbourne (where riots in Dili, East Timor, have so focused Australian media interest that there's no chance of Kabul, Afghanistan, scoring a column inch).

Mobin's morning report probably sums it up pretty well.

'It was a military convoy coming in to the city from the Shomali Valley', he reports. 'They were driving too fast [ah, just like the UN] and they had already hit a bus and another car before they arrived in the city. It was accident-accident-accident.'

This had a ring of truth to it. The Guardian's website had talked of simmering anger due to aggressive driving tactics and the US defence that this style of driving is 'necessary for security'.

I could picture where the accident had happened. 'Was it coming down the hill into the city, where the dual highway ends at the big roundabout where we've fuelled up and where all the taxis and buses pick up passengers?' I ask.

'Right', confirmed Mobin. 'The truck ran right over a taxi [I'd seen the flattened vehicle on TV] and hit a whole line of cars. They killed four people and injured many others.'

Which is where the confusion starts. It's pretty clear on day one that seven or eight people were killed (the number later rose to 11), but was it one, or four, in the initial accident? And were the rest killed by panicked Americans (they only fired over the crowds, an American spokesman declared) or by panicked Afghans? As usual it's irrelevant. What's relevant is that the anger is out there and it's driven by all sorts of things – government corruption and government inefficiency, and the fact that plenty of international money sloshes around yet so much of it goes to the peacekeepers and NGOs and so little trickles down to the Afghan people.

The aggressive driving certainly doesn't improve things. 'And it would help a lot if they jumped out and provided medical assistance after an accident instead of pointing guns at people', suggests Rodney Cocks, an Australian UN worker I meet on the flight home.

• • • •

My enforced stay at the British embassy means I never get to the Kabul Museum and Mobin deems the lookout point we'd planned to climb to on our last morning at least temporarily unsafe.

Perhaps there is one little find I can make in my final hours in Kabul. I'll go looking for the Titanic. The movie *Titanic* – released 1997, directed by James Cameron and starring Kate Winslet and Leonardo DiCaprio in a steamy romance among the icebergs – was a huge hit worldwide including in Afghanistan. The Taliban were in power and, of course, movies were banned, but nothing prevents videos reaching their audience and Titanic-the-movie soon morphed into Titanic-the-wedding-cake. Titanic after Titanic, impressive confections of cake and icing sugar, sailed out of Kabul bakeries into the dusty heat of the Afghan summer.

'People identified with the film', Mobin explained as we went in search of a Titanic bakery. 'They liked the story, the young couple searching for love, not directed by their parents. The people on the ship were facing disaster, just like Afghanistan. They looked at the Titanic, but they thought of Afghanistan. They wanted a wedding cake that symbolised not only love, but also our country's problems. It made you realise that we were not the only people in the world who were unhappy.'

Fashions come and go and the Titanic has clearly sailed away. There are no Titanic cakes in sight.

'They are no longer popular,' explains one wedding cake baker, 'but there is a photograph of a Titanic cake in my photo album.' He pulls a dishevelled album out from under the counter, but there are no Titanics in sight.

'It must be in the other album', he explains, hauling an even more time-worn album from its hiding place.

Again there are no Titanics. How long before Afghanistan can shake off its Titanic status and sail into ice-free seas?

ALBANIA

SERBIA & MONTENEGRO

MACEDONIA

ADRIATIC SEA

Kruja

Durrësi

TIRANA

Ardenica

Apollonia

Berati

Fieri

ITALY

GREECE

Tepelena

Jal Beach

Gjirokastra

Himara

IONIAN SEA

Saranda

Butrint

I encountered my first bunker before we'd driven a kilometre from the Mother Teresa International Airport. Of course the airport itself was a pleasant curiosity – how many countries have an international airport named after a nun, even if she is the world's best-known nun as well as the most famous Albanian? Apart from a few postcards, I didn't encounter Mother Teresa again until my departure day, but Albania's bunker collection was an oddity that would follow me all around.

In the 1950s Albania was already well advanced on the single-minded path that would take it via Stalinism and Maoism to its final position as the most isolated and least-visited country in Europe. Even when the Berlin Wall crumbled and Communism collapsed in the rest of Eastern Europe, the party stumbled on, like a chicken with its head chopped off. Then in February 1991 an angry mob hauled down the gigantic bronze statue of Enver Hoxha from its plinth in Sheshi Skënderbej, the main square of the capital, Tirana, and 45 years of one of the world's weirdest governments came to an end.

The bunkers were the ultimate symbol of Hoxha's paranoia – a symbol not likely to disappear in a hurry. Unlike the Berlin Wall, Albania's obsessive dictator built things to last. The bunkers are also an indicator that Albania was a very inward-looking Bad Land, quite harmless to anyone else in the world, but utterly convinced that the outside world was a major threat to them.

You can imagine the scene in the early 1950s as Enver inspects the first of the 700,000 concrete mushrooms that will eventually dot the tiny country.

'You're sure it's strong enough to withstand a tank attack?' Hoxha queries the prototype bunker's creator.

'Absolutely', declares the bunker designer, who is quickly shoved inside as Hoxha signals for a tank to trundle forward and blast the shelter with its gun. The shaken engineer eventually emerges, relatively unscathed, physically at least, and Hoxha orders the country's concrete makers to step up production. By the time Hoxha died in 1985, Albania had a bunker for every fourth person in the country. They dotted every strategic point from mountain passes to remote beaches, harbour entrances to airport approaches, consuming three times as much concrete as the French used in the construction of their equally useless pre–World War II Maginot Line.

The Maginot Line didn't hold up the German invasion of France, but Hoxha's bunkers never had to withstand an attack. After all, why would anyone want to invade Albania? Today the bunkers stand in virtually undiminished numbers. They are not easy to demolish and the Albanians have to live with them. It's hard to find a new use for the squat little domes. Many were tiny affairs, barely big enough for a couple of cramped people and pretty useless for anything today other than an extraordinarily solid dog kennel. Farmers have turned some into animal shelters. Beach bunkers are often filling up with drifting sand, but probably the most common bunker use is as a handy place for quick trysts. Albanian virginity is lost in a Hoxha bunker as often as American virginity was once lost in the back seats of cars.

. . . .

An hour later I'm standing with pretty much the same viewpoint as Hoxha's statue used to have, except my eyes are 15 metres closer to ground level. To my left the National Museum of History is fronted by a huge mosaic mural owing some debt to the art of the Cultural Revolution in China. I can almost picture Mao front and centre, leading the workers, soldiers, revolutionaries and assorted historic figures towards some bright Marxist-Leninist future. In fact it's a woman, rifle held aloft, who leads the charge, although the Albanian flag flying behind her has been reworked to remove the Communist Party star.

Across the square to my right is the statue of national hero Skanderbeg astride his horse, and beyond his statue are the Et'hem Bey Mosque and the Clock Tower, both lucky survivors from Hoxha's 1967 campaign to convert Albania to an atheist state by destroying all its mosques, churches and monasteries. Directly in front of me is the Palace of Culture, but the most interesting sight is directly at my feet. If the Hoxha statue were still around, it would be gazing down at a fine indication of the total victory of capitalism in Albania. Lined up around the pedestrian area is a varied collection of electric and petrol-driven toy cars, motorcycles and other child-size devices with happy children at the wheel zooming dangerously back and forth across their little playground. It's a fine preview for Albania's even more dangerous roads.

The most prominent Hoxha relic is a stone's throw from my hotel. The 'pyramid' is just that – a tattily built, white-tiled pyramid that started life as a museum to the long-term dictator. Opened in 1988, three years after his death, it was designed by his architect daughter, Pranvera Hoxha. I'd encounter another Pranvera Hoxha homage to an Albanian hero right at the end of my visit. In the spate of Hoxha-deletions that followed the end

49.

of Communist rule, a Hoxha museum was clearly unwanted. The giant marble statue of the seated Hoxha was chopped up and the museum's contents ('more or less everything he ever touched or used', according to the Blue Guide) were removed. Today the pyramid is officially known as the International Centre of Culture, but it's also had a spell as a discotheque and kids find it makes a very usable playground slide.

The word 'pyramid' has a special resonance in modern Albania. The capitalism-run-wild period that followed the fall of Communism ended with a dramatic nationwide pyramid-banking scheme. It's estimated that 70 per cent of the population lost all their savings as, inevitably, the scam ground to a halt in an orgy of rioting and violence that nearly slid the country into civil war. Remarkably it marked the bottom of the slide and the economy has been steadily improving since 2002. After bankruptcy the only way is up, the cynics might say, and it's going to be a while before Albania is invited to join the EU.

That evening I bar-hop through the city's Blloku area, which, until 1991, was shut off to the general Albanian proletariat. This was where Hoxha and the other high-ups of the Albanian nomenklatura hung out. Hoxha's home may have been the best Albania could muster, but compared with the residences of some other Bad Land leaders it's a conservative suburban villa. Today Blloku has become Tirana's bar, restaurant and café centre. If Hoxha were still alive, he could pop straight across the road for a cocktail in the Buda Bar. I continue on down the road to Effendi, a restaurant where the 'Ottoman cuisine' reflects the long Turkish influence from when Albania was one of the furthest outreaches of the Ottoman Empire.

One of my dinner companions is Nevila Popa, who works for EDEM, the USAID-supported Enterprise Development and Export Market organisation. A few weeks previously I'd been wandering Washington DC with Scott Wayne, an American tourism consultant and former Lonely Planet guidebook writer. Scott's Lonely Planet assignments had even included several visits to Sudan, a country fully deserving Bad Land status today. I'd told Scott that I was planning to visit Albania and he'd put me in touch with EDEM, one of his consultancy clients.

Nevila had worked at a hotel in Grand Rapids, Michigan, and she's the first example of what I soon decide is an Albanian norm – people who have gone abroad for a spell and returned with enthusiasm, skills and excellent English. My other dinner companions include Kliton Gërxhani and Armand Ferra, two young men who've done their time abroad and come back to set up websites, book hotels, dispense advice and organise tours in the new Albania.

Tirana has been a much brighter, livelier and more orderly town than I'd expected. The potholes in the street haven't been as big as I'd been looking forward to and on the walk back to my hotel even the street lighting is better than it should be if Albania was still a Bad Land disaster zone. I've also been surprised not just that so many people speak English, but that they speak it so fluently.

'We are a small country', Kliton (or Tony as he told me to call him) explained. 'We have to be able to speak other languages.'

'And we have an aptitude for them', Armand confirmed.

Well, Albanian is not a language that trips off the tongue. Even the name of the country comes out as Shqipëria.

• • • •

Just as Gaddafi never saw a revolution he didn't want to support, Hoxha never found a branch of Communism he didn't eventually fall out with. Euro-Communism, despite that French style (good enough as a finishing school for Pol Pot and Ho Chi Minh), was quickly discarded. Yugo-Communism got the boot equally as fast. Tito may have been good at whipping fractious Balkan states into line, but his brand of Communism quickly faded from bright Marxist-Leninist red to a wishy-washy revisionist shade of pink.

51.

Joseph Stalin was much more to Hoxha's liking and under Uncle Joe's guidance Albania settled in for a long spell as the leading exponent of hard-left Stalinism. That was until Khrushchev, with his pinko revisionism, came along and Hoxha was forced – forced, mind you – to abandon the Soviet Union for the stricter rules of Maoism, as best expounded during the Cultural Revolution. And then, unhappy day, the Chairman took the really long march and before you knew it the Chinese had embarked on revisionism as well.

In *Two Friendly People*, a handy collection of Hoxha's speeches on Albanian-Greek relations, the Albanian leader sets the world straight on that one.

'It is not true', he declared, 'that we "broke away" from China. No. It was the Chinese revisionist and capitalist leaders who undertook anti-Albanian actions and unilaterally breached the agreements on economic co-operation with our country and they did this because we tried to convince them that they were applying a counter-revolutionary foreign policy and sliding ever more deeply into reprehensible actions and alliances with American imperialism.'

Well, what could you expect? Poor Albania had been through this all before, Hoxha continued, when 'we denounced the treacherous actions of the Khrushchevite revisionists'.

It was a tough world out there and it had been left to tiny Albania to stay true to the essentials of Marxism-Leninism. 'We thought that the Yugoslavs and the Soviets, and later the Chinese, were our friends', Hoxha sighed.

And what did they do? Why, they 'behaved like betrayers, revisionists of Marxism-Leninism, and sabotaged and damaged our economy'.

The USSR and China had been warned that they were going astray. What more could poor little Albania do? The only choice was to abandon the misguided great powers to their fate and stay on course by itself. So with the Chairman dead, embalmed and on display in Tiananmen

Square, and Joe ditto in Red Square, Hoxha set out to lead Albania down its solitary path. North Korea and Cuba were also staying true to real Communism, but neither was in a position to lend a little impoverished European a hand. Ties with China were cut in 1978 and for the remaining seven years of Hoxha's life Albania became more isolated. And poorer. Hoxha retreated into his Tirana villa and rationing became steadily stricter.

'My father needed to drink milk for his stomach condition,' Nevila explained, 'so we had to get up at 3.30am to be near the front of the queue at 6am when they started to dole out milk.'

Hoxha died in 1985. Ramiz Alia took over and moved an infinitesimal step to the right, but essentially nothing changed. Until in 1989 everything changed. The Berlin Wall came down, the Iron Curtain rusted away, the Soviet Union went into retreat and, finally, but not until two years later, Albania kicked over the bad old days as well. On 20 February 1991 the unbelievable happened. An angry mob hauled down Hoxha's statue in the centre of Tirana and dragged it away to be cut up and melted down. Within a remarkably short period not a statue, image or inscription of the dictator remained anywhere. Even his grave didn't survive. He was exhumed from his place watched over by the statue of Mother Albania in the Martyrs' Cemetery and whisked off to somewhere much more common.

In fact, I'm told by an anonymous source at the museum, there are Hoxha statues left and one day, when the anger has subsided, one will be hauled out to be put on display as a reminder of that crazy, but terrible, era.

• • • •

With Artur Haxhi at the wheel, Nevila and I travel south to Berati, whose definition as a 'museum city' protected the town's churches and mosques from Hoxha's atheistic destructive urges. They're perched on a fortified hilltop looking down at the newer (though still Ottoman-era) town below. The walls of the 14th-century citadel stand on foundations that date back to the 4th century BC. Inside the citadel, winding cobbled streets lead to old stones houses and churches.

The Onufri Museum, housed in the Church of the Dormition of St Mary, is the citadel's main attraction. Dormition is the Orthodox equivalent to the Catholic Church's 'assumption', the Virgin Mary's direct transfer to heaven. Onufri was a local master of the art of painting religious icons, and the old church is stuffed full of his icons along with works by other painters and a host of other religious art. Thank God, you might say, that Hoxha restrained himself from trashing this little collection, because it's terrific. The church itself is a wonder – ancient choir stalls, a gilded golden glow to everything and some ostrich-egg hanging lamps to add a nicely exotic touch to the whole ensemble.

We've met with Martin Heusinger, a German Albania enthusiast who has set up a travel company with his Albanian wife, Enkeleda Olldashi, to promote Berati. Together with an American resident who has joined us we wander the winding streets past the remains of the dozen or so churches and couple of mosques that survive, clamber up on to the citadel walls to gaze down at the Chapel of St Michael clinging to the hillside below, and then head down to the Mangalem quarter for lunch.

At the Bujari Restaurant I extravagantly grab the bill for our party of six. I've already had too many cups of coffee, snacks and meals paid for by my Albanian companions and I definitely feel it's my turn to pick up the tab. We've had hearty bowls of soup, plates of robust bread, bowls of the usual fresher-than-fresh salad, side plates of almonds and cheese, more plates of lasagne, a collection of bottles of Tepelena mineral water, followed by bowls of early-season cherries and slices of honeyed cake. The bill for the six of us comes to 1000 lek – let's call it US$11 with a tip.

After lunch we clamber up the narrow streets below the citadel. The fine old houses gave Berati the name 'the town of a thousand windows'.

A threesome – grandmother, daughter, grandson – emerge from one of the houses to check us out. They're bemused by Martin, clearly a foreigner, speaking Albanian when they ask us where we're from.

'Albanians are wonderful people, they have so many unique qualities', announces the cheerful old lady.

'So if we're so wonderful, why are we behind everywhere else in the world?' asks Nevila.

'Well, there were 50 years of Communism', is the reply – an explanation I'm already realising is a catch-all for Albania's problems.

'And why does nobody like us?' asks Enkeleda.

The poor Albanians do seem to have got themselves on the wrong side of everybody, blamed for everything that goes on in the neighbourhood, but I'm beginning to feel that's ancient history or 10 years out of date at least.

We wander across the seven-arched stone bridge to the Gorica quarter, but the threatening clouds deliver a downpour and Martin ferries us back to the hotel where I take an afternoon nap. When I emerge an hour or so later, the view from the rooftop is amazing. The sky has cleared to reveal a superb backdrop of snow-capped mountains rising up behind Berati's minaret-studded skyline.

Nevila, Artur and I stroll through the Mangalem quarter to join the evening *xhiro*, the Balkan custom of walking, as in Italy, a *passeggiata*, a circuit of the town centre en masse, but the weather must have curtailed the stroll this evening. I'm pleased the custom continues. I remember seeing walkers performing a similar ritual in Yugoslavia back in the early 1970s. As we walk back to the hotel for dinner, I'm amused to note that the Leaden Mosque (for its lead-coated dome) shares its compound with the Misisipi Bar, close to where the *furgons*, intertown minibuses, congregate.

• • • •

Heading south from Berati we pass a huge Chinese-built steel foundry. A Turkish steel-maker tried to revive it, but today it's near derelict. Further down the road there's Albania's biggest oil refinery during the Communist period. Naturally it's guarded by an assortment of bunkers.

For a country that faced serious hunger in the early 1980s after it disowned its Chinese benefactors when they turned soft on Communism, Albania today has an absolute overload of bars, cafés and restaurants. You cannot walk down the main street of any decent-size town without tripping over them, and along the highways and byways they pop up every few kilometres – almost as often as the roadside memorials to traffic deaths. They're often attractive places – clean, neat, tidy and, in the case of the roadside places, often with umbrellas (provided by Biria Stela as I jot my notes) and shady trees. The food is generally straightforward, hearty, well prepared and fresh.

'Of course, our food is all organic,' Nevila explains, 'because our farmers can't afford chemicals and fertilisers.'

Even the toilets are usually clean (even if they are often squat-style) and for English speakers they may be conveniently labelled B and G, although the letters stand for Burra and Gra not, as I first thought, though with equal accuracy, Boys and Girls.

We've stopped because Nevila has just had a phone call (modern Albania's mobile phone coverage is phenomenal as opposed to in the Communist years when only the elite had access to a telephone) from Auron Tare who, it turns out, is only 10 minutes behind us and also heading south to Gjirokastra and Butrinti. When he turns up, it's quickly clear he's as big a character as his Wikipedia entry, which launches its description by announcing that he's an 'Albanian journalist, historian, and adventure traveller'. It goes on to reveal that 'he is the head of the Albanian National Trust Foundation' and then talks of his work as the founder of the Butrinti National Park, his recovery of artwork stolen in the post-Communist chaos, his spell as a journalist with the British ITN television team during the Kosovo crisis, and his Indonesian post-tsunami efforts. And that's only the serious stuff. He also played for the Albanian national basketball team.

I abandon Nevila and our cautious and careful driver to ride with Auron in his Land Rover. Auron drives with much more appropriately Albanian verve. I've already noticed that any worthwhile corner will have at least one memorial, if not a cluster, to those who died when their Mercedes collided with the guard rail, shot over the precipice and plunged into the river, or simply rammed head on into an oncoming vehicle. There are so many that it's probable a certain percentage of the victims met their end by colliding with the memorial to the preceding fatal accident. On some corners the memorials are lined up so densely a guardrail is clearly unnecessary.

Albanians have not had long-term driving experience. If you weren't in the government or a friend of Hoxha, you needed a special permit to own a car during the Communist years and the permits were not dispensed in great numbers. In the whole 45-year Communist period precisely two were issued. Once the doors opened, the cars quickly flooded in and Albanians have clearly been crashing them like a Project Gotham Racing video game. To have filled up so many wreckers yards in just a decade and a half is clearly an achievement. The number of cars bearing the word *autoshkolle* (driving school) indicates that many more Albanians plan to take to these dodgy highways.

A quite ridiculous percentage of the vehicles are Mercedes and it was widely suggested in the first years after Albanian independence that they were being stolen to order from all over Europe. It's an idea that Auron indignantly pooh-poohs.

'How would they get them here?' he queries. 'If there was a procession of stolen Mercedes coming down through Italy to be shipped to Albania, wouldn't the shipping companies be looking out for them?'

The stolen-Mercedes affront may annoy Albanians, but that's nothing to how they feel about British author Robert Carver and his mid-1990s travel book *The Accursed Mountains*. Carver travels around the country convinced that every other person he meets is eyeing him with cheating, stealing, robbery or murder on their minds. The $30 he's charged, or rather overcharged to his eyes, for dinner (a 'fish dinner' readers are frequently reminded) for three puts him in a sour mood that pervades the whole book.

'Albania wasn't like that when he was here and it certainly isn't like that today', Auron avows. 'When he wanders around Gjirokastra he imagines people are following him intending to rape him. It's ridiculous.'

I check the book's Gjirokastra chapter and Carver announces in the opening line that 'the first attempt to murder and rob me' took place in the castle. He then slinks back to the place he's staying to shave his beard off to look less like a foreigner. Despite people constantly edging towards him, knives drawn and hands ready to pickpocket, it never happens. Nobody else meets Carver's standards either. When he gets to the Greek site at Butrint, where I'm heading the next day, British archaeologists have ruined 'the delicate atmosphere by erecting large, ugly and quite unnecessary signboards' and the view is further despoiled by a party of 'waddling, elderly American Midwesterners, each wrapped in characteristic brightly coloured flannel baby-clothes'.

We zoom through Tepelena, birthplace of Ali Pasha. Depending on whom you trust, Pasha was either an Albanian national hero or a 'cruel and bloodthirsty tyrant' (Wikipedia again). There's a roadside memorial here to the son of Albania's president Alfred Moisiu. His four-wheel drive skidded off the road and into the river in 2004. I have a bottle of Tepelena mineral water in my daypack, bearing the useful commendation that it is 'The Water of the Albanian National Football Team' – *Uji i Skuadres Kombetare Shqiptare te Futbollit* if you want it in Albanian. A further line of type reveals that the water 'suffled how it gush from the source of the woods of Tepelena'. It's the appropriate brand to be carrying since Auron's brother is Igli Tare, an Albanian football star who plays in one of the world's top football leagues for the Rome Serie A team SS Lazio.

• • • •

I take an instant liking to Gjirokastra with its corkscrewing, roller-coaster laneways and its dark, brooding stone buildings. The whole town is overlooked by an even darker and more brooding castle. Down below the old town is the modern Communist-era town. We don't bother going to see it.

Unfortunately many of the fine stone buildings in the old town are crumbling with age and neglect. We have a look around a particularly magnificent Ottoman-period example. The owners live in a nondescript modern house fronting it and it's easy to see why they're not using the old place. It's huge, draughty and leaky, and would undoubtedly cost a small fortune to light, heat and maintain. Gjirokastra needs some wealthy Western mansion restorer and would-be writer to move here, do up one of these stately homes and write *My Year in Gjirokastra* or *Under the Gjirokastra Sun* about the experience.

Gjirokastra is the hometown for Ismail Kadare, far and away Albania's best-known author and the winner of the inaugural international Booker prize in 2005. It's not so proud of its other famous citizen – Enver Hoxha. His birthplace is now a museum, but an ethnographic one. There's no mention of the Hoxha connection and indeed the house was burnt down in 1916 when the future dictator would have been eight years old.

Despite enjoying a long, boozy lunch before we explored Gjirokastra, there's still room for another serious dinner after our explorations, where Nevila talks of the absurdities of life in Hoxha's Albania.

'I wanted to study economics at university,' she explains, 'but I was told I had to do physics. A year later my younger sister, who had no interest in economics, was told that was what she had to study.'

'The thing was,' she went on, 'we knew nothing about the outside world; we simply accepted our lives. Looking back it seems absurd what we put up with.'

Albania had its own equivalent of the USSR's KGB or East Germany's Stasi. Every third Albanian citizen had either been interrogated by the Sigurimi or actually served time in one of Hoxha's prison camps. A large section of the National Museum of History in Tirana is dedicated to the horrors of life under Hoxha's thumb, including a labour camp prison-cell you can try out for size. Sigurimi informers were known as '80 lek men' for the monthly 80-lek pay bonus they received for spying on their neighbours.

The next day we drop down to the coast at Saranda and turn south to Butrinti. Auron Tare is justifiably proud of these Roman ruins in their own little national park. The site is topped by a small fortress housing a brand new museum. Saranda is one of Albania's most popular beach resorts, helped by its proximity to Corfu. In the Communist era, holidaymakers on the Greek island would sit in beach cafés at night sipping their ouzo looking across the Ionian sea at the searchlights scouring the beaches of Albania, wondering what dark deeds were being performed there. Today day-trippers from Corfu are Albania's biggest international tourist contingent.

The town is a curious mix of Ottoman, Italian and Communist-era influences and, unhappily, it's now being overrun by lots of cheap and nasty developments. Illegal development is a big problem for Albania. During the capitalist free-for-all interlude, all sorts of buildings were put up without any permit or permission; remarkably some of the owners are now being forced to demolish them. A Tirana restaurant, known as 'Taiwan' because it's like a little island, is in the middle of a park that was once covered by illegal buildings.

Saranda even features a town-centre archaeological site with the foundations of a basilica, which at one stage functioned as a synagogue.

Even this site was threatened by illegal developments, but they've been held at bay.

The coast road south actually hangs back from the coast for many kilometres – slow kilometres because Artur proceeds with exaggerated and painstaking care. I was happy with that on the open road from Tirana through Berati and Gjirokastra, but on this stretch it gets exasperating proceeding at 15 to 20 kilometres per hour as if we were in something with no suspension movement and minimal ground clearance, not in a big, hunky four wheel drive. A month later I'll be on a road in Afghanistan where a similar speed feels much more appropriate to the road conditions.

Eventually we stop for the night at Himara. My guidebook notes that, with fine beaches and a couple of Greek tavernas, Himara has 'tremendous potential as a holiday spot', but warns that 'strolling past rusting car wrecks and a tidal line of plastic may not be quite what you'd expected in a beach'. The Albanians have come late to plastic packaging and the detritus of Western consumerism, but they've adapted to it with considerable enthusiasm. So much so that many Albanians spend a lot of time apologising for what a mess their country has become. Unhappily I can console them that I've seen far worse. Libya, for one, is way ahead of them.

Before we retire to a restaurant for another fine and filling Albanian repast, we continue down the coast to Himara's decaying castle, overlooking the old part of town and the coastal headland just south of the modern port. We continue further south and well off the road, which by this time has climbed into the hills, to visit Jal Beach, a beautiful little arc of white sand spoilt, once again, by some hideously ugly half-built developments. Claims that Albania has the last undeveloped stretch of coast along the Mediterranean may soon be history. There are a couple of very picturesquely sited bunkers guarding the bay and Himara has a fine collection along its beach, all filling up with windblown sand.

Sitting on my toilet in the Himara guesthouse, I could see this bathroom had clearly been designed by a plumber rather than an architect. You could use the shower to simultaneously flush the toilet and rinse out the sink that my chin was resting on. Architecture is clearly not a topic of great interest to Albanians. There are some beautiful buildings – the stone houses of Gjirokastra, for example – but they're old. There's one word that fits almost everything built under Hoxha and, even more so, after the great leader: ugly. In fact, 99 per cent of the buildings seem to have come off precisely the same dreary drawing-board. There's one slab floor plonked on top of another until the builder ran out of energy or money, but the steel reinforcing rods are left sticking out the top just in case he finds more energy (or money) and decides to add an extra floor or two.

• • • •

The road climbs away from the coast, zigzagging up to the Llogaraja Pass – the coast falling away below, while snow appears on the peaks above. Down the other side we soon return to sea level and drive through Fieri to reach Apollonia and the country's other notable Roman ruins. Apollonia has clearly not had the attention that Butrint has enjoyed. In particular, it's crying out for some rubbish bins and someone with a large stick to whack anybody who decides to throw plastic wrappers, soft-drink cans and empty Tepelena mineral-water bottles on the grass around the Agora.

The ruins climb up a hillside and there are fine views of the surrounding countryside, which, for some reason, is dotted with yet more of Hoxha's bunkers. Perhaps they'd simply run out of strategic sites to protect and decided that keeping invaders away from the ruins was a good idea!

Heading north, we're following the old Via Egnatia, the great Roman highway that led from Durrësi on the coast across the Balkans to Thessaloniki in Greece and on to Constantinople. Hungering for lunch, we pull off the road to climb up to Ardenica, a hill popping up from

the flat plains. There's a restaurant with great views right at the top of
the hill, but there's also the Ardenica Monastery, which doesn't appear
in any of the tourist material I've read but definitely should. Like the
museum-church at Berati, the monastery's church is a gilded treasure box.
It survived the regime's 1967 war on religion solely because the bishop
at the time managed to persuade the demolition crew, who sounded
remarkably like the student vandals of China's Cultural Revolution,
that the monastery's historic importance required its protection. A
Skanderbeg connection helped – the 15th-century national hero might
have been crowned or even married here. Even the Communists revered
Skanderbeg, something that would be underlined for me the next day.

Durrësi, the final stop before we return to Tirana, is Albania's old
capital, major port and second city after the capital. It also has the best
bunker reuse I'll encounter on my short visit. At the beachside Bunkeri
Restaurant you don't really dine in a bunker – even a big bunker isn't
really restaurant size – but it does make a cosy little bar for a pre-dinner
drink, so long as you don't stand up too quickly and crack your head on
that tank-proof concrete ceiling.

The town also has a very fine archaeological museum, a stretch of
Byzantine-era city walls and a crumbling though impressively large
Roman amphitheatre. There's also a well-kept Martyrs' Monument to
members of the Albanian resistance who died in the struggle against
the Germans in World War II. We have to squeeze through a gap in the
fence to get in to look at it. There's no chance of getting in to check King
Zog's former palace, now occupied by the military.

Love him or hate him, King Zog was quite a character; with a name
like that you'd have to be. He started life as Ahmed Zogilli, changed
his family name to Zogu (Albanian for 'hawk') and became prime
minister and then president before deciding that being king was more
to his taste. Crowned King Zog in 1928, he spent the next 10 years
modernising Albania, admittedly from a fairly basic starting point.

Reflecting his early warlord status, he also made plenty of enemies: he survived 55 assassination attempts. They became so predictable that there were occasions he even drew his own gun and shot back at the would-be killers. The National Rifle Association would have loved him.

Unfortunately his modernisation projects were often funded by Italy, and Albania soon became so indebted to Mussolini's fascist state that it became a de facto Italian colony. In April 1939 Mussolini decided to completely take over and King Zog fled to Britain, the start of an exile that would last the remaining 22 years of his life. He took with him his bride of just 388 days, Queen Geraldine, and most of the gold from Albania's treasury (it paid for a floor of London's Ritz Hotel for a spell). The daughter of a Hungarian aristocrat and his American diplomat wife, Queen Geraldine was only 22 years old when she married King Zog. Her family was so penniless, she'd been selling postcards in Budapest's National Museum before King Zog, scouring Europe for a suitable bride, spotted her photograph (taken when she was 17 at a Hungarian society ball) and summoned her to Tirana. Ten days later they were engaged. Their glittering wedding featured presents from all over Europe, including a bright red supercharged Mercedes from Adolf Hitler.

Queen Geraldine stuck with King Zog through his long exile in Britain, Egypt and finally France (where he died), then lived in Spain and South Africa before finally returning to Albania shortly before her death in 2002 at the age of 87. Their son Leka Zog, only three days old when King Zog fled the country in 1939, has attempted to restart the Albanian monarchy, but without success.

• • • •

64. From Tirana the road hairpins up into the mountains to Kruja, a popular day trip from the capital and my last stop in Albania. In the town's old castle stands the Skanderbeg Museum, probably the best-kept building in all of Albania and a potent Hoxha reminder, since it was designed by his daughter and her husband. Albania's national hero soon becomes a familiar sight, particularly in his horse-riding mode as in his square in the centre of Tirana.

Back in the 15th century, Kastrioti, the son of an Albanian prince, was held hostage by the Ottoman Turks, converted to Islam and took the name Iskander, from Alexander the Great. When he rose to the rank of bey, or governor, under the Ottomans, he tagged that on to his adopted name to become Skanderbeg. In 1443 the Turks suffered a defeat by a Hungarian force and Skanderbeg read this as a signal to abandon the Ottoman Empire (and Islam), return to Albania and kick out the occupying force.

From his stronghold at Kruja he defied the Ottoman powers until his death, withstanding sieges in 1450, 1466 and 1467. Albanian resistance weakened after his death in 1468 and 10 years later another siege was successful and the country once more fell to Ottoman control. It would remain that way until the final collapse of the empire after World War I. The Albanians take Skanderbeg very seriously and the museum is full of paintings and dioramas of his struggles with Turkey and reminders of how often his name pops up on statues and squares around Europe.

The traffic crawling back in to Tirana after the Kruja excursion is appalling. The city's a melange of roadworks and bridges, much of it lagging far behind the growth in traffic. That evening I wander the bars and restaurants of Blokku one more time before retiring to the revolving Skytower Bar to watch all of Tirana spin beneath me in a leisurely 40 minutes. It's not a bad view and not a bad carafe of red wine for less than three dollars. Not a bad country either – I've enjoyed my short circuit of a Bad Land that only gained that status by resolutely cutting itself off from all the outside world, and is now frantically trying to get itself back on the same wavelength.

BURMA
(MYANMAR)

'We'll call an election', commanded the military dictator.

'We'll have to give the Tatmadaw [Burma's army] a political party name. I think State Law & Order Reform Council sounds good', he continued, not realising that in English its acronym, SLORC, didn't sound so good at all.

'Then, when we get elected, I'll be president and everything will be under control again.'

It was a neat plan. Twenty-five years of military rule would end with the army still firmly on top. The thousands of students who had died in pro-democracy protests would, General Saw Maung concluded, be quickly forgotten. The economy? Well, democracy might do something good for the economy. Certainly nothing the Tatmadaw had done for the economy had done much good. From being the rice basket of Asia, Burma had spiralled steadily downwards to its present position as the basket case of Asia. Meanwhile arch-rival Thailand had sprinted equally as steadily ahead until the average Thai's per-capita income was 10 times the average Burmese's. And for every tourist who came to Burma, there were probably a hundred in Thailand.

Nevertheless, it was inconceivable that the army wouldn't win. After all, every issue of the *New Light of Myanmar* (formerly the *Working People's Daily*), the government-controlled daily English-language newspaper, carried stirring stories of how much the people of Burma loved the Tatmadaw and how much good the Tatmadaw did for the country and the people. All of it illustrated with photographs of one army general or another announcing a new project, cutting the ribbon to open a new road, being welcomed with rapturous applause by school children or listening intently as some new scientific wonder was explained to him. The Tatmadaw loved the people, the people loved the Tatmadaw – apart from a few thousand students and they were all dead now. Who else could win the election?

Well, there was Aung San Suu Kyi and her ragtag National League for Democracy (NLD) Party, but for a start she wasn't eligible to run for office. Her own father, the heroic Bogyoke Aung San, had thoughtfully written a clause into the constitution banning anybody married to a foreigner from politically powerful positions. Aung San Suu Kyi, quite apart from having spent most of her life overseas, was married to an English academic.

Anyway, in situations like these the opposition was always fragmented while the Tatmadaw was nothing if not unified, quite apart from controlling all the media. The election result was a sure thing.

Such a sure thing that it appears General Saw Maung, the SLORC and the Tatmadaw didn't even bother rigging the election in 1990 by double-counting votes or intimidating voters if they looked like casting their ballots incorrectly. Zimbabwe's Mugabe could have shown these hapless losers a thing or three about how to run an effective election. In fact Burma's first election in 25 years was, it appears, a remarkably fair fight. So fair that the end result was the NLD as a knockout winner, the SLORC an abysmal loser. No less than 392 of the 485 parliamentary seats went to the NLD.

'Let me clarify what I meant when I said we'll have an election', General Saw Maung quickly announced. 'Now the election is over, we first have to rewrite the constitution, then we'll decide if whoever won the election gets to take over.'

Nothing moves fast in Burma and heading on towards 20 years later the daily struggle to complete the new constitution still goes on. Fortunately for the military, however, having an election did have a very important side-benefit. It clearly identified the traitorous individuals who did not love their country and its wonderful army. There were at the very least 392 of them – the 392 newly elected NLD members, for whom a spell in prison was clearly a very good idea.

That's where Burma, or Myanmar as the military rulers have renamed it, still stands. Most NLD members have been released from their period of re-education – some of them only after they signed agreements not to engage in any further political activity – but some still languish behind bars. Aung San Suu Kyi has been in and out of house arrest (and worse) ever since the elections and although for many Burmese the economic story is far better – the once-empty shops are now full of consumer goods and the country is once again a rice exporter – Burma is certainly no Asian tiger.

• • • •

From Rangoon's (Rangoon is now called Yangon) ramshackle airport a Singapore taxi whisks us into town. The modern cars that now clog Rangoon's roads were one clear indicator of change. In the 1970s, when I'd first visited the reclusive country, there was hardly a traffic jam's worth of cars in the whole city and most were rusting, rattling relics of the British era. Today's taxi fleet certainly isn't showroom new – their signposting indicates they've all enjoyed a previous incarnation on the streets of Tokyo, Bangkok or Singapore – but one thing hasn't changed. They all have their steering wheels on the wrong side.

It's all Ne Win's fault. Most things in Burma are Ne Win's fault.

During World War II, when he was known as Shu Maung, he was one of the 'Thirty Comrades', the group of idealistic young nationalists led by Aung San Suu Kyi's dad, Aung San, who had slipped away to Japan, looking for help to unseat the British colonialists. With Japan's entry into the war they'd marched triumphantly back into Rangoon where the Japanese had announced that colonialism was over, the evil British were defeated and that Burma was now an independent country. Aung San and Shu Maung were now the leaders of the Burmese army – the name went from the Burmese Independence Army (BIA) to the Burma Defence Army (BDA) before settling on the Burma National Army (BNA). The army wasn't the only one to have a name change. Shu Maung had renamed himself Ne Win, 'Brilliant like the Sun'.

Despite being whisked back to Japan to be presented with the Order of the Rising Sun, Aung San soon began to doubt the wisdom of siding with the Japanese. If the British had treated the Burmese like bullocks, he concluded, under the Japanese 'we are treated like dogs'. It would be an improvement 'even to get back to the bullock stage'.

Furthermore, the war wasn't turning out to be such a foregone conclusion after all. The British and their Indian troops had been pushed right out of the country by the victorious Japanese, but then they'd turned round and started to march back towards Rangoon. They'd mounted an imaginative 'behind enemy lines' campaign, air-dropping small groups of guerrilla forces known as Chindits. Not everybody in Burma had welcomed the Japanese with open arms either. The Burmese-speaking people of the central plains, the Bamar, had, at first, gone along with the Japanese occupiers, but Burma wasn't a simple homogenous country. There were the Muslim Rakhaing people of the far west, along the border with what is today Bangladesh. To the south there were the Mons, who had at various times been a buffer state between Burma and Thailand, or even struggled with the Burmese for control of the great kingdom of Bagan.

To the east and northeast, in the hills that rose up towards the borders with Thailand, Laos and China were a host of hill tribes, many of them closely related to the hill peoples of Thailand and Indo-China. They included groups like the Karen, predominantly Buddhist like the majority of Burmese, but with an influential Christian minority. Wary of the Burmese's loyalty, the British had never incorporated them into their army – unlike the Indians in India – but they had trusted the Karen and now many former Karen soldiers cooperated with the British guerrilla forces. Soon, Aung San, Ne Win and their Burmese comrades found themselves fighting a proxy war for the Japanese. Their battles with the groups in Burma who had not willingly accepted Japanese rule stirred up a bitterness that would cripple Burma for many decades after the Japanese left.

As the British and their Indian allies marched ever closer to Rangoon, Aung San and the BNA hastily switched sides.

'Go on, Aung San. You only came to us because you see we are winning', joked Lieutenant-General William Slim, commander of the British forces.

'It wouldn't be much good coming to you if you weren't, would it?' countered Aung San.

So when the bombs fell on Hiroshima and Nagasaki and the war came to a rapid conclusion, Aung San and his companions were once more in the front-row seat to lead an independent Burma. The rush to Burmese independence concluded at the auspicious time of 4.20am on 4 January 1948. To this day nothing gets done in Burma without calling in the astrologers and fortune-tellers. That middle-of-the-night hour may have been the right time for independence, but it was too late for Aung San. In July of the previous year he'd been assassinated by a political rival. He'd

71.

left behind three children. His daughter, Aung San Suu Kyi, had just turned two.

Independent Burma was not so much a unified nation as a buzzing hornet's nest and at times the government's powers barely extended beyond the Rangoon city boundary. Certainly there were elections, but Burmese democracy never reached far and in 1958, not long after the 10th anniversary of independence, the economy was on the floor, the political situation was up against the wall, and the prime minister, U Nu, called 'time out'. In marched Ne Win, still at the head of the Burmese army, to establish a caretaker military government, which managed to restore law and order and if not completely halt, at least partially curtail, the uprisings devastating the country.

In 1960 the military returned to the barracks and new elections were held. Once more U Nu was elected prime minister and once more the country tumbled into chaos. This time when Ne Win marched back into power in 1962 it was for keeps. U Nu was slung into prison and Ne Win announced that the country would now embark on the 'Burmese Road to Socialism'. Perhaps he was trying to outflank the Communist Party of Burma, one of the principal rebel groups and strongly supported by the Maoist Chinese, but the Burmese Road proved to be a strictly downhill path.

Soon the economy, which had never really recovered from the destruction of World War II, was all but comatose. The Chinese and Indian traders, who controlled much of Burma's retail trade, were kicked out of the country and large banknotes were 'demonetised' on the theory that if you were rich enough to have them you were too rich for the country's good. The doors were firmly slammed shut to any would-be foreign visitors and before long the only way you could find anything was on the black market.

Which is why our airport taxi was, like nearly every vehicle stuck in the traffic jam around us, on the wrong side of the road relative to its steering wheel. Until 1970 the Burmese drove on the left, like England and like Burma's neighbours to the west (India and Bangladesh) and to the east (Thailand and Laos). Then the rules were suddenly changed and the Burmese took to driving on the right. It made no sense at all, firstly because the country was completely isolated, so it made no difference which side the Burmese drove on; secondly because if the government ever did open the land borders to Thailand (the most likely place), the two countries would be driving on opposite sides; and thirdly because almost all the cars in the country came from drive-on-the-left nations. They were either left behind by the British or imported from Japan.

So why had this utterly pointless change taken place? It was back to Ne Win and his faith in astrology and fortune-tellers. When his favourite astrologer was asked what he should do to improve Burma's collapsing economy, the soothsayer, who clearly had a much better grasp of economics than the dictator, struggled to find a polite way to tell him that his crazy economic strategies were bankrupting the country and that easing up on his leftist policies was the only answer.

'Move to the right', suggested the medium, thinking politically.

Ne Win immediately ordered Burmese drivers to switch sides.

•   •   •   •

I am sipping a cold Mandalay Beer beside the swimming pool at the Pansea Hotel. It's hard to believe this is an all but bankrupt country run by an evil military dictatorship. The stylish French-owned hotel, built in a colonial-era teak mansion, once housed the employees of a British timber firm when they were in the city on business. It is certainly very unlike the places I'd stayed on my first few visits to the country decades earlier.

On those occasions I'd been an idealistic young backpacker, kicking around the region with my wife, Maureen. In 1978 we'd arrived in Rangoon and taken a backfiring old Humber taxi to the YMCA.

Halfway into town we encountered a traffic light. There certainly hadn't been any traffic jams to slow us down prior to that point. In fact the streets were almost empty with just the occasional old, overcrowded World War II–era bus with dozens of Burmese hanging precariously from the sides. Male or female, they were elegantly dressed in sarong-like *longyi* and that, at least, hasn't changed. Jeans have still made no inroads into the Burmese dress code.

When those late-1970s traffic lights shifted to green, a horrible graunching noise indicated that the ancient 'Britmobile' was not slipping smoothly into gear and the reason for our push-start at the airport became clear – our battered banger was clutch-less. Our driver had hoped for a smooth, stop-less passage all the way from terminal to terminus, but the traffic light had thrown a spanner in the works. We disembarked to help him push, but this time it wouldn't start and we eventually abandoned the hiccupping Humber for an Austin almost as ancient.

The YMCA was nearly as decrepit as our taxi and we spent a sleepless night squashing mosquitoes that had zoomed in through the gaping holes in the wire-mesh window-screens and hoping that our antimalarials were effective. Our seven-day visas were a distinct improvement on the 24-hour visas that were all that was on offer only a few years previously, so six days later we were back in Rangoon and this time we abandoned the Y for the greater comforts of the Strand Hotel. Built in 1901 the Strand was one of the three great Asian hotels established by the Armenian Sarkies brothers and in the late 1970s all three hotels were run down and overdue for major renovations. Run down in Rangoon was on a wholly different plane from what run down meant in Singapore at the Raffles or Penang at the E&O.

74.

In the early 1990s the Strand enjoyed a comprehensive overhaul, courtesy of the Dutch-Indonesian hotel wizard Adrian Zecha, creator of the Aman chain of super-luxury resorts, but in the 1970s it was a picture of decaying splendour. Outside was a line up of elderly Chevies, crumbling but still in far better shape than their English equivalents. One of these lead sleds could, with the underhand application of a handful of US dollars, convey you all the way to Pegu, 80 kilometres northeast of Rangoon. Any further than that was likely to lead to trouble with the authorities. Inside the hotel the reception area sported a glass-fronted lost-and-found cabinet containing never-to-be-claimed items, such as greying ladies' gloves, a single Cinderella-like high-heeled shoe, and a mildewed top hat, clearly abandoned at some British officer's formal affair a half-century earlier.

Our second-floor room was blissfully mosquito free, but the water pressure didn't seem to have enough 'oomph' to get that far above sea level and late that evening the Strand's lobby proved to be just as rat-infested as most other areas of the city. We'd been sitting around discussing Burma, travel and other important topics with a young Dutchman, a Mexican couple (20 years would pass before I encountered any other Mexicans travelling anywhere outside of Mexico) and a few other assorted travellers. The bar had shut down at 10pm. When it was open it dispensed nothing better than Mandalay Beer and a curious clear spirit called *tinle*, which you could mix with other ingredients to make a *tinle* and tonic or a *tinle* and Coke, if there had been such a thing as Coke in Burma, of course.

The bar's closure was not a problem – the front desk still had an icebox full of cold bottles of Mandalay Beer, stashed away for exactly such late-night gatherings. What was a problem was that at 10pm not only did the bar shut, but also the rats came out to play. Soon they were bounding across the lobby, leaping from sofa to table to chair. Occasionally they'd short-cut right across your lap, which reduced our Dutch friend to crouching on top of his chair with his feet drawn up, uttering unhappy squeaks.

A quarter of a century later the Strand was clearly not the same place.

The lost-and-found cabinet was gone, replaced by a jewellery shop
– American Express, Diners Club and Visa happily accepted – with the
better pieces easily marching into the four figures (in US dollars) range.
The bar was now open for as many hours as any guests were willing to
stay up and as for the rats… well, they could still be found on the streets
of Rangoon, but in the Strand? Not a chance.

• • • •

The elderly Chevies had disappeared from the front of the Strand as
well. So had the city's old Humbers, Hillmans, Austins and Morrises,
replaced by much newer, and more reliable, Toyotas, Nissans and Mazdas.
They'd go much further than Pegu as well.

Getting fuel when travelling 'up country' could still be a problem,
but with application of the requisite number of US dollars, which no
longer had to be handed across surreptitiously, you could drive pretty
well anywhere in the country. Well, pretty well anywhere in the country
controlled by the central government and not by some random rebel
group.

Our driver, U Zaw Naing Oo, had worked for the construction division
of the Korean *jaebeol* (business conglomerate) Hyundai when they built
a major dam project. Like every Burmese I was to meet he was polite (he
spoke excellent English), competent (he certainly knew all the short-cuts
and all the best roadside noodle stops) and very communicative. Not
far out of Rangoon we paused at the Taukkyan Commonwealth War
Cemetery. Endless rows of small memorials in the beautifully maintained
cemetery mark the last resting place for over 6000 British and Indian
troops who had pushed the Japanese out in the longest, and probably
least-known, land campaign in the war against Japan.

Nowhere else did Allied troops slug it out with the Japanese in such
a protracted fashion. Much of the Pacific War was conducted from

30,000 feet by endless formations of US Air Force bombers raining thousands of tonnes of explosives down on Japanese cities until two atomic bombs brought everything to a rapid conclusion. Other clashes on land were often short and sharp, if brutally hard fought. The US troops at Guadalcanal, in the Solomon Islands, took six months to despatch the Japanese forces, but the painful assault on Okinawa lasted just 82 days. From when the Japanese took Rangoon in March 1942, it took over three years before their abrupt withdrawal in April 1945.

Further north, in the small town of Shwedaung, a sign indicated, in outdated English, that the Shwemyetman Paya was just one furlong off the road. The 220-yard side-trip took us to the 'Paya of the Golden Spectacles'. Buddhism, for all its noble truths and eightfold paths, often seems to be strongly based on Buddha-image one-upmanship. There are numerous claims to the biggest, longest, tallest or most heavily gold-plated Buddha, but no tape measure was required to check this huge seated image's claim to fame. Perched on the smiling Buddha's nose was a giant pair of gold-rimmed spectacles. Originally, so the paya's helpful brochure informed us, the image was 'devoid of spectacles' and it's a little unclear when they made their first appearance. What's more certain is that in 1886 they were stolen. King Thibaw, the last Burmese king to rule from Mandalay, had just been overthrown and shipped off to India by the British, and disrespectful activities, like stealing a Buddha image's glasses, were not uncommon.

The current pair of glasses was popped on during the colonial period when an English officer stationed in Prome donated them in the hope of fixing his wife's eye troubles. Naturally she was cured. The quite stylish, and very large, circular-lensed glasses are removed once a fortnight for a quick polish and clean – an operation that requires nine monks. A spare pair sits at the ready in a glass showcase, just in case the originals are dropped.

We overnighted in Prome, recently renamed Pyay, on our way north.

Prome had been totally off limits on my first few visits to Burma, but in 1983 there were rumours that you could rent a vehicle in Rangoon and get to some of these forbidden places, even though the seven-day visa limits were still in force. On that occasion, on my first night in Rangoon I tossed up between taking the train to Mandalay early the next morning or trying to find someone with a pick-up to rent. I wandered over to the tourist office in the centre of town to see what time it opened in the morning and before you could say 'Psst, wanna rent my Toyota Hilux?' I'd been approached by a Burmese gentleman hanging around in a nearby doorway and we were negotiating a one-week rental.

We set off before dawn the next morning with my original English-speaking contact as a guide, plus the driver and his assistant. In the back of the pick-up truck was a stack of five-gallon fuel containers, since you needed a special permit to buy petrol outside of your area of residence. The other important piece of equipment in the back was a large tarpaulin. When we passed checkpoints I would lie down in the back of the truck with the tarpaulin spread over me. On that first visit to Prome, I entered and departed the town hidden under the cover, but once inside it was easy to wander around the Shwesandaw Paya and gaze across to the gigantic Buddha image, gazing back at us across the trees at eye level with the hilltop pagoda.

This time staying in Prome was no problem, although visitors were clearly few and far between. We ventured beyond the town to the ruins of the ancient city of Thayekhittaya. Burma has so many of these forgotten sites that only the really big ones, like Bagan or Mrauk U, attract more than the most enthusiastic of visitors. We strolled around the crumbling ruins and through the villages that dot the site. By the time we got back to the car park beside the site museum, the sun was about to set. As we drove back towards the main road we passed a long line of men and boys marching out of the village with long poles slung over their shoulders and lamps swinging from the end of the poles.

'What are they doing, where are they going?' we asked our driver.

'Killing rats', he said. 'The rice fields are full of rats. They'll set up their lamps in the fields to attract the rats and when the rats come out they'll kill them. They'll be in the fields all night.'

The next morning we found another Westerner breakfasting on the roof of the hotel. Richard Forrest was an Australian tour leader who had led adventure travel groups around the country until the Burma boycotters persuaded his company to shut down their Burma operations.

'Actually, I'm doing exactly the same thing as before they withdrew', he explained. 'People come to me independently rather than through the company. There probably aren't as many of them, but it's exactly the same sort of people. Funnily enough back in Australia the vote on whether to withdraw or not depended completely on whether people had been here or not. If they had visited Burma and made friends here, they certainly didn't want to abandon them. If they'd never been here, then it was easy to say no.

'I'm carrying on partly because I think it will open up', Richard continued. 'There are lots more places opening up so I'm spending some of my time checking out the new areas. I've just been on a trek through the Shan states.'

We carried on north. The roads were narrow, but neither as potholed or as overcrowded as I'd become used to in India or other Third World countries. Our lunchtime noodle halt was in a busy little truck-stop village where I wandered into a covered market beside the road and admired the heaped piles of vegetables and fruit. If the Burmese economy was on its last legs, the farmers still seemed to be doing their jobs. In comparison the markets in Cuba were miserable affairs and if we'd seen a market in North Korea, we probably wouldn't have believed it.

• • • •

Our northbound trip took us via Inle Lake to Mandalay from where
we would catch a converted old Irrawaddy ferryboat down to Bagan. Inle
Lake is outrageously picturesque and famed for its leg-rowers, who stand
at the back of their flat-bottomed boats, looking much like an English
Oxbridge punter, but then propel the boat forward by twisting a leg
around a single oar and leg-rowing it along. On my first trip to Inle Lake
the government was only reluctantly opening up to private enterprise and
although visitors were emphatically steered towards the government-
owned hotel at Taunggyi, 25 kilometres from the lake, I managed to stay
at U Ohn Maung's pioneering guesthouse at Nyaungshwe, right by the
water.

'We were still operating without a licence', he explained. 'If
government officials dropped by we would herd our guests over to one
side of the courtyard and hang *longyis* from a clothesline so they weren't
seen.'

Over a quarter of a century later U Ohn Maung had been elected to
parliament in 1990 on Aung San Suu Kyi's NLD ticket, been bundled
off to jail by the military government as a result, and emerged from
imprisonment to put more effort not only into lake tourism, but also
into a roll call of projects to improve life in the villages around the lake.
Nyaungshwe is now packed with guesthouses, restaurants, travel and tour
agencies and, inevitably, internet cafés. The action has also moved out
to the lake and U Ohn Maung's luxurious lakeside Inle Princess Resort
is right at the top of the price scale. The dining room and bar, with a
dramatically soaring ceiling, are modelled on a wooden monastery at
Kengtung.

We make a series of excursions across the lake, winding up the river to
Indein, on the west side, with its mouldering old complex of shrines and
dropping in to Nga Hpe Chaung, the famous Jumping Cat Monastery.
Clearly there's only so much meditating any monk can stand. Between
times they've devoted themselves to training the monastery's 13 resident

felines to leap through hoops. I note that the reward is a handful of Whiskas and not just any Whiskas – it's the French variety. These are clearly choosy jumping cats.

Right down at the southern end, the village of Kyauk Taung is entirely devoted to pottery making. Everywhere are lines, heaps and piles of pots in every size from tiny flowerpots to giant water-storage pots. The big pots are so beautiful and the whole village is so picturesque it's almost sad to contemplate that one day reticulated water, plumbing and taps will arrive. Water will no longer be stored in big ceramic pots and the world will move on.

Many of the houses around the lake are actually built out over the lake, on stilts. On our last visit to Inle Lake we were shown plans for a long bridge to connect the 'floating village' of Maing Thauk with its 'land village'. The bridge would let children walk to school and old people get to the village health centre without waiting for someone to transport them by boat. It was another of U Ohn Maung's pet projects and Maureen and I agreed to finance the building materials. This time we got to walk along our 300-metre bridge. It had even had its first birth when a woman didn't get to the health centre quite fast enough.

U Ohn Maung takes us by another of his projects, a village orphanage, and past the site where he wants to build a real hospital. The village has a forest monastery and the faint remains of the British Fort Steadman and an old British cemetery.

It's a harrowing drive north to Mandalay. The traffic has become much worse over the years, although the road is also somewhat better. Soon after my last visit the Moustache Brothers had been reunited and I'm keen to touch base with them. The two brothers and a cousin are *a-nyeint pwe* performers, a traditional Burmese blend of dances, music, jokes and slapstick. Back in 1996 the jokes got them into serious trouble. Burma's military rulers are nothing to joke about and when the brothers poked fun at them, U Par Par Lay and U Lu Zaw, brother and cousin, received seven years of hard labour. U Lu Maw kept the family going, performing with his wife mainly for foreign visitors.

'We're no longer allowed to perform', says U Lu Maw, resignedly. 'So we just give "demonstrations"', he laughs, painting large apostrophes around the word.

'This was Mandalay's Broadway', U Lu Maw continues, pointing down 39th Street. It may look less than Broadway-like, but for visitors it's certainly one of the city's big attractions.

The next day we're forging down the Ayeyarwady River at a stately eight knots in the RV Pandaw, a teak-and-brass Raj-era fantasy. In 1920 the Irrawaddy Flotilla Company (IFC), the Scottish-owned 'fabulous flotilla', was the largest privately owned ship fleet in the world. In 1942, with Japanese troops flooding into Burma, all 650 ships were scuttled. In the late 1990s another Scot, Paul Strachan, revived the IFC name and took over the RV Pandaw.

The 46-metre vessel was built in Glasgow in 1947 to the same steam-powered, stern-paddlewheel design as the pre-war flotilla ships. She was actually sailed out to Burma from Scotland. Although her sides were boarded up for the voyage to make her more seaworthy, it would have been an amazing feat to sail a vessel with just a metre draft across the open seas. For nearly half a century the Pandaw plied the rivers of Burma carrying passengers and cargo.

The Irrawaddy Flotilla Company's old Siam Class steamers carried 4200 deck-class passengers and 40 more in staterooms. They were 100 metres long and only recently have present-day government boats managed downriver speeds faster than those monsters travelled upriver! The captains of these mighty riverboats were so important that a Mandalay shop once had a sign announcing they were 'Silk Mercers to the Kings and Queens of Burma and the Captains of the Steamers'.

The new operators stripped the old Pandaw down and rebuilt it with modern luxuries – the 16 cabins all have attached bathrooms and air-

Date 20 Apr 07
www.truprint.co.uk, 1981557901, 1923963449.

Date 20 Apr 07
www.truprint.co.uk, 1981557901, 19239469948.

conditioners – but with a decidedly old-fashioned feel. The ancient steam engine and paddlewheel had already been replaced with modern diesels driving outboard propellers. Lounging outside your room in a cane armchair or sipping a gin and tonic in the bar, it's hard to avoid humming that old Kipling ditty:

> *Come ye back to Mandalay*
> *where the old Flotilla lay*
> *Can't you 'ear their paddles*
> *chunkin' from Rangoon to Mandalay*

We enjoyed lunch as the stately ship passed the old capital of Sagaing and sailed under the Ava Bridge, just south of Mandalay. That evening it was sundowners on the upper deck as the sun sank below the horizon, and dinner after we moored for the night near the town of Myinmu.

The next morning the Pandaw is on its way before dawn and by breakfast time moors beside the village of Yandabo. It was under a tree on the riverbank at Yandabo that the treaty was signed ending the first Anglo-Burmese War (1824–1826) when the Burmese ceded Arakan, Assam, Manipur and Tenasserim to the British and allowed a British resident to set up at Ava. The village is not connected to the road network so its contact with the outside world is principally by river. Almost everyone in the village is engaged in making pottery and during the dry season there are thousands of pots lined up at various stages of manufacture. The pots are traded up and down the river and even exported. The IFC has sponsored the rebuilding and operation of the village school.

There's a steady flow of traffic up, down and across the river. Sometimes approaching ships carry a couple of bowmen, sounding the river depth with long red-and-white striped poles. There is always a pilot on board the Pandaw, each of whom knows his own stretch of river with its constantly shifting shallows and sandbanks. Periodically the riverboat pulls in at some small settlement to drop off one pilot and pick up another.

Late that afternoon, the Pandaw moors at Pakokku, a busy little provincial town only 25 kilometres north of Bagan. A fleet of chartered trishaws takes us to the town's colourful little market, to a blanket-weaving workshop and to a cheroot manufacturer, all the while pursued by a cheerful posse of bicycling women intent on selling blankets and other crafts.

I manage to drop in to the Mya Yatanar Inn, which for many years has been a favourite overnight halt for backpackers making their way to Bagan on local ferry boats. 'It's an old place run by old people', explain the owners, U Tint San and Daw Mya Mya. The fact that the facilities are rough and ready doesn't seem to worry the guests who have filled a collection of notebooks with effusive praise.

• • • •

That night the Pandaw moors only a few kilometres south of the town and by the time breakfast is over the next morning she's in Bagan. My first two visits to Bagan bracketed the devastating July 1975 earthquake. There had been a great deal of repairs over the next five or 10 years, but in the mid-1990s a frenzy of renovation and rebuilding kicked off, much of it to the great displeasure of archaeologists who had been involved in far more painstaking work. The new-century restorations, in contrast, were 'anything goes'. Every stupa acquired a new gold-leafed finale and, just as Jurassic Park dinosaurs could be cloned from a single cell, so were towering temples being recreated from a brick height or two of foundations.

84.

We floated over this gigantic construction project in a hot-air balloon. Balloons over Bagan was run by Khin Omar Win and her Australian husband. Just as with Aung San Suu Kyi, it was an ailing matriarch who had brought Khin Omar back to Burma. In Khin Omar's case it was her grandmother, but just as Aung San Suu Kyi stayed on after her mother's death so Khin Omar stayed on after her grandmother died.

Khin Omar left Burma in 1975 at the age of five, not long after I made my first visit to the country. At that time her father was a medical student. In 1974 U Thant, the Burmese UN secretary-general, had died and Ne Win reluctantly allowed his body to be returned to Burma for burial, setting off a tragic series of events that in other circumstances might have been almost comic. For some reason Ne Win decided that the much-revered Burmese elder statesman should be put to rest quietly and obscurely. Offended, an alliance of students and monks seized the coffin, performed their own funeral ceremony and buried him on the politically charged site of the university's Students' Union building. During Ne Win's violent takeover in 1962 the building had been blown up, along with the students inside at the time. Once more, troops marched in to the university campus, snatched the coffin and poor U Thant – his dead body playing a much bigger political part than his live one ever did – was buried yet again. In the subsequent rioting, between 16 (the official figure) and hundreds (probably much closer to reality) of people died and Khin Omar's family departed for Britain.

From her new home she had maintained contacts with her homeland, returning several times to visit family members. At the age of 18, she went to see her ailing grandmother and stayed in the country for six months before going back to England where she went to university and became involved in Burma activist activities. After finishing university she again returned to Burma, but this time she decided to stay, meeting and marrying an Australian, Brett Melzer, who worked for Premier Oil.

'Oh, so you married the forces of evil', I say.

'Yes', is, of course, the only possible reply.

Together they set up their hot-air ballooning business. Effectively she'd switched sides from the 'boycott Burma' activists' stance to her own pro-tourism activities.

'Sure I could stay away, live in the West, get a comfortable job,' she explained, 'but I decided to stay here and work for a better Burma from within.'

Establishing the operation took some time and required facing questions like, 'Are women allowed to be higher than the highest pagodas?' 'Well, they're already flying over them in aircraft coming in to Bagan airport' was the obvious response. That question of Buddhist religious protocol was particularly important for several seasons when the balloon pilot was a woman.

'And what about shoes? Should they be removed when you fly above a pagoda?' When an important monk was taken for a demo flight his feet were watched closely and his sandals stayed on.

The sparkle of gold stupa spires seen when floating across the ancient city was clear evidence of the sweeping rebuilding, and no stupa had enjoyed more lavish treatment than the Dhammayazika Paya. The extravagant restoration clearly bore little relation to the original.

'It's not surprising', said U Tun Naing Shwe, the guide showing us around the site later in the day. 'The Dhammayazika was a Khin Nyunt project when he was Secretary One.

'Now that Than Shwe [the army's top general] has kicked him out, it's unlikely to get such careful attention', he laughed. 'They acquire merit by rebuilding or refurbishing pagodas and they have acquired so much bad karma they need lots of merit', U Tun Naing Shwe explained. That was why all the pagodas were being tarted up in Bagan.

'It's a real waste of money', he went on. 'The archaeologists hate what they're doing. So many of the pagodas and temples are being rebuilt from bare foundations when they have no idea what the original construction was like. Or there are renovations like this one – crazy lavish gold-gilding jobs – that bear little relation to the original.'

It was hardly surprising that this particular pagoda had enjoyed such profligate spending. When Secretary One decided to slap on the gold leaf and lay out the marble flagstones, all sorts of local dignitaries felt obliged to climb on board and make their own contributions as well.

'Soldiers and pagodas are all we ever see in the papers', complained U Tun Naing Shwe.

It was certainly true. Every issue of *The Rising Light of Myanmar* devoted half of the front page to a story about some general opening another pagoda (or hospital, school, technology institute or rice mill), illustrated with photos of him inspecting rows of assembled monks (or nurses, school children, engineers or farmers). If a second-level general was elevated to page one, the first-ranking one would drop back to page two. By the time all the other generals and all their other appearances had been covered, you were generally halfway through the paper. The stories always included neat little summaries of the people's enthusiasm, the Tatmadaw's kind concerns and the overriding importance of working against enemies of the state – that is, anyone who didn't agree with military rule and the lousy job they had been doing for so many years.

There were clearly much better ways of donating money and time and much more pressing needs than restoring and rebuilding yet another ancient temple. We'd seen plenty of construction projects from our balloon ride, but the passengers included three German plastic surgeons and the leader of their Interplast team. This group of volunteer doctors and nurses made annual visits to the country, setting up surgery workshops. Many of their operations were for cleft palates, a problem easily fixed at an early age in the West, but devastating in the Third World.

'These children are locked away, hidden from the outside world', explained U Aung Nyunt, the Bagan restaurant owner who hosted the medical group on their visit. 'After their operation they can come out, join the other children, become part of the world. It's astounding how their lives change.'

87.

Treating young burn victims was another common operation for the visiting surgeons. In Burma, as in much of the Third World, many children have disastrous encounters with cooking fires and the disfiguring burns not only make their lives incredibly difficult, but also far too often simply cut them off from the outside world. The surgery workshops can change all that.

'So why don't they donate money to something like that?' U Tun Naing Shwe queried. He had his own answer: 'Because a gold-capped stupa is much more visible than a child with a repaired mouth.'

• • • •

Our visit to Bagan featured one of those curious coincidental reconnections that happen with travel. We'd been very impressed with U Hlau Maung, the driver-guide showing us around the ruins. Realising we were already familiar with all the main sites he proved to be an expert at leading us to unusual lesser-known temples and always seemed to know who would have the keys to unlock them.

'How did you get into this business?' I asked him towards the end of the afternoon.

' My family were very poor,' he said, 'so they sent me to a monastery because there I would get some education and I would be fed. But I hated life in the monastery and as soon as I could I left and got a job as a pony cart driver. I started to take tourists around the ruins and I began to learn English from them.

'The Israelis always asked so many questions. They were a big help with my English simply because they made me work so hard at it. The strange thing was that talking to the tourists I began to get interested in all the questions about Buddhism that I was not interested in when I was a monk. So I started going back to the monastery to learn more.

'Then a guidebook recommended me', he continued, reaching in to the minibus glove-box to pull out a timeworn copy of my Burma guidebook! There was mutual amazement – mine to see his name in the book, his to see mine.

'After my name appeared in the book,' U Hlau Maung went on, 'people began to ask for me to guide them. Eventually I went to Rangoon to study to be an official guide.'

Today his cart had become an air-conditioned minibus, but he was still very clearly a guide who knew his stuff and enjoyed imparting his wisdom. He was equally keen to see other young people make good. Outside our hotel the next morning he explained that his rise from the ranks was known and admired by other young pony cart drivers who in turn were working on their English and hoping to become tourist guides. People like U Hlau Maung are going to make it no matter what, but our book gave him that little extra boost, a small helping hand that he was very aware of and very grateful for. Later that day he introduced us to U Maung Maung, another pony cart guide made good, whose path to an education and later success also came from his contacts with young travellers. Today he owns four lacquerware workshops, employs 70 people and exports to Europe and North America.

• • • •

It's impossible to exaggerate just how big a mess Burma has been almost continuously since World War II. Describing it as a repressive military government, oppressing a calm and resilient people with a handful of quarrelsome border regions thrown in, is a gross oversimplification. So I'll compare it with another utterly confusing modern chaos-nation.

In the late 1990s, I made a brief visit to Lebanon, a country recently emerged from a brutal 17-year civil war. Before I arrived in Beirut I thought I had a fairly good couple-of-sentences synopsis of what

happened: the delicate balance between Christians and Muslims fell apart
when Palestinians flooded in from Jordan after the Israelis took the West
Bank. The end result was an endless civil war, which only ground to a halt
through utter exhaustion.

A week later I understood far less about Lebanon. My simple outline
had completely fallen apart. In fact the Lebanese situation was never just
Christians versus Muslims. There were dozens of Christian and Muslim
militias as well as the Christian Lebanese Army. Then there was the
Palestine Liberation Organization and assorted other Muslim groups,
including Hamas and the Iranian-backed Hezbollah, along with the
Syrian army and the Israelis together with their surrogate Lebanese forces
– even some American marines for a spell.

It certainly wasn't just one side against the other.

Edgar O'Ballance's *Civil War in Lebanon, 1975–92*, a fascinating
year-by-year account of what happened during that period, reported
that 'at one time or other… each one of the dozen or so major armed
groups fought against each other…'. In between punching it out with the
Muslims, every Christian militia took potshots at every other Christian
militia, every Muslim group fell out with every other Muslim group and
nobody got on with the Israelis.

On one occasion a fragile ceasefire fell apart when 'Lebanese Forces'
militia clashed with elements of the Lebanese army. Shooting broke out
because of 'a scuffle over queue-jumping on the ski slopes'. Both groups
of military skiers 'called for armed assistance', and before long the rocket-
propelled grenades were arcing over the Green Line again. Central
American countries may have soccer wars, but has anybody else ever had a
ski-lift shoot-out?

Take out the chairlift and extend the timeline from 17 years to more
than 50 and the Burmese story has just as many unlikely twists and turns.
The country was falling apart even before the British handed it back.
No sooner had the new government taken over (withdrawing from the

British Commonwealth was almost their first action) before everything collapsed. For a spell it was dubbed the 'Six-Mile Rangoon government', for that was as far from the capital that its control extended.

There were not one but two Communist insurrections, the Red Flag and White Flag sections of the CPB, or Communist Party of Burma. There was the PVO (People's Volunteer Organisation), Aung San's private army, which, after his death, decided it would make its own pitch for power rather than support the central government, plus all the regional minority groups from the Buddhist Mons to the Muslim Rohingya. For a time the Karen, or Kayin, the biggest non-Burmese ethnic group, supported the central government, but even that soon went wrong. When Karen troops successfully stormed through CPB-controlled areas, it simply stirred up old resentment from the Burmese – even the Burmese who had been trying to put down the CPB insurrection.

As if a variety of Burmese groups and a kaleidoscope of minority ethnic groups were not enough confusion, the Chinese KMT (Kuomintang) appeared on the scene in late 1949. Pushed out of China by the steady advance of Mao's communists, remnants of the KMT set up shop in the northern Shan and Kachin region. Heavily armed, by the CIA no less, the KMT soon proved even harsher than the Japanese had been less than 10 years earlier. However, the arrival of Burmese troops to shoot it out with the KMT proved even less popular and soon there was a Shan rebellion under way as well.

This confusion has seesawed back and forth from the end of World War II right up to the present day. Brutal campaigns like the 'Four Cuts' programme of the 1970s, closely modelled on the British 'New Villages' strategy during the Malaya Emergency in the 1950s and the American 'Strategic Hamlets' policy in Vietnam, brought more of the country under central control, but only for a short time. Inevitably something else would come along and shift things into reverse.

Remarkably, the Burmese Way to Socialism not only pushed the country to the brink of bankruptcy, it also financed the border regions' struggle against the central government. Ne Win's ill-conceived economic policy backfired twice. As the economy went down the drain, and the Indian and Chinese traders were chased out of the country, everything from rice to soap to medicine to car parts disappeared off the shelves. Soon the black market controlled everything, paid for by a steady stream of smuggled rubies, teak and opium, most of which passed out of the country through the rebel-held border regions, paying taxes and tolls on the way. As the black-market goods flooded back in the opposite direction, the rebels charged more taxes and tolls and this new wealth helped to finance the ongoing battle with the central government.

By the time of the democracy protests in 1988, the Burmese had endured 25 years of Ne Win's quixotic route to socialism and were completely fed up. Socialism had become synonymous with government corruption and economic idiocy. Democracy might have been a rallying call for the protests, but it was the military government's economic ineptitude that really drove people onto the streets. The demonstrations were put down with typical ferocity and brutality and the subsequent elections were completely ignored, but economically there has been progress.

'Life is hard,' said one hotel owner, 'but it was much worse during the socialist times.'

My driver-guide U Ba Maw concurred.

'Don't think it was all rosy before Ne Win took over', he warned me. 'Before 1962 it was complete chaos. That was why Ne Win was able to take over.'

I was well aware of that. The Burma activist groups in the West painted a picture of an energetic, orderly, democratic nation from independence right through until Ne Win's grab for power in 1962.

92.

Burmese socialism has been consigned to the trash bin even more comprehensively than Communism in post-Mao China. Simply dumping the wilder excesses of economic mismanagement, however, hasn't solved all the problems. Ignoring the 1990 election results, continuing to engage in the use of forced labour and generally not being very nice to the assorted border region and minority groupings have made Burma a pariah state. Its military dictatorship has been charged by the United Nations with a 'crime against humanity', for its systematic abuses of human rights, and Western campaign groups have tried to increase economic pressure on the regime by discouraging investment and tourism.

Any Western company that invested in Burma was likely to find protesters turning out at AGMs or bombarding them with 'please explain' emails. As a result, investment dried up and even the line-up for foreign aid was likely to find Burma pushed to the bottom of the list. There'd been some ups, but it was mostly downs and the late 1990s Asian meltdown certainly hadn't helped.

The mere fact that U Ba Maw was so open about failings past and present was another indicator that what I'd heard from the activist groups – that people would be afraid to talk – wasn't necessarily the whole truth. I found it never took more than a little prompting to get a Burmese to open up about the government and how much they hated it. Sometimes it took no prompting at all for people like U Myint Swe, who had barely slid the minivan door closed before he launched his attack. The government hotels were hopeless, he reported, the staff were bored and disinterested and he tried to avoid taking tourists to any government-run establishment.

'It's not surprising', he explained. 'They are paid so little, so very little, and even then the government cheats them. For example if a tourist pays in dollars and the service charge is 10 per cent, the government converts it into kyats at the pathetic official rate before passing it on to the staff.'

He was equally pessimistic about the hope for change.

'They are criminals. They have committed crimes, a long list of crimes. They are afraid that if a new government comes in they will be convicted and made to pay for their crimes.'

93.

I'd heard the same analysis from many other people: 'The generals look at what has happened to Soeharto and his family and they are afraid, very afraid. When Milosevic was arrested and sent for trial that really scared them', a visitor at our hotel explained. 'If he can be tried for his crimes, why shouldn't the generals in this country?'

•   •   •   •

Having two currencies running simultaneously is always confusing, but many of the Bad Lands seem to like the idea. Of course, people in many countries, good countries as well as bad ones, may find it convenient to have a second currency to hand. When your own currency is falling through the floor, putting any ready cash into something more stable can be a very good idea. There are many countries whose citizens are inclined to keep the bare minimum of their own currency, certainly have no intention of depositing money in the bank, and wherever possible stash it under the mattress in the form of greenbacks. And never mind what their government may say about the Great Satan. The Great Satan may be the devil incarnate, but the Great Satan's money is always just fine.

The Deutschmark used to perform much the same function for many Turks, who would take plenty of marks back home after spells of working in the Fatherland. It was a big question mark in the introduction of the euro whether Turkish mattress-marks would be converted into dollars or euros when the mark disappeared. In other places gold may be the reserve currency. Indian women's love of gold jewellery is in large part simply a convenient way of keeping cash at hand in a more trustworthy medium than the rupee. For many years Dubai earned a large slice of its income as a smuggling centre from where gold blocks were carried by dhow to the subcontinent.

Even in countries where the currency is strong and trustworthy another currency may often be readily accepted. Throughout the world today's

exchange rate from the local currency, whatever it may be, to the US
dollar is often common knowledge. For a spell Burma took the two-
currency game one step further: Burma had three currencies. As soon as
you arrived, right after immigration, and before you headed over to the
baggage carousel, you were intercepted at a bank counter and required to
change US$200 into 200 things that looked remarkably like Monopoly
money (perhaps they used the same printer) and were known as FECs
– Foreign Exchange Certificates. Advocates for a tourism boycott claimed
that this compulsory transaction was just the first way a foolish tourist
kept the nasty government afloat, by paying US$200 simply to enter the
country. Really the stupid FEC was only a way station en-route to real
money, the kyat (pronounced chat). You could quickly convert your FECs
into kyats at pretty much the same exchange rate as the US dollar.

So why introduce this extra complication if it didn't really signify
anything? Beats me. Like a lot of other strange things about Burma, the
useless FEC was a mystery and eventually it was dumped.

. . . .

'They didn't have to change Rangoon', explained U Tin Maung Oo,
a metallurgy student I'd bumped into in Pathein (formerly Bassein).
'Rangoon was quite all right. They didn't need to change it to Yangon. It
was because of the engineering students.'

In most places in the world, engineering students are famed for being
resolutely apolitical. When their fellow students are propping up the
barricades, engineers are more likely to be found propping up the bar.
Not in Rangoon, where the engineers were reputed to be especially fiery
and always ready to appear at the front line of every protest. Furthermore,
their college, the Rangoon Institute Of Technology, had a most
unfortunate acronym.

'Change Rangoon', ordered the general-in-charge-of-name-changes.

'I don't care what you change it to, but I don't want to hear anything more about the students from RIOT rioting.'

Switching Rangoon to Yangon, and turning RIOT into YIOT may have pleased the generals, but all around Burma, now officially known as Myanmar, I'd been perplexed by the name changes. Mandalay had stayed Mandalay, thank God, but everywhere else had acquired a new name, starting with the country itself. Interestingly, that name change was one of the very few military moves that enjoyed some general approval.

'Calling the country Burma would be rather like calling Britain England', Tin Maung Oo went on. 'Certainly England is a very large part of Britain, just like Burma is a very large part of Myanmar, but nobody from Scotland or Wales wants to be called English. We may call people from Myanmar Burmese, but the real Burmese are the people from the central plains who speak Burmese. We call them the Bamar. The country of Myanmar includes lots of people who aren't Bamar, people like the Shan, the Karen, the Mon or the Rakhaing.'

The name Myanmar may have been accepted in the country itself, but that certainly isn't the case beyond its borders. I don't expect the Burma Action Group is ever going to become the Myanmar Action Group and, from their perspective, using the term Myanmar is likely to label you as a supporter of the regime.

Myanmar I could live with, and I was glad Mandalay had stayed that way, but most of the other changes had lost a certain flavour. To my ears Prome sounded much better than Pyay, Pegu than Bago, Pagan than Bagan. On my 1970s visit, a trip up to Maymyo (effectively 'May-town' after the British Colonel May) to stay in the time-warped old Raj-era relic Candacraig had been a real highlight. A town called Pyin U Lwin certainly didn't have the same ring, although it was simply reverting to its pre-colonial name tag. And as for renaming the mighty Irrawaddy River the Ayeyarwady…

• • • •

It was our final night in Burma and we sipped cold beers and G&Ts on the lawn running down to the Inya Lake from the lakeside house. Our host worked for a Swiss engineering firm and their sundowner guests included Bill Keats, an English architect who was making a useful living out of being virtually the only resident Western architect in the country. Hotels, embassies and offices were all part of his portfolio, but it was houses he really specialised in – houses for generals and drug lords.

'English colonial is what they like', he explained. 'They're not concerned that they're castigated in the English media. And I'm not concerned about taking their money either. The SLORC-itect, that's what I am.'

'This is a great location', our host expounded, gazing across the lake to the setting sun. 'Everybody who's anybody in Rangoon lives around the lake. There's the Inya Lake Hotel', he said, pointing at the huge Russian-financed, Israeli-constructed hotel, which when it was first built was something of a Southeast Asian joke, but after recent renovations had reached a rather higher standard.

'Down there is Khun Sa', he went on, indicating the home of the Shan state drug-lord who had traded his heroin trading fortune for a peaceful retirement, despite the CIA million-dollar price on his head.

'Over there's the Ne Win mansion', he continued, pointing towards the secluded mansion of the late military dictator, failed economist, astrological fanatic and all-round bad guy.

'And, down there,' he concluded, pointing towards the south end of the lake, 'is Aung San Suu Kyi's home.' His gaze ran down the lake, towards 54 University Avenue, the home and detention centre of the Nobel Peace Prize winner.

CUBA

Florida Keys (US)

STRAITS OF FLORIDA

BAHAMAS

GREAT BAHAMA BANK

HAVANA

Varadero

Santa Clara

Trinidad

Camagüey

Guardalavaca

Playa María
la Gorda

Holguín

Baracoa

Guantánamo

CARIBBEAN SEA

Santiago
de Cuba

JAMAICA

So why do the Americans have it in so bad for poor old Fidel and the Cubans?

Look what he's done for the place. Kicked out a vicious dictator (nobody has a good word to say for his predecessor, Batista), established a secure government (none of those continual revolutions that have plagued so much of Latin America), ploughed money into education and health (Cuba's infant mortality and literacy figures are not just way ahead of anywhere else in Latin America, they're right up there with the USA) and certainly not made himself rich. If Fidel were ever to get the boot, he wouldn't be retiring to a mansion overlooking the Costa del Sol. Sounds like a thoroughly good guy. So how come he's so unpopular in the USA? Or in Miami at least?

Or conversely how come so many Cubans are so dependent on Miami?

'If you don't have relatives in Miami, you're fucked', said a Cuba-expert friend I bumped into in London just before I flew to Havana. 'The place is like Warsaw in the 1980s, back in the Solidarity days, but transported to the tropics.'

He was only half-right I thought, as I walked along a typically schizophrenic Cuban city street.

The shelves were full.

The shelves were empty.

All of the full shops could easily have been 7-Elevens anywhere in the world, well stocked with soft drinks, confectionery, instant foods, tissues, shampoos, toothpaste and more. There was an entry ticket to these shops – convertible pesos – Cuba's hard currency. Common Cuban pesos aren't good enough.

The empty shops were strictly for the locals and it was hard to tell what the handful of goods on display even were. There were never more than a half-dozen different items spread thinly across the shelves. Some mysterious liquid in a plastic bottle, some strange substance wrapped in shiny paper, not much choice, not much of anything and nothing likely to coax the pesos out of your pockets.

Outside, women would ask, politely, for soap. Always soap. There was plenty of it in the hard-currency shops and lots of those familiar miniature hotel soap-bars in the hard-currency hotels and resorts. It was the same everywhere in Cuba – one world and another, the world of plenty and the world of shortages.

I have never seen a country so devoid of street food. There are no food stalls, no street markets, no vending machines. Walking through the back streets of the beautifully preserved colonial town of Trinidad one day, I was surprised to see a couple of boxes of tomatoes sitting on the sidewalk. Already this sight of food – food simply sitting there in the street – was so astonishing I stopped walking and reflexively reached for my camera before realising that this was nothing special, just a box of tomatoes.

• • • •

'There are more tourists in Cuba right now than at any time since the revolution', said Jonathan Wordsworth, an American architectural writer Maureen and I bumped into in the lobby of the Hotel Riviera.

'And the architecture is wonderful. It's not just the old Spanish colonial stuff that everybody knows about. It's also places like this', he indicated with a sweep of his hand taking in the vast lobby.

'This place is pure late-1950s Las Vegas. It was built by Meyer Lansky, the Jewish Mafia guy, in 1957, just before the revolution and since then it's been virtually untouched. Have you seen the executive floor? Wow, it's pink, totally pink, the carpets, the walls, everything. We don't make them like that anymore.'

Jonathan could visit Cuba legally. Government business, study tours or journalism are official reasons for Americans to visit Castro's kingdom. Or, more correctly, to spend dollars there. Despite sanctions, the trade embargo and the strange diplomatic relations between the US and its tiny neighbour, it's quite OK for Americans to visit Cuba. Of course, they can't fly there directly. To make the 250-kilometre trip between Miami and Havana means, for most American visitors, a long detour north to Canada or a circuitous trip via Mexico. There's also a more direct, but underhand, flight via Nassau in the Bahamas. Ostensibly you're just flying to Nassau, but after a short stop the plane continues straight on to Havana, on a totally separate ticket, of course. You can play much the same 'fool the American government' game via Jamaica.

The legal twist for American Joe Tourist comes after he's made his way to the Caribbean Bad Land: he can't spend money. If somebody looks after him, pays for his room, food and transport, then that's fine, but if Joe Tourist spends his hard-earned US dollars in the enemy state, then he's broken the law and can be fined when he returns to the land of the free.

Now how does Uncle Sam know you've spent greenbacks in Castro-land? Well, he doesn't, of course. Joe and Jane Tourist have flown to Toronto and two weeks later come back, perhaps with a rather better suntan than you'd normally expect to pick up in Ontario midwinter, but there's no law against that. Of course, if Joe and Jane went via Cancun – the Mexican mega-resort is a popular gateway to Cuba with flights several times a day – even the suntan wouldn't be suspicious.

Official US figures are that 160,000 US citizens legally visited Cuba in 2002 – the US seems to take an awfully long time to process their Cuban tourism statistics. Although the US government has been working to reduce that figure, and claims that visitor numbers have dropped, you can be certain a lot of Americans drop in on Havana unofficially and probably spend some dollars while they are there. Theoretically that terrible crime could result in a fine of a quarter of a million dollars and 10 years in jail. Of course, nobody has ever been put behind bars for flying to Havana and buying a Coke (Coke and other familiar American soft drinks come to Cuba via their Mexican subsidiaries), but in recent years the number of Americans fined for being bad tourists has been steadily climbing. One estimate, and everything to do with the US and Cuba seems to be either an estimate or a guess, is that the slap-on-the-wrist rate for visiting Cuba has quadrupled during the Bush administration.

How do you get caught? Well, not by the FBI checking your credit-card records. Visa and MasterCard credit cards issued by American banks cannot be used in Cuba and American Express cards cannot be used at all, no matter where they're issued. Which is not to say Visa and MasterCard are not happily accepted in Cuba – an Australian, British, French, German, Canadian or Mexican version will do just fine – but there will be no incriminating credit-card slips to catch out unwary Americans unless they also have an overseas bank account.

A wad of Cuban hotel bills and restaurant receipts will do the trick, however. So will a nice boxful of those Cuban cigars, which, so it's said, JFK was careful to stock up on before he slammed the embargo doors shut. Or simply not having a ready answer when the immigration officer asks exactly where did you go and stay during that little Canadian vacation. And how come you managed to get such a good tan when it has been overcast and snowing for the past 10 days?

Americans who do get caught are likely to get an official letter demanding to know how many of those oh-so-pure greenbacks were spent for Fidel's benefit, followed by a second letter with a fine of, typically, about US$7500. Equally typically the fine can be bargained down to something between US$700 and US$2500. There are regular murmurs from Congress about repealing these crazy restrictions. Opponents of the sanctions insist that they're unconstitutional but, if anything, President Bush has an even harder-line stance on Cuba. After all, it was Florida that squeaked him in to the presidency on the first occasion.

So if you are planning a holiday in Cuba, have some answers ready. Of course you didn't leave Canada for somewhere warmer. There are no stamps in your passport (the Cubans are very understanding that way) so who's saying you've been strolling down the Malecón in Havana? The fact that you have no credit-card slips or paperwork from Canadian hotels or restaurants is easily explained: you stayed the whole time with your good Canadian friends, the couple you met in Spain a couple of years ago and always promised you'd visit.

In fact, for Cuban Americans and Americans on official business, you can fly directly from Miami to Cuba. American Airlines operates several flights a week between Miami and Havana or Santiago de Cuba. Of course, the flights depart anonymously from Miami International Airport. The flight won't appear on the departure monitors, there'll be no announcements about its imminent take-off and no flight number and destination will be posted at the boarding gate.

At the other end, however, everything will be totally normal. The American Airlines flight number will appear on the arrivals screens, the flight will be shown at the arrivals gateway, there may even be posters suggesting you 'Fly American' posted around the airport.

Technically, foreigners could get into expensive trouble by flying to

103.

Cuba. There's no way you could buy a London–Miami–Havana–London ticket without the US government's blessing, but what's to stop you getting a London–Miami–Cancun–Havana–London ticket? You're not flying between the US and Cuba so what's the problem? Well, the US government doesn't like Cuba and the USA appearing on the same ticket. Get a ticket written that way and they could confiscate it when you showed up in the US.

Even those officially permitted American visitors have all sorts of restrictions imposed on them that would seem totally ridiculous anywhere else in the world. Just because they're allowed to spend dollars in Fidel-land doesn't mean they can spend too many of them. There's a daily limit of US$167 plus phone calls. Journalists do have an out, however. They can spend more so long as it's expenditure 'incidental to journalist activities'. That's US$167 in Havana, incidentally. Drop in on Guantánamo Bay and your per diem drops to US$78. The orange-clad Gitmo residents stay for free, although for longer than they might wish.

• • • •

What really fascinated me about the Hotel Riviera is what happened to it between 1959 and now. It opened on 10 December 1957, so it must have had just 12 months in operation before the revolution. Was it just put on ice, locked away for the next 40 years? Or did comrades from Eastern Europe and the Soviet Union enjoy this American decadence through the 1960s, 1970s and 1980s? Through that period tourists in Cuba were predominantly from the eastern side of the old iron curtain. For many years it was all but impossible for Westerners to get a visa, but gradually carefully selected tourist groups, many of them from Canada, started to slip in. Then the Berlin Wall fell, the Soviet Union collapsed and the Eastern European tourists simply dried up. There was a painful hiatus, the worst years of the 'special period', the *período especial,* before Western

Europeans started to flood in – attracted by sun, sand (in some cases sex) and low, low prices.

Gangster-chic is not the only architecture of note in Havana. As well as the classic American resort buildings of the 1950s, there's also wonderful colonial architecture from the 19th-century Spanish period. Elsewhere in the world much of it might have disappeared, demolished to make way for newer buildings, but in Havana everything was frozen in time from 1959 onwards. For decades it rotted away, but in recent years there has been a huge effort to restore and renovate the old parts of central Havana. Much of it is already beautifully restored, but every year it simply gets better and better.

In complete contrast there's also an enlightening selection of 'people's architecture' – grey and crumbling apartment blocks that could just as easily be East Berlin or Warsaw leftovers, and brutalist Soviet-style heroic monuments, particularly in the Plaza de la Revolución.

Then there are the cars. Cuban cars come in three eras. Right now glossy new Peugeots and economical new Hyundais dominate the streets. Rent a car in Cuba and that's what you'll get. Prior to that there's a 20-year hiatus to the Russian Lada era from the 1970s and 1980s, all of them looking a bit battered and bruised from the dings and narrows of outrageous traffic. And then it's 20 years back again to the American cars of the 1950s, only a few of them newer than 1958. Clearly there was a big buying binge in the last two years before the Americans lowered the boom. Havana's streets rock and roll with 1957 Plymouth Furies, 1956 Oldsmobile Rocket 88s and 1958 Chevy Bel Airs.

Isn't it weird that the world's true enthusiasts for American automobiles – the people who would drive their 'Chevy to the levy' any time – are the Syrians and the Cubans? Why would two countries so high up on America's Bad Land list love those icons of American culture so wholeheartedly?

Havana may have plenty of Detroit iron still circulating, but the number of lead sleds is not excessive. Part of the city's charm is that you can stroll across any street at any time without glancing twice for oncoming traffic and if you're driving there's always a free parking space.

Cuban music, on the other hand, fills every available space. The Buena Vista Social Club has a lot to answer for. Nowhere can you pause for two minutes without another band materialising out of thin air, setting up shop and launching into another shoulder-shaking number. This is definitely shoulder music. The rest of the body can stay absolutely stationary, but the shoulders show the beat. At Café Lambada one night there's not only an eight-piece band, but also a dancing couple to go with it. His beard and beret seem to say he fought the revolution with Che, Raul and Fidel, but the business card Wilki Arencibia drops on our table announces he's a 'maestro de Salsa'.

• • • •

I pick up a rent-a-car, a new and well-kept Hyundai, in Havana, and Maureen and I drive clear to the western end of the island then U-turn and drive all the way back to the eastern end. Driving around Cuba is no problem, in daylight at least. Driving at night is an entirely different story, as I would soon discover. The roads are generally in pretty good shape. There's even a real divided-lane freeway, or *autopista*, running about half the length of the long, skinny island. The traffic is generally light and generally well behaved. For foreigners getting fuel is no problem. In most towns there's at least one clean modern petrol station selling fuel for convertible pesos. The Cuban peso stations, for Cubans only, are grubbier and quite likely to be sold out.

Of course there are a few problems. You'd be disappointed if there

wasn't something to make driving worth talking about. Overtaking trucks or buses can be a little nerve-wracking due to the low-quality diesel fuel they use. Most of them seem to belch out enough black smoke to hide an Allied World War II ship convoy from a fleet of pursuing U-boats. As a result, overtaking can be entertaining.

The big problem throughout Cuba, however, is signposting. There isn't any. Once they'd used up the annual paint budget for the obligatory 'Socialism or Death' billboards, there was nothing left for anything else. Living without the Western advertising onslaught is one thing. Not knowing whether to turn left, right or go straight-on every time you come to a junction is quite another.

Leaving Havana we soon cross what has to be the Pinar del Rio Autopista, but can't work out how to get on to it. Eventually we bump down what feels like a farm laneway and find our way on to the road.

Most of the time, we soon discover, the lack of signposting is no problem. For at least three quarters of the distance we cover there's a hitchhiker or two in the back and they always ensure we take the correct turn at every junction. For the average Cuban, hitchhiking is how you get from one place to another. You certainly can't afford your own car and there definitely aren't enough buses for everybody. So you stand by the roadside and stick out your thumb. There are even official hitchhiking points complete with platforms and stairs to make getting into trucks easier. We pick up engineers, architects and lawyers, young men and old ladies, couples and mothers with their children. The back seat is rarely empty.

• • • •

One day we end up in Varadero, partly out of interest, mostly because we can't get any further that night. Driving from the western end of the island we'd intended to skirt around Havana and then head off further east, but the Cuban disdain for direction signs catches us out and we end up on a very nice looking freeway – but the wrong very nice looking freeway. Fortunately we soon pick up a friendly young couple, a pair of recently qualified lawyers, hitchhiking on the *autopista* slip road, and they explain where we went wrong, suggest we try Varadero for the night and get us off the freeway at the correct (unmarked) exit, pointing in the right direction for Cuba's mega-resort.

By this time it's getting dark and we soon find ourselves travelling very slowly and very cautiously. Few vehicles can afford the expense of having lights after dark and it's eminently possible to overtake a smoke-belching truck only to find a completely blacked-out bullock cart coming in the opposite direction. Even vehicles travelling in the right direction can be dangerous, we discover, when we suddenly find ourselves bearing down on a totally unlit old American car, its driver crawling along the edge of the highway, trying to see where he is going by the faint glimmer of moonlight. From behind not even a reflector hints at his location.

Eventually we emerge on the coast, on the busy, well-lit Via Blanca, which runs 140 kilometres from the capital to the Torremolinos, the Surfer's Paradise, the Miami Beach, the Cancun of Cuba. Varadero is the biggest resort in the Caribbean, the place where one out of every three foreign visitors to Cuba ends up. For a large slice of that visitor population Varadero is all they will ever see of Cuba.

The fact that there are tens of thousands of hotel rooms along Varadero's 20-kilometre stretch of beautiful beach hasn't prevented most establishments from hanging out their 'full' signs, and even getting in through the front door to ask at the reception desk is, we quickly discover, not easy. Each of the big hotels seems to have a small posse of bouncers at the front door, all paying exceptional interest to your wrists as you approach. It is not a keen interest in what the time is and how long before their shift ends. Every guest is equipped with a plastic wristband, rather like an elderly hospital inmate. The band proves they are a hotel guest and qualified to indulge in the hotel's all-inclusive offerings.

Varadero is all-inclusive, pre-paid, cash-unnecessary on a grand scale. Once the happy European (or Canadian) vacationer has paid for the trip, nothing else is needed. From the breakfast buffet to the beer at sundowner time to the midnight mojitos, everything is included. The only time the Varadero visitor is likely to venture out of this carefully corralled little paradise is to make a day trip to Havana, where they are easily distinguished from other Varaderian groups on day-release by their different coloured plastic wristbands.

For the Cuban government this is tourism in its most perfect form. The visitors are neatly sequestered in one little enclave where their only contact with everyday Cubans is with a carefully vetted squad of workers, most of whom are bussed in at the beginning of their shift and bussed out at the end. There is no chance that any entrepreneurial Cuban individuals will dirty their hands by making money out of the tourists either. The businesses are all owned by the government or by joint Cuban–foreign-owned enterprises. Many of the hotels are owned by the same Spanish tourist operators who have learnt their trade along the beaches of the Costa del Sol, Costa Brava and Costa Blanca.

In other, lower key tourist enclaves, a little private enterprise is grudgingly permitted so long as it is severely circumscribed. Casas particulares, small family-operated bed and breakfasts, or the restaurants known as paladares, are allowed to operate as long as they don't take away business from places owned by the government. To ensure that this doesn't happen there are rules restricting how big a sign can be displayed, how many seats a paladar can provide (no more than 12), and even what dishes can be served. In a seaside restaurant, lobster and shrimp can only feature on the menus of the government establishments, and ditto for beef, since the government owns all the cows. Most important, employment had to be strictly limited to family members – in Castro-land you certainly don't want one comrade having to work for another. If after surmounting all these hurdles a hard-working comrade should contrive to make an unseemly profit, the taxes, charges and licence fees can be quickly jacked up to bring things back into perspective.

None of these gentle relaxations of the rules apply in Varadero. In Cuba's mega-resort, business is strictly a government prerogative. There are no casas particulares or paladares in Varadero. It is quite OK for the Spanish Sol Meliá group to turn a profit from its hotels on the beach, but heaven forbid that a native Cuban should do the same thing. Let capitalism dirty the Spanish, not the locals. Sol Meliá is the biggest foreign hotel-operator in Cuba. In 1996, when the US Helms-Burton legislation was trying to bully foreign companies out of Cuba, the company decided to forget about the American market. They sold up their hotels in Miami and Orlando and concentrated on Cuba instead.

Economics isn't the only thing that grates at Varadero.

As we load up our trays at the lunch buffet, call for another all-included cocktail at the bar, open another bar of soap in the bathroom, we contemplate that none of this is available to the smiling waitress restocking the breakfast counters, the smiling barman mixing the mojitos, or the smiling maid tidying up the bathroom. At the end of their shift they'll be paid in Cuban pesos, a currency that won't buy any of the goodies lavished upon the foreign visitors. They'll be bussed out of Varadero to their homes, well away from the international visitors, where the shelves in their peso shops will be bare.

• • • •

We had an educational window-shop down República, the main shopping street running from the railway station to the city centre in Camagüey, Cuba's third-largest city. The occasional glossy, well-lit shop aimed at foreigners punctuated a string of peso shops loaded with cheap tat, low-quality junk, horrible fashions and general rubbish.

My favourite – I was so intrigued by it that I walked past it a half-dozen times trying to gauge if there was a local reaction – was a miserable-looking window with a crumbling and bald dress dummy

wearing what looked like something recycled from World War II.
Next to this example of the wonders of the Cuban rag trade was a sign
proclaiming the glories of all those years of socialism. Was this serious?
Or was this window display simply a not-so-subtle comment on the
failures rather than the glories of Cuban socialism?

Every other woman walking by was wearing the standard Cuban
fashion statements: short, tight, low, high, stretched. Preferably in Lycra.
That string of one-word diktats sums up Cuban fashions, and the more
you've got to stuff into it the better. In Cuba no women can be too big,
too wide, too round for Lycra. 'Thrusting femininity' was the two-word
definition of the Cuban approach to fashion, according to one visiting
travel writer. Every Cuban woman has style and it's none of this 'white is
this year's black' bullshit.

Actually Cuba is full of style. Even the Museo de la Revolución,
essentially a museum to document what bastards Batista and his
imperialist puppet masters the Americans were, and the contrasting
heroism of the Cuban people, is full of style. Castro always looked
stylish. Wasn't it Fidel who started the whole revolutionary combat
fatigues thing? Didn't he always have a photographer on hand to record,
in stylish-looking black and white, the whole revolution from start to
glorious finish? Didn't he (and nearly every other Cuban revolutionary)
remember to keep their boots (and shirts and trousers) from every stage
of the struggle so they could be preserved in museums? A pair of Italian
boots I'd bought on impulse from a Paris shoe shop a few years before,
thinking they looked stylish, were clearly just the Fidel Mark 1 boots
from the first stage of the struggle. If someone would tell me the shop to
buy the Mark 3 boots, I'd pop out and buy a pair right now.

And Che... well, what can you say? A rock-star (Buddy Holly and
dozens since), movie-star (James Dean), royalty-star (Princess Di) death.
Do it while you still look perfect enough to launch a million T-shirts.
Che is simply the Cuban souvenir – Che T-shirts outnumber five to one

any other Cuban memento.

In fact Che, not Fidel, is the Cuban icon. El Jefe may be the undisputed leader, but visually Fidel is not often to be seen. There's no Fidel personality cult; it's Che's gigantic neon-lit portrait that gazes out heroically across the Plaza de la Revolución in Havana. Even Camilo Cienfuegos, the revolutionary hero who died in a plane crash in 1959, pops up more often than Fidel.

Nowhere is the Che cult displayed with more energy than in Santa Clara, where a gigantic statue of the superman towers over the museum dedicated to his life. Che was captured in Bolivia in 1967 and murdered at the CIA's behest. His remains were returned to Cuba in 1997 and interred here. The museum shows another side of Che's life: his comfortable Argentinean childhood and his adventures as a young medical student when he explored South America by motorcycle and encountered the grinding poverty that was to propel him into his life as a revolutionary. In 1954 Che was in Guatemala and witnessed the CIA-backed invasion that toppled the elected government and installed the repressive military regime that was to blight Guatemala for nearly 50 years.

It was Che Guevara's capture of Santa Clara on 29 December 1958 that spelt the end for Batista's despotic regime. Using a cobbled-together bulldozer, Che's rebels cut the railway line into the city, derailing an armoured train sent to reinforce Batista's troops. Despite being overwhelmingly outnumbered, Che's guerrillas soon defeated the 3000-strong garrison and, late on 31 December, Batista realised that Santiago de Cuba, the second largest city in Cuba, was about to fall. In the early hours of 1 January 1959, Batista fled to the Dominican Republic, taking US$40 million with him to finance his comfortable retirement in Franco's Spain. He died in 1973.

• • • •

Our travels around Cuba have been a curious blend of organised (you can't get more organised than staying in a resort filled with European package tourists) and disorganised (our visit to the scuba-diving haven of Playa La Gorda, right at the western end of the island, was short-circuited by a serious room shortage – we could only stay for one night). We've stayed in dull, ordinary hotels and fancy old colonial-era hotels and in casas particulares, one of which reminded me of a particularly old-fashioned English bed-and-breakfast. We've been completely lost once or twice due to the serious lack of signposting and on one occasion stopped some foreign cyclists to ask where the hell we were. Sometimes we've found it very difficult to find food and then felt guilty knowing we were eating in places where effectively Cubans are not welcome.

In Guardalavaca, where I try Cuban scuba diving again, Maureen and I have one of those ludicrous over-dinner arguments, the reasons and causes for which disappear as soon as you stop shouting at each other.

'Maybe we're both in a bad mood because neither of us is really enjoying Cuba', I suggested.

'Well, Havana was great', Maureen disagreed. 'It looks wonderful. There's all the music, the revolution and so on.'

'Sure,' I allowed, 'the revolution is certainly interesting historically, but after you've seen a half-dozen revolutionary museums (was any revolution ever so well documented, so well photographed? God, they even kept the boat Fidel arrived in in 1957!) they begin to pall. After a thousand kilometres you begin to feel that a bit less energy into "Socialism or Death" billboards and a bit more into some other things could make a difference.'

'And nothing else does it for me', I continued. 'The other towns are OK, but essentially dull. So far the best has been Trinidad, but it's just a watered-down version of Antigua in Guatemala. Not as well kept, not as colourful, not as interesting, not as anything.'

'Yeah, I guess so,' Maureen agreed, 'and in between there are beach resorts like Varadero that are the pits, all-inclusive resorts where the locals are totally shut out.'

Which was where I'd really had enough. In this 'glorious socialism, wonders of the revolution, Alice-in-Wonderland', the workers are excluded by guards and by money.

'And I really hate those plastic wristbands they put on their guests'. Maureen concluded. 'You look as if you're an asylum inmate or somebody in a hospital.'

•   •   •   •

There was a final sightseeing stop on our way to Santiago de Cuba – Guantánamo Bay, favourite US station for captured Taliban and Al-Qaeda members. How did this chunk of Cuba come to be in the possession of its arch enemy?

Well, in 1903 the USA grabbed it, fair and square.

After the Spanish-American war in 1898, the US decided not to hand control of Cuba over to the Cuban rebels who had been fighting for their independence from Spain for years. Instead they set up a US military occupation, which was withdrawn, reluctantly, in 1902, but only after saddling Cuba with the Platt Amendment, a law that gave the US the right to intervene militarily any time they didn't like what was going on. In 1903 the US decided they didn't like the way the Cubans were running Cuba and annexed 116 square kilometres at the mouth of Guantánamo Bay, to use as a naval station from where they could keep a close eye on things.

In 1934 President Roosevelt deigned to change the control to a 99-year lease so Cuba could look forward to getting their land back in 2033, except that it requires both sides to agree for the lease to be terminated and for nearly 50 years the US has been extremely reluctant to agree to anything with Cuba.

Following the revolution in 1959, Fidel asked for Guantánamo Bay to be returned. The US refused, of course, and in turn Castro has subsequently refused to accept the annual rent, all of about US$4000 a year. For a time the base served a useful purpose protecting the approaches to the Panama Canal, but its principal use today – apart from its recent function as a more convenient prison than Afghanistan – is as an irritant to Castro. As well as being home to the 7000-odd US personnel and the current batch of prisoners from Central Asia, the base has also housed far larger numbers of refugees. In 1992 there were 11,000 Haitians holed up here after they attempted to escape from their country's collapsing economy. In late 1994 they were followed by over 30,000 Cubans, intercepted by the US Coast Guard en route from Cuba to the bright lights of Miami. Most of them eventually ended up in the US. Clearly there's no shortage of facilities to house unlimited numbers of Taliban and Al-Qaeda n'er-do-wells.

Of course, there's no way to visit Guantánamo Bay from the rest of Cuba, although a handful of now elderly Cubans have kept their jobs on the base since the 1950s and still cross the border every day. They'd better take care since the base is encircled by trenches, fences, watchtowers and the largest minefield in the Western Hemisphere. No less than 75,000 mines stand ready to deter any thoughts Castro might have about unilateral lease terminations. Afghan arrivals would probably feel quite at home, since their own country has the unfortunate distinction of being one of the most heavily mined in the world.

Although we couldn't drop in to check out the golf course, yacht club, supermarkets, cinemas and the only McDonalds in Cuba, the Cubans do make it possible for us to have a peek into their unwanted visitors' home. At a military checkpoint on the road we drop off our current hitchhikers, leave our passports in the checkpoint office and drive 15 kilometres to the Mirador de Malones, a 320 metre-high viewpoint looking down on the base. Fortunately our CUC$5 admission charge includes a cold drink because there is nothing to see, even with the 25-cents-in-the-slot telescope. The base shimmered in the heat far below us and it's hard to make out anything. Amnesty International won't be able to check up on the holding conditions for Al-Qaeda terrorists from up here.

Then, Amnesty International doesn't need to check up on the conditions. No matter how bad they are, they can hardly make the US government's image any worse than it is already. So why did the Bush government decide to establish the USA's own gulag in Cuba?

Three reasons: US law doesn't apply here, international law doesn't apply here and it's impossible for independent observers to see what the hell's going on. Which hardly contributes to Cuba's Bad Land status. Guantánamo Bay may be in Cuba the island, but effectively it's in the USA and not the regular holier-than-thou USA. It's in the Bad Land USA.

Back on the main road our hitchhikers are still waiting for a ride so we take them on board again for the final few kilometres to their destination.

• • • •

A rickety old twin-engine Antonov AN-26 rattles us back to Havana. From the departure lounge at the Santiago de Cuba airport I had spotted a nice new Aerocaribbean ATR-42 outside and concluded we'd be zipping back to Havana in comfort. Half an hour later that aircraft flies off to the Dominican Republic and all that's left is the old Russian rust bucket. It's after dark and we are well over an hour late before finally being ushered out to the aircraft. There are no reading lights and the general cabin lighting is too weak to read by, so there's nothing to distract you from the aircraft's strange vibrations and noises.

At least I have a seat and my seat has a safety belt. My last Antonov flight was way back in 1992 in Cambodia, when the national airline was still called Air Kampuchea. When we'd all crowded on board and grabbed a seat there were still two or three passengers standing, so cane chairs were provided for the extras. On that occasion my seat was provided with both ends of a seat belt, but unfortunately they were both the same end. In comparison this Antonov is virtually showroom-new, although the entire flight, with a short intermediate stop at Holguìn, seems to be a process of accelerating until a speed is reached where the whole aircraft starts to vibrate and rattle, then coasting back to a smoother velocity before speeding up to the vibration point again.

We spill out at the domestic terminal in Havana, grab our bags, emerge into the gloomy car park and pile into the capacious back seat of a fine-looking old Chevy. Fine looking, but not fine running. We are only halfway to the car park exit before terminal noises from up front announce some sort of major mechanical failure and we are transferred to a Russian vehicle, an elderly Moskvich in much worse shape than our superannuated Antonov. Compared with this rust bucket the aircraft was a paragon of modern engineering and fine maintenance. Most of the windows are broken, the window winders don't work, the floor and the roof are bare metal and heat pours in from various gaps to the engine compartment. Simply having us in the back seat clearly makes our driver and his sidekick very nervous. Only the glossy modern taxis in Cuba are licensed to convey foreigners. There wasn't one was at the domestic airport that night and it's pretty clear that having us on board is illegal and worrying.

To compound the difficulties our driver doesn't know where our hotel is, but fortunately by this time we know our way around Havana enough to point him in the right direction. He eventually drops us off round the corner from the hotel entrance, well out of view.

• • • •

There's one final pilgrimage to make in Havana. The Hemingway pilgrimage. I've already been bumping into Ernesto all over town. I've sipped a mojito – rum, lemon juice, sugar, soda, a big sprig of mint leaves, ice cubes, stir – in La Bodeguita del Medio, irrespective of the fact that my guidebook author has clearly taken a major dislike to the place. I've actually developed such a taste for mojitos (they are delicious) that I've probably indulged in a few too many of them in La Bodeguita, among other Cuban hostelries.

Scrawled on the wall of La Bodeguita is a message from the great writer himself that this is the place for mojitos, but that he prefers to take his daiquiris at El Floridita. We dutifully continue on to the elegantly old-fashioned El Floridita for dinner. The décor may have been old world, but the bill, when it comes, is right up to date. After two weeks in Cuba we've learnt to check the prices carefully since there's clearly a policy in touristy places of marking things up from the menu. Here a CUC$17 bottle of wine gets elevated to CUC$27 and although I am inclined to let the little elevations go (I can live with the CUC$4 meals that became CUC$5) this is a bit too much.

We'd also looked in at the Hotel Ambos Mundos, where Hemingway usually stayed in room 511. With his second wife, Pauline Pfeiffer, he was here on and off for six years during the 1930s. Even though the plot for *For Whom the Bell Tolls* was mapped out in this Old Havana hotel, the holy grail is Finca la Vigía, the house he bought in 1939, just outside of town. The name means Watchtower Farm and a taxi driver whisks us out there, explaining on the way the complicated paperwork he had to fill in for each trip, a government policy to ensure he doesn't make too much money.

'You can't go inside' is the first thing I'm told after I've paid the entry price, but that, it turns out, is unimportant. The house is surprisingly small and has plenty of windows so it's easy to see inside. What's even more surprising is that it's packed full, as if Hemingway had just popped out for a few bottles of rum, planning to be back in five minutes. The bookshelves are chock-full, the magazine racks are bulging, his clothes still hang in the closet, his Royal typewriter (he typed standing up) still rests on the stand by the bed.

Outside, the swimming pool is empty, which makes it hard to imagine Ava Gardner doing a few naked laps. Hemingway's fishing boat, *El Pilar*, is also on display, just like *Granma*, the ship that Castro used to return to Cuba to launch the revolution. *Granma* stands in a glass-walled showroom right in the centre of downtown Havana, along with many other items of revolutionary armoury. Hemingway had remarkably little to say about the revolution and, although a famous photo shows the revolutionary and the writer shaking hands after Castro won the cup that Hemingway had awarded for an annual game fishing tournament, he left Cuba soon after, never to return. A year later in Idaho he put his shotgun barrel in his mouth and it was all over.

Ernest's and Fidel's boats are a reminder that boating deaths are not uncommon for Cubans. They drown when their leaky craft go down en route to Florida. And would-be escapees don't just die on the 150-kilometre boat trip from Cuba to Miami. On Christmas Eve in 2000 the body of a teenager was discovered in a field near London's Gatwick Airport. He had fallen there when the undercarriage of a British Airways Boeing 777 was lowered as the aircraft was on its final approach after flying from Havana. The young Cuban had been hiding out in the wheel compartment. It wasn't the fall that killed him – he'd died from the cold and lack of oxygen many hours before he tumbled into a British field.

Nor was he alone. On Christmas Day, as the same aircraft took off to fly back across the Atlantic to Cancun in Mexico, the body of another Cuban teenager spilled out on to the runway. Freezing to death certainly hadn't featured in the escape plans of Alberto Vazquez, aged 17, and Michael Fonseca, aged 16. In fact they hadn't even intended to stowaway to Europe. What they had planned to do was certainly very risky, but not necessarily fatal. They'd climbed over the airport fence and hidden in the long grass beside the runway waiting for the departure of the American Airlines flight to Miami. When the aircraft turned for the start of its takeoff run the two boys intended to run across and climb up into the undercarriage compartment. The short trip to Miami would only take half an hour and the aircraft would not climb to its normal cruising altitude. It would be uncomfortable, it would be very cold, it was certainly stupidly dangerous – they could easily be crushed by the retracting wheels or fall out when the undercarriage was lowered – but with luck they would have got away with it… if they hadn't made the fatal error of mistaking one Boeing jetliner for another.

Thirty minutes to Miami was survivable, nine hours to London certainly wasn't. Cruising 10,000 feet higher than the summit of Mt Everest, there was almost no way they were going to survive the lack of oxygen and temperatures as low as –50°C. Stowaways do occasionally get away with such foolhardy escape attempts. In 1996 an Indian teenager fell from another British Airways aircraft as it approached Heathrow, but his brother survived the 10-hour trip from New Delhi. In 2000 a Tahitian stowaway managed to make it alive to Los Angeles in the undercarriage compartment of an Air France 747. Far more frequently, however, Third World stowaways die en route and their bodies are found aligned with some airport runway. The deaths of the two Cuban teenagers were the third known case of Cubans dying en route to Europe in 12 months.

• • • •

I have one more encounter with Cuba. Given the way everything about the place picks you up or drops you down, I'm happy that this final meeting should be another example of the Cuban upside. In March 2006 Maureen and I are in Pakistan, checking the post-earthquake situation with an aid group. As we head back down to Islamabad, the capital of the country, from the mountains, we pass a string of buses, packed full of Cubans.

120.

They're Cuban doctors and medical staff, departing Kashmir after months of work treating post-earthquake injuries. The huge earthquake hit northeastern Pakistan on 8 October 2005, killing 73,000 people, damaging or destroying 80 per cent of the buildings in large parts of the earthquake zone and leaving three million people homeless. The first Cubans arrived less than a week later – there would eventually be 2300 of them at 44 hospitals, the largest international contingent to come to Pakistan's aid.

There's no question the Cubans did a terrific job under extraordinarily difficult working conditions and hardly surprisingly there were some culture clashes between the freewheeling Cubans and conservative Islam.

'The Kashmiris were a little shocked at the male-female handholding and bare flesh at first,' said Marc Preston of Australian Aid International, 'but the Cubans soon fitted in and the cold weather loaded the clothes on.'

'What was more relevant was how strict Muslim attitudes affected the delivery of healthcare,' Conner Gorry, an American Cuba expert who went to Pakistan with the Cuban team, told me. 'I witnessed many examples of husbands denying permission to their wives for surgical procedures (sometimes life-saving) or taking them from intensive care units against doctors' orders, emergency medical triage consisting of men first, followed by children and finally women regardless of the severity of injury, or of women lying to male translators about medical conditions because religious-cultural norms prohibited them from talking to men about personal matters.

'What was most amazing to me was that the Cuban doctors and surgeons, nearly half of whom were female (precisely because of the religious restriction regarding female patients seeing male caregivers), treated so many quake victims in spite of all the differences (and the cold!).'

Amusingly, Castro had offered to send this same Cuban medical team in to another huge natural disaster just a month earlier: Hurricane Katrina in New Orleans.

'No thanks', said Mr Bush.

• • • •

Overall I didn't warm to Cuba. Oh, sure, Havana was every bit as beautiful as promised, the music was terrific, the people were friendly, travel was easy. And there was so much to be admired about what had been achieved in Cuba since the revolution – higher literacy and lower infant mortality than just about anywhere else in Latin America for starters. The literacy and infant mortality figures are not just good for a Third World country, they are right up at First World standard. Cuba's infant mortality figures compare more than favourably with the USA, but then there's no deprived underclass in Cuba. It's simply that nobody is very rich.

It's interesting to track the infant mortality figures over the years. It started to drop as soon as Batista got his marching orders and has fallen consistently ever since, except for a short rise when the Soviet Union collapsed and the Cuban economy went into free fall. There was probably some CIA operative watching those infant mortality figures rising and rubbing his or her hands with delight: 'See, the blockade is really working.'

On consecutive days in Baracoa and Santiago de Cuba our thoughts about the country were pulled in one direction then another.

'It's the 1950s American dream', we thought as we strolled Baracoa's streets one evening. Music, dancing, small groups talking animatedly in the central square, everything a long way from the counter-view of America as a place of schoolroom massacres, urban drug problems and drive-by shootings. Of course, everything was a little run-down and rough at the edges, but there's a price for anything.

I really liked Santiago de Cuba. We whiled away the evening listening to a band play in the bar of our elegant old hotel and even bought a CD of their music. Round the corner I got the cheapest haircut I've had in years.

The next day two women, one a doctor and one an architect, brought the downside of the Cuba story home to us.

'There are shortages of everything', complained Ana Moreno.

'And so often there's no real work, but you have to spend endless hours scrabbling for hard currency', continued Mireya Quiroz. 'You have to get dollars to make life liveable. And there's no fish because it's all sold to tourists.'

This was the division that I really disliked, that made me edgy about the whole Cuban experience. The Cubans in their miserable cafés lining up to pay pesos for miserable-looking food while next door our place is air-conditioned and brightly lit and, while the food we (and the richer Cubans) pay for with real money may not be brilliant, it's a hell of a lot better than they're getting.

The beaches? I'd rather not think about them. The 'us and them' nature of Cuban beach resorts really made me feel uncomfortable. Dollar-paying European and Canadian tourists on one side of the fence, Cubans resolutely kept on the other. At the end of the day that was the aspect of Cuba I most disliked. Bright lights, air-con and stacked shelves for those with dollars to spend; gloom and Eastern Europe in 1950s ambience for everybody else.

Who is to blame? Well, America could certainly shoulder some. It is the only country that really thinks of Cuba as a Bad Land. Sure, Cuba is Communist, but so is China and America goes out of its way to be nice to China. So is Vietnam, and they'd won the war – but Vietnam is back in the good books. Certainly Cuba is a military dictatorship, but nobody ever said you have to be democratic to get the US seal of approval. It's hard to think of a less democratic nation than Saudi Arabia and there have been plenty of very nasty dictatorships in Latin America that have not just enjoyed American approval, but have also been installed or propped up with American dollars and American military might. Terrorism? Well, that's never been a Cuban policy and the days of Cuban troops acting as Soviet surrogates in Angola or Somalia are long gone.

In fact it's American policy that has kept Castro in power. The Cubans may have their doubts about their government, but they sure as hell don't want George Bush telling them how to run the place. If Bush made friends with Fidel, he'd probably fall over the following week.

All in all it's very hard to figure out exactly why the US government bears such a grudge against Cuba, but then just how effective is the US grudge in any case? There are plenty of European, Asian and Latin American companies ready and willing to do business with Cuba. Nobody misses Chevies and Fords when they can get Hyundais and Peugeots. There are plenty of Spanish hotel companies ready to build hotels along the Cuban beaches and no shortage of European and Canadian tourists ready to stretch out on the sun lounges. The Golden Arches may not have appeared in Havana, but if you want a Coca-Cola the Mexican bottling plant has had no trouble providing the pause that refreshes.

Perhaps you can blame 25 per cent of Cuba's plight on stupid American policies, but the other 75 per cent? That's all down to Fidel.

IRAN

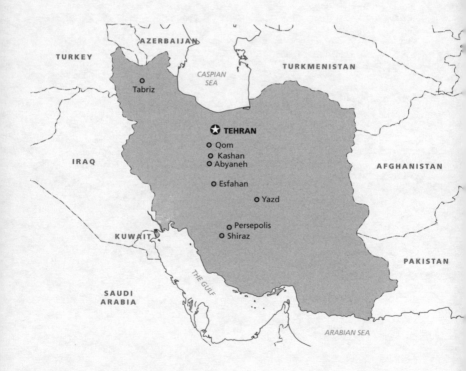

TURKEY

AZERBAIJAN

CASPIAN
SEA

TURKMENISTAN

Tabriz

⭐ TEHRAN

IRAQ

Qom
Kashan
Abyaneh

Esfahan

Yazd

AFGHANISTAN

KUWAIT

Persepolis
Shiraz

PAKISTAN

THE GULF

SAUDI
ARABIA

ARABIAN SEA

The Paykan swerved to the side of the road and a portly gentleman levered himself out from the driver's seat and steamed across the pavement towards me, like the Titanic on a pressing engagement with an iceberg.

I was in Iran and I was about to be kidnapped.

'I am a guide. I speak English', announced Ahmad Pourseyedl as he grabbed my arm. 'Come, we will go to the Fin Gardens.'

There was no arguing. The fact that I had only arrived in Kashan half an hour earlier and was on my way out to dinner only allowed me to put off the inevitable for 12 hours. The next morning I belonged to Ahmad. In fact I had become part of Ahmad's family. At each of the beautiful traditional homes for which Kashan will, one day, be justifiably famous, the ticket seller was expected – no, commanded – to offer me the family discount.

It was a typically Iranian encounter. I cannot remember the last country I visited where there was such an overwhelming urge to make you feel welcome, to roll out the Persian carpet, to include you in the family gatherings. That night, in the Khan-e Tabatabei, a fine old house where the central courtyard became a restaurant for the evening, the family at the next table introduced themselves. 'You are by yourself – why don't you join us?'

Walking through the park beside the Zayandeh River in Esfahan a couple of days earlier an older woman had called out from her park bench: 'Do you speak English? Come talk with us.' In Yazd I was intercepted by three young men and ushered back, after I walked straight past the entrance to the Bagh-e Doulat Abad gardens. One of them was keen to practise his already excellent English and when I told them I lived in Melbourne I was reminded, yet again, that the best thing Australia ever did to foster better relations with the Islamic Republic was not to win a football match. In late 1997 Iran drew with Australia in a World Cup preliminary in Melbourne, thus ensuring a place for Iran in the 1998 World Cup. Repeatedly the mere mention of the word 'Melbourne' brings a smile to an Iranian face. That night three old women, comfortably seated feasting on a watermelon on the roadside in a narrow laneway in the old city of Yazd, offer me a slice as I pass by.

This is what life is like on the Axis of Evil.

• • • •

Apart from Albania, all of my Bad Lands put you through hoops of some sort before you can get in the door. Even Cuba requires you to have a 'tourist card'. Why is it that I can just front up in the United States, Japan, France, Italy and many other countries that half the world would dearly like to call home, while countries from which half the population would simply like to escape, and where nobody is queuing up to find a way in, go to all this effort to restrict your entry?

On paper – or on my computer screen – Iran wasn't all that bad. You could even download their visa application form from the embassy website, and issuing a visa would only take five days. Or so the website claimed. Ten days later I phoned the embassy to ask what was happening.

'We have sent the application to Tehran', the helpful official explained. 'You must wait at least two weeks.'

'So much for five days', I thought as I asked to have my visa-less passport returned. I had to go to Japan at the weekend.

'I've got a British passport as well', I suggested. 'If I applied for a visa with that passport, you could be preparing it while I am in Japan next week.' Their website had indicated that British passport-holders needed to allow two weeks for their visa applications, as opposed to the fictional five days for Australians.

'Oh, you should not do that', the still-helpful official replied. 'We have a great deal of difficulty getting visas for British citizens. You will probably have to wait two months. But we will process your application while you are away. If you send your passport back when you return, we will only have to stick the visa in the passport.'

And they were as good as their word.

A couple of weeks later I board a shiny new Emirates Airbus from Dubai, zip across the Gulf and head almost directly north to Tehran, sipping a glass of wine, which I assume, wrongly, will be the last alcohol I'll see for a couple of weeks.

In Tehran I grab my bag off the carousel, my passport is stamped, I clear customs and I'm in Iran. I have made absolutely no plans, not even booked a hotel for the night. I'm just going to cruise into the city and see what happens.

The three young women at Tehran airport's tourist desk have their hair discreetly covered, but otherwise we could have been at Heathrow or JFK. Clearly tourists don't turn up every day, certainly not without even a hotel booking. They joke about not doing this too often, comment that they don't know the hotel I've pulled out of my guidebook, phone through to book me a room and finally wish me a pleasant stay in Iran. It's the first of many contacts I'll have with the opposite sex in Iran and a firm reminder that this is not the Arab world. The very idea that you might be asking a woman to book a hotel in Saudi Arabia is inconceivable.

I'm intercepted at the terminal door. 'You need a taxi? Come, I will take you into Tehran', he announces in good English.

'OK, what's the fare?' I reply.

'The usual fare', he evades, trying to grab my bag to seal the deal.

'Ten thousand', he eventually allows, when pushed.

I've got a lot of ten thousands. Back in the baggage-claim area I'd changed US$100 into rials and quickly realised it was a good thing I'd not changed US$200. The biggest rial note is 10,000, worth a smidge more than one US dollar. So I had a pocketful of ten thousands – 84 of them to be precise.

'No, 10 like this', he admits, holding a finger over the final zero to indicate that he was performing the most standard Iranian 'confuse the foreigner' trick, quoting prices in *toman*. For some reason many prices in Iran are not in rials, but in a totally imaginary unit known as a *toman* or 10 rials. So prices can always be out by 10 and my would-be-driver's 'usual fare' of 10,000 is really 100,000 rial.

The next day, with my price sensitivity not yet keyed in, I'm amazed at how low the prices are in a fancy restaurant until I notice the T after each figure. Suddenly main courses are US$12 to $15, not $1.20 to $1.50. Even a week later I am still occasionally getting tripped up. 'That's remarkably cheap', I think, then rapidly conclude that at 10 times the cost it wasn't such a bargain.

'There's your driver', says the taxi-kiosk dispatcher, taking 35,000 rials from me and writing out a chit.

We sling my bag in the back of, disappointingly, a Peugeot rather than a Paykan, and head out into Tehran's terrible traffic. Nothing written about Tehran can avoid mentioning that this is a contender for any 'world's worst traffic' award, so let's get it out of the way. The traffic in Tehran is appalling. It's not just the volume, it's also the crazily exuberant driving style and the often-battered vehicles challenging for their space in the jam. It seemed bad on my first visit to Tehran, way back in 1972, but it's undeniably far worse now. Seoul, Bangkok (before it was cleaned up), Manila, Cairo, Riyadh, you name it – Tehran is always the winner.

I have a special affection for Iran's national car, the Paykan, or 'Arrow'. Thirty-five years ago, in what seems like a previous life, I was a young engineer with the Rootes Group car manufacturers in Coventry. I worked on the old Hillman Hunter, a project known in-house as Arrow. Rootes, taken over by Chrysler just before I joined them and bankrupted not long after I left, managed to sell not just the car but a whole car-manufacturing plant to the Iranians during the Shah's era and in a remarkably short time the sturdy Paykan flooded the Iranian market.

In Britain production of the old Hillmans and their assorted clones ground to a halt decades ago, but in Iran they just kept rolling off the assembly line. By the 1990s the old Paykan was years out of date – a clunky, polluting, unsafe menace and completely gutless compared with modern vehicles. Every year the government announced that Paykan production was about to end and a year later they were still going. Now it finally looks like the Paykan era is about to finish, but there are so many out there they will remain the most popular car for many years.

There's something else blended into the traffic maelstrom. Apart from the piss-weak Paykans, a mix of more modern cars, lumbering buses and weaving motorcycles, there are also suicidal pedestrians. There seems to be a simple trade-off agreed to between wheeled and foot traffic. The wheeled stuff will totally ignore pedestrian crossings and in return the pedestrians will totally ignore traffic lights. In fact pedestrians totally ignore traffic. They simply walk out into the road, barely glancing at the cars, buses and motorcycles bearing down on them (often from both directions since one-way signs don't stop Tehrani drivers from proceeding in the wrong direction). Crossing the road is strictly dog-eat-dog. Even a stooped-over little old lady will be ignored – there's absolutely no compassion. Yet if you march out blindly, they'll stop.

Sometimes you'll see little informal groups gathering by the roadside, waiting for a critical mass to form before they surge collectively out into the turmoil. 'If there are enough of us, we're less likely to be mown down' seems to be the theory.

I have a hotel to head to. The last time I was in Tehran was way back in October 1978, in the tumultuous slow-motion months as the Shah tumbled in freeze-frame off his throne and the Ayatollah and his cohorts marched back in after a long vacation in neighbouring Iraq (although the actual return was from France). On that occasion my taxi dropped me outside the Amir Kabir Hotel, a long-term backpacker favourite, around midnight. The streets were eerily deserted (empty streets are always much more threatening than crowded ones) and the Amir Kabir was equally empty – shuttered, closed down, out of business.

I had wandered the streets and quickly found a slightly better substitute for the threadbare old Amir Kabir. This time I know what to expect. The Atlas Hotel is a comfortable midrange place, although the toilet in my quite modern bathroom is squat style.

• • • •

The next morning I stroll a couple of blocks east from my hotel to the 'Den of US Espionage'. The former US embassy was seized by the revolutionary Iranians in 1979 and held for 444 days, substantially contributing to Jimmy Carter's re-election defeat. Today it's occupied by a hard-line militia group and the wall around the compound is decorated with anti-American slogans and murals including a painting of a skull-faced Statue of Liberty.

132.

The den of espionage moniker may sound like overheated Ayatollah rhetoric, but beneath the ex-embassy building is the basement bunker where, in 1953, CIA operatives, led by Kermit Roosevelt, grandson of Theodore 'big stick' Roosevelt, plotted to bring down the elected government of Mohammad Mossadegh and install the last Shah, Mohammed Reza. In 1951 Mossadegh had been *Time* magazine's Man of the Year for standing up to international oil companies to protect his people's rights. The 1953 coup attempt flopped and the Shah had to flee to Rome, but more money changed hands and three days later a second go ended democracy in Iran for the next quarter of a century. It was hardly the CIA at its most effective, but then we've become used to seeing the CIA at its least effective in recent years.

In subsequent years the CIA got better at overthrowing democratically elected leaders and installing somebody more in line with the US view of the world. Patrice Lumumba of the Congo went in 1960, Salvador Allende in 1973 and many people also blame the dismissal of Indonesia's Soekarno in 1966 on the CIA. Those attempting to whitewash the takeover of the US embassy insist the Iranians feared the embassy was plotting another coup to reinstall the hated Shah.

I have a contact at the British embassy (let's call him Graham) and after checking my emails at an internet café across the road I zigzag through the concrete barriers and enter the fortified embassy compound.

'We're the American embassy proxy', Graham explains.

'If there was an American embassy, they'd be stoning them and chanting "death to America" outside their walls. Unfortunately we stand in for them.

'Of course, the protests are all very well organised', he continues. 'The police could easily stop them completely and as it is they always move in before things get too heavy. Although we did have 80 windows broken last week.'

Despite which there is a long visa-applications queue.

'That's a bit of tit-for-tat', he explains. 'If we're fussier about the visas we issue, you can be certain they'll make it more difficult for Brits to get visas for Iran.'

As we cross the compound he points out the house where Roosevelt, Churchill and Stalin held their famous conference in November–December 1943, a meeting that began the process of dividing the world into competing spheres of influence through the Cold War years. It was Germany's invasion of Poland in 1939 that kicked off World War II, but in Tehran in 1943 Poland was abandoned to Stalin's tender mercies.

Over dinner one evening Stalin proposed that the German problem could be permanently resolved by simply executing 50,000 to 100,000 of the top-ranking German military once Germany was defeated. Roosevelt, not realising that Stalin's proposal was deadly serious, countered that perhaps 49,000 would be enough.

'The table they sat around for that discussion is still in the room where they met', says Graham.

I spend the rest of that first day and most of the second wandering the city, at times somewhat haphazardly, although I do manage to fit in the National Museum, the Islamic Museum, the Carpet Museum and the Contemporary Arts Gallery. Tehran is really not as bad as its reputation. Sure, the traffic is chaotic and the pollution can be throat-burning, but there's lots of green. The city has plenty of parks and almost every street seems to be lined with trees and the jube, the water channel that is a feature of so many Persian cities. Even in the July heat the mountains to the north of Tehran are still snow-capped.

After a couple of days in Tehran I'm also beginning to get a feel for the female fashion question.

On the one hand there are very definite rules about what women must wear. They not only stipulate the rules for chador design (nearly knee-length and baggy), the colour (black) and even the thickness (winter weight) but also the rules for shoes (black, clumpy) and socks (black, thick). We don't want to see any sexy ankles peeking out from below a chador.

In reality liberal interpretation of the rules seems very possible. Of course, there is safety in numbers. When there are lots of people (and there are certainly lots of people in Tehran), then an individual can get away with more. So, although black predominates, there are sudden splashes of colour. And as long as they wear something that covers them up, even a sweatshirt, these fashionistas seem to be OK.

There are many women in trousers and long, tight-fitting versions of the tunics known as manteaus. The headscarf solution is particularly interesting. I notice some women in caps, rather like the cap with a sun-protection back-flap that someone might wear in the West, and another with what looks like a bathing cap. This is a long way from Saudi Arabia!

One woman goes striding by in an orange coat, with matching orange scarf and orange shoes, looking very chic. If I'd seen her in New York or Paris, I might have thought 'Hey, an interesting look', certainly not 'Islamic dress-code'.

It's funny. In France girls and women fight to be allowed to wear scarves. Here many women would like the right to discard them. Well, if Iran can force foreign women to wear a scarf covering their hair, why shouldn't France require schoolchildren not to wear them? It would be amusing if there was something silly for men to wear, a spiky, frilled collar perhaps, or if men were compelled to wear a winter overcoat all the time. Beards are definitely out, I've been told. Makes you look as if you're sucking up to the mullahs.

Before I arrived in Tehran I'd made an Iranian contact through a university course in Australia and I've been invited to a party this evening. It's in a classy area of Tehran and dress-wise, once we're indoors and the doors are closed, things are immediately very different. The men look the same, but the women, Iranians as well as foreigners, suddenly ditch the scarves and appear in jeans, T-shirts, singlets. Hair and bare arms, never seen on the street, suddenly appear.

This could easily be a party in the West. There's even a bar... and booze. **135.**

'Where does the beer come from?' I ask Mansoor.

'One of the religious militia groups', he explains. 'We have several different militia groups apart from the regular army. This one has the monopoly on beer imports from Turkey. They'll bring in a container of "arms", which is actually Efes beer', he continues, handing me another cold can.

It could easily be the same revolutionary guard militia group that shut down Tehran's new Imam Khomeini Airport 10 minutes after its long-delayed opening in 2004 because they didn't like the Turkish-Austrian consortium that was going to run the airport. They thought the consortium might have connections to Israel. It was a storm in a teacup remarkably like the American concern about a Dubai company running US container ports two years later.

I'm being so charmed in so many different directions by the people I've met in Tehran that it brings me up short when an Irish woman explains in colourful detail what a hassle the men can be and how she has put a great deal of effort into learning Farsi insults to hurl back at the men who come on to her.

'Telling them "Go fuck your mother, it's cheaper" works pretty well,' she explains, 'or "I'd rather sleep with your sister". If all else fails, there's always, "You've got a willy – I'd like a penis".'

None of this sounds like particularly good advice. Perhaps like me she's had a few too many cans of Efes tonight. It's 2am by the time the taxi drops me off at my hotel and I have trouble walking an absolutely straight line up the stairs to my room.

• • • •

When Omar Khayyam wrote 'a loaf of bread, a jug of wine and thou', he was probably dreaming about a jug of Shiraz. Sadly, although Shiraz, that dark, peppery red, is popular worldwide (and particularly in Australia), you won't find any Shiraz in Shiraz. Or, openly at least, anywhere else in the strictly teetotal Islamic Republic of Iran. Fortunately

I did sample some Shiraz Shiraz way back on my first visit, sitting in the back of a VW Kombi at an Esfahan campsite.

Shiraz may be off the wine list, but Omar Khayyam was never the favourite poet in any case. His popularity in the West – all that 'moving finger moving on' verse – is in part due to Edward Fitzgerald, who put a lot of effort into translating and promoting him. In Iran Omar Khayyam's reputation rests on his mastery of maths rather than his prowess as a poet. Sa'di and Hafez, both of whom are buried in Shiraz, are the big names in a country where poetry is still important.

I start my short tour of Iran in a new Iran Air Airbus, which zips me south to Shiraz. The ticket for the London–Paris, San Francisco–Los Angeles or Sydney–Melbourne equivalent distance costs about US$30. It was a late night and an early start and I've got a fine hangover to go with it. Something I had not expected in the supposedly alcohol-free Islamic Republic.

Quite apart from the two poets' tombs, Shiraz has a fine old fort, some interesting mosques and mausoleums and the Bagh-e Eram or 'Garden of Paradise'. By lunchtime I've made my way to Hafez's tomb, which stands in a beautiful garden and features a popular teahouse where you can sit around, puff on a *qalyan* (water pipe), sip *chay* (tea) and quote the master. Sipping *chay* is definitely an important activity. Much of life takes place around a teapot. I trace my 30-year love affair with tea straight back to my first visit to Turkey and Iran in the 1970s. Tea was a stewed, milked, sugared affair until I discovered it could come in tiny glasses and, while sugar was on offer, it wasn't necessary.

I'm lunching on a healthy bowl of *abgusht* – ab means water and gusht means meat – and that's essentially what this utilitarian meal consists of: a clear broth with meat, potatoes, tomatoes and beans or lentils. *Abgusht* has a reputation as the poor person's meal, but it also provides the basis for the popular Iranian saying, 'Add more water to the *abgusht*', because if unexpected guests turn up you can always stretch the abgusht by diluting

137.

it. Like any popular dish, it has its subtle charms; correct seasoning and long, slow stewing are what makes a stand-out *abgusht*. It's also known as *dizi*, from the earthenware pot it's served in, and often, as here, it comes with a pestle-like device to mash up the ingredients.

That afternoon I visit the Bagh-e Eram gardens and then, with what seems like half the population of Shiraz, take a leisurely stroll out to the west of the city along Dr Chamran Boulevard. It's Friday night and it's a Shiraz ritual to picnic in one of the parks lining this long street.

Iran may not have many tourists – there were far more in the early 1970s when I made my first visit – but that hasn't stopped Iranians putting a great deal of effort and money into restoring old buildings as hotels and restaurants. I'll find more in Yazd and Kashan, but my first encounter in Shiraz is impressive. The Hammam-e Vaikal is an old bathhouse, or hammam, restored as a teahouse and restaurant. The beautiful octagonal room has a pool bubbling in the centre, and there's a musical trio playing a violin, a tabla-like drum and a strange stringed instrument to one side. The food is excellent, the setting is wonderful. Nor am I the only tourist. There's a cheerful group from Hong Kong, half-energetic Hong Kong Chinese, and the rest an assortment of Western expats.

Shiraz is interesting enough, but the real attraction is 50 kilometres away where the ancient ruins of Persepolis perch on a plateau below a cliff face. Darius I (the Great) began construction of his showpiece city in 518 BC. Its glory days ended in 330 BC when Alexander the Great invaded Persia, sacked the city and for good measure burnt it down. Historians are uncertain if the destruction of Persepolis was the unfortunate result of a drunken party that got out of hand or deliberate revenge for Xerxes' destruction of Athens 150 years earlier.

Today things move faster. It took less than two years from the destruction of the Twin Towers to the trashing of Baghdad. Alexander may have been slower in exacting revenge, but he was also somewhat more organised than our modern-day Middle East invaders. He cleared

Persepolis out before it was burnt. Signs at the site note that emptying the Treasury took 3000 camels and mules to cart off '12,000 talents' of silver. I've no idea how much a talent is worth, but it certainly sounds impressive.

It's the bas-reliefs that really tell the Persepolis story and the impressive Apadana Stairway has the best of them. The 23 subject nations who turned up to show their respects march in line after bas-relief line, with gifts like a lioness and two cubs (from the Elamite delegation), two humped camels (from the Bactrians among others), a buffalo (from the Babylonians), a humped bull (from the Gandarians of the Kabul Valley, the Buddhist folk who carved out the Bamiyan Buddhas), two horse-chariots (from both the Lydians and Libyans), bags of gold (from the Indians of the Sindh – even then gold was important in India) and a small giraffe and elephant tusks (from the Ethiopians).

Apart from Persepolis, we also visit the ancient city site of Pasargadae and the impressive rock tombs of Naqsh-e Rostam and Naqsh-e Rajab with their beautiful bas-reliefs cut into the cliff faces. It's been a long day even before I take a taxi to the Yord Restaurant near a village outside of Shiraz that night. The restaurant is named after the traditional nomad tent set up to house it during the summer months. My hotel is uncertain it exists at all, then has trouble working out how I should get there and my taxi driver has a great deal of difficulty finding it even with their written and verbal instructions.

The good food and traditional music performances make the effort worthwhile, but getting back is even worse. There are no taxis so I stumble along a path through the forest until I get to the village where there are also no taxis. I'm not even certain which direction it is to Shiraz, but as usual Iranian kindness kicks in. When I stick my thumb out to try to hitch a ride, a Paykan pulls over almost immediately and the driver takes me not just back to Shiraz, but right to my hotel door.

• • • •

I'd intended to take a bus for the 450-kilometre trip to Yazd, but Hassan, my Persepolis taxi driver, had been such a friendly guide I decide the US$70 splurge for air-con comfort and the opportunity to make some stops en route was justified in the 40°C heat. We cruise off with his Chris de Burgh tape providing the wholly inappropriate soundtrack and his nine-year-old daughter along for the ride.

Yazd features a Zoroastrian fire temple and Zoroastrian Towers of Silence where, once upon a time, vultures would pick over the dead bodies. A few days later in Esfahan I'll encounter another interesting reminder that there are other religions in the Islamic Republic.

Water features everywhere in Iran, flowing along street edges in the jube (open drains), cascading down channels in gardens and parks, sprinkling in fountains and appearing in pools in the open courtyards found in so many traditional old houses. It's also dispensed with remarkable civic generosity. In museums, parks, mosques – even along every length of street – there's usually a public refrigerated water dispenser, an Iranian version of a drinking fountain. In the big cities piped water is safe to drink (I certainly got through plenty of it in my summer visit to Iran) and a happy consequence of this ready availability of cold drinking water is that Iran is not afflicted with the litter of empty plastic water bottles that plagues so many developing countries.

Yazd is a centre for the underground irrigation channels known as *qanat* and there's even a Water Museum, which explains all about them and, of course, features a *qanat* running through a subterranean chamber.

The city's water channels may be hidden from view, but examples of its other traditional architectural feature are very evident. Any worthwhile old home is topped by what looks like a cross between a stylish chimney and a lookout tower. This is a *badgir*, a wind tower cunningly designed to catch a passing breeze and funnel it down over a pool of water in the house to provide a surprisingly effective form of natural air-conditioning. Standing under a *badgir*, you can feel the cool downward breeze and, at the appropriate spot, the upward return flow. They are found not only in this area of Iran, but also on the Arab side of the Gulf (they feature in some fine old houses in Dubai), in some villages in western Afghanistan and in the Sindh region of Pakistan. Every old house of note around the town is topped by a fine example, and a small reservoir, where the wind cools the water, is known as Shesh Badgir, from the six towers that ring the domed reservoir.

Restoring and reopening traditional old *badgir*-equipped houses as hotels and restaurants has become a local craze. I stay at the handsome Malek-o Tojjar, a fine example of one of these old houses. That afternoon, sipping tea in the courtyard café and reading *Reading Lolita in Tehran* (I had to use that repetition somehow), Azar Nafisi's novel about a reading group dipping into forbidden Western literature, I'm invited over to join a real reading group. The four Yazd university students, three of them female, are keen to practise their English and talk about the English language books they're studying.

This so clearly isn't Saudi Arabia. Young couples openly hold hands, women shake hands with you, talk to you and smile at you. In Saudi not only is there virtually no opportunity to talk to a Saudi woman – even if you did you'd see no more than her eyes, and possibly not even those.

Despite (or perhaps because of) their should-be-camouflaging attire, Iranian women are always eyeing you off. It's all shy smiles and seductive glances. While I was photographing the passing traffic in front of a mosque that evening, a woman, sitting behind her boyfriend on a motorcycle, tosses me a wink and a wave; later that evening three old ladies chorus 'hello' from their late-evening watermelon feast in an old city back alley.

Dinner tonight is at the Silk Road, another photogenic hotel in a renovated traditional old house, like the one I'm staying in. Once again the courtyard centres around a pool, the architecture is beautiful, the evening light glows, and the *badgir* rises up as a backdrop to one end.

Some of the guests and diners sit at tables, with some of the tables at knee height and others at a normal level. Others, like me, lounge back on wide, carpeted, sofa-like affairs, sitting cross-legged and sideways, leaning back against the armrest. When your meal is served it's arrayed in front of you, in the centre of the 'sofa'. If there are two of you, then you face each other. The sofa is wide enough to accommodate four.

I'm served some tea and sweets, but no food emerges from the kitchen until well after 9pm.

The Iranians clearly rival the Spanish when it comes to eating late. It's no problem because simply watching what's going on is a delight. There's a buzz of happy activity – families, individuals, a handful of tourists but mostly Iranians. Occasionally people climb upstairs for the view and we can see them silhouetted on the flat-topped roof. Lots of people smile over at me, stop to exchange a few words, inquire about my impressions of Iran or offer a 'welcome' if nothing more. These people are so energetic, so cheerful, so unlike what the media would have us believe about Iranians.

• • • •

I skipped the bus trip from Shiraz to Yazd, but I do opt for bus travel on the next leg to Esfahan. The bus is air-conditioned, comfortable (it even has an on-board toilet) and costs about US$3 for the 300-kilometre trip.

This single city alone could justify a trip to Iran, but it's hard to decide whether the prime attraction is the magnificent sweep of the Imam Square, with its perimeter of shopping arcades and its breathtaking blue-tiled mosques, or the gentle curve of the Zayandeh River with its multi-arched bridges and fringing parkland.

Five of the 11 bridges that span the river are elegant old affairs. One of my favourite photographs from the trip Maureen and I made across Asia in 1972 is of Maureen sitting on the river edge with the double-level Khaju Bridge in the background. She is in an outfit, quite respectable though it was, that would have got her instantly arrested by the Morality Police in 21st-century Iran.

I wander down one side of the river, pausing for tea in the middle of the-river teahouse built into the Chubi Bridge. Sipping tea and puffing a waterpipe in a teahouse is a favourite Esfahan activity. The Chubi Bridge teahouse is decorated with carpets, pictures and an eclectic collection of lamps and lights hanging from the arched ceiling. It's easy to see why it's reputed to be the most appealing in the city.

I sit in a window alcove where a tray of tea is instantly brought to me, equally quickly followed by the standard Q and As from the waiter.

'Where are you from?'

'Australia.'

'What is your name?'

'Tony.'

'My name is Mohammed. Do you like Iran?'

'Iran is wonderful, especially Esfahan.'

'Welcome.'

Mid-afternoon the teahouse is busy. The waiter quickly returns to my end of the bay with a waterpipe for the attractive young woman in the next alcove who, like me, is scribbling in a notebook.

An hour or so later, walking up the other side of the river, I make another tea stop in the island teahouse just downriver from the Si-o-Seh or Bridge of 33 Arches. The riverside parks are busy with people sitting on the grass and young couples strolling along the riverbank holding hands.

An old woman waves me over to the park bench where she is sitting with some friends. 'Do you speak English?' she asks. 'Come talk with us.'

Finally I walk back past my hotel to the main square for yet another pot of tea, this time in a teahouse perched beside the bazaar entrance gate at the north end of the square. A family asks me to pose with them in a photograph, standing on the teahouse balcony with the long sweep of the square as a backdrop.

As the sun drops lower and the temperature cools, the square is full of evening activity. Once again that Persian passion for spreading out a rug on any patch of grass and having a picnic comes into play. The French, with their equivalent passion for 'keep off the grass' signs, would totally disapprove.

The next day I start with the square, walking past the shops, dropping in to the Sheikh Lotfollah and Imam Mosques and exploring the Ali Qapu Palace. The 'square' is actually a long rectangle and cars are strictly restricted to the northern 20 per cent. The remainder is vehicle-free.

The Sheikh Lotfollah Mosque is a little jewel box, so intricate and detailed it's hard to believe it's a building, not something you can just pick up and carry away. There's the trademark Persian blue and turquoise tile-work, but it's also tiled in green-white-gold. In contrast the Imam Mosque is the whole damn Tiffany's. Big and slightly odd, the entrance forms the end of the square, facing straight down the plaza, but inside the building skews off to the right in order to face Mecca. The front is just a front.

On the balcony of the Ali Qapu Palace, with the square spread out below us, I meet a young Iranian-American couple. Hassan and Sanaz live in Los Angeles, a city with probably the biggest Iranian population in the USA. He left Iran when he was a child, before the revolution, and has never been back before. She left 18 years ago, after the revolution.

'I was expecting it to be much worse', Sanaz admits. 'I think it's actually improved since I left.'

'But everybody complains', Hassan adds. 'I was expecting some people to dislike the system, but everybody I speak to – taxi drivers, farmers, you name it – complains. In some ways they've just swapped a crown for a turban.

'Of course, people always want change. Last Thursday we went to Jaam-e Jam in North Tehran. It's a shopping centre, very popular with young people and on Thursday afternoon they come out to show off.'

I have this immediate vision of Yoyogi Park at Harajuku in the centre of Tokyo, where on Sundays the cos-play-zoku (the costume-play-tribe) appears.

'It's weird', ponders Hassan. 'Young guys with rings in their eyebrows and girls clearly pushing it as far as they can, with very tight and almost transparent manteaus, scarves falling off to show their hair, lots of make-up. I'd like to have taken some photographs, but they'd probably not want their sins recorded.'

I swap hotels, moving across the road from an economical backpacker place to the expensive, if not exactly luxurious, Abbasi Hotel, occupying an old caravanserai. Last time in Esfahan, over 30 years ago, the Abbasi was way out of my price range and I certainly wanted to try it this time.

After changing hotels I do a long walking tour from the Chehel Sotun Palace through to the Jameh Mosque, then back through the bazaar to the main square to make the requisite visit to some carpet shops, followed by a visit to the Hasht Behest Palace before jumping in a taxi to cross the river to visit the group of Armenian churches in the affluent Jolfa area with its elegant cafés and glossy shops. This quarter of the city is a reminder, like the Zoroastrian temples in Yazd, that the Islamic Republic is not exclusively Islamic. Once again it underlines how different Iran is from Saudi Arabia. Only the Mary Church in Jolfa is open so I'll have to come back tomorrow to visit the Vank Cathedral, but I stop in at a surprisingly edgy shopping centre with lots of hot fashions, make-up and music.

I've done so much running around I'm exhausted and it's heading towards sunset by the time I get back to the Imam Square. At the south end of the square the sun is down and the floodlit blue tiles of the huge Imam Mosque have an eye-catching glow. A carpet dealer intercepts me and after a short sales pitch switches to tour guide and suggests I should have another look at the mosque.

'If you have seen it in daylight, you will find it quite different now that night has fallen,' he suggests, 'and you can go in now for free. They don't charge tourists in the evening.'

Unfortunately a guard stops me entering.

'It's prayer time', he explains. 'You cannot go in.'

Instantly an animated discussion starts up among the men sitting around him. Within minutes he relents. 'They all say you must see the mosque by night', he explains. 'If you keep over to one side, you will not disturb anybody. Go ahead.'

They're right. The floodlit blaze of blue, turquoise, yellow and gold stands out with razor-cut clarity against the inky sky.

• • • •

The next morning there's the shaking minarets to quake at, an amazing old pigeon-house sited in the middle of a traffic roundabout to see, and the extravagantly painted frescoes of the Vank Cathedral to admire before I head off to Kashan.

I have a car and driver again because there are some stops to make en route to Kashan. Today's major diversion is to Abyaneh. The old village's twisting lanes and mud architecture have brought it Unesco recognition, but not yet many tourists. If it was in some exotic corner of France or Spain, every other house would be a café or craft shop. Here the mosque is closed, there's one solitary little counter selling a handful of souvenirs, and there are no other shops, no place selling drinks, no restaurant.

Between the village and Kashan there's a brief encounter with that other Iran, the one that features in the press and TV much more often than beautiful hotels and friendly people.

146.

'It's a nuclear research centre', my driver explains as we pass anti-aircraft gun emplacements beside the road and half-buried buildings.

In Kashan the driver drops me off at my hotel, a mundane affair after my luxurious interlude in Esfahan and the beautiful old houses of Yazd, and I emerge to take a pre-dinner stroll. I only take a few steps before a Paykan swings in to the side of the road. A portly gentleman leaps – or would do, if his bulk hadn't prevented him – out of the car and grabs my arm. Ahmad Pourseyedi, my Kashan kidnapper, has me in his grip. Arguing is out of the question. I can put him off, but he is an irresistible object, impossible to simply reject.

'OK, we'll meet right here at 9am tomorrow', I finally agree. I am very reluctant to tell him which hotel I am at. 'If I don't turn up, then you know I can't make it,' I continue, 'but I'll definitely try to be here at 9am.'

My kidnapping postponed for 12 hours, I dine at the Delpazir Restaurant. It's become the restaurant in Kashan that all overseas visitors go to because it's run by Englishwoman Jane Modarresian and her Iranian partner. They still have the Persian restaurant they established in the London suburb of Mitcham, but they decided to move to Kashan because they thought it would be a better, safer environment for their three children, two boys and a girl. Sounds remarkable? Well, I heard precisely the same story from an American woman and her Iranian husband when I met them in Tehran.

When the American-Iranian couple's son, born in the USA and growing up there for the first eight years of his life, returned to the States 10 years later, he travelled around the country, stayed with relations, worked in various odd jobs. And then returned to Iran, because he preferred it.

Coming out of my hotel in the morning, Ahmad's trusty Paykan is parked right outside. He'd clearly deduced I must have been staying close to where he'd found me the previous evening.

'Ahmad, you're right on time', I announce.

'Yes,' he agrees, 'but how do you know my name? I didn't tell you my name last night.'

'You're Ahmad Pourseyedi', I counter. 'Oh, I have ways of knowing these things.'

At our morning reunion I have managed to provide him with a puzzle that would intrigue him for our whole time together. Completely by accident I'd bumped into the 'charming old rogue' recommended in my guidebook as the town's best guide and for the next 24 hours he does charm me.

Everyone we meet is either Ahmad's friend or relation and all of them are expected to let me in at half price. Even the tollbooth operator at the end of a stretch of freeway is an acquaintance who can be persuaded to drop the price. By the end of the day I've even been round to his house, where his wife brings us lunch while we take a break during the midday heat. Lunch over, we stretch out on the Persian-carpeted floor for an afternoon nap before we recommence our sightseeing.

We start with the Tappeh-ye Seyalk archaeological site where, naturally, Ahmad is friends with the resident archaeologist Abbar Etemad Fini, busily reconstructing a pot, just as you'd expect an archaeologist to be doing at a site noted for its pottery finds. Further along the road is the Fin Garden with ponds, pools, springs and all the other attributes of the Persian view of paradise. This was also the place where the 19th-century Iranian hero Amir Kabir (the former chancellor of Persia and reformist; his name pops up all over the country) was treacherously murdered. He died in the garden's bathhouse, which has a waxworks-style recreation of the event. Allowed to choose how he would die, he opted to slash his wrists although the tableau seems to show him sitting back calmly while the villain is about to plunge the knife into his wrist.

Our circuit of the city stops by the remnants of the city walls and drops into a number of mosques, but it's Kashan's superb collection of old houses that deserves the most attention. Before and after photographs in a number of the houses illustrate just how much work has gone into the restorations. In one house I bump into a big extended family, several members of which speak excellent English.

'It must be very difficult to restore a place like this', suggests the daughter who is perhaps 12 years old, still sporting braces on her teeth. 'They have so little to work from, just some of these old pictures.'

Her father is more concerned about the outside world's view of Iran than Kashan's architectural restoration problems. If the Western world's media isn't fretting about the latest wild pronouncements from President Mahmoud Ahmadinejad, there's always a threatening bearded Ayatollah in the background and the underlying concern that all that research to peacefully produce electricity from nuclear power may really be just another step towards joining North Korea, Pakistan, Israel, India and all those countries with atomic Weapons of Mass Destruction.

'How can we give people a better view of Iran?' he asks. 'When people visit they realise this is not a bad place', he reflects. 'I can't understand why they have these ideas about us.'

Well, carrying on about 'death to America' and preserving all those paintings around the walls of the old American embassy building in Tehran doesn't help, but my impression is that so much of this is just play-acting. Wander through any park full of picnicking Persians, endure another barrage of 'welcomes' and accept another glass or two of tea, and you begin to realise that these are not the rabid extremists some segments of the Western media would have us believe.

As we're leaving the house the matriarch of the group asks if I'd like to join them on their tour of the town. There's space in one of their cars, but I explain that I already have a guide and car.

There's a final stop before Ahmad leaves me to my own devices for the evening. Wandering around the old bazaar he turns down a derelict alley and leads me through an anonymous door into a beautiful old caravanserai. It's neglected and dilapidated, but with its towering multi-domed ceiling over an octagonal pool (with real water!) and typical Persian tile work, it could be exquisite. I can see it as a restaurant, wonderfully revived with tables around the pool. My mind zips back to a poolside lunch (with rather nice white wine) in a Beverley Hills hotel a few months earlier.

There are more encounters with Iranian hospitality come dinnertime in Khan-e Tabatabei. Built in 1834 for a wealthy carpet merchant, it's one of the houses I visited earlier in the day. To get there I jump in a share taxi heading in more or less the right direction. A local would make sure it's going exactly where he wants, but I often just hop aboard anything heading the right way and if it's not going right there, well they're not expensive and I can easily take another one. This one stops part way towards the restaurant and lets all the other passengers out. The driver then ascertains exactly where I'm going and takes me straight there without any suggestions about increasing the standard 5000-rial (60-cent) fare.

• • • •

The next morning Ahmad is waiting outside the hotel to take me on one final excursion to some sites outside the city. Finally my Kashan kidnapper drops me off at the bus station, but only after checking exactly what time my bus will depart for Tehran. I've enjoyed cruising around Kashan in Ahmad's Paykan and he seems genuinely sorry to see me go. He's still scratching his head, wondering how on earth I knew his name.

'Lizard city', announces the young man sitting next to me as the bus rolls through Qom, Iran's religious centre.

The film *Marmoulak* (*The Lizard*, 2004) has been a controversial box-office hit and, almost inevitably, has ended up being banned. Reza Marmoulak is in jail for his exploits as a petty thief able to climb buildings with lizard-like agility. He escapes from a spell in hospital by stealing a mullah's robes and then ends up in a small village where he's mistaken as the village mosque's new mullah. He soon becomes a major hit with his off-the-top-of-his-head advice and Koranic interpretations. Of course, the mullahs began to get really pissed off when people began to refer to them as lizards, so it was almost inevitable that the film was proscribed.

'Mullahs are no good,' my seat companion insists, swirling his hand vertically round his head to indicate their turban and then his finger horizontally beside his head: 'they're nuts.'

Mullahs are famed for curious 'what the Koran would say' elucidations. Khomeini himself was once asked for a ruling on what should happen to a chicken if a man had sex with it. Could the chicken violator then barbecue the buggered bird? No, thundered Khomeini. Certainly not. Nor could his family. Or their neighbours.

How about somebody who lived two doors away? Well, that was OK. Fried fornicated fowl is all right further down the street. Ditto for poached poked poultry?

• • • •

Back in Tehran the bus stops at the frenetic Southern Bus Station and I head out for another round with the city's madhouse traffic. On the bus I'd been talking to Paul and Carolyn, the first American travellers I've met who are not of Iranian descent. They've had no problems exploring Iran, although Carolyn has had to grapple with the dress question.

'I don't think a Western visitor is necessarily respected for going the whole [chador] way', she concludes. 'I think we probably get more kudos for being locally "correct", but stylish at the same time.' I've heard similar conclusions from other travellers, male and female, elsewhere in the region.

'In the back blocks of Afghanistan, wearing local clothing can help to fit in,' suggested one intrepid visitor I met in that country, 'but wearing exactly the same thing in Kabul can have precisely the opposite effect.

It either looks like you're trying too hard or suggests that you're an American spy. In Kabul I always wear inconspicuous Western attire.'

There's a curious artificiality about the dress question. Watching a TV soap in a hotel lobby a few days before, I'd pondered the living room scenes, the young wife chatting with her husband with her hair still discreetly covered by a scarf. Of course in real life – not Iranian TV soap-opera life – she'd have discarded the scarf the instant she stepped inside.

I emerge from the bus station, check my guidebook and work out that I need to cross to the other side of the road to hail a taxi heading in the right direction. Halfway across the highway I'm hit, not by a car, bus or motorcycle, but once again by the realisation that Iran can be a surprisingly sophisticated country, well aware of the outside world and how they connect to it.

'Hey, Lonely Planet!' yells the cop directing the traffic and simultaneously pointing at my open guidebook. 'Which way you going, man?'

• • • •

'That was a golden era', Mohamad, a tourist guide I'd encountered in the stunningly attractive restaurant housed in the old Hammam-e Vakil in Shiraz, responded when I told him I'd driven through Iran so many years earlier, during the Shah's era. 'There were problems, but we had so much more freedom in those days.'

'Not quite', I thought, thinking of the dreaded Savak, the Shah's secret police, who were every bit as capable of exacting terrible revenge on the regime's opponents as the religious police are today.

'After every revolution there are winners and losers', muses Mansoor, back in Tehran. 'The Shah thought Iran ended at the boundaries of Tehran. He completely neglected the country and the villages. People outside Tehran are much better off than in the Shah's era.

'Look out on the street', he indicates, pointing at the traffic turmoil that boils all around us. As usual the mayhem would be a gold-medal contender in any 'world's worst traffic' Olympiad.

'You see plenty of women driving, don't you? That wouldn't have been true in the Shah's era.'

Not only do Iranian women drive, but in a country where bad driving is a given they sometimes seem to drive particularly badly. As if in confirmation, a women clips the back of the car in front of us as she pushes in to the roundabout turmoil. Not looking in your mirrors is standard procedure in Iran, but how can you see what's going on when you have a scarf billowing around your face?

'Recent elections may have been a disaster for the progressives, but look what's happened since', Mansoor continues. 'Legislation either ended up in deadlock or if it got passed the clergy immediately vetoed it. Now the conservatives control the parliament, but things are actually happening. They're even letting through legislation that they would have barred if the progressives had passed it.

'And it's quite true they constantly shut down newspapers,' he says, as the traffic surges past a newsstand, 'but the staff walk out the door, move three buildings down the street and start another newspaper.'

It certainly seems credible. I'd counted 23 broadsheet newspapers, 14 tabloids and 12 sports papers at a newsstand that morning. At less than 20 cents each I'd usually buy all three English-language papers and it seemed to take the average Iranian newsstand browser half an hour just to decide which paper to buy. I'm still wondering what an Iranian page-three girl would look like in the local tabloids? Lifting a chador for a glimpse of ankle?

Omid, a friend of Mansoor's, arrives soon after we've sat down in Mansoor's apartment and produces a letter, which is handed around the room.

'What do you think it means?' he asks.

153.

It's pretty clear to me what it means and there are nods of agreement around the room when I give my interpretation.

'Well, it's written in the sort of confusing legalistic language you'd expect from any immigration department', I start. 'Essentially it seems to say that your immigration status is OK and will not be changed. You can stay as long as you like, but if you ever leave the country there is no guarantee that you will be let back in and they don't plan to change that.

'So you're stuck in the US,' I presume, 'which is where I get confused, because you're not in the US, you're here in Tehran.'

'Yeah, yeah, I know', Omid responds. 'I came back to Iran eight years ago. I'm not even planning to go back to the US at the moment. I'd just like to be able to return if I change my mind.'

'Yet US immigration still thinks you're there?' I query.

'Of course,' he agrees. 'I always write to them from my friend's address so they think I'm still living there.'

'Didn't they notice when you left?' I ask.

'Nah,' Omid concludes, 'I just crossed the border into Canada. Nobody noticed.'

• • • •

I've had a great time in Iran. I've had a lot of interesting encounters and met a lot of people quite apart from the amazing places I've seen. Repeatedly I've been reminded that Iran today stands with millennia of culture, education and sophistication as a background. There have been more translations of German philosopher Immanuel Kant into Persian than any other language in the last decade, according to the *New Republic*. Iranians are people with opinions and broad-minded attitudes, irrespective of what their fundamentalist religious leaders might insist.

'We're not like Pakistan' is a statement I've heard more than once from Iranians. So much of Iran is window-dressing and appearances, whether it's waving fists at America or even segregating the sexes. The religious rule-makers may insist on it and there's no denying that gender inequality is a big factor, but this is not Saudi Arabia.

On the flight out of Tehran I'm suddenly back in the worst of the Arab world. Across the aisle is a Saudi couple, their two young children sitting a row in front. The couple are both traditionally attired; she's in full-covered-face mode. So how do you eat when your head's in a bag? You take food in one hand, grab your face covering in the other to pull it above your mouth, pop the food in and pull the covering back down. Awkward and ridiculous looking? Absolutely.

IRAQ

We've spent over an hour wandering from office to office in the pouring rain. At one, Husni Tutug reluctantly slips a banknote into the pages of my passport before he hands it over the counter. It seems to work. The passport comes back within minutes with a stamp inside. I'm finally out of Turkey. We drive over the bridge and stop in a car park just beyond the sign announcing 'Welcome to Iraq'.

● ● ● ●

I had several bites at Iraqi tourism before I finally crossed the border in 2006.

Way back in 1989 Iraq ghosted on to my guidebook radar screen. Getting into Iran or Iraq had been all but impossible when the two countries were slugging it out in what correctly could be defined as Gulf War I. The Kuwait Gulf War is really Gulf War II and the current get-rid-of-Saddam disaster is Gulf War III. When the eight-year Iraq-Iran slaughter, in many ways a reprise of the worst trench-warfare-stalemate years of World War I, finally ground to a halt, intrepid travellers started looking at these two fascinating countries again.

There were plenty of reasons to be interested. Iran had the great ancient city of Persepolis (built by Darius the Great from 518 BC and sacked by Alexander the Great in 330 BC) and the exquisite beauties of cities like Esfahan. Iraq had Babylon, Nineveh, Nimrud and Ur. Who wouldn't want to go to either country? Back in the 1970s getting into Iran was fairly straightforward. Iraq was much more difficult, but post–Gulf War I the doors to the Islamic Republic of Iran remained firmly shut. So intrepid travellers began to pay more attention to Iraq and for a brief spell at Lonely Planet we began to ponder the economics of an Iraq guidebook.

In 1989 we sent Rosemary Hall, an intrepid English travel writer, off to Iraq to investigate its tourism possibilities. Her research provided the Iraq chapter of our West Asia guidebook and we began to think about expanding it into a stand-alone Iraq guidebook. Then in 1990 Iraq invaded Kuwait, leading to Gulf War II in 1991, and all ideas of Iraq travel went into the freezer.

Meanwhile I had another Iraq tourism taster – many miles away from Iraq.

In October 1991 at the Frankfurt Book Fair, Jens Peters, Stefan Loose and Renate Loose had been regaling me with stories of life in Berlin when the wall came down.

'We were just about to have dinner,' recalled Stefan, 'and Misha called out from the living room, "Mum! Dad! People are crossing the wall".'

'We didn't believe him, even though there had been so much change in the East in recent weeks, but when we saw what was happening we immediately decided to hold dinner and go straight to the wall.'

The Looses lives in Kreuzberg, only a stone's throw from the wall, and East Berlin.

'We didn't get back home until the next day', continued Renate.

They went on to tell me of the passion with which they attacked the wall.

'For months you could not find a hammer or chisel in Berlin', Jens said. 'You could tell which way the wall was by the constant chipping noise.'

'Amazing,' I said for the nth time. 'I really must visit Berlin one day.'

'No, not one day', they replied in unison. 'Right now. The wall hasn't been down for two years yet. Today it's still east and west, but every day the differences are fading. If you want a taste of what East and West Berlin used to be like, you've got to come right now.'

So a week later I was sleeping on the couch in the Looses' Kreuzberg apartment and, like any serious East Berlin visitor, I made the pilgrimage to the Pergamon Museum where, like any Pergamon visitor, I was blown away by the Ishtar Gate, which had been spirited away from Babylon by German archaeologists.

• • • •

Yet I still didn't get to Iraq. A handful of strictly policed Iraq tours took place, but I was waiting for real travel, independent travel, to become possible. With the new century more Iraq comments and thoughts ghosted past. Looking out over the glittering lights of Dubai from the sky-high bar of the Emirates Towers Hotel one night in 2002, I found myself sitting next to a cheerful South African rugby enthusiast. He'd recently visited Iraq, partly on business, but much more, I thought, out of interest. And he'd found it fascinating. He raved about its attractions, the Biblical sites, the age-old history.

Only a few weeks later, talking with Eugene Mall, a German expat working in Japan and an inveterate traveller, we kicked around the concern that if we didn't get there soon there might not be an Iraq to visit.

'I really fear the Americans will invade Iraq,' he explained, 'and if they blunder in, everything could be destroyed. I've always wanted to see Iraq – perhaps I should go there right now, before it's too late.'

In early 2002 the approaching war seemed inevitable even though it was still a year away. Somehow we couldn't believe Bush would be crazy enough and somehow it seemed he couldn't resist. In London I had dinner with Charlotte Hindle, Lonely Planet's UK manager for many years, Simon Calder, her husband who also happens to be the travel editor of the *Independent*, and Jonathan Glancey, a writer for the Guardian. Jonathan was convinced Bush and Blair would soon launch their war and was working overtime to get a visa to get into Iraq before it was wrecked.

A couple of months later Jonathan did get there and wrote of visiting the ancient Sumerian capital of Ur, near Nasiriyya, 375 kilometres southeast of Baghdad. A year later, when Iraq had been comprehensively shocked and awed, and before the conquerors had settled in for their own long-term period of being horrified and harried, Jonathan pointed out that air attacks on the unfortunate Iraqis were nothing new.

Like many countries in the region, Iraq was a fall-out from the collapse of the Ottoman Empire. The Ottomans had kicked off in the late 1200s, established themselves in Constantinople (today's Istanbul) in 1453, and reached their peak with Sultan Süleyman the Magnificent knocking at the gates of Vienna in 1529. By the time of his death in 1566 the Ottoman Empire incorporated most of the modern Middle East, the North African coast all the way to Morocco, the Balkans and a healthy slice of eastern Europe.

From there it was steadily downhill, culminating with choosing the wrong side in World War I. Even the Turkish heartland of the old empire might have disappeared if Mustafa Kemal, aka Ataturk, had not rallied the disheartened Turks and thrown out the invading Greeks during the Turkish War of Independence from 1920 to 1922.

Other fragments of the Ottoman Empire either found their own independence or traded one colonising power for another. Which was precisely what happened to Iraq in 1920 when Britain grabbed its slice of the old empire, an area encompassing everything from the old Mesopotamia – the Greek term meaning 'between two rivers' and

AFGHANISTAN

(**1.**) → TONY IN FRONT OF THE MINARET OF JAM
(**2.**) → FEEDING THE FAMOUS WHITE PIGEONS AT THE SHRINE
OF HAZRAT ALI (**3.**) → THE EMPTY NICHE OF AN ANCIENT
BUDDHA DESTROYED BY THE TALIBAN IN 2001
(**4.**) → POSTERS FOR SALE, MANY OF NORTHERN ALLIANCE
HERO AHMAD SHAH MASSOUD

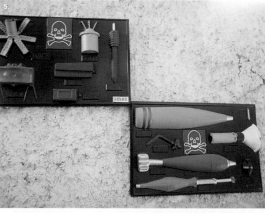

(5.) → AN UGLY ASSORTMENT OF LAND MINES
(6.) → THE JAMSHADY BROTHERS RUN A
TRAVEL AND TOURISM BUSINESS (7.) → ANOTHER
TANK ABANDONED BY THE ROADSIDE (8.) → TONY
AND THE ELDEST JAMSHADY, MOBIN, AT THE
SHRINE OF HAZRAT ALI

ALBANIA

(**1.**) → A STATUE OF NATIONAL HERO SKANDERBEG
STANDS IN THE CENTRE OF TIRANA (**2.**) → GREAT VIEWS
AT A RESTAURANT ON THE TOP OF ARDENICA'S HILL
(**3.**) → A BUNKER LOOKS OUT TO SEA AT JAL BEACH
(**4.**) → THE RUINED AGORA OF THE ANCIENT GREEK
AND ROMAN CITY OF APOLLONIA

(**5.**) → A DETAIL OF THE HUGE MOSAIC MURAL COVERING
THE FAÇADE OF TIRANA'S NATIONAL MUSEUM OF HISTORY
(**6.**) → KRUJA'S SKANDERBEG MUSEUM, BUILT IN THE
TOWN'S 6TH-CENTURY CASTLE (**7.**) → A HOXHA BUNKER
MAKES A COSY BAR IN THE SEASIDE BUNKERI RESTAURANT,
DURRËS (**8.**) → THE FORMER ENVER HOXHA MUSEUM,
AKA 'THE PYRAMID', IN TIRANA

BURMA

(**1.**) → MONKS PLAY VOLLEYBALL IN FRONT OF THE SHWE INN THAIN PAGODA, IN INDEIN AT INLE LAKE (**2.**) → THE MOUSTACHE BROTHERS, TRADITIONAL *A-NYEINT PWE* PERFORMERS (**3.**) > THE STRAND HOTEL IN YANGON (**4.**) > THE SHWEMYETMAN PAYA'S DESPECTACLED BUDDHA

(**5.**) → THE 'BALLOONS OVER BAGAN' COMPANY'S BUS
(**6.**) → THE GILDED SPIRE OF THE DHAMMAYAZIKA
PAYA STUPA (**7.**) → THE *RV PANDAW*, MOORED ON
THE AYEYARWADY RIVER (**8.**) → THE BRIDGE TO
CONNECT THE 'FLOATING VILLAGE' OF MAING
THAUK WITH ITS 'LAND VILLAGE'.

CUBA

(**1.**) → CHE SOUVENIRS OUTNUMBER EVERY OTHER
CUBAN MEMENTO (**2.**) → ONE OF THE MANY
'HOMELAND OR DEATH' BILLBOARDS ON THE *AUTOPISTA*
(**3.**) → AN AMERICAN CAR – *DE RIGUEUR* IN HAVANA
(**4.**) → AN ARTISTIC 'EXPLOSION' MARKS WHERE CHE'S
REBELS CUT THE TRAIN LINE INTO SANTA CLARA

IRAN

(**1.**) → TONY WITH HIS KASHAN TOUR GUIDE, AHMAD POURSEYEDI (**2.**) → THE BEAUTIFUL COURTYARD RESTAURANT AT THE SILK ROAD HOTEL (**3.**) → BAS-RELIEFS ON THE APADANA STAIRWAY IN THE PALACE OF DARIUS, PERSEPOLIS (**4.**) → THE 1972 PHOTO OF MAUREEN WHEELER IN FRONT OF THE KHAJU BRIDGE

IRAQ

(**1.**) → TWO *PESHMERGA* SOLDIERS POSE FOR A PHOTO ON TONY'S ARRIVAL IN IRAQ (**2.**) → THE HISTORIC PIRA DELAL (BEAUTIFUL BRIDGE) IN ZAKHO (**3.**) → SIPPING TEA BESIDE THE BOSPHORUS IN THE ANCIENT KADIKÖY DISTRICT, ISTANBUL (**4.**) → THE ARBIL CITADEL'S HUGE IBN AL-MISTAWFI STATUE

(5.) → ONE OF DOHUK'S PLETHORA
OF APPEALING JUICE STANDS (6.) → A GENEROUS
LUNCH WITH DRIVER ADRIS ON THE WAY TO ARBIL
(7.) → SUPERSIZED BUSTS OF KURDISH HEROES
LINE THE PATHS IN A SULAYMANIYAH PARK (8.) → THE
CITADEL OF ARBIL TOWERS ABOVE THE TOWN CENTRE

LIBYA

(**1.**) → STORAGE CHAMBERS IN THE INTERIOR WALL OF KABAW'S *QASR* (FORTIFIED GRANARY) (**2.**) → A CAMEL RIDES IN THE BACK OF A PICK-UP TRUCK, EN ROUTE TO FEZZAN (**3.**) → A TYPICAL GADDAFI BILLBOARD (**4.**) → SCOPING OUT A ROUTE THROUGH THE UBARI SAND SEA, FEZZAN

(**5.**) → A BARBERSHOP ADVERTISES AFRICAN HAIRSTYLES
IN TRIPOLI'S MEDINA (**6.**) → SCHOOLCHILDREN
PUT ON AN IMPROMPTU PERFORMANCE AT LEPTIS MAGNA
(**7.**) → A SUPERB PREHISTORIC ROCK CARVING OF A GIRAFFE,
WADI METHKANDOUSH (**8.**) → TRAVELLERS ENJOY THE VIEW
FROM THE BALCONY SEATS OF LEPTIS MAGNA'S
AMPHITHEATRE

NORTH KOREA

(**1.**) → PYONGYANG-BOUND – TONY OUTSIDE A SLEEPER
CARRIAGE (**2.**) → A REALLY GOOD BILLBOARD OF KIM IL-SUNG,
WITH KIM JONG-IL AND TWO GRATEFUL FARMERS
(**3.**) → FROZEN LAKE CHON, IN THE CRATER OF MT PAEKDU,
STRADDLES THE KOREA–CHINA BORDER (**4.**) → THE
CHARMING AND TINY MISS LEE, OUR TOUR GUIDE AT THE
PAEKDU SECRET CAMP

(**5.**) → THE IMPOSING DEMILITARISED ZONE BUILDINGS
(**6.**) → A VISIT TO THE 20-METRE-HIGH MANSUDAE
STATUE OF KIM IL-SUNG IS OBLIGATORY
FOR VISITORS (**7.**) → THE DANCING ARMY PERFORM
DURING PYONGYANG'S ARIRANG MASS GAMES
(**8.**) → TONY'S NORTH KOREA TOUR GROUP STRIKE
A CHEERFUL POSE

SAUDI ARABIA

(**1.**) → AL-FAISALIAH CENTER – DESIGNED BY UK
ARCHITECT SIR NORMAN FOSTER AND BUILT BY THE
BIN LADEN GROUP (**2.**) → THE RESTORED HEJAZ
RAILWAY AT MADAIN SALEH, SAUDI ARABIA'S PETRA
(**3.**) → THE *DIWAN* (MEETING ROOM) OF MADAIN SALEH
(**4.**) → TONY WITH SAEED JUMAAN, HIS NAJRAN GUIDE

(**5.**) → A DOOR IN QASR AL-MASMAK, WITH THE FAMOUS BROKEN SPEARHEAD EMBEDDED IN IT (**6.**) → NAJRAN'S FAIRYTALE CASTLE, IN THE MIDDLE OF THE SOUQ (**7.**) → QASR AL-MASMAK, RIYADH, BUILT AROUND 1865 (**8.**) → THE NATIONAL MUSEUM OF RIYADH

defining the ancient Sumerian region between the Tigris and Euphrates
Rivers – to the mountainous Kurdistan area of the north.

The Iraqis, a mishmash of Arabs, Kurds and Assyrians following
both the Shiite and Sunni divisions of Islam, quickly revolted against
British rule and as a result found themselves facing some aerial shock
and awe, 80 years ahead of the repeat performance in 2003. Iraq became
an aerial-bombardment testing ground for Arthur Harris, the RAF
squadron leader who two decades later would oversee the destruction
of the German cities of Hamburg and Dresden in massive raids, with
death tolls sometimes said to rival Hiroshima or Nagasaki. In Iraq in the
1920s Harris reported that 'within 45 minutes a full-sized village can be
practically wiped out, and a third of its inhabitants killed or injured, by
four or five machines which offer them no real target, no opportunity for
glory as warriors, no effective means of escape'.

While the RAF was getting Iraq under control from above, the
British army was also showing how to do things at ground level. Saddam
Hussein's famous gas attack on the Kurds at Halabja in 1988 was not a
first. The British had tried out gas on Iraqi rebels in 1920 'with excellent
moral effect'.

• • • •

The US assumption seemed to be that the Iraq choice was black and
white, black being Saddam of course, white being democracy. Preferably a
democracy just like America's – that is, not the sort of democracy you find
next door in Iran or the sort of democracy the Palestinians would opt for
a few years later.

In fact this was never a coin toss with the odds heavily weighed in
favour of heads (democracy) over tails (Saddam). It was much more like
tossing a pack of cards up in the air then picking out the ones that
landed face up and tossing again. There were clearly multiple alternative

end-games to the pre-liberation situation, some of them even less pleasant than what we started with.

First, of course, there was straight back to the status quo, black followed by black. Until his death sentence actually resulted in Saddam dangling from the gallows we could have ended up with Saddam's Iraq Version 2. All we had to do was bust Saddam out of jail and the statue makers could be melting the metal for another round of heroic images. There's still the possibility of black followed by another shade of black – another Saddam-style dictator could end up at the top of the heap after all the shooting and voting finishes.

Or we could end up with an Iran-style theocracy, ranging all the way from something fairly democratic (but with Islamic state trimmings) to a real mullah-run operation that would, presumably, be not at all fond of the Great Satan and all it stands for.

Then there's the Arab tribal option, a country run by the biggest sheikh around (Saudi style) or with power shared between a bunch of them (like the United Arab Emirates). There's nothing particularly democratic about this option, but the end result could vary all the way from the Saudi end of the spectrum (greedy rulers who turn a blind eye to all sorts of things so long as they stay in control of the purse strings) through to UAE pragmatism.

Then there's the straightforward chaos option. Iraq could fragment into a Middle East Balkans with the Kurds hiving off their northern enclave, to the considerable displeasure of Turkey and Iran, neighbouring states with big Kurd minorities. Meanwhile the Shiites (backed by Iran) could be slugging it out with the Sunnis. Presumably part or all of a chaotic Iraq could be the new Afghanistan, home for whoever needs a nicely secluded base from which to operate.

Why was installing democracy in Iraq so important anyway? Lack of anything like democracy has never endangered Saudi Arabia's most favoured status. And back in 1953, when the Iranians looked like opting for the wrong sort of democracy, a democracy that would hurt Western oil interests, democracy was quickly given the boot and a friendly-to-Western-interests dictator, the Shah, installed on the throne.

• • • •

Once the shock and awe phase was over and George W made his 'Mission Accomplished' visit to an aircraft carrier off the California coast, dressed up military fashion so he looked like he'd done it all himself, people started to turn up in Baghdad. Virgin was talking about soon starting London–Baghdad flights and the Thorn Tree, Lonely Planet's travellers' chat area on the website, was full of discussions about how much a seat in a car should cost from Amman in Jordan to Baghdad and which hotel to go to in search of that Baghdad-bound taxi. Even 'Is it safe for solo women travellers?' was a topic of discussion for the next few months.

'Kirkuk and Mosul look quite good', reported Peshmarga, and 'Things are fine in most areas (be careful around Fallujah, Saddam City etc)', said Vaughn, both on 11 June 2003. The next day Scott Filtenborg was fretting about backpackers 'who couldn't tell the difference between Bangkok and Baghdad' and suggesting it would be better to 'wait till things settle' even if it was 'a year or more'. That same day ransomc22 suggested that 'If you're a woman, I would just suggest covering your hair to make you look less western.'

If you couldn't get to Iraq itself, where to track down traces of Iraq in other countries was another topic of conversation at that time. Of course, the Pergamon Museum's collection in Berlin topped most lists, followed by the Louvre's collection of Assyrian material from Khorsabad. Or there were the Nineveh and Nimrud collections in the British Museum and the sculptures from Ur at the University Museum in Philadelphia.

Very soon, however, Thorn Tree discussions of 'how to do Iraq' tapered off and dried up, because it was very clear nobody was going to be doing Iraq unless they had a death wish. Through 2004 the situation steadily

worsened. In a December 2004 interview *Time* magazine's Baghdad
bureau chief, Michael Ware, discussing the Fallujah attack, described
Iraq as an 'absolute disaster' and underlined the obvious fact that far from
containing terrorism the ill-thought-out invasion was creating brand new
terrorists like an assembly line. If the Soviet invasion of Afghanistan had
inspired one generation of Jihad, then this crazy misadventure was the
follow up, he figured.

Recruits who last the distance go through four stages, said one book
I read. In the first stage they think, 'The war is proceeding on a normal
course.' If only there were more men, the problems could be solved. A
few months later it's, 'Since we've already gotten ourselves in this jam,
we should get the fighting over with as quickly as possible.' Which
again means add more men. Then it's the realisation that 'Something is
desperately wrong here. What a mess!' And finally: 'We'd be wise to get
the hell out of here – and the sooner the better.'

Of course history repeats itself, or our leaders don't learn from it, for
that neat little four-step analysis was not written about the Iraq debacle at
all. Vietnam? No, not that one either. It's from *The Hidden War* by Russian
journalist Artyom Borovik, an account of the Soviet Union's disastrous
intervention in Afghanistan. Like Vietnam, the USSR's Afghanistan
adventure ended up with ignominious withdrawal, which is how most
unbiased observers believe the Iraq catastrophe will also conclude.

• • • •

In early 2006 events in Iraq, already going steadily downhill, take a
distinct turn for the worse. There's talk of the mess descending into all-
out civil war with the USA standing to one side, unable to do anything.
So I decide it's time to go there.

Not to central and southern Iraq – Nineveh, Nimrud, Babylon, Ur and
all those other ancient centres are going to have to wait, as is Baghdad.

There is no way I am going to see Iraq properly in the foreseeable future, so I'll settle for seeing Iraq improperly – I'll just have a taste of the accessible part of Iraq. Most of the country may be a disaster, but there's one part of the country that is accessible and fairly safe: Kurdistan.

I'm going to a tourism conference in Washington DC. If I make a nice little transit of northern Iraq, entering from Turkey and exiting to Iran, I can arrive in Washington direct from two of the three Axes of Evil. I fly to Istanbul from Singapore and Dubai early one morning and soon get into the swing of Turkey by taking a ferry across the Sea of Marmara at the mouth of the Bosphorus to Kadıköy, the commuter seaport on Istanbul's Asian side. My next flight doesn't leave from Istanbul's secondary airport, named after Sabina Gökçen, the Turkish air force's first female combat pilot, until mid-afternoon, so I have plenty of time to sip a leisurely glass of tea at a harbourside café and watch the world go by. I'm flying to Diyarbakir, in the heart of Turkey's Kurdish region and well over in the eastern part of the country.

Stepping out of Diyarbakir's modern little airport terminal late that afternoon, I'm greeted with a chorus from the waiting crowd of taxi drivers: 'Iraq, Iraq, you want to go to Iraq?' they ask in unison.

'Well, yes, but not tonight', I explain. All I want to do tonight is find a hotel and get some sleep.

'Don't mention Kurdistan', a Kurd I met in London had advised me. 'You want to go to Iraq. As far as the Turks are concerned there is no such place as Kurdistan.'

I dump my bag in the Balkar Otel and set off to explore the town, quickly deciding that Diyarbakir is not likely to hit my favourite towns list. The town has an impressive six-kilometre city wall dating from the Byzantine era, 1500 years ago, but the wall itself is dark and foreboding and everything about the city is either modern and tatty, like a run-down Communist-era Soviet centre, or old and decidedly decrepit. There's also a lot of broken glass around and some very attentive-looking

165.

IRAQ

military checkpoints.

Later I discover there were clashes between the local Kurdish population and the Turkish security forces just a few days previously.

By the time I've strolled across the old town to look at a hotel converted from an ancient caravanserai, the weather is shifting from overcast and threatening to drizzling and then to bucketing down. Of course, I'm also pretty jet-lagged after my overnight flight from Singapore, so I grab some food, duck into an internet café to get out of the rain, and then head back to the hotel. I've just got off to sleep when the front desk phones to ask me to come downstairs to talk with my driver. It turns out he's handed the job on to someone else, Husni Tutug.

Next morning Husni is there and ready to go at 7am. We travel via Mardin and Midyat (with an impressive collection of Syrian churches), and pause to look at the Morgabriel Monastery before stopping for lunch at Silopi, just before the border. For eight solid kilometres before Silopi a nose-to-tail line of trucks waits to cross the border into Iraq. There's some paperwork to complete in Silopi, which I wouldn't have known about, but I've been wondering why it's necessary to take a driver right across the border rather than just get dropped there. I'm about to find out.

Syria's directly across the river from the road for the next few kilometres, but the truck line-up continues for another 10 kilometres and now it's often two, three or even four trucks wide. There must be thousands of them. With most of them it's impossible to tell what they're transporting, but there are transporters full of new cars and pick-up trucks, and trucks laden with construction equipment, pipelines, reels of wire and bags of cement. Clearly there's a lot of building work going on across the border.

What I don't see – and I know I'm going to be asked about this – are endless rows of trucks carrying Australian wheat. It's been an ongoing scandal in Australia that the AWB (the Australian Wheat Board) funnelled $300 million in to Saddam's pockets to ensure Iraq bought its wheat from Australia rather than Canada, the USA or some other supplier. It was a

166.

king-size bribe and the politicians have been dancing the 'didn't happen on my shift' tango overtime. It's also prompted a storm of cartoons and jokes in the Australian press and provided a neat explanation for why the Australian government was so easily convinced about those fictitious Weapons of Mass Destruction (WMDs): they thought they'd paid for them.

The border is a chaotic, muddy mess and it's raining solidly again. Husni seems to know exactly which door to head for, which window to bang on, which queue to barge to the front of and exactly whom to bribe. I spot him slipping a note into my passport before he hands it over to one official. Nevertheless it takes over an hour of zigzagging from one ramshackle building to another before we make the short drive across the bridge that conveys us into Iraq.

Arriving in Iraq is like a doorway to heaven. Suddenly I'm sitting in a clean, dry, mud-free waiting room being served glasses of tea while we wait for the passports to be processed – Husni's too. He has to exit Turkey, enter Iraq and then repeat the process in the opposite direction to get me through. The officials decide to put me through hoops, however, and I have to spend 20 minutes explaining why I want to visit Iraq and what I do for a living. Finally they relent, hand my passport over, and welcome me to Iraq. I've already been welcomed by half a dozen *peshmerga* soldiers, photographed with two of them and had a chat, in French, with one.

Husni drops me in a car park, over two hours after we arrived at the border, and I take a taxi to Zakho to look at the town's ancient bridge before continuing on to Dohuk for the night. This little trip is a foretaste of my next few days in Iraq: there's a certain amount of communication confusion. I can't get across to Adris, my driver, where I want to go; 'bridge' doesn't seem to appear in my Kurdistani phrase list, riffling through the handful of books in my daypack doesn't turn up a picture of a bridge and the quick sketches I make of bridges in my notebook don't produce a glimmer of recognition.

'Take me to a hotel', I finally request and, sure enough, there's

167.

somebody at the front desk who knows exactly what I'm looking for, even if he is a little disappointed that the first tourist for a while doesn't actually want a room.

Known as the Delal Bridge, Beautiful Bridge in Kurdish, Zakho's number-one tourist attraction is said to have been built by a local Abbasidian ruler, which dates it anywhere from AD 750 to AD 1258, although there are suggestions it might date back to Roman times. Whatever, it's an impressive multiple-arched bridge over a rocky river and clearly very old. Zakho is also said to have a stretch of old castle wall but nobody at the hotel knew about that so we press on to Dohuk.

It's not far, along a freeway dotted with advertising billboards, and as we drive in to the centre there are a surprising number of hotels. The Sulav Hotel might be one of the biggest (and most expensive) in town; my room costs US$36. I take an instant liking to Dohuk. It's bright, energetic and crowded and has lots of fruit-juice stands. I wander around the town, try out an internet café – it had such a tangle of wires leading in to the building, I concluded it had to be the centre of the World Wide Web – search inconclusively for Dohuk's bit of decaying castle wall, look in various shops in the bazaar, check out the money-changing quarter (there are no ATMs that work and credit cards don't function either) and take quite a few photographs. Everybody is very enthusiastic about being photographed, a sure sign that there aren't many tourists around.

The weather, however, is still miserable and after a very agreeable meal in a restaurant I repair back to the hotel. It's still raining when I get up and, as I leave Dohuk, I've taken on Adris as a driver again. It starts to bucket down. The rain continues all the way north to Amadiya, which I am expecting to have hints of a Kurdish hill town but in the rain it looks like a miserable dump more than a mountain escape. Perhaps it all looks better when the sun's shining and, as I head south again, glimpses of snow-dusted peaks appear. Before long the sun is shining and everything does indeed look much better.

Travelling east towards Arbil requires lots of diversions, presumably to avoid approaching too close to Mosul. There's lots of security although it centres on a visual check of each vehicle's inhabitants. I expect Arab passengers get more than a cursory glance. Only once today (and once yesterday) do I have to produce my passport and explain what the hell I am doing in Iraq. Along the way we stop for a hearty roadside lunch (the Kurds like to eat well) and I take some photographs of the restaurant and staff, which delights everybody.

Arbil is a delight as well. I'd always thought that Damascus was the world's oldest continuously inhabited city but Arbil (or Erbil or, in Kurdish, Hawler or Hewler) disputes that claim. The modern city crowds around the ancient citadel, which surmounts a hill in the middle of the town, so as soon as I've found a hotel room I head towards that prominent landmark. A stairway ascends to the citadel entrance, guarded by a huge seated statue of Ibn Al-Mistawfi. Who was he? An important government official back in the 13th century, I later discover, and he wrote a book titled *History of Erbil*. It's a fine-looking statue, especially with kids clambering over it and sitting in the local hero's lap.

Just inside the citadel entrance should be three large 19th-century Kurdish houses, turned into museums according to my 15-year-old guidebook report. Sadly it turns out Saddam trashed them. Back in 1991 in the Kuwait Gulf War, George Bush Senior had encouraged the Kurds to rise up against Saddam, but then failed to follow through, halting the allied advance well before it got to Baghdad. Saddam suppressed the uprising with customary brutality, sending huge numbers of Kurdish refugees fleeing into the Kurdish regions of neighbouring Iran and Turkey. The beautiful old houses were gutted.

Not finding the houses was a disappointment, but there's a surprising substitute. A sign announces the Kurdish Textile Museum. Recently opened and very well presented, the museum displays an eclectic collection of carpets, kilims, saddle bags, baby carriers and other local crafts along with well-presented displays and information about the Kurdish people and nomadic tribes. Lolan Mustefa, who established the museum, is a mine of information on Arbil and the surrounding region. I'm enormously impressed that he has put so much effort into creating an excellent tourist attraction, when Iraq today has so very few tourists.

From the museum I continue to the citadel's mosque, visit the hammam (or bathhouse) and enjoy the view over the city from the citadel walls on the other side. Back down below the citadel walls I explore the bazaars, inspect the kilim shops, joke with the shoeshine guys, check the selection of papers on sale at the newsstands, photograph the photographers waiting for customers outside the citadel, snack on a kebab and drop in to a fruit-juice stand for an orange juice. It seems ridiculous, but I'm really enjoying Iraq.

• • • •

Funny how things always look darker at night. I wake up in the middle of the night worried about how the crossing to Iran might go and that unease colours the rest of the day. Before departing Arbil I waste some time tracking down the small, rather dusty and forgotten archaeological museum. Finding things that nobody seems to know about is never easy and having language difficulties to grapple with doesn't help.

Coming back into the Sheraton car park, halfway through my museum search, I encounter a couple of burly Western guys checking over their armoured Land Cruiser. One of them sports a T-shirt announcing that sleeping soundly in bed is only an option for some people (presumably his clients) because some other people (presumably wearing T-shirts like his) are ready to exact extreme violence upon some other unspecified people. It's a slightly enhanced version of the quote attributed to George Orwell that 'people sleep peaceably in their beds at night only because rough men stand ready to do violence on their behalf', but it fits the situation well.

170.

I don't expect for a second they're going to know where the museum is (they don't), but I ask anyway and at least get some advice about safety.

'You haven't got a driver? Take care. This may be Kurdistan, but it's still Iraq. It's dangerous out there.'

Which I guess it would be with a T-shirt like that.

At the hotel desk, after some discussion, since most of the staff also aren't aware there is a museum, I'm given instructions: straight up the way I was going, but driving distance rather than walking. With Kurdish written instructions in hand I flag down a taxi, set off up the road, stop to ask bystanders, U-turn and eventually end up right back where I gave up in the first place. I was standing right outside the museum when I was directed back past the Sheraton and, remarkably, it's exactly where my ancient guidebook said it was, just past the Hamarawan Hotel.

I've arranged another car and driver and soon after we're heading south, with Arvan sporting his Beijing 2008 Olympics sweatshirt at the wheel. The road towards Sulaymaniyah is fast and fraught, a straight road with lots of traffic and lots of hairy overtaking manoeuvres. In northern Iraq driving is probably the most dangerous activity. Frustratingly none of the names on my Iraq map pop up and when there is a name it isn't on my map. I have a suspicion that cartographers working on maps like this simply put in the big places we all know about – Arbil, Kirkuk and Baghdad along this route – and then make up a bunch of names to scatter in between.

So between dodging oncoming trucks we're heading down the highway towards Kirkuk, although I'm expecting we'll turn off to the east sometime before we get there.

A few months earlier Geoff Hann, an Englishman who ran tours through Iraq back in the 1970s and was looking at the place again, had also set out from Arbil towards Kirkuk, 'despite being strongly warned against it'.

'What town is this?' I ask as buildings and a flyover appear ahead.

'Kirkuk', replies Arvan, in what sounds like an unhappy tone.

I thought we were going to skirt around Kirkuk, as we'd done with

Mosul, and Arvan is instantly looking for a way out again. The first road we try deteriorates into a construction zone and then is blocked completely. We U-turn, and continue on our original route, presumably sticking to the Kurdish southern fringe of the city. Speeding through is not an option. The road is interrupted by a series of speed humps so big that we virtually come to a halt to tip over them without grounding.

I'm relieved to come through another comprehensive roadblock and we take a fast divided road heading straight east to Sulaymaniyah.

Like me, Geoff Hann also soon found himself hurrying east. 'As we entered the city and crossed the last checkpoint, still in the Kurdish part of town, my driver picked up bad vibes, deemed that wisdom was the better part of valour and we left rapidly, passing through the slums of Kurdish refugees towards Sulaymaniyah. It was not for me to argue given the latest round of killings there. You have to trust these people's instincts as much as your own.

'So I still have not visited the tomb of the Prophet Daniel', Geoff regretted.

• • • •

The conclusion of the Kuwait Gulf War in 1991 and the proclamation of No Fly Zones shackled Saddam Hussein and allowed the Kurdistan region to effectively declare independence from Baghdad. Correction: regions rather than region, because northern Iraq promptly split into two statelets. Massoud Barzani and the Kurdistan Democratic Party ran northwest Kurdistan from Arbil, while Jalal Talabani and the Patriotic Union of Kurdistan ran southeast Kurdistan from Sulaymaniyah.

In 1998 an American peace deal stopped the two Kurdistan parties from actually shooting at each other, but it was not until mid-2006 that they finally unified the two halves of Kurdistan. Talabani is now the president of all of Iraq, while Barzani is the president of the Kurdistan region of the country.

Kurdistan's peacefulness and relative independence is a double-edged sword for the rest of Iraq. The positive viewpoint: if Kurdistan can be peaceful and stable, why can't the rest of Iraq? The negative one: if Kurdistan can cut itself off from the rest of Iraq, why can't the Shiites and Sunnis divide up the rest of the country? 'Doing a Slovenia' is an ongoing topic in Kurdistan. Slovenia managed to abandon the rest of Yugoslavia and cut itself free before the fighting in the Balkans really began. As a result Slovenia is one of the success stories of the old Eastern Europe and comfortably better off than Croatia, Serbia and the other pieces of the Yugoslavia jigsaw puzzle.

Iraq without its northern Kurdistan region might still be a viable state, but Iran and Turkey, both with substantial Kurdish minorities bordering the region, certainly don't want an independent Kurdistan inspiring their Kurds to demand greater autonomy or, far worse, independence. Nor would the rest of Iraq be a pretty sight if it split into independent Shiite and Sunni entities. Under Saddam the Sunni minority had the power, but not the oil. That's predominantly in the Shiite regions of the country. Split southern Iraq into the two Islamic divisions and the Sunnis would be left with nothing more than palm trees, sand and a big chip on their collective shoulders.

For Iran a divided Iraq might not be so bad. After all, they're Shiites and could be expected to get on well with a Shiite lesser-Iraq. Saudi Arabia might not find it so agreeable, since that country's Shiite minority has always been treated as second best by the Sunni majority and where is Saudi Arabia's oil? In the northeast of the country where Saudi Shiites predominate.

My first task in Sulaymaniyah is to find the museum, which I have been told is much better than the one in Arbil. It's already closed for the day, but fortunately it's close to my hotel. I have no idea what else Sulaymaniyah has to offer, but wandering the park with its collection

of busts of Kurdish heroes and the bazaar area, with its mosques and
more Kurdish hero statuary and portraits, uses up the rest of the day
very satisfactorily. I also look in to a couple of more modern shopping
centres and check out (although I don't dine there) the town's MaDonal
restaurant, an Iraqi-Kurdish interpretation of the golden arches. Finally I
return to the Ashti Hotel, which is definitely not up to the high standards
of Dohuk and Arbil.

There's not a lot to do in Sulaymaniyah at night. I hang around in the
lobby for a while and drink more tea, but eventually I drift up to my
dreary room, check the security guys at the rear entrance to the hotel
from my window, flick through the TV channels (chancing upon the
Lonely Planet TV programme on Sydney on the way), read a little, write
up some notes, fall asleep.

I sleep badly. Again I wake up in the middle of the night running
through the logistics of this trip. I have to get to Tabriz in Iran by
tomorrow night in order to fly out the next morning to Istanbul and on
to the USA. It looks like the drive from Arbil to the Iran border could
take four or five hours. Add a similar time from the border to Tabriz and
it's going to be a push to get it done in one day, especially if there are any
delays at the border. And what if I can't get across the border at all? That's
going to be a huge hassle.

Of course these sort of problems always seem bigger at 3am than they
do in daylight but eventually I come to the decision not just to simply
head back to Arbil in the morning, but to continue straight through and
try to get across to Iran that day. Then I'll have all the following day to
make my way to Tabriz.

In the morning I have a look around the surprisingly good museum. It
doesn't open at 8.30am (according to the guard at the front entrance last
174. night) or 9am (the guard at the rear entrance), but at 9.30am. While I'm
waiting I chat with Jalal Kakeyi who works at the museum as a chemist,
dating finds, he informs me. It's a surprisingly good museum and it

certainly didn't get trashed in the post-invasion chaos, like the Baghdad museum.

The museum has a big collection of reliefs, statues, steles, pottery, jewellery and tools dating right back to the Palaeolithic and Mesolithic eras. There are small pottery figures from the Old Babylonian period, ivory plaques and small delicate pottery from the New Assyrian period, and glazed pottery and gold coins from the Abbasidian period. Even the comparatively recent Ottoman period is covered.

Museums seem to have hit hard times in quite a few cities around my Bad Lands wanderings. The destruction of the Baghdad Museum was a sorry tale, although not unexpected. After all, Saddam's men had done a thorough job of sacking the excellent Kuwait Museum as well as setting all the oil wells alight before they headed home in 1991 after the Kuwait invasion and Gulf War. Having carted away the contents of the museum they also smashed and burned the building for good measure. It's the one building in Kuwait that has been left unrestored.

The unfortunate Kabul Museum in Afghanistan, at one time probably the finest museum in the region, suffered multiple attacks. First, every Mujaheddin mob that took Kabul took time out to loot the museum, so anything valuable and portable soon departed Afghanistan and today probably resides in the homes of affluent art collectors in more peaceful parts of the world. Then the Taliban turned up and after ignoring the collection for the first five years finally got around to trashing it in early 2001 – at the same time as they destroyed the great Buddhas of Bamiyan.

Remarkably it appears there were survivors from the Kabul's museum collection inspection by the Taliban. The museum's director had taken the precaution of hiding, even burying, some statues and as the museum reopens they are being returned to display.

Unfortunately it isn't just Muslim iconoclasm. In the first days of the Iraq invasion in 2003 it was Americans doing the looting and vandalising just as much as the Iraqis. Watching the Saddam statue fall in Firdos

Square – helped by a contingent of Marines who roped up the statue
to an armoured recovery vehicle – reminded me that the Hungarians
cannily kept dozens of their unwanted statues of Marx, Lenin and other
Communist-era heroes and collected them together in the Szobor Statue
Park just outside Budapest. The collection now attracts 40,000 visitors a
year who happily pay to see it.

Another piece of Saddam-era artwork that I'd quite looked forward
to seeing in some future museum also fell to American destructive
urges. On this occasion a group of soldiers demolished the famed mosaic
portrait of George Bush Senior that visitors to the Al-Rashid Hotel
walked over as they entered the lobby.

The entrance mosaic was created after a cruise missile damaged the
hotel and killed a receptionist and a guest from Jordan in January 1993.
Only a few months later 23 US cruise missiles hit the city in the early
hours of the morning of 27 June. One of the missiles killed Leila al-
Attar, who was staying at her sister Suad al-Attar's home because her
own home had already been destroyed by an earlier US attack. For one
woman to have two homes destroyed in bombing raids was too great a
coincidence, Iraqi conspiracy theorists decided. Leila al-Attar must have
been deliberately targeted because, as the director of Baghdad's Museum
of Fine Arts, she was responsible for the Bush mosaic.

A collection of Saddam statues and portraits of George Bush Senior
could have made a useful starting point for a museum of recent Iraqi
history, along with a big exhibit of the Weapons of Mass Destruction
(always capitalised) or at least pictures of what they were supposed to look
like. The museum souvenir shop would probably have done a good trade
in T-shirts bearing the smiling face of former Iraqi Information Minister
Mohamed Saeed al-Sahhaf with a voice balloon saying 'Tanks? I don't see
any tanks.'

. . . .

Arvan turns up and we head off to Arbil and then to the Iran border. My map seems to indicate that you could head directly north, cutting a lot of distance off the trip and avoiding dicey Kirkuk completely, but the map has been pretty much a work of fiction so I'm not at all surprised when this idea is abortive. After another fuel-bargaining session on the edge of Sulaymaniyah, we're soon speeding down that familiar freeway, skirting round far-too-familiar Kirkuk and then heading north on the Baghdad–Arbil road.

Arvan seems mildly surprised at my change in plans, but we skirt around Arbil and turn off east towards Iran. The road starts to climb almost immediately and soon we're high above the town on a surprisingly good road. Salahuddin is a good lunch stop and after a long northward stretch at the foot of an endless ridge we turn east again through the Rowanduz Gorge. This is the 'Hamilton Road', a fine piece of British colonial road building by Archibald Hamilton, a young New Zealand–born engineer, between 1928 and 1932. He wrote a book about it, *The Road Through Kurdistan*, which after nearly half a century out of print was reprinted recently and which I'm reading at the moment.

The road up through the gorge is quite spectacular with a number of bridges that I presume are Archibald Hamilton's handiwork, although I don't manage to match the actual bridges with the old black-and-white photographs in his book. There's a group of young people at the Gali Ali Beg waterfall, crowding together to be photographed at one of the prime attractions in the gorge.

Beyond the gorge the road continues to climb and I begin to get more concerned about the crossing. This is nothing like the busy road from the Turkish border. The traffic is getting lighter and lighter, the road is climbing and winding, and it's all taking much longer than I'd anticipated. It's clearly a very remote region surrounded by snow-covered peaks and little else. It's now late afternoon and if the border is closed for the evening, what am I going to do until morning? Stand in the rain?

Yes, the rain has started again.

Finally we arrive at the Kurdistan border control and my worst fears are realised. I'm not sure what it is that I'm told at great length, but the general message is that I'm not going to get into Iran. Perhaps the border is closed to anybody who is not Iraqi or Iranian? A week later I discover that this is actually no longer the northern border crossing between Iraq and Iran. There are still three crossings between the two countries, two further south in regions I definitely do not want to venture into, but the third crossing, the northern Kurdistan crossing, is now east of Sulaymaniyah at Bashmakh, crossing from Penjuen (or Penjwin) in Iraq to Marivan in Iran. If I'd known, I could have arrived there this morning!

What a drag. Here I am right at the border, about the same distance from Tabriz as Arbil, but that's where I'm heading back to. Still the sun breaks through to provide a nice clouds-over-the-snow sunset as we hurtle back downhill. It's a scary ride, a nine-hour Arbil–border–Arbil round trip by the time I arrive at my hotel. En route we've got lost twice. Once, I realise Arvan has gone wrong and tell him to U-turn, the second time my trusty GPS tells me that we're heading in the wrong direction.

There are flights out of Arbil – I'd checked that possibility before I left – but tomorrow the only option is to Beirut. It looks like my best bet is to retrace my steps to Diyarbakir in Turkey, where I started my Kurdistan foray, but are there flights tomorrow and can I get there in time to fly to Istanbul to pick up my flight to the USA the next morning? It's nearly 10pm when I dump my bag in the Arbil Tower Hotel and race to the internet café next door, where I'm told they close in five minutes. Which, it turns out, is plenty of time to get on to the Turkish Airlines website and check their flight schedules. Isn't the World Wide Web wonderful? Even in Iraq it works. If there's a seat available and if I can get across the border fairly quickly, I should make it.

• • • •

I grab a quick meal in the hotel's restaurant and even treat myself to a beer before heading for bed at midnight. Just before 5.30am I tiptoe into the lobby. Assorted staff are asleep on the sofas, but the security guy outside still seems to be awake although he doesn't notice my arrival. Arvan doesn't turn up at 5.30am, which is probably just as well as the first hint of dawn only shows after 6am, when he does arrive. He's brought his brother Alan along for the ride. Then there are thick patches of fog to slow us and we get lost once, just after I decide we are heading straight in to the Mosul no-go zone, and for a while we seem to be travelling in totally the wrong direction.

I'm relieved when something familiar pops up and pleased when we stop for a late-breakfast–early-lunch at exactly the same roadside restaurant I'd stopped at en route from Dohuk to Arbil a few days ago.

We arrive at the border just after 10am and I'm immediately pounced on by a gang of Turkish drivers keen to take me to somewhere, anywhere, in Turkey. I quickly negotiate a price with one dapper gentleman and it's less than half what I paid for the same trip heading to Iraq. Then it's the excruciating departure procedures, including a fine tooth comb search of the car for smuggled cigarettes. Some vehicles seem to spew cigarettes out of every cavity, but the three cartons my driver has are not found.

Altogether the paperwork, rubber stamps, racing from office to office, standing in line and car searching (out of Kurdistan as well as in to Turkey) consumes almost three hours. The line of trucks waiting to cross the border seems even longer than at the beginning of the week, well over 20 kilometres long.

Finally we're on the road and what a road it is. The sun is shining and the countryside looks beautiful. Later in the trip snow-capped mountains spread right across the frame. The town of Mardin looks like a postcard (wish I had time to stop for a day or two) and we even pause for an excellent lunch, which also includes a car wash and shoeshines for both of us.

We arrive at the airport at 4.45pm for the 5.45pm Turkish Airlines flight, but it's full. Diyarbakir's modern little airport (excellent wi-fi reception throughout) has one curious omission – there is no departure or arrival board anywhere so the only way you can find out if any of the four airlines represented (Pegasus, Sun Express and Onur Air as well as Turkish Airlines) have flights and when is to ask at each desk.

There are some no-shows, so I get the last seat on the flight, but there's one final amusement. Out on the tarmac we have to identify our bags before they're loaded on board and mine isn't there. Some more last-minute bags arrive, but mine still isn't there. Finally somebody looks at my baggage tag and boarding pass and points out that I'm standing beside the wrong aircraft. The Airbus over there – waiting for one final passenger and with a lonely blue travel pack sitting beside it – is where I should be.

• • • •

So was there an alternative to the shock and awe performance? Did we have to bomb the shit out of the place and then march in to knock the statues over and search for Saddam's hidey-hole? Well, two other places in this book – one right up on the Axis and one a clear contender for a position, until its leader shaped up – received very different treatment.

North Korea, that other evil axis podium placer, hasn't been shocked and awed, bombed, invaded or even really threatened. Isolated a bit perhaps, leaned on heavily, pilloried in the press, but certainly not comprehensively wrecked the way Iraq has been. If you compare the two countries on internal evil, external evil, WMDs and terrorist threats, it's clear that North Korea comes out well ahead. The North Korean government has been just as horrible to its own citizens as Saddam, falls behind Saddam's Iraq when it comes to belligerence to its neighbours, but pulls ahead when it comes to support for terrorism.

IRAQ

In the all-important WMD category, North Korea is a clear winner.
Iraq didn't have any, North Korea most probably does, makes no secrets
about it (especially after its recent nuclear tests), probably helped other
countries (Pakistan, Libya) towards developing their own WMDs, and
boasts missiles as a major export, along with fake dollar bills, drugs and
drink, although they supplied Scuds not to Iraq, but to Iran. The 39 Scuds
Iraq launched against Israel in 1991 were home-made, and essentially
they were duds, wildly inaccurate and prone to breaking up in flight.
Two Israelis were killed by the Scud barrage and, although the 50-odd
Scuds launched against Saudi Arabia did more damage, it was more by
luck than accuracy. They didn't need Patriot missiles to shoot them down.
Just as well since the initial Kuwait Gulf War claim that Patriots brought
down 80 per cent of Iraqi Scuds was later scaled back to 70, 40, 10 or
perhaps even 0 per cent.

Nevertheless North Korea gets cold-shouldered rather than invaded.
The Kim Il-sung/Jong-il combo are clearly Saddam Hussein competitors
when it comes to undesirability, so how come they escaped?

There's a third alternative to invasion or isolation and that's the carrot
and stick routine that has winkled Libya's Gaddafi out of his self-imposed
seclusion. Gaddafi isn't up to Saddam's standards for rotten treatment of
his own citizens, but he has thrown his weight around locally and been
a keen promoter and actual instigator of terrorist attacks. Plus Libya
definitely did work on WMDs, although the new, reformed Libya has
washed its hand of those nasty activities.

That's all history. Libya gets pushed and pulled, North Korea gets
isolated. Only Iraq gets invaded and occupied.

LIBYA

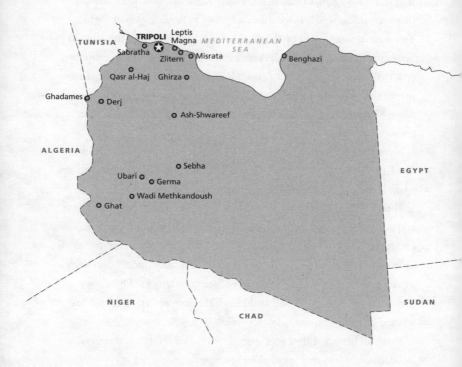

TUNISIA

TRIPOLI ☆ Leptis
Magna *MEDITERRANEAN*
Sabratha ○ *SEA*
Zlitern ○ ○ Misrata
Qasr al-Haj ○ Ghirza ○ Benghazi ○

Ghadames ○ ○ Derj

Ash-Shwareef ○

ALGERIA

Sebha ○

Ubari ○
Germa ○ EGYPT

Wadi Methkandoush ○

Ghat ○

NIGER

CHAD SUDAN

In the mid-1990s Colonel Muammar Gaddafi suddenly decided the Great Socialist People's Libyan Arab Jamahiriya needed something other than the oil business and socialism to keep the population occupied. It wasn't like they needed the money – there was plenty of that, enough to both look after everybody and print as many copies of the Colonel's little Green Book as necessary while still leaving some spare cash in hand for fomenting international terrorism.

'What about tourism?' the Colonel mused, forgetting for a moment his government's unpleasant practice of blowing up French DC10s over the Sahara Desert in Niger, American 747s over Scotland and the odd discotheque in Berlin.

Nasty habits apart, it was not an unreasonable thought. There's no question that as a tourist destination Libya could be huge. Greek history, Roman history, the battlefields of World War II, the old camel caravan towns, the rock-art sites in the desert and the romance of the Sahara and its remote oases. Egypt, immediately to the east, and Tunisia, just to the west, were also desert countries and not unlike Libya in many respects.

Egypt had millions of tourists every year, despite the occasional tourist massacre. And while Egypt had all those Pharaonic ruins and some fine scuba-diving possibilities in the Red Sea, didn't Libya have Leptis Magna, the finest Roman ruins outside of Rome itself? And didn't Libya have beaches every bit as good as Tunisia's, where every year millions of European tourists flocked to Club Med resorts and other sun-sand-and-sex attractions? In contrast to the millions flocking to Egypt and Tunisia, Libya didn't even manage 100,000.

'Why shouldn't Libya have at least a measly little million of them?' Gaddafi reflected before dispatching a minion to London, not with instructions to snipe on London police from the safety of the Libyan Embassy – another little slip-up from the bad old days – but with orders to contract a tourism research organisation.

A few months later I bumped into Rowan Sutherland at a tourism conference in Malaysia.

'He turned up at our door,' said Rowan, a researcher at a London-based tourism consultancy, 'and said that Gaddafi wanted to know what he needed to do to get Libyan tourism off the ground. We said that would be £20,000 please. He wrote the cheque and we're working on the project now.'

'First, however,' Rowan continued, 'we said we needed the answers to three basic questions. For starters, would there be any flights? Libya was still on the "most wanted" list. No self-respecting Western airline would fly there and not only was Libyan Arab Airlines very restricted in where they could fly, they also had difficulty even keeping their planes in the air due to trade sanctions. Not many Libya visitors were likely to arrive by land or sea.

'Secondly, would Libya issue visas for tourists? They'd always been notoriously tight-fisted with visas. It's very difficult to get anybody to come inside if you keep the front door locked and don't answer it when somebody knocks. We quickly found out that it was virtually impossible to get a visa for Libya if you weren't going on official business.

'Don't laugh', Rowan went on. 'There are lots of countries, like India, where the tourist department works hard at attracting visitors while the immigration department works even harder at keeping them out.'

'And the third question?' I asked.

'That was to do with booze', Rowan concluded. 'Libya is staunchly Islamic and alcohol is banned. Lots of those laze-on-the-beach visitors in Tunisia expect to get a cold beer at sundowner time. All those Club Med enthusiasts expect unlimited free wine with their meals. A dry beach holiday wasn't going to attract the beach resort hordes no matter how white the sand or how warm the water.'

. . . .

A decade later, when I finally arrive in Tripoli, Libya's capital, only one of Rowan's questions has been resolved satisfactorily. There are indeed lots more flights into Libya, including the Emirates 777 that brings Maureen and myself in from Dubai. The night before, we'd dined at the Glasshouse, a trendy restaurant in the hyper-stylish glass-chrome-wood Dubai Creek Hilton. Our meal was accompanied by a very pleasant, if rather expensive, bottle of French Bordeaux.

Earlier we sipped a cold beer on a sightseeing cruise up and down The Creek. The tour beers and that bottle of wine would be the last alcohol we'd see for two weeks. Like Saudi Arabia (but unlike Syria and some other hard-line Islamic states) Libya remains a staunch prohibitionist. The Glasshouse meal would also be many Michelin stars better than anything we'd eat in Libya.

So flights, tick; booze, cross. What about visas?

Forget it.

For a start you can't make a solo visit to Libya. Lots of wanted and unwanted sub-Saharan Africans may traipse in across the border, legally

185.

and illegally, but for would-be Western visitors the only way to get in is to sign up for a group tour.

I'd got the names of a couple of reliable agents in Tripoli who could organise a two-person group tour for Maureen and me and sort out the visas. Getting the visas was not straightforward. The agent had to apply. Once this pre-application had been sorted, 'the visa invitation can be faxed to you within three to four days', emailed our agent Saif.

Then we just had to send the invitation to the Libyan embassy (or the Libyan People's Bureau as they tend to be called), get the official visa form (no photocopies or internet downloads available), get the important passport information translated into Arabic and written into our passports (although most people we would bump into in Libya could read our script perfectly well) and then apply for the visas.

There was, however, one more serious obstacle.

'There is a new law which makes it obligatory for travel groups to be at least four people', Saif's email continued. 'If you are just two people, you have to apply with two additional passports, even though only two of you will be actually travelling.'

'Well, the visa situation is certainly strange!' I emailed back. 'So I have to find two people who don't mind applying for a Libyan visa even though they are not going to Libya?'

Precisely.

We would only have to pay for the tour for two and we would only be charged for the work in making two visa applications, but there was no way around applying for four visas. Maureen and I both have dual nationality – could we each apply twice?

Not possible; it had to be four different people.

'Surely you have friends or relatives who hold valid passports and who would not mind having two pages of their passport stamped with the Libyan visa plus the translation of the passport?' queried Saif.

Some people might not find a Libyan visa in their passport too attractive, but eventually my 80-year-old mother volunteered to apply and we 'volunteered' our son.

At this point another obstacle popped up. Australia, we belatedly discovered, did not have a Libyan People's Bureau. The visa forms would have to come to us from the London bureau and our passports would have to be sent back and forth to Europe. The visa forms, however, did not come. Eventually I emailed Saif again and received an effusive apology for his delayed reply and the good news that a Libyan People's Bureau had just opened in Australia. Sure enough there was, but when I phoned the office a polite official apologised and said they could not yet issue visas. He suggested I apply to their diplomatic office in Kuala Lumpur, Malaysia.

By this time I had made the flight bookings to Libya, tagging the visit on to the end of a business trip to Europe. Time was rushing by. I emailed Saif: 'I've phoned the Libyan People's Bureau in Canberra and they are not yet issuing visas and do not know when they will be able to start. So we will have to make the visa application in London.'

Right, said Saif. I went off to the USA on another trip, expecting the forms to arrive while I was away. They didn't, and when I emailed Saif again he was 'terribly sorry for the long delay which is due to a long week of religious holiday we have had recently'.

He went on to explain that 'the London option is now too risky because of the time factor', but there was a new solution. The visas could be issued from Berlin because his agency had 'excellent relations with the Libyan Embassy there'.

OK, do it through Berlin I replied, but again nothing happened. Finally, with time getting right down to the wire, Saif emailed me again to say Berlin was no longer necessary because the Australian Libyan People's Bureau could now issue visas. I phoned the bureau again and guess what? They still couldn't. I sent a final email to Saif: 'It seems to me that this is proving impossible to complete. Perhaps it is not possible

187.

for Battuta Tours to obtain a visa and I should approach a travel agent in London and see if they can organise this for me?'

There was no reply. I may have failed in Tripoli, but tours from London were quite easy to organise – given sufficient time, which I no longer had. They did cost about twice as much for precisely the same tour, but doing it through an agency in Tripoli wasn't intended to be a money-saving operation. I simply wanted to experience it that way. The forms arrived from London, I couriered the passports, forms and photographs back and 48 hours later followed them to London myself, travelling on my second passport. I still had nearly two weeks before I was due to leave Europe to meet Maureen in Dubai and then, a few days later, continue to Libya. Despite which the Libyan People's Bureau contrived to run me right down to the line. There were still no passports in my sweaty hands when I flew out of London. They caught up with me in Dubai.

• • • •

There is love at first sight. I still remember waking up in a train from Talaimannar on the Jaffna Peninsula down to Colombo (we'd somehow snared one of the limited number of sleeper compartments), pulling the blinds up, looking out at this Arcadian vision of rice fields and palm trees, and instantly falling in love with Sri Lanka.

Tripoli doesn't do that.

The immigration official copies our passport data straight from the original page. The expensively procured Arabic translation does not get a glance. I'm watching. Then we're hanging around at the tail end of the passenger huddle, beginning to wonder whether our bags have been lost en route, when the conveyer belt reluctantly coughs them out and immediately grinds to a halt. The reason for their tardy appearance is plainly obvious. The straps have been pulled off my travel pack and someone has been trying to pull the zip open. The padlock on Maureen's bag has been ripped off, taking half the zip slider with it, and the bag is open, although the only sign that somebody has been inside is that the medical kit has been rummaged through. We're still seething as the minibus picking us up merges on to the airport freeway and immediately dials up warp speed for Tripoli. Twenty minutes of computer game highlights follow as we scream up behind taxis, dodge around Mercedes and slalom from one side of the freeway to the other. When I can drag my eyeballs away from the oncoming mayhem, the view from the freeway is not too exciting. Dusty apartment blocks draped with clotheslines seem to be the architectural statement for Tripoli. Satellite dishes (and big ones, not those dinky little things used for Sky TV in Britain) seem to adorn every apartment balcony. 'They're cheap and everybody's bored by the two Libyan channels', our guide in the minibus informs us. 'They'd rather watch Egyptian TV.'

As we approach the centre we pass what looks like a very modern and rather high-tech prison complete with guard towers at every corner and halfway along each wall, but also with a grand entrance.

'What's this – is it a prison?' I ask the guide.

'No, that is the home of our leader', is exactly the reply I expect.

Our hotel is a glossy new five-star affair. It opened as the Corinthia Towers, but the name was quickly changed to the Corinthia Bab Africa, the 'gateway to Africa', an indication of the Colonel's current Africa fixation. It's Tripoli's biggest, brightest, brashest new tourist trap, or it will be as soon as the tourists start to arrive.

Tourists or not, 'we're already running at 100 per cent occupancy', reports Tony Trabone, the dapper little Maltese chief concierge. 'Now if only I could get my staff to arrive on time', he complained. 'They think nothing of arriving three hours late and leaving three hours early.'

A relaxed attitude towards life can be a good thing. We hail a taxi outside the hotel to go to a restaurant just past Green Square for dinner.

'Great music. Who's the guitarist?' I query as the taxi drops us off at

189.

the restaurant.

'I have no idea. A friend made the tape for me', the driver responds, in perfect English. 'Here, have the tape', he continues, ejecting it from the player.

'No, no', I say, pushing the proffered tape away, and making a mental note to take those tales of Arab hospitality a little more seriously before I offer any more casual praise.

Walking back to the hotel we pass Green Square where the whirl of traffic still looks like Grand Theft Auto running at high speed, an impression underlined by a police car, a tow truck and an ambulance lined up side by side at the edge of the square waiting for the inevitable accidents to occur. The bus and shared taxi stations and a gaggle of restaurants, cafés and market stands cluster just beyond our hotel. The long-distance taxis are all Peugeot 504 or 505 station wagons, the 'car' of Africa.

I like Tripoli.

• • • •

The Jamahiriya Museum is magnificent, just as promised, even if four of the five floors are closed the first time we drop in. We do get everything from prehistory through the Punic, Greek and Roman periods with interesting models of the ancient sites and some superb Roman mosaics; I'm a sucker for mosaics. A big map of the country lights up to show prehistoric settlements, the Punic, Greek and Roman advances, and the trading routes into Libya from east and west and across the Saharan wastes to the south, but nothing happens when I press the button for 'Islamic Conquest'.

190.   We don't get the Revolutionary Libya galleries, with all the images of 'the Man', 'the Colonel', the 'father of African unity', the 'knight of the revolutionary phrases' (according to Yasser Arafat), a 'mad dog' (according

to Ronald Reagan) or simply the 'Leader of the Masses' (in his own humble opinion). We do get the battered green (everything to do with Colonel Gaddafi is green) Volkswagen he was beetling around in at the time of the great revolution. A few years ago I had a Beetle of much the same era as the Colonel's, although I'm pleased to report that mine was in much better nick.

The Colonel never saw a revolutionary movement or independence struggle he didn't like. His support for the IRA was notorious; he probably did more for terrorism in Ireland than anybody apart from the Irish of New York and Boston. Even the Welsh nationalists, a group principally known for their attempts to inflict unspellable and unpronounceable place names on the British, got a boost from the Colonel. Despite his enthusiasm for exporting revolution to the West, his greatest efforts were always reserved for pushing Arab nationalism and unity, in the name of which Libya entered into all sorts of completely impractical bonds with neighbouring states. The Federation of Arab Republics with Egypt and Syria in 1972 lasted in some fashion for five years, but others were much shorter. The merger with Tunisia in 1974 was probably a record: the Tunisians pulled out after two days.

There were plenty of other equally unsuitable tilts at Arab unity including one with Morocco in 1984. How was revolutionary Libya (led by the charismatic, if somewhat erratic, Colonel) ever going to hitch up with utterly conservative Morocco (led by a boring king)?

After 30 years of failing to unify the Arab world the Colonel switched horses and trained his sunnies on the south. If he couldn't guide the Arab world to unity, he'd give Africa the benefit of his leadership. In 1999 Gaddafi rolled out his grand plan for a second USA – the United States of Africa. Although it looks likely to be a long time before an African Union rivals the European one, the Colonel's African embrace quickly resulted in accelerated African immigration. Migrant workers from sub-Saharan Africa, particularly Mali, Sudan and Niger, have always found their way

191.

to Libya and the Libyans, happy to have somebody do the menial work they weren't interested in performing, were generally unconcerned. When people from Cameroon, Chad, Ghana, Guinea and Nigeria also started to pour in, the welcome quickly dried up. Riots in 2000 probably led to over 100 deaths and were followed by mass deportations of illegal immigrants.

'We didn't get anything for all the money we put in to the other Arab countries', complained Abdel Chiouch, a young Libyan I met in the teahouse by the Ottoman clock tower in the medina.

'It was a complete waste. When we were hit by the embargo [UN sanctions were unrolled in 1992] nobody stood behind us. The prices of everything went up and none of the Arab states we'd supported did anything for us.

'After more than 10 years we're finally getting away from the embargo, but I think Africa is going to be the same mistake all over again.'

Wandering back from Green Square through the medina towards our hotel we seem to meet half the sub-Saharan population of Libya. There are an absurd number of barber shops down Sharia Homet Gharyan offering an exotic blend of 'Black Men's Haircuts'. Somebody somewhere in English-speaking Africa is turning out a great range of haircut posters. One cheerful hairdresser offers to cut my hair in any of the 40 or so styles on offer, but none of them suits.

Record shops offer pirated CDs of all the current American hip-hop, rap and pop chart-toppers as well as Kenny G. Pirated DVDs are equally popular and there's an interesting collection of West African titles, some of them labelled 'for sale in Ghana only'. I'm tempted by *Reckless Babes* (available as edition one or two) or *God Loves Prostitutes* (well, so does an awful lot of Africa), but *Emergency Wedding* sounds like it could be a big hit. The Western collection includes plenty of pop music video-clips, Hollywood blockbusters and sometimes a whole shelf devoted to Mr Bean.

There are a surprising number of internet cafés and passing travellers are not their main clientele. There simply aren't enough of them. I look into one café where every computer is in use, about a third of them for playing games, some of them for surfing the net, but most for dealing with emails. One guy is on something called Sudan Online, looking at what looks like a Sudanese dating chatroom. Two other guys seem to be composing one of those 'I need to get $17 million out of Nigeria and if you give me your bank account details we can split the proceeds' scams.

. . . .

Having got our visas through a British tour company, we then had a tour to go on. We tagged along on their standard one-week tour, but added our own little two-person tours before and after. Apart from Maureen and me, our group are 100 per cent British and even the two of us, with dual Australian-British nationality, are slightly British. Neither of us is very used to group travel – apart from heading off with a bunch of friends on trekking trips or renting a house somewhere – but in some places a group is inevitable. North Korea, for example. Hardly surprisingly our tour companions are a well-travelled bunch. Nobody heads to Libya on their first trip abroad.

Although, by God, they are British to the core. There's eccentricity – Richard is the prime example and as a result is also our group's clown, tall-tale teller and naughty schoolboy. Naturally there are class issues. With the British there have to be little frissons of tension across class lines. And there's plain old British twitter. All the world may laugh about the insincerity of a Californian's 'have a nice day now', but after a week of l-u-u-u-vlys, w-u-u-u-nderfuls and a-m-a-a-a-zings, a simple 'have a nice day' seems like complete reality.

To hustle the nine of us around Libya takes four people. Abdul Shalgam is the guide, a quietly spoken, small and studious-looking man in his early 70s, but looking much younger. He spent 40 years working in

193.

the Department of Antiquities and clearly knows his stuff.

Salah Adem is the fixer and minder, making sure everybody is on the bus and has their room keys, and generally attending to all the other little problems forgetful tourists seem to generate. He's in his 30s, prematurely balding, very energetic and blessed with a permanent smile. Like Abdul he's from the Cyrenaica region to the east.

Sam-the-driver pilots the bus and is a model of smooth calm, always there and ready to go, never in a hurry, but equally never hanging around. And then there's Issei. At first I think he's Sam's offsider, the driver's general assistant, which seems to be a necessity in so many countries in the developing world, but then it's clear he doesn't actually do much assisting.

'He's our policeman', explains Salah. 'Every group of seven or more has to have one.'

'So what does he do?' There seems to be remarkably little for our very own policeman to accomplish, given that we're processed through checkpoints at regular intervals along every highway by Salah who has a stack of photocopies of his passenger list, detailing our names (in Arabic as well), our professions (either 'retired' or 'working'), dates of birth, passport numbers and nationalities.

'If we have any problems or the bus breaks down,' Salah explains, 'then he will help.'

I can't imagine what he would do. He doesn't have a weapon in the unlikely case we need protecting from somebody, he doesn't have a phone in case we need help and I'm positive if the bus broke down he'd be completely useless. In reality, Issei is just another example of Libya's huge programme of government make-work – somebody else who has been given a useless job to keep them busy.

194.

Some of the group were already finding the trips too long, the toilets too dirty or the food too dreary, although to be honest we all soon found the food lived up to Libya's reputation for 'the dullest cuisine in North

Africa'. The only real dispute comes right at the end and of all things it's over tipping. A couple of Americans on board would have sorted it out immediately. It's partly word from above that we should tip and partly some feelings that tipping the secret policeman is definitely not our responsibility. I fall between the two extremes, happy to tip, but feeling no compulsion to tip the secret policeman – I didn't want him, he didn't do anything and if Gaddafi wanted to send somebody along to spy on me that was his responsibility.

• • • •

What is it about dictators and having their portraits – or better still their statues – everywhere? The Colonel's pictures are pretty ubiquitous in Libya, but they're a long way from high art. Quite often they're set up as revolving billboards, so two or three different likenesses are recycled every 30 seconds. There's a distinct style to Gaddafi portraits. The favourite is standing with arms folded, gazing upwards, so you always seem to be looking up his nose. Quite often he's wearing sunglasses, so that you can't tell if he's peering myopically at something – perhaps written on the ceiling? Some older photographic portraits show him dressed in the HMS *Pinafore* school of naval attire, always a favourite with dictators. The portrayal I like best, however, is on the one-dinar note, where he stands with one hand to the side of his face, looking like he's auditioning for a part in the Libyan production of *Queer Eye for the Straight Guy* and about to announce that this week's nerd has taste that is just too awful.

Like a surprising number of other dictators, Gaddafi soon realised that the brilliance that had led him to the seat of power had to be recorded for the benefit of the citizens of less-enlightened countries. In North Korea forests fell for the numerous books Kim Il-sung wrote to explain the earth-shaking importance of the *Juche* Idea, his formula for economic independence and wellbeing. China had Mao's *Little Red Book*, and in the mid-1970s Gaddafi retreated into the desert and came back with *The Green Book* – a slim volume easily available in a variety of languages from bookshops in Tripoli. Explained in just 120 pages, Gaddafi's 'Third Universal Theory' will, if we only take the trouble to apply it, solve all the world's problems. Presumably Libya's have already been sorted out.

The Green Book is divided into three handy sections, starting with 'The Solution of the Problem of Democracy'. The problem, so it seems, is that there isn't any out there. Democracy is all about representing the people and since we end up electing somebody else to represent us we aren't representing ourselves, ergo we don't have democracy. Political parties, parliaments, plebiscites and the press are all undemocratic and the solution, which you'll see posted up widely around Libya, is 'committees everywhere'. Once everything is decided by committees, we'll all have democracy, just like in Libya.

Having solved the democracy question Gaddafi goes on to sort out economics in Part Two, 'The Solution of the Economic Problem'. In a word it's socialism with the catchy slogan 'partners not wage-workers'. There's a detailed explanation of why getting paid for work is no different from slavery, a handy little example about producing 10 apples but not being happy unless you get to keep all 10 and some serious warnings about the dangers of employing domestic servants. It's also suggested that everybody needs to own their own land and their own house and preferably their own car. Since a surprising number of people in Tripoli own shiny new BMWs, Audis and Mercedes, this could be the kind of socialism we can all live with. Not Hertz or Avis, however. Gaddafi warns us that we should certainly not 'possess private vehicles for the purpose of hiring them out', because that's pretty much like enslaving the people who rent them.

196.

Finally Gaddafi really gets into his stride when he lays out 'The Social Basis of the Third Universal Theory' in Part Three. First of all he explains the pros and cons of 'Families', 'Tribes' and 'Nations' before getting down

to a serious think about women and why they're different to men. Part
of it is that 'woman menstruates or suffers feebleness every month, while
man, being a male, does not'. Having made this shattering discovery he
quickly moves on to conclude that another big difference between the
sexes is that women can get pregnant, in which case they are 'feeble for
about a year'. Perhaps this is because men are 'strong and tough' while
women are 'beautiful and gentle'. Much is made of the more liberated role
of women in Gaddafi's new Libya, but in fact there's remarkably little of it
to be seen. Women may not be invariably veiled and shrouded, but they're
generally well covered up and what is much more noticeable is that they
are simply not visible. In so many situations the crowd (in a teahouse, in
an internet café, even on the streets) will be 100 per cent male. Gaddafi's
'female bodyguards', a favourite in most tales about the Colonel, are really
just another little piece of showmanship. The real weaponry is packed by
men.

Discovering how men and women are different and deciding what to do
about it takes up the longest section of the book, but there's still room to
ponder 'Minorities', 'Education', 'Melodies and Art' and, in some of the
best gobbledegook in the book, the question of 'The Blacks' and 'Sport,
Horsemanship and Shows'.

Sport could easily be sorted out if we all played it rather than wasted
our time watching it. Then we'll all be down on the field kicking the ball
around rather than sitting in the grandstands and as a result 'stadiums
will be vacated and destroyed'. The black race is going to solve its own
problem by the simple process of out-populating everybody else, due to
the fact that 'their low standard of living has protected them from getting
to know the means and ways of birth control and family planning'.
Population increase is also lower among other races because they work
too damn hard, unlike 'the blacks who are sluggish in a climate which is
always too hot'.

Travel-writing friend Jennifer Cox said that Gaddafi's *Green Book* ideology also included the promise that everyone in Libya should get at least the basic essentials of life – a loaf of bread and a bottle of olive oil. I never saw it, but Jennifer said she saw piles of bread being dumped under half-built overpasses in Tripoli, left there to feed the hungry.

• • • •

Heading south from Tripoli into the desert, it's a couple of hours before we pull off at Qasr al-Haj, a wonderful fortified granary. The huge mud-built circle encloses 114 separate chambers, one for every chapter in the Koran. They were once used to store grain on the upper floors and olive oil in the basement level and are arranged in a charming higgle-piggle of ups and downs, looking like something that came from a child's scribble-pad rather than an architectural drawing-board. Further south there's another fortified granary at Nalut, a town perched on top of a plateau reached by a zigzag road from the plain.

The road runs through progressively more barren country – 'featureless' and 'waste' spring to mind. The imminent arrival of the occasional bleak little settlement of flat-roofed, block-shaped buildings is signposted by the litter of plastic bags and bottles, tin cans of varying ages, and general junk and rubbish that coats the roadsides in most populated parts of Libya. *The Green Book* may have set out to solve most of the world's problems, but it's clear the Colonel never got round to writing the chapter about keeping the Great Socialist People's Libyan Arab Jamahiriya tidy. Libya is one of the most comprehensively trashed countries I've ever visited.

We stop for lunch at a roadside filling station a little south of Sinoun. By this time the *ghibli*, the 'hot, dry wind from the south', is blowing at gale force and the usual overcast sky has taken on a uniform beige shade. Venturing out of the bus, you feel your eyes start to burn and the gritty sand on your teeth. Every couple of minutes through lunch the wind bursts the door open and one of us has to jump up to push it shut again. A small souvenir shelf offers a nice series of 'American Aggression' postage stamps, Gaddafi wristwatches in male and female models, and the first Gaddafi T-shirt I've spotted in Libya.

There's a final brief pause at Derj, a grotty little junction town brightened only by two excellent king-size Gaddafi billboards. I have to lean into the sand storm to run back down the road to photograph them. Meanwhile our group huddles in the Tsawa Company for Tourism café and watches what looks like 'Arab Idol' broadcast from Cairo. The weedy teenager from Syria wins and bursts into tears. On the final stretch to Ghadames, sand dunes have blown across the road in a couple of places.

At first glance Ghadames, the 'jewel of the Sahara', is just another jumble of block-shaped buildings and the Khafila Hotel is straight out of the cheap-and-nasty school of construction. Our ugly little room, with its squeaky metal door, is furnished with a collection of shoddy chipboard furniture including two lumpy beds. The bathroom features a shower but no shower curtain, so the floor is quickly awash and there's neither a fan nor air-conditioner. In late winter that's no problem, but the room must be uninhabitable in summer.

In contrast the old town, where Maureen and I head as soon as we've left our bags, is a Unesco World Heritage–listed delight. With one small problem: it's utterly deserted. Even tourists are absent for our impromptu evening circuit, although we're intercepted at the Bab al-Burr, the main entrance to the old city, by an utterly charming French-speaking guide who gives us a short introduction to what we'll experience at greater length the next day.

That night dinner (for the fifth meal in a row, French fries are a feature) is followed by a surprisingly good Tuareg 'cultural performance' for the predominantly Italian and Japanese guest list. Jerry-built or not, the Khafila has 100 per cent occupancy. A sextet of drummers beat tune to a wailing flute player's lead while six men (one of whom we'd chatted to earlier outside the Ghadames internet café) work through a repertoire of high-stepping, fast-paced, perfectly synchronised dances. There's a costume change between every dance and the exuberant ensemble's nifty footwork is emphasised by the beautifully embroidered slippers that are a Ghadames speciality. Next day Maureen buys a pair. The final energetic whirl, featuring one dancer dressed up as some wild beast, even convinces our skinny police minder Issei to join in.

The next morning the old city is populated by tourists, if not the citizens of Ghadames. In the 1980s the Libyan government decided to build a new town, presumably in the same building blitz as our tatty hotel. Within five years the old city's 6000 inhabitants had shifted to their new home.

'Voluntarily', insists Mohamed al-Houni, our local guide, who is just as charming, though English- rather than French-speaking, as the previous evening's equivalent.

'Nobody was forced to leave, but the new houses had electricity, running water and toilets,' he explained, 'so everyone kept their old homes and still sometimes visit them, but they all moved to the new city.'

That afternoon I track down Abdulgader Abufayed, the UN's project manager for the old city rehabilitation project. 'Moving out was purely voluntary,' he confirms, 'but a city without people is a monument. We have to find ways of bringing the city back alive.

'We are investigating many ways of doing that. I think in the end it will be a combination of handicrafts, tourism and investment. We have to find ways of making the city self-propelling. It has to be capable of sustaining itself. There is no taboo on new ideas. Some people may move back in but it will not be completely repopulated. The old city could not provide the facilities people demand today.'

200.

Lack of running water and sewerage are the key missing components, but there's no reason the old city could not be plumbed and have sewers installed without losing its character. The restoration that took place around 2001 is easy to appreciate at street level, but looking across the rooftops from our lunch stop it was easy to pick out the white-painted houses that had been restored among the other crumbling rooftops and towers. The beautifully decorated old house where we have lunch is clearly kept for just such occasions; it's a real highlight.

'What has happened is not so bad', Abulgader concludes. 'It's not like the new city was built on top of the old and destroyed it. The old city is still all there.'

Richard and I had already kicked around one idea. 'A company like Aman Resorts could turn a series of the houses into a wonderful hotel. I can just see the tables and umbrellas set out on the roof terraces.

'Then we'll make a sunset drive to Algeria at gin and tonic time', Richard continued. 'We'll set up a little enclave just across the border.'

The Algerian border is not much more than 10 kilometres away and indeed we do head in that direction for sunset. Salah collects our passports before we leave – in case we stray across the border?

Close to the border we stop to climb to the summit of Ras al-Ghoul, the evocatively named Mountain of Ghosts. From the top of this crumbling desert castle we gaze down at the campsite where an Islamic force besieged the castle in AD 668. Just beyond the camp is a graveyard and from there the spectacular views roll away to the west. The sand dunes we can see are actually across the border in Algeria and we can also see to Tunisia, just to the north.

Descending from the castle, we drive a few more kilometres to a series of towering sand dunes, where our drivers engage in a bit of dune bashing, racing up the hills in our Land Cruisers although with less success than on a similar dune-hooning trip near Dubai a few days earlier. Our Land Cruiser in particular is arthritic and asthmatic.

Maureen, Salah, Issei-the-secret-policeman and I clamber up to the top of the topmost dune, floundering up through the fine sand to the summit. The afternoon wind is whistling up over the edge and abrading us with

the windblown sand. We get back down to the cars just at sunset – our
drivers have built a fire and are baking bread and making tea. Give us a
billabong and we could be in Australia making damper and boiling the
billy.

• • • •

'*Buongiorno!*' A volley of greetings ricochets across the breakfast
tables; Italians are far and away Libya's biggest tourist contingent, which
is not surprising given it's only 500 kilometres from Syracuse in Sicily
to Tripoli, only a two-hour flight from Rome. It is, however, also very
surprising, given Italy's dismal colonial record. Like Belgium, that other
European power that got into the empire game late in the day, the Italians
didn't prove very good at it. Libya and Ethiopia both paid the price.

At the turn of the 20th century, Libya was another part of the rapidly
decaying Ottoman Empire, which by the end of World War I would
totally implode, leaving Turkey as its forward-looking replacement. By
the end Iraq, Syria, Lebanon, Jordan, Palestine, Egypt and Libya had all
gone their own ways or, more often, been gobbled up by somebody else.
In unlucky Libya's case it was the Italians who did the gobbling. When
the Italians booted the Ottomans out in 1911–12, they claimed it was
to liberate the Libyans, ignoring the cold reality that the Libyans had
been working very hard at liberating themselves from Ottoman rule for
many years. It was nothing new. The USA had claimed to be liberating
Cuba and the Philippines from Spanish rule in remarkably similar
circumstances after the Spanish-American War in 1898.

For the next 30 years the Libyans struggled against Italian rule, most
notably under the leadership of Omar al-Mukhtar, the 'Lion of the
Desert'. Al-Mukhtar was finally captured and executed by the Italians in
1931. Today his statue tops one of the columns outside Tripoli Castle at
the corner of Green Square. In the late 1930s Mussolini began to ship in

Italian settlers by the boatload and Italian control finally began to extend
to all corners of the country. Italian domination came at enormous cost
to the Libyans. It has been estimated that up to a quarter of the Libyan
population died during the three decades of Italian colonialism.

Then World War II arrived and Libya became the battleground
where the Afrika Korp of Rommel (the 'Desert Fox') slugged it out with
the Eighth Army of Montgomery (the 'Full Monty'). When the sand
settled in late 1942, the Germans had suffered their first major defeat
of the war and by early 1943 it was the British rather than the Italians
who controlled things from Tripoli. The war ended with the British
Empire heading for rapid downsizing. There was certainly no incentive
to add an impoverished and disgruntled new stretch of desert to the
Commonwealth. The French had a go at grabbing a chunk of southwest
Libya to weld on to Algeria, but Libya finally became independent in
1951.

For the rest of the 1950s Libya struggled to repair the damage of
Italian colonialism and World War II, but the discovery of oil in 1959
quickly made it a very different place. Libya suddenly became the richest
country in Africa and a succession of governments proved incapable
of coping with the new-found wealth. The Six Day War in 1967 and
the shock waves it sent through the Arab world probably triggered the
upheaval that brought Gaddafi to power. Quite apart from popular anger
with governmental excess, corruption and favouritism, there was now
anger at a government that had paid loud lip-service to Arab nationalism,
but in fact had done nothing to support the front-line Arab states.

The revolution in 1969 was remarkably peaceful (there were very few
deaths) although initially a little puzzling (it was nearly a week later
before Colonel Gaddafi popped up as the new leader) and then went
charging off at high speed. Gaddafi quickly nationalised businesses
(proving his socialist credentials), redistributed wealth (pleasing the large
percentage of the population who resented Libya's wealthy elite, which

had profited from the oil boom) and set out on his quixotic campaign for Arab unity (pleasing those who thought Libya wasn't doing enough for Arab nationalism).

He also kicked out the remaining Italian settlers, dispossessed Libya's Jewish community and took an each-way bet on Islam by closing churches or converting them into mosques (which pleased religious hardliners), but then stacking the mosques with compliant clergy (which didn't).

With his penchant for dressing up, Gaddafi was always the Peter Pan of dictators. One day he was taking his lead from Hollywood (desert sheikh followed by safari suit) and the next it was rock music (military uniforms from the Sergeant Pepper dress-up box followed by a lounge-lizard outfit from Bryan Ferry). Since Libya often seemed to be Neverland and the Colonel's behaviour was often as erratic as his wardrobe choices, there was also a definite flavour of Michael Jackson about the place. One day he was welcoming another terrorist group to Tripoli (although the IRA were never happy with a place where beer was unobtainable), the next day he was banning shops (all of Tripoli was briefly serviced by just seven government-owned supermarkets and Yasser Arafat flew in to cut the ribbon at the opening ceremonies). Then he was launching the Great Man-Made River project to turn the desert green or even changing the name of the country from simple old Libya to the Great SPLAJ, the catchy acronym for Socialist People's Libyan Arab Jamahiriya. Jamahiriya translates somewhat like 'state of the masses'.

In the 1980s Gaddafi's revolutionary impulses started to make him very unpopular outside of Libya. Part of the problem were the 'revolutionary committees', which, like Mao's Red Guard, began to have a life of their own. No Libyan who spoke out against Gaddafi was safe from these firebrands, not only in Libya, but also abroad. Assassination attempts took place all over Europe, reaching an extreme in London in 1984 when a sniper in the Libyan embassy fired on Libyan protesters outside on the street and managed to kill a police officer. The Libyans in the embassy were all sent home and Britain severed relations with Libya. America had done so three years earlier.

More assassinations, an expensive (in cash and lives) and ultimately unsuccessful border dispute with neighbouring Chad, attacks on passengers at Rome and Vienna airports in 1985 by Libyan-aided and Libyan financed Palestinian extremists, and finally the Pan Am and UTA airliner explosions in 1988 and 1989 all elevated Libya to the top of the international most-wanted list and in 1992 the UN instituted sanctions, which would make life very difficult for the next 10 years.

Of course, as with all the Bad Lands, things weren't all one way and Reagan's missile strike at Benghazi and Tripoli in 1986 wasn't the only occasion the Libyans have been attacked. In February 1973 Libyan Arab Airlines flight 114 departed Tripoli to fly via Benghazi to Cairo. The aircraft was chartered from a French operator and although the co-pilot, the flight attendants and most of the passengers were Libyan, the captain was French. Approaching Cairo the 727 flew into a sandstorm and the pilot lost sight of the usual visual approach markers and at the same time overshot a radio beacon. Air traffic control in Cairo warned him that he was approaching the Sinai, still under Israeli control following the 1967 Six Day War. The aircraft made a hasty U-turn and headed back towards Cairo, but not quickly enough to evade two Israeli Air Force Phantoms, which intercepted the airliner and shot it down, less than a minute's flying time from Egyptian air space. From the black box voice-recorder it appeared the crew did not realise they had strayed into Israeli-controlled air space and only realised the aircraft were Israeli, not Egyptian, at the last moment.

There were only five survivors from the 113 passengers and crew.

Of course, when trigger-happy military personnel shoot down civilian aircraft it's never a good look. So did the Israel government do some quick explaining and apologising? Over to you, Golda Meir: 'I want to tell you that I don't just appreciate you, I admire you!' she said to Israeli

Chief of Staff Dado Elazar, who had ordered the airliner shot down.

Well, they were only Libyans.

• • • •

It was Roman ruins that first attracted me to Libya. Of course, every visitor to Rome inspects the Coliseum and the other ruins at the centre of the empire, but at its peak Rome extended not just across Europe, but east into Asia and south into Africa. Years ago I walked across Britain from east to west, following Hadrian's Wall, which marked the northern extreme of the empire. I loved the feeling that the centurions stationed here were living life right on the edge, guarding the outer boundaries of the empire against the Scottish wild men to the north. One account I read commented how this was undoubtedly a hardship posting, but also tied up with excitement and danger. To the Romans, Scotland in those days was the equivalent of darkest Africa to the Victorian explorers.

Africa and Asia, on the other hand, offered warmth, wine and more than a touch of civilisation. I've been to the superb ruins of Ephesus in Turkey, Palmyra in Syria and Volubilis in Morocco, but Leptis Magna, on the Libyan coast about 100 kilometres east of Tripoli, is regularly cited as the most magnificent site around the Mediterranean.

Although Leptis Magna was first settled from the 7th century BC, it only became really important around the time of the birth of Christ, under the Emperor Augustus. The city became an important port and began to acquire those architectural symbols that distinguished an important Roman city, including a market and a theatre. Olive oil was a lucrative, although mundane, export through the port, but the trade in wild animals to appear in the Roman spectacles was a much more exotic activity. When Septimus Severus, 'the grim African', marched on Rome in AD 193, the centre of gravity of the Roman Empire shifted southwards and for a spell the new emperor had visions of Leptis Magna rivalling Rome itself. A long peaceful spell accelerated the city's growth, but then war returned and in AD 211 Severus was killed in battle in England.

For another century Leptis continued in undiminished splendour before floods, earthquakes and Roman neglect began to take their toll. The city fell into Byzantine hands in the 6th century and the construction of a wall around the city forewarns of the Arab invasion that followed a century later. By the 10th century the once-splendid city was deserted and disappearing beneath the sand.

We're certainly not disappointed with the ruins. Because no modern city was built nearby or, worse, right on top of the ancient Roman site, Leptis Magna is very well preserved. The triumphant Arch of Septimus Severus, the luxurious Hadrianic Baths, the Nymphaem – the 'Temple of Nymphs', the huge marble-floored Severan Forum with its many remarkably expressive Gorgon heads and the grand theatre all speak of the city's glory days. A party of school children arrive at the theatre at the same time as our group and, spotting the Western visitors, they line up on the stage to launch into that Disney number 'It's a Small World'.

We walk further east to inspect the extraordinarily well-kept 16,000-seat amphitheatre and the circus or hippodrome where wheel-to-wheel chariot races were once staged in front of up to 25,000 cheering spectators.

Despite its fine state of preservation, Leptis Magna still faces grave risks from the modern world. Exploring the market area Abdul Shalgam is dismayed to discover a missing piece of ancient balustrade. He's certain that it was there the last time he visited and tyre tracks across the paving to the spot underline his concerns.

'Look,' he points out, 'they've backed a truck up here, levered it out and taken it away. It looks like it's only happened in the last few days. The guards are simply not taking enough care.'

Of course sites like this are always threatened by greedy collectors and regrettably the danger is not a new one. Back in the late 17th century Claude Le Maire, the French consul to Tripoli, ransacked the site, shipping off huge numbers of marble columns to France. The Versailles chateau and the St Germain des-Pres church both feature pieces plundered from Leptis Magna.

Although Leptis Magna is Libya's most important Roman site, it's not the only one. We had already ventured east from Tripoli to visit Sabratha, a Roman city with an even more magnificent theatre than Leptis Magna (although without a troupe of school kids to sing to us). If our visit to Libya had been longer, we could have continued east towards the World War II battlegrounds of Tobruk and visited the ancient Greek ruins at Cyrene and Apollonia.

At lunchtime in Leptis Magna my soft drink comes from the 'African Bottling Operation, Tripoli, Great Socialist People's Libyan Jamahiriya under the supervision of Pepsico Inc'. US trade embargo? What US trade embargo? Pepsi is clearly the market leader in Libya, although Coke is also available. The principal Libyan soft drink is Bitter Soda, which looks and tastes remarkably like fizzy red mouthwash.

We finish Leptis Magna with a visit to the excellent museum. The penultimate room is a very unimaginative collection of pressies to the Colonel. 'It's all nothing', a young student who had attached himself to Maureen for some English conversation announces, with a dismissive wave of his hand.

'A revolution? We have not had a revolution', he continues, clearly unconcerned that any of the Gaddafi memorabilia was bugged. 'A revolution has to come from everybody. This was not a revolution, this was him taking over.

'But he has the weapons', he concludes thoughtfully.

208.

The museum itself concludes with a huge two-storey-high cut-out image of the Man with arms raised exultantly and the happy throngs crowding at his feet. It would be fun to pose our contingent for a group

photo on the balcony, gathered around him, peering over his shoulders
and round each side of his head.

That night we continue a little further east along the coast to overnight
at the port of Zlitern. Wandering back through the town to our hotel,
I pause to gawk at the sheer number of satellite dishes tacked on to the
tatty apartment blocks. In one shop I spot a 'super luxury size beach
towel' sporting the English Arsenal football club badge so I buy it for
my Arsenal fan son. As in shops all over Libya, lots of the outlets here
are fronted by large displays of footballs. Clearly there's a big demand
from local soccer players. Gaddafi's son actually captained Al-Ahly, one
of the two major Tripoli football teams, and the Libyan national team,
which still hasn't made Libya into one of Africa's great football nations.
Even football can be political in Libya. In 1996 fans began chanting
anti-government slogans during a game in which he was playing. His
bodyguards proceeded to open fire on the crowd and killed at least 20
spectators.

The next day there's another foray into the desert before we return to
Tripoli. We follow the coast for a stretch beyond Misrata to the east,
then turn inland and finally on to a gravel road that runs beside the Great
Man-Made River for 80 kilometres before finally turning off again to
ancient Ghirza.

It's a minor site, a collection of tombs built in the Roman style, but
probably by Libyans who had profited from serving in the Roman army.
We picnic under acacia trees close to the larger group of tombs and wash
our food down with bottles of 'Water from the Great Man-Made River'.
Then we drive on a couple of kilometres to a smaller assortment of tombs,
picturesquely perched close to the edge of a deep wadi with beautiful
acacias scattered across its sandy floor.

At both sites Abdul frets that nobody is looking after these
irreplaceable sites properly. Yesterday's discovery of the damage at Leptis
Magna was a shock. Today there's a lintel fallen from the roof of a tomb.

209.

'I'm sure that was there last time', he worries. There have been so many police roadblocks. Why couldn't they pull some of them off that time-waster of an occupation and put them on duty looking after the ancient sites?

• • • •

The rest of our group has gone back to England when Maureen and I head south to the Fezzan. In early spring the countryside is unexpectedly green and fertile for the first 100 kilometres out of Tripoli, then it starts to dry out and before the 200-kilometre line it's utterly barren – only at the occasional wadi is there much vegetation. The scenery is never without interest. The road climbing through dramatic rocky hills, then running across equally desolate plains but the view always punctuated by distant ranges, flat-topped mesas or curiously eroded pyramidal hills. Occasionally there's a scatter of camels or a telecommunications tower. At one point what looks like a Burmese pagoda pops up on the horizon only to resolve into another communications device, a bizarre stepped-structure fronted by a bank of solar panels. The infrequent settlements – always preceded by a denser roadside crust of plastic bags, frayed tyres, crushed water bottles and rusted tin cans – are dusty, drear little eruptions of half-built breezeblock buildings, a petrol station, a couple of teahouses (in one of them the proprietor is watching *Spartacus* when we drop in), a shop or two, and the inevitable police checkpoint. The roads are smooth, the traffic light, the speed limit 100 kilometres per hour. The speedo needle sits at 150.

Further south, there's a lunch stop at Ash-Shwareef. After we stumble through a confusion of Arabic, English and French (the French works best) the meal is the usual salad-soup-chicken-rice-chips, but it's a cheerful place – it would be a good highway truck-stop in the US or Australia. Afterwards the country becomes extraordinarily barren. At times there is not a leaf or blade of vegetation as far as you can see, but the road parallels the Great Man-Made River for a stretch and crosses it a couple of times. After Brak we sail into the Idehan Ubari, the Ubari Sand Sea. This is serious sand-dune country and the afternoon *ghibli* whisks a film of sand across the road just a few centimetres above the road level. A dragon's backbone of dunes, regular as a sine wave, ripples away to the southeast.

Finally there's Sebha, a bustling metropolis with an old Italian fort and the airport. Just beyond the town is the truck park where grossly overloaded trucks labour in after long hauls across the empty desert from sub-Saharan Africa. In Australia almost every year a battered pick-up truck of Aboriginals grinds to a halt somewhere in the outback and before help arrives half of the five or 10 passengers have died of thirst. When disaster hits these African truckfuls of economic immigrants the numbers are likely to be 10 times as large. In 2001 a broken-down truck was found with 96 dead passengers. And 23 survivors.

From Sebha the road runs along the extraordinary Wadi al-Hayat, a green mirage in the heart of the Sahara. For 150 kilometres it's stony silence along the south side of the road and an intensively farmed strip along the north while massive sand dunes parallel the road only a few kilometres away. After the long, empty road south from Tripoli, this stretch is comparatively heavily trafficked. Finally we turn into the Dar Germa Hotel in Germa to be met by the equally extraordinary sight of Hassan Sharif, looking like a Tuareg garage mechanic, his *ashaersh*, the Tuareg turban, making a strange contrast with his Ferrari-red overalls.

Hassan learnt his English during a year-long spell in Dublin. The weather? 'Yes, it was terrible. There was rain, even snow!' Later he confides that it gets bloody cold in Germa during the winter as well.

The next morning Hassan is dressed Tuareg-style from the neck down as well as the neck up, his pale, mauve turban contrasting nicely with a black *galabiyya*, the full-length loose-fitting robe worn by men. Properly

LIBYA

attired he looks even more dashingly handsome, ready to stride across
any desert that presents itself. His endlessly cheerful offsider Mohammed
sports a gold-brown turban and a purple robe. Mohammed is from Niger
and speaks French, so for the rest of the day the conversation is a three-
way Arabic, English, French melange.

We cruise a few kilometres back down the road towards Sebha, turn
off through the farmed strip, stop to let air out of the tyres to cope with
the sand, and almost immediately disappear into the sand dunes. Within
minutes all directions disappear and I'm secretly glad I've brought my
GPS along and set the co-ordinates for Germa before we left. For the
next hour we swoop up and down over the dunes, sometimes stopping
for Hassan or Mohammed to clamber up a nearby dune, possibly to
reconnoitre the route, possibly simply to spy out a patch of *fish-fash*, the
patches of ultra-fine sand that can bog even a carefully driven Land
Cruiser.

If you've got a 'children's book' view of the Sahara – endless rolling
sand dunes, the only sign of life a camel caravan plodding across the
lifeless sand (of course, Toyota Land Cruisers are substituted for camels)
– then this is it. We're even heading towards the postcard-perfect desert
oasis – pools of clear water surrounded by green palm trees and then by
the golden, burning sands. In fact the Ubari Lakes number more than a
dozen. At Maharouba, the 'Burning' Lake, we come across a small party
of Germans, two couples with some very small children. They've been
dropped off here to camp by this little-visited lake for a week or two.
Continuing west, with more stops to look around, we labour to the top
of a particularly high dune and nudge our nose over the sharp edge of the
sand ridge. The deep blue Gebraoun Lake appears directly below us.

'Ooooh', breathe Hassan and Mohammed in unison, as if they're
amazed to have tumbled upon it.

'*Une bonne casquette*', announces Sher, the manager of the Winzrik
campsite beside the lake. He's from Mali and he's spotted his home

country on the map of Africa on my cap. It's easy to imagine the caravans pulling in to this desert oasis and in a sense they still do, except today the distant tribes are from Italy, the Netherlands or France and their camels have 'morphed' into Toyotas.

The village of Gebraoun itself has gone. The inhabitants were relocated to new apartments by the main road in 1991. At Ghadames I was told that everyone went voluntarily, but here's there no question that it took force to move some of the villagers from their remote homes by the beautiful desert lake. Today some visitors only stop for lunch and perhaps a quick dip; others hang around, perhaps renting a pair of skis or even a snowboard from Sher to try a little sand-skiing down the dunes.

• • • •

The next day we head a few kilometres directly south from Germa, climbing up through the dark, stony range that backdrops the view. Then we turn west and for the next two hours race across a wide, featureless plain. Far to the south the view ends at a range of towering sand dunes, the start of the Murzuq Sand Sea. Later the dark trace of the Msak Settafet range emerges to the north. There's no trail to follow. The route could be a hundred or even a thousand lanes wide, despite which there is a police checkpoint in the middle of nowhere. Finally we leave the plain to make a short traverse of another stretch of textbook Sahara desert, race across some more featureless plain, and finally rock and roll over a corner of the Ocean of Stone before coming to a halt at Wadi Methkandoush.

The walls of the wadi and its southern extension, the Wadi In Galghien, form a remarkable gallery of rock art of the 10,000–6000 BC 'Wild Fauna Period'. It's a significant site for its remote location and for the extraordinary quantity of artwork, but also for the history so vividly illustrated. Global warming and climate change are such current topics that it's easy to forget how recently the Sahara was very different from

213.

LIBYA

the arid sandbox we've been cruising around. When the artists chipped out their illustrations on the wadi walls the Sahara was populated with animals that today are only found in the less extreme climates of countries far to the south.

The history of change the rock art illustrates is an eye opener, but the exceptional quality of much of the work is equally amazing. Elephants, ostriches and a variety of cattle and antelope appear regularly. There's at least one notable rhino and an equally impressive crocodile, but it's giraffes that really inspired these ancient Sahara artists. Even the complex patterns of the animal's hide are faithfully reproduced on some of the wadi's giraffes. My favourite, and it's equally popular on postcards, shows two giraffes and an elephant in a novel transparent style so you effectively see all of all three animals at once.

Driving back to Germa, we take a longer detour into the sand-dune country. Once again we're in picture-book Sahara, where sand rolls away in every direction and even a hubcap-high bush is a rarity. And once again we nose out over the top of a high dune and look down upon a lake, except this lake has disappeared, leaving just the rocky white pattern of its drying death throes. Once upon a time it must have been just like the Ubari Lakes. Now, like the water, the surrounding vegetation has totally disappeared. As we gaze out over this scene of utter emptiness, there is absolutely no sign of life between us and the horizon until, from behind a fold in the distant dunes, the tiny figure of a camel emerges. It's quickly followed by six more, trudging across the landscape towards some far-off water source known only to thirsty camels and their drivers.

It's a pleasure to get back to the Dar Germa Hotel and shower off the sand and dust that quickly coats you and everything else in the car. It's a particular pleasure in our room's extravagant bathroom. Although the hotel was described as 'very basic', a step down from the merely 'basic' hotel in Ghadames, in fact it's neat and tidy and illustrated with all sorts of Sahara photographs, pictures and maps. The bathroom is the same

214.

size as our entire room at Ghadames and equipped with a sink, toilet, bidet and a variety of fittings in an extravagantly kitsch gold-trimmed style. This is nicely counterbalanced by utterly utilitarian and completely exposed plumbing, which snakes and writhes its way from the wheezy water-heater mounted high on the wall. It seems to be a one-off; other rooms have much less extravagant bathrooms. The hotel's food is also several notches above 'very basic' – perhaps a function of the Sudanese cook, the staff from Mali, Niger and Egypt and the Italian woman who manages the show.

The following day we venture into the Ubari Sand Sea again. It's the same routine: down the highway a few kilometres, turn north through the farmed strip, stop to drop the tyre pressures and disappear into the rolling dunes. It's clear Hassan loves plotting a path through the dunes, careful never to drop too low into depressions, exhilarated when we top a big one. Once again we suddenly emerge at the top of a ridge to find a green-fringed lake below us. Mandara, like Gebraoun, once had a village, which was forced to relocate in 1991. Here the village would soon have had to leave anyway. In the early 1980s the lake started to dry up until today it's just a collection of pools and puddles.

'I think it's because of the agricultural projects', announces Hassan. 'They take too much water.'

Yesterday we'd driven by one of the projects. Its enormous irrigated circles of grain are fed by wells tapped into the underground desert aquifers. Is there any connection between that project's launch in the early 1980s and Mandara Lake starting to dry up at the same time?

Dried up or not, it's still an idyllic scene from the top of the sand ridge, but 20 years ago we would have been gazing down at a lake famed for its changing colours while the sounds of children playing drifted up to us. Now it's completely quiet. Down at the lake the pools and puddles are crusted with thin ice-like skins of salt.

'Too much water for agriculture', repeats Hassan.

We pause at the abandoned village mosque and Mohammed shins up a dead tree to break off some firewood. I have this absurd vision of driving through Los Angeles in our admirably beat-up Toyota with its Arabic licence plates. On the roof there's a line of jerry cans for extra fuel along with the pile of firewood; a goatskin full of water is slung on the side, while at the controls are two wild-looking Tuareg tribesmen with voluminous turbans swathing their heads.

It's only a few kilometres to Umm al-Maa, the postcard Ubari Lake and one that still has plenty of water. Long and narrow with dark blue swifts flitting between the palm trees and over the water and sand, the 'Mother of Waters' is even more picturesque than its predecessors, if that's possible. While Hassan builds a fire to bake bread and Mohammed fixes lunch, I go for a swim. Like the other lakes it's as salty as the Dead Sea although digging a well nearby always provided fresh drinking water. I glisten with salt crystals when I dry off and my swimsuit dries completely stiff, as if it had been hung out on a sub-zero winter day.

'I was bobbing around like a bathtub rubber duck', I explain to Maureen.

'You looked more like a rubber tyre to me', she sweetly replies.

Cruising back across the dunes in the late afternoon we finally meet a dune that beats Hassan. Despite surveying the route beforehand and breaking down the ridge top, we still end up teeter-tottering on the edge with all the wheels off the ground. Ten minutes of shovelling gets us back in control.

'That place is always difficult', Hassan grumbles. '*Fish-fash* too much.'

There's a final dried-up lake on the way home.

'There are wolves here', Hassan explains and as if on cue something emerges from behind a dune and trots down towards the lake on the other side. The animal spots us at the same instant we spot it and we all stop. There's plenty of time to study it through binoculars and although its large erect ears look more fox-like than wolf-like, that's the way wolves are around here.

Our final morning in the Fezzan we drive west as far as the town of
Ubari, where Hassan lives. His wife and some of his children are away in
Tripoli.

'Beyond here there is nothing for 240 kilometres until Ghat', Hassan
explains. 'Or you can turn north and drive across the dunes for two days
and then through the mountains for another two or three days until you
reach Ghadames. I have done that trip several times, but you must have
three or four cars. Today we navigate with GPS.'

We drive up to the top of the range overlooking Ubari, where we're
perfectly aligned to look down at all the satellite dishes dotting the
rooftops of the town far below. From here it's like the town is covered in
white polka dots.

'I was born in Ubari,' Hassan muses as we look down on his home
town, 'but then my father moved to Algeria and I lived there until I was
13. Then when Algeria became free all the Libyans had to move out.'

'Did your father work there?' I inquire.

'No, my father did not work. He had animals', Hassan replies
somewhat enigmatically. 'He had camels. We brought them back to Libya
to sell.' This was before cars, when camel caravans still travelled across the
Sahara, ignoring the borders that now divide the sands.

'The trip took about 15 days each way', Hassan continues. 'Sometimes
he did the trip twice in a year.'

• • • •

So where is Libya going? The Colonel has taken a step back from
terrorism and a step towards a market economy, but where has 30 years of
following *The Green Book* taken Libya? Not very far in some respects. For
all the money poured into a multitude of revolutions the Israelis are still
in Israel, Arab unity is still a nonstarter, African unity is unlikely to be

any easier to create, and very few of those revolutionaries he funded have managed to achieve their revolutionary aims.

As for the economy, *Green Book* or not, Gaddafi's recipe for a managed one has proved no more successful than any others. Libya still overwhelmingly depends on oil (and would be a sorry mess without it), the public sector is bloated and inefficient, and the private sector is not only tangled with restrictions and bureaucracy, it also suffers from the straightforward difficulty of interpreting what the hell Gaddafi means in his *Green Book* meanderings. Like Saudi Arabia and other oil-rich Arab nations, Libya has a native population that is remarkably unenthusiastic about a hard day's work. They crowd the public sector (lots of opportunity for sitting around there) and are notably absent in other areas, particularly in fields like tourism where slacking off isn't an option.

On the other hand, Gaddafi has made Libya a much more independent country and clearly made huge efforts to raise the general living standard and distribute the benefits of the country's oil wealth more equitably. From our perspective shifting people out of their charming, if ill-equipped, old houses and villages may look unfortunate, but we're being chauvinistic, patronising romantics if we try to ignore the attraction of running water, flush toilets and electricity. Unfortunately Libya seems to have inherited the public housing curse of creating instant slums on a nationwide scale, but that's another story.

Dishevelled, tatty buildings and the nationwide problem of garbage and litter make Libya look a much poorer country than the statistics indicate, but even the statistics aren't too exciting. Like Saudi Arabia, Libya is a country with so much money sloshing around that it clearly should have better figures in everything from infant mortality to literacy. So Gaddafi's school report isn't going to be a glowing one: 'tries hard, but easily distracted and end results not impressive'.

218.

· · · ·

Hassan drives us out to the airport to fly back to Tripoli. To the very end he's effortlessly charming. I don't think I've ever met anyone who looks so serenely calm, relaxed, dignified and competent. He waves away the money I try to offer him as we part – tipping clearly does not fall into the Tuareg code of conduct.

We'd heard that British tour groups could not use Libyan Arab Airlines because British travel insurance companies won't cover their flights, but for the first time in the Fezzan the tourist numbers are not almost entirely Italian – there's a healthy minority of Brits as well.

It's hardly surprising I miss the Tripoli pre-boarding announcement, it was probably only made in Arabic: 'We are now pre-boarding women with veils. Men and other women please wait for the general boarding announcement.' Twenty or so women and an assortment of children obediently head for the plane. The general scrum begins soon afterwards.

The next day we fly out. I'd met Donald Yorke, an old university engineering friend, at a party the year before. He worked in the oil industry in the post-revolution but pre-embargo era of the 1970s. 'When you left Libya you could fly with Libyan Arab Airlines or Alitalia', he recalled. 'There would be two flights departing simultaneously for Rome: one empty, one packed. Everybody on the Alitalia flight would be hanging out for a drink and the moment the door was shut, that was it. We were out of there, we'd left Libya – the flight attendants would be racing down the aisle handing out drinks before we'd even got out to the runway.'

We're well in the air and heading towards Egypt before the drinks trolley comes past us.

●　●　●　●

219.

On our last morning in Tripoli there was one final surprise in an often very surprising country. I go for a last wander around the medina and drop in to the old cathedral. One of Gaddafi's first moves after the 1969 revolution was to turn it into a mosque, but today it's mainly used as a gallery. There's an exhibition by the French artist Marie-Elisabeth Mathieu titled Memento, sponsored by the old city of Tripoli and the French cultural association. There's no catalogue or explanation, but it's pretty clear what this exhibition is all about. It is memories of September 11 and would be a sadly evocative piece of art anywhere in the world. Here in Libya it's strangely moving. The centrepiece is an eight-metre-high World Trade Center tower, constructed of the little flat wooden trays used in Libya to transport and display vegetables and fruit. They're wired together with the plastic ties used to bundle electrical cabling. The centre of the tower is floodlit from below and pieces that look like aluminium foil origami – people, planes? – float down inside.

NORTH KOREA

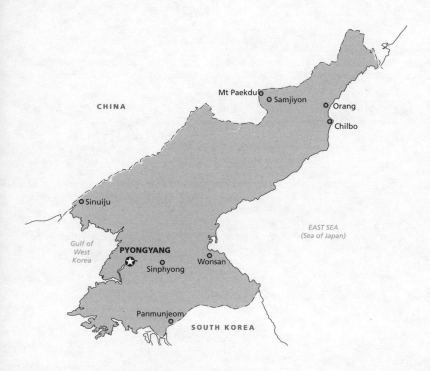

CHINA

Mt Paekdu○   ○ Samjiyon

○ Orang

○ Chilbo

○ Sinuiju

EAST SEA
(Sea of Japan)

Gulf of
West
Korea

PYONGYANG

○ Sinphyong   ○ Wonsan

○ Panmunjeom

SOUTH KOREA

'You guys really *are* the axis of evil', our guide splutters over his stein of beer in the Pyongyang duck restaurant.

'You're always leaning out of the windows and taking photographs when I tell you not to. You wander off without a guide to keep an eye on you. You giggle – giggle! – when the local guides are making speeches about the accomplishments of the Great Leader. I know there'll be a report made after this tour. I could lose my job. At the very least I'll be sent to Lake Chon to lead local tours for six months next winter.'

We fell about laughing. True, we had demanded that the bus stop every time we came to another really good billboard of the Great Leader, the Dapper Despot as I'd dubbed him, or his son, the Dear Leader, aka the Tubby Tyrant. Perhaps we were the tour group from hell, but what the hell? This was the country for suppressing giggles and our guide, Kim Myong Song, or 'Mr Kim' as I always called him, was always joking.

It's easy to fall for the international media's portrait of North Korea as a place alternating between horror and comedy, a Stalinist theme park, a gulag run by Monty Python. In fact it's hard to argue that any portrait of the country and its leadership could be too far-fetched when reports of the population facing starvation are counterpointed by tales of the leader's son trotting off to visit Tokyo Disneyland using a fake Caribbean passport. North Korea's recent elevation to the nuclear club has underlined that the antics inside this super-secret Communist state are no laughing matter.

• • • •

My relationship with this enigmatic nation began by accident. I was in a lift in the former Portuguese colony of Macau updating my *Southeast Asia on a Shoestring* guide. The door slid open on the wrong floor and almost immediately I realised the office I wanted wasn't there, but it was too late, the doors had shut, the lift had already departed. I pressed the button to recall the elevator and glanced through the glass frontage of the Korean Tourist Office as I waited for its return. Fortunately the lift didn't return instantly because it took me a few minutes to realise what was wrong. This was not an ROK, Republic of Korea, tourist office. This was a DPRK, Democratic People's Republic of Korea, tourist office.

The word 'Democratic' in a country's name is always a giveaway. By definition any country that proclaims itself democratic is definitely not democratic and the DPRK is a fine example of that maxim. North Korea shut itself off from the outside world after the Korean War ended in 1953. Its only real supporters were Russia and China, both pretty reclusive places themselves.

'Hello,' I said to the smiling young lady, 'are you really a North Korea tourist office?'

'Oh, yes,' she happily replied, 'would you like to visit the Democratic People's Republic of Korea?'

224.
———

'I certainly would', I shot back. 'I didn't know you allowed visitors. What do I have to do to make a visit?'

'There are no problems,' she went on, 'just fill in this form.'

I felt like I'd chanced on a wormhole into another universe, but my schedule was crowded and 10 years passed before I finally got around to joining a group visit to the Magic Kingdom. I am not a group travel person, but for North Korea there is really no choice. Technically you can make your own one-person tour, but you're still going to be stuck with guides and minders and have very little choice of what you see and how you see it. Going with a group at least gives you other people to bounce ideas and impressions off. And with a bunch of you running around, it's a little more difficult for Big Brother to be watching every minute of the day.

I meet my group at Beijing's main railway station. It's fitting that a place as isolated as North Korea should take a long time to get to. There had been a night at the airport hotel in Hong Kong, another overnight in a Beijing hotel, and finally an overnight train journey.

Rolling out of Beijing in the late afternoon, we pull into Dandong, the China–North Korea border town, the next morning. The Chinese town sprawls back from the north bank of the Yalu River. On the south bank is Sinuiju, the greyer, quieter, poorer North Korean sister city. There's the usual Chinese hustle in Dandong, with neon signs and new buildings surrounding a giant statue of the Great Helmsman in the square directly in front of the station. The Mao cult has faded remarkably since its 1960s Cultural Revolutionary heyday and this survivor seems a brave relic, a signal from the citizens of Dandong that despite everything they've still got a soft spot for the old boy. Giant statues, as we would soon see, are definitely not an endangered species on the other side of the border.

We do some last-minute shopping at the food stands in the station entrance, but regrettably I don't go looking for a Kim Il-sung badge from the sidewalk vendors purveying North Korean maps, postcards and other tourist goodies. Almost everybody in North Korea wears a small, discrete Kim Il-sung badge but we soon discover they are impossible for an outsider to procure.

It takes a couple of relaxed hours to complete the border formalities
on the China side. Meanwhile, the two Pyongyang-bound sleeper
carriages, which had been hooked on to a standard train from Beijing, are
disconnected, mysteriously rolled away and equally mysteriously reappear.
We reboard them for the short shunt across the border where they'll be
connected to a North Korean train for the journey to the capital. A few
minutes after leaving the Chinese station we're rolling across the bridge,
paralleling another bridge that was brought down during the Korean
War. The Chinese chunk of the partially destroyed bridge has become a
café and lookout point where Chinese tourists eye North Korea through
binoculars.

'Cameras away', shouts Nick, our Beijing-based English tour organiser,
comedian and all-round North Korea expert. It's the first rendition of
what will become the standard North Korean order. The North Koreans
are extremely touchy about what gets photographed in the workers'
earthly paradise. Nothing that looks slightly unparadisiacal is to be
recorded.

A children's fun park is our first sign of North Korea; it's dusty and
disused – clearly nobody has been having fun here for a long time.
Minutes later we're in the station at Sinuiju, where North Korean
officials board the train and embark on an immigration and customs
arrival process just as laid-back and relaxed as the Chinese on the other
side of the bridge. Our first Kim Il-sung portrait gazes down at the
platform. Two of our group have mobile phones, which are taken away
and returned, much later, carefully wrapped and stamped with a customs
seal to ensure they are not used in North Korea. Quite how they would be
used is unclear.

After half an hour of poking around our bags, inspecting passports
and visas (our visas, collected in Beijing, are assembled on one big sheet,
not stamped into our passports) and chatting amiably, the officials allow
us to ramble around the station, just as long as we don't go outside. We

wander up to a rather sparsely stocked snack bar (all the drinks are from Singapore) where we can look down on the square in front of the station. A Kim Il-sung statue looks out over the square, which is hardly bustling but nor, on the other hand, is it deserted.

In our whole two-week trip we will see no fainting soldiers, no starving children, no obvious signs of the famine that has racked the country for years. Nevertheless on the six-hour journey from the border to Pyongyang there are plenty of signs that not all is well. The roads are empty. At one stage, a road parallels the railway and for an hour I only see one vehicle moving, a Mercedes Benz. Throughout my visit I will never see a bus carrying North Koreans outside of the cities and even the occasional trucks packed with people will look like they're on short trips only. Perhaps the government's tight control on movements plays a part. You don't go anywhere in the people's paradise without having a permit.

There are no goods on the go either. Empty highways tell tales of a country shut down, but there are also clear signs of the problems down on the farm. The North Korean countryside looks like one big disaster area. All the way to Pyongyang we're running through farming country and it's obvious the land is overworked. Every tiny patch is being used and it's clear a lot of it shouldn't be. When you start growing things on the sloping sides of riverbanks and drainage ditches you're asking for erosion problems. In Pyongyang I will pick up a booklet by Kim Jong-il titled 'Improving the Layout of the Fields is a Great Transformation of Nature for the Prosperity of the Country'.

Our train stops and people get off and line up to have their paperwork checked. Our North Korean guides, who will stick close to us for the next week, are waiting on the platform. There's the bespectacled Mr Kim, a fluent English speaker, who would make a good computer nerd in the West. His occasional exasperation (why can't we just accept that we shouldn't be taking photographs?) rarely overpowers his sense of humour. He's also very aware. We've been instructed to bring presents for our guides, but I soon see the kangaroo tie I present him with disdainfully passed on to our bus driver. The kangaroos aren't necessarily déclassé, but it's clear if a tie gift isn't silk it isn't worth having.

Mr O's English isn't as good and I soon begin to wonder if he's really a guide at all. Perhaps he's there to keep an eye on the real guides, just as they're there to keep an eye on us. Ms Park, on the other hand, is new to the job and a cheerful delight. She's young, sometimes slightly worried looking, but her English is just as assured as Mr Kim's. Physically and fashionably, if you'd whisked all three of them away to Seoul, they would have blended in without a hitch.

Our group is a curiously mixed bag. For a start they're not old. Sometimes 'last' destinations like this attract an older audience, people with money and time who've already been everywhere else. In fact half of this group is quite young and nobody is ancient. Are they anoraks, as the British refer to nerds with curious obsessions? The real surprise is how many are second-time visitors when I would have thought this was a 'been there, done that' destination.

Eugene, a solid, efficient-looking German engineer and long-term Japan resident, probably is a real travel junkie and Subrapta's Madras-based leather export business clearly gives him an excuse to travel widely. I guess I have to slot myself into that unhealthily addicted category as well.

Ivan and Jeanne-Pierre, on the other hand, are simply inquiring young travellers. They're both postgraduate students and you get the feeling they're here purely because they like going to unusual places. Ivan is really an American, but is travelling on a Slovakian passport, and Jeanne-Pierre is a French-Canadian, although the French connection comes courtesy of Belgium. Ian, a Scot, is also young and almost Japanese in his enthusiasm to be photographed everywhere. The rest of the British contingent are all unusual. John, from Northern Ireland, is in fact an anorak anorak, not even a travel one, while Camilla is not only very English (with a name like that she'd have to be) but also very very earnest. She has been in Beijing studying Chinese and this is her second visit to the DPRK. She's returning because her previous trip didn't coincide with the Mass Games. Also second-timers, Phil and Jaqueline soon become the weirdest of our weird little ensemble. Their enthusiasm for all things North Korean is so unshakeable that I find myself glancing over at them to see if they really are wearing those fabled rose-coloured spectacles. Digby, an Australian, is also a repeat offender.

Subrapta is the only Asian in the group. 'We don't need to visit North Korea', Jinghui, a Chinese friend, had commented in Beijing. 'Anyone who remembers China in the 1970s has already been there.'

The sun is just setting as we make our first, obligatory, stop en route to our hotel. Nick has thoughtfully brought a large bouquet of flowers from Beijing, their fragrance floating along the train's corridors. It saves queuing to buy a bunch from the flower-seller close to the foot of the giant Mansudae statue, a 20-metre-high bronze figure of the Great Leader looking out over the capital city of the dreamland he created. We're lined up to bow respectfully before this personality cult classic. 'If you can't hack doing it, then you should think twice about coming to North Korea', Nick had warned us.

The hotel lobby doesn't look enormously different to any other 43-storey international hotel's entrance foyer. The time at different international cities dances in lights above the reception desk and the cashier is ready to change your US dollars into North Korean won. The only immediate giveaway is the black-and-white photo exhibit to one side of the desk, detailing atrocities committed against the Korean people by the Japanese Imperialists (during the 1905–1945 occupation) and by the American Imperialists (during the Korean War, which remarkably was not labelled with its better-known name, the Victorious Fatherland Liberation War). Oh, and this week's bestsellers in the bookshop included page turners like *Japanese War Crimes Past & Present* and *Kim Jong Il – Selected Works*.

A sign above the bookshop reminds us that the *Juche* Idea 'is exerting a great influence on the ideological life of humanity', and at the same time 'gaining a strong sympathy from people all over the world'. Around midnight I finally crawl into bed, after one last look out my 40th-floor window. Across the Taedong River, the pyramid shape of the 105-storey Ryugyong Hotel dominates the city's skyline. The lights of a car cruise along the riverside road. It's the only vehicle moving in the city.

• • • •

Korea has always been the Hermit Kingdom. Today, under the absolute rule of the late 'Great Leader', Kim Il-sung, the man who single-handedly inflicted defeat on both the Imperialist Aggressor Japanese and the Imperialist Aggressor Americans (not to mention the Puppet Stooge South Koreans), the President for Life-and-Beyond, North Korea has become a modern version of that old nickname. It's an apt description for a country that manages to be isolationist and Stalinist and behave like a monarchy.

Squeezed between China and Japan long before they found themselves squeezed between Russia and America, both Koreas have suffered from being Big Power surrogates. In the late 1800s the Koreans panicked that their old enemies, the Chinese and Japanese, were being supplanted by even more frightening new enemies from Europe, America and Russia. Their response was to slam the doors shut. It proved hopeless. Poor Korea found itself battered between Russia and Japan until, with the defeat of Russia in the Russo-Japanese War of 1904, the country came under even stronger Japanese influence. By 1910 the Japanese were in control. By the start of World War II, Korean schools were forced to teach in Japanese and the study of Korean history was banned. Korean men were conscripted into the Japanese army, Korean civilians were shipped to Japan as virtual slave labourers (a large proportion of the atom bomb casualties at Hiroshima were Koreans working in the factories) and Korean women were forced into prostitution as 'comfort women' for the Japanese army. It's scarcely surprising that the Koreans, north and south, still carry a large chip on their collective shoulders against the Japanese.

At the same time, a divide started to open between the northern and southern halves of Korea. North Korea is colder, drier, higher and less fertile than the south. If a famine struck, it was always more likely to hit the north than the south, and during the periodic struggles with the Chinese it was the north that always bore the brunt of the onslaughts. The arrival of American Christian missionaries also played a part in the division, convincing many northern converts that their problems were caused by the effete Confucians in the southern capital of Seoul.

The guerrilla struggle against the Japanese during World War II was principally a northern endeavour. It may not have been quite as exclusively northern as the North Koreans will insist, but there's little question that, when it came to battling the Japanese, Kim Il-sung, even if he did not defeat them all by himself, played a major part. During the war the southerners continued to be better fed than their northern brethren, although it was the north that became the cog in the Japanese industrial tool.

After 40 years of Japanese occupation, the war's conclusion did not bring independence. The Russians only declared war on Japan on 8 August 1945, after the first atomic bomb had been dropped and less than a week before the war ended. Now they marched into Korea from the north at the same time as American troops entered from the south. Korea was divided at the 38th parallel. The unfortunate Koreans became the first Cold War pawn.

Both countries had been devastated by the Japanese occupation during World War II and then by the Korean War, which lasted two years and was fought out on almost every square centimetre of land. Fighting broke out on 25 June 1950 and the North Korean troops soon marched all the way to Busan in the southeast corner of the country. A couple of months later the South Koreans, with their American support (and the support of a small number of other nationalities), fought their way back north as far as the Chinese border before Mao sent his army in and pushed them back to the 38th parallel, exactly where the whole mess had started. The line has been the uneasy border between the two Koreas ever since.

With the Korean War, it's really irrelevant who fired the first shot – the South (according to the North) or the North (according to our side of the argument). Both sides were itching to start trading blows and America and Russia – paying the bills, supplying the arms and handing out the advice – were clearly ready to unleash things as well. The end result was not unlike what happened between Israel and the Arab world 20 years later. It's easy to forget that in 1967 it was Israel that invaded its neighbours, not vice versa. Of course, if they'd waited a few more days the Egyptians and Syrians might well have been marching across the border, but the truth is the Israelis fired first. The Korean War was going to happen – it didn't matter who fired the first shot.

After the war the Russians poured in aid to the North and created a Soviet-style economy of collective farming and gigantic state-run industrial concerns. The workers marched forward, led by the ideals of *Juche*, Kim Il-sung's home-grown blend of Marxism and self-sufficiency. For a while they were better off than their brethren in the south, but when the South Koreans put the pedal to the metal in the 1960s *Juche* was shown to be useless and South Korea pulled away from the North like a hotted-up Hyundai overtaking a worn-out horse cart.

• • • •

232. Our visit doesn't – like most – kick off with a tour of the Pyongyang sights. This is the 'mountain tour', and we've chartered a small Air Koryo aircraft to take us to the north of the country for a couple of days. Our

bus pulls up at the Pyongyang International Airport terminal building
and we all start to laugh. It's the natural reaction when you're confronted
with the capital's international airport and find the car park deserted.
To be honest, there were two vehicles, our bus and a car. It's OK to
photograph it, so we scatter in all directions to record what an empty car
park looks like.

Later that morning our bus winds down the dirt, but comfortably
smooth, coastal road from the military airport at Orang to the mountain
town of Chilbo. The coastline is beautiful with tiny bays, picturesque
little fishing villages (which we're emphatically not allowed to
photograph), soaring cliffs and mountains rising up further inland. Any
place where land meets sea in anything less than a sheer, unclimbable
cliff there's a continuous concrete wall, topped with spikes or broken glass
and surmounted by a double-strand electric fence. Supposedly this anti–
Imperialist Aggressor (and Puppet Stooge) fence continues right down
both coasts, but the fear of invasion is clearly shared. Similar barriers line
the coast in South Korea.

At the Outer Chilbo lookout there are beautiful pillar-like rock
formations and our first encounter (there will be more) with Kim Il sung
rapture. A local guide pops up, something we will soon get used to, and
launches into a description of the scenery, translated from Korean by
Mr Kim. There is a standard routine to any description whether it's of a
natural feature, historical site or monument. First there's a brief account
of what you're looking at, then there's a longer report on when Great
Leader or Dear Leader visited it. If they dropped by more than once
then there will be a tale about each visit. If it's some sort of work site
– a collective farm, for example – then you'll hear how Dear or Great
instructed the farmers (or workers, fisherfolk or soldiers) how to grow
more, produce more, catch more or kill more, this information being
gratefully received with open-mouthed awe.

Here it was the mountains and the climate itself that were awestruck.

233.

When Kim Il-sung turned up the weather was lousy, but the mountains, clever mountains that they were, realised that their important visitor had a close connection to a more important mountain. After all, the Great Leader and Mt Paekdu, legendary birthplace of the Korean people and the highest mountain in the country, are good friends. So, recognising just how important the visitor was, it's hardly surprising that the weather cleared up instantly. This tale is recounted with such rapturous fervour and translated with such deadpan conviction, it's hard to suppress the giggles that become the norm for any North Korean tour.

Our hotel comes with a fairly standard feature outside Pyongyang – no running water. The bathtub was full of cold water and a plastic bowl is provided to scoop it out. Mix a couple of scoops of cold with the hot water from the vacuum flask, provided Chinese-style for making tea, and you have the ingredients for a shower. There's another very nonstandard feature – other guests. They're from a town in the northeast of China and by the time we get back they are already making serious inroads into the restaurant's beer supply. By dinnertime the all-male party is getting to the uproarious song stage and the restaurant staff begin to move a series of dividers between our tables to protect us from the sight, if not the sound, of Chinese party animals. Nick, whose fluent Chinese has already provided plenty of amusement in the train's dining car from Beijing, will have none of this. Leaping from his seat he seizes one of the dividers and pulls it aside, yelling 'We will have no divisions here!' A roar of approval goes up from the Chinese band, glasses are raised to our international group, and we're requested to add our songs to the festivities. Subrapta Das wins the contest with what he describes as 'a bawdy Sri Lankan number'. Subrapta vies with Olaf, one of the German trio, as the group clown. 'Beneath my coffee-coloured complexion,' he shyly announces **234.** when we compliment him on his winning song, 'I am blushing pink.'

The next morning, after breakfast – which was remarkably like the rice, fish, vegetables and kimchi of lunch and dinner the night before – we board the bus and head back along the empty, winding road, requesting stops for photo opportunities and repeatedly being told not to take anything with people or villages in the frame. A half-dozen of the Korean War vintage Mig-15s at the airport are flying circuits. As our bus pulls on to the runway to take us to our waiting aircraft I look out the back window to see one of the elderly Russian fighter planes making its final approach. Presumably fuel is too precious to allow second circuits and our driver hurriedly pulls off the runway.

We fly north to Korea's most revered (and highest) peak, Mt Paekdu. Samjiyon Airport is not a purely military operation like Orang, but it's even quieter than the capital. Pyongyang International Airport had no passengers, Samjiyon has nobody. We unload our own baggage and march over to the empty terminal. The Tupolev on the apron has just flown in with an army contingent who are currently lunching at our hotel. There's not room for both army and tourists so we're ushered into the airport's VIP room (overstuffed chairs, side tables, the usual portraits) and handed what looks like a DPRK Japanese bento box prepared several days ago.

Beijing just two days ago was cooking, Pyongyang and Chilbo were warm. Samjiyon is distinctly chilly and as our bus carries us up towards Mt Paekdu it turns from chilly to cold to icy. By the time we've climbed above the tree line it's bloody freezing and I'm glad I stuffed a sweater and ski jacket into my bag. Mt Paekdu is a spectacular volcano crater with a lake straddling the North Korea–China border. In 1998 a young British backpacker in China set out to walk around the 14-kilometre circumference of Lake Chon unaware (his British guidebook hadn't warned him) that he would march straight across the border and into a North Korean diplomatic incident. No way I would want to be walking anywhere near the lake today. At the end of May it's still iced over and a bitter wind shrieks up the inner slope of the crater and spills over the edge with such ferocity that only a couple of us venture right up to the top of the lookout.

Back in the bus, we roll down into the forests to investigate Mt Paekdu's Great and Dear Leader connections. This was where the Great Leader mounted his guerrilla attacks on the Japanese occupiers and where, in a humble log cabin, the Dear Leader was born in 1942. Except there are no records (outside of North Korea) of any anti-Japanese action here and, despite the tales of Kim Jong-il's arrival while shells whistled past and bombs exploded, the evidence is that he was born in Khabarovsk in Russia. The Western information is that Kim Il-sung was in Russia for most of World War II and returned to Korea on board the Russian warship Pukachev on 19 September 1945, well after he'd finished off the Japanese. Never mind, like any capitalist PR firm the North Koreans have never let the truth stand in the way of a good story and the Paekdu Secret Camp site is fronted by a magnificent billboard-sized mosaic of Great Leader and wife, with Kim Junior in her arms, all smiling warmly from the snowy scene with the log cabin standing cosily in the background.

Our attention is focused on our local guide, the charming Miss Lee, who is so irresistibly cute in her khaki outfit and so tiny (even her Kim Il-sung badge looked bigger than normal) you could have wrapped her up and taken her home as a Korean People's Army Doll. Once we've torn ourselves away from the mosaic, there is the Great Leader's log cabin from where he directed military operations and the family log cabin where little Kim theoretically greeted the world. Fortunately we later came to the rotting foundations of the 'real' log cabin where it is revealed the Disney-esque cabins we've just inspected are just rebuilt replicas. The slogan trees, however, are undoubtedly real.

Perhaps.

They're safely encased in Perspex cylinders and covered by canvas condoms, which, one day, will wrinkle back at the touch of a button to reveal tree trunks bearing anti-Japanese slogans. In between ambushing the Imperialist Aggressors, the Great Leader's well-trained guerrillas took time out to burn patriotic slogans on to the trees. Since nobody had

236.

yet managed to wire up the electric motors to pull back the covers we are
reluctantly allowed to pull them up manually. As if leaving tree graffiti
wasn't careless enough, the guerrillas, clearly not too concerned about
covering their tracks, were also inclined to leave the remains of their
campfires to be found. At another possibly not-so-secret camp we are
proudly shown countless campfire sites, each one encased in a tent-shaped
glass box.

• • • •

The modern army contingent had moved on from the dining room by
the time we arrive at the Pagaebong Hotel, a hidden-in-the-forest DPRK
Fawlty Towers complete with 50 rooms, no guests (God knows how long
since there had been another group) and once again no running water – to
the sink at least. My room also has a TV, no doubt tuned to the DPRK's
single channel, but since it has no power lead it's impossible to check.
The fridge is similarly deficient, but at least one of the two bedside lights
works. Much of the hotel (not all of it, curiously enough) is freezing cold.
Half seems to be closed off, with piles of old furniture heaped along
the corridors. The stairs and public areas are laid with fraying, badly cut
carpet, which loops and sags down the stairs. Beside the second-floor
bar is a pool room with a pool table, with no balls or cues, but the bar
itself is well stocked with cans of Heineken for just 1.50 won, 75 cents
in US currency. Where in the world can you buy a can of Heineken beer
for less than a US dollar? The theory is that it's imported for the political
elite and since nobody except that tiny group could afford anything so
extravagant as a can of beer it's provided to them at cost.

We repair to the bar after dinner and proceed to have another raucously
bizarre North Korean evening culminating in a game of musical chairs.
Did I ever imagine I would end up playing musical chairs in a key centre
of the evil axis? Remarkably we only manage to break one of the chairs

and in the final round I take control of the cassette player and manage to rig the results so that the final chair is disputed between our charming Ms Park and the bar's equally charming Ms Kim. Clearly neither of them has experienced this Western children's game before and find it invigorating.

In the morning there's a visit to the Rimyongsu waterfall with a crumbling concrete pavilion plonked in the middle of it. The hotel dining room had a romanticised painting of the scene, everything magnified until the waterfall became Niagara in size. The visit has an unexpected bonus. The village by the falls has been turned into a huge housing construction site. It looks remarkably similar to suburban tract housing projects in the West. I half expect to see a display house decorated with flags and a sign offering 10 per cent deposit and low monthly payments, but second glance indicates that this is definitely a Third World project with everything being done by hand and large groups with hammers squatting by the roadside converting rocks into tiny pebbles.

'Would it be possible to see inside a house?' I ask Mr Kim, not expecting for a moment that it would be. The senior guides confer, Mr Kim goes off and returns 10 minutes later to say it's been arranged. Even more remarkably, we find ourselves not in an almost completed or recently finished house, but in one that's actually inhabited. It's not going to win any architectural awards, and if you were over six-foot tall you'd be scrunching down under the low ceilings, but it's actually quite cosy, if bare. There are no chairs or tables. A long storage cabinet is all there is in the main room. The glass-fronted doors reveal quilts and blankets. They're rolled out on the floor to convert living room to bedroom, just like a traditional Japanese house.

The smaller second room just has a storage shelving unit. The floors are lino covered and the only decorations are the standard pictures of Dear and Great in one room, and a framed photograph of the dynamic duo in the other. There's a smaller storage room and a kitchen where everything is clearly prepared from scratch. There is nothing packaged or tinned, but everything is very neat and tidy, with stacks of pots and dishes in a cabinet. The sink and cooking equipment is all at floor level, the middle of the floor is at a lower level – you climb down to put yourself at waist level to the coal-fired cooking equipment. There's no running water – a tin bucket sits by the sink. The final room is the washing and laundry room, again without running water, or for that matter, a toilet.

After lunch some of us join in an impromptu football match with the construction workers labouring on an extension to the empty hotel. After a stop to pay our respects to another gigantic Great Leader statue, we fly back to Pyongyang and the Arirang Mass Games.

There's a dramatic 'clack' as 20,000 children slam their card books open on another page and, on the other side of the 150,000-seat May Day Stadium, the face of a gigantic Kim Il-sung pops up. There's a roar of approval while, down on the stadium floor, the dancing army proves they can march as well and stride off the grounds. I'm watching the Arirang Mass Games – or more correctly the Mass Gymnastic and Artistic Performances.

One side of the stadium is taken up by those carefully choreographed children, flipping open the pages of their card books to make patterns and pictures, including that huge face of the Great Leader. The activity is equally precisely timed and the numbers are nearly as big down at ground level where the evening kicks off with thousands of women in pastel green, yellow and purple dresses swooshing out on to the grounds. 'Mass' is clearly the appropriate word. A dozen or a hundred carefully coordinated hula-hoopers is one thing; a thousand of them, all dressed in blue, is visually quite another. Now feed in another thousand rope skippers (in pink) and yet another thousand tennis-racquet wavers (in white) and the effect is astonishing.

The effect can also be beautiful, when a sea of women in white swirl their blue cloaks to produce a shimmering then storming sea across

239.

which a red ship swiftly sails, mirrored by a second red ship moving in a flickering blaze of opening and closing card books across the stadium seats. It can be amusing, when rabbits, rice plants, chickens and (what came first?) eggs dance across in the 'increase production' number. Or it can be simply cute, when thousands of children, all toting flotation rings, race out on to the grounds while beach scenes materialise behind them.

And then there's the incredible dancing army. If a war's ever decided by which army does the best mass dancing, my money is on the North Koreans.

●　●　●　●

For such a secretive society, North Korea has made a success of attracting global headlines. Giving the world the middle finger – the US and their southern neighbours in particular – has been a favourite pastime of North Korea, using somewhat unconventional foreign policy tactics such as assassinations, suicide missions, drug running, counterfeiting, kidnapping, missile launches and, in late 2006, nuclear tests.

In November 1987 Kim Hyun Hee, a 26-year-old woman from North Korea, boarded KAL 858, a Korean Airlines 707, in Baghdad. The flight continued to Abu Dhabi in the United Arab Emirates and then departed for the South Korean capital, Seoul. On board were 115 passengers and crew, 93 of them Korean workers returning from the Middle East. Unfortunately for those on board, Kim Hyun Hee and her 70-year-old 'father' had deplaned in Abu Dhabi and carelessly left some of their hand luggage in the overhead locker. Hours later, over the Bay of Bengal, KAL 858 exploded and plunged into the sea. There were no survivors.

Meanwhile Kim Hyun Hee and dad, travelling on forged Japanese passports, had flown from Abu Dhabi to Bahrain and were about to board a flight to Jordan when the immigration authorities became suspicious about their circular journey. Realising they were about to be arrested, the pair decided to have a last cigarette. It was indeed a last drag for Kim Sung Il, the father figure, for as well as the bomb, packed into a radio they had left on board the Korean aircraft, they were also equipped with cyanide-spiked Marlboros. Kim Sung Il, no relation to the Great Leader Kim Il-sung, died instantly, but his 'daughter' survived and was flown to South Korea for some extensive interrogation.

It turned out that she'd been recruited and trained in North Korea before starting her international activities from Macau, the centre of North Korea's most popular export — fake US hundred-dollar bills. In one four-month spell in late 1998 to early 1999, they were reputed to have funnelled more than half a million in counterfeit US bills through a front company based there. It also provided cover for Ms Kim's bombing operation.

In South Korea Kim Hyun Hee confessed (Kim Jong-il made me do it) and was pardoned on the basis that she was young, foolish and pretty and the nasty North Koreans had brainwashed her. So why had the nasty North Koreans, and Kim Jong-il in particular, dreamed up this crazy plan? To undermine the 1988 Olympics, due to be held in Seoul, of course.

The aircraft bombing wasn't the first crackpot plot designed to destabilise the South Koreans. In 1983 a South Korean government mission paid a visit to Rangoon (now Yangon) in Burma (Myanmar). North Korean agents left three bombs in the roof of Rangoon's Martyrs' Mausoleum. It was South Korea's president, Chun Doo-hwan, and his cabinet officers who were the focus of the assassination attempt, but the North Koreans mistook the South Korean ambassador, arriving in a large car, for the president, who was stuck in a traffic jam. Only one of the three bombs went off, but 21 people were killed including South Korea's foreign minister, deputy prime minister, two other ministers and a host of advisers, journalists and security personnel, all except four of them Koreans. Two days later a suspect was arrested, but in what seems to be the norm for North Korean agents when found out, he tried to commit suicide, using a hand grenade. Two more suspects also tried the hand

241.

grenade routine later the same day, one of them succeeding and killing three Burmese policemen as well.

In the 1990s North Korean activity shifted to submarines and fishing boats, although suicide remained part of the game plan. In September 1996 a North Korean submarine ran aground off the coast of South Korea and the heavily armed crew of 26 made it to shore, sparking off a manhunt that lasted 53 days and involved 60,000 South Korean troops. Rounding up the North Koreans led to the deaths of three South Korean civilians and five soldiers, but eventually 25 of the 26 were accounted for. One escaped, one was captured, 13 were killed and the remaining 11 committed suicide.

Remarkably, after initially threatening 'merciless retaliation' for the South Korean round-up, the North Koreans eventually apologised. The expression of 'deep regret' did, however, come at the end of a news round-up concentrating on the activities of the 'US imperialists' and branding South Korean President Kim Young-sam a 'ruthless tyrant', a 'puppet' and a 'traitor'. Visitors to South Korea can see the North Korean submarine on display just north of the east-coast resort town of Jeongdongjin, otherwise noted for featuring in a popular South Korean television soap opera. Despite those 'deep regrets', two years later a North Korean miniature submarine got itself knotted up in a South Korean fishing boat's nets, well inside South Korean waters. When the crew of nine were unable to disentangle their vessel they all committed suicide.

In contrast to all the murder and mayhem of bombing missions, Kim Jong-nam's 2001 scheme to visit Tokyo Disneyland was light-hearted comic farce. The 29-year-old eldest son of Kim Jong-il looked like a younger version of his chubby pop when he – along with two women and his four-year-old son – were marched out to a China-bound plane from Tokyo's Narita Airport. Since there are no direct flights between Japan and North Korea (or almost anywhere else and North Korea for that matter) it wasn't possible to send the naughty lad straight home.

By the time he 'sauntered nonchalantly', according to the reports, out to his All Nippon flight, the 'Little General' had been enjoying the Japanese government's hospitality for three days. The Japanese maintained a diplomatic silence about the affair, possibly to avoid inflaming relations with their touchy neighbours (next time the missiles might land right in Disneyland), but equally likely out of embarrassment for not noticing that a certain visitor from the Caribbean island of Dominica was more likely to dance to the rhythm of *Juche* than calypso. Kim confessed to paying US$2000 each for the passports for himself and his companions, but it wasn't a complete waste. The stamps in his passport indicated that this was his third stay in Japan in a 12-month period.

So why had he dropped by for visit number three? Reportedly so his son could enjoy that all-American Mickey Mouse experience, but cynical DPRK watchers noted that the Little General was a member of the North Korean intelligence service and believed to be a computer expert. The Disney excuse might have been simply to cover up some more sensitive pursuits.

Very little is known about Dear Leader's family life, but he is believed to have three (possibly four) children by three different women. Kim Jong-nam was born in 1971, but Dear Leader didn't bother to marry the Little General's mother, Sung Hae Rim. The Little General was followed by his half-sister, Kim Sul Song, born in 1974, and his half brother, Kim Jong Chul, born in 1981. Kim Sul Song is clearly the black sheep of the family. There were tales that she'd defected to South Korea, although it's now believed that she is in Moscow, being treated for depression.

In April 2003 Australian surfers at the popular Victorian beach resort of Lorne were witnesses to another North Korean botched operation. Wallowing in the waves dangerously close to shore was the Tuvaluan-flagged, 120-metre, 4000-tonne bulk carrier *Pong Su*, operated by the Pongsu Shipping Company in Pyongyang. The rusty vessel was just a few hundred metres off the notoriously tricky coast and had just dispatched a boat to shore. While trying to land through the heavy surf, one crewman drowned and the police turned up just in time to grab another, along with 50 kilograms of high-grade heroin. The *Pong Su* promptly sailed off and a comic-book four-day chase commenced up the east coast of Australia before the ship was finally boarded by commandos and sailed into Sydney.

Meanwhile the police had found another 75 kilograms of heroin, hidden close to the road outside Lorne, and presumably awaiting collection. Local treasure hunters took to scouring the woods around the resort, but who knows – the rust bucket had probably sailed right around Australia before the Lorne debacle, quite possibly dropping off shipments all over the place. It was all 'a sinister trick to tarnish the image of the dignified Democratic People's Republic of Korea', North Korea's official news agency reported. The shore party of four, from Malaysia, Singapore and China, were convicted, but remarkably all the North Korean crew from the captain down got away with it, including a 'political officer' who had worked in the DPRK's Beijing embassy. Somebody had fooled them into believing they were coming to Australia to pick up a shipment of BMWs for re-export to Malaysia. The final four were released in early 2006 and the 'unseaworthy' *Pong Su,* which had been costing the Australian government A$2500 a day for three years to look after, was towed out to sea and sunk by RAAF aircraft.

In 2002 kidnapping was added to the charge sheet. For years there had been sensational stories in Japan about abductions, backed up by testimony from captured North Korean spies and reports of sightings of the missing Japanese citizens in Pyongyang. Then, out of the blue, Kim Jong-il suddenly confessed that the wild rumours were true and 12 (a number later raised to 13) people had been kidnapped, although it is still believed that the numbers could have been much higher. The abductions took place in the late 1970s and early 1980s and included a 13-year-old girl, seized as she came home from school, and a courting couple strolling along a deserted beach. The people captured had no security, military or espionage value. They may have been taken to serve as Japanese-language instructors for North Korean agents, or to provide identities for North Korean spies.

During the intervening years, eight of the kidnapped Japanese had died by natural causes or in a variety of accidents, a remarkably high death toll even in a country like North Korea. Furthermore most of their graves had been 'washed away in floods'. When remains of two of the kidnapped Japanese were returned to Japan, DNA tests proved they were not the people the North Koreans claimed so it's hardly surprising that years later this case is still running hot.

South Koreans were also kidnapped by the North, most notoriously the noted movie director Shin Sang-ok and his actor wife, Choi Eun-hee. In early 1978 she was kidnapped by North Korean agents while working on a film in Hong Kong. Six months later the director was also captured and whisked off to Pyongyang where he was told by Kim Jong-il himself that he had a new career awaiting him in the North. When he refused he was chucked into Prison No 6 to enjoy a four-year grass and rice diet. In 1983 he was hauled out for a second session with the Dear Leader and reunited with his wife. Kim Jong-il even apologised for taking so long to get back to him. He'd been 'busy at the office'.

This time the director decided that making North Korean movies might not be so bad after all, particularly when he was provided with a Mercedes and a salary of $3 million a year. There are 'fewer restrictions than is commonly believed', he would later tell a South Korean interviewer. In the next few years he directed five North Korean films and became so trusted that in 1986 he was allowed to pay a visit to Vienna, with his wife, where they escaped to the US embassy. He spent the next 14 years in the US, directing movies as 'Simon Sheen' and died back in South Korea in 2006.

• • • •

North Korea's background music, vaguely stirring patriotic sort of stuff, doesn't play in elevators, but drifts across the city, particularly early in the morning, and materialises from within bushes and trees at important sites. In the morning it greets me when I pull back the curtain to look out the window across the river. Despite the light traffic on its six- and eight-lane boulevards, Pyongyang is not as pollution free as promised. A smoky coal-fired power station belches a cloud of black smoke across the city. The unfinished Ryugyong Hotel's pointy shape wavers in the morning haze. In a command economy like North Korea's, where everything gets done from the top, building hotels and attracting tourists are two entirely unconnected operations. So huge hotels, like the one I'm in, stand three-quarters empty while even huger hotels, like the one I'm gazing at, stand half-built.

The massive Ryugyong Hotel is the supreme example of what happens when a command economy goes into meltdown. From almost anywhere in Pyongyang and for many kilometres outside the town, the 105-storey failure rises like a giant inverted ice-cream cone. If it had been finished, it would have been one of the world's largest hotels and added another 3000 empty rooms to the city's quota of unused bed nights. It would have been the ultimate symbol of the 1980s, when buildings and monuments sprouted like rice shoots, all designed to hide the fact that the emperor was really naked. In 1989, with the Soviet Union disintegrating, the flow of easy money suddenly stopped and so did construction. The Ryugyong remains an empty shell, which tourists are hustled past and discouraged from photographing.

We are billeted at the Yangakkdo International, which sits on an island in the middle of the river. Attractions here include a Chinese-staffed karaoke bar and a basement casino, also run by the Chinese, and with a 100 per cent Chinese clientele. At the bottom of the stairs leading to the second basement the entrance takes sharp descending twists and turns until anyone tallish has to walk hunched over. Eventually it leads to a host of attractions including a massage parlour, sauna, swimming pool, shop, hairdresser and shoe repairer.

At the end of this curious complex an exchange counter displays a sign with the prices for everything from a massage (including an 'itinerant massage'), every haircut you could imagine (bun, bob, loose hair) plus hair dyeing with a lower price quoted for 'guests who bring their own hair dye'. Men can opt for a regular shave or haircut or a rather cheaper 'hair trimming', which despite the lower cost still includes 'shaving behind the ears'. Finally there's a complete run down on shoe repair costs including 'sticking down what has come off' with a price per centimetre of whatever it is that has to be stuck down. The grand finale, for both shoe repairs and this sign, is 'when fixing the men's heels to those of women's shoes'. This feat will set you back 4.70 won, a bit over US$2.

You can't step out of your hotel without a minder at your shoulder, except here. Since it's on an island it's safe to allow us out, so long as we don't try to cross the bridge. Or perhaps they only intended we wander around the hotel grounds at one end of the island. I decide to take an early morning stroll. When I try to walk along the riverside walkway I come up against a metal fence at the hotel boundary. I take the vehicle exit route and am firmly turned back at the security station, busily clocking in hotel workers for the morning shift.

I find another way out and walk along the riverside, past the Pyongyang International Cinema Hall (a festival due next month) and the Yanggakdo Football Stadium (they could have held a round of the 2002 World Cup here, but never bothered to even acknowledge South Korea's invitation), right up to the end of the island. Down here the land is divided into tiny strips of garden and two well-dressed women, front-desk staff from the hotel perhaps, arrive carrying bags and gardening tools. They pull out overalls from the bags to protect their office clothes while they tend their vegetable patches.

On the other bank, a greying rusting vessel is a floating symbol of

'Imperialist Aggression'. It is the USS *Pueblo*, captured while on an intelligence mission off the coast of North Korea in 1968. The 'Armed American Spyship', as the video shown on board calls it, was, according to the Americans, a marine research vessel, 'seized in international waters'. Despite US threats of retaliation, which included bringing the 'nuclear-powered', as the North Koreans underline it, aircraft carrier *Enterprise* up to the front line, nothing happened. Eventually the crew of the *Pueblo* went through the usual rigmarole of writing the sort of Communist-bloc confessions that Communist-bloc captives are always expected to write and nobody believes, the US made an official apology and after nearly a year's captivity the ship's 82 officers and crew (one was killed in the original capture) were bussed down to Panmunjeom in the Demilitarised Zone (DMZ) and, one by one, got off the bus and walked across the border, all of it filmed by North Korean cameramen.

• • • •

Usually DPRK tours launch straight into Pyongyang propaganda, but our mountain interlude means we're four nights into the tour before we get our first bout of brainwashing. At the Victorious Fatherland Liberation War Museum the little lights are soon dancing down the map to show how, after the Imperialist Aggressors and the Puppet Stooges launched their unprovoked attack on the north, the People's Army soon crossed the border, liberated Seoul and advanced southwards liberating more and more of the country. They'd almost completed the job (move on to the next room and map at this point) before the Imperialist Aggressors shipped in vast numbers of troops and made their bumbled landing at Incheon. With the People's Army horribly outnumbered, the Great Leader made a rapid strategic withdrawal to the north and then turned round and, with a little Chinese help, pushed the imperialists and their traitorous southern compatriots back to the south. Then there

248.

was a long stalemate during which time the monsters bombed the north unrelentingly and committed countless atrocities before finally, realising they were never going to win, admitted defeat and surrendered.

Next stop was the Great People's Study Hall, where the Great Leader's statue, sitting rather than standing for once, gazes out over the entrance lobby looking remarkably (except for the missing beard) like Abraham Lincoln's statue in his Washington DC memorial. The library has, we are told, 30 million books in 60 different reading rooms. We're shown the one dedicated to the thoughts of Kim Il sung; in between defeating imperialists and advising farmers, workers and soldiers, he also found time to write hundreds of books. We're also shown one of the computer rooms, which, although it's not connected to the Internet, follows that capitalist maxim that nobody went wrong by buying Big Blue. All the computers are IBM, although in this context it must stand for Imperialist Business Machines.

Like every other Pyongyang attraction there's a tourist shop in the Great People's Study Hall, but from a souvenir point of view the DPRK is turning out to be remarkably poorly stocked. Apart from the severe lack of badges, there's an equally great shortage of anything portraying the revolutionary kitsch that confronts you at every corner. Images of any of the countless Kim Il-sung statues that tower over odd corners of the country are unavailable, ditto for reproductions of any of the thousands of billboards that dot city and country alike, portraying father and son in a wide variety of images from the 'post-realist, neo-pop epoch of socialist romanticist art', also known as 'Commie kitsch'. It's the badges we really miss. Virtually the only North Koreans who don't sport a Great Leader badge are those fashionistas who have moved on to the double-portrait Great-and-Dear-Leader badge. Repeated shuffles through the postcard collections at every hotel, bookshop and tourist site finally yields one of the Arch of Triumph ('it's bigger than your petit Arc de Triomphe', I gloatingly inform a French friend) and a couple of the Monument to the Party Foundation, three gigantic hands holding up a hammer (the workers), a sickle (the farmers) and, convincingly one-upping the old USSR, a calligrapher's brush (the artists). Until that lucky find I was concerned that a 3-D view of the Pyongyang Maternity Hospital might be the best on offer.

Daydreaming of the avid market waiting for the first capitalist to produce the Great Leader statue snow dome, I embark on a search for interesting stamps for my postcards. Even the Princess Di commemorative issues (the DPRK was no more immune to Di-mania than any other Asian country from Bangladesh to Bhutan) are only available through the stamp collectors shop and that's where I finally track down Kim Il-sung stamps for the cards I am going to send to Imperialist Aggressor Land.

'Where did you get these stamps?' the clerk at the hotel post office inquires when I go to mail the cards.

She seems content with my explanation – she should be, they cost twice their face value – but, it turns out, sending postcards portraying the country's dead (but still reigning) president is not so simple. North Korea may have a president for eternity, not just for life, but postage-stamp images of the Great Leader are clearly far too important to be used on postcards.

'After you left the post office there was a discussion about what to do', reported Camilla, who had been queuing behind me. 'They finally decided to put the postcard in an envelope with a box cut out to show the address. That way the Great Leader stamp wouldn't be displayed or defaced.'

• • • •

Pyongyang's metro is a subway designed by HG Wells. It looks and feels like a Victorian-era vision of the future, with huge platform areas surrounded by a heavy diet of revolutionary art and topped by kitschy chandeliers. Every station has an inspiring name that bears no relation to its actual position and on a ride from Reconstruction to Glory I board the carriage and, shock horror, realise someone has been scratching words on the windows!

Is this North Korean graffiti? The first sign of youthful dissent?

The guide quickly brings me down to earth: 'We bought all the carriages secondhand from East Germany. They came that way.'

We have half an hour to explore the consumer delights of Department Store No 1, five storeys of the output of the DPRK's finest factories and workshops, and just a stone's throw from Kim Il-sung Square. This is *Juche* self-reliance at its best. Nothing is imported. Like the metro, it seems to come from another era, the time when shops had counters and everything was kept behind them. If you want something, you ask for it.

I peruse the toy department, the record section (more 33 ⅓ LPs than CDs), the sports section (heavy on table tennis), the pen display (remember fountain pens and removable nibs?) and a surprising large space for stuffed birds and animals. The staff, strictly female and all in bright blue outfits, outnumber the shoppers, but they're friendly, greeting me with hellos and even, from the sports counter, an inquiry on my home country. Tour guides and the party elite are virtually the only people who speak any foreign language. What use would a foreign language be? Nobody's going anywhere. Yet you often hear 'hello' and 'where are you from?' In fact the North Koreans could easily be Californians; they'd quickly learn to say 'have a nice day now'. They're certainly not dour and unsmiling.

The musical instruments section offers everything from pianos to a double bass to a selection of the DPRK's finest electric guitars (I guess George W would call it an evil axe). It's the bike department that I find most interesting. Almost everything on sale in Department Store No 1 is crude or rough or outdated, but the bikes are on another strata of shoddiness. At first glance they look just like the classic men's single-speed, rod-brake machines turned out in their millions by Flying Pigeon or Phoenix in China or Hero in India. Close up it's a different story. These are the nastiest, crudest, roughest, most badly made bicycles I have ever seen. Everything about them looks inferior, from the rough welding to the bent brake rods to the uneven paint. Back at the hotel for lunch, I head straight for the employees' bicycle park. Contrary to many Pyongyang visitors' reports, the city is not bicycle free. Some of the bike park machines are Japanese, most of them Chinese. There's not a DPRK bike to be seen.

Musing about those shoddy bicycles, I can imagine the DPRK missile salesman at work: 'Mr Hussein/Gaddaffi/Musharraf/Assad, we have an Axis-of-Evil special this month. With every Rodong 1 missile we're throwing in 100 of our finest bicycles.'

'That's how you make bicycles?' queries the potential weapons-of-mass-destruction customer. 'Look, I think I'm going to have to cancel that missile order.'

Our shopping interlude over, it's back to the monuments. We whisk by the Arch of Triumph (commemorating the Great Leader's defeat of the Japanese in 1945), the Monument to the Party Foundation and the tower of the *Juche* Idea (complete with a wall of plaques put up by *Juche* admirers from all over the world – there's even one from New York City). Then it's out to visit Kim Il-sung's humble peasant home on the outskirts of town. Somehow it alone survived the Japanese occupation and the destructive power of the Korean War, which flattened Pyongyang, and Seoul too for that matter.

It's the obscenity called Mangyongdae School Children's Palace that really does it for me. Our group is led around a half-dozen rooms (and one Olympic-size swimming pool) where smiling, rosy-cheeked children dance, play accordions, strum the curious stringed instrument known as a *kayagum* (its sound is 'tender, elegant, but plaintive' according to my local guidebook), work on their calligraphy, embroider or, in the swimming pool, plunge from the high board.

These rooms are only a selection, a tiny sample, we are assured, of the 500-odd rooms in the palace, where every day 5000 pampered school kids hone their skills and sing the praises of the Great Leader. And those 500 rooms are only an adjunct, a side game, a mere appendage to the grandiose, over-the-top, ostentatious, obscenely extravagant horror of this marble-pillared, soaring-ceilinged, sweeping-stairwayed, statue-tiered monstrosity of a building.

When the fat cats in Pyongyang decided to construct this ugly symbol of their arrogance, how many farmers did they decide to leave planting their fields by hand and ploughing them with an old cow? How many road workers did they decide to leave by the side of the highway breaking rocks with a hammer? It's no wonder aid workers pull their hair out when they're confronted with this contradiction. In the country people starve while in Pyongyang their masters play games in palaces. The idiots then let us gather the evidence for their conviction. They're so ashamed of what they've done to the workers that they have a fit if a tourist photographs someone doing real work, but photographing another colossal stone and bronze monument to the tubby tyrant is OK. So aid workers try to feed the starving, living in textbook Third World conditions, while children dance in a marble palace a whole world away.

That night some of our group embark on a tour of Pyongyang by night, which essentially means looking at monuments by floodlight, although in Kim Il-sung Square the Great Leader's illuminated portrait turns off at precisely 9pm, just as we arrive. Some of us end up at the Taedonggang Diplomatic Club, which seems to be run by the North Koreans, not the diplomats, since it has all the standard North Korean signs: portraits of the deadly duo, photos of recent events in Pyongyang with the dumpy despot's face smiling from the centre, no running water in the bathrooms and so on. There's a video room, cinema, restaurant and karaoke bar as well as the billiards room and bar where we repair to.

Arabic music is oozing out of the speakers. 'Sounds Libyan', says Camilla, an identification quickly confirmed by Digby who recognises one of the billiard players as someone from the Libyan embassy, having met him in the basement Egypt Palace Karaoke Bar at our hotel. Libyans seem to lose their distaste for alcohol once they're outside their own country. The other billiard players are from Laos and Pakistan and for once every fluky shot I make goes in, so it's a fine DPRK evening.

• • • •

We're off across country. The road to Wonsan sweeps across the central mountains, diving through dark tunnels, the last one of which, the Rainbow Tunnel, is 4 kilometres long. The highway activity is just like I observed from the train down from the border: nobody and nothing is on the move and there are clear signs of a highly stressed environment with fields cut into steep hillsides, erosion and deforestation.

Overuse is a short-sighted approach, but 'North Korea has always been very short-sighted', a Western diplomat I bumped into at the Diplomatic Club had mused. 'Before the collapse of Communism, Russia and China paid for everything. The Koreans didn't need to worry about rice production because China covered any shortfall. While other Asian countries were double-cropping and introducing new improved varieties of rice, they didn't worry about raising production. Having full employment was more important than how much they produced.'

Just past halfway there's a pause at Sinphyong where, according to the guidebook I bought in Pyongyang, Yellow Serpent Liquor is the specialty. 'The nonpoisonous yellow serpent is tasty and effective', the guidebook declares. 'A yellow serpent is put into over 60% alcohol and buried until the medicinal elements come off. The liquor makes the organs of the body work smoothly. It is said to do wonders for ageing male virility.' A bottle of this potent stipple costs US$10.

A long pedestrian causeway, punctuated by a couple of swaying suspension bridges, leads out from beside our hotel to Jangdok Islet. At night it's populated by fishermen toting quite professional rods. In the morning they've been replaced by a solitary snorkeller and a large collection of women foraging around for shellfish. Some fishermen are floating their lines out with the aid of square wooden floats topped by sails, but my favourites are young guys paddling energetically out to sea on inflated truck inner tubes, trailing a long fishing line baited with hundreds of small lines dangling below. A fellow fisher pays the baited line out from a neat box on shore. These guys are miniature long line trawlers.

Regrettably we don't get to wander the traffic-free streets of Wonsan – lack of city wandering time is the number-one complaint for the whole group – but we do visit a fine old temple ('extensively damaged by American bombers during the war') and the Chonsam Collective Farm where there's another local home visit. This one is clearly pre-selected, but it's remarkably like the house to which we'd made a spur-of-the-moment visit. There's the same kitchen with a sunken central area, the same coal-fired cooking range, the same sparsely furnished rooms, the same double portraits as the only form of decoration.

· · · ·

The DMZ is in fact the world's most heavily armed frontier. On the drive south to Panmunjeom in the DMZ, our bus stops in what would be a freeway service centre in the West, except there are no fuel pumps. The building, complete with restaurant and souvenir shop, straddles the six-lane freeway and from the balcony I take a photo of the empty highway. I have to wait 10 minutes for a vehicle to come by, otherwise the image would be totally traffic free.

255.

Can we visit the North's DMZ village, just to confirm that the southern puppet's lies that it's actually uninhabited are indeed an outrageous slander? No, sorry, that won't be possible. We can, however, make an excursion to see the Korean Wall, the solid concrete structure that extends 280 kilometres from one coast to the other.

'They claim it is an anti-tank wall, but if that is true why is it so high?' proposed the DMZ soldier-guide. 'To stop a tank you only need a wall 50 centimetres to a metre high.'

'Is it true that there's also a 30,000-volt electric fence on the North's side of the DMZ?' we bounce back.

'Perhaps', comes the enigmatic reply.

And what is that designed to stop? It won't hold up tanks, will it?' we persist.

In fact fences, walls, concrete obstacles and electric wires are completely unnecessary when it came to shutting the South out. The crippled state of the North's economy provides all the restraint necessary.

The bus pulls into the Armistice Building, something DMZ tours from the south are never going to see. These are the buildings where the protracted negotiations took place – they went on for two years, nearly twice as long as the entire first stages of the war – and where the armistice was finally signed. They are firmly in the northern sector of the DMZ.

Our soldier-guide gives us the standard spiel: the American imperialists arrived in Korea on 8 September 1945, claiming they had liberated the country from those other imperialists. 'This was clearly a lie since the Great Leader Kim Il-sung had already liberated the country on 15 August.' Then the Imperialist Aggressors and their Puppet Stooges built up their strength for the next three years before launching their assault on the North. Fifteen other countries joined the one-sided attack on the DPRK (there's conspicuous silence on Russian support and the flood of Chinese 'volunteers') before finally the American warmongers, realising the hopelessness of their situation, begged for peace. From the starting point of the negotiations in mid-1951 the mess could have been sorted out in a couple of months, but instead the imperialists dragged it out for two years and 718 separate meetings before they finally admitted defeat.

Well that's one interpretation.

•   •   •   •

There are always two sides to every story and, wherever we are, one side is always much louder. Not many of us get to visit these pariah states, so it's hardly surprising we've taken the standard Western perspective on board. North Korea is so clearly a Bad Land – forget any blather about Weapons of Mass Destruction and terrorist activities, the way the DPRK treats its own citizens is shocking.

The government Kim Il-sung installed in North Korea may not have been very nice (even before the shooting he was the one who shut the border to stop an exodus south), but nor was the system the US installed in the South. For the best part of 40 years the South was saddled with a series of dictatorial, draconian and decidedly undemocratic governments.

We hear a lot about the North's million-plus troops, more than half of them within 80 kilometres of the DMZ, and how they outnumber the South Korean army nearly two to one. Yet if the North's energies are so focused on plans to invade the south, what are those walls and electric fences along the North's coast all about? Is it possible the North is equally frightened of an invasion from the South?

There certainly are North Korean incursions into the South, but the traffic is not one way. There was the USS *Pueblo* in 1968, which I'd seen moored on the riverside when I'd made my early morning stroll from my Pyongyang hotel. And was the EC-121 reconnaissance aircraft shot down in 1969 an innocent victim of North Korean aggression? There doesn't seem to be much question that other US aircraft flew over North

257.

Korea in subsequent years and the Fatherland Liberation War Museum in Pyongyang has a whole basement section for shot-down aircraft of the American Imperialist Aggressors. There's even a mint-condition helicopter complete with a photograph of the offending machine with its American crew standing beside it, hands raised and looking very surprised about the whole matter.

We hear a lot about nuclear weapons the North may have, far less about the nuclear weapons the US definitely did have (and, who knows, may still have) in the South. Back in Washington, Dubya musing loudly about the virtues of 'regime change' and calculating the costs of just marching in and changing things for countries that haven't got the sense to do it themselves is hardly encouragement for a little disarming.

When Kim Il-sung met with US negotiator Selig Harrison in 1994 he announced, 'What would be the point of making one or two nuclear weapons when you have 10,000-plus delivery systems that we don't have?'

Whether they need nuclear weapons for defensive (or offensive) purposes, the North Koreans certainly know how to use them as bargaining chips. Eight years before the 2006 crisis, the Pentagon decided there was an underground nuclear-processing facility under construction at Kunchang-ni near the Chinese border and demanded to have a look. 'Sure,' said the North Koreans, 'you can come and have a look, that'll cost you US$300 million.'

Eventually the price was bargained down to 600,000 tonnes of food, and a team of 14 American nuclear inspectors turned up and spent three days looking round no less than 10 kilometres of tunnels, none of which, it turned out, had anything to do with nuclear weapons. The suspicion about this nonexistent facility had screwed up relations on the peninsula for the best part of 12 months, but nobody at the Pentagon got their knuckles rapped. The economy may be in tatters, they may have trouble feeding the population, but there's no question the North Koreans have an admirable ability to perform one feat. The *New York Times* recognised it clearly in a March 1994 article: 'They have mastered the art of dangling Washington on a string.'

So, what about unification. Could it work? First of all the Americans have to leave the South, that's clearly the starting point from the Northern perspective. Jimmy Carter suggested doing exactly that way back in 1975, even before he was elected, but was eventually shot down by the Pentagon sabre-wavers. Simply pulling all the American troops out is hardly likely to make everything instantly OK, but it would help.

For a decade at least, the South has adopted an official policy of rapprochement but the two Koreas would face a huge information, understanding and attitudes headache. Nobody from the North travels south and for years anybody from the South who travelled north, via a third country or whatever, had committed a criminal offence and could expect to be imprisoned when they returned.

'The two sides would elect a Supreme National Assembly', our guide explains. 'It would handle international diplomacy and the military, but everything else would be administered by the two regional governments. They don't want to change their system and we don't want to change ours so we would have one country, but with two different forms of government and two different economic systems.'

'Would there be freedom of movement between the two halves?' I ask.

'Of course', he responds. However, he's much less certain when I ask if the North will be able to access world news, southern media, mobile phone systems, the internet and all the other avenues of communication and information that are so rigorously blocked off at present. After all, if the North was really genuine about opening up to the outside world, there's no reason they couldn't stop jamming the South's radio and TV broadcasts right now.

'Aren't you interested in outside news?' I asked one of our guides. 'Wouldn't you like to hear the news from South Korea?'

'That does not interest us,' he staunchly replied, 'it does not meet our

259.

socialist standards.'

'Well, when the Dear Leader's son was arrested in Japan, trying to visit Disneyland on a fake passport, did you hear about that?' I queried, knowing very well that he had not.

'I do not know if the Dear Leader has any children', he replied.

Nor, it turned out, did he know where the Dear Leader lived. 'You do not know where your leaders live, do you?' he countered. The White House? Ten Downing Street?

The Dear Leader's Pyongyang hideaway may be really hidden, but it would have been hard to miss the Great Leader's humble abode. On the way out to the zoo (for some of our group) and the Revolutionary Martyrs' Cemetery (for others) we'd passed the Kumsusan Memorial Palace, the mausoleum where the remains of the Great Leader, like other Communist heroes from Beijing and Hanoi to Moscow, are preserved like a wax model at Madame Tussaud's. Prior to his departure to the workers' paradise in the sky this was his personal palace and, as befits one of the great heroes and inspirations of the century, it was considerably bigger than the White House or other lesser leaders' official homes.

'And what about photographs?' I continue. 'We can photograph anything we want in the South. Will that change in the North after reunification?'

'It's not just the government', he answers. 'You ask those people out there,' he says, waving at the pedestrians on the roadside, 'they don't want to be photographed either.'

'Oh, sure,' I shoot back, 'they're certainly told they shouldn't want to be photographed, but why should we believe they really don't?'

There's no answer.

From what I've seen, it's crystal clear what the fate of 'one country, two systems' would be, if it actually happened. Within days the South Koreans would have filled North Korea's shops with the spoils of the consumer society. Who would be shopping for the shoddy products of the North's earthly paradise when the glittering prizes of the South's jaebol (business conglomerates) were on offer? How long would Air Koryo last in competition with Korean Airlines? How long before the North's handful of secondhand Toyotas had been replaced with shiny new Hyundais, Kias and Daewoos?

* * * *

'What does surreal mean?' asks Mr Kim. We have made that final dawn trip to the giant statue of the Great Leader and while we'd been photographing the early morning pilgrims he'd read the line in my guidebook that visiting North Korea was 'too surreal to be believable'.

I proceed to dig myself into a hole that proves difficult to get out of. 'Surreal means something that, on the surface, looks very realistic, but when you look more closely you realise that it is not real at all', I explain. 'It's a word often used to describe a style of art in the West.'

'So how does it apply to North Korea?' he continues.

'Well, it's like all the exploits of the Great Leader and the Dear Leader that we're told about', I say, strolling nonchalantly out on to very thin ice.

'We're told the Great Leader visited a farm and taught the farmers how to grow more rice, that he went to a factory and instructed the workers how to increase production, how he meets fishermen and they quickly discover, with his expert tuition, that they could be catching more fish. Obviously this is not true, nobody can be an expert on everything.'

'When did you meet Kim Il-sung?' says Mr Kim and I can see the veil drop, surrealistically, across his eyes. 'If you have not met him, how do you know he is not an expert on all these matters?'

It's the final surreal experience of a decidedly surreal trip.

Of course the North Koreans are not dull automatons, characters from a real-life Orwellian 1984 – they're people who laugh and play and want a better life – but what we see is what their government wants us to see and

261.

any attempt to sneak a peek at anything else, or worse photograph it, is energetically circumscribed.

The next day we fly back to Beijing: Air Koryo to Shenyang, Air China from there. As we taxi in to Shenyang's big, glossy new airport terminal (a steel, aluminium and glass construction that could be anywhere in the affluent West) a Korean Airlines flight from Seoul rolls in right behind us. The governments of the North and South may be barely talking to each other, but minutes after clearing immigration the Seoul bags are spilling on to the carousel, mixed in with the Pyongyang ones. I toy with the idea that you could jump on the Seoul flight when it returns to the South Korean capital and 24 hours later be right back on the DMZ, toeing the line from the opposite side.

SAUDI ARABIA

'Swap oil for carpets and it might all be different', said Don George, Lonely Planet's US-based global travel editor. 'If Afghanistan had oil and Saudi Arabia had carpets, which country would have been bombed?'

There's no question that having a barrel or two of oil around the place does ensure you get treated with some respect. What was Afghanistan after all? Just the post office where the letter bomb was sent from and where, foolishly, the letter-bomber hung around after delivery.

When somebody mails you a letter bomb do you attack the post office or the place where the letter bomb was put together? September 11's letter was written in Saudi Arabia, the letter's author was from Saudi Arabia, its contents (15 of the 19 hijackers) came from Saudi Arabia and the cash for the postage came from Saudi Arabia. So why did Afghanistan get bombed and not Saudi Arabia? Carpets versus oil may have something to do with it.

I knew Saudis weren't the most popular people in the Arab world. Nobody in the Arab world likes the Israelis, but once that dislike is out of the way they can concentrate on not liking each other very much either.

Only the Kuwaitis challenge the Saudis for most unpopular Arabs. It's partly wealth: the Saudis have it, most of the Arab world doesn't, and many Egyptians, Palestinians, Syrians and other less-wealthy Arabs end up working in Saudi Arabia where they're often poorly paid and badly treated. It's partly Islamic arrogance: Saudi Arabia has the two holy cities and Wahhabism is the purest, most conservative form of Islam (it's what the Taliban modelled themselves on). The Saudis look down their noses at everybody else's Islam. Even the 7 or 8 per cent of Saudis who are part of the Shiite sect rather than the mainstream Sunni sect are severely discriminated against.

Finally, though, it's sheer hypocrisy. How austerely pure can you be when you're spending up on every luxury brand from Armani to Ermenegildo Zegna? Nor are the Saudis quite so Islamically pure once they venture beyond their borders. The Arabian Gulf city-state of Bahrain is joined to Saudi Arabia by a causeway and every weekend Saudis flock in for a short spell of R&R. A wave of political liberalisation in Bahrain in 2001 raised the prospect that religious clerics might push to ban alcohol. Unlikely, thought the more cosmopolitan Bahrainis, 'We make too much money from being the closest bar to the world's thirstiest country.'

• • • •

You don't whine about being misinterpreted and misunderstood, but then keep the doors firmly shut to anybody who might want to come in and do a little understanding. The Saudis keep their house locked so securely it's hardly surprising that the outside world believes they're ashamed of what goes on indoors. This is a country that beheads, mutilates and flogs people; that keeps women locked away and disenfranchised in almost every way possible; that has zero democratic rights, zero religious freedom and strict state censorship and media control. As Geraldine Brooks points out in *Nine Parts of Desire,* if Saudi

Arabian society were divided into blacks and whites rather than women and men, there would be international trade sanctions and worldwide outrage at the appalling treatment of one half of the population by the other. As she also points out, if there were 90 million small boys who were forced to have their penises amputated, there might be an outcry about that as well. Clitoridectomies remain a predominantly Muslim rite.

Saudi Arabia is not just two holy cities and a whole lot of desert, and it does get some tourists. What we think of in the West as tourists that is, not just the three million Muslim pilgrims who make the haj to Mecca each year, or the umrah, which is a Mecca pilgrimage made out of season. A small number are Gulf-state Arabs, who don't need a visa, or *umrah* pilgrims who take advantage of visa regulation that lets them stay on after their pilgrimage.

There's not a lot of domestic tourism. 'When Saudis travel they want what they can't get at home, so nightlife and shopping are the most important things', said a hotel manager. Considering the amount of shopping available in the kingdom it scarcely seems necessary to go overseas to look for name brands, but the Saudi shopping instinct is well known. When the king did a 45-day trip around the world in the 1990s, his two 747s didn't have enough shopping capacity. A Saudi Air Force Hercules flew out to each stop to cart purchases back to Riyadh and would then catch up at his next stopover.

'Nor are they very interested in anything pre-Islamic, so you won't see many Saudis at Madain Saleh for example', my hotel manager informant continued. 'If the prophet's not involved, they couldn't care less.'

Nevertheless some tourists are nonbelieving foreigners, not just pilgrims. There are lots of foreigners in Saudi Arabia. Perhaps six or seven million of the population of around 21 million are expat workers and their families. The greatest number are from the Third World, including over a million each from India and Egypt, and large numbers from Pakistan, the Philippines and Bangladesh. Few will have their families with them and they often only get home to see their wives and children for a month or so every couple of years. In contrast, the First World workers are highly paid and often bring their families and take time off to travel around. After all, there's plenty to see – great desert and mountain country for off-road camping trips and the Red Sea for scuba diving.

There are probably also a handful of tourists like me, business visitors who stay on after they've done their business. Once you are inside you can pretty much go wherever you want, although if you're not a Muslim you have to stay out of the two holy cities. I'd had a previous incarnation as an engineer so it was a fairly simple job to find a friend with an air-conditioning company in Jeddah who could arrange for his company to 'sponsor' me – that is, to ask the Saudi embassy to issue a visa.

Prior to September 11 there had also been a limited number of tightly controlled and fairly expensive tours for Westerners to Saudi Arabia. September 11 certainly scared that contingent away.

'We used to get 10 to 15 tour groups a month', lamented the hotel manager. 'In the six months afterwards we had two.' Today that limited and fairly exclusive business looks like it may be kicking into gear again, but you can forget about joining one of those rare tour groups if you're a 44-year-old orphaned widow, divorcee or spinster. Women are not allowed if they're under 45 unless they're accompanied by their husband or father. A responsible male is required to keep an eye on them and make sure they behave themselves.

Absurd? Well, a lot of things about Saudi Arabia are absurd. Presumably once women reach 45 they're sterile, dried up, on the shelf and unlikely to pose a serious danger to the stability and morality of the kingdom. A 35-year-old unaccompanied woman, on the other hand, could be a real danger. The prophet might turn in his grave, the Kaaba in Mecca could shatter, the kingdom could fall.

There are lots of problems for foreign women quite apart from the need to have a man to watch over them. For a start there's the *abaya*, the all-enveloping black shroud that all women are obliged to wear. Technically non-Saudis are not required to wear the *abaya*, but if they don't the *mutawwa* are likely to get them. The 'Committee for the Propagation of Virtue and the Prevention of Vice', which is more or less what *mutawwa* translates as, are 'a squad of moral vigilantes out to enforce Islamic orthodoxy as they understand it', according to my guidebook.

After my first couple of days in Riyadh I was disappointed I'd still not seen a *mutawwa*. 'How do I find one?' I asked an Indian expat.

'Wear shorts and you'll find one very quickly', he replied.

In fact the *mutawwa* are recognisable by their short ankle-revealing *thobe*, or robe, their full bushy beards and long hair and the fact that they do not wear the usual *gutra* or headcloth. They also carry around a stick to whack wrongdoers. A website on the miserable state of human rights in Saudi Arabia commented that they are 'empowered to investigate, search, arrest and detain citizens and foreigners, and their abusive practices, including physical attacks and beatings, have been widely noted' (Human Rights Watch – http://hrw.org/backgrounder/mena/saudi/). The Australian foreign affairs department warns their citizens, 'particularly females', that 'incidents of assault have been reported' and that they should end any encounter 'as quickly as possible – if necessary by leaving the area immediately'. 'Steer clear of them', suggested my guidebook.

So if a woman doesn't wear her *abaya*, a *mutawwa* is likely to attack her with a stick.

'"Close your face!" they'll shout, "Close your face!"' a Sudanese taxi driver had demonstrated in Dubai.

'It's part of the government's method to keep down dissent', suggested one liberal Saudi I spoke to. 'If people are worrying about being hassled by the *mutawwa*, they have less time to worry about the profligate spending of the wealthy.'

In mid-2002 a government official announced that the *mutawwa* would be cracking down on manufacturers whose *abaya* did not come up to standard. The regulations for 'decent women's cloaks' required that they be 'thick and not revealing, loose so they do not show the body, and open from the front only. The black dress should cover all the body, be devoid of decoration, drawings, writing and other marks and different to male dress'.

In fact *abaya* and the necessity to wear them vary quite considerably. A Saudi woman is likely to wear the whole head-to-toe outfit with the face completely covered or with only a slit for the eyes. Wearing your glasses outside the slit can look quite comical. Really serious Saudi women even wear black gloves so if they have to hand money out, or take something in, not a square centimetre of flesh will show. Foreign women can get away with showing their faces, but not their hair. Even a wisp of hair is completely verboten.

Riyadh – the capital, in the religiously conservative heartland – is 100 per cent *abaya* country. Certain other centres are also very conservative, but some cities are much more freewheeling and although foreigners will still have to wear one they may not have to cover their heads. Get out in the desert or way off the beaten track and foreign women (none of this applies to Saudis) can dress conservatively, but pretty normally. There are unlikely to be any *mutawwa* poking around the un-Islamic ruins of Madain Saleh. The strictly foreign 'compounds', where most Western expats live, are also much more free. Even Wilfred Thesiger, the Englishman who crossed the burnings sands of the Empty Quarter soon after World War II and wrote the desert-crossing classic *Arabian Sands*, pointed out that it was principally a city extravagance. In the desert women have to work and they can't do that in an *abaya*.

Apart from branding women, the *abaya* is also uncomfortable, hot and quite possibly dangerous. Perhaps it's just as well women are not allowed to drive. Saudi roads are unsafe enough already without people trying to drive with a black bag over their heads.

'The Japanese tourists are amazing', said a Moroccan tour guide I spoke with. 'They actually get *abaya* made in Tokyo so they can get off the plane already wearing them. Other visitors don't buy one until after they arrive and then they're always asking, "Do I have to wear it now? Can I take it off now?" I think Japanese women even wear their *abaya* in their hotel rooms.'

The Saudis not only keep a tight grip on who comes in to the country, they also tightly restrict the news that filters in. While the *Arab News*, the principal English language newspaper, daily rails about the 'Jewish dominated' American media, the Saudi censors are busy blacking out anything that offends them in publications from outside the country.

'Religion, politics and sex are the three things they don't like', said a bookshop manager. 'The trouble is the responsibility for wielding the black marker-pen on incoming publications goes to the most junior staff and they can get into trouble for letting something through, but they won't be reprimanded for censoring too much.'

Of course, it's pictures that are more likely to get blacked out than text, so in a liquor ad on the back cover of *Outside* magazine, the bottle is blacked out along with the two blondes' cleavages and legs, but Hugh Hefner escapes untouched. In another magazine a picture of the Sex in the City stars requires heavy blackout work on arms, legs, navels and cleavages.

The absurdity is that, while countless marker-pens run dry covering up Britney Spears' navel in magazines, she can flaunt it at will on MTV. With so much satellite TV beamed down, the Saudis have simply given up trying to keep questionable TV out. Once upon a time the *mutawwa* were likely to stone offending satellite dishes so owners either hid them away or stone-proofed them with wire fences. Eventually satellite dishes were simply banned, and then the ban was not enforced. Today there are even 'dish *souq*,' – markets devoted to satellite dishes and their paraphernalia.

In early 2002 the *mutawwa* determination to ensure no women went out uncovered contributed to a tragedy in the city of Mecca. A fire in a run-down, badly designed and overcrowded girls school led to the deaths of 15 girls and injuries to many others. As the girls attempted to escape from the blaze they were pushed back inside by the *mutawwa* because they were not covered by their *abaya* and there were no responsible males to accompany them out. Furthermore when police and firemen tried to enter the blazing building they were blocked by the *mutawwa*, since men, even firemen, should not be mixing with unrelated women. The Interior Minister Prince Nayef said that the *mutawwa* had only been there to 'stop the girls being mistreated', but people I speak to do not think it unlikely that they would have been quite capable of such idiocy. 'They're the most hated people in the kingdom', is a sentiment I hear expressed more than once.

. . . .

I've heard that getting through immigration and customs can be tedious so I'm not surprised when there's an undignified scramble for the door before the 777 has even come to a halt at Riyadh's King Khalid Airport. The haste is even more evident inside the terminal, but I'm fairly well placed in the line until, when I'm just two from the head of the queue, our immigration official stands up and walks off the job. After 15 minutes another official comes by and tells us he ain't comin' back, so it's back to the end of another line. After a while I start timing how long it takes to process each passenger – about two minutes – which means a 30-person line takes an hour to work through, nearly as long as the flight from Dubai.

272. The Englishman in front of me goes through in less than 30 seconds, however, and I follow suit, grab my bag and get whisked through customs with equal alacrity. After all the stories about zealous officials going through women's fashion magazines looking for 'pornographic' bra ads, I was wondering if they'd check what you had stored on your computer.

The speed-up continues when I emerge because my hotel has sent a driver and a few minutes later we're zooming along the freeway towards Riyadh, the speedometer warning-chime occasionally informing us we're exceeding 120 kilometres per hour. Despite my Indian driver complaining about death and carnage due to speed and simple craziness, the drive into town is actually fairly calm. Sure, a few cars zoom by at what must be closer to 200 than the 110-kilometre-per-hour speed limit, but we only encounter one accident all the way to the Al-Khozama Hotel.

Right next to my hotel, and a useful landmark for my next few days in Riyadh, is the new Faisaliah Tower, looking like a slightly pregnant version of San Francisco's Transamerica Pyramid. It's the work of English über-architect Norman Foster and discreet engravings both sides of the entrance doors reveal that it was built by the bin Laden group. Riyadh's other signature skyscraper, the Kingdom Centre, has a hole right through it. 'It's used for practice flights' is the Saudi joke.

Having dumped my bag, I find an ATM and soon I am in the Faisaliah Shopping Mall. The flashy centre has lots of familiar Western brands, including labels such as Miss Selfridge, Harvey Nichols, Donna Karan, Etam lingerie, Liz Claiborne, Hugo Boss, United Colors of Benetton, Mango, Guess and even French Connection UK, with its racy acronym proudly displayed across the back of the shop. Do those all-enveloping *abaya* wandering out of the shop enshroud teenagers with 'FCUK' inscribed across their T-shirted breasts I wonder? The Western kids, with their jeans emerging from the bottom and their faces on display above, look like they're appearing at some engowned graduation ceremony, but the Saudi women, totally covered up, resemble a scene from *Star Wars*.

I walk down the next street stopping for a cappuccino in a Dr Café, which feels just like a Starbucks except there are no women either side of the counter and the exclusively male clientele is more than 95 per cent

273.

traditionally dressed. A few doors down I discover that the standard red-and-white check *gutra,* which makes Saudi men look like they've just had a collision with a French bistro's red gingham tablecloth, isn't so standard at all. A menswear shop advertise that they have Valentino, Dunhill and Givenchy *gutra.*

· · · ·

I quickly discover that the capital's taxi fleet is almost without exception piloted by Pakistanis – and a nicer, gentler bunch of subcontinental taxi drivers you could not ask to meet. Many of them speak at least some English and are keen to talk about cricket (Pakistan's team is doing pretty well) and, quite unlike the way taxis work on the real subcontinent, none of them is at all pushy about the fare. They use their meters without hesitation and often seem keen to round fares down to the nearest five riyals!

Between taxis I walk, particularly around the Al Baatha old city area. I go there in the early afternoon to visit the Masmak Fortress only to discover the Saudi siesta can really stretch. The fort's closed from noon to 4pm. I return just after four only to be told that today is family day and since my family aren't with me I'll have to come back tomorrow, which is a men's day.

The fortress plays a key role in modern Saudi history and at least I get to see one clear piece of evidence to demonstrate just what a dramatic day 16 January 1902 was. Less than a century earlier in 1818 the Al-Saud family's rule came to a disastrous end when the Turks, who reckoned the sandy wastes of Arabia were just another part of the mighty Ottoman Empire and that these local upstarts were getting too big for their *thobe,* decided to reassert their authority. Dir'aiyah, the Saud family capital just outside Riyadh, fell to the Turks and it looked like it was all over for the Al-Sauds.

274.

Not quite. Within four years they'd regained control of Riyadh, but for years internal squabbles sapped the family's power and finally in 1891 Riyadh was taken by their rivals the Al-Rashids, strongly supported by the Turks. To this day Turkey is not very popular in Saudi Arabia. The 12-year-old Abdul Aziz ibn Abdul Rahman al-Saud was smuggled out of Riyadh, hidden in a saddle-bag on a camel, so the legend goes, and grew up in Kuwait intent on restoring his family's power and getting rid of the Al-Rashids and their Turkish patrons. Ibn Saud, a shorter version of his name popular in the West, rode back across the sands in late 1901 leading a band of just 60 supporters on what would undoubtedly be the most successful raid in Arabian history.

Hiding in a house near the Masmak Fortress, Ibn Saud and 40 of his warriors waited until the fort's commander left the stronghold at dawn. Rushing out from their hiding place the Al-Saud band overpowered and killed the commander and soon controlled the fort. In the melee a spear hurled by one of the band lodged itself so firmly in the wooden fortress door that the broken spearhead can still be seen today. I take a photograph of that notable chunk of metal before departing to wait for men's day. It's an arresting thought that if the fort commander had managed to get back inside and slam the door shut the Al-Saud raid might have failed and today the country might be named after an entirely different family. I'd be in Rashid Arabia.

The fortress isn't Riyadh's only piece of history. The next morning I grab a taxi soon after dawn. I see a lot of dawns in the next 10 days. The first couple of hours of daylight are cool and delicious before the heat starts to pound on you like a white-hot sledgehammer. On the outskirts of Riyadh are the ruins of Dir'aiyah, the Al-Saud's capital until the Turks destroyed it. Much of the dried mud architecture is picturesquely crumbling, but there are a couple of palaces and the old bathhouse that have been restored along with most of the extensive city walls and some of the guard towers. Wandering around this spellbinding ruined city in

275.

the morning cool, I also experience something that will become very familiar in the days ahead: I have the whole place to myself. Repeatedly in museums, forts, palaces and ruins I will be the only person there.

Having Dir'aiyah all to yourself is great and the previous day I'd also been the sole visitor in Riyadh's magnificent new National Museum. Saudi Arabia's near total inexperience with tourists is not so convenient when you need a permit to go somewhere. Officially you must have a permit from the Ministry of Antiquities to visit any archaeological site, but Dir'aiyah is permit-free and it's very unclear which other sites need permits or even where they are. Madain Saleh, my next stop, definitely needs a permit, and later in the trip I come across another permits-only site and I'm simply not allowed to see it, even though I might have been the only visitor for weeks.

After inquiries, phone calls and shuffling from desk to room to office at the museum, I'm eventually led to a large, spacious office where half a dozen men lounge around looking bored. It's unclear what gets done here, if anything, but having a solo tourist turn up to apply for a permit is clearly not part of the everyday agenda. Not much English is spoken, but eventually I'm told to apply in writing and the letter, preferably in Arabic, should be stamped by my sponsor. I patiently explain that I'm not working here, I'm just a business visitor and my office is on the other side of the world so I can't go back there to get the letter written. Can't I just write the letter right now?

Eventually this proposal is reluctantly agreed to and I tear a page out of my notebook, note down my name and passport number and write 'please give me a permit to visit Madain Saleh'.

Come back tomorrow I'm told.

The next day there's no discernible change in the office and the official I spoke to before isn't around, but, remarkably, my permit is found and after a long delay while somebody important enough is found to sign it, I go away clutching it tightly.

That evening, after my men's day visit to the Masmak Fortress, I continue on to the Murabba Palace. Unfortunately men's day at Masmak is family day at Murabba. Fortunately, even though I have no wife or children to give me respectability, I am allowed in.

The men and family ruling causes lots of complications. Unless a restaurant has two separate areas —one for men and one for families — women are simply not allowed in. It's understandable. Women are not allowed to uncover their faces when unrelated men are around and eating when you've got a bag over your head would not be easy. At lunchtime I'm in a quite respectable, but male-only, Lebanese restaurant when I notice a woman outside waving what looks like the same menu I'm holding. She's come to order food to take away, but she is not allowed inside to order it. My waiter in his coat and bow tie goes outside to stand in the sun on the busy pavement and take her order.

Furthermore 'men' does indeed mean 'men', but 'family' doesn't necessarily mean 'women'. At the entrance to the family room at a branch of an American fast-food outlet, a sign announces that no single women are allowed in. Of course men by themselves are banned, but so are women either solo or with just another woman. She needs a man or child to be allowed entry.

'It can get very confusing', said an American expat. 'I was taking a friend's daughter out for a pizza before I met the rest of our group. She hadn't reached puberty so she didn't have to wear an *abaya*, but as a man with a child did I qualify as a family, even though it wasn't my child?'

The answer was no. They were not allowed in.

• • • •

At 6am, the sun just up, I'm boarding a flight to Medina, probably the only nonbeliever on an MD90 full of Muslims. It's one of the two Muslims-only holy cities, but the airport is outside the infidel-free zone so it's OK to fly in. I'm then going to rent a car and drive north 400 kilometres to Madain Saleh. The airport is actually the other side of Medina and I'd been concerned about accidentally straying into the city, but everybody, including the rent-a-car desk, assures me there's no chance I'll do that. Sure enough a few kilometres down the road an exit sign announces 'All Non-Muslims Take Next Exit'. I peel off and head north.

Never heard of Madain Saleh? Well, if you've seen Petra in Jordan or even its appearance in *Indiana Jones and the Last Crusade*, you'd certainly recognise Madain Saleh. The stone-cut tombs, which are all that remain of the ancient Nabatean centre, date from 100 BC to AD 100, when this was a great city on the frankincense-trading route and second in importance only to Petra itself. Today there's one major difference between the two ancient cities. Petra is overrun with tourists (or at least it is when the Israelis aren't shooting it out with the Palestinians and scaring everyone away) and has over 70 hotels. Madain Saleh has hardly any tourists at all and just two hotels.

I no sooner arrive at my hotel than I'm adopted by a little group of Canadians, two of them Riyadh-based expats, the other two visitors from back home. They're being guided by Hamim, an extremely capable young Moroccan guy. Moroccans are well regarded as guides in Saudi Arabia because they're used to dealing with tourists and they generally speak English and French as well as Arabic.

The ruins are superb. The stone-cut tombs are not as ornate as at Petra and instead of being concentrated along a narrow ravine they're scattered in a variety of outcrops. The iconic Madain Saleh tomb, the Qasr Farid, stands isolated, a single mighty lump of rock swelling up out of the sand. We arrive just before sunset and sit atop a nearby dune to watch the sun sink beyond the hills off to the west, dappling the red rock of the tomb an even deeper colour.

Earlier in the afternoon we'd stopped at the old Hejaz Railway station at the northern end of the site. Once upon a time this was a station on the line that carried pilgrims from Damascus to Medina. Opened in 1908 the line was a favourite target for Lawrence of Arabia during World War I although his railway-sabotaging activities never got this far south. The crippled line never recovered from the war and was finally abandoned in 1924. There were some half-hearted attempts to revive it during the 1960s and 1970s, but today it's quietly and picturesquely rusting away.

At the hotel that night I meet Patrick Pierard, a longtime French resident in the kingdom who has written a book about off-road trips in the Hejaz region and is the local expert on the line, the old Turkish forts built to protect it, and the solid-stone station buildings that pop up beside the road about every 20 kilometres to Medina. The next day, on my way back south, he leads me off the road to the ruins of a fine old railway fort and later, following his instructions, I divert to another abandoned station with a locomotive and line of carriages still standing outside.

Flying out of Medina includes one of those weird little experiences that has you scratching your head and wondering if it was something cultural you'd missed or some deeper misunderstanding. I get back into Medina earlier than I expected, early enough that it seems possible I might get a flight out to Jeddah that evening and not have to wait for the flight I'm booked on the next morning. I've got no urge to stay in a city I'm not even allowed in, even if there is a hotel just outside the Muslims-only ring of protection.

So I drive to the airport and leave my bags in the rented car in case I can't get on, and go to the check-in desk. It's 6.15pm, there's a flight at 7pm, but I'll have to go standby. Come back in 15 minutes. I go back to the car park, retrieve my bag, hand the keys in to the Budget desk and clear up the paperwork and I'm back to the check-in desk at 6.30pm. They still don't know if there's a seat available. Come back in another 15 minutes. At 6.45pm I'm told the flight's in final boarding and it's full. I'm not worried, there's another flight at 9.30pm and I can hang around the airport and grab some food.

At the ticketing counter my ticket is taken and the agent goes into such an interminable bout of keyboarding I'm beginning to think there's something wrong with it, but finally he emerges from behind the counter, tells me to come with him and marches off through security and into the departure area. I trail behind, still toting the bag I intended to check in as well as my carry-ons. At the gate desk the agent goes into another marathon bout on the computer, but finally (by this time it's about 7.10pm) hands me a boarding card and tells me I can get on the 7pm flight after all. So up the steps I run, still carrying the bag I intended to check in.

Business class is half-empty. If they'd have upgraded me, I could have got on easily. It's only a short flight and I would probably even have offered to pay the extra if they'd asked. However, when I step into economy I'm mildly shocked. Where are all the passengers? This plane is not full. Around 100 of the 250 or so seats are empty. So why was I told to wait 15 minutes, and then another 15 minutes, and then told it's full and to try my luck on a later flight?

• • • •

There's a definite Indian flavour to my Jeddah hotel. The check-in clerk asks for my 'good name' and the porter is then told to 'do the needful' with my bag. The hotel turns out be part of a subroutine of the Indian Oberoi chain.

Jeddah's importance as a Red Sea port made it the big city of Saudi Arabia until Riyadh finally overtook it when air travel ended the capital's desert isolation. Not until then did the foreign embassies relocate from Jeddah and Riyadh become the national capital in more than just name. The historic port city is still a more cosmopolitan place than straight-laced Riyadh, and Al-Balad, the old town centre with its multistorey houses, although dwarfed by the relentless expansion of the new city and distanced from the sea by land reclamation, remains one of the most interesting city areas in the country.

With its intricately fretworked wooden windows and coral-rock construction, old Jeddah's architecture is instantly recognisable although many of the Al-Balad buildings are like dishevelled, pot-bellied drunks. A couple of storeys up, the walls lean precipitately backward to counterbalance their bulging lower storeys, swelling out closer to street level like overhanging beer guts. At the same time the whole building sways drunkenly to one side or the other while the windows lean sideways or fall forward like the torn and peeling coat pockets on a drunk's jacket.

Wandering round the *souq* – the generic term for a market – I ask one stallholder, his wares limited entirely to Saudi-style sandals, if I can take his photograph and I'm invited in to sit and sip a cup of tea. It turns out he's from Yemen. I've been warned so forcefully about the dangers of taking photographs in Saudi Arabia that I have, to date, been very cautious about taking my camera out of my daypack. There is no question that taking photos of women is totally off-limits. I think even taking pictures of streetscapes with women in the frame would be off-limits. The few requests to take photographs of men have not been welcome either. In a square near a mosque I was amused to see the park benches had signs, in English as well as Arabic, insisting that you did not use them during prayer time. Two young Saudi boys were sitting on a bench beside the sign, but when I asked if I could photograph them they refused.

I'm the only passenger on the Red Sea Palace Hotel's bus tour of the city's further flung sights and it's a pretty perfunctory affair: 'there's the king's palace, there's another palace, there's the old airport, this is the Corniche', and finally, just before we got back to the hotel on the edge of Al-Balad, 'this is chop-chop square'.

Every Saudi city has a chop-chop square, where capital punishment is administered in Saudi style. There's no advance announcement, but on the appointed day the executioners come to the square and spread out a blue plastic sheet. The condemned man or woman arrives in a police car, hands bound, eyes covered, tranquillised. He or she is led out to the execution spot, made to kneel down and is beheaded with a swift sword stroke. It's usually just chop, not chop-chop. Nor is murder the only crime that leads to beheading. You can also pay a one-way visit to chop-chop square for rape, armed robbery, drug smuggling, sodomy or even witchcraft. In 1996 a Syrian citizen was executed for sorcery although it's believed his real crime was knowing too much about the questionable business practices of his employer, a Saudi prince.

Chopping hands off (for theft) and floggings (for drunkenness or homosexuality) are other popular Saudi punishments and in 2002 Englishman Gary Nixon was sentenced to eight years imprisonment and 800 lashes for running a booze business. Now that might have dissuaded Al Capone in the prohibition era. Usually the lashes are administered 50 or so at a time with 15 days between instalments. Nixon can be thought lucky he got off so lightly. A few years before, nine transvestites were sentenced to between 2400 and 2600 lashes each.

My second night in Jeddah I eat at Abou Shakra, an Egyptian restaurant overlooking the Corniche. It's Thursday night, the equivalent of Saturday night in the Christian West and it seems half the town has come to the seaside for a stroll.

The Arab world loves its mobile phones. Earlier in the day I'd passed a coffee bar where a group of Saudis were sitting around a table, their mobiles piled in the centre like logs on a boy scout campfire. Tonight the restaurant doesn't need muzak, there's a constant jangle of ring tones. Sometimes the jingles harmonise, sometimes they clash, but nobody is willing to answer the bloody things until their selection has played right through to the bitter end. I'm happy to leave and join the other weekend strollers along the Corniche. In a car park between the road and the beach, families have spread rugs on the tarmac and are having picnics. It seems a strange place to picnic, but further along the feasts are taking place right on the sidewalk with six lanes of traffic whipping by just a parked car's width away.

In the distance I can see strange lighted objects moving back and forth just out to sea. Jeddah is noted for its peculiar 'sculptures', which seem to pop up at every junction, in the middle of every roundabout and in any other sufficiently conspicuous position. My first thought is that this is some sort of mobile, illuminated sculpture.

The moving sculptures turn out to be horse-drawn carriages parading the beach, each festooned with strings of Christmas-like coloured lights. In between the carriages are camels and horses, taking beach-goers for a ride. The beach is also lined with rows of swings womaned by a chorus line of *abuya*-clad mothers pushing their children. So there's noise, colour, confusion and camels, enough to make the complete Saudi experience as soon as one more vital ingredient is added to the mix: danger. A couple of hundred miniature versions of those fat-tyred four-wheeled motorcycle devices supplies that. Some of their pilots are adults, but many more of them are children. Some simply hurtle along the pavement or beach, crouched low over their machines; others race around the beach, weaving in and out of the horse-drawn carriages, horses, camels and strollers. Others perform high-speed slaloms along the front.

This is clearly an accident begging to happen yet somehow it doesn't. In the half-hour I sit and watch this bizarre scene, doing my best to keep out of the line of fire, no high-speed racers collide head-on or chop a camel off at the knees; no beach moto-crosser mows down a strolling family; no slalom-ace spins out and wipes out an entire picnicking group. One day they will!

There's a final touch of Saudi surrealism back at the hotel. Usually the lobby reflected the country's cosmopolitan mix, with a group of Indian expats at one table, a party of British engineers talking loudly about 'Saudi-fucking-Arabia' at another, and a mix of Saudis and Western businessmen at a third. Tonight all the foreigners have been swept out and the lobby is wall-to-wall white *thobe* dotted with red-check *gutra*.

Regrettably Jeddah's most famous long-term expat resident was relocated even before he died in 2003. Big Daddy Idi Amin ended up in Saudi Arabia after his despotic rule of Uganda ended in 1979. His conversion to Islam had made him friends like Libya's Gaddafi and Saudi Arabia's King Faisal although it was unlikely that Faisal's successor, King Fahd, was so happy about his long-term guest. Idi may have been a lousy human being but he was a good Muslim, so the Saudis provided him with a home and swimming pool in Jeddah, a late-model Chevrolet Caprice, and a monthly allowance of about US$1500. Although he gave occasional interviews to African newspapers, he knew the deal depended upon keeping a low profile – trying to ship arms to northern Uganda in 1998 didn't fit that bill. He was promptly relocated from sophisticated Jeddah to straight-laced Mecca.

• • • •

'It's good business', said the manager of the Jeddah internet café I ducked into. He didn't seem concerned about government censorship and hadn't even heard of women's internet cafés being closed down, although I looked the story up on one of his computers. Like everything else in Saudi Arabia, internet cafés are sex-segregated. The 'women's café shut down' story didn't make it clear why it was shut down. Using the café as a meeting place? Looking at sites they shouldn't have? Accessing banned sites is a likely reason for a Saudi café to be shut. The government's censors have blocked off over 400,000 websites because they're 'anti-Islam' or they are a 'danger to state security'.

My next stop is Taif and a quick surf for hotels turns up an unbeatable 'one night only' bargain at the Taif InterContinental. When I get there it turns out to be not such a great deal because the hotel is way outside the town.

'We can call a taxi from town', suggests the doorman, but adds that I might find a taxi on the road outside. It's more freeway than road, but a couple of taxis flash past so I venture down the slip-road where Osama bin Laden's miniature twin brother in a beat-up old Peugeot stops almost immediately. Grow a bushy beard and slap on a *gutra* and almost any Saudi looks like Osama. His driving is very un-Saudi – he's slow and cautious, for which I'm most grateful, and he seems quite happy with what I pay.

Prayer time pops up five times a day and although the pre-dawn one, Fajr (sunrise), doesn't interrupt much (apart from perhaps waking you up) the other four – Dhuhr (noon), Asr (afternoon), Maghreb (sunset) and Isha (night) – certainly can. Since the times are determined by the time of sunrise and sunset, wherever you are they differ from day to day and from place to place and are listed for main centres in the paper each day.

At prayer time everything is supposed to stop, but that seems to be open to some interpretation. Planes don't stop flying, buses don't stop driving, taxis don't stop picking up fares, but shops and restaurants do close their doors. At prayer times you'll see the McDonalds staff lounging around outside, waiting for the 'all clear' to sound from the mosque, 20 minutes or half an hour later. Or sometimes longer. If you're hidden away inside, some places will let you carry on with your meal, but if you're in plain view you're likely to be hustled out on to the street. Dreaming over my coffee one day I didn't notice the café empty and, when I stood up to pay, discovered I was not only totally alone, I was also locked inside. The staff were grabbing a smoke outside. Hearing noises upstairs, I climbed the stairs to investigate and found a pool hall with all tables in action.

• • • •

Looking down the Abha-bound bus, there are half a dozen Saudis, but the other 50-odd passengers are probably a representative selection of Saudi guest workers. Developing world guest workers that is – wealthy

Western workers would be flying or driving. There are no women either, although the previous day's bus had half a dozen, including a couple of brazen older Filipinistas with uncovered hair. Today's passengers mainly come from the hard-working Middle Eastern neighbours or the subcontinent, apart from a scattering of Africans.

The first 100 kilometres from Taif pass by at suitably rapid Saudi-freeway pace, but then the road narrows and begins to twist and climb. The countryside also becomes noticeably greener, hardly lush Irish-green, but the sort of green that would not be out of place in parts of Italy or Greece. It's also surprisingly densely populated. One scattered small town is quickly followed by another, places that could boast a bank or two with ATMs, a car dealer and a host of shops and workshops.

In between the more modern buildings – square, flat-roofed places whether they are smaller homes, bigger ones or four- and five-storey buildings – are square watchtowers, signs of an earlier unsettled age when tribal feuding was common. They go on for hundreds of kilometres, sometimes popping up every kilometre or so. Fortress-like homes or even groups of buildings like small walled villages also appear from time to time.

I've had remarkably few real conversations with Saudis over the past week. So much of the everyday tourist contact is not with Saudis, but with Egyptians, Syrians, Indians, Pakistanis or Western expats. This time, however, I find myself sitting next to an English-speaking Saudi. Eventually I steer the conversation around to September 11 and its effect in Saudi Arabia.

'Nobody wants to talk about it or even think about it. They want to close their eyes', he says, gesturing with his hands across his eyes.

'Nobody knows why they did it, although most of the hijackers came from Asir', exactly where we are heading towards. 'We saw their pictures on the television.'

'What you are saying to me, you should not say to anyone in Riyadh', he concludes. 'It's OK to talk with me this way, but in Riyadh you must be very careful who you talk with.'

The man in the street wasn't the only one with an *abaya* on when it came to seeing what was going on. When the Saudis finally and reluctantly admitted that 15 of the 19 hijackers were Saudis – although Saudi newspapers still tend to say 'were alleged to be Saudis' – the Interior Minister Prince Nayef claimed 'Saudi Arabia bears no responsibility at all' for September 11. As for the whereabouts of that well-known and much-searched-for ex-Saudi all the prince had to say was, 'we have no information and we have no interest in this subject'.

In fact I'm going from one hijacking centre to another. At least one of the hijackers hailed from Taif, but it was the Asir region, and most particularly Abha, where most of them came from. Abha was the home town for four of the 15 and it's speculated that the town's firebrand cleric Safar al Hawali may have helped to convince them of their holy mission. So it's remarkable that hordes of high-powered Western journos hadn't taken this same bus south. This should have been the town where packs of reporters from the *New York Times*, *Time* magazine or the *Daily Telegraph* descended to doorstep the families of the September 11 multiple murderers. Abha was 'ground zero' for hijacker recruitment, but had there been any Western reporters on this bus, intent on chasing the story back to its starting point? I don't think so.

The trip to Abha had been 'guesstimated' from six to nine hours, but by late afternoon it looks like even nine hours is wishful thinking. Apart from the winding road, there is also a subcontinental routine to the stops. Someone would shout for the driver to stop, would get up and farewell his friends, the driver's assistant would swing up the luggage compartment doors and retrieve the passenger's bags and off we'd go again only for the process to be repeated a hundred metres down the road.

Just when boredom was really setting in we get there, right on nine hours. Though we're not at Abha. Somehow we'd zoomed by Abha half an hour previously and I end up 25 kilometres further along at Khamis. A taxi whisks me back to Abha for precisely half of what it has cost to get all the way from Taif. My guidebook says there's only one hotel in the centre of town. It turns out to be a dive, but I'm too exhausted to care. When I wander out for food – chicken shwarma yet again – I find three other hotels.

If I have one superstitious travel fear, it's tied up with grubby hotels like this one. I'm not particularly worried about my bus falling over a precipice, or my boat going down soon after I discover there are no life jackets on board. I hate the thought of dropping dead in some nameless dive. It's stupid, because if you're dead you're not going to care, but when I'm travelling alone the thought of having a heart attack or dying in my sleep in some dismal hole like this one really freaks me. The next morning I shift hotels, although my bill turns out to be somewhat less than I was quoted at check-in, which makes it seem not quite so dive-like.

I go in search of a rent-a-car. Jamal, an Egyptian, offers me a choice of battered Mitsubishis and points out that the rate doesn't include insurance.

'Can't I pay extra for insurance?' I ask.

'Sorry, we don't have insurance. Don't worry about it, you're not going far from Abha.'

Well, *enshallah,* nothing will happen, but Saudi driving comes from another universe. It's not aggressive like Italy, it's not flat-out speed like Spain or Germany, it's not utter chaos like Cairo or Delhi, nor do Saudi drivers display the sort of pig-headedness you can encounter in the West from Manchester to Melbourne. No, Saudi drivers are completely random. They'll overtake and then simply not pull back in until they're suddenly surprised by somebody approaching head-on. They'll hurtle up behind you at warp speed and either try to squeeze past or decelerate a centimetre behind your back bumper.

288.

All too often Saudi drivers discover warp speed is too big a figure for the next corner, as the black rubber streaks on the way in and battered guard rails and coloured concrete on the apex repeatedly illustrate. On the road from Taif there are regular sightings of battered vehicles far down the hillside below those traumatic corners.

The keynote driving manoeuvre, however, is the unsignalled multi-lane change. Using indicators is never popular with Saudi drivers, but it has a special frisson of excitement when a driver suddenly decides he wants to turn off to the left and he's three lanes over to the right. No problem, he simply turns and most of the time everybody misses him.

'Double zero', announced my Pakistani taxi driver in Riyadh as a Saudi Chevy swung abruptly across our bows.

'Their *agal* [the double-looped cord that holds their *gutra* in place] makes two zeros,' he explained, 'and that's how intelligent they are.'

Their driving may be erratic, but they're remarkably tranquil about the sort of driving that would inspire road rage in the West. The only time Saudis consistently use their horns is the instant a traffic light turns green, even if they're 10 cars back. My Saudi driving technique is simply to give every other car a lot of space. And I constantly watch my rear-view mirror for anyone about to ram me from behind.

'Don't have an accident, you'll always be at fault', an English resident had advised me.

'Even if the local driver is going too fast and not looking when he runs in to you from behind it's still your fault', he went on. 'This is his country, he belongs here, you don't and if you'd not been here the accident wouldn't have happened.'

Everywhere in Saudi Arabia there are plenty of Mercedes and BMWs and in the big cities like Riyadh and Jeddah it's clear how important this market is to companies like Rolls-Royce, Ferrari and Porsche. It's also one of the last places outside North America where Detroit can still flog its wheels, although curiously all the Chevrolet Luminas so popular with the Saudi police force are really from Australia. Ditto for the ubiquitous Toyota taxis. The real Saudi car, the one you'll see parked side-by-side-by-side in town-centre parking lots, or gathered by the

289.

dozen at Bedouin encampments in the middle of the desert, is the Toyota pick-up truck. Sure a Nissan or Mitsubishi will do, but, just like the Taliban, oh-what-a-feeling the Saudis have for a Toyota Hilux, so long as it's in the standard Saudi pick-up colour scheme that is – white with an orange flash down the side. It's said the king dispensed thousands of them to the Bedouin at the start of the Kuwait Gulf War, to ensure their loyalty.

My Mitsubishi is not only battered, it's also worn out I realise as I chug up the first hill heading south to Habalah. The road climbs up to the very edge of the escarpment, from where the mountains tumble down to the Red Sea. Some of the villages I drive through have more of the characteristic square mud houses with their sloping walls and decorative slate ledges. They're interspersed with watchtowers, but unlike the square ones between Taif and Abha these are round, with stone for the lower section, mud for the upper. The house and the watchtower design elements are reflected in much of the modern architecture around Abha.

At Habalah an abandoned village clings to the steep rock face, 300 metres below the plateau top, but still hundreds of metres above the dry valley bottom, which slopes away towards the coast, disappearing in a shimmering grey heat haze. It's a fantastic sight and once again I have the whole place to myself. If I'd come at the weekend, however, I wouldn't have been so alone. Perched at the top of the escarpment is an amusement park, a Luna Park as the Saudis (and Australians) call them, complete with a cable-car running down to the abandoned village. A row of stone enclosures allows Saudi families to picnic and enjoy the view without seeing each other. To complete the desecration there's a dense coating of soft-drink cans, mineral-water bottles, plastic bags and other modern debris over everything. Great view, though.

290. In the afternoon I take another direction out of the city and drive to another escarpment-edge view. It's only as I reach the top I realise why my rent-a-car is so gutless – the altitude is just under 3000 metres, which also accounts for my breathlessness when I climb a little hill. On the way back into town I divert off the road looking for a view down on Abha and find myself, judging from the armed military guards at the front gate, at the entrance to some Saudi prince's weekend mountain escape. Saudi Arabia is littered with the royal family's many princes' many palaces, escapes, weekenders, retreats and hideaways. The high walls around this one seem to stretch for about a kilometre and what I took to be a neat row of pine trees turns out to be an equally neat row of furled green garden umbrellas peeking over the wall, presumably on a terrace where you could sip a nonalcoholic sundowner at beer-o'clock and watch the last rays dapple the town below.

Keeping the extended royal family in palaces, executive jets and limousines consumes a large part of the budget (King Ibn Saud had 44 sons from his 22 wives, for example), but Saudi Arabia still manages to get by without any income tax although a modest (perhaps 2.5 per cent) tax on foreigners is mooted from time to time. After all, they send home around US$18 billion annually so they could presumably pay a bit to their hosts.

I'd had a glimpse into the spending habits of Saudi princes and their entourages over a cup of coffee at a ski resort in Colorado. I'd met a British executive aircraft dealer on the chairlift and he'd given me a brief background on the used-jet market.

'I don't deal in the little stuff like Learjets,' he started, 'I handle G5s and up.'

Usually he didn't buy and sell like a used-car dealer either. His business was more like a real-estate agent, the middleman. Sometimes, however, it was worth putting up his own money.

'It was an about-to-be-deposed dictator's DC9', he explained. 'Low hours, forced sale, a great buy. I had to find a crew, get them into country X and get the aircraft out before the mob at the palace gates got too restive. Eventually I found a buyer for the plane in Saudi. The king has a

747, with an operating theatre downstairs just in case he has a heart attack at 30,000 feet. The top princes will also have widebodies and then as you move down the royal pecking order it's smaller passenger aircraft before you get into the executive jet territory. Members of a top prince's entourage would also have their own aircraft and I eventually sold this one to the Lebanese business adviser of one of the high-level princes.'

A popular myth held that the king's 747 not only had an operating theatre, but also a live transplant donor on board each flight, ready to be sacrificed just in case a fresh heart was needed.

• • • •

Stephen Ulph, the editor of the Jane's Information Group's Islamic Affairs Analyst, wrote that, 'a staggering two-thirds of Saudi PhDs are now awarded in Islamic Studies – a qualification that leaves their bearers effectively unemployable, disenchanted, and in many cases with little else to do but go in search of a "higher calling".'

On my final Saudi excursion, in Najran, just north of the border with Yemen, I test that research on the ground. Once again I find myself sitting next to an English-speaking Saudi, a university student on holiday from the US and, presumably, slumming it travelling by bus. When I query him on the statistics he agrees.

'The percentage is probably even higher', he suggests, but then pops up with the old Arab world Coca-Cola-and-the-Zionists urban myth. 'Ten per cent of the price of every can and bottle of Coca-Cola goes straight to Israel', he announces. 'The fact is suppressed in the West so you don't hear about it, but in the Arab world everybody knows.'

At lunchtime we pause in Zahran, a small town where I'm told some of the September 11 hijackers had connections. Nobody seems to be looking for would-be pilots today and a couple of hours later I'm in Najran. It's a curious place, essentially one long main road stretching for 15 kilometres from the isolated Holiday Inn at one end to the fairytale castle in the heart of the *souq* at the other.

The next morning I am picked up by Saeed Jumaan, quite the most charming tour guide you could ask for. As a young boy he went off to work for Aramco, the Arabian American Oil Company that propelled Saudi Arabia to the top of the petrodollar charts. He learnt English with Aramco, but returned to his home town, still a teenager.

'One day in the market I saw this Western woman having difficulty making herself understood', he tells me. 'I offered to translate and she immediately asked if I wanted a job. I ended up working for her company for the next few years, but that first afternoon she asked me to come back to her company's encampment. I went with her, but I remember being terrified. I had no idea what was going to happen to me, whether this was the end of my life.'

In the shadow of Najran's enchanted castle is the basket *souq*, full of baskets and curious stone turned pots from Yemen, and close by is the 'ladies *souq*'. Special dispensation allows women to work in this market. The goods spill out of the stalls and across the wide, dusty aisles – baskets of spices, heaps of kitchen utensils, piles of pottery, incense burners, boxes of tribal jewellery, all of it jumbled together with no discernible order, much of it piled up on boxes and stands that give the whole *souq* the look of a rolling, colourful hillscape, dotted by the black peaks that are the women, squatting among their wares. It is absolutely the most disorganised, chaotic, untidy, higgledy-piggledy market I have ever seen. There's no way they can pack things away at the end of the day's business, a tarpaulin or a plastic sheet is simply hauled across the goods.

One women is selling goat skins sewn up at the head and anus with a stopper plugged into one of the legs to be used as a water container or, in this case, to carry cooking fat. I can't imagine anything I'd less like to carry home with me, but my 'what the hell is this' interest prompts her to offer a lower price every time I pass her position. Later I see a man

293.

making larger ones, strictly for carrying water with a tap shoved up the opening where the anus would have been.

. . . .

Queuing up for security at Najran Airport, I peek surreptitiously over the shoulder of the woman in front. What would her identity card show? Clearly if a Saudi woman went overseas she must have her photo on her passport. Other countries are not going to accept a picture of someone disguised as a black sack. Here the question of photo identification on a driving licence never arises, but what do they show on their local ID?

Answer: their husband's picture.

The flight to Riyadh skirts the edge of the Rub Al-Khali, the Empty Quarter. I'd toyed with the idea of making a foray out into the Empty Quarter from Najran, but it's two hours each way before you really get into the sand dunes, too long for my short stay. Halfway to Riyadh the desert – generally beige, featureless with occasionally black, rocky outcrops – suddenly gives way to a huge agricultural project. The circular irrigated fields (technically known as centre pivot irrigation systems) look like someone has sat down with a stack of giant CDs and slung them out one by one on to the sand. The Saudis used a big chunk of their oil wealth to build up a major agricultural sector, proving that if you pour enough water on a desert you can grow grain even if it isn't necessarily a very ecologically or economically sensible idea. This realisation is beginning to sink in and some cutting back is going on.

The Empty Quarter may be the world's biggest sand desert, but in fact it isn't that big. The state of Western Australia, which is nearly all desert, is 25 per cent bigger than all of Saudi Arabia – in *Dirt Music,* Australian author Tim Winton described his home state as being rather like Texas, 'only it's big'.

In the Riyadh boarding lounge, waiting for my flight to Dubai, I'm suddenly not the sole nonbeliever in sight and some of the Western women have already cast their *abaya* aside.

'I have this vision of expat women dropping their *abaya* at the departure gate when they finally leave Saudi', I'd said to one of the Canadians in Madain Saleh.

'I'm burning mine at my going-away party', she'd replied. 'I'll be on my way out, they can't do anything then.'

. . . .

So much of the Saudi experience revolves around women: their presence, their exclusion, their appearance, their restricted lives. This is the country that taught the Taliban how to treat women and much of women's role in Saudi Arabia is well documented. They can't drive (which introduces a whole new category of guest worker to the equation, the women's guest-worker-chauffeur), they can't work except in strictly controlled female-only situations, they can't go into certain shops (CD shops and video shops are both strictly forbidden to the fairer sex), they can't even ride on a bus without a responsible male to keep an eye on them.

They can't even get a haircut. Saudi Arabia is overstocked with barbers, but hairdressers for women simply don't exist. A woman can't have her hair cut by a man and working as a hairdresser is not an occupation open to women.

'It's not a problem for the rich Saudis,' said a British expat, 'they'll fly in a hairdresser from Paris when they want their hair done. Of course, there are secret hairdressers, the taxi drivers know where to find them.'

'What about Kingdom Tower?' I asked. Riyadh's new super skyscraper included a pioneering women's floor with shops purely for women and operated by female staff. 'Why couldn't they have women's hairdressers in a women-only environment like that?'

'Well, Kingdom Tower is still pretty experimental', she said. 'Anyway there are female *mutawwa* as well. They've been in there trying to ensure that women keep their hair covered.'

In fact I do see women working. In smaller towns, further from Riyadh, there were often women selling things in a *souq*, but not in the shops themselves. While the men lounged back in the comfort of stalls, the women squatted on the ground, often on the pavement or out in the sun. The special ladies *souq* in, remarkably, ultra-conservative Najran was the one exception.

The most unusual thing about the women was that most of the time they just weren't there. Early in the morning you might see the occasional woman, but most of the time in most of the country they simply disappeared for the rest of the day, reappearing like black-cloaked vampires as the sun went down. For much of the day you could almost forget this was a country that treated women like enslaved second-class citizens, only to wake up with a start as their sinister forms reappeared in the evening. Like 'death out for a walk' as French author Guy de Maupassant famously described them.

So why do Saudi men treat their women so abjectly and why do they brand them with this absurdly uncomfortable and impractical outfit? It's not like the ritual tattooing of the Pacific, the stretched lower lips of the Surma women of Ethiopia, or the long necks (actually depressed collarbones) of the Padaung women of Myanmar. Those ritual appearances are looked upon locally as a sign of beauty, not something to be hidden away and disabling.

There was, however, another time and place where women were deliberately handicapped, just like in Saudi Arabia today – China. Every time I go back there the speed of change seems to have kicked up another notch. In Guilin the hustle, the bright lights, the crowds, the fashions, the traffic and the restaurants would have had Mao spinning in his grave faster than a CD. In the restaurant I went for dinner (busy, noisy, very

Chinese, terrific food, especially the noodle-thin stir-fried potatoes with green peppers) the next table had three young guys and a girl. Shortly after I arrived a second girl turned up – she was stunning, wearing very tight, faded blue jeans and a silvery top. Then the sixth member of the group rushed in, looking equally à la mode and finishing a phone call on her mobile as she pushed through the door. A couple of days later I was leaving the country and at Beijing airport I was suddenly whisked back to a much older China. A small group of Chinese were moving towards the check-in counter, gently helping a very old lady who was hobbling painfully. I realised instantly why she was having such trouble walking – she had bound feet. I'd seen the shoes, read the description of how it was done, but surely it was centuries ago, something associated with the opium trade, something that had died out long, long before Mao or even Chiang Kai Shek? Yet here we were, at the start of the 21st century and there were still people alive with bound feet.

That's what *abaya* remind me of. They're the Saudi equivalent of bound feet, something that ties people down, makes them helpless, deprives them of freedom, restricts them, binds them, hobbles them.

And black. Why would anyone want to wear black under that pitiless Saudi sun?

'So why did the men end up all in white and the women in black?' I asked a Saudi.

'Well, we men had the first choice, of course,' he replied, 'and in this climate you'd be crazy to wear black.'

Given that women can't work, except under the most constrained circumstances, and are severely restricted in what they can do and where they can go, how do they pass the time? Things aren't all that great for men either. You're certainly not going to meet your friends in a bar (since alcohol is banned), male or female you won't be going out to the cinema (they're banned too) and as for clubs, dancing and discos… So Saudis do what lots of people do when there's nothing else to do. Make babies.

Fertility rates have come tumbling down in many countries. In Japan and Italy the average number of children per woman has dropped below the 2.2 generally reckoned to be what's needed to keep the population static. In Bangladesh, once looked upon as an international basket case, the fertility rate has dropped to just over three children and even Kenya, the world's fertility horror story in the late 1970s when the average Kenyan women had eight children, has brought its rate down to around five children.

For all the BMWs and Mercedes Saudi Arabia is definitely Third World when it comes to contraception, birth control and fertility. The average Saudi woman now has more than six children.

The resulting population boom means 60 per cent of the population is under 18 and unless oil stays at sky-high levels, simple demographics will eventually undo things. The post-oil-boom baby bulge is looking for jobs and in turn creating its own baby boom. Eventually something has to give. New job-seekers appear on the market far faster than new jobs are created and it will inevitably get worse if the government does not institute big changes but the Saudi government has never moved fast. A continuing fall in per-capita income and a drop in living standards could lead to some emancipation of women, a window could crack open to a democratic breeze. Or it could lead nowhere at all. There's still a lot of oil and at current price levels the government has lots more breathing space.

So the government seems to be edging towards real employment change in only the most gentle and delicate fashion. My guidebook discreetly notes that, 'two generations of generous public assistance have not inculcated the country's youth with a strong work ethic'.

That's putting it mildly. It was a joke during the Kuwait Gulf War that you'd get a thousand-dollar prize if you spotted a Saudi carrying anything

heavier than money. When I queried why the 'no women working with men' rule didn't seem to apply to Saudi Arabian Airlines' female flight attendants I was told: 'They're probably Moroccans, you certainly couldn't have a Saudi women employed as a flight attendant. Anyway if you see anybody working, they're probably not Saudis.'

Saudis dominate the government jobs. About three quarters of the million or so people employed in that sector are Saudis, but there are an awful lot of non-jobs in that sector, a lot of offices full of people pushing paper from one side of a desk to the other and then having another cup of tea. Meanwhile in the harder-working private sector, the proportions are reversed. The sector is much bigger, employing over six million people, but over five million are expats. That's a tough statistic for the government to live with when unemployment among Saudis is already conservatively estimated to be 15 to 20 per cent and set to go much higher.

The government has instituted a policy of Saudisation. Seventy-five per cent of a company's employees should be Saudis unless, of course, there are not enough 'competent nationals' available. 'Some firms employ Saudis to sit around to meet the numbers', an Indian business manager in Riyadh told me. 'We can't afford to do that, but it can be difficult to find Saudis who'll stick with a job. They're keen to be managers, but they don't want to start at the bottom and work their way up. If they speak good English, they're likely to be paid more in a government job as well.'

Indians, making up 1.5 million of the expat-worker pool, have recently been subjected to a blanket ban except in certain categories. Osama al-Kurdi, Secretary-General of the Council of Saudi Chambers of Commerce and Industry, in trying to get the recruitment ban lifted, stated that 'all studies on Saudisation emphasise that there are certain areas which Saudis do not like to work in, while in other sectors the number of Saudi workers are far fewer than the number required.'

Of course, spurning the menial jobs isn't unusual in most First World countries. Would a table get cleared in the US without Mexican bus boys? Is there still a Brit employed in a London hotel? Even Japan depends heavily on its frequently illegal arbeits to keep its economy functioning. In Saudi Arabia, however, the problem isn't just at the bottom of the job basket. 'They simply aren't turning out enough graduates with the right qualifications and until they do they'll have to keep importing labour', said an expat doctor.

• • • •

There's a lot I don't like about the country, but everybody I met, Saudi or expat, was polite, helpful and often friendly, and it was an intriguing place to visit. There have been so few visitors and so little written (and even less filmed or photographed) that places often came as pleasantly jolting surprises. If the Saudis were to free up their visa requirements, they could easily have many more visitors – there's plenty to see, getting around is quite easy and the facilities are more than adequate. The jobs created could also help reduce their mounting unemployment problem. More importantly, though, it could form a channel of communication in both directions. And that's what Saudi Arabia badly needs. For all the whining about how unfair the world is to Islam it's the country's inward-looking, tightly constrained, narrow-minded view of its religion and its position in the world that is the real cause of the Saudi problem.

THE EVIL METER™

Measuring 'badness' is not an exact science. Countless times in my Bad Lands travels I was reminded that every story has two sides and very often one country's terrorist is indeed another country's freedom fighter. Balancing up the varying perceptions of what constitutes immorality or wickedness is like trying to compare rotten apples with bitter oranges. Nevertheless I'm going to have a go at it. I've devised my very own 'Evil Meter™' and I'm going to run it over each of my Bad Lands to gauge which really is the baddest of them all.

Three things give a country marks on my Evil Meter™ – how it treats its own citizens, if it is involved in terrorism and if it is a threat to other countries. We'll look at how each measures up to those requirements and rate them from zero (perfect treatment) to three (evil personified).

In a perfect world people should have a say in who rules them. So if they have no access to democracy and decisions about their lives are made at the whim of a monarch or a dictator, that's going to rack up points. As well as the right to vote governments in or out, people should also be allowed to criticise them and not risk getting thrown in jail, or worse. They should also be allowed to get on with their lives without undue government interference. Sure the government can tax you, fine you if you drive too fast or drink too much, require that your kids go to school and generally make you jump through dozens of other hoops. If, however, you want to start a legitimate business, move from town A to town B, marry or take up a weird religion, then you should be allowed to do so. Finally you should expect to be treated fairly by the government. If you do something wrong, you should get a fair trial and the punishment, if you're convicted, should fit the crime. My Evil Meter™ records up to 3 points in this category.

Terrorism, and how a country handles it, also includes a number of factors. A country may be an outright supporter of terrorism. There are places that think for various reasons terrorism is a good idea and support it directly. That might mean training and financing its own terrorists. Or it might mean offering support in some form for an independent terrorist group or a terrorist group in another country.

Supporting terrorism doesn't have to be direct in my point count. It can be a result of some other policy or it can even be completely inadvertent. Pouring too much military equipment into a country for one reason or another can easily result in excess equipment spilling over the edge and getting into the hands of a terrorist group. Or the government can turn a blind eye to support from the general population for various forms of extremism. It may see this as a way of allowing people to let off steam or exercise their free will, but the end result may be support for terrorist activities. My Evil Meter™ can also record up to three points in the Terrorism category.

Finally there's External Threats – outright national aggression towards another country. For some reason country A simply decides it has to bomb, attack or invade country B. Three points are available in this category too, making nine points available thus far.

Of course, nothing worthwhile is measured on a scale of nine. We all know 10 is the number to aim for so my Evil Meter™ also dispenses a bonus point for a good Personality Cult. No Bad Land can be really awful without a superlative collection of statues and portraits of the leader. A strong personality cult isn't a prerequisite for Bad Land status, but a decent collection of statuary and portraits of the great leader certainly helps. Iraq clearly ticked that box during the Saddam era and Libya still has a nice collection of Gaddafi billboards, but I was very disappointed in my visit to Albania to find that Enver Hoxha statues had totally disappeared.

Far and away the best Bad Land statue collection is, for now at least, in North Korea and I desperately hope the fall of that regime won't also lead to the fall of all those Dear Leader and Great Leader figures and portraits. The Chinese could show them how to let the political artwork gently fade into the background. Big Mao images remain – they're simply in the shadows; either the spotlights have been turned off or statuary is simply lost among billboards for mobile phones, cold beers and pricey perfumes.

Working from bottom to top, the merely slightly bad to the outright appalling, here are the scores.

CUBA
1.5 POINTS

Poor old Cuba is an also-run when it comes to evil. The only place Fidel is tough on is Cuba. There's only ever one candidate to elect (the maximum leader, of course), there's no chance you can say anything critical about him, and the only free-enterprise is prostitution. The US may have worked hard for nearly 50 years at impoverishing the country, but Fidel's worked even harder at the same task.

On the other hand when it comes to public health and education Cuba doesn't do so badly – infant mortality figures in Cuba are comparable with the far wealthier USA. This pulls the two points Cuba would score for being thoroughly bad to its own people back to a 1.5.

Externally the country is no threat to anyone. Apart, that is, from the Cuban national baseball team's ability to beat almost anybody, including

303.

the USA, and Fidel's ability to bore anyone to death with his endless speeches. Once upon a time aircraft hijackings were pretty much a 'take me to Havana' speciality, but terrorism is really not a Cuban talent.

Despite those trademark military fatigues, the bushy beard and the big cigars, Fidel doesn't get off the ground in the Personality Cult bonus category. Images and statues are almost all reserved for the even more photogenic Che Guevara.

BURMA
2.5 POINTS

Despite all the fingers pointed at it, Burma is really nowhere when it comes to evil on my meter. There's no evidence the generals have ever tried to foment revolution, export terrorism or invade other countries although their slack attitude towards opium poppy cultivation means they're a major supporter of First World drug problems.

When it comes to grinding down Burma's own population, however, the generals are champions. They've slaughtered students, imprisoned a Nobel Prize winner, devastated minority ethnic groups, beaten up democracy campaigners, flattened and relocated villages and forced children to work building roads and railways. Twenty years ago, when their policies also included mad socialism, they could have scored a full three points in this category, but shops full of electronic gear and streets jammed with Japanese cars indicate that mad socialism has been consigned to the economics wastebasket.

The generals do score a half-point in the Personality Cult bonus category. Apart from dressing up in Ruritanian military outfits and pinning ridiculous numbers of medals across inflated chests, they wouldn't look like contenders. Although, given there are those billboards proclaiming what a wonderful job they're doing, how much everybody loves them and how all the country's problems are the fault of 'that woman', for sheer outright delusion they get a half-point.

ALBANIA
DURING THE ENVER HOXHA ERA
3 POINTS

Today Albania is a reformed nation, simply waiting for the outside
world to realise all those image problems are part of the distant past. Even
in the worst years of poor deluded Enver Hoxha's regime, Albania was
really a nonstarter in the evil stakes. To the outside world it was simply
reclusive; it was certainly no threat to anyone either through terrorism or
directly. Actually, scared little Albania was convinced the outside world
was a threat to it, hence all those bunkers scattered around the country.
Britain and America probably did plot to help Albanian opposition forces
overthrow Hoxha in the early 1950s, about the time he kicked off his
bunker-building spree.

Internally, however, Hoxha ensured that Albania was right up there
in the evil stakes. You didn't vote, you didn't criticise (unless you wanted
a lengthy stay in a prison modelled on Joe Stalin's gulag originals), you
enjoyed the most impoverished lifestyle in Europe and for entertainment
you could help build those crazy concrete bunkers. Or enjoy a spell in the
chrome mines.

Plus Hoxha-era Albania scores a bonus point for a good Personality
Cult. Unfortunately the statues and busts have all disappeared. The only
hint of the bad old days is Hoxha's awful (in architecture, design and
construction) pyramid ex-museum in the centre of Tirana.

SAUDI ARABIA
4 POINTS

Well, the Saudis certainly aren't going to invade anybody. Back in the
Kuwait Gulf War it was a standard joke for coalition military that the
only thing you'd ever see a Saudi soldier lift up was a bag of money. Nor
is a country so dedicated to hiding statues, pictures, films, drawings,
painting and any other depiction of the human form going to have a

305.

chance of scoring a Personality Cult bonus point.

When it comes to terrorism, however, the Saudis are right up there. Encouraging terrorism may not be government policy, but the Saudi government is hand-in-glove with Wahhabism, the extremist form of Islam, which believes that it's right and anybody else is an infidel deserving death with no virgins lined up in the afterlife. Add that to an educational and economic system in large part dedicated to turning out Islamic scholars and then having to spend the oil money on importing people to do the hard work, and you're heading towards a situation where the only calling for too many bored young men is a spell of jihad. That could mean trotting off to Afghanistan to help the Taliban oppress women, or trotting off to the USA to hijack aircraft and fly them in to buildings. The Evil Meter™ reads two points.

Saudi activities may not be too much fun for other countries, but it's not much fun if you're a woman either, having to put on a black sack anytime you go outside, not being able to drive, only being allowed to work under extremely limited circumstances – in fact not being able to do most things without a 'responsible male relative' to keep an eye on you. Many of the country's guest workers don't get treated too well either. Throw in near zero democratic rights, a medieval punishment system, strict government censorship and the morals police wandering around waving big sticks and Saudi Arabia scores another two points for not being very nice to its own people.

LIBYA
BEFORE GADDAFI REFORMED
4.5 POINTS

Today it's an all-new user-friendly Libya, although they've still got a long way to go before the doors are really open to Western visitors. Visitors from other (poorer) countries in Africa, planning to turn up as refugees in Europe as soon as possible, don't face anywhere near as much difficulty getting in to Libya. It's hardly surprising, since Gaddafi has given up on unifying the Arab world and now concentrates on unifying Africa, with himself at the helm of course.

Libya's treatment of its own citizens has not been terrific. In the bad old days Gaddafi was prone to chasing his opponents wherever they went. The most notable downside of this policy was in London in 1984 when a Libyan sniper, firing on Libyan protesters in the streets outside the Libyan embassy, managed to kill a London bobby instead. Complaining isn't a good idea in Libya either. In 1996 a riot broke out at a football match in Tripoli and when the shooting stopped there were at least 20 dead. The shooting had started after spectators had started shouting slogans against either the Gaddafi government or, equally possibly, Gaddafi's football-crazy son Saadi Gaddafi, who is said to have ordered his personal security guards to fire on those foolish fans. Of course, the slaughter wasn't widely reported in Libya so it's hard to tell exactly what happened.

The positive side of the equation? Well Gaddafi does believe in his socialist duty to feed and shelter his people. A visitor reported seeing bread dumped under bridges and underpasses every morning for the hungry as part of this programme. Nevertheless Amnesty International continues to have grave reservations about the human rights situation in Libya so even today the Evil Meter™ scores would give him a point in this category.

Terrorism? Well, the reformed Gaddafi wouldn't think of that sort of thing, but in his bad old days he not only funded any terrorist organisation who wandered by Tripoli with their hands out, he also did some terrorising of his own, most famously by sabotaging a French DC-10 and an American 747. So although the new good Gaddafi may not go in for that sort of thing, the old bad Gaddafi certainly did and scores two points.

Gaddafi wasn't above making the odd direct external threat and sending the Libyan troops in when he felt they were needed. Fortunately for the outside world they weren't too effective. His support for Uganda's Idi Amin didn't save that notorious bad lad, although his escape to Saudi Arabia was probably engineered by Gaddafi. He supported a variety of other African hopeless cases including the Central African Republic's Bokassa and Liberia's horrific Charles Taylor, but it was in Chad where Libyan military might played its longest-running role. When the French Foreign Legion turned up, however, they soon scooted home to Libya. So despite his efforts Gaddafi only scores one as an External Threat. He might have liked to be threatening, but he wasn't.

Finally Personality Cult bonus points: a good effort, but not up with the best is probably the most you can say for Gaddafi's billboard collection. The problem is he always looks like he was trying out for a position on *Queer Eye for the Straight Guy*: not the ideal look for a Great Bad Land Leader role. Half a point.

AFGHANISTAN
UNDER THE TALIBAN
4.5 POINTS

Outside the Taliban's own ranks and the equally misguided enthusiasts of Wahhabism (the Taliban with credit cards), nobody has much enthusiasm for the Taliban and their treatment of the long-suffering citizens of Afghanistan. It's hard to find anything nice to say about people who hate music, art, film, kite flying and women. Plus they were so completely focused on forcing their interpretations of how the world should work upon everybody else that simple little things like feeding people just didn't come on to their screens. Those things could be left to Allah (or the UN, or foreign NGOs) while they concentrated on stoning adulterers, burning books and blowing up Buddha images. So a solid three points for being horrible to the people of Afghanistan.

Sadly it has to be admitted that the Taliban were not all bad. They came into existence as a reaction to how much bad was already out there.

The mujaheddin may have helped to topple the Soviet Union, may have several nice positions in the new democratic government of Afghanistan and may have created a genuine poster-pinup national hero in Ahmad Shah Massoud, but the reality is that much of the time rape, pillage and destruction were their chief talents. The Soviet Union may have trashed the Afghan countryside, but it was the mujaheddin who trashed the cities and heaped more years of suffering upon the already long-suffering Afghan people. So we'll pull the Taliban back half a point, horrible though they were.

Which is remarkably like how I feel about the Western world's best-known Taliban: Australian David Hicks. Anybody who supported all the ridiculous stuff the Taliban believed in can't be a very pleasant person. If he'd turned up back in Australia, I would definitely have wanted to cross the street if he was strolling by. If he'd been handed over to a bunch of radical feminists for a little re-education after he returned home, that would have been entirely fitting, but getting shoved into a no-charges, no-communication, no-defence, no rules-of-law, utterly wrong prison camp like Guantánamo Bay is just as bad. Worst of all, when your own government does the Pontius Pilate act and washes its hands of you and says some other country can do whatever it pleases with you, then definitely the Evil Meter™ has to balance things up. So, unhappily, I have to say David Hicks' sins are balanced out by the sins against him.

Given a clean, uninfluenced reading the Evil Meter™ would probably produce the same result for America's best-known Taliban, John Walker Lindh.

Irrespective of which, the Taliban can rack up another two points in the Terrorism category. They may not have engaged in it themselves, but they put up with and sheltered people who did. They took in a bunch of people who not only used Afghanistan as a launching pad for the September 11 attacks on the USA, but also brought their particularly single-minded hatreds to bear on parts of the Afghan population like the

Hazara. And women in general.

Personality Cult bonus score? A big fat zero. The Taliban didn't like images of anybody and they were so reclusive there's hardly anything known about Mullah Omar apart from the fact that he only had one eye.

On the other hand Osama definitely generated a Personality Cult, but he was a Saudi, not an Afghan…

IRAN
5 POINTS

Like many visitors to Iran I've come away with some passion for the place. As a tourist destination it's fantastic and the people can be terrific too. They have the right blend of enthusiasm and cynicism and they're smart enough to have thought-out opinions about their position in the world, what the world thinks about them and what they think about the world.

'You can talk to the man in the street and you'll get a thoughtful judgment', mused Andrew Burke, a Lonely Planet writer who has covered the country. 'That wouldn't happen in, say, Laos. The average man-in-the-street in Laos wouldn't have a clue what was going on and certainly wouldn't think it was his right to say something about it.'

It's called democracy and, while democracy Iranian-style certainly isn't up to the standards we're used to in the West, it is probably ahead of any other country on my Bad Lands list apart from today's Albania. Even Iraq, despite its good-as-it-gets-under-the-circumstances brand of democracy, is realistically a long way behind Iran. The Iranian reality is that lots of people may be a long way from 100 per cent enthusiastic about the ayatollahs and the religious influences on their life, but they're definitely 100 per cent unenthusiastic about the USA (or anyone else for that matter) nosing in and suggesting that 'regime change' should be on their agenda.

So, although the Iran government is a long, long way from being nice to its citizens, it's also far from the worst around: score one point in the first category.

Where Iran is definitely not nice is the Terrorism category. Although they've probably not become directly involved, they have certainly supported lots of organisations who have put their Iranian money to bad use. They put much more effort into promoting terrorism than Iraq and, what's more, they're proud of it. Two points.

External Threats? Well, there's lots of talk about destroying Israel because the Holocaust never happened so for hot air alone they score a point here. In fact, despite their 'we'll make a bomb if we want to' threats, they don't have the wherewithal to turn all this posturing into bad actions so no more than a point here.

Remarkably Iran can scratch up a half-point in the bonus category. Given the Islamic abhorrence of graven images it would seem unlikely, but in fact, as any visitor to Iran can confirm, the country is well stocked with some very artistic Khomeini billboards.

Finally, since it's my Evil Meter™, there's going to be another half a bonus point for the Ayatollah's fatwa on Salman Rushdie. I don't like to see writers being threatened, particularly for books the threateners have not even read.

IRAQ
UNDER SADDAM HUSSEIN
6 POINTS

No question about it: Iraq under Saddam was not a nice place. He slaughtered and gassed his own citizens, murdered his political opponents, set his son Uday loose on a losing football team and killed thousands more Iraqis by sending them off to fight ridiculous wars. The Evil Meter™ reads two in the first category.

For External Threats Saddam scored even higher, a perfect three. He launched a war against Iran that went on for eight long years and then repeated the feat with his invasion of Kuwait. In the course of the Kuwait Gulf War he also hurled a bunch of badly aimed Scud missiles at Saudi Arabia and Israel. Having Saddam as a neighbour was clearly not a good idea.

On the other hand, despite the Coalition of the Willing invading Iraq as part of the War on Terrorism, Saddam scores a big fat zero in the Terrorism category. If Saddam didn't like you, he'd launch the Mother of Wars – he didn't mess with mere terrorism.

Saddam does score a solid bonus point for Personality Cult. He built statues and posted portraits with the best of them. If bad taste could earn another point for a Bad Land, then Saddam would have scored with every good-taste magazine from Architectural Digest to Wallpaper for his collection of over-the-top palaces.

NORTH KOREA
7 POINTS

No way round it, the DPRK is the only country to score points in every category including a clear Personality Cult victory.

The unfortunate citizens of North Korea have no choice about their government and absolutely no right to say anything about it. There's minimal economic freedom, no choice in where you live or work, and religion simply doesn't exist (apart from worship of the Great Leader and his progeny of course). Plus countless North Koreans have starved to death in recent years and if you try to escape and get caught, things can turn really bad. So three points.

Terrorism: with blown-up aircraft, kidnapped schoolchildren, fake US hundred-dollar bills and assassinations on its scorecard, North Korea fully deserves two points in this category.

External Threats is a difficult one. After their 2006 nuclear test (if it really happened) North Korea is more likely to have those dreaded WMDs than Iraq (of course, these days we all realise Lichtenstein was more likely to have WMDs than Iraq). It also has a penchant for driving tunnels under the DMZ towards South Korea and there are those provocative missile-tests and submarines full of suicidal commandos. Plus there's all the bragging about exacting terrible revenge upon imperialists and puppet stooges. On the other hand the coastal defences indicate that they're just as frightened of being invaded and how effective would a North Korean attack be in any case? Their air force dates from the Korean War, their army is half-starved and half a head shorter than their South Korean equivalents and from what I saw in Pyongyang they can hardly build a bicycle, let alone an accurate missile. So the Evil Meter™ only scores them one point in the External Threats category.

The bonus point, however, is clearly theirs. There is no Personality Cult like the North Korean Personality Cult and I really hope we can all one day enjoy the great Dear Leader/Great Leader Statue & Billboard Amusement Park.

SOME CONTROL COUNTRIES

Any good instrument needs a control test to make sure it's working properly so let's think about how my Evil Meter™ would react to some countries that don't feature as a Bad Land: like the USA.

You'd be hard pushed to complain about American treatment of American citizens. Come the next election you know whoever is in power will pack up and depart if he or she is voted out. There is no way an American president is going to call in the army to extend a stay in the White House. Plus you can certainly say whatever you like about any politician including the president and get away with it. Just imagine what would have happened to Michael Moore or Graydon Carter (the editor of *Vanity Fair*) in, say, Singapore.

Starting up a business and making a lot of money is an American birthright, marrying who you want (well, perhaps not if they're the same sex in some states) is also a right and you can certainly join any

313.

religion you choose. You can even dream up your own nutty religion and encourage others to join up. Anything new in the religious line, from Mormonism to Scientology, seems to be an American invention.

Of course, you're far more likely to end up in an American prison if your skin is black or your language Spanish. And when it comes to prisoner numbers the USA is a world leader per capita or in outright statistics. Capital punishment is also a US favourite, but overall the Evil Meter™ would still have trouble giving the USA a reading in this category.

Unhappily, despite George W Bush's War on Terrorism, the USA is not lily-white in this field. There's plenty of evidence of direct US support for terrorist activities – remember Ronald Reagan, Colonel Oliver North and undercover arms sales to Iran in order to fund the Nicaraguan Contras terrorist group? And didn't the CIA try to blow up Fidel with exploding cigars?

What about all the civilian deaths from the US military's trigger-happiness and bad aim as well? Quite apart from civilian deaths in Iraq the 290 crew and passengers on an Airbus flying in to Dubai in 1988 discovered the US military could be as trigger-happy as any real terrorists when the guided-missile cruiser USS *Vincennes* shot the aircraft down with the loss of all on board.

Then there's indirect US support of terrorism. A large slice of the financial support for the IRA's terrorism in Ireland came from hats being passed around in Irish bars and clubs in New York and Boston. Most of the dollars collected no more went to Irish widows and Irish education than the Saudi equivalent ended up supporting peaceful study of the Koran in Pakistani madrasahs. The War on Terrorism has, at least, stymied that sort of terrorist support.

Unfortunately the USA today is an outright winner when it comes to encouraging and recruiting terrorists. Driving down a freeway in Tehran I saw some wonderful terrorist recruitment billboards: ad agency, the US

Army; studio, Abu Ghraib; model, Lynndie England. Could Al-Qaeda
have produced anything better even if they'd had J Walter Thompson
working for them?

Furthermore every image of the USA's own gulag, Guantánamo Bay,
encourages more jihad supporters. Every story about 'rendition flights',
grabbing suspects and flying them off to a nameless destination for a little
incarceration and torture, inspires a few more suicide bombers. Every
time a US government spokesperson like Colleen Graffy opens her mouth
and says something so incredibly stupid as her description of a triple
suicide by Guantánamo detainees as a 'good PR move', terrorism chalks
up another win.

Or perhaps not. Perhaps Colleen Graffy and Rear Admiral Harry
Harris, Guantánamo Bay's commander, with his equally asinine
comments about hanging yourself with clothing and bed sheets being 'an
act of asymmetrical warfare waged against us', had another aim. Perhaps
they were simply trying their best to make the place so distasteful even
the most blindfolded neo-cons will campaign to close it down.

So overall I'm pretty sure the Evil Meter™ would score some points for
the USA in the Terrorism category.

Finally I suspect my Evil Meter™ might go off the scale if the US was
tested in the External Threats category. Just run through the Bad Lands
and think what has happened to them, courtesy of the USA.

Afghanistan – flooded with arms that fuelled the devastating years of
mujaheddin turmoil, bombed by Clinton and Bush, bombed and invaded
by Bush.

Albania – nothing much, although Hoxha must have built all those
bunkers because he was terrified somebody was going to invade.

Burma – boycotted.

Cuba – almost 50 years of isolation, boycotts and embargoes and plenty
of threats, although the Bay of Pigs affair probably fits the terrorism
rather than the invasion category.

Iran – any number of threats to try the Iraq regime-change experience again.

Iraq – bombing, invasion, boycotts, embargoes, more bombing, another invasion, occupation.

Libya – boycotts, seclusion, embargoes, bombing.

North Korea – war, invasion, threats, boycotts, embargoes.

Saudi Arabia – now there's a country the US has always loved. OK, they're somewhat democracy-free, they do treat women rather shabbily and they did finance, plan and man the September 11 attacks but, hey, any country can make mistakes.

Of course, any story has two sides, so we should try not to forget that although the US may be a serious danger to any country it doesn't agree with that can still be a good thing. The European nations would still be sitting around twiddling their thumbs and saying 'oh dear' as ethnic cleansing went on in the Balkans if the US hadn't led the way in Kosovo.

Personality Cult? Well, it's true that portraits of the president do seem to be a much more common sight as you're lining up to clear US immigration these days, but there's certainly not enough of them to score a point in the bonus category.

How would the Evil Meter™ react to some other 'good' countries, like Australia, the UK or France?

Australia and the UK were both willing to join in when it came to rounding up the forces for the Iraqi mayhem so they're in there with the US on that one. On the other hand neither has been quite as keen as the US on throwing out centuries of well-founded laws or in kidnapping people and flying them off for a spell of electrics-to-the-genitals treatment.

316.

Australia has, however, remained the only country in the Western world, apart from the USA of course, that continues to believe that Guantánamo Bay is a good thing. It's worth noting that Britain insisted that none of its citizens were left in a Caribbean gulag and Major Michael Mori, the US Marine lawyer for Australia's Guantánamo inmate David Hicks, has correctly pointed out that in the US there would be national outrage if any American citizen was being subject to the sort of treatment meted out to his legal client.

France, of course, resolutely said 'non' to the Iraq idea, but I'm fairly certain my Evil Meter™ would produce a reading if it was applied to *la belle France*. After all, France has had a long tradition of propping up nasty African governments so long as they made an effort to speak a little *français* or invest the money they'd beaten out of their population in chateaus, champagne and Concorde charters. And if things began to look really bad for some of their Bad African Land clients, France had the Foreign Legion always ready to ride in to the rescue, successfully keeping the rebels away from the palace door.

Finally, even the worst of the Bad Lands would have trouble competing with France at getting caught red-handed in the state-sponsored-terrorism competition. In 1985, spooked that Greenpeace might disrupt French use of the Pacific as a convenient nuclear-testing spot, a batch of French agents were dispatched to Auckland, New Zealand, to sink the Greenpeace vessel *Rainbow Warrior*. The ship sank and a Portuguese photographer on board died, but the French agents were clearly not James Bond material. Two of them ended up on trial, but New Zealand was curtly reminded that it was Paris who pulled the European Union strings in Brussels and economically things wouldn't be very nice for the small Pacific nation if the incompetent French agents weren't promptly released. They were.

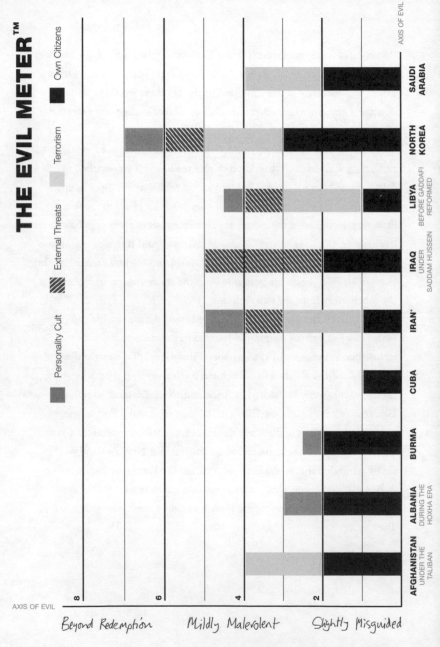

THE EVIL METER™

■ Personality Cult   ▨ External Threats   ▨ Terrorism   ■ Own Citizens

AXIS OF EVIL

8

6

4

2

Beyond Redemption

Mildly Malevolent

Slightly Misguided

AFGHANISTAN UNDER THE TALIBAN   ALBANIA DURING THE HOXHA ERA   BURMA   CUBA   IRAN*   IRAQ UNDER SADDAM HUSSEIN   LIBYA BEFORE GADDAFI REFORMED   NORTH KOREA   SAUDI ARABIA

AXIS OF EVIL

* Iran scores an extra 0.5 bonus points for issuing fatwas

OTHER
BAD LANDS
THE EXTENDED LIST

I described my journeys through nine Bad Lands, but of course there are many other places in the world that could easily qualify for that status. Here is my 'Top Ten' extended list of countries that, like the others already chronicled, derive their Bad Land status from an assortment of causes ranging from colonial-era mismanagement, involvement in other countries' proxy wars and governmental failings to outright corruption.

Somalia defines better than anywhere the description 'failed state' and has been effectively written off and forgotten since the 'Black Hawk Down' disaster in 1993. Forgotten, except that over the following years many of Somalia's warring warlords have been quietly funded by the USA, because the alternative, an Islamic state that might become a new home for Al-Qaeda, was too horrible to contemplate.

The end result? In June 2006, after 15 years of anarchy, an Islamist force took over Mogadishu, the capital, and kicked out the assortment of warlords. Why? Because the general population was completely fed up with endless violence and, as a result, no government, no schools, no health care, no life. Inevitably the Afghanistan comparisons have been made: for squabbling Somali warlords read squabbling Afghan mujaheddin and for Somali Islamists read Afghan Taliban. Don't forget the Taliban were, perhaps reluctantly, welcomed at first and the Somali Islamists might have learnt some lessons from how the Taliban squandered that welcome.

Remarkably Somalia has a Kurdistan-like northern region, known as Somaliland, which has cut itself off from the rest of the country, elected its own government and been relatively stable and safe. You can visit Somaliland from Eritrea and be fairly confident of getting home to tell the tale. Despite the chaos and lawlessness, Somalia as a whole also has one modern business: mobile phones. There's a workable and reliable cellular phone system, just like in Afghanistan and assorted other Bad Lands.

With the mess in Darfur regularly popping up on our TV screens and in newspaper editorials Sudan, separated from Somalia by Ethiopia, could also join my list. But there are plenty of other African Bad Land candidates including Congo/Zaïre, the country that two centuries ago defined the term 'darkest Africa' and remains one of the blackest black holes in a continent well endowed with disaster stories. From 1867 until 1908, this great slab of central Africa was known as the Congo Free State, with Belgium's King Léopold II as the utterly ruthless ruler. International outrage over the king's mindless brutality – he knew all about terrorism – led to the creation of the Belgian Congo. Independence arrived in 1960, but Patrice Lumumba, independent Congo's first elected prime minister and to this day a hero of African independence, was deposed only 10 weeks later, imprisoned, brutally beaten on more than one occasion and finally killed in early 1961. Belgium played a part in his overthrow and, naturally, the CIA are also accused of lending a hand.

Joseph Mobutu, the chief of staff of the army when Lumumba was deposed, soon took over and ruled for the next three decades. For the full story read Michela Wrong's *In the Footsteps of Mr Kurtz*, accurately subtitled *Living on the Brink of Disaster in Mobutu's Congo*. Mr Kurtz was

Joseph Conrad's character in *Heart of Darkness*.

The reader alternates between horror and laugh-out-loud amazement as Mobutu, who ran Zaïre as his personal fiefdom for 32 years, leads France, the USA and the World Bank down every blind alley on offer. While his people starved, Mobutu chartered Concordes from Air France so he could zip to his chateau in France at supersonic speed. In the last swirls of the final downward spiral, as his international friends abandoned him and the rebels closed in, Mobutu discovered he couldn't even call in his air force. The fancy supersonic Mirages were never going to return from a visit to France for maintenance – they'd been surreptitiously sold off to finance a Zaïrean air force commander's European retirement.

Mobutu departed in 1997, but never got to enjoy his own retirement in France. Within months he died of prostate cancer in Morocco. Congo/Zaïre has abundant natural resources, including huge diamond deposits, and it's one of the most important sources of tantalum, a vital ingredient in the manufacture of mobile phones and computer chips. So with Mobutu gone things soon improved, right?

Sure things improved, just like getting rid of that nasty dictator Saddam Hussein made things much better for Iraq. Far from improving the country's hopeless situation, Mobutu's departure made things far worse. Laurent-Désiré Kabila, the new dictator, proved equally rapacious and it soon became clear that Mobutu's overthrow was simply an excuse for a proxy war between rebel groups supported by Rwanda and Uganda.

Soon other African nations joined the melee including some, like Zimbabwe, that did not even share a border with the Congo. Kabila was assasinated in 2001, only to be followed by another Kabila, his son Joseph. Africa's First World War, as the civil war has been described, brought a soaring death toll, as many as four million by 2006, which has made it the most deadly war anywhere in the world since World War II. A ceasefire between the assorted rebel groups and elections in late 2006 may have brought some stability to the unhappy country, but after nearly

50 years of unremitting post-independence misery it's hard to believe.

Further south, Zimbabwe is not quite such a disaster area as Congo/ Zaïre, although it clearly could be if President Robert Mugabe has his way. Once upon a time Zimbabwe was fairly well-off by African standards and one man has managed to piss that all away. I have to admit that on the first occasion I went to Zimbabwe – back in 1989 – I was told Mugabe would eventually wreck the place and I dismissed that view as ex-colonial paranoia. They were right; I was wrong.

Poor Angola had the bad luck to be a Portuguese colony and become another of the world's proxy battlefields when the Lisbon dictatorship collapsed in 1974. Marxism-Leninism would have won, but the US certainly didn't want that domino falling and through the 1980s the CIA poured military aid into the country, often via the apartheid government of South Africa. The greenbacks went to Jonas Savimbi and his UNITA (National Union for the Total Independence of Angola) rebel group while on the other side the USSR financed Cuban mercenaries for the MPLA (Popular Movement for the Liberation of Angola). Just like Israel in southern Lebanon, South Africa itself was ready to shift troops into southern Angola anytime the struggle seemed to be going the wrong way. The result was death, injury or refugee status for hundreds of thousands of unfortunate Angolans.

The collapse of the Soviet Union should have terminated the endless struggle and in 1992 the UN supervised an election, won by the MPLA. Savimbi promptly reneged on the agreement and went back to war, funding his operations by control over Angola's rich diamond deposits. Diamonds, it turned out, could also be a terrorist's best friend, and for another 10 years Angola stumbled from crisis to crisis, outrage to outrage. UN representatives pointed out that if dealers in the West refused to buy Angolan diamonds, which were funding Savimbi's army, his power would have quickly melted away. UNITA's response was to shoot down UN aircraft carrying humanitarian aid.

Government troops finally managed to kill Savimbi in February 2002, which decisively concluded his long reign of terror. Angola is a Bad Land that just might be emerging from 30 lost years although unhappily the MPLA is hardly corruption free. I made a brief visit to Angola in 2005 although I didn't venture out of the capital, Luanda. In 2006 the Angolan football team qualified for the World Cup in Germany, an event that for the first time created a real feeling of national unity.

Surely Latin America can produce a competitive Bad Land? Argentina might have qualified during the generals' rule, but the little squabble with Maggie Thatcher over the Falklands/Malvinas scrubbed up that country. Kicking the Argentineans out of the Falklands in 1982 not only converted the Iron Lady's shaky political position to the solid control that allowed her, for better or worse, to comprehensively overhaul the British economy – it also terminated Argentina's military dictatorship.

Colombia definitely has Bad Land potential and will continue to face problems as long as the demand for high-quality Colombian marching powder stays strong in the West. Want to sort out Colombia's problems? Well, forget about stamping out the drug trade and just legalise the stupid stuff is my suggestion. Sure you'll have some new addicts who wouldn't have been addicts before, but they won't have to turn to crime to fund their addiction and Colombia (and other drug-producing countries like Afghanistan and Burma) won't have their own internal problems as suppliers. In fact let governments handle sales and marketing and cocaine and heroin could easily lose their forbidden flavour and become boringly mundane.

So I'll leave Colombia off my extended Bad List, move north into the Caribbean and put Haiti on instead. Now there's a nice failed state – all that beach paradise potential, some of the world's best naïve art, French as the national language and total bloody chaos as the end product. Looking at Haiti you wonder how Fidel's Cuba ever deserved to be a Bad Land.

323.

Check the stats. Infant mortality? In Haiti it's around 100 deaths per 1000 live births (among the worst in the world); in Cuba it's less than 10 (right up with First World standards). National income per person? It's only about US$3000 for Cuba, even when adjusted for the low cost of many subsidised essentials, but that's still two to three times the amount the average Haitian has to live on. Literacy? Close to 100 per cent in Cuba, more like 50 per cent in Haiti. Life expectancy? If you're born in Cuba, you can expect to live to your late 70s, just like Americans and other First World citizens. Haitians are lucky to see their 50th birthday. Government? Well, Haiti does hold elections from time to time, even if whoever gets elected never manages to stay in power for more than five minutes. That must be the reason Haiti has not been subject to economic sanctions and attempts to destabilise their government for the past 50 years, unlike neighbouring Cuba.

How about the Pacific – any Bad Lands there? Unfortunately there's lots of potential. The Solomon Islands, Papua New Guinea and East Timor have been labelled Australia's 'arc of instability': three countries that cannot get their acts together and in recent years have all needed outside assistance to try to clean things up.

Papua New Guinea, a vast and colourful nation with huge economic and tourist potential, is probably the biggest danger simply through its size and, therefore, the size of the problem. The great colonial carve-up of the island was strictly on the map – none of the colonial powers actually explored the territory where they so nonchalantly drew borders. First a north–south line was drawn in 1824 to separate Dutch territory to the west from British territory to the east. In fact Britain took virtually zero interest in their holdings until the Germans appeared and an east–west line was hastily drawn to separate German New Guinea to the north from British Papua to the south. It was nearly 50 years later before the first explorers, arriving in the New Guinea Highlands by air, discovered the border had been drawn not through an uninhabited wilderness, but through the most densely populated region of the whole island. By that time the Germans had lost World War I and the British had handed over management to Australia.

The Dutch retained their half of the island even after the rest of the Dutch East Indies became independent Indonesia in 1949. When independence came for Australian Papua New Guinea in 1975 it should, logically, have joined with Dutch New Guinea to create an island nation. Instead in 1962 the Dutch half had been handed over to Indonesia in what was seen as a US-pressured attempt to placate Soekarno, who was leaning heavily towards the USSR. Soekarno's control only lasted two more years, but the Indonesians have stubbornly held on to what became Irian Barat, then Irian Jaya and now Papua, despite ongoing resistance from the Papuans who are ethnically and culturally totally unrelated to the Indonesians, but closely related to the citizens of Papua New Guinea.

Since independence, democracy has had a tough time in Papua New Guinea because allegiance is directed towards one's tribe, not towards the country as a whole. Constantly shifting alliances make for regular changes of government and high levels of corruption. Ongoing local violence, driven by low employment and fuelled by tribal machismo, has led to large slabs of the country falling into the control of quaintly named 'rascals'.

So we'll add Papua New Guinea to the Extended Bad List and move north to a tiny nation that is Sad Land as much as Bad Land: Nauru. The tiny equatorial island had the misfortune to be deeply covered in phosphate, aka guano, aka bird poop. For the best part of a century the phosphate was dug up and shipped out, a bounty that briefly made the citizens of Nauru among the wealthiest in the world, right up with the Arab oil states. Then the phosphate ran out, the birdshit investments turned out to be, well, shitty, and Nauru went bankrupt. Even their Melbourne skyscraper, locally known as Birdshit House, was repossessed and today poor little Nauru depends on half-hearted money laundering and a role as Australia's own Guantánamo Bay. Just as the USA uses its

Cuban enclave as a prison far from the reach of lawyers and the eyes of journalists, so has Australia used Nauru as a place to closet away would-be refugees as part of the country's 'Pacific Solution', intended to deter would-be refugees arriving from real Bad Lands like Iraq or Afghanistan.

Back in Asia, Pakistan is a strong contender for Bad Land status. After all, this was the only country that really supported the Taliban apart from Saudi Arabia. Any terrorist event in India is likely to be blamed on Pakistan and it was also the conduit for all those dollars heading to Afghanistan's mujaheddin warlords. A large slice of that weapons money leaked out of the pipeline and ended up supporting a roll call of Pakistani ne'er-do-wells, from international terrorists to local gangsters. Plus, and it's a big plus, Pakistan today is probably home for Osama bin Laden, if he's still alive.

In the Middle East there's no stronger candidate for a Bad Land listing, from the US perspective, than Syria. It's the conduit between Iran and the Hezbollah militia in Lebanon, it's done some terrorising off its own bat, it was Saddam's best pal before his downfall and it's not been very nice to its own citizens. It also has extraordinarily friendly people, good beer and wine, great food, wonderful Greek and Roman ruins, fascinating reminders of the early years of Christianity, Crusader castles and a positive passion for beautifully restored old American cars. The dry desert air ensures that Syria's fine collection of antique Detroit iron is in far healthier shape than the better-known relics in Cuba. You cannot, however, cruise down the Biblical 'Street Named Straight' in Damascus in an elderly Chevy. It's pedestrian only.

Last, but far from least, there's the combo that is arguably the baddest Bad Land of them all. For what would Iran have to rant and rave about or Al-Qaeda to mount terrorist attacks over if Israel/Palestine didn't exist? If it wasn't for the ongoing death, destruction and unhappiness, the Israel-Palestine or Israel–Arab-world conflict would look uncannily like the equally never-ending struggle between the cartoon characters Tom and Jerry. Jerry, the troublesome mouse, taunts Tom, the fat cat, until Tom, aka Israel, loses his temper and sets out in mass destruction mode to destroy Jerry, aka Palestine (or Hamas or Hezbollah or whatever part Jerry is playing this week). Tom never manages to flatten Jerry, who inevitably pops up to continue the game next time round, but he certainly smashes plenty of vases, furniture and anything else breakable along the way.

Or think of the Palestinians (or Hamas or Hezbollah) as the obnoxious drunk hassling the pumped-up bouncer until, predictably, the bouncer flexes those steroid-enhanced biceps and beats the miserable little troublemaker to a pulp. The winners and losers are utterly predictable, but it's equally unsurprising who wins the sympathy vote in many of the next morning's papers. Bouncers should have some self-control, one paper will editorialise. Drug suppliers shouldn't be nonchalantly handing out steroids to bouncers, another will accurately observe. Of course, some papers will, correctly, point out that obnoxious little drunks should learn better behaviour. Yet as soon as he's off his crutches he'll undoubtedly be hassling the bouncer all over again.

If I was going to add just one more Bad Land to my main list, Israel/ Palestine would have to be it.